# Charming Billy

# Alice McDermott

—

# Charming Billy

BLOOMSBURY

First published in Great Britain 1999

Copyright © 1998 by Alice McDermott

The moral right of the author has been asserted

Bloomsbury Publishing Plc, 38 Soho Square, London W1V 5DF

A CIP catalogue record for this book
is available from the British Library

ISBN 0 7475 4433 6 (Hardback)
ISBN 0 7475 4661 4 (Paperback)

10 9 8 7 6 5 4 3 2 1

Printed in Great Britain

## Author's Acknowledgments

I am grateful to the Virginia Center for the Creative Arts for providing a quiet place; to Kevin E. McDermott for research assistance; and to Harriet Wasserman and Jonathan Galassi for friendship, wisdom, and infinite patience.

For Will, Eames, and Patrick

# Charming Billy

SOMEWHERE IN THE BRONX, only twenty minutes or so from the cemetery, Maeve found a small bar-and-grill in a wooded alcove set well off the street that was willing to serve the funeral party of forty-seven medium-rare roast beef and boiled potatoes and green beans amandine, with fruit salad to begin and vanilla ice cream to go with the coffee. Pitchers of beer and of iced tea would be placed along the table at intervals and the bar left open—it being a regular business day—for anyone who wanted a drink.

The place was at the end of a sloping driveway that started out as macadam but quickly diminished to dirt and gravel. There was an apron of dirt and gravel in front of the building, potholed, and on the day of the funeral filled with puddles, and the first ten cars parked here, including the black limousine Maeve had ridden in. The others parked up along the drive, first along one side, then the other, the members of the funeral party walking in their fourth procession of the day (the first had been out of the church, the second and third in and out of the graveyard), down the wet and rutted path to the little restaurant that, lacking only draught Guinness and a peat fire, might have been a pub in rural Ireland. Or, lacking dialogue by John Millington Synge, the set of a rural Irish play.

How in the world she ever found this place was a mystery, despite the question being asked again and again as Billy's friends and family filed in—the women, in high heels, walking on tiptoe down the sloping path, the men holding their wives' arms and umbrellas that had already been well soaked at the side of the grave. All of them, in their church clothes, giving a formal air to the gray day and the ragged border of city trees and wet weeds. All of them speculating: perhaps the undertaker had suggested the place, or someone from the cemetery. Perhaps a friend or relative on her side (few as they were) who knew something about the Bronx, or maybe Mickey Quinn, who had his territory up here. But Mickey Quinn denied it, shaking his head, if you can believe there's a bar in any of the five boroughs that he hasn't been to.

The place smelled slightly of mildew, understandable in this weather and with this thick (even in April) bower of trees, but the red-and-green tile floor was immaculate and the wooden bar gleamed under the fluorescent light. One long table draped with white tablecloths and set for forty-nine cut diagonally across the entire length of the room. One large window showed the parking lot full of cars, the other a wood that no doubt ended at a narrow side street or a row of dumpsters behind a row of stores, but seemed from in here to be dark and endlessly deep.

Maeve sat in front of this window, at the head of the table. She wore a navy-blue dress with long, slim sleeves and a round neckline, and anyone in the room who had not thought it earlier thought now—perhaps inspired by the perfect simplicity of what she wore—that there was a kind of beauty in her ordinary looks, in her plainness. Or, if they didn't think to call it beauty, they said courage—more appropriate to the occasion and the day—not meaning necessarily her new-widow's courage (with its attendant new-widow's clichés: bearing up, holding on, doing well), but the courage it took to look out onto life from a face as plain as butter: pale, downy skin and bland blue eyes, faded brown hair cut short as a nun's and dimmed with gray. Only a touch of powder and of lipstick, only a wedding band and a small pearl ring for adornment.

Of course, they'd thought her courageous all along (most of them, anyway, or—most likely—all but my father), living with Billy as she did; but now, seeing her at the head of the table, Billy gone (there would be time enough throughout the afternoon to say it's unbelievable still), her courage, or her beauty, however they chose to refer to it, became something new—which made something new, in turn, of what they might say about Billy's life. Because if she was beautiful, then the story of his life, or the story they would begin to re-create for him this afternoon, would have to take another turn.

My father sat to her right. Although Maeve had made all the arrangements herself—had found the place and chosen the menu and requested the fruit salad be served as soon as all the guests had arrived so there would be no long interval for speeches or toasts, only a quick blessing from one of the priests, he was the one the waitresses spoke to, and the owner of the place asked every now and then if anything was needed. He was the one who would settle the bill at the end of the afternoon and tip the waiters and the girl who took the coats and the umbrellas. He was the one who asked Maeve, after he'd already poured her a glass of iced tea, if she would like a drink, and then got up to fetch it for her, nodding to the undertaker and the driver, who were having their lunch at the bar.

She said, "Thank you, Dennis," when he placed the martini in front of her and then waited just a moment, her pale hand just touching the stem of the glass before she lifted it. "Good luck," he said, raising his own glass of beer. She nodded.

There's not much sense in pointing out the irony here—or even in trying to determine if everyone was either oblivious to it or so keenly aware that it no longer bore mentioning. Billy had died an alcoholic. Last night, in his casket, his face was bloated to twice its size and his skin was dark brown. (Dennis himself, my father, when he had identified the body two days ago at the VA, had said at first, momentarily relieved from the fact that Billy was dead, "But this is a colored man.")

Billy had drunk himself to death. He had, at some point, ripped apart, plowed through, as alcoholics tend to do, the great, deep, tightly woven fabric of affection that was some part of the emotional life, the life of love, of everyone in the room.

Everyone loved him. It was Mickey Quinn saying this, down at my end of the table. Mickey Quinn, who also worked for Con Ed, his territory being here in the Bronx, although he'd never heard of this place before. Mickey with a beer in his hand, and the irony either lost on him or too obvious even to bear mentioning. "If you knew Billy at all," he said, "then you loved him. He was just that type of guy."

And if you loved him, we all knew, you pleaded with him at some point. Or you drove him to AA, waited outside the church till the meeting was over, and drove him home again. Or you advanced him whatever you could afford so he could travel to Ireland to take the pledge. If you loved him, you took his car keys away, took his incoherent phone calls after midnight. You banished him from your house until he could show up sober. You saw the bloodied scraps of flesh he coughed up into his drinks. If you loved him, then you told him at some point that he was killing himself and felt the way his indifference ripped through your affection. You left work early to identify his body at the VA, and instead of being grateful that the ordeal was at long last over, you felt a momentary surge of joy as you turned away: This was not Billy, it was some colored man.

"He had the sweetest nature," another cousin, yet another Rosemary, said at my end of the table. "He found a way to like everyone, he really did. He always found something good to say, or something funny. He could always get you laughing."

"He was funny, though." It was agreed. "God, wasn't he funny?"

"Everyone loved him."

Not missing the irony of the drinks in their hands and the drink that had killed him, but redeeming, perhaps, the pleasure of a drink or two, on a sad, wet afternoon, in the company of old friends, from the miserable thing that a drink had become in his life. Redeeming the affection they had felt for him, once torn apart by his willfulness, his indifference, making something worthwhile of it, something valuable that had been well spent, after all.

The fruit salad was canned but served with a little scoop of lime sherbet, which was refreshing, everyone agreed. It cleared the palate. The rolls were nice. There was some soda bread in one of the bread baskets, someone must have brought it. "Not as good as mine, but then I prefer it with caraway seeds, the way my mother used to make it . . ."

You could not redeem Billy's life, redeem your own relentless affection for him, without saying at some point, "There was that girl."

"The Irish girl."

"Eva." Of course, Kate, his sister, would remember her name.

"That was a sad thing, wasn't it? That was a blow to him."

"A girl he met right after the war. Right after he came home. Out on Long Island."

"An Irish girl," Kate said, "visiting her sister, who was a nursemaid for some wealthy family from Park Avenue. He wanted to marry her, even gave her a ring. She had to go back home first, her parents were elderly, I think. But they wrote to each other. Billy was a great letter writer, wasn't he? He was always scribbling notes and mailing them off."

"He'd write a note on anything, wouldn't he? A paper napkin, a train schedule, and mail it off to you."

"I have one," Bridie from the old neighborhood said. She dug into her patent-leather purse and found a greeting-card-sized envelope with two stamps that showed a harp and a fiddle. She looked at the postmark—June 1975—and then extracted a limp paper square of a cocktail napkin that contained Billy's looping hand. "He sent it from Ireland," she said. "From Shannon Airport." And there was the Aer Lingus logo in the corner. With a blue ballpoint Billy had written: "Bridie: Just saw your face pass by on a twelve-year-old girl in a navy-blue school uniform. Said her name was Fiona. She was meeting her father's plane from New York. Your smile, your eyes, your very face at that age—second edition. Love, Billy."

The napkin was circulated, held as delicately as a fledgling, some even reaching into a purse or a breast pocket for reading glasses so as not to miss a word. All the way up the table to Maeve, who read it with a smile and a nod, and all the way back down again. Bridie took it back and read it once more before placing it into its envelope and back into a side, zippered compartment of her Sunday pocketbook.

Other letters from Billy were being mentioned: a note scribbled on a *Playbill* page, on a business card. The long missives he'd sent home during the war, whole lines blacked out by the censors but the homesickness coming through. He was so homesick. The postcards from the Irish trip, the place mats and napkins from various Long

Island restaurants and diners, that summer he and Dennis
were out there, fixing up Mr. Holtzman's little house. You
remember Mr. Holtzman. Dennis's mother's second husband. The shoe-store man.

Which was the same summer he met the Irish girl. Eva.
The one he had hoped to marry.

"She went back to Ireland at the beginning of the fall,"
Kate would remember. "And not long after that, Billy took
the job with Mr. Holtzman—Saturdays all day and maybe
Thursday nights, I think it was. Dennis had arranged it
for him. Billy was trying to put together enough money to
send for his girl, to bring her back here, and Dennis set it
up with Mr. Holtzman that Billy work at the shoe store
when he wasn't at Con Ed."

"He was a great salesman," her younger sister, also
Rosemary, said.

"Well," Kate explained, "Mr. Holtzman had lost some
business during the war—I don't know if it was rationing
or his being of German extraction or what. Anyway, he
was glad to get Billy, an ex-GI with that handsome face
of his. Those blue eyes."

"He was a good-looking young guy," Bridie from the
old neighborhood said. "Maybe a little shy."

"And that's where he met Maeve, wasn't it? In the
shoe store?"

"Later on," Kate said. "She used to come to the store
with her father, and I remember Billy telling me how patient she was with him because, you know, her father was
a drinker, too."

"A redheaded W. C. Fields," sister Rosemary said. "I
remember him at their wedding." Rolling her eyes.

"Poor Maeve has had her share of it."

A pause as a waiter reached between them to remove the fruit-salad bowls, every one of them whispering, Thank you, thank you, and then Thank you again as another waiter leaned in to put down the lunch.

"Doesn't this look good?"

"And the plates are nice and warm."

"They're doing a nice job, aren't they? I wonder how she found this place."

"The undertaker, I'm sure. He probably gets a commission."

"He sent her the money," Kate continued. "Eva, that is. The Irish girl. He sent her about five hundred dollars, I think."

"Which was a lot of money in those days." Someone was required to say it.

"It certainly was"—and to second.

"He sent her the money in the spring sometime, this would have been in '46. And she wrote back to say she was busy making plans, you know, arrangements for coming back over. Lord, he was like a man waiting for a bus in those days. The sun couldn't rise and set fast enough. He was hoping she would come over before the summer ended, so they could spend their honeymoon together, out on Long Island, in the little house, Holtzman's house, out where they'd first met. I don't know where he thought they were going to live after the honeymoon—remember what it was like, trying to find an apartment then?"

It was remembered. It was also noted that the roast beef was very tender, very moist. Better this splash of juice than a thick gravy.

"Rose and I were already living at home with our husbands and I had the baby, too," Kate said. "I don't know where Billy thought he was going to put her."

"I don't think," her sister Rosemary said, "he looked beyond her coming back to the U.S. and their getting married and going back out to Long Island."

"Maybe that was good," cousin Rosemary said.

Dan Lynch said, "Maybe it was just as well."

"Because he didn't hear another word from her all through the summer," Kate went on, "though I think he must have written to her two or three times a week, maybe more.

"In September, Dennis got a call from her sister, the one who was still minding the children on Park Avenue. He went into the city to see her and then came rapping at our door at about nine o'clock on a Sunday night. He asked Billy if he wanted to take a drive out to Long Island to check on the little house. I think he said there had been a storm out there. Anyway, Billy was always game. I remember he went out with his suit on a hanger because they were going to drive back first thing in the morning and go straight to Irving Place. I remember my mother ran after them with a sackful of rolls and butter and some sliced ham for their breakfast. All the way down the stairs.

"So it was dinnertime the next day before Billy got home, and that's when he told us that Eva had died— pneumonia. She was twenty-six years old. I'd like some tea instead," and the waiter with the stainless-steel coffeepot leaned away. "With lemon, please."

"Tea for me as well, please," Bridie said. "I'd almost forgotten this."

Mickey Quinn said, "None for me, thank you, maybe later," and then added that he thought only Midwesterners drank their coffee *with* their meals. He said he remembered how it was in the service, the Midwesterners guzzling coffee with every meal, it was a wonder they could taste anything. He paused to see who would rise to the bait, pick up the conversational thread, turn the talk away from Billy's lost girl to the Second World War.

But Dan Lynch said again, "It was a blow."

"I honestly thought he'd never get over it."

"But he stayed on at Holtzman's store, didn't he?" Dan Lynch said. "I mean, afterwards. Even when he didn't need the extra cash anymore. He stayed on. That was Billy all over, wasn't it? Loyal like that."

"Well, see," Kate said, "the money he'd sent her wasn't all earned. Mr. Holtzman had advanced him a good deal of it, and when Billy wrote to the girl's parents, to extend his sympathy—can you imagine that letter?"—Bridie shivered audibly—"naturally he told them to keep the money to pay the funeral expenses and to keep a fresh wreath on her grave."

"Like Joe DiMaggio," Bridie whispered.

Kate's eyebrows disapproved of the parallel. "For a while," she went on, "he talked about going over himself, but we discouraged it. Even Dennis said it would be awkward, maudlin. I was afraid it would just break his heart. Thank you. But working at the store was good for him, in the long run. It filled up one or two nights a week. And Saturdays. And, like I said, Holtzman was glad to have him."

"Billy told great stories about that place," Mickey

Quinn said. "You know, the kids screaming and the women squeezing their toes into size fours or leaning down into his face when he was trying to fit them, nearly smothering him with their furs and their perfumes. I remember him telling me about one, some big-footed woman who said to him when he measured her, 'Young man, I've always been told I'm a five and a half,' and he says, smooth as silk, 'That's five if it's halved, madam.' "

"A woman bit him on the ear once," Dan Lynch said. The information might have been on the tip of his tongue for twenty years.

"No."

"You're joking."

"Good Lord."

"It's the truth!" Delighted to finally get it out. "Billy must have blushed every color of the rainbow when he was telling me, down at Quinlan's. It seemed he was leaning over to pick up some of the shoes this woman had been trying on when she reached down, too, as if she was going to help him, and took a nip out of his ear. Can you imagine it?"

"He was good with the children," Bridie from the neighborhood said quickly, steering our thoughts down a more wholesome route. "He fitted all of mine, from infant shoes on. He had a way with children."

"And he met Maeve there," cousin Rosemary said.

Sister Rosemary confirmed it. "He met Maeve there. She always came in with her father. Getting him shoed, Billy said, was like fitting a mule, and no sooner would she be in to buy him a pair than they'd be back because he'd lost one of them. It didn't take Billy long to realize he'd lost one under a barstool somewhere."

"But Billy managed to ask her out," Bridie said.

"To the movies. You could have knocked me over with a feather when he told me he was taking her out to the movies. It had been what, Kate? Four or five years since the Irish girl?"

"Five years. It was 1950 and they were married three years later, in 1953."

"Thirty years, then," Mickey Quinn said.

Kate nodded. "It would have been thirty years in September."

"That's a good long run," said Mickey Quinn.

And all eyes went to Maeve, who, it seemed, had not touched her food but with her hands in her lap was leaning to listen to Ted, another of Billy's cousins, as he crouched beside her chair, speaking earnestly.

"She never had an easy time of it," sister Rosemary said, "especially recently. You know, toward the end."

"Toward the end it was a foregone conclusion," Kate said. "I think it was worse for her at the beginning, when she had her father *and* her husband to keep track of."

"She's doing beautifully today."

"Oh, she's strong."

"You have to hand it to her. She's got a lot of courage."

And a certain beauty, perhaps, looking up now to say something to my father, and to Father Ryan beside him, her pale hand in a fist on the white tablecloth. And if courage also meant beauty, then her presence in the shoe store was Billy's salvation, or at least his second chance that through willfulness and indifference he had let slip. But if she was as plain as they'd always said her to be during all the years Billy was alive, a plain girl approaching thirty with an alcoholic old father to take care of and no prospects—if Eva had been the beauty—then Maeve was only a faint consolation, a futile attempt to mend an irreparably broken heart. A moment's grace, a flash of optimism, not enough for a lifetime.

"I didn't know," cousin Rosemary whispered. "Was Billy having trouble even in the beginning? Even when they were first married?"

We all turned to Kate, whose memory had already proven keen. She was the older sister, the only one of them gathered here who had attained real wealth (although it had already been well noted that her husband wasn't here today, hadn't come last night), and so she could speak with some authority, while the rest might only venture a guess.

"Well, he always drank," Kate said. "But for a very long time it seemed he drank harmlessly. I remember him feeling no pain when he was on leave, before he went overseas, but that was understandable. I remember the night he came home and told us that Eva had passed away. He went straight to bed afterwards and I called Dennis to see if I could learn anything more and Dennis said they'd both had quite a lot to drink the night before, which was understandable, too. It was probably as hard for Dennis to tell him as it was for Billy to hear the news."

His sister Rosemary said, "I remember he had one too many at Jill's christening. I was worried about him riding the subway home."

"But for years he never missed a day of work," Kate told us. "And he was there to open the shoe store every Saturday morning from the time he started into the early sixties, when Mr. Holtzman finally sold the place to Baker's. I don't think Mr. Holtzman ever knew he drank. Certainly no one at Edison knew until near the end."

But Mickey Quinn held up his hand. "They knew," he said wisely.

"But not until fairly recently," Kate said. "Maybe when he went into the hospital in '73, the same year my Kevin graduated from Regis."

But Mickey Quinn frowned and shook his head slightly, apologetically, as if over something that was only slightly askew. "They knew," he said again. "We all knew. I left Irving Place in '68 and the fellows in the office knew Billy was a drinker even then. They covered for him, mostly in the afternoon. He'd go out on a call after lunch and not come back to the office and they'd cover for him. Everyone liked him. They were glad to do it."

"I think Smitty might have covered for him, too," his sister Rosemary said. "In the shoe store. Do you remember Smitty? Mr. Holtzman's assistant—the little bald man?" He was remembered. "I went in there one Saturday, we were looking for Betty's First Communion shoes, and Billy was just coming in from lunch. I had the feeling he'd had a few. I mean, he was fine, and the kids were always happy to see him, but I noticed Smitty did all the measuring and got out all the shoes. Billy mostly sat. Which wasn't like him. He was sucking a peppermint."

"When was this?" Kate asked as her wealthy husband, trained at Fordham Law, might do.

Rosemary paused to calculate. "Betty was in second grade. 1962." Almost in apology: "He was drinking in '62."

Dan Lynch raised his hands. "Well, what does it mean? He was drinking before that, too. Down at Quinlan's. Saturdays after work. Sunday evenings. Hell, I was always there, too, and my liver's fine."

"So when did it become a problem?" cousin Rosemary asked.

"He started AA in the late sixties," Kate told her. "And then again around '71 or '2."

"He took the pledge on that Ireland trip. That was '75."

"What good did it do?"

"I thought it would stick. Maeve did, too."

Dan Lynch was chuckling, his hand around his small glass. "I remember Billy saying that AA was a Protestant thing, when you came right down to it. Started by a bunch of Protestants. He said he didn't like the chummy way some of them were always calling Our Lord by his first name. I drove him to the first meeting and waited to take him home, 'cause Maeve didn't want him driving, and when he came out he said you could tell who the Catholics were because they'd all been bowing their heads every ten seconds while the Protestants bantered on about Jesus, Jesus, Jesus."

(And sure enough, up and down our stretch of table, heads bobbed at the name.)

Sister Rosemary said, "He didn't like them calling God a Higher Power, either—which I guess was the official AA term. Nondenominational, you know. He said it only proved that none of them had a sense of humor. He said you'd have to be God Himself to get higher than most of these guys had been."

There was a bit of low laughter. "Billy had an irreverent streak," Mickey Quinn said. "I liked that about him."

"The way Father Joyce explained it to me," Dan Lynch went on, "the pledge was the Catholic take on AA. He said it was like Holy Orders itself—you signed on and there was no going back. An unbreakable oath never to take another drink. Billy thought it was the real thing."

"But he broke it."

"There's plenty of priests that break their Holy Orders, too," Dan Lynch told them.

"Well, it got him over to Ireland, anyway," cousin Rosemary said. "I tried to talk him and Maeve into going over any number of times, but I never could do it."

"Maeve isn't one to travel," sister Rosemary said. "She's a homebody. Always has been."

Kate leaned toward us all, folding her hands on the table: a tasteful ring of diamonds, a gold bracelet, a professional manicure. "I often wondered," she said slowly. "I never had the heart to ask him, but I wondered if Billy went to visit the town Eva came from. While he was there."

Her sister shook her head. "Billy would have said so if he had. He wasn't one to keep things to himself."

Kate paused only a moment to consider this. "But he might not have wanted it to get back to Maeve, you know," she said. "He might have thought she wouldn't want to hear about a pilgrimage like that."

"Who would?"

"She knew about Eva?" Bridie said, whispering too, adding, "Thank you," as the waiter took her empty plate.

"I'm sure," Kate said. "Thank you." And then: "Actually, I don't know. I'd imagine she knew something about her."

"He must have told her something."

"Dennis would know," Mickey Quinn said. "They were always real close."

But Dan Lynch objected. "I was the best man at Billy's wedding," he said. "We were pretty close, too."

"Well, did he tell Maeve about the Irish girl?"

Dan waved his hand impatiently. "I'm sure he told her something. You know, it's not the sort of thing men talk about. And I'll say this for Billy, you never heard him mention that girl again, once he married Maeve."

"Ask Dennis," cousin Rosemary whispered.

The selected dessert was brought in: two scoops of vanilla ice cream in cold stainless-steel bowls. Hands in laps to make the poor man's job easier as he reached between their shoulders. Thank you.

"I remember watching Maeve come down the aisle," Dan Lynch said, lifting his spoon, holding it like a scepter. "She was on her old man's arm, but it was clear as you watched her that she was shoring him up, you know, keeping him straight. She was smiling as sweetly as any bride, but there was a determination in the way she walked, you know, the way she held her shoulder up against his, like it was a wall about to topple. She took hold of his arm when they got to the first pew, I mean a good grip, right here." He demonstrated, taking hold of his own forearm, spoon and all. "The old man banged his foot against the kneeling bench—you could hear it all over the church—and for a minute it looked like he'd go down headfirst. But she got him in there and got him seated. She maneuvered him. By sheer force of will, I'd say. And then she gave a little nod, as if to say, Well, that's done, and came up the steps to marry Billy." He sipped his beer. "Ready to take him on, is what I remember thinking. She was a plain girl, but determined."

"Very quiet," Mickey Quinn said. "Go over there for dinner and Billy would do most of the talking."

"He was lucky to find her," sister Rosemary said. "My mother always said there's nothing more pathetic than an old bachelor who's not a priest. That's what she thought Billy would be, after the Irish girl. An old bachelor. No offense, Danny."

And Dan Lynch laughed, blushed a little across his bald dome. Sipped his beer and shrugged. None taken—the story here being that Danny Lynch was such a connoisseur of beauty and behavior that no flawed wife could have pleased him and no flawless one could have been found.

"Did you ever meet her?" Bridie from the old neighborhood whispered. "The Irish girl?"

The two sisters exchanged a look across the table—the kind of look they might have exchanged had they been eyeing the last bite of a shared piece of cake. "She came to the apartment," Kate said, scooping it up. "It was just before she went back home. Billy borrowed Mr. Holtzman's car to go into the city to get her."

"She was very pretty," Rosemary added, taking a crumb. "Like Susan Hayward."

"Oh, I didn't think so," Kate said. "But she had nice hair, dark auburn. And big brown eyes. She wasn't very tall, even a little chubby. Billy brought her for Sunday dinner and then couldn't eat a bite himself. He was so— I don't know what—so delicate with her. The way he spoke to her, and watched her and listened to her. She did have a nice voice, you know, the poor girl" (a reminder to us all that she had died young), "with her brogue and all. My mother's brogue got thicker just listening to her. They were good-looking together, Eva and Billy. A handsome pair. Better looking together than singly, somehow. He was lovestruck, that's for sure. We kidded him when he got home, after he'd taken her back to the city. We put his plate out on the dining-room table when we heard him coming up. We'd saved it. He'd hardly eaten a bite. We said, 'What was wrong with your dinner, Billy?' " She began to laugh. "We said, 'How are you going to marry this poor girl if her mere presence takes your appetite away? Billy,' we said, 'she'll be at your dinner table every day, breakfast too, when are you going to eat? You'll starve. You'll waste away to nothing. You'll have to sneak over here just to calm down enough to have your dinner.' We gave him such a hard time."

"And do you remember what Momma said?" sister Rosemary asked. Kate swallowed her smile, looked blank. Professional makeup, too. "No."

Well pleased, Rosemary said to my end of the table, "You know my mother thought herself a kind of psychic."

She was getting her share of the story, after all. "She read cards and had dreams. And she said after Billy left that when she touched the girl's hand she felt four quick pulses in her own stomach, like baby kicks, which meant they'd have four children."

"Or that your mother had indigestion," Mickey Quinn said.

"More likely," Kate said. "You know how my mother cooked."

"She wasn't a much better prophet."

But Bridie shook her head. "I don't know," she said. "It might have been true. I mean, you could say if the girl had lived, that's how many children they might have had."

Dan Lynch said solemnly, "Which would have made this a different day."

"It would have been a different life," Bridie said.

Mickey Quinn shook his head and leaned back in his chair, as if to avoid all such speculation. "I'll have that cup of coffee now, please, when you get the chance," he said to the waiter's back.

"A different life," Dan Lynch repeated, and raised his beer.

The light through the window behind Maeve had begun to change now. A trace of shadow coming between the dark trunks of the trees, the clouds breaking up, perhaps.

"I don't agree with that," sister Rosemary said softly. "I've done a lot of reading in this regard, with Billy the way he was. Alcoholism isn't a decision, it's a disease, and Billy would have had the disease whether he married the

Irish girl or Maeve, whether he'd had kids or not. It wouldn't have been such a different life, believe me. Every alcoholic's life is pretty much the same."

"Now I don't agree," Dan Lynch said under his breath, and Kate added, "It's not always fatal."

"I say it's a matter of will," Dan Lynch said, speaking up, keeping Kate from running away with the talk once again. "I drank side by side with Billy Lynch for nearly forty years. My liver's fine. Billy never had the will to stop."

Sister Rosemary frowned, shaking her head. "That's not fair. When he went to Ireland, when he took the pledge, he was truly determined. He told me so. You know what faith Billy had. And you know how seriously he took that trip. He was truly determined that time. But the disease had him in its grip." She raised a fist, showing them.

Dan Lynch poured himself and Mickey Quinn another beer. "Well, let me tell you what he told me," he said. "Down at Quinlan's, maybe a year or two after the Irish girl died. He told me," he said, lifting his glass, pointing around it, "that every year was a weight on his shoulders. Every hour was, he said." He pointed to Kate. "Remember when you said he was like a man waiting for a bus, when he was waiting to get her back here? Well, when you said that I thought: It never changed. He was still waiting, years after she'd died. But he was waiting to go to her now. Ever since the night Dennis told him the news, he was waiting to die. I'm sure of it."

"But there was Maeve," Bridie from the neighborhood cried.

"That's not fair to Maeve," sister Rosemary said.

Dan Lynch shook his head. "I'm not saying a word against Maeve. She had a lot to handle, that's for sure. But if you ask me, Billy had a foot in the hereafter even before he met Maeve." He glanced up the table and then leaned forward, lowering his voice because the guests were beginning to thin out, Billy's friends and relatives getting up to have a few more words with Maeve, to go to the bathroom, or to get another drink before departing.

"We went to Mass together once. Feast of the Assumption. August 15. We'd both stopped into Quinlan's after work, a blazing hot day if there ever was one, hot as Hades, and both of us realized at the same time what the date was. We hightailed it over to 6:30 Mass at St. Sebastian's and, I don't know, I glanced at Billy, just after Communion. It struck me that it wasn't any thought of Our Lord or the Blessed Mother that put that look on his face. It was the girl. The Irish girl. When he turned his eyes to heaven, that's who he saw."

"Oh, nonsense," sister Rosemary whispered.

Mickey Quinn studied the ceiling. Down the table, a few heads turned, perhaps sensing a fight.

Dan Lynch took a sip of his beer, pursed his lips around the taste. "What's nonsense is all this disease business," he said. "Maybe for some people it's a disease. But maybe for some there are things that happen in their lives that they just can't live with. Things that take the sweetness out of everything. Maybe for some it's a sadness they can't get rid of or a disappointment that won't go away. And you know what I say to those people? I say good luck to those people." He raised his glass, raised his chin. "I say maybe they're not as smart and sensible and accepting as every one of us," indicating every one of us with a sweep of his beer, "but they're loyal. They're loyal to their own feelings. They're loyal to the first plans they made—just like Billy was loyal to Holtzman and the job he gave him. And like he would have been loyal to her if she had lived and come back here and they'd gotten married. Just like he was loyal to Maeve: Billy never breathed another word about that girl after he married Maeve. But the girl was first, and for Billy she would always be first. That's the kind of guy he was. Maeve couldn't change him."

"I think he went to her grave when he was in Ireland," Kate said suddenly. "I just have the feeling that sometime while he was over there he went to the town she was from and visited her grave. I think it was the whole reason he made the trip."

Rosemary shook her head, appealed to Mickey Quinn, who was intent on dissolving the sugar in his coffee. "He went with Father Ryan to take the pledge," she said patiently. "To make the retreat. To quit drinking."

But Kate said, "Oh, Rose, think about it. Ireland's not the only place that has retreats for alcoholics. He could have made one over here. Maybe he thought if he went to her grave he could put something to rest, finally. Put his feelings for her to rest so then he could quit drinking."

"But he couldn't," Dan Lynch said sadly, and poured another little beer.

"He couldn't," Kate agreed. "Which is why it didn't stick, as determined as he was."

But Rosemary's mouth was set. "No," she said firmly. "Look, there are faster and more pleasant ways of killing yourself. I tell you, I've read everything there is about this. Alcoholism is a disease, it's genetic. Our own father ruined his liver as well and probably would have died the same way if he hadn't gotten cancer. And Uncle John in Philadelphia was an alcoholic. And two of his sons—Chuck and Peter—go to AA. And Ted. And Mary Casey and Helen Lynch. And Dennis's father was no teetotaler either."

"Uncle Daniel died of cancer," Dan Lynch said indignantly. "He was no drunk." He turned to Bridie and Mickey Quinn. "He brought his six brothers and a sister over here and God knows how many other friends and relations. All on a motorman's salary."

"He was a saint," Bridie from the neighborhood said, nodding. "My mother always said so."

"Okay," Rosemary said. "God bless Uncle Daniel, but my point is that our family has what they call a genetic predisposition to both cancer and alcoholism. Billy had it in his genes."

"When he came back from Ireland," Kate said softly, stroking the stem of her glass. "June of '75—I remember because my Daniel had just graduated from Fordham— he went straight out to Long Island. Out to the little house. Dennis was there, it wasn't long after he'd lost Claire. Remember how he used to rent the place back from his mother's tenant so he could spend his vacation? Well, Billy wasn't home for more than a day when he took the train out—and he hadn't been there in years."

"Meaning?" Rosemary asked coolly.

"Meaning he went back to the place he first met her. Eva. He was trying to work something out."

"Oh, honestly," Rosemary said. "It had been nearly

thirty years. What was there to work out? It was a shame that she died, but Billy had had thirty years of living since then. I mean, come on, name me anything that's going to stay with you that strongly for thirty years."

Which seemed to silence our end of the table for a moment, as if the thing we would mention had only momentarily slipped our minds.

Cousin Rosemary poked her swizzle stick into the remaining ice in her glass. "It's all water under the bridge," she said, as if water from under the bridge was the very thing the tall glass contained. "What's the point of even discussing all this now? Billy was here and now he's gone, and I for one just can't believe it. Despite his troubles." Tears now. "I'll miss him. I'll miss his voice over the phone. I'll miss his smiling face."

"Hear, hear," Mickey Quinn said.

But Dan Lynch raised his beer again. He was whispering, his voice fierce. "I just don't think it credits a man's life to say he was in the clutches of a disease and that's what ruined him. Say he was too loyal. Say he was disappointed. Say he made way too much of the Irish girl and afterwards couldn't look life square in the face. But give him some credit for feeling, for having a hand in his own fate. Don't say it was a disease that blindsided him and wiped out everything he was." He bit off a drink, his face flushed. "Do the man that favor, please."

The clouds were indeed breaking up and a feeble bit of sunshine was striking Maeve's hair—you couldn't say lighting it up, but striking it and revealing it for what it was: a dull brown getting coarser with gray, and yet showing what it was so clearly that you could see a kind of

appeal in it. Maybe it was just the honesty of it. A kind
of beauty that was not a transformation of her simple features but an assertion of them, an insistence that they
were no more than what they appeared.

My father stood beside her, his napkin in one hand,
reaching behind her to say goodbye to another cousin, Ted
from Flushing, who went to AA in order to die of cancer,
not cirrhosis. Ted's little wife was right behind him, one
hand on his back.

In the next half hour, my father would pay the bill and
distribute the tips and take Maeve's arm when she walked
out to the limousine that would carry her home to Bayside.
He would promise to stop in to see her later in the evening, just to make sure she was all right. He would shake
hands with everyone, thanking them for coming, agreeing
it was unbelievable, unbelievable still. In our car, crossing
the bridge, he would listen with a slight smile when I told
him about the debate that had gone on at our end of the
table.

"Well, here's the saddest part," he would say, finally,
wearily, as if he were speaking of an old annoyance that
time had nearly trivialized, but not quite: "Here's the
most pathetic part of all. Eva never died. It was a lie. Just
between the two of us, Eva lived."

TELLING THE STORY, my father easily slipped from
past to present: Billy was, Billy is, Billy drank,
Billy drinks. Billy sets his heart on something.

In the front seat of Mr. Holtzman's car, on Seventieth
Street, just off Park Avenue, my father watched Mary,
Eva's sister, worry a small handkerchief, Irish linen (naturally), embroidered in one corner with three small shamrocks. Emblematic, sure, now, looking back, but in truth
the children, her charges, had sewn it for her. She had
shown them how to make the stitches. They had made
one for their mother and their aunt. And one for her.

Her fingernails were round and white and always made
him think that she had just come from giving all seven of
them their baths, as she probably had. It was late September, late afternoon. The light the same that hung over the
city now as we crossed the bridge into Queens.

"They're shamrocks," she said, showing him because he had asked her. She spread out the damp fabric. Her skirt was good wool, her sweater cashmere, hand-me-downs from her employer. "The children made it for me. I showed them the stitch. They made one for their mother and one for her sister up in Riverdale. And then they made one for me. Shamrocks."

"I know what they are," he said. And then added, "God, you're a silly woman."

The look on her face told him she was anything but. "Don't kill the messenger," she whispered.

It was Mr. Holtzman's car, an old humpbacked Ford: the wide cloth front seat, the old rationing sticker in the corner of the windshield that asked, Is this trip necessary? Something of the smell of the man's hair pomade on the back of the seat and the fabric around the window.

She said, "What will you tell him?" and if you're looking to blame someone for the lie, then you could as well blame her for putting it just that way: What will you tell him? As if there were options to choose from.

"I'd like to tell him she's dead," he said.

"She's dead to me."

This was Irish hyperbole, of course. This was the Irish penchant for pursuing any mention of death, any metaphor, any threat, the way a seal goes after a tossed mackerel. Because he'd had no real intention then. No plan. This was just talk.

"I knew about Tom," she said, the hometown boy Eva had married. "But I knew she liked Billy, too. She always said how sweet he was. She always talked about his great letters. I never would have believed she'd steal his money." To make a down payment, she had said, on a gas station on the convent road outside Clonmel.

He leaned across her lap, across the good wool skirt, the soft cashmere, the still-lovely dregs of her employer's bottle of Chanel—and pulled at the bone-white handle of the car door. The handkerchief was in her hand, balled in her fist again. The tears starting again.

"I wish she had died," Mary said. "It would have been better." It was the Irish penchant for the word, sure, but also the fact that she was young enough to think that such talk proved her feelings were profound. "She's as good as dead to me now."

Leaning, he pushed the car door open with his fingertips. He still had one hand on the steering wheel. She put her hand on his arm, the linen handkerchief between them. "Will you call me?" she said.

He said he would. He kissed her. And then leaned to push the door open again, all the way now, so that it swung out over the sidewalk. So that there was nothing else for her to do but to get out, unassisted, and to walk with her head bent and her handkerchief to her eye, unescorted, back to the building's service door, where she'd been waiting for him just half an hour before.

Such rudeness meant something in those days. It's all ignorance now, but then it was intentional and it meant something to both of them. It meant the end of the thing.

EVEN CLIMBING THE STAIRS to Billy's apartment that evening, he had no real plan. He only knew he didn't want to deliver the blow with Billy's two sisters and their husbands and Aunt Ellen, his mother, around. Imagine the night: your life's plans blasted, the baby crying in the next room, your sister and her young husband stirring in their bed, your widowed mother tapping at your bedroom door hour after hour saying, "Are you all right? Would you like a cup of tea?" Saying from behind the closed door, "Billy, there'll be plenty of other girls, believe me."

When Dennis had left Mary in the city that evening, he first went home to Jamaica, where earlier in the day Holtzman had wondered out loud if the little Long Island house had done all right in last night's storm. He'd grabbed his Dopp kit and a suit, a pressed shirt and a tie, and then told Holtzman he would drive out there tonight, just to see how the little house had fared.

Surprised, Holtzman licked his lips and ran a hand down his belly. He was a jowly German with slick hair and earlobes that could have held an entire thumbprint. *My mother's husband.*

"That's awfully kind of you, Dennis," Holtzman said slowly, full of hesitation. Wondering, no doubt, if there was a girl involved here, perhaps the very same girl who had called the house that afternoon. Wondering, no doubt, about the miles driven and the wear and tear on the machine and how many more years of accommodating her grown son would have to go into this marriage.

Dennis's mother was on the other side of the living room, going through the Sunday papers, smoking. She paused to watch the two of them.

"I'll take Billy along," Dennis said—no doubt killing the light in the projector that showed Holtzman some

pretty young blonde stark naked against the brown up-
holstery of his car. There would be no such nonsense if
Billy went along.

"Billy always loves a ride out there."

And Billy, opening the apartment door, grinned to see
Dennis. There was a fountain pen in his hand, he was just
getting off a note. He wore the trousers and the white
shirt he had worn to Mass that morning. A drive sounded
great, come in, come in. His sister Kate on the living-room
couch with the baby, whispering that her husband had the
bedroom, he was studying. Rosie and Mac, her husband,
out to the movies because Kate's husband (shhh) was
studying. Billy's mother coming from the kitchen with a
book in her hands, whispering hello, reminding them to
keep it low because poor Peter was in there studying.

The lie—still the only lie he'd intended to tell that evening—forming itself nicely around its little grain of truth:
the storm last night. Mr. Holtzman, he said, had asked if the
two of them would take the time to drive out there tonight
to check on the place. They could spend the night and
drive back in the morning, go straight to the office.

At the curb, they turned to see Billy's mother running
down the stairs and into the vestibule with a brown paper
sack full of rolls and butter and slices of the overcooked
Sunday ham. What will you eat in the morning, way out
there?

Dennis put the bag on the floor of the back seat, next
to the bottle of vermouth and the bottle of rye he'd borrowed from Holtzman's cabinet. They both got in, the
green light of the dashboard catching Billy's glasses.

His mother's vision of eastern Long Island, Billy said, was of wild black ducks and desolate potato fields and a mad, foaming sea. She'd never understand what he saw in it.

"Maybe she has a point," Dennis said.

He set landmarks for himself, places at which he would begin: once they reached the Jericho Turnpike, the Sunrise Highway, once they crossed into Suffolk. "I saw Mary today," he would say. "She had a letter from Eva. She got married, Bill, last month. To a boy she'd known since she was a child. She's spent your money. Put it into a gas station, if you can imagine. Probably hocked the shoes you sent her. Probably hocked your ring. It's a damnable thing, Billy, a damnable thing."

But his courage failed him. His thoughts, to be frank, going more and more to the other people he would have to tell once he'd given Billy the news. His mother first and foremost, who would say, What a shame, with that light in her eyes that would say, as well, I knew it all along. Who would then ask about Holtzman's money.

There was Holtzman. The man had already composed a long list of things that he believed Dennis and Billy and most of their generation were incapable of doing: running a business, making a fortune, shaking free of the lesson they'd learned in the service that having someone take care of you was equal to taking care of yourself. Creating a future.

Writing the check he had given to Dennis to give to Billy to send to Eva so she could come back before the summer was over, Holtzman had said, "You boys will never have any money if you spend everything before it's earned."

"This is an advance, sir," Dennis had told him. "Billy will earn it back in no time at the store."

Holtzman had looked wise, a maddening look in a man so dull. "But first he'll spend it," he had said.

Holtzman would have to be told.

And the fellows in the office. All of them knew about Eva, Billy hardly able to go twenty minutes without working around to saying her name. The girls in the office, too, many of whom (your mother included) had once had an eye for him. Many of whom, no doubt, would find the story of Eva's betrayal slowly changing the way they saw him: if she preferred Tom, might not I?

(His mother telling him through his closed bedroom door, "Billy, there will be plenty of other girls.")

The rest of the family would have to hear about it, and Billy would have to endure for some months, maybe years, both their sympathy and their studied silence whenever the subject of love and marriage arose. The neighborhood would have to know, too. Including Bridie, whom Billy was talking about now as they passed through Speonk— another point at which he had promised himself he would begin.

Bridie, it seemed, was engaged at last, to be married to a fellow named Jim Fox, from Staten Island, around Christmas. Which would make . . . Billy counted out loud, naming each couple off . . . the seventeenth wedding he'd been to this year.

"Everyone always thought she was holding out for you," Dennis said.

But Billy shook his head. Kate said Bridie would have married Tim Schmidt if he'd lived. They'd had an understanding, Kate said. Kate herself had sat up all night with Bridie the day the news came that he'd been killed. In Italy, in the winter of '43. Kate's own husband in the same division and unheard from for six weeks or more. Wasn't it easy to forget sometimes what the war had been like for the people at home? You know, Mike Breen was in the Battle of the Bulge as well. Saw him at Quinlan's. He had a hell of a war . . .

The night grew deeper and the headlights showed just the one dark stretch of road that carried them toward that mad sea. Better she had drowned in it, Dennis thought. Better the women gather around Billy in real mourning, sit up with him all night if they liked, moaning about fate and loss and the inevitability of death, than have them turn their gummy sympathy, their studied silence on him every time there's a mention of love and marriage. A gas station on the convent road. Better he be brokenhearted than trailed all the rest of his life by a sense of his own foolishness.

He told him the lie in the rutted, rain-filled driveway of the little Long Island house. The headlights showed only a single branch, its leaves already touched with color, that had fallen across the side yard. (He was surprised to see it, as if he had made up the fact of last night's storm as well as Holtzman's request that they come out here to check its effect, as if, were he to touch it, he would discover it was made of paper and paste.) Everything else around them was in utter darkness. Billy had just gotten the flashlight from the glove compartment. It was the roof he was most concerned about, he said. Considering all the ceiling plaster he'd slapped around last summer, the last thing he wanted to see was that it had all ended up on the floor.

"I saw Mary today," Dennis began. "She had a letter from home. About Eva." The details came easily enough, without much planning. Pneumonia, he said, the country being as damp as the relatives always said it was. She'd been sick for weeks, he added, which would explain why she hadn't written him for so long.

Billy sat for a moment, stunned, and then pulled his glasses off from around his ears and touched thumb and forefinger to the bridge of his nose. And then he blessed himself and cursed and said quietly that it was a damnable place, a piss-poor primitive country. He asked if they had at least gotten her to a hospital.

"I don't know," Dennis said, meaning, of course, that he hadn't thought the story through that far. He was stunned himself, at the audacity of what he had done, was doing. The breadth and depth of the lie he was telling, the world he was creating that even now he saw he would not be able to sustain. There would be a tremendous number of details, a tremendous number of opportunities for mistakes, misjudgment, for a sense of falsehood, inaccuracy, to creep in and bring the whole thing down. Billy would get a letter from her (let's hope with a check inside), or he'd run into Mary on the street, or Mary's employer, or he'd rush over to Ireland to throw himself on her grave, or she'd come back here with her husband and feel compelled to give him a call, to apologize. It was an audacious, outlandish thing he was doing, and he knew the workaday world, the world without illusion (except Church-sanctioned) or nonsense (except alcohol-bred) that was the world of Irish Catholic Queens New York, didn't much abide audacious and outlandish. Not for long, anyway.

He took the flashlight, told Billy he'd give him a few minutes alone. He reached into the back for the food and the drinks and made his way across the muddy path to the little house.

All was intact, no water stains that he could see, no inordinate dampness. No mildew yet, which might or might not be because of the lumps of charcoal his mother had scattered along the baseboards when they'd closed the place up after Labor Day. Just three weeks ago now. When they were still saying Billy and Eva would be back before winter for their honeymoon.

He mixed a pitcher of drinks, made some sandwiches with the stringy slices of ham. At one point he heard the car door slam, but it was some minutes before he heard Billy's footsteps on the path. He didn't come in. He sat on the front steps as they had done nearly every night when they were first back from the war. The light from the living room shone through the screen and onto Billy's white shirt.

Dennis carried the drinks outside then, the plate of sandwiches balanced on top of one of them. He pushed the screen door open with his foot and Billy moved a little to make room for him. Billy took the drink. Dennis put the plate of sandwiches on the steps between them.

He asked Dennis to repeat the details, the letter, the pneumonia, the length of her illness—which Billy himself said would explain why he hadn't had a letter from her all summer.

"Her parents would have written to you themselves," Dennis added, looking into the darkness of the yard and the road, covering his tracks, "but they thought it would be better if they told Mary first and Mary thought it best that I tell you. She'll be going back over herself now, I suppose."

"You'll miss her," Billy whispered, and Dennis shook his head. Nothing he could say in that regard struck him as authentic.

He put his hand to the back of Billy's neck at one point. Refilled both their glasses more than once. Later, he led him into the house and put him to bed.

It was the next morning, on their way back to the city, when Billy said he couldn't understand how Dennis had managed to keep from telling him the news the whole time he was at their apartment the night before, the whole way out to Long Island. How he'd managed to drive and chat, to keep from telling him until they had reached the place. He didn't say he admired or even appreciated Dennis's restraint. He simply said he couldn't understand how he'd managed.

We were in our own driveway by now, and again my father was smiling, shaking his head at that old annoyance. He said it was a very long time ago. They'd been younger than he was now capable of remembering them.

"Did he ever find out?" I asked him. "That you lied about it?"

He nodded. "In 1975," he said. "When he was over there. He met her again. Had a cup of tea with her in the little shop she'd added to the gas station. I guess it had turned into quite a successful operation. She had four kids, too. All grown by then. He said she was still good-looking."

"Did she pay him back?"

"I guess she offered to. More out of embarrassment than anything else. Of course, he wouldn't take it."

"Was he mad, when he found out?"

"At her? Never."

"At you."

He considered this. "On the one hand," he said, "she was back from the dead. There was that. On the other, he'd lived thirty years with a mistaken belief. With that grief. But no, he wasn't angry. He ended up kidding me about it almost. We realized that it had all happened a long time ago."

He pulled open the door.

"Do you wish you'd told him the truth?" I asked.

"Yes," he said, without hesitation. "I suppose." He smiled again. "It's a bad business. A lie like that." And then he was climbing out of the car, the thin gray cloth of his suit jacket buckling between his shoulders. We went in the side door, into the kitchen. Our coffee cups and juice glasses were still in the sink. He'd left the radio on; it had become a habit, I think. I followed him through the kitchen into the dining room, where he stood before the mirror over the sideboard, pulling off his tie, raising his chin to unbutton his collar.

"Did you ever tell Mom?" I asked.

"I never told anyone," he said. "And Billy never told anyone, either, as far as I know. That was his choice, I thought. When I went down to the VA Tuesday morning, though, I was glad it had come out, back in '75. I was glad he didn't go through his whole life deceived about it. Didn't die thinking about some lovely reunion in the sweet hereafter."

"You think he would have? That's what Dan Lynch was saying, that he was waiting all his life to meet her in heaven."

Working with two hands, my father pulled off his tie, unknotted it, folded it in thirds, and placed it on the lace doily that covered the sideboard. "That's Danny Lynch for you" was all he said. He turned, leaned his two palms behind him, on the edge of the server. He spoke as if providing an antidote to Dan Lynch's utter nonsense. "I shouldn't have done it, I suppose. I should have told him the truth. He would have gotten over it and met Maeve anyway. He would have found something else to moon about when he drank. Rosie was right, an alcoholic can always find a reason but never needs one. I thought I was preserving his innocence, I guess. But I should have re-membered that when Billy sets his heart on something there's no changing him. He's loyal. He's got this faith— which is probably why he drinks. The problem is, it's hard to be a liar and a believer yourself, at the same time. I didn't see it until your mother died, and it gave me some trouble then. I don't know if you remember."

I lowered my head. I remembered. And my father pushed himself away from the server, where he'd been leaning. Too much said. He headed upstairs to change. I went to the kitchen to stand there for a minute looking for something to do. I put the kettle on—a genetic trait. When I called up to him, he said he'd just have a piece of toast or something before he went over to Maeve's.

THE LONG ISLAND HOUSE was my father's inheritance from a mother who, in a recapitulation that must have left even the heavenly host momentarily voiceless, decided during the closing days of her life to make an end run at heaven. It was not that she had been a bad woman until then. She had simply been indifferent, to her two husbands and her son, to her grandchildren, to most of the simple and complex joys of the life she had been given.

The house became hers during her second marriage, and according to my father, the only pleasure she ever got from it was her ability to withhold invitations to visit. The house itself was a modest affair, updated by my father and Billy right after the war, and except for an occasional dusting, an occasional coat of paint, hardly touched again until the early eighties. It had a single room divided into a living room and kitchen, with three tiny bedrooms stuck like postage stamps along the side. The small plot of land it sat on was mostly scrub, but there was a bay beach within walking distance and, especially at night, the tang of sea salt in the air, and for my grandmother's friends and family from Brooklyn and Queens it was a toehold in a world of spacious lawns and famous artists and summer colonies where wealthy people had once called their mansions *cottages*—of days at the shore that did not involve changing trains for Seagirt or waiting in line for two hours at the Jones Beach tolls.

The man she had inherited it from, Holtzman, her second husband, had bought it during the Depression from another city dweller down on his luck and then with money problems of his own had all but abandoned it for nearly a decade. Toward the end of that decade, a petite redhead somewhere in her late forties began to visit his store on Jamaica Avenue, looking for size fours. With her tiny heel resting in the palm of his hand, he learned she was a widow with a son overseas. He took her phone number in order to call her when something new in her size came in. He took her to lunch, allowing her to leave her box of shoes behind the counter while his assistant ran the store. He gave her some stockings, and a handbag. He took her to dinner and, driving past the house in Jamaica that had been his childhood home, had said that he also owned another place, a little bungalow out on Long Island.

She mentioned the house in a letter that reached my father while he was overseas. A regular laundry list, he said, of reasons why she should remarry. The house on Long Island was right up there near the top.

He said there wasn't anything at all about love.

She was, according to my father, the most unsentimental woman he had ever known or even heard of. He blamed this mostly on her childhood. The only child of Scottish immigrants with delusions of grandeur, she had been raised in genteel poverty, given ballet and riding lessons, lessons in deportment and French and violin, until tuberculosis made her an orphan at twelve. She spent the next six years being passed from one already-overburdened relative to another and at eighteen had married a forty-four-year-old streetcar conductor so full of blarney (as my father told it) and wild verse, of Tennyson and the Bard and Gilbert and Sullivan, that he'd had to import every brother and sister, cousin uncle niece and nephew from the other side simply to have enough ears in which to deposit it all. Which made him Holy Father to a tenement's worth of Irish immigrants but kept his wife and son mostly impoverished and never—what with one wetback mick after another being reeled in from the other side and slapped down on their couch—alone in their own home.

My mother might have been different, my father was fond of saying, if her life had been different (I was a teenager before I began to point out that this was true of us all), and I think that throughout his own life my father harbored in his heart a vision of his mother as a happy and pampered child whose bright eyes saw only the purest intentions.

As it was, as he knew her and as I knew her, she was a Geiger counter for insincerity, phoniness, half-truths. She could dismantle a pose with a glance and deflate the most romantic notion with a single word. She had no patience for poetry, Broadway musicals, presidential politics, or the pomp of her religion—although my father, his father's son, loved these things in direct proportion to her disdain—and she sought truth so single-mindedly that under her steady gaze exaggeration, self-delusion, bravado simply dried up and blew away, as did hope, nonsense, and any ungrounded giddiness.

Her philosophy of life seemed to be to get to the bottom of things, the plain, unadorned, mostly concrete and colorless bottom of things, and from there to seek to swat away any passing fancy that might cloud the hard-won clarity of her vision. Because she was also intelligent and witty, and because all her cynicism was bolstered by a keen logic, she gained in her later years a reputation as a sage, but one whose advice friends and family would seek only at the tail end of some experience when they were ready to be either reconciled to their disappointment or disabused of any vestige of hope for some unexpected change.

When Holtzman died in 1964, she found a year-round tenant for the Long Island place, because it was at the time the economically sensible thing to do. (Swatting away any sweet recollection of summer weekends spent there with her husband and her young grandchildren since—swat—the one was dead and the others growing so quickly that such weekends wouldn't be continuing much longer anyway, and if they were to continue, at the expense of the steady income a year-round tenant could provide, they would really be more of the same, wouldn't they?—days at the beach and cookouts on the back-yard grill, taking strolls through the village, marshmallows to the campfire, bread heels to the duck pond, and really, when you got to the bottom of it, how many memories of pleasant summer days on Long Island does one person need? Isn't enough as good as a feast?)

Eventually, all mention of the house seemed to disappear and my parents began to suspect that she had quietly sold the place to her year-round tenant and found some far more practical and profitable way to store the money that had been tied up in it for so long. We had begun to spend our vacations in the Adirondacks by then, had even stopped reassuring ourselves that the mountains were far preferable to the shore. Children of a certain age are pleased to encounter nostalgia, I think, and the summer days we had spent with my father's mother in the Long Island house moved easily into our family's short but expanding list of things we used to do but did no more.

And so it was with some amazement that I learned on the afternoon of her funeral in 1971 that she had left the Long Island house to my father. My mother told me the news as we left the restaurant where her funeral luncheon had been held. I remember the greedy triumph I'd felt: a house, a piece of land, all unexpected and unsought and, most satisfying of all, unearned—the greedy and self-satisfied triumph of a lazy heir.

But my mother's triumph was that the inheritance was part of a package of changes my grandmother had made to her estate in the weeks before she died, a part of her deathbed conversion. The Long Island house, it turned out, was the only thing my father was getting. The rest of my grandmother's money, which was really Holtzman's money, was to go to the Church she had had, until then, no use for, to a number of charities whose mailings and TV solicitations she had always held up as proof positive of their misappropriation of funds, and even to her mixed-race former neighbors in Jamaica who took in foster children—for profit, she had always claimed. My mother was Catholic enough to be grinning as she told me all this, as if the satisfaction she felt in learning that my grandmother did, indeed, fear God was well worth the substantial sum of money that she had just described away. Money that otherwise would have been our family's alone.

My brothers and I saw it differently, of course. We saw our college tuitions dispersed. We saw her surprising change of heart not so much as a deathbed conversion but as a final-hour placing of bets, a closing-time rush (as my oldest brother, the philosophy major, put it) to get a piece of the action in Pascal's wager. A woman as clear-sighted as my grandmother would not go to meet her maker empty-handed, sure. But, we were certain, a woman as clear-sighted as my grandmother would know, too, that what she was going to meet might just as well be the void of a spent body and a finished mind. She was merely covering her options.

My father claimed it was an indication of the soft, even romantic heart she had carried and hidden all along. In support of this, he described how in those last days, after she had made her sweet intentions known, she had also said one morning when the hospital chaplain left her room, "Don't they send them to hospitals because there's something queer in their pasts?" Still her ornery self. But she had added, too, when she told him he was to have the Long Island house, "Get Billy to visit you there. He's avoided the place for too long."

I knew that in life she had pretty much ignored Billy, although with no more passion or purposefulness than she had displayed in ignoring us all, and so, by way of explanation, my father told me, perhaps for the first time and in a much abbreviated form, the tale of Billy's brief romance, and engagement, to a girl he'd met out there, right after the war. A girl who died of pneumonia before they could marry.

Billy was for me then merely one of my father's legion of cousins, distinguished not so much by his alcoholism (it had seemed to me that there were more alcoholics among them than there were Republicans, or even redheads) as by his wife, Maeve, who without many relations of her own relied so heavily on my father whenever Billy was giving her trouble. I suppose I made some connection, or that as my father told the story there was some connection implied, between that ancient disappointment and Billy's current need to drink, but as I said, that side of his family was full enough of alcoholics who had as far as anyone could tell married the girls of their dreams to make such a connection compelling.

"You think he's been avoiding the place?" he'd said to his mother, more intrigued by the fact of this kind of conversation, at this late date, than by any observation she might make about Billy.

"I think you know he has," she said. "And I'm sure you know why."

"Revenge," my father told us now. "Stubbornness."

So he could say, whenever he was asked out there or whenever someone else had come, "I won't go back myself," and wordlessly remind them all of what he had suffered, found and lost, all those years ago. He never had to say the girl's name. He merely had to hold up a hand when he was invited and whisper a gracious No, no, in order to remind them all.

"Get Billy to go out there again," my father's mother said. "Make him bring his wife."

"My mother understood," he said, proving further that she had not been all she had seemed, that her cool exterior had hidden all along a warm heart. "She had Billy on her mind. Billy and Maeve, and that summer he'd spent out at the Long Island house, all those years ago. My mother had thought about him without ever seeming to. She'd thought about any number of things we never knew."

Of course, what he did not say then was that she, too, had been deceived. That despite her lifelong disdain for delusion and romance and teary-eyed reminiscence, she had ended her life recalling Billy's summer idyll on Long Island and his pretty (or so the story went), much-loved girl who had died; she had sought a remedy for him, even as she went about securing her own soul.

BILLY DID RETURN to the Long Island house, in the summer of 1975. It was early July and my father and I met him at the train station in East Hampton. I was on a break between summer semesters at college. Having, perhaps, inherited my grandmother's distaste for too much of a good thing, I had decided to get through college in the shortest time possible and had taken courses during every summer and winter break. I was due to finish that December, a year and a half ahead of time.

Since my grandmother's death, my father had spent two weeks every summer at the Long Island house and then rented it back to Mr. West, the man he still referred to as "my mother's tenant," for the rest of the year. The understanding was that when my father was ready to retire in another eight or ten years, he would sell our house in Rosedale and move here permanently. The joke was that Mr. West would then return to his wife and three sons, whom he had deserted a dozen years before.

My own mother had died of lung cancer in the spring of '73. The solitary life my father now led could still, at times, strike my heart (my arms, my shoulders, the pit of my stomach) with an unbearable weight, but each time we were together I saw, too, that the life suited him well enough. He had always had a tremendous capacity for accommodation and contentment, whether alone with a newspaper or at a dinner table filled with friends and family. I suppose his mother had taught him not to expect much from life and so it was easy enough for him to see each day as an endless parade of unexpected pleasures. She said it as a caution against excess, but my father said it with a kind of amazed gratitude: enough *was* as good as a feast.

I suppose there's not much sense in trying to measure the breadth and depth of your own parents' romance, the course and tenacity of their love. Your parents' or anybody else's, for that matter. I know an older couple who have so convinced their grown children of the charm and endurance of their passionate history—married young and poor, separated by war, reunited to become dedicated and hardworking young parents, loving partners in the building of a business, patient guardians of teenagers, payers of tuition, and finally (looking proudly into each other's eyes) grateful, rich, and still passionate retirees and grandparents—that their children have had nothing but disappointment and grief in their own love lives and now, in middle age, look at their aging and still smug progenitors with envy and despair.

My parents, I have to believe, had a marriage that ran the typical course from early infatuation to serious love to affection occasionally diminished by impatience and disagreement, bolstered by interdependence, fanned now and then by fondness, by humor. That they loved each other is a given, I suppose, although I suppose, too, that there were months, maybe years, when their love for one another might have disappeared altogether and their lives proceeded only out of habit or the failure to imagine any other alternative.

A good-enough, a typical kind of mid-twentieth-century marriage that suddenly blossomed into something else in the year she was dying. I hesitate to use the word about a time that was filled with so much pain, that was for me only awful, but I think it was during my mother's illness that my parents became passionate about one another. Their meeting, their courtship, their years raising children, every ordinary day they had spent together until then all became merely the running start they had taken to vault this moment. To sail, gracefully and in tandem, across the abyss.

It made it easier that they both believed in the simplest kind of afterlife—that my father could say to her, even in those last days, joking but without irony, "You're going to get tired of hearing from me. I'll be asking you for this that and the other thing twenty-four hours a day. *Jesus*, you'll be saying, here comes another prayer from Dennis." And my mother would reply, her voice hoarse with pain, "Jesus might advise you to take in a movie once in a while. Give your poor wife a rest. She's in heaven, after all."

It was a joke, but they believed it, and they believed, too, I think, that their love, their loyalty to one another, was no longer a matter of chance or happenstance but a condition of their existence no more voluntary or escapable than the pace of their blood, the influx of perception. There was, I thought, a perverse joy about their closeness in that year, as my father, for the first and only time in his life, turned his back on the scores of friends and relatives who had come to depend on him as they had once depended on his father and thought only of her. (Refusing even Billy's calls. Putting a pillow over the phone in our upstairs hallway before he went to bed and telling me to ignore the thing should I hear it ringing in the middle of the night.) There was, in their anticipation of what was to come, a queer self-satisfaction. It was clear now that they would love each other until the last moment of her life— hadn't that been the goal from the beginning? They would love each other even beyond the days they had lived together; was there any greater triumph?

At eighteen, I was not so sure. At eighteen, I wanted only a mother who would be there in the flesh to see me graduate and get married and have children of my own. Who could keep my father from living the rest of his life alone, nagging his dead wife with a thousand daily prayers.

ON THE MORNING BILLY ARRIVED, my father and I had our usual breakfast on the front-porch steps. We were careful in those days to do everything in a usual way. It was different when I visited him at home, when he had his job to go to and I had my room and my friends, enough vestiges, for both of us, of our lives as they were before my mother died to help us through an hour or two without missing her. But out on Long Island our being alone together served first and foremost to remind us of her absence and we clung to routine (or I clung to what I was certain was my father's routine when I was gone) as if it had been prescribed.

Every morning he would wake at seven and do Army-issue calisthenics either in his room or out on the back porch. He would shower and dress and then go to the kitchen to get breakfast. I would get up when I heard him put the kettle on. By the time I was showered and dressed, the cereal would be poured and the juice squeezed and the tray ready to be taken outside, where we would sit on the front steps if the weather was fine so I could dry my hair in the sun.

The property was not much, but at that time of the year the weeds and brambles that edged the front lawn were full of Queen Anne's lace and black-eyed Susans and the honeysuckle along the side yard was lush. Across our mostly untraveled street there was a vacant field, also a tangle of weeds and wildflowers, that held at its center the crumbling cinder-block foundation for a house that was never built. Beyond that, there were some trees, the bay, the blue sky.

The grass at my feet was as green as it would get and the sandy soil was already warmed by the sun. I leaned back against the step, resisted flicking off the piece of cracked green paint at my elbow (my father was on the step above me, watching). I tilted my head back to catch the sun on my face, recognizing as I did the perpetual hope of a sun-shot transformation that certain young men might notice when I returned to school next week—the tan, the sun-streaked hair, the slimming effects of a daily swim . . .

When I opened my eyes again it was to the sound of a car pulling into our gravel driveway. It pulled in only far enough to get its rear bumper out of the road, and even the way its engine died and the driver's door opened seemed tentative. Slowly, Mr. West climbed out and walked toward us, looking all the while like a man on the verge of retreat. He was lanky, older than my father, I thought, but muscular and well tanned. He carried a cigarette cupped in his palm and held close to his thigh, and this made him seem even more furtive and cautious as he approached. I had met him only two or three times since my childhood, once down at Montauk, where he kept his boat, once on the street in Amagansett, although the matchbooks and magazines and mementos he'd left in the house each year made me feel I knew him better. He was, as my father liked to say, a Bonacker, a real Bonacker; a colloquialism that for my father meant Mr. West was a hick.

My father called good morning even before Mr. West had quite reached us, and when he touched his dark captain's hat and apologized for interrupting our breakfast, my father cried, "Not at all, not at all," jovial, friendly, sitting on the top step with his cereal bowl and spoon like Old King Cole. "What can I do for you?"

Mr. West pointed to the back of the property, to the clapboard garage where each year he stored his spare clothes and personal things for the two weeks of my father's vacation. "There are a few odds and ends I need to get at," he said politely. "If you don't mind." And my father waved his spoon. "No, no, no, of course not, go right ahead. No need to ask. Have you got your key?"

Mr. West nodded, holding up a ring of them in the palm of his hand.

"Then go right ahead. Take your time." Ever the benevolent landlord.

But as Mr. West crossed the side yard and unlocked and opened the wide door and began to rummage through his things (we heard him whistling, mumbling to himself), my father sat stiffly, uneasily, without sipping his tea or finishing his cereal or saying a word, more tenant himself than landed gentry. The house and property still more his mother's tenant's than our own.

And then a sudden blast of music came from the car at the end of the driveway, a sudden zipping riff of talk and static, violin, rock. Both my father and I looked over, but I know I saw him first, through the sunlight and shadow that played across the windshield: a boy in the front passenger seat, leaning to adjust the radio. As he sat up again, he put his arm out through the open window to tap the car's roof. But then he stopped and suddenly raised his hand, the fingers spread, a dark band, braided leather, slipping down his wrist, in a gesture that seemed first and foremost to say: No harm. I raised my hand in the same way.

And there it was: our greeting. Our own children, in that first eternity, must have pricked up their ears.

"One of his boys," my father said. Cody or John or Matt, I knew from the names penciled on the back of the pantry door. Matt the tallest in 1967. "He's staying with his wife."

It was my father's belief that Mr. West would not have left his wife and three sons in 1964 if on the day he stormed out of their house in Amagansett my grandmother had not been there offering a furnished rental at a year-round, reasonable rate. What he would have done, what he should have done, my father claimed, was to storm out of his house, drive to the IGA, pick up a six-pack, drink it on his boat, which was then in dry dock in Three Mile Harbor, fall asleep, and then crawl home the next morning, hungover and remorseful and chilled to the bone. But what changed this scenario, changed forever the lives of Mr. and Mrs. West and their three children, was the index card on which my grandmother had written *Year-round rental, reasonable, furnished,* and stuck to the bulletin board just inside the entrance to the store, the index card that Mr. West had grabbed on his way out, six-pack under his arm, setting the thumbtacks flying.

Whatever guilt my father felt about evicting Mr. West in eight or ten years' time when he sold our house in Rosedale and moved out to Long Island permanently was assuaged by his belief that as soon as he did so Mr. West would return to his wife and now-grown children.

The man emerged from the garage carrying a jacket and some loose papers under his arm. He called a thank you and got into his car and backed out slowly, his son turning toward the window only briefly as they passed the house again.

Inside, as was our routine, my father and I did the dishes and straightened up. We briefly debated what to do with the wine and beer in the refrigerator, the Scotch in the cupboard, and then my father, with a wave of his hand, said, "Let them be. It's up to him, not us." But then he added that it wouldn't hurt us to lay off the stuff ourselves until Billy was gone.

As was our routine, we drove to the A&P in East Hampton to pick up the ingredients for tonight's dinner—something to grill outside and something sweet for dessert. Then we headed for the train station, twenty minutes early.

It was one of those perfect eastern Long Island days. It was mid-week and so the village had settled into that polished lull it always acquired in the time between Sunday night and Thursday afternoon, when the weekenders began to arrive again. The sky was a beautiful, oceangoing shade of blue, with perfect white puffs of clouds, and the geraniums and impatiens planted around the stationhouse were lush. There was the sweet smell of hay and grass in the air, a touch of salt ocean. On the platform, I leaned to look down the tracks and saw the place, flocked by dark green trees, where the earth curved and merged the two black lines of tracks: *infinity*. How could anyone who had seen the illustration in grammar-school textbooks fail to think of the word?

A woman joined us on the platform, a tall woman in a thin dress, a bouquet of wildflowers held in the crook of her arm. And then two young men, tanned and sockless and dressed in expensive shades of pale yellow and pink. Then three girls in tennis whites and gold jewelry, another textbook illustration, but this time the caption would have read *Hamptons Debutantes*.

I wore cutoffs and sandals and a university T-shirt, my father a well-worn polyester polo shirt and gray gabardine suit pants, a beige baseball cap stained at the bill and around the sweatband, so that I suppose our illustration would be marked *Natives of Queens*.

"He'll notice a big difference," my father was saying about Billy. "After thirty years." And then: "He sure as hell better be sober."

"So what if he's not?" I asked. "Now that he's made this pledge. He goes straight to hell?"

My father glanced at me, seeing the apostate that I was. (Seeing, too, I suppose, his mother's one-cornered smile.) "I don't know," he said, to spare himself my sarcasm. We had long ago given up arguing about the niceties of our Church.

We felt the change in the air before we heard it confirmed by the far-off whistle of the train. Now all of us on the platform became attentive. Those at the back stepped forward, those at the edge stepped back. There was another blast of the whistle and then the black engine blotting out the light. There was the screeching of the brakes until, in what might have been mistaken for silence, the train came to a full rest before us, panting, it seemed, huge. We heard the conductor's voice, saw the shape of him moving past the windows. Another swung out of the middle car and looked up and down the platform as if he had arrived in an uncertain and hostile environment. Then he let go of the handrail and stepped out, turning to assist the passengers who had already gathered behind him.

Billy descended sideways, his black satchel coming first, black shoes and white socks and a Southern gentleman's pale blue seersucker suit. He smiled and waved and then placed his suitcase on the ground and waited for us to meet him.

He was taller than my father, but slightly stooped. He'd been thin all his life and the heaviness, the bloatedness, that age and alcohol had brought to his frame seemed irrelevant somehow; he still held himself like a thin man. You would still describe him as such. His dark hair was combed straight back from his forehead, still marked by the impression of his wet toothcomb. He wore the rimless glasses that you once saw only on priests and nuns, and his blue eyes were pale gray, nearly pearl. He smiled a little as he waited for us to approach him, touched his red tie, as elegant as a pope, but then, just as my father put out his hand and said, "Hey, Googenheimer," a wicked humor tumbled into his face. He grinned, they both grinned, shaking hands, laughing even, although neither had said any more than that yet. His cheeks and nose were bright pink with broken capillaries and spider veins, marks of his dissipation, sure, but, on Billy, subtly charming, almost intentionally so—like a touch of rouge and powder on a handsome actor's face.

"How was the trip?" my father was saying, laughing still as if in anticipation of a punch line.

"Behind me now," Billy said, grinning.

He took my hand, his was cold, and I gave him a quick kiss on the cheek, which was cold, too, and still smelling of Ivory soap and Sensen.

As the train pulled out again, he waved to someone inside—"Barney Callaghan's son," he told my father. "Can you imagine? A conductor on the Long Island Railroad." He turned to me and winked. "The children," he said, "are taking over the world." His face was all brightness, small white teeth, blue eyes, pink cheeks, and red lips, flashing lenses catching the changing light.

At the car, we put Billy's suitcase in the trunk—glimpse of my father's tackle box and fishing pole and the green army blanket dusted with sand.

My father offered lunch at the restaurant across the street, and Billy glanced at the place over his shoulder, nodding as if it was something he remembered. The intersection at that hour was nearly empty, and the sudden stillness that followed the departure of every train made the sunlight seem anticipatory, somehow: Dodge City at noon, a showdown pending.

"It's all the same," Billy said, even as the midday stillness began to fray around the edges: a light changing somewhere, cars once more headed our way.

"No, it's different," my father said. "It's not like the country anymore, more like any other suburb. We'll go for a drive, you'll see."

Inside the restaurant, the air was frosty and dark, and although nearly every table was taken, there was a hush about the place. I shivered as I sat down, and rubbed my bare arms. Billy leaned toward me. "I'll tell you what's happening," he whispered. He held up one finger, lecturing. His lips were remarkably smooth. His eyes red-rimmed but clear. "Everybody here's been complaining about the heat all summer long and now they can't bring themselves to complain about the cold." He sat back a little, a smile working at the corner of his mouth. "Doesn't that tell you something about getting your heart's desire?" Then he motioned to the waiter. "Do you think you can adjust the air a bit?" he said softly, with just a touch of a brogue, a souvenir, no doubt, of his trip to Ireland.

"We're working on it," the waiter said, exasperated.

When he walked away, Billy pushed out his chair, stood, and then made a great show of swinging out of his suit jacket and draping it gallantly over my shoulders, saying to the people around us who had lifted their eyes to him, "A bit chilly in here, isn't it? Don't you think?" Getting each one to agree. Forming a union, it seemed. "Well, see now, you brought a sweater," he said to the older lady right beside us. "You're the clever one." The jacket smelled of Old Spice and the Long Island Railroad. Shivering, I pulled it over my elbows and felt as I did a small square weight in one pocket—a breviary or a flask.

By the time the waiter came to take our orders, Billy had learned that the old lady with the sweater had lived out here since 1952 and wouldn't leave the place for a winter in Florida for all the tea in China. And that her companion, who had spent her childhood in Sag Harbor, felt much the same, although she still had her home in Yonkers.

"Well, I haven't been out here for nearly thirty years," he told them. The way he said it, this might have been his childhood home as well. The women were sufficiently sympathetic. Sufficiently puzzled. "My wife enjoys the Rockaways, you see, or used to, anyway, before it changed," he went on. "She likes a place with a boardwalk. And you know how it is, one summer passes and then another and you find yourself saying, 'Next year, let's go out there.' It's the prettiest spot on earth as far as I'm concerned, but you know how it is, suddenly it's been thirty years, even though it seems like yesterday."

As he spoke, he rolled up his shirtsleeves—his pale forearms were sandy with the remnants of a winter psoriasis—took a fountain pen from his breast pocket, and began to scribble a note on the corner of his paper place mat, all the while seeming to give the ladies beside us his undivided attention. He folded the place mat in half, then in quarters, and then folded a neat triangle at the top and tucked it inside. He wrote a quick address on the white front—Father somebody or other, it seemed, Albany, New York. He slipped a finger into the breast pocket of his shirt, extracted a single stamp, licked it, and put it in the corner. He placed the envelope at the edge of our table as if a courier might momentarily snatch it away.

"Oh, it's changed out here," the woman with the sweater told him. "It's not like it was in the forties."

"It is in my dreams," Billy told them. "Just the same." He winked, ran his hand through his hair. "But then again, so am I."

"Oh, aren't we all?" the sweater lady and her friend both said at once.

Billy smiled at them with something like gratitude, as if he could not imagine being seated beside two more pleasant and perceptive women. He raised his water glass. "God bless dreams," he said, and the ladies returned his toast. If there were shoes to be had, I suspect he could have sold them a dozen.

When the waiter brought our sandwiches he looked at the empty space before Billy with some perplexity and then quickly shifted the extra place mat at our table to Billy's place. Throughout the letter writing and the simultaneous conversation with the ladies, my father had been sitting back, grinning, watching his cousin be himself and delighting in it—there was no other word—delighting in him. I glimpsed for the first time what it must have cost my father, during all those years of my childhood when Billy was banned from our home until he could show up sober, those same years when my father's voice would wake us all in the middle of the night, as he shouted into the phone, "Billy, you're killing yourself" or, more tempered but more desperate as well, "Just let me know where you are, Billy. Just tell me where you are."

I moved my elbow against the weight in Billy's jacket. If it was a flask, it was empty. If it was a breviary, it was rather thin.

"So how's everyone?" my father asked, leaning forward to lift his sandwich.

Billy launched into a familiar litany: his sister Rosie's kids (Holy Cross and Katherine Gibbs, Queensborough Community and the telephone company) and Kate's kids (Regis Fordham Notre Dame Marymount Chase Manhattan) and his mother at eighty, who still liked her nightcap.

And who he had seen from the old neighborhood and the office and who had invited them out to Breezy Point next weekend and did you hear Kate's husband is now CFO of the entire organization, which means another addition to their house in Rye, which is already big enough for anybody, if you ask him, so he said to her, Why not take some of that money and feed the poor rather than redoing a house that's already well done. It's not like she's happy with her life or ever has been, if you know what I mean. She told him she could very well feed the poor and put a new guest wing on her house at the same time, which only goes to show she's not only missed the point of charity but become as addicted to spending money as her husband is to making it.

"And how was Ireland?" my father asked.

"Cold," Billy said, shaking his head as if the weather were a moral deficit. "And wet. A miserable place to quit drinking."

My father smiled, indulgent. "But you quit." It was not a question.

"I signed on," Billy said, nodding. "And the day after I signed on I got a car and drove out to County Wicklow. All by myself. To Clonmel."

"And how was that?" my father asked—I have to say he asked it casually.

Slowly, Billy put his sandwich on his plate and sat back, his fingers touching the edge of the table. "Eva runs a gas station there," he said. "With her husband. She has four kids." He paused. "Eva does."

My father was stirring his iced tea with a long spoon. He nodded, carefully lifting the spoon and placing it on the tiny plate beneath his glass. He touched the lemon wedge beside it. "I knew that," he said.

Billy raised his eyebrows and smiled a little. His teeth were perfectly straight and even. Dentures, I remembered my mother telling me once, courtesy of Uncle Sam. "She told me you did," he said.

My father fiddled with the spoon. Had I asked earlier in the conversation who Billy Sheehy was or Marge Tierney or Eddie Schmidt or Tony D'Agostino I might have been inclined to inquire here about Eva and her gas station and her four kids. But the chicken salad had walnuts in it that I was thinking I really could have done without and it was easy enough to guess that Eva was someone from the neighborhood, from the company, from my grandfather's sprawling legacy of immigrants and immigrants' children. Someone Billy might send place-mat letters to.

"I did know," my father said. "I'm sorry to say."

And Billy blew some air from between his lips and shook his head and glanced at the cold ceiling above us. Then he winked at me. "When you were christened," he said, "your father drove us over to the church from your house. Your mother, God rest her soul, stayed at home— women did that in those days, didn't they"—to my father—"missed out on their own babies' christenings to stay home and get things ready for the party?"

"They were supposed to still be in confinement," my father said, and then, acknowledging the truth: "But they were usually getting things ready for the party."

"So your aunt was holding you," Billy went on, "your

mom's sister Louise, and she and I went on in with the others while your father here parked the car. You were brand-new to that parish, weren't you, Dennis? To St. Clare's?"

I saw my father beginning to grin, anticipating what was to come. "We'd just bought the house the month before."

Billy turned back to me. "Well, he must have gotten confused parking, because he took longer than we thought he would, and next thing you know, we're all standing at the baptismal font, waiting for him. And in he comes, at a run, and when he sees us standing up there with the priest he does a little leap to get to us—I guess he thought we were going ahead without him—and splat, lands right on his face at our feet."

My father was grinning now, looking at his lap, shaking his head.

"I've heard this," I tried to say, but Billy went on.

"Well, everybody says, Good Lord, and when the priest bends down to help him, your father looks up all red in the face and says, 'I'm just so loaded.'"

"With happiness!" my father said now. "I meant to say, I'm just so loaded with happiness . . ."

Billy shook his finger at him. "Yeah, but what you said and what everyone heard was 'I'm so loaded.'" To me again, his eyes suddenly wet with tears, although only my father was laughing. "And just a week later I go into a diner up on Linden Boulevard and there's the priest who did the baptism—what was his name, Dennis, he was an older man?"

My father shook his head to show he couldn't recall. "I should remember," he said. "He gave me such a talking-to when the christening was over."

"Anyway, there he is in this diner and he comes over to me and he asks, 'How's that unfortunate brother of yours?'—he thought we were brothers—and I told him, 'Still full of the same stuff, I'm afraid.' " And now Billy, too, began to laugh, a deep, quiet but irrepressible laugh, his eyes shining with their unshed tears. " 'Still full of it,' I said." He glanced at my father. "Not exactly a lie, you might say. More a matter of interpretation."

My father bowed his head again, as if to concede something, but when he looked up his smile showed a shadow being lifted. "All right," he said, as if he were ready to stand corrected. "All right." As if he believed he was being forgiven.

WE TOOK HIM on the usual big-home tour through the estates of East Hampton and he seemed to remember every one of them from his single summer here after the war. One he identified as the Appleton residence—he had bought a postcard of it way back when. Mosler, Eastman, Bouvier. His favorite was a place on the edge of the beach, above a potato field. "Where's Pudding Hill Lane?" he asked, and my father turned down it for him, driving slowly. "They called these their cottages," Billy said at one point, turning to me in the back seat. "Yes." I nodded as if the irony of it was still interesting. We had the windows open and Billy had one arm raised, holding on to the roof; the other hand was in the left, empty pocket of his jacket.

"Well, it's still beautiful," he said as we headed back to the village and the little house. "Nothing's changed."

"Just us," my father said, but Billy had begun to recite slowly, softly, like a man humming a tune to himself, letting the words get caught in the breeze from the window. " 'I will arise and go now, and go to Innisfree...' " It was a matter of some pride to my father, to Billy's friends and family in general, that he had carried a volume of Yeats with him all through the war. Not that my father, or most of his family, read the poems themselves; more that Billy's interest absolved them from any interest of their own. When my generation of cousins began to come back from college with copies of Ginsberg and Ferlinghetti and Sylvia Plath, our parents could sniff, "Oh, poetry, sure. Billy Lynch loves that Irish poet, Yeats (or Yeets)"—with a proud nonchalance that seemed to hint that the poet was a friend of a friend. " 'And I shall have some peace there,' " Billy said.

At the house I quickly changed into my bathing suit and headed out for my daily, transforming swim, stepping past the two of them on the front steps, short glasses of lemonade in their hands and *Time* magazine on my father's knee: an article about Nixon, poor man (they were saying), poor hounded man, caught in his tangle of lies. Billy had left his jacket and tie in the guest bedroom.

The bay was about a mile and a half away, through streets that were, as my father had said, becoming more and more suburban. As he'd pointed out each time we'd walked this route together, thirty years ago there was hardly a house between ours and the bay, and the road that was tarred now was mostly dirt then. He and Billy himself that first summer they were back from overseas had widened part of it with the scythe Mr. Holtzman had lent them.

Now there were as many houses, as many cars on the tarred road as you might find in any of Long Island's greener suburbs. And although most of the houses here, with their leanto carports and decorative lobster pots, with nautical flags and badminton sets in sandy tree-shaded yards, were clearly summer homes, beach cottages in the less ironic sense of the word, there were a number as well that had pale aluminum siding and custom-made drapes in bay windows and full two-car garages, as sturdy and suburban and dull as any in Rosedale or Franklin Square. Places for year-round living, for six o'clock dinners of macaroni and cheese and hurried mornings of getting to work and meeting the school bus. Suburban sprawl overtaking summer romance, as far as I could see. The chances for any of us living that rare two weeks in high summer, in a wild place by the sea, a hiatus, as Billy and my father had called it after the war, diminishing and diminishing.

When I heard a car behind me, I moved to the dusty edge of the road, as I'd gotten into the habit of doing on this walk. I shot an angry look over my shoulder when I felt the warmth of its engine on the back of my legs. It was, after all, my life coming at me, my future that was threatening to run me down—who wouldn't give it a dirty look?

I slowed further, even stepped onto the sandy edge of the road, into the tall weeds and the grass. Finally, I turned. It was Mr. West's car and Matthew or Cody or John was driving, leaning across the front seat to call out the window and offer a ride.

He (Matthew, you) was due to meet a friend at the lobster dock in twenty minutes, so we were spared the memory of a first conversation on the same sunny bay beach where Billy met Eva in those first weeks he was home from the war. We sat in the car instead, the broad front seat. There was the scent of stale cigarettes and old joints and the sweet smell of the beach towel I held on my lap. You were tan and wore the leather band around your right wrist. Just out of Stony Brook. Worked a charter fishing boat all summer. Wanted to own one of your own. Wanted to see the West Coast. Never went into the city, didn't like it. Couldn't imagine living in a place like Rosedale, going to college way up in Buffalo. A Bonacker, a real Bonacker. But your mouth was wry and your eyes dark brown. I suspected you would age into your father's face exactly, but without the furtive brows. You ducked your head when you laughed, like someone who has flubbed his lines onstage, someone needing to correct himself.

We agreed to go out that night. Walking back from the bay—I'd stayed longer than usual, accruing benefits, I thought—I wondered if my father would be offended. I knew what my mother would have said: a date was for her my primary social obligation and superseded all other claims. Even in her final days she insisted I go out if someone asked me. "Go," she had said, frowning as if she could not believe my hesitation, as if to say, Haven't I taught you anything? When she couldn't speak, she merely waved her hand, sweeping me out: *go*.

They were sitting on lawn chairs now, my father and Billy, on the sparse grass in front of the house. As I came down the road, my father was leaning forward, his forearms on his knees, his head bent, listening like a diligent priest. Billy was leaning forward, too, but with his arms folded across his chest and his back straight. They both looked up when my sandal hit the gravel driveway, but they were too lost, it seemed—in conversation? in the past? in recrimination?—to fully notice or recognize me until I was almost beside them. Or close enough to see that my father was shaking his head, ever so slightly, refusing, refusing something that Billy wanted him to take. And that Billy, holding himself carefully, speaking slowly, softly, even as he turned to smile at me, had already had quite a bit to drink.

O F THE (LET'S FACE IT) half dozen or so basic versions of the Irish physiognomy, they had two of
them: Billy thin-faced with black hair and pale
blue eyes behind his rimless glasses; Dennis with broad
cheeks, eternally flushed, and dark eyes and fair hair that
had only begun to thin under his combat helmet, somewhere, he claimed, in northern France. One every inch
the poet or the scholar, the other a perfect young cop or
barman. The aesthete priest and the jolly chaplain.

But in fact they had both gone to the RCA Institute
before the war and had left steady jobs at Con Ed to enlist.
In July 1945, they both had plans to return there in the
fall, or as soon as the Long Island house was finished, as
soon as they were ready to end this hiatus—they called it
that—between their lives as they were and whatever it
was their lives were to become.

Their charge had been to make the place livable again

after nearly a decade of abandonment. To update the plumbing and the electrical, chase out the mice and the wasps, repair or replace whatever parts of the floor or the ceiling, the windows or the doors needed repair or replacement. The directive had come from Holtzman, the shoe salesman, as if an afterthought, over dinner the second night Dennis was home (although it was not home to him, it was the salesman's house, even though he sat at his mother's dining-room table). He offered the project as if in a burst of inspiration, even said something like "Here's an idea for you boys . . ." although Dennis knew that in his kit in an upstairs bedroom (not his room, although the bed was the one he had slept in as a child) he had the letter his mother had sent him, the laundry list of reasons to remarry. He knew by the anxious glance Holtzman shot her, even as he pretended to be inspired, that the project had been his mother's idea all along.

On the afternoon of their arrival, they parked the car in the rutted and overgrown driveway and in shirtsleeves and fedoras and army boots cut through the knee-high grass and the weeds with the scythe and the clippers Holtzman had lent them. City-bred, they made quite a show of it, testing their arms and the heat and their resolve, and sending the tall grass, the bees and grasshoppers and zithering beetles every which way as they made a good path across the sandy soil to the three peeling steps at the front door. They pulled the screen off its hinges with the first tug.

The key Holtzman had given them was attached to a chain that was attached to a metal shoehorn engraved with the name and the address of his Jamaica Avenue store. It was only this, this awkward key chain, that made them fumble a bit. The door itself opened easily, the way it would in a movie or a dream, as if the lock hadn't been real at all, or as if the hinges had been well oiled. The place was musty and warm and you could see dust motes in the sunlight that came through the kitchen window as clearly as you could see the sink and the stove and the sagging gray couch.

Now the vague thoughts Dennis had been having about every place he'd been to since his return from overseas took form and he said to Billy, "This has been here," as if Billy would know what he meant. What he meant was, this house has been here, just like this, all the while he had been locked in the adventure and tedium of the war. This had been here, just as it was (like the Chrysler Building, his mother's new home, the Jamaica Avenue El), all the while and at each and every moment he had been away.

"Since the twenties, I suppose," Billy said, not getting it.

"Forever," Dennis told him.

But Billy got it later, after they'd found a restaurant in East Hampton for dinner and then, because neither of them had been here before and because the charm of the village gave them the sense that the roads that led from it offered something more, they toured the place in Holtzman's car. It had all been here. The elegant trees that lined the broad streets, the great green lawns that grew, even as they were slowly passing, greener and deeper in the twilight so you could almost make yourself believe that night was seeping in through their roots, not moving across the sky above them. The houses—when had they ever seen such houses, how was it they hadn't known they were out here? Grand and complex palaces, *cottages* wood-shingled or white, with gazebos in their gardens and great pillared porches that curved like bows and widow's walks and gabled attic rooms from which you could probably glimpse both the silver spires of the city and the black ocean edge of the earth.

They moaned to see the darkened places that had not yet been opened for the season—"No one even there"—and whispered, "Take a look at that," when one was lit like a steamship from stem to stern. But what killed them, what really killed them, were the houses that looked out over the ocean, that had for their front or back yards a dark lush carpet of beautifully mown grass and then, running down from the other side, as if front and back had been built on different planets, magnificent dunes, sea grass, white beach and sea.

"Leave me there when I'm dead," Billy said of one of them—a large house on a wide lawn with a starry backdrop of sky that even in near darkness seemed to contain the reflected sound and sparkle of the ocean. "Prop me up on the porch with a pitcher of martinis and a plate of oysters on the half shell and I'll be at peace for all eternity. Amen."

They made their way home in darkness, under the thick leaves along Main Street and out toward the sandier and less elegant regions of the Springs and Three Mile Harbor. They made several wrong turns and even in the driveway sat squinting at the little house for a few minutes before they decided it was the right place, after all.

They agreed to sleep in the car that night, since the mattresses were mildewed and the mice well ensconced. With GI resourcefulness they hung T-shirts over the opened windows and secured the edges with electrical tape in order to keep out most of the bugs.

They smoked for half an hour, Dennis in the front seat, Billy in back. "I never knew," Billy said at one point, his glasses in his hand, his hand resting on his forehead, "I never knew what it was like out here." It was what he would write on his postcards tomorrow, creating artifacts. "Isn't that something? I had no idea those places were out here."

"It's something," Dennis said. "Bridie was here once," he added. "She came out to Southampton with someone. She said it was really something."

"It is," Billy said. He paused. "It almost makes you wonder what else you don't know about yet."

Dennis frowned for a moment and then said, "Plenty," with a laugh. But although Billy looked the part he was no poet or scholar and could not explain: what else did he not know about yet that would strike him as the village tonight had struck him—strike him in that very first moment of apprehending, of seeing and smelling and tasting, as something he could not, from that moment on, get enough of and could never ever again live without.

By the end of their first week they had a routine and a sufficient knowledge of the roads to find the dump and the bay beach, the cheaper restaurants and the hardware stores. They did the heaviest work early in the morning and then ducked inside before noon to wire and paint and plaster. Around four or five, when the sunlight began to edge from white to yellow, they took their towels from the clothesline they had rigged between two trees out back and walked with them draped around their necks the mile and a half to the bay. They cleared a shortcut with Holtzman's scythe. The beach there was rocky at the shoreline, littered with shells, but the water was warmer than the ocean, and since neither of them was much of a swimmer, they both welcomed the chance to just float and dive and touch their toes to the bottom at will.

Some nights they stopped into a bar off the Springs road. They both drank too much the first and second time, but only Billy, engaged in long conversation with the bartender and an ugly old Bonacker who could not hear enough about the war, drank too much the third and fourth.

Billy drunk, in those days, was charming and sentimental. He spoke quietly, one hand in his pocket and the other around his glass, his glass more often than not pressed to his heart. There was tremendous affection in Billy's eyes, or at least they held a tremendous offer of affection, a tremendous willingness to find whomever he was talking to bright and witty and better than most. Dennis came to believe in those days that you could measure a person's vanity simply by watching how long it took him to catch on to the fact that Billy hadn't recognized his inherent and long-underappreciated charm, he'd drawn it out with his own great expectations or simply imagined it, whole cloth.

They talked about the war: the characters in their divisions, Midwesterners always the crudest, didn't you notice, something to do with living around farm animals, no doubt; the officers good and bad, the morning just before they returned, when a group coming out of first mess claimed they were serving cake for breakfast, which turned out to be only bread, fresh bread. The tar-paper shack Dennis and two other fellows had constructed, warmer than the tents, the Pilsen Hilton. Their luck in avoiding the Pacific. Their quests for souvenirs. Patton and Ike and F. D. R., the lying old smoothy. The kids begging chocolate and chewing gum. The French girls, all of them beautiful, one coming to Switching Central in Metz, where Billy was operating near the end, to ask if a message could be sent to her fiancé, another GI gone north. She said she even knew his code name, Vampire, which made two or three of the other boys laugh out loud. She was a dark-haired girl with great big dark eyes. She wore a white handkerchief knotted around her neck, as lovely as diamonds. The message she asked Billy to send was simply: "I am still here."


THEIR SHOULDERS AND ARMS and the backs of their necks burned and freckled and peeled, and after dinner each evening they walked through the village with toothpicks in their mouths or drove past the great houses on the surrounding streets, noticing the changes in them, how they looked in the rain, in clear twilight, how well they bore even the oppressive air of the hotter days and marveling, marveling still, that this Eden was here, at the other end of the same island on which they had spent their lives.

One afternoon just before VJ Day a family was spread across a blanket on the widest crescent of bay beach—at least they thought it was a family as they approached from the road. But as they dropped their towels and bent to unlace their already loosely laced boots, to slip off the socks they wore under them and the pants they wore over their swim trunks, they quickly changed their assessment. Six children, the oldest no more than nine, and two women, girls, actually, who were not old enough to be mothers to them all.

They nodded a greeting to the girls and the children as they made their way to the water and then, swimming out with as much form as they had ever shown for as much distance as they dared to go, floated a bit under the paling sky, glancing as they did, in subtle, sidelong glances, at the group on the shore, at the girls especially, one standing now at the water's edge, a pail and shovel in her hand and two little ones at her feet. The other, only a little plumper, on the blanket still and wearing an old-fashioned swim cap over her curly hair that from the water's distance—at least for Billy, whose glasses were in his pants pocket on the sand—seemed like an aura of royal-blue light.

Five of the children were knee-deep in the water now, dipping their outspread hands just as the one girl was instructing them to do, fingers splayed like starfish, washing off the sand. Then one of the children, the tallest boy, stepped out of the water with his splayed hands held high, as if he were a surgeon, as if the sand might leap up at any minute and cover them again and called, "Eva," toward the blanket, "Eva," although it was impossible to tell if he meant the girl in the swim cap or the sixth child, who sat beside her, because at that moment a huge black touring car pulled up from the road and in a sudden gath-

ering of pails and shovels and shells and picnic baskets
and cover-ups and blankets—a sudden momentum that
died the minute everything was off the sand and they
made, in incredibly slow motion, the trek from beach to
car—they were gone.

The two swam a little closer, to a shallower, more comfortable distance from the shore, and then climbed out of
the water completely. They reached their towels and in
an economy of terry cloth that they had learned in the
service dried face and arms and shoulders with one end,
chest and legs with the other, and then sat on the dry
middle on the sand to smoke a cigarette and then, flicking
their feet with one sock and then the other, put on socks
and boots for the walk home.

The road was hot and Dennis had both his pants and
his towel draped over his shoulders to protect his latest
burn. He could feel as he walked the salt drying on his
legs and on his face and arms. He could see a line of it
on the pale hair of his cousin's calf.

They were virgins, both of them. Before the war, all
the girls they'd known had seemed to be another cousin's
schoolmate or the daughter of an aunt's best friend, and
while desire had presented itself often enough, the tight
quarters and the rigorous decorum of that time and place
had failed to offer opportunity for more than an accidental
brush or a chaste kiss. And later, when opportunity did
abound, when they were handsome in their uniforms and
perfectly fit, they were only weeks or days away from shipping out and the looming possibility of their own deaths
made even the desire to commit, at this late date, that
kind of mortal sin seem as foolish and as fleeting as the

mad longing to hurl yourself, willy-nilly, from some great height—the parachute jump at Coney Island, for instance, or the observation deck of the Empire State Building—or to raise your head from the mud during a live ammo drill at boot camp, just because you had the urge.

They had bruised girls' lips with kisses then, had learned the pleasure of encircling a waist or running a hand along a stockinged leg, of feeling a heartbeat behind a breast, but the Paulist Fathers had gotten them at an early age and they had studied heaven and hell long before they knew that at the top of a stocking there was only bare flesh, and boys they had known from the basketball court or the K. of C. had already gone over and lost their lives. And even in Manhattan, at midnight, in uniform and as drunk as the girls on their knees, they saw through the bold music and the laughter and the smoky air their foreshortened lives, the nearness of eternity, and so always rode the subway home alone, reeling and laughing and helped by the hands of innumerable smiling strangers, to sleep it off under their mother's own roof.

THE NEXT AFTERNOON the two girls and their six charges were there again, the thinner one in the same dark blue bathing suit that cut squarely across the top of her thighs in the front but in the back relented a little and followed the sweet lines of her bottom; the other in yet another swim cap, a pale yellow one this time, a halo now as Billy squinted at her from across the sand. They had a beach umbrella with them today, green with yellow stripes, and in its shade they had both a lunch hamper and a wicker laundry basket.

The children were in the water already when the two of them arrived, the younger ones equipped today with red and blue inner tubes, and so it was easy enough, after they had shed their boots and their socks and their khaki pants, to nod at the ladies once more and then to say to the children as they walked past them into the gently lapping surf, "The water's very wet today, don't you think?"

There was a pause of children's stares.

Billy winked. "It wasn't quite as wet yesterday, was it?"

The four children gazed at them, four towheads with blue-green eyes and a red bandage of sun across each nose. "No," one of them, the tallest girl, said. "It couldn't be."

"Sure," Billy told them. He rubbed some water between thumb and forefinger as if he were feeling cloth. "And one day last week it was hardly wet at all."

"Didn't need a towel," Dennis said.

"Didn't need a towel," Billy agreed. "Went in for half an hour and came out dry as a bone."

The older girl was still looking at them skeptically, but the younger ones had begun to giggle, the laughter bobbing up to their throats much as they were bobbing inside their swim tubes. "No," they said. "You're making that up."

"It's the truth," Dennis said indignantly, and then Billy pointed to the smallest girl, who, because she could not touch the bottom, moved with more abandon as she laughed.

"Look at this little one here," Billy said. "She looks like a buoy."

Dennis shook his head gravely. "No, she's a girl."

The little one looked to her bigger sister and the sister said, "She's a girl."

"But she looks like a buoy," Billy said again. "A buoy, a buoy." He pointed out to the bay, to the black buoys that dotted the horizon until the children saw what he meant and began shouting, "A buoy, a boo-eee, one of those."

But Dennis continued to shake his head. "How could she be a boy with all that hair piled up on top of her head? You're a girl, aren't you?"

And the little one, uncertain of the joke but delighted by the attention, merely giggled and bobbed and let the other three cry for her, "Yes, she's a girl, but he means a buoy, a buoy."

The commotion had the desired effect (blessed, blessed children) and slowly, the young woman in the navy-blue suit sauntered toward the water with a toddler on her hip, a smile beginning, Dennis was certain, if she would only raise that coyly bent head.

This she did as she entered the water and with her free hand splashed some of it on the baby's plump leg. "Hello," she said, meeting their eyes just long enough to show that hers were gray and darkly lashed.

"Hello," they said, one after the other, with as much gallantry and graciousness as they could, being bare-chested and thigh-high in water. Had they been wearing hats, they would have tipped them.

"Isn't the water wet today, Mary?" the older girl asked.

Mary continued to sweep up water languidly with her fingertips and to brush it onto the child's legs. "Yes, isn't it?" she said. The poor child looking down into the bay with something nearing terror, clinging to her shoulder and the neck of her suit, pulling it down just that much to show an inch of pure white flesh just below a delicate suntan. "Wetter than yesterday, I think," she said.

And there it was.

"You're Irish," Dennis said, and Billy asked, "Where from?" at the ready with the information that his own father was from Cork and his mother Donegal.

She was from a place in County Wicklow, although she'd been over here since before the war. Since before Jonathan, the oldest boy, who was now stretched out under the umbrella with a magazine and an apple, was born. And of course, looking up at Jonathan on the blanket, they could not help but see the other girl, too (although Billy saw her as a mirage of smeared color, pink legs and a dark suit, pink shoulders and arms and face, and a yellow cap like a low flame, a mirage that perhaps only wild hope and great imagination could form into a solid woman).

"That's Eva, my sister," Mary said. "She's only visiting. She's on her way home."

The family they worked for had a place on Park Avenue and a house in East Hampton and money, Dennis gathered, that poured down like sunlight. The man of the house had spent the war in Washington, D.C., but not so much of it that the babies ever stopped coming, all six of them born in the past decade, and the seventh, the newest, now asleep in the wicker basket.

"It was really too much for me," Mary said. "So I

asked if my sister could come for the summer. She'd been with a family in Chicago. She'll be going home in the fall."

Billy squinted and nodded and stirred the water around him with his hands. It might have been quicksand, he seemed, at the moment, so mired in it. It was not that Mary herself wasn't pretty enough, with her gray eyes and her dark hair and her boyish and direct way, but Dennis already had the greater part in the conversation and she herself seemed to like it that way. And he wanted to swear no allegiance until he had considered both options carefully, and he sensed, perhaps because she was still a blur of colored light, that the girl on the blanket was the one for him.

But how to get to her? How to end this conversation here (he and Dennis, after all, hadn't even swum yet) and get up on the shore and near enough to the blanket where she sat in the partial shade of the umbrella to say, "Well, hello, Eva."

And then the infant in the basket began to cry. At first he thought it was the cry of a gull and he looked toward the sky, but then he saw her kneeling beside the basket and lifting the child—another blur—to her shoulder, then standing, rocking, beginning to pace. The other children were oblivious to the crying, as no doubt they had to be in a family where year after year another baby arrives to bump them that much further into adulthood, but Mary and Dennis were oblivious, too, talking now, just the two of them, about certain lucky investors who had done nothing but profit from the war.

Billy walked past them, through the water and over the rocky edge of the shore. He had not swum and so only his trunks and legs were wet and even his hands seemed to dry as he made his way toward her. The baby was crying full blast now, hot and sleepy and desperate against her shoulder. She had a hand behind its head and was hushing and clucking, but as soon as he was close enough to see her better, he knew she'd had her eyes on him all along. The boy with the magazine turned his slim back to them, as befit a magnate's son.

She smiled ruefully. The blossom of curly hair above her forehead was dark, dark red, and the yellow cap that hid the rest of it had been partially knocked back, a dishevelment that made what at a distance was the illusion of an aura, a halo, seem, close up, only childish and adorable. Her eyes were brown, her cheeks smooth and broad, and because her teeth were crooked her mouth was crooked, too. She was shorter than her sister and indeed plumper. And the shoulder the poor babe was wetting with saliva and tears was whiter than the sand, scattered with dark beauty marks as delicate as distant stars.

"Can I take him?" Billy said, holding out his hands. He stood at the edge of the blanket, darkening the sand with the water from his suit.

"If I can just get him his bottle," she said—her accent, too, was plumper than her sister's, and there was a tremble in it, a kind of panic, set off, no doubt, by the child's insistent misery.

"I'll take him," he said.

If he had been more self-conscious, it wouldn't have worked. Or if he had been more calculating. If, when she handed him the screaming child he had noticed the movement of her breasts, the size of her waist, the shape of her legs and her thighs as she quickly turned to the lunch hamper to find the bottle of milk, the child would have stiffened in his arms and screamed all the more and he would have been forced to hand him back to her and perhaps even, awkwardly, make his defeated way back to the water, matters far worse for his interference.

But the child was as light as a feather in his hands and the lightness took his breath away. The baby wore a seersucker sunsuit that left his tiny arms and shoulders bare, and Billy covered these with a cupped palm as he rested the child against his chest. The flesh was as sweetly warm as if the hand of God had just formed it. He blew softly across the child's downy hair and closed his eyes to say, "Now now, little fellow. Now now."

The child was lighter than the sun-warmed air. The miracle of it, for him, was the perfection of the tiny head and spine, ear and hand. The miracle was that the child quieted immediately in Billy's arms, placed his cheek to Billy's heart, and heaved one deep and restful sigh even before she had turned from the cooler with the bottle of milk in her hand.

"Will you look at that now?" she said, showing her crooked smile, her flashing eyes. "You must have a way with children."

And he could see from the start (her eyes were not so much brown but a kind of mahogany, the exact color of her hair) that there was nothing she more admired in a man.

"Have you got lots of brothers and sisters?"

What better way to begin? He held the child and they talked together until the wet sand at his feet had dried again, and when the child next woke she handed him the bottle and he lowered himself and the baby onto the blanket, under the umbrella's shade, and fed him there while the other children ran up and back and Dennis and Mary, now standing at the edge of the water, talked and talked.

When did he fall in love with her? Probably it was the day before, before she had even come clearly into his view. But that afternoon he fell in love with the rest of his life, and that was better still. The days ahead when he would come to the beach here and the child he held, the children who ran to them, wet and trembling, would be theirs and when the flesh of her arms and her throat and her sweet breasts would be as familiar to him as his own.

It was there, that life, that future. It had been there all along. He simply hadn't known it until now, or had the capacity to imagine just a month ago that something like this might be his. That this golden future, this Eden, had been part of the same life he'd been living all along. Wasn't that something? He hadn't known until now that it was there.

They met again the next afternoon and the next. Dennis and Billy began to quit work a bit earlier each day, and at times it was nearly dusk before they left their boots on the steps by the front door.

The Mr. and Mrs.—or so the girls called their employers—were in Washington for the week, and so it was easy enough for them to tell the driver not to come until six or so, then seven. The children were glad to be out late and to have their supper at the shore, with the candy Billy brought them for dessert.

At night the boys still made their slow circuit of the

stately homes, but now with a keener interest and intent, to discover the house the girls lived in. Although they tried gentle questioning for the first few afternoons ("You're not in one of those places on the beach, are you?"), it was only by direct inquiry that they learned which house it was exactly and then were rewarded that same night with the sight of Eva, glimpsed through the only opening in the high hedge that until now had made the house uninteresting, crossing the front path, barefoot, and going up the steps to the porch.

Late in August, a Tuesday night, they met the girls at the house itself. It was nine o'clock. The Mr. and Mrs. had said the girls could go out, but only after the children were asleep, and the girls told them to come around to the back and knock at the kitchen door.

At deep blue twilight they passed through the village and down the now-familiar streets. They were newly showered and shaved and they wore the white shirts they had washed out in the morning and left to dry in the sun all day long and then ironed themselves, with an ancient, secondhand Proctor-Silex, on a towel under a pillowcase spread out on the kitchen table. They turned in, as they had been instructed, past the tall hedge, and the crackle of their slow wheels on the gravel drive was enough to set their nerves drumming, the way the fanfare did in the moment before a curtain was raised on a stage.

They parked, and now locusts and the hush of the ocean filled the air along with the odor of honeysuckle and salt water. There was a line of windows across the back of the house and each of these was warmly lit, and on the nearest side a simple set of steps led from the driveway to a darkened door.

These they climbed, whispering, "Is it here?" and peering in before they knocked to a small square hallway lit by a rectangle of curtain-filtered light from the room beyond. There were the familiar shovels and pails, the swim tubes and the hamper. They heard Mary's voice, and then the inside door was pulled open and there she was in a pale dress, opening the door to let them in.

"We'll need another minute," she said. "There's a mutiny in progress."

The room they followed her into was huge—easily as large as the apartment where Dennis had been raised. A kitchen with a table as big as a bus and an icebox that could have housed a short family. The room was softly lit now and quiet, but it was possible to imagine the chaos there must have been just an hour or two before. You saw it in the two wooden high chairs, still slightly askew, at the far end of the table, in the five empty milk bottles lined neatly on the metal drying board, the scattered children's books and crayons and paper airplanes on the window seat at the far end of the room. You smelled it in the pleasant odor of dishwashing soap and coffee and the lingering scent of some kind of roast.

Eva sat at the near end of the table, her back to them, and as she turned at their entrance they saw she had Sally, the five-year-old, on her lap. Eva, too, wore a dress. It had capped sleeves and a rounded neck and there was nothing more beautiful than the way she turned in her chair and smiled up at them over the little girl's head. There was a glass of milk and a half-eaten cookie on the table before them.

"All in bed but this one," Mary said.

"Oh, but she's going now, isn't she?" Eva whispered, leaning around to see the little girl's face. "Now that the boys are here."

She was a bony little angel in her thin cotton nightgown and her braid. A sprite. And too small, Dennis thought, to be at home in a house this huge. But she nodded and said yes, clearly exhausted, and put her feet to the familiar linoleum.

" 'Down by the salley gardens,' " Billy said in a light brogue as Eva stood and took the little girl's hand, " 'my love and I did meet...' "

The child smiled up at him, recognizing the poem he had recited to her before, on the beach. " 'She passed the salley gardens with little snow-white feet.' " He put his hand to his heart, emoting. " 'She bid me take love easy, as the leaves grow on the tree; But I, being young and foolish, with her would not agree.' " He winked at Eva over the little girl's head. " 'She bid me take life easy, as the grass grows on the weirs; But I was young and foolish, and now am full of tears...' "

"Say good night to the gentlemen," Mary told her, and Sally whispered good night and waved shyly.

"Good night, dear," they both said, and then watched as Eva led her down a darkened hallway, lit at its far end by the lights in other rooms, and then up the back staircase.

Had he been a poet or a scholar, Billy might have remarked how, in any house, children asleep in far rooms add a sweetness to the air. But he would save the remark for Eva alone, when the children and the house were theirs.

SINCE IT WAS TOO LATE for supper, they went into South-ampton, to a place Dennis remembered Bridie mention-ing—a bartender there the brother of a friend from Woodside. But the bartender this night was a stranger, although an amiable one—another GI who'd been lucky enough to watch the war from an air base in England. He'd seen Glenn Miller there, just before he boarded the plane he disappeared on. And married a girl from Corn-wall, who hadn't joined him yet but was already saying in her letters how much she was going to miss bloody En-gland.

Mary and Eva clucked their tongues. Poor girl.

The bar was cool and dark and it gleamed in sundry places like a jewel; like a jewel it caught light along its polished surfaces, in its brass rail, in the mirror that ran its length and the various glasses and bottles that lined the heavy, stately counter across its back. There was only an-other couple at a table in the corner and the four of them, until the door opened and a single young man walked in. He sat opposite them, at the far end of the bar, and be-cause the bartender was in the middle of a funny story about a crazed airman and one unloaded bomb, the man sat unserved for a good while, until Dennis, when the story was finished, pointed and nodded.

The bartender wiped a tear of laughter from his eye, threw the bar rag over his shoulder, and turned toward the new man, and then, just as abruptly, pulled the rag down and began slowly to polish an empty foot of bar.

"But I was sorry to miss seeing Paris," he said. "That's my one big regret about the war." He moved in front of them again. "We had this one fellow," he said. "Another pilot." He began to lean his elbow toward the bar, to launch another story, and Dennis, thinking he was either nearsighted or lazy, pointed again and said, "There's a man who's been waiting."

Still leaning down, the bartender looked over his shoulder toward the man, and the man—he was no older than themselves—lifted his hand and raised a finger to indicate he was there, as if he were in a crowd of patrons and not alone at the end of a mostly deserted room.

The bartender turned back to them. "This guy went to Harvard, this pilot I'm talking about, but he was a nice guy just the same, regular. And he comes up to me one morning and he says . . ."

Now Billy, beginning to feel parched in sympathy for the man (although his own glass had twice and quite generously been refilled), interrupted to say, "I think there's a man who needs a drink."

This time the bartender didn't turn around, just bowed his head and smiled a bit—he was a good-looking guy with a strong chin and thick hair—and picked up his story again.

The girls exchanged a look of both surprise and concern, and then Eva looked at Billy in a way he imagined he would someday find familiar, looking for him to explain. While the bartender continued with his story, the man sat, impassively, his hands folded one upon the other on the bar, and then, without a single look of impatience or anger or disgust, only perhaps a single deep breath, a defeated movement of his shoulders, he swung off the barstool and pushed out the door.

The boy from Harvard, it seemed, would have flown the bartender to Paris after the liberation, as a wedding present, if he'd survived the war.

He straightened up again. "This is my round." But Dennis put his hand over his glass and pointed to the place where the man had been.

"What is he, a boozer?"

The bartender turned casually, the cocktail shaker in his hand. He seemed unaware until then that the man had gone, and still maddeningly indifferent to having lost a customer. He shook his head, selecting rye for the girls' old-fashioneds. "We don't serve Jews," he said, as neatly as he poured the drink and placed it on the bar before them.

THEY WERE GRATEFUL to get outside, and more grateful still to get back into the salesman's car and return to the dark and elegant roads of East Hampton. "Well, I think it's a shame," Mary said from the front seat. "Good Lord, what did you boys fight for anyway? Has he read about the camps? What was the war all about—that poor man."

And the other three shook their heads, yes, poor man, but unwilling to let the shame of it, the sluggish, sickening sense of false hope and false promise, invade their idyll in this lovely place.

Billy leaned down toward Eva's lap, pointing out her window. "Look there," he said. "That one. That's my idea of heaven."

They parked at the Coast Guard beach, and the girls sat together on the bumper while the boys found driftwood and built a small fire. While they were gathered around it, the beach became vast and black, and the thud of the invisible ocean, even with its predictable rhythm, seemed relentlessly startling.

They each put an arm around their girl's shoulders, and then Dennis lifted the dimming flashlight and asked Mary to take a walk with him down to the shore. Billy and Eva watched the swaying beam as it moved through the dark and then disappeared over the seawall.

Eva had her shoes off and her white toes were partially buried in the sand. She had her knees raised under her skirt, the skirt's hem pulled down around her ankles. She leaned forward when the other two had gone, moving out of his arm to stare at the burning wood and say, "When I was a child, I used to pretend I was a little person caught down there, inside the fire. A lost soul." She moved a finger to trace an imaginary path. "I'd see myself running, up one log and down the other, to escape the flames."

She turned to him, the firelight on her cheek and her bare arms. "I was certain I was going to hell and I thought it was a good way of practicing—you know, planning how I'd manage in there, how I'd outsmart the devil."

He laughed. Her eyes were marvelous. "What made you think you weren't going to heaven?"

She pulled down the corner of her crooked mouth. "Don't all children think they're going to hell?"

He shook his head. "All children think they're going to be saints—probably martyrs. I did."

"Well then," she said, raising her head so that for a minute he thought she was addressing someone else, perhaps Dennis and Mary returning, some third person out there in the darkness. "There's the difference between you and me."

Kissing her was like inhaling the essence of some vague but powerful alcohol. He recalled his poetry: like taking the wine breath but not the whole wine. He knew it was the literal commingling of her whiskey and his gin, of the smoke from the fire and the sea spray that was too fine to dampen their skin but that had made a delicate veil for her soft hair, one that broke as he moved his fingers through it, perhaps too roughly. But he knew it was something else, too, something that could not be distilled from its parts; that was the dark flavor of desire, but a desire for something he couldn't give a word to—for happiness, sure, for sense, for children—for life itself to be as sweet as certain words could make it seem.

"I wish you would marry me," he told her, surprising himself not because he had broached the subject but because he had not said, "You will."

"Oh, Billy," she whispered, and laughed, straightening his glasses and then, coyly, taking them off completely. "End of September and I'm back home."

Now the darkness around her, and the firelight itself, had softened—even the threatening bang of the ocean had dimmed. "But you'll come back," he said.

She held the glasses between them, against her heart. "It costs a lot of money to go back and forth," she said.

"Then stay," he told her. "Can't you just stay?"

She shook her head. "My parents are there," she said.

"But your sister is here."

"And three more over there."

"Then send for them. Send for your parents, too."

"Oh sure," she said with a laugh.

"I mean it. That's how my father's family did it. Dennis's father came over first and then brought over his six brothers and his sister, and Lord knows how many more."

Her head was bent low now; she was tracing his glasses with a finger, holding them in her lap. "I have to go back," she said. "They're expecting me."

He could see the line of her parted hair, her scalp so white against the rich darkness. "I'll send for you," he told her. "Can I do that? You go home for a while, and as soon as I save the money I'll send for you. I'll bring you back. Can I do that?"

She shook her head only slightly and, with her chin still lowered, whispered, "There's still my family."

"I'll send for them, too," he said, and because he heard her laugh a little, perhaps saw her smile, he added, laughing as well, "I'll send for them all, your parents and your sisters and the next-door neighbors if you want me to. Does your town have a pastor—I'll send for him. A milkman? Him too." She was laughing now. "Is there a baker you're particularly fond of? Any nuns? Cousins? We'll bring them over. We'll bring them all over." It was what his life had held for him all along.

Laughing, she raised her shining eyes, her dark brows that nearly ran together above them and proved, as far as he was concerned, that Nature in her overprotectiveness understood what a glorious pair of eyes She had created. "You're planning to rob a bank or two, are you?"

"Sure," he said. He took her face in his hands, but even this close he couldn't tell if it was firelight or tears that made her eyes shine so, or maybe his own muddled vision. He pulled her to him, but carefully this time. There was a vast darkness beyond them and the indifferent pounding of the sea, and adrift in the same world that held their fine future there was accident and disappointment, a sickening sense of false hope and false promise that required all of God's grace to keep at bay.

Fifty yards away, the dimming flashlight lit a yellowed inch of sea foam and then rolled a little toward the ocean with the water's retreat. The next wave crashed with such a sound it might have been the great iron door of perdition closing behind him. But Dennis hardly flinched.

He would have something to tell the priest at St. Philomena's on Saturday.

TWO WEEKS LATER, Holtzman and his mother came down by train to assess the boys' progress and, for the shoe salesman's sake, to get some idea of just when they might return to the city and their real jobs. Holtzman was a generous man in his way, and he appeared to love his petite wife to distraction, but while half a century of bachelorhood had made him more than ready to indulge her, it had also made him wary. A nation's gratitude was all well and good, but it, like his, was not to be taken advantage of, and should not be expected, he told his wife at the Jamaica station, to outlast the first gesture. The gesture had been made, they had had their hiatus on Long Island. Uncle Sam might be offering twelve for twelve, but he himself put more stock in a young man's financial independence.

And yet the sight of the restored little house elated him. Billy acted as tour guide, and as he pointed out each improvement they had made, Mr. Holtzman congratulated them both for their skillful way with plaster and paint and fresh wood. He patted his heart with forefinger and thumb—it was a gesture of his that always made Dennis think of someone feeding coins into a machine—and told them how, fifteen years before, he had bought the house on impulse, after seeing an ad in the nether reaches of the newspaper. He'd had no idea then what he'd do with it, he said, he only knew it was a good price, an incredible price, as much as the woman who sold it to him—daughter of the now-bankrupt builder—might once have paid for a new dress. Less. He touched his heart. He only knew that he shouldn't pass it up, just as you wouldn't pass up a dime you saw on the sidewalk, even if you had a mason jar filled with them at home. Just as you wouldn't pass a pile of junk at the curb if you saw something, a chair, a table, a three-legged telephone stand, that was usable and whole. (Which explained, Dennis thought, the one in the hallway of the Jamaica house.) She was throwing the house away; he picked it up.

Dennis's mother, in the meantime, strolled through the tiny rooms as if she'd expected no less than smooth walls and fresh paint and new fixtures in the tiny bath. "We're going to have to do something about this furniture if we're going to rent next season," she told her husband, and

Holtzman said, "Sure," in a way that even Dennis could tell—and he hardly knew the man—meant he had no intention of renting at all.

They drove to the bay, passing as they did the newly risen frame of another bungalow. "I think this place is going to get popular," Billy told him. "Long Island's going to start booming, Mr. Holtzman," he said. "You're lucky to have your foot in the door." And Holtzman nodded, fed some more coins to his heart. So well pleased with himself that Dennis couldn't help but say, glancing into the rearview mirror, "There're two sides to lucky, aren't there? There's the guy who picks up the dime and the guy who drops it, isn't there?"

But Holtzman wasn't the sort to imagine himself into anyone else's life. "You boys did a fine job," he said again, as if a compliment was what Dennis was fishing for.

At the beach, they watched him hop awkwardly over the shells and rocks that edged the water and then dive into the bay. Was there another GI in America, Dennis wondered, who had returned from the war to find that a fat German had married his mother?

His mother sat beside him on the blanket he had spread out for her, the wool field blanket he had carried across Europe. She watched her husband from under a straw hat and behind dark glasses, inscrutable.

The day was warm and humidly overcast. Mary and Eva were at a Firemen's Fair with the children. They wouldn't see them today—which he was beginning to think was just as well. Billy was standing at the foot of the blanket, still wearing his T-shirt and pants and his boots, staring out at the water. He had not said Eva's name since they had met his mother and Holtzman at the station, which was either a remarkable display of restraint or a devastating string of opportunityless hours. Either way, Dennis thought, that, too, was just as well.

He had learned at an early age to be careful about what he brought his mother—odd paintings or dreams, fanciful plans—not because she had no interest in him (he was her only child and she was in her way an adoring mother), but because in an instant, he knew, she could show him that the painting was unintelligible, the dream nonsense, the plans intemperate or illogical, or fatally incomplete. She would not do so cruelly or blindly or with any sense of mean-spiritedness, but rather in the same careful and loving way another mother might tell a child that the aspirin was not candy and the laundry bleach not fruit punch.

Growing up, Dennis knew that whenever his father left the kitchen table or walked out of the room, he had only to glance at his mother to learn that whatever story the man had just told them was a lie, an exaggeration, a rehearsal for or a rehash of a story he would tell or had told someone else—the passengers in his car or the men in the saloon or whoever happened to be living in their parlor. Dennis had only to glance at his mother to learn that the man, for all the people in New York City who worshipped him, was flawed, difficult, full of too many other people's lives and not enough of their own, of her own.

What his mother would make of Billy's rabid infatuation he could only guess, but his sense was that it would grow thin under her steady gaze, become a childish delusion, perhaps even to Billy himself. She would, he knew, put it into perspective for him, remind him that it was summer and he'd just returned from the war; that this girl, this Eva, was a stranger, after all, with plans of her own, back to her own country in another few weeks and, when you came right down to it, on fifty a week from Con Ed (minus train fare and clothing and the rent he'd have to pay his poor mother), how likely was it that he'd be sending for her anytime soon? His mother would, Dennis knew, open Billy's eyes for him, diminish things.

But of course two hours without Eva's name crossing his lips was far more than Billy could stand.

He sat heavily at the foot of the blanket and began to unlace his boots. "Where did they say they were going today?" he asked Dennis over his shoulder. "Montauk?"

Dennis glanced at his mother, who had inclined her head toward them ever so slightly.

"A Firemen's Fair," Dennis said.

Billy nodded and smiled. "The children will love that, won't they. Let's hope Mary and Eva can keep up."

Now his mother turned her face, the blind eyes of her dark glasses, fully toward him. Love, Dennis thought, had made Billy not rude but insidious. He knew the discourtesy of this private exchange—the violation of that primary, schoolboy rule of social intercourse, "Is there something you'd like to share with the class?"—would force Dennis's hand. Force him to explain.

"Some children we met here at the beach," he told her. "Seven of them, steps and stairs. They come here every afternoon with their nursemaids so they can paddle in the bay. They have a house in the village, but they like to come here because one of the little girls . . ."

"Sally," Billy added, unable to resist. He was in love with all of them.

"Sally," Dennis continued, "is terrified of the waves."

His mother smiled a little under her dark glasses. She was sitting erectly on the blanket, holding one knee. Her skin was ivory white and downy and scattered with pale freckles. In the shade of her hat she could have been twenty.

"They have a fabulous house," Billy went on, the opportunity here at last. "Nearly a mansion, and they just use it in the summer. Pudding Hill Lane is the name of the street. Like something from a nursery rhyme, don't you think? Seven children in a house on Pudding Hill Lane."

"You've been there?" his mother said pleasantly. Billy blushed from his throat to the roots of his hair—no, from his waist to the roots of his hair; even his white T-shirt seemed to turn pink. "We've taken the girls out," he said. "The nursemaids, what, Dennis, two, three times now?"

"About that," Dennis said, and pulled his own shirt up over his head. "Are you going to swim?" he asked Billy, cutting short a sentence that began "They're Irish girls . . ." Billy still had his glasses on and so had vision enough to catch Dennis's look.

"All right," he said, reluctantly pulling off his shirt, reluctantly closing the marvelous door that for a moment had allowed him to say Eva, Sally, Mary, Pudding Hill Lane . . .

As they waded into the water Dennis said softly, "Don't tell her any more about the girls."

Billy looked at him with innocent, myopic eyes. "All

right," he said, and then could not help but add, "Guilt must be a terrible thing."

Dennis felt the reproach but laughed. It was, after all, Billy's sweet romance he had thought to preserve.

"Guilt is glorious," Dennis told him with a wink. "When it's well earned." And then dove into the same salt water Holtzman was floating in—making, when you thought about it, a fine stew.

HIS MOTHER ALWAYS IRONED Holtzman's shirt first, down in the basement of the Jamaica house, on an ironing board she set up once, in April of '45, and never took down again. She washed their shirts by hand in the sink down there and then ironed them the next morning. Holtzman's first, she said, because he was, after all, her husband, the owner of this spacious house, sponsor of the feast. Her son's second, because the iron would be hotter by then and so make a neater collar. Loyalty, to blood or to water, being a complicated thing for his mother.

The routine they fell into after he and Billy returned from Long Island that summer was a balancing act. She'd be in the kitchen when Dennis came down in the morning, making his coffee and buttering his toast, but she'd never eat anything herself. She'd wait for Holtzman. Instead, she'd lean against the counter and watch her son, assessing: the cut of his suit, the knot in his tie, the prospects for his future. Although at that time in her life she had held only two jobs herself—one in a bakery in Brooklyn, one in the mailroom of the gas company—she had a considered opinion about what the workaday world could do to you, and it wasn't a very high opinion, either, despite her Protestant blood.

In part, she objected to the monotony of nine-to-five, the tedium, the hours and days you ended up wishing away, swinging from one Saturday morning to another like a monkey at the zoo. In part, it was the anonymity: Forget what dreams you'd dreamt the night before, forget the adoring eye that beheld you over breakfast, or even the grief that had been wringing out your soul all night long, because the way she saw it, once you boarded the subway or the bus or joined the crawling stream of automobiles or found your space in the revolving door, the elevator, behind the desk or the counter or the machine, you became what you really were—you became, when you got right down to it, what you really were: one of the so many million, just one more.

As a boy, Dennis had been made to recite "The Village Blacksmith" for every guest and boarder and drinking partner his father brought to the house. He would stand in the middle of the parlor or, in summer, when the place was stifling with immigrants and heat, in the middle of a circle of them up on the roof, and emote: "Under a spreading chestnut tree . . ."

Whenever he reached the lines

> *Each morning sees some task begin,*
> *Each evening sees it close;*
> *Something attempted, something done,*
> *Has earned a night's repose.*

his old dad's eyes would fill with tears—a full stanza be-hind the tears that had already sprung to the eyes of every other Irishman in the room as soon as he figured out that the blacksmith's wife was dead—and when the poem was finished, those were the lines his father would ask him to repeat.

Dennis had only to glance at his mother to learn that she found no charm in the words, that it sounded to her like monotony. A slow march to an unremarkable end.

The job at Edison, in fact, had been a gift to his dying father from Bart Carroll and Uncle Jim, who already worked there, back in '37, when Dennis was eighteen. "The greatest city in the world will always need electric-ity," his father had said, well pleased, his face under the hospital lights already a death's-head. The death's-door smell of ether. The other visitors around him—brothers, cousins, friends—had agreed. "Dennis will do all right," they'd said, touching his shoulder, patting his back, turn-ing him a bit so he would not see the way his father drew up his knees under the thin sheets, so he would not see his father, who had loved life, being pulled from it, writh-ing, by a miserable death.

"Any one of the utilities would be a safe bet," they told him, turning him away. "But you can't do better than Edison, Dennis. There's security, if you stick with them. Stick with the company and you'll be fine."

At home, his mother said, Cooper Union, City College, the RCA Institute if electricity's what you're interested in. A public-speaking course then. The service, officer's training. Something else. Something more.

He had humored her, sitting through night classes when he could, joining the Army in '41, telling her, to her consternation, that there wasn't much he wanted in the long run. That when he got right down to it, he was happy enough with what he had.

Now, on these mornings after he and Billy had returned from their hiatus on Long Island, she watched him get ready to go to the office, forever ordinary, as far as she was concerned, forever out of uniform and in suits that she thought could have been better tailored (although his shirt was well pressed). She watched him eat his breakfast, adjust his hat in the mirror in the hall, lift his briefcase and his umbrella, and head out to the bus that would take him to the subway that would take him to the office, precisely as she knew he would be doing for the next forty years, and she would not be able to disguise her regret. He could see it in her face as she watched from the front window: good-natured son, loyal employee like his father, one of the so many million. Just one more.

Holtzman would come down the stairs as Dennis went out the door, and he'd always take his time saying good morning to her and putting on his hat and his coat, making sure that Dennis was a good three or four blocks ahead of him before he himself set out to pick up his morning paper at the corner store. If the bus was late, Dennis would see him there, tossing a nickel into the cigar box where Dennis had just tossed his. They'd both raise their respective copies, intent on three-inch headlines and at the ready with an expression of complete surprise (Well, hello, didn't see you) should either one of them acknowledge the other, which of course neither one of them ever did.

Back at the mansion, Dennis knew, his mother would have the eggs boiling and a plate of sliced bread set out on the stove. When Holtzman came in, he would pin each piece to a long fork and toast it perfectly over the open flame of the gas burner. He did the same for Dennis on weekends. Dennis imagined that it had been the bane of the man's long bachelorhood: having no one for whom to demonstrate this technique.

("And you ask me," my father said, "if I think Danny Lynch is a lonely soul.")

Every morning, Holtzman and his mother sat catty-corner at the old kitchen table where Dennis had once done his homework, where his father had once sat, recited, sung, put his forehead to the bare wood when the night had been long and the sun too quick to rise. Sitting catty-corner, Holtzman and his mother talked about money: investments they had made, bills that were owed, profit from the store, and the wholesale price of shoes. Every once in a while Holtzman would reach under the table to pat her knee or she would touch his hand, still talking, so that anyone watching from behind the kitchen's thick-paned windows would think they'd been pledging love for half an hour over their cooling eggs, not determining the limits of their inventory.

She was a continual marvel to Holtzman, as far as Dennis could see, this tiny woman who had arrived so unexpectedly into his late middle age. She seemed to think of him as the embodiment of good sense, practicality, relief, the soundest investment she had ever made.

When they had eaten, he would take the paper and a second cup of coffee into the living room or, more discreetly, up the stairs to the hall bath, while she did the dishes and then went down to the basement to start the wash. It always gave her enormous pleasure to consider how her marriage had brought her not merely a house but a basement. A basement all her own. It struck her as a great luxury not to have to maneuver around the baby carriages and footlockers and the deplorable armchairs of a dozen neighbors but to be able to sail, unimpeded, from stair to washtub to clothesline and ironing board—which she had set up in April of 1945, when she first moved in, and would never be required to take down again.

Of course, Holtzman's basement wasn't empty, but what it contained was mostly hers—her footlockers and garment bags and end tables. As she had said in her letters to Dennis overseas, Holtzman was terribly reasonable about her things, insisting that since she was the one giving up her apartment (her home, he'd called it), then she should not give up her furniture as well. It hadn't taken much to accommodate it all: his house had three times as many rooms as the apartment, and what became redundant, his dining room and kitchen set, for instance, a number of lamps, a bed, he had generously allowed her to offer to her late husband's relatives. With the war ending, there were plenty of takers among the various cousins, even among those who hadn't found homes of their own yet, or even spouses. Holtzman's old kitchen chairs, for instance, ended up in Mary Lynch's bedroom in Astoria, piled in a column against the wall for what must have been at least three years, maybe four: a monument to hope her father, Uncle Jim, used to call it, until Mary met Jack Casey just in time (she was nearing thirty herself) and the chairs became kitchen chairs once again.

For Dennis's mother, these excess bits of furniture not only established her new role as benefactress (she, who for so long, throughout her first marriage, in fact, and well before, had been supplicant); they also paid off a debt. She was, to a great extent, beholden to her first husband's people, who had supported her so generously during the period of his illness and her widowhood and especially in the years after Dennis joined the service. And throughout those years, try as she might to pay them back, or even to temper their generosity with the insistence that her widow's pension was sufficient, her needs few, they would only hold up their hands and respond with some long and often exaggerated tale of what selfless and bighearted miracle "her Daniel" had once done for them, tales that would more often than not end with tears and a "God bless his soul," or a "We won't see another one like him again," until she, Sheila Lynch, the impoverished widow with the soldier son, would find herself brewing them a cup of tea or pouring out a drop of vermouth or putting an arm across their shoulders to whisper, "There there."

My father would say this much for his mother: she never distanced herself from her first husband's family after she married Holtzman. As much as she might have liked to.

In the basement, she would plug in the iron and pause to see if the lights would flicker—they did, something to ask Dennis about. She'd fill her sprinkler bottle at the sink and take the shirts from the line and iron them: her husband's and then her son's.

HE HAD BEEN, WITHOUT question, Holy Father to the entire clan, her Daniel. Forty-four years old when she met him, with a shock of dark hair falling down into his homely face. Holy Father to the world, if it had let him.

The story went that she had been living at the time off Nostrand Avenue in a small and airless apartment that belonged to her Great-uncle Robert and Aunty Eileen, his dour wife. They didn't want her there—she had seen the man bite his lip when she reached for a second piece of toast and grip the table, as if he might at any minute leap up to stay her hand if she poured more than a splash of milk into her oatmeal. But their only son had left for Europe and news of his empty bedroom reached Washington Heights, where she had been living with another, younger aunt and uncle, sharing a bed with an eight-year-old cousin—a boy with limbs of lead and the odor of a wet overcoat.

Aunty Eileen had resisted the idea of some sixteen-year-old girl occupying her son's room (drilling the scent of her hair into his pillow, scattering undergarments, bleeding onto his mattress—she thought of everything, that woman) and relented only after she swore never to dress or undress in the son's room. She was instead directed to leave her bags in a corner of the pantry and to change her clothes there before her uncle was up in the morning and after he went to bed at night. This she did willingly—her cousin's wide feather bed, all to herself, was such a luxury—and seeing her up and all ready for school just as he was shuffling into the kitchen must have given her uncle an inspiration.

She wasn't there long when he announced that he'd found a little something for her to do. A couple he knew, countrymen of his, had a bakery on DeKalb, and since the wife was troubled with back problems, they could use a girl to come in first thing in the morning to set out the breads and the cakes. He never said how much she would be paid and she understood without asking that whatever money she made would go straight to him. Her uncle knew that it had been her parents' dying wish that she stay in school, and he himself had enrolled her at Manual Training the very day she left Washington Heights, but the morning job was a nice way of offsetting what the care of her would cost him without compromising whatever reluctant pact he had made with the dead.

The day before she was to start, she went by the place after school. Only the baker's wife, Mrs. Dixon, was there, but she was rosy-cheeked and merry and cried out when she saw her, "Oh, but you're a wee little thing!"

It was like a fairy tale, that first morning. The streets were wet and dark, full of reflections. Somewhat ominous, sure, so early in the morning that it was nighttime still, but also full of promise, adventure. When she came into the empty shop it was warm and dimly lit and full of the scent of baking bread.

All the light came from the back, where the ovens were, but there was enough light to see by, and she found the cap and coat she was to wear folded neatly on the counter. She thought of the elves and the shoemaker. She covered her hair and slipped into the smock. Yesterday, when Mrs. Dixon had showed it to her, it had buckled over her shoes. Now it was hemmed to just the right length, ten inches above her ankles.

Hesitantly, but ready to begin, she peered into the light of the back room. She felt the heat of the stove like a warm hand on her face, and then she saw the baker sitting on a stool beside one of the wooden tables. His shoes and his pant legs beneath his apron were covered with flour; his shoulders were slumped and he had his hand around the glass that was resting on the table beside him. He was a dark-haired man with black brows and a broad, flushed face.

He looked up at her from under those brows and then waved his free hand and said, not unkindly, "Well, come in, come in. I'm not going to bite you."

She stepped in. The wooden floor seemed soft and it, too, was covered with flour. On another huge table just opposite the great cast-iron stove there was a sheet of scones not yet baked and a wicker basket full of small brown loaves.

"My wife showed you what to do?" he asked.

She nodded. "Yes," she said, but there was little voice in it.

She had to rise up on her tiptoes to get a good grip on the basket and then nearly crashed into the doorframe as she carried it out, feeling him watching her. When she returned, he was standing, slipping the sheet of scones into the oven; another sheet, golden brown and redolent, was on the wide table. He looked at her over his shoulder as he closed the oven door. "You're a little bit of a thing, aren't you?" he said pleasantly, friendlier than he'd been before.

They were standing together in the narrow space between the oven and the table, and the empty basket in her hands made the space seem narrower still. He suddenly reached out and pulled at her earlobe with a floured hand. "A wee thing," he said. He wasn't much bigger, really only a head taller, than she, but his chest was broad and had begun to press against the basket and her arm. He tugged at a strand of hair near her temple, poked at her cap. By now she could smell the drink on his breath but didn't know enough then to recognize it for what it was.

"A wee baby doll in her dress," he said, and pulled at the collar of her smock. He chucked her chin. She only grinned, blushing. He was old enough and she was young enough; she believed he was playing with her the way you would play with a young child, admiring her, making friends.

He told her to take the empty basket to the kneading table. She was grateful to be free of that tight space, free of his attention. She could feel her face begin to cool.

He was on her so fast she thought for a moment that the lights had gone out. He had her head in the crook of his arm and so startled her that he caught her opened mouth with his own and she could hear the click of their front teeth. It was not a kiss, it was all teeth and wet bone, and she could feel the low laughter in his chest in the moment before he released her. Laughing still, he turned casually back to his work.

Out in the shop, she dropped half the scones and had to wipe them off on her new smock. She rubbed her mouth with the sleeve. In the back, he had begun to sing. Pieces of folk songs and of lullabies. Some of the songs her own father had sung—a beautiful maiden much loved by a young boy going off to war, a sea captain bound for his last voyage, kissing his wife at the garden gate. When she returned with the empty tray, he merely glanced at her over his shoulder, his mouth now gently shaped for his tune. He had a good voice, soft and sweet, although the words gave him some trouble.

When she left the shop that morning, the sun was up and the street, newly washed, smelled like the coming spring. The world was populated again, with people whom she might, in time, come to know. On the way, she met a plump girl from her class, Alma, who was delighted to accept the bag of warm scones Mrs. Dixon had pressed upon her as she left the store. "I don't like them," she told Alma by way of explanation. "Never did."

She lived the next year not so much in a nightmare as on the verge of one. Because there was no telling. Days would go by and he wouldn't touch her. Then there would be a jolly morning: he might be singing, icing a cake, and in an instant he'd have her by the throat. Or worse, she'd come in to find him morose, mostly silent, hardly moving from his stool. She'd keep her eye on him then, avoid him whenever she could—even taking things out of the oven herself, which Mrs. Dixon told her never to do, so she would not have to disturb him. Sometimes it would work, and she'd slip out of the shop at eight o'clock like a fish released to a stream. Sometimes he would raise his heavy brows and say her name again and again—"Shee-la, Shee-la"—wagging his great head, until she had come close enough for him to grab her wrist or her skirt or her sleeve and aim his murderous yellow teeth toward her breasts. Sometimes he would just appear behind her and take hold of her hair. He'd back her up against the alley door or press her into a wall.

("A filthy, dirty man," she said, telling the tale. This would have been in their kitchen in Woodside at the crumb-scattered table, just Dennis and his mother alone in the apartment now. Dennis just beginning his career with Con Ed. What was lucky, she'd said, was that the man was a drinker, or else who knows how far he might have gone. "A man can't, you know," she'd said. "After too many drinks. I don't suppose your father ever told you.")

Child that she still was, she began devising rituals that might protect her, or at least predict for her how the morning would run. If she could walk from her uncle's building to the bakery without lifting her eyes, he wouldn't touch her that day. If she saw the street sweeper's cart at the corner, he would.

Then there came a morning when she handed Alma her bag of treats and Alma said, "I'm going to miss these."

She had a job, at an office building downtown. Her father had put her onto it. She was leaving school at the end of the week. Two hours later Sheila herself sat in front of the man Alma had described. He was a balding man with a mustache and a bow tie and an old-fashioned high collar. The cubicle he met her in was small, with one window wide-open to let in the breeze. He began by talking a little about the war and the patriotism of American youth and asked if anyone near and dear to her was over there, carrying her picture.

She said no. Had she leaned any farther back in her chair she'd have been out the window herself.

He gave her the job, no doubt because he thought she was a serious and steady young woman bound for spinsterhood. She didn't go back to the bakery. She didn't finish school either. She knew this part of it would have been a blow to her parents, who had been mad for education, but in the nearly half dozen years since they had both—one within four months of the other—taken sick and died (her mother not taking nearly so long to go about it, hurrying to join him, someone had said), she had received very little aid from them and even less comfort. At twelve she had imagined two hovering angels to guide her for the rest of her life, but she had since lived too many desolate nights in rooms where she was not wanted and did not belong, eaten too many bitter meals, every bite and every sip counted and resented. She had tasted Mr. Dixon's breath, smelled the sharp, lingering scent of his saliva on her cheeks and lips even as she bowed her head and asked them to deliver her. Had they lived, she knew, they would have been sorry to see her leaving school, but they hadn't and that was all.

("That was all," she had said in the tiny kitchen in Woodside, in the middle of her dark fairy tale. Something else his God-fearing, ghost-hearing, saint-loving father hadn't told him: they hadn't lived and that was all.)

Her uncle frowned to disappoint his friend, but since she would turn her salary over to him, he was reconciled.

On a Monday morning, she joined Alma on the train. She figured she had pulled herself from the edge of hell, and even if the job proved dull (which it did) and Alma, without her daily bakery bribe, disloyal (she did not), there was the luxury, anyway, of this gray purgatory.

At Borough Hall, she followed her friend's wide rump up the steps of the streetcar. Eclipsed by the great expanse of black gabardine that was Alma, she heard his brogue first, that loud and laughing voice. And then, climbing aboard, she got her first glimpse of his homely, happy face.

WHEN SHE WENT UPSTAIRS again, Holtzman would have opened the window and sprayed the bathroom with cologne. She'd give him his pressed shirt and hang Dennis's in his room. (Another luxury her marriage had brought her: closets to store things in, closets to step into.) When Holtzman was dressed and ready, he would find her again and kiss her goodbye. He would always have the newspaper under his arm and, without fail, it seemed, a shoebox. He was daily finding new shoes for her in her size (it was, after all, the way he'd wooed her), and more often than not she found them lacking—a harder sell as a wife, my father said, than she had ever been as a customer.

Holtzman took the bus to the store in those days, and as soon as he was gone she would put on a housedress and wrap her hair in a duster and clean. You have to understand what the house meant to her, a woman who had spent so much of her adolescence as a guest in already overburdened households, sleeping on the edge of beds, keeping her clothes in a box out in the pantry or the hall-way. Who had spent her first married life in one- and two-bedroom apartments that also served as permanent way stations for an endless string of penniless Irish immigrants.

He was a character. This was the word the passengers on the trolley said to one another, or so the story went: men in straw hats and bowlers (in those days), women in their dark office costumes. They'd lean toward one an-other in their seats, smiling over something he'd said or, more likely, cried out. "Isn't he a character?"

"Is it spats you're wearing today, Mr. Ellsworth?" he might ask the frail old gentleman who had just, cautiously, seated himself. "Aren't they handsome? Now, if you die in those today, you know, the undertaker will be dancing in them tomorrow."

Mr. Ellsworth would grin, "Oh, I won't die today, Mr. Lynch,"—the passengers all around them smiling in an-ticipation as if they were watching a couple of vaudeville comedians—"not until I hear what happened to Paddy at Asbury Park."

Daniel would lift his cap and brush back that shock of thick dark hair. "Jaysus," he'd tell them, "there's a tale."

He was a legend—at least in that part of Brooklyn at that hour of the day. He talked constantly, pointing out as he did some fellow on the street, or a cop he knew, or a building that was a part of another story. Eventually, the talk always came around to Paddy—and sometimes Paddy was a brother and sometimes Paddy was a cousin and sometimes an uncle or a friend. Paddy making the crossing and Paddy on Ellis Island and Paddy taking the wrong train to Pittsburgh or Vermont.

"Paddy's in Philadelphia. My brother put him onto a job there, making cre-aam cheese, of all things. He's staying with some relations who have a cat as big as a suitcase, and when Paddy comes home the first day at the factory, he smells for all the world like a six-foot bottle of milk . . ."

There were passengers who waited on the street, letting other cars pass, in order to board Daniel's. Others who timed their commutes simply to be able to ride with him.

Sheila began to do the same. Not because she cared for his stories—too many of them, she said, were either impossible or absurd—and not because he called her by name or tickled her fancy each day with some sly running joke (old Mr. Ellsworth had made it through another night, and sweet-faced and asthmatic Mrs. Timoney, always huffing and puffing, was being sought by the police, and Saul, a hunchbacked office boy, was a colonel just back from the front, even fat Alma, who carried an umbrella no matter the weather, was a prognosticator of disastrous storms—"Tornadoes today, miss?" "Is there a typhoon in the air?"). She waited for his car because she silenced him.

Her life had slipped into its tedious routine. Out of the son's bed by dawn (and always with a shudder to recall what other early mornings had brought) and a quick wash and dress in the tiny space of the pantry. Breakfast for herself and her aunt and uncle and then the washing up, the walk to the train. In the mailroom she was corraled like a horse with an unending number of envelopes and packages, twenty minutes for lunch, ten for coffee . . . one of the many million, just one more.

But once or twice a day, if she caught the right car, she was a rarity, a sphinx. She was watched for. She silenced him.

He who had something to say to everyone could only stammer and blush as she walked by, could only say, "Good day, miss," and not even that if she looked him straight in the eye. The other passengers saw it, even Alma saw it, and the initial surprise it had engendered gave way to curiosity and then a sympathetic awe. He was in love with her, they whispered, had to be. And she giving him nothing in return, not even the time of day. In that odd moment of silence that always followed her boarding, she was the one who had everybody's attention, not Daniel.

And that was what she couldn't get enough of—after the life she had led. To be noticed, to be singled out. To be recognized as someone unlike any other.

It was midsummer the morning his car pulled in, but he was not on it. There was a general backing down the stairs. "Where's Daniel?" someone asked, debating whether to go forward or to wait.

"Out today," the strange man said.

Resignedly, they boarded, and just as they were seated, Daniel himself swung up into the car, looking ridiculous in a brown suit and a straw hat with a green-and-yellow-striped band. He was flushed and breathless.

The other passengers greeted him as if he were a returning hero, but he ducked his head shyly and took the seat just behind her.

"Any hurricanes?" he asked Alma, but with unutterable sadness, as if he had just been gutted of all humor

and all resolve. She giggled and squeezed her arms together, turning in her seat to see him. "Not yet," she said.

His brown eyes were on the back of Sheila's neck.

"Your day on the town, Daniel?" a passenger asked
him.

"You might say that." But nothing more for them. Not
this day.

"Out and about with Paddy?" a woman asked from
across the aisle.

"No," he said softly. "Not me."

When she got up to leave the car, she turned to him—
what a lost soul he seemed, in his brown suit and his good
hat. She saw that whatever it was he had imagined he
would say or do had been washed out of all possibility,
just the way the color was washed from his face.

The next day, he was himself again, although he red-
dened even before she passed him. His cousin Paddy was
getting married, he told them. Lucky man. To a redhead,
no less. Not very big, but with a fine face. He was having
some trouble with the ring, however—he's thick, is
Paddy—with the size of the ring, and so he took a two-
cent washer and a ham bone down to the jeweler . . .

Everyone's eyes going to her as he spoke. She watching only the street: a girl unlike any other.

In September, the women in the office were warned
that they might have to make way for the returning veterans. On a Friday night in October she came home to
find Mr. and Mrs. Dixon in the living room, him with his
suit on and his hair slicked back as if he had come court-
ing, her heavier than she had been, her moon face hanging
wider and lower than usual over its cushion of soft chins.

When she went into her bedroom to take off her hat, she saw that the mattress had been stripped, the pillows and blankets heaped across the opened window.

The son was coming home (on Aunty Eileen's yellow face, joy looked like a stomach disorder) and she would have to find another place for herself. The Dixons had a little extra room in their apartment above the store—tiny, Mrs. Dixon said, but neat—and with a child on the way (Mrs. Dixon touched her wide waist) they would need someone to help them full-time. So it could all work out very nicely.

Over dinner, Mr. Dixon moved his black little teeth to say, "You're not eating."

And Uncle Robert laughed and said she usually ate plenty.

On the trolley car that Monday, she followed Alma's swaying backside up the stairs and then said, "Hello, Daniel," with an angel's smile. "How are you today?" There was a pause (she was certain) and then, from somewhere in the car, a smattering of applause.

"I'm fine, thank you, miss," Daniel said. "It's a lovely day, isn't it?"

"Yes, it is," she told him, although it was cold and damp with a spitting rain. "Just lovely." Passing old Mr. Ellsworth in his seat, she swore she saw a tear in his eye. Not dead yet, after all.

The rest of the story went that on her second morning as a young bride she stepped out of her bedroom and found two characters asleep on the living-room floor. They wore mismatched parts of dirty suits and used their battered satchels for pillows and they slept with their hands tucked between their thighs, like hobos. There was a warm, barnyard odor in the air.

She stepped back, startled, and bumped into Daniel ("your dad," she said in the kitchen in Woodside when the word alone was enough to make Dennis's heart ache with his own loss), who was right behind her. "Who are they?" she had asked.

"Paddy" was the answer.

She claimed she never again had the place all to herself and would not have it to herself until Dennis went off to Fort Dix.

She never had his attention all to herself again, either, my father said, not even when he was dying and the parade of Paddys in and out of the ward where he lay so impressed all the nurses that one of them had asked—or so he'd heard told—Is he a politician?

But now she had this sturdy house, all brick, three bedrooms upstairs and a full basement and foot after foot of baseboard to dust and floor to polish. A tiny garage out back, a small yard with a tree, a front hedge. You could say it was the influence of her tidy German husband that transformed her from the indifferent housekeeper she had been while Dennis was growing up into the cleaning dervish she became as Mrs. Holtzman, but the more likely explanation seemed to be that cleaning Holtzman's house was her way of pacing off her acreage, tallying her assets, running her hands through her pile of gold doubloons. There was a laundry list of reasons why she had married again and not one of them had anything to do with love, but with enough space (when you came right down to it), enough baseboard and yard and empty room, enough heat in the winter and sufficient windows to open for a cross breeze in summer, love was an easy thing to do without.

For some of us, anyway.

IN THOSE DAYS, Billy was at Irving Place, too—and it wasn't unusual for Dennis to run into him in the morning, on the subway or out on the street. Strangers watching them in those days would have thought they were long-lost comrades-in-arms, a couple of ex-GIs, maybe brothers, who had not seen each other since before the invasion. Dennis would catch a glimpse of light off Billy's glasses and shove his way through the standing commuters in his car to shout, "Hey, Bill!" Or he'd hear his own name out on the street and turn to see Billy bobbing through the traffic, heading toward him. "How are you?" "How's things?" Shaking hands and slapping their fresh newspapers on each other's back. "Good to see you."

It would take an act of will to picture him now as he was then: to put aside every image that had come in between, including that dark, stiffly bloated remnant of his face that was Billy in death, and remember him clearly: thin and handsome in those days, the dipped brim of his fedora over the blue eyes and the rimless glasses, a nick of dried blood on his smooth cheek, a red blush from the cold. A lingering scent of the church he had just come from on his overcoat, and a taste of the Eucharist still on his breath as they stood together in the crowded subway car, hand over hand on the same white pole, exchanging shouted bits of news or falling into silence as the train rattled and screeched and tried to knock them off their feet. As glad for each other's company as if they'd long been deprived of it.

("The way your brothers used to be," my father said. In their teens and early twenties, when a buddy or two would come by the house and they'd all stand in the living room for a few minutes before they went out, grinning, knocking shoulders, laughing at everything because the world that just moments before had seemed the source of only aggravation and concern had suddenly become easy and diverting, theirs for the taking. " 'Pity the girls,' I used to tell your mother when they'd gone"—tires screeching out of the driveway and the furniture they had dwarfed beginning to crawl out of the corners again. " 'Pity the poor girls,' " as my parents went back to their newspapers or Friday-night TV shows and tried to keep the smell of the boys' aftershave in their nostrils, because they could not, as they would have preferred, stand out in the street to look after the taillights. " 'The girls,' your mother would always say, 'can take care of themselves.' ")

The daily Masses were a new thing with Billy, and tied up with Eva no doubt, although the relatives thought it had something to do with the war. He would not have been the first in the neighborhood to have come back with a new need for religion, a new sense that only the daily, formal petition for mercy would get them through the rest of their lives.

But what Billy was asking for in those days was not mercy, or maybe it was mercy of another kind. The mercy of time. He needed time—weeks at work and bits of his salary tucked away and saved—but he needed to stop time as well. He needed the world to hold its breath for a while; for all affections, all hopes, all plans for the future to stop in their tracks for a while, to remain as they were, all across the city. For all of us to be true to our own intentions.

The church itself would have obliged: the good sound of the familiar Latin, the same women every morning saying their beads, the red sanctuary lamp, and the candles beneath the statues of the Virgin and St. Joseph, steadfast and true.

Even old Father Roche, an insomniac who said the six o'clock Mass every morning, because, Billy knew from his own days as an altar boy, he would be sound asleep in the sacristy by eight. Unchanging.

And yet: from his sister Kate's bedroom at any hour of the night there came her husband's hushed and angry voice, and more often than not when Billy left for Mass she would be on the couch in the living room with Danny, her baby, in her arms. She would be crying softly.

"Are you all right?" Billy would whisper, awkwardly, embarrassed for her.

She would wave him away. "I'm fine."

The poor child, nearly two but wrapped like an infant against the drafts, wide-eyed, watching them both.

On the drainboard in the kitchen, shades of his father when he was alive, there would be a bottle of gin and an empty glass, his mother's antidote for a widow's long nights.

After Mass, on the platform at the Woodside station, among the pressing crowd of strangers headed toward the train, Billy would hear his name called out and turn. Or, walking toward the office, he'd see a hat on a head and above a pair of shoulders that he would recognize as Dennis's. They'd slap each other with their newspapers and grin madly at the not-at-all-unlikely happenstance of meeting. "How are you?" "What's up?" "How's Mary?" "What do you hear from Eva?" "Eva's fine, had a letter on Tuesday." At last and the first of the day: "Eva's fine." Even the mention of her name, the shouting of it over the subway's roar, an act of courage, a reaffirmation of faith.

THESE WERE THE DAYS when everyone they knew was getting married or having babies. When it was not unusual for the hat to be passed around the office two or three times a day, a big diamond glittering on the finger of the girl who handed out the card and the pen.

"Is this for you?" Dennis would always kid her before he signed. "Come on, when is it going to be for you?"

She was a pretty blonde, round-faced and small-mouthed. A great white smile that had a kind of bonus in it: the electric click of snapped gum. She was engaged to her high-school sweetheart, who was still in the Navy.

"What do you want to marry a sailor for?" he'd ask her as he signed his name to the card. "Who's going to be the Sunshine Girl when you leave?"

She'd grin (snap, snap) and lean over to take the card and the pen from his hand. "I want to marry a sailor," she'd say. "So I'm not the Sunshine Girl when I'm sixty-three."

Claire Donavan was her name. From Brooklyn via Stenography.

That fall and all through the winter and spring they

visited more churches and synagogues than Dennis could have imagined—following hand-printed maps or hastily copied instructions, riding the subway in good suits or driving with Billy or Danny or Mike, or with his mother and Holtzman in the old car. Or crowded into a taxi with a group from the office, dry-mouthed and laughing over what they couldn't remember about the night before. There was always the smell of bay rum and Vitalis and Chanel. The hangover breaking up like dark ice in the fall sunlight or a bracing winter rain, or in the triumph of finding St. Charles Borromeo in Brooklyn or Faith United Methodist in Hastings or Beth El in Little Neck, Queens, with twenty minutes—time for a quick cup of coffee—to spare.

And then the stepping inside, resisting the habit, in the Protestant churches, of reaching for the holy-water font (although, more often than not, they blessed themselves anyway, the ushers in their morning suits smiling to see it: with a face like that how could he do otherwise?), and slipping the yarmulke on in the synagogues, self-conscious but game (the jokes in the Yiddish accent would come later), the point of the ceremony, of their gathering like this in their best clothes and their polished shoes being everywhere the same.

For Billy, it was sustenance. Even the churches and synagogues themselves provided sustenance: crowded among apartment buildings or brownstones, sitting among trees or parking lots, appearing as you climbed up out of the subway or made the last of a dozen wrong turns through suburban streets or flipped the map upside down and looked through the windshield to say, "It should be here." The number and variety of them sustained him. The sense that in every town, up to the Bronx and out to Staten Island and even far into New Jersey, the need for faith, for that which was steadfast and true, had given rise to these holy places. These cathedrals and sanctuaries and catering-hall altars before which Grace from Stenography might stand, or Jack from Service or Peggy Lynch, Uncle Mike's pretty daughter, or her sister Rosemary, who was not the pretty one, or Tommy from the neighborhood or cousin Ted (straight as an arrow in his morning suit, you had to hand it to him, considering how comatose with drink he'd been the night before). Stand and say, "This will not change."

On Sunday evenings while Dennis was going into Manhattan to meet Mary (taking the subway when he had resolved to sin no more, Holtzman's car when just one more was the current resolution), Billy wrote to Eva. Still in his suit pants and the clean shirt he'd worn to Mass. His mother—God help her, she was a miserable cook— would be toughening up a roast in the oven and cooking the color out of Brussels sprouts and green beans (figuring that flavor was not inherent in the vegetables themselves but acquired after long simmering when they were doused in their serving bowls with butter and salt). Rosie and Mac, her husband, would be at his mother's or the movies, Kate down to Uncle Ted's with the baby so her husband could study.

"Dear Eva," he would write, and no doubt he could have filled a page with it, the way he loved to repeat her name: "Hello, Eva. How are you, Eva?"

He told her how he spent his days, writing as well as

he could, but being careful, too, he said, not to go on too long about ordinary things. He knew better than to say everything he felt. But he also knew that the listing of too many ordinary details was worse. To say what he felt would have been to stifle with one sentence a thousand others. But to say only what he'd done would be like describing a city that blocked out the sun.

He must have thought of the girl in Metz—"I am still here"—because surely it was all he meant to write to Eva, every Sunday as his mother put out her wedding china and Mac and Rosemary bustled in and Kate returned with the baby to timidly knock on her own bedroom door. As somewhere some church rang a distant bell and a bus spit exhaust on the boulevard and Mary took Dennis's arm as they crossed Park, headed toward Lexington and a bar-and-grill owned by an Irishman who'd been brought over by his father. As the water struck the sand that led to the great house on the hill that Billy and Eva would marvel at again, together, his idea of heaven, before returning to their idyll in Holtzman's little place, an idyll that would begin whenever the money he was putting away each week, which was increasing itself incrementally, even now, over at East River Savings, had grown sufficient enough to bring her back.

Unwavering faith: This will not change. I am still here.

But the money was slow in growing.

There were all the wedding presents, after all, the baby gifts and bachelor parties and the office collections and cab fares and cleaning bills. There was the money he gave Kate when she needed a lift after a night of the baby crying and Peter, her scholar of a husband, shouting about the exam he had to take the next day, the studying he'd not yet done. There was the money he lent his cousin Ted when he smashed his car on Queens Boulevard—so his new wife wouldn't know—and the money he gave his mother when she broke her bridge. There was the special collection for Father Roche's fiftieth year as a priest.

"You're more like my father than my father was," Dennis told him one night at Quinlan's when he was crying in his beer that he would not have the boat fare by summer, much as he tried.

"In this family," Billy said, his glass to his heart, "you couldn't say a kinder word."

Danny Lynch raised his own drink. "Amen to that," he said, ever the keeper of the flame.

IN THOSE DAYS, Dennis had his territory on the Lower East Side, from Broadway to the river, Houston to Canal, shops full of Jewish and Chinese merchants, streets littered with bums. The bums would pull themselves out of doorways when they saw him coming, rise from the edges of curbs to say, "We're moving, Officer, we're moving"—as if any round-faced Irishman in a topcoat and a hat had to be a cop. They'd salute like old soldiers, or hunch their shoulders and cower like serfs in the Middle Ages, like men who more than once had felt a nightstick crack upon their backs. "We're moving, Detective." Dennis would raise a fist at them, touch his overcoat as if he indeed carried a pistol and a badge. "You'd better move, fellows. And keep moving." Drunks, bums, booze hounds. What you thought of, in those days, when someone said alcoholic.

Four steps down and into a dingy little shop that he'd remembered being closed up even before the war. The door propped open with flattened cardboard boxes, not for air—it was a cold gray day—but light, since the power hadn't been turned on. There was a narrow counter filled with haphazard piles of shirt boxes, another dozen or so large containers filling all but a thin passageway through the store. There was a barrel spilling straw, an odor of old damp brick and roach powder. He rapped on the counter and called out, and a man appeared from the back. A small, short man in a wool jacket that was too big for him and a fur hat that was too small. His hands were bare and he held them together. They were bright white in the gray place and he rubbed them together because it was cold, of course, but the effect, with his hooked nose and his stooped shoulders, made Dennis think "Shylock."

"Edison," he said, warily, because he knew this was a guy who would not take anything he said at face value. The man moved his head like a turtle, getting a better look at him in the gloom of the store. "You the Edison man?"

Dennis put his hand out to introduce himself and saw that the man was missing the middle three fingers of his right hand, and the tips of the last three on his left. He was a Polish Jew, not long in New York. A tailor, he said, before the war, and without indicating his hands gave a vaudevillian shrug. Now a shopkeeper, ladies' and children's apparel. Or anyway, as soon as he had the power he would be.

As Dennis had predicted, the man didn't want to hear anything he said, and end of next week was too long for

him to wait. He was not an old man, not as old as he'd
first appeared, but he seemed shrunken inside his big coat
and he had a lousy set of dentures that slipped as he spoke
and made his breath stale.

"Mr. Lynch," he said—once he got hold of Dennis's
name he was like a dog with a bone—"consider my situation."

"Mr. Leibowitz," Dennis told him, "consider your wir-
ing. Consider your shop going up in smoke."

The man pretended to be resigned. He looked around
the place as if all his struggle, through the war, through
the camps, through the long crossing over, had come to
this cold pathetic end. He shook his head, as if he was
familiar with this, this mundane disappointment delivered
by this mundane, earnest, broad-faced man, a disappointment as pervasive and as terrible as the world's more famous evils. He shrugged and then suddenly turned and
gently took Dennis's hand, holding his wrist in the space
between his pinky and thumb on the left. He drilled a
folded bill into Dennis's palm with his right.

"Anything you can do," Mr. Leibowitz said.

Dennis objected and tried to hand the money back,
but the man turned away, waving his gaped hand beside
his ear, swatting at the words. He might have said, "It
can't hurt."

The folded bill was still in his pocket when he got back
to the office. He rode the elevator up with Claire Donavan
and three other girls, just back from lunch, their fur collars
smelling of perfume and cigarette smoke, their bright lipstick fresh and the powder on their cheeks and noses like
a dusting of sugar.

"You're quiet, Mr. Lynch," Claire Donavan said into his ear as they watched the lights moving behind the numbers for each floor.

"I'm praying for a power failure, Miss Donavan," he said, moving only his eyes to look at her, her bright white smile and the gum cracking like sparks behind it. Peppermint. Sugar. Lilac perfume. The war was far enough behind them now: bread was bread once again, not cake. He had a hankering for cake.

Billy got on at twelve. "Dennis!" he said, and Dennis said, "Billy boy," as if he'd spent the morning looking for him. They nearly shook hands. But the eyes of the four women were on them, on Billy more accurately. He was the only one of them not wearing a hat and a coat, and it made him seem finer, somehow, in his gray suit and white shirt and simple tie—the way a priest all in black can seem the more elegant in the midst of brightly colored wedding guests.

"You've been out in the field?" Billy asked softly.

"Till just now," Dennis said.

When they got to their floor, the girls stepped out, but Dennis pinched Billy's sleeve and made him stay on.

"Who is he?" they heard before the door closed on them again, and Claire Donavan answered, "Cousins."

Dennis reached into his pocket and pulled out the folded bill. He was surprised to see it was a ten. He handed it to Billy. "Put this in your happily-ever-after fund."

Billy looked at it sheepishly. "Where's it from?"

The elevator stopped and Dennis pushed another button for a higher floor. He told him. He said he was going to put it into the poor box at St. Brigid's but the door was locked. "I think the bums have been coming in and stealing the Communion wine."

"Catholic bums," Billy said.

Dennis nodded. "The worst kind. So take it and put it in your happily-ever-after fund."

Still, Billy hesitated. He told Dennis to put it in the collection basket on Sunday. Dennis said he'd have it spent by Sunday. Billy said, Spend it. Dennis said he had a rich mother, he didn't need to spend it. Finally, he pushed the money into Billy's palm as Mr. Leibowitz had done to him. He said when the time came, when Eva was back here and they were snug in their little cottage in East Hampton, Billy could buy all their baby clothes from Mr. Leibowitz.

"Will it ever happen?" Billy said wistfully, even as he folded the money into his pocket.

Dennis said, "I don't see why it shouldn't." Although, in truth, he saw: indistinctly as yet and as if from the corner of his eye. Think of those ruined, ragged men in the street, Billy among them, in the unimaginable future. Think of Leibowitz's butchered hands. Think of the promises he had made to Mary at moments when the girl had every right to believe him. When, for as long as it took, he managed to believe himself. With so many other forces at work in the world, brutal, sly, deceiving, unstoppable forces, what could be more foolish than staking your life on an ephemeral feeling, no more than an idea, really, a fancy, the culmination of which is a clumsy bit of nakedness, a few minutes of animal grunting and bumping, a momentary obliteration of thought, of conscience?

Indistinctly, and as if from the corner of his eye, he saw what Billy's fine dream, Billy's faith, was going to come to. But he also saw, in his own (his own father's) romantic heart, that its consummation would become a small redemption for them all.

HOLTZMAN'S HEAD WAS HUGE when you came upon him from behind, in the dim back corner of his shoe store, bent over his inventory sheets and fresh from the barber's, so the only way of telling where his neck stopped and his head began was the seemingly arbitrary place where a shadow of tiny hairs began to sprout from that Germanic column of red-and-purple flesh.

The stockroom smelled of shoe leather and cardboard and, as Dennis came closer, dill pickles and mustard. The overhead lights were remarkably dim; the only brightness came from the single gooseneck lamp that sat on his desk. His sandwich in its wax-paper nest rested on the corner of the desk, just outside the circle of light, and when Dennis saw Holtzman's fat hand reach for it and lift it to his mouth, he knew for certain that the man still hadn't heard him come in and that if he cleared his throat and called Holtzman's name or came a few steps farther and touched his shoulder, he would startle the old Kraut, perhaps send that plug of ham on rye with butter and mustard right into his esophagus.

So Dennis paused, long enough to see Holtzman return the sandwich to the desk, long enough to see that it was chewed and swallowed (he turned an inventory sheet over and sighed and lifted a finger to his mouth to dislodge something from between cheek and gum). Long enough, too, to reconsider what he was doing and to turn around, get back on the train, get back to work. Let Billy's sweet romance follow its own course.

But the road to hell . . . and Dennis said, "Excuse me, Mr. Holtzman. I'm sorry to interrupt."

The man turned, his big head like an old buffalo's, peering over his flank. And then, when he saw it was Dennis behind him, he swiveled his chair around and wiped his mouth and began to stand.

Dennis held out a hand. "Don't get up," he said, although Holtzman was already standing, already saying, "Dennis," and then, "Is everything all right?" the chubby hand to the heart, the heart lacking even the courage to let him say, "Is your mother all right?"

Dennis knew then that he'd had the right idea, coming here, to him.

Holtzman offered him the metal chair beside his desk. "Please, sit," he said after Dennis had assured him that his mother was fine, that he had only come to ask a favor. Even in that dim light, Dennis saw two things pass in quick succession over the man's face: one was the relief that there was no bad news. Second, the sudden suspicion that he was about to be asked for money.

Which Dennis, did, of course, and without too much beating around the bush. He said he wanted to borrow five hundred dollars to give to Billy so he could send for his girl and her mother by summer, find an apartment for them all, and get on with his life. He said Billy would be glad to work in the store on the weekend so that the money would be an advance against salary, not a flat-out loan, and that Billy, and he, would be sure all of it was paid back in a timely manner, with interest.

He said he was certain that Billy would eventually save what he needed himself, without anyone else's help, but it could take him another year, and a year was a long time for a young girl to wait all alone on the other side of the ocean.

"You met her," Dennis said. "Last summer. On Long Island. Outside St. Philomena's."

Holtzman nodded. "A pretty girl," he said, and already Dennis could see that he was forming an argument against him: prettiness was a virtue. She would wait for Billy to earn the money himself.

Dennis nodded. "Pretty enough," he said, countering what he hadn't spoken. "But for Billy, the moon and stars encircle her head. I don't know that he can wait."

Holtzman shrugged a little, touching thumb and forefinger to his chest. Dennis saw his eyes glance longingly at his thick sandwich.

"Eat, please," he said. "Don't let me stop you."

Eagerly, Holtzman took hold of the sandwich, sending, as he did, another longing glance toward his inventory sheet. Dennis began to wonder if he should have gone to his mother instead. But he'd been certain that his chances with Holtzman were better. The man had, after all, given up what had seemed a comfortable and complacent bachelorhood to take on a penniless wife and her grown son; he had opened his home to them, his cottage on Long Island; he had moved his ancestral furniture to the basement or distributed it to her relations in order to accommodate her secondhand junk. He had readjusted his morning routine, rewritten his will, instituted what was called a "family discount" at his store (which was essentially 20 percent off for anyone who was identified as part of Daniel Lynch's sprawling legacy), and increased his own grocery bill by at least 50 percent. He had complicated his life. All because a tiny woman had entered his shoe store looking for size fours. All because she had placed her stockinged foot in the palm of his hand.

He had, according to Billy's mother, who was there, wept copiously, gratefully, as he recited his wedding vows in the dim front room of the rectory.

Holtzman took another bite of sandwich, passed his tongue over his teeth, chewed, put the napkin to his thin lips. He never had managed to look Dennis straight in the eye. *My mother's husband.* Finally, he said, "I'm not a wealthy man."

Dennis nodded, murmuring like a priest. He understood that, he said.

"I'm not made of money," he said. Dennis understood that, too. "It's an awful lot of money," he added while Dennis continued to nod. "I don't know that I have access to that much money myself."

Dennis pursed his lips sympathetically. He was always struck by the irony of it. His father's wealth, which was purely figurative, had always been boldly proclaimed. Holtzman's, a literal fact, was relentlessly denied.

"The business is still recovering from the war years," he said. "Long-time customers came in and told me that they wouldn't shop here anymore because of what went on in Europe. There was leather rationing, you know. I had these damn corduroy shoes to sell. I lost a lot of business."

He looked at the big sandwich in his hand, seemed to consider whether or not it contradicted his lean-times story, bit into it anyway.

"Billy might be an asset, then," Dennis told him as he chewed. "It might impress your customers to know you're helping out a former GI."

Holtzman considered this, seemed to like it, but then shrugged it off lest Dennis begin to think he had an advantage.

"He's a good-looking guy," Dennis went on. "Soft-spoken. People like him. Women like him."

Holtzman shrugged again as if to say Dennis didn't understand the shoe business.

"If you would think of it as an investment, not a loan."

"It's a lot of money," Holtzman said.

"It's what I figure he really needs."

"And when would he be in here? Just Saturdays?"

"Isn't Saturday your busiest day?"

Holtzman shook his head. "He'll take a long time to earn back five hundred dollars just working on Saturdays."

"He'll be paying you off from his salary at Edison, too," Dennis said. "And I'll be helping him out."

Holtzman put the sandwich down, daintily wiped his fingertips and then his mouth. Turned a little in his chair, as if, Dennis thought, he was about to dismiss him. But then he said, working that tongue into his cheeks, looking over his papers, "I'm thinking of staying open Thursday nights. Gimbel's does it."

"Billy could be here Thursday nights," Dennis said. "Billy could be here by 5:30 easy."

Holtzman sucked his teeth again, turned to another inventory sheet on the desk before him. It was clear he was becoming more and more interested as he feigned growing indifference. Not nearly as sly as he believed himself to be. "What does he know about shoes?" he said.

Dennis laughed. "How much is there to know?" and then quickly amended it. "Smitty can show him what he needs, I'm sure."

Holtzman looked up from his desk. "He's willing to do this?"

Dennis grinned. He hadn't mentioned any of this to Billy yet. "Are you kidding?" he said. "He's dying to do this. He's nuts about this girl. It'll be nearly a year. He's dying to see her."

Casually Holtzman leaned down to slide out the bottom drawer of his desk. "I'll give him a dollar an hour to begin. Thursdays till nine. Saturday nine to six. Twelve-fifty a week. Fifty dollars a month." He lifted a heavy check ledger from the drawer, tossed it onto his desk. Flipped it open. "He adds whatever he can from his regular salary once a month."

"What kind of interest do you want?" Dennis said.

Holtzman waved the pen he had lifted. "This is family," he said. And then he added as he wrote, exacting another kind of payment, "You boys will never have any money if you spend everything you make before it's earned." He might have been talking to a child.

Dennis felt the warmth in his cheeks. "This is an advance, Mr. Holtzman," he reminded him. "Billy will earn it."

Holtzman lifted his head to give Dennis a shrewd look—a skin-deep look if there ever was one. "But first he'll spend it," he said.

BILLY WAS AT HIS DESK when Dennis got back to the office. He put the check in front of him. "Here you go," he said, and understood for the first time why it was that his father had bankrupted himself and estranged his wife and filled their tiny apartment with far-flung relatives from the other side: simply to know this power, this expansiveness. Simply to be able to say, as he said to Billy that day in the office on Irving Place, "Here you go." Here's your life.

Full of himself, and of Billy's sweet, blushing gratitude, he decided that day, too, that he would marry Mary when Eva came. Make a good confession for a change, say yes and mean it, rather than have it turn into another instant sin when the priest behind the dark screen asked him if he planned to marry this girl he was having his way with. He'd give her a ring on the day Billy married Eva. Find them a place of their own. Get his life started. Why not? He could afford it, he had a rich mother. Why not? Bread was what you wanted over the long haul, when you got right down to it. When you got right down to it, you wouldn't want a lifetime of cake. And it would make for a fine summer.

BILLY WIRED THE MONEY to Eva in April and in his next letter asked her to send him her shoe size and the sizes of her younger sisters so he could pick up something for them at the store. This she did, including in her last note to him a folded sheet of butcher paper that contained a tracing of her right foot and each right foot of her three younger siblings. She said she knew that shoe sizes were different in the States and thought this was the best way to be sure of a good fit. She said, too, that she was making this letter a short one—she wanted to catch the postman—and would write more later. She said she was busy making plans.

In the shoe store that Saturday morning, Billy spread the brown paper out on the counter so Smitty, Mr. Holtzman's assistant, could determine each size. Smitty advised oxfords for the sisters, and by lunchtime Billy himself had selected a pair of tan-and-white spectators for Eva. He had sold a pair to a woman that morning, a young woman who had come in intending only to get her old father fitted with a pair of wingtips. The shoes had made even her thick ankles seem elegant and sporty.

The same girl returned twice that summer, once more with her father, once with a talkative girl friend who did all the trying on and buying. This was the summer that Billy, holding his breath, was going through the mail his mother had left out on the sideboard each evening and finding nothing, as he told them down at Quinlan's, nothing at all from Eva. The same summer that Dennis had begun to keep a tally of all the simple things a Brooklyn-born girl knew that an Irish-born girl had to have explained to her.

Like the prohibition against a girl calling a fellow on the telephone. On a Sunday afternoon in late September of 1946, Holtzman told Dennis there was a young lady on the phone and with a disapproving shake of his head handed him the receiver. Dennis sat beside the three-legged telephone table Holtzman had once retrieved from a pile of junk at someone else's curb. An hour later he met Mary at the service entrance of her building, on Seventieth Street, just off Park. He was thinking that if she was expecting a child, then he would, of course, marry her immediately, and tell himself that it was the hand of God (his father consulting) moving him toward a future that he only understood now he never honestly wanted. A future in which his own bad luck was the other side of Claire Donavan's sailor's opportunity.

But what Mary had to tell him was all about Eva.

This was the same week that Maeve, trying to orches-

trate her own fate, came into the store by herself. It was
a Thursday night, just beginning to get dark, and Smitty
was working alone. By way of making conversation, he
told her that he wasn't sure if he'd lost his young assistant
or not. Mr. Holtzman had simply told him this morning
that Billy wouldn't be in tonight. "We'll have to see if he
shows up on Saturday morning," Smitty told her, releasing
her heel and allowing her to place her foot on the ground
and wiggle her toes a bit, leaning over her lap to look at
the new shoes and to tell him, finally (no surprise here),
that perhaps she wasn't that fond of them, after all.

Gently holding her ankle, he removed the new shoe
and returned it to its box. To save her more embarrassment (she was already blushing to the hairline) he didn't
even offer to show her another pair. He simply said as he
slipped her foot back into the tan-and-white spectators—
well worn now and out of season—that there were always
new styles coming in. She should stop by again sometime.

He pushed his footstool aside and held out his hand to
help her up, thus lending her—it was a favor he did for
every female customer—a moment of regal grace as she
stood.

"Try us again," he said gently.

He was a dapper little man with thinning hair and a
dark mustache. She was twenty-eight or so, in a brown
tweed three-quarter-length coat and a gray skirt and shoes
that should have been retired after Labor Day. She had
combed her hair into fluffy curls that just brushed her
shoulders, and her lipstick was fresh enough to have left
a mark on her front tooth. Smitty had been selling shoes
for twenty-five years, ten at A&S, fifteen with Holtzman.

He was married with no children and, at this stage of the game, little love, but he had memory enough to know what it had cost her, walking in all by herself, no preoccupying old man or bold girl friend to hide behind. He asked Dennis later if it didn't seem to him to be the exact way of the world that the very night she decided to take the risk, to throw the dice or spin the wheel and see just what might come out of being by herself in the shoe store with Billy, the two of them (with any luck) all alone, would be the very night, the first so far, that Billy didn't show up.

Smitty thought to tell her as he walked her to the door that there was a girl over in Ireland who had his diamond ring, but who could heap that kind of humiliation on anyone? There was no time for it anyway, because once she had gotten through the obligatory trying on of just one pair, once she had discovered that Billy was not, indeed, in there, she was out the door. Perhaps believing that the time saved on this fruitless visit could be added to the next when, surely, by the law of averages if nothing else, she would not miss him again.

It was the very next morning when Holtzman came in that Smitty learned the reason for Billy's absence: his fiancée in Ireland had passed away. Pneumonia. It was just like the man to mention the news only after it had had some effect on the running of the store. Holtzman himself, and Billy, it seemed, had known since Monday or Tuesday.

"He won't be back working here, then," Smitty said. "With no wedding to save for."

But Holtzman shook his head. "He'll be back." He

patted down a hiccup, touching his heart, the gesture making him appear to be soothing himself, reassuring himself. He liked Billy, knew the ladies liked him as well. Business was booming. "He just wanted last night off. He'll be here Saturday. He'll stay on."

Confirming what Smitty had begun to suspect, watching Holtzman carefully record Billy's hours but never seeing a pay envelope pass between them: Billy was working off a debt.

"What a blow for him, poor fellow," Smitty said.

Holtzman turned his hand back and forth, as if there were a number of ways to look at the situation. "Life goes on," he said.

As promised, Billy was in the store again that Saturday morning, paler perhaps, perhaps thinner. Maybe a new puffiness around his eyes, a whiff of alcohol on his breath. "I'm sorry for your loss," Smitty said, and Billy gripped his arm just above the wrist and said, "Thank you, Mr. Smith. I wish you had met her," before his voice broke. There was such perfect trust, such perfect helplessness in Billy's brief touch (Smitty had felt something like it only once before when he'd given his arm to a blind woman on the subway stairs), that Smitty, although he barely came to Billy's shoulder, immediately placed his hand under Billy's elbow, as if to offer more support. "He was at odd ends," Smitty told Dennis when Dennis next came by the store. "I've always said that it's the ones who are always joking who feel things more deeply than the rest of us. It's something I've always said."

Smitty began, in the next months and years, to step back whenever a young woman came into the store while

Billy was there, certain that sooner or later, the urge to live being what it was (he winked when he said this to Dennis, as close as he could come to indicating that he was talking about sex), the grief would pass and one of the young women who came in would catch his eye.

When Maeve returned sometime in January with her shuffling old father once more in tow, Smitty ducked into the stockroom until Billy was finished with his current customer, and when he peeked out onto the floor he saw that Billy had the old man's shoe off and was trying to get him measured—the man grumbling all the while, the girl cajoling. Billy patiently lifting the man's thick foot onto the wooden measure and watching it slide off again.

"He's a piece of work," Smitty said when Billy stepped into the stockroom to pull the man's size.

"You can smell the beer on him," Billy told him. "He must have had a quart with his corn flakes."

There was a bit of business with the shoehorn: the old man making an awkward circuit of the store with the silver shoehorn still stuck into his heel, up under his pant leg, and Billy going after him in a loping, stoop-shouldered run, trying to retrieve it. The girl watching, beginning to smile. Billy catching her eye and smiling as well. A start.

But of course it was the old man he befriended first, Maeve standing by like some storybook princess awaiting her fate as Billy discovered that the old man's family on his mother's side was from Mallow as well and that he himself had more than once ridden on the streetcar in Brooklyn with that storytelling Irishman everyone was so fond of—that was your uncle, was it? There was the war to discuss and the Yankees and the Dodgers. The radio sermons of Bishop Sheen. The inconvenience, for a man his age and with his stomach problems, of the midnight fast before Sunday Mass and the people he'd known, over the years, who had worked for Con Ed, had worked two jobs the way Billy was doing, had worked for the NYPD, as he himself had done. "When Maeve, my girl here," indicating her downcast eyes and the parted brown hair, "was eight years old, her mother passed away on us"— and you can imagine the boundless sympathy in Billy's blue eyes, boundless and unhesitating and, best of all, untempered by the count of intervening years, the years since that everyone else the old man knew handed to him like a shot of diluted whiskey, a cup of tepid tea, as if the time passed since her dying was a kind of comfort. Billy, of course, understood that there was no comfort, not when the love you'd felt had been fierce, and true.

They sat almost knee to knee, Billy on his footstool, the box of new shoes in his lap. The old man in the worn red-leather chair, his hands on the cool steel of the armrests and the tears springing to his eyes—always red-rimmed and rheumy—the handkerchief going to the nose—always swollen and cherry-red—as he repeated the story of his wife's life, his own insult and devotion, while Billy, with all the patience, all the time in the world, listened with the attentiveness of an avid apprentice, an admiring acolyte, listened as if he were receiving instruction, if even then he needed any instruction, in the perseverance of grief.

Looking on, Maeve saw her father's future with this kind and attentive young man before she had the courage to imagine her own. Or rather, being nun-taught, lives-of-the-saints—saturated (the quiet, handmaiden saints who, if they had not chosen the better part, were freed by their bustling about with food and drink and dishes from ever having to form a sentence, or even a clear thought, about how they loved Him and why), she saw that only through her father's life, which was all the life she had planned to know, would he gain any part in hers.

MAEVE'S, OF COURSE, was not an unusual case. "Unusual for your generation now," as my father put it, "but not for ours." The girl child wedded to the widowed father. Speaking of Maeve, my father had once said that although the joke is always the Irishman, the Irish bachelor, ever faithful to his dear mother, take a look at an unmarried Irishwoman's attachment to her old dad if you want to see something truly ferocious. It was, I suppose, the very image I'd fought against myself, in the years after my own mother died, when I went off to Canisius instead of staying at home and going to St. John's or Queens or Malloy, when I took only short breaks during the summer so that my father would know I had a life of my own, despite him, despite the weight that hit my heart stomach chest bones every time I thought of him alone, waking alone, going off to the office, shopping, eating, coming into the house at 4 a.m. after getting one of Maeve's calls, after getting Billy off the floor or out of his car or into the hospital, if that's what was needed. Even when I married Matt and we headed for Seattle. Lives of our own, we said. Self-sacrifice having been recognized as a delusion by then, not a virtue. Self-consciousness more the vogue.

Maeve was only eight when her mother died—my father getting the story in her tiny kitchen, over all those
cups of tea and slivers of cake she had served him after
they'd gotten Billy into bed, over all those nights she had
summoned him. There had been another child, an older
sister, who died of lead poisoning when Maeve was very
small. A policeman's daughter, Maeve had gotten some
sense early on of the precariousness of life, the risk taken
by simply walking out the apartment door. Her mother,
all false courage, touched her father's back, the hem of his
coat, as he went out, saving the intake of breath, the sign
of the cross, for the moment she saw him gain the street.
Anything might happen, and did, and Maeve felt the
heavy weight of her grieving father's hand on her shoulder. He might have shipped her off to female relatives,
but he managed instead to trade in his beat for a desk job
so he could stay alive for her. The nuns at her school were
more than happy to take the child in for as many hours as
he needed them to, and Maeve spoke often—or as often
as she spoke of anything—of the pleasant afternoons she
had spent in the tiny courtyard of the convent beside her
school (vine-covered walls, a single oak, a statue of St.
Francis above a concrete birdbath, one of the Virgin in the
crook of the tree) or in its seldom-visited front room,
where the silence was palpable, luxurious, punctuated as
it was by the soft steps of the sisters going through the
hall or up the stairs or stopping in to bring her a glass of
ginger ale and some digestive biscuits on a saucer. There
would be frost on the windows, her schoolwork spread
before her on a narrow, lemon-scented desk, her hand-

writing, the lovely round perfection of it, her greatest vanity.

There was no question, when she finished school, of
having to find a job—which made her the envy of most
of her girl friends, who were struggling with stenography
and switchboards, and getting to the subway by eight.
There was no question, either, that she would join the
nuns for good. She did the shopping and cleaned the
house and cooked his meals. Lipstick was for weekends,
a movie with the girls, a Saturday afternoon at the stores
along Jamaica Avenue. Her father drank most evenings,
but it was a man's right and, with a wife in her grave, his
only solace. And when things got out of hand—when, in
his cups, he growled at her or cursed her or waved his
arms about as if her love and attention were cobwebs she'd
draped around him—there were the nuns to go to, who
would listen quietly and advise prayer, but also make sure
that the pastor crooked his finger at the old man next time
he and Maeve were at Mass. So she had the attention of
men, too; her father when he was feeling fond of her and
the priests when he was giving her trouble, and the
butcher and the fellow at the newsstand, and even on occasion some boys she had known from school, not the
best-looking ones, of course, the homely mostly, the
bad-skinned and wet-palmed, the untalkative (which
meant a long night of short questions and short answers
for them both) who saw in her plainness, her lack of prospects, their own advantage. Billy she first laid eyes on as
he leaned to place a pair of new shoes in Holtzman's window on Jamaica Avenue, his hand held over his heart to

hold back his tie. He looked up and smiled, but she knew even then that he would have smiled at anyone.

Bringing her father to the store was her way of showing Billy her life in one sweeping glance. Bringing her girl friend was a flirtation with despair—if he fell in love with her talkative friend, Maeve would, at least, in her lifetime, know him. Walking in alone was a dream, but as it turned out, it was another girl's dream. She was the plain one with the father, the one who without him would have become a nun. She was the one who, having chosen this part, must stand steadily by as his future was formed for her.

No one gathered in Maeve's living room that evening could have recalled it either, not accurately anyway: how young they had been then. How much these things had mattered.

Mac, Rosemary's husband, who had once been as young himself (in the cramped apartment, in the childhood bed of his young bride), sat on the brocade-under-plastic-slipcovers couch, his shirtsleeves rolled up, his pant legs neatly tucked above the knee. He had assigned himself the task of cracking the walnuts that had been set out in a porcelain bowl on the coffee table and spreading the pieces of meat out on a paper napkin. He leaned over his work like a watchmaker. He had already walked down to the corner deli once for more rolls, and again for a bottle of ginger ale. He had stood on a chair to change a lightbulb in the kitchen and swept the wet walk with a broom from Billy's garage, and now he cracked walnuts as if to keep up with a relentless demand, although the pile he had accumulated had already begun to overflow the paper napkin.

Billy's sister Rosemary was moving back and forth from the kitchen to the living room, pausing at intervals to glance out the front windows, hoping to intercept any visitor—as she had intercepted us—who might ring the doorbell or knock on the door and disturb Maeve. There was another couple in the living room with Mac, next-door neighbors, and Kate was there, although still without her wealthy husband. Two women friends of Maeve's from the Legion of Mary had installed themselves in the kitchen.

An Indian couple from across the street stopped by with a covered dish, but couldn't be convinced to stay. Two men from Edison and their wives were just leaving as we walked in. Dan Lynch arrived by bus with a box of bakery cookies. He was changed out of his suit but looked that much more polished in a pressed sport shirt and tattersall pants. He took a seat in the living room as well and placed his teacup and saucer on his knee.

The narrow house was a gallery of Billy's life that evening—how could anyone help but think it? From the curb where we parked to the three brick steps to the cool hallway, dim as a church, that led past the living room and the staircase to the kitchen and the back yard where Shortchange, Billy's motley mutt, had begun to whine as soon as she heard my father's voice.

How could my father keep from thinking of it: the sight of Billy's car pulled up over the curb and the berm or left fishtailed out into the street, of the brick-edged gash above Billy's eye, the pale soles of his shoes as he sprawled in the dim hallway, of Maeve standing over her husband in her pink chenille robe: "If you can just get him under the arms, Dennis."

How could he help but think of her maddening calm on those nights when she went into the kitchen to put the kettle on after they'd managed to drag Billy into bed— the drunk hauled up the stairs and pulled out of his clothes, wounds dabbed at with a cotton ball soaked in peroxide, shoes wiped clean with a wet cloth and set out on the front steps to dry, just another housewifely task completed.

"Would you like a little sliver of cake with that, Dennis?"

(How could he help but think of my mother on those nights, at home, still healthy, sound asleep in their bed while he sat with Maeve and discussed a solution, a cure. Or of all the nights in the past decade when he came back to our house after Maeve had summoned him, and found himself there all alone.)

It had always been my father's contention that Maeve was as satisfied with the appearance of sobriety as she would have been with the sobriety itself, more so, actually, since real and permanent sobriety would have meant the end of these mad nights, these long days of nursing him and waiting for him, and then what would occupy her time?

From the phone that hung on the wall in the tiny kitchen, she would tell my father when he called, "Oh, Billy went up to bed already, Dennis. I'm sure he's asleep by now . . ." or "He just left to take Shortchange for a walk," letting an hour or two, or even the rest of the night, go by before she called him back to ask if he would please come over and get Billy out of the street or off the floor or, once, away from the door of her bedroom, where she had barricaded herself against him.

Or he might hang up, convinced she was lying (turning to my mother to say so), and suddenly the phone would ring while the receiver was still under his hand and there would be Billy's voice, a little breathless but still sober: "Just got in," the rattle of the leash behind him and the click of the dog's paws against the linoleum. "Let me just get her her biscuit."

Billy's voice over the telephone, this telephone: how could he help but think of it?

We'd been in the house only a few minutes, had walked only from curb to front hall and into the kitchen, when my father reached for the leash that hung from a hook by the back door and said he'd take the poor animal for a walk.

Upstairs, Maeve was resting. Rosemary and the two women from the Legion of Mary made it clear that she had insisted no one leave on her account—that everyone should stay, have a drink, eat up all the food. She had insisted that it was a comfort to her to have people in the house, but she needed half an hour or so to put her feet up, to rest her eyes in a darkened room. To take the measure, perhaps, of how she felt now that the ordeal was at long last over.

On the wall above the tiny kitchen table that was covered now with casserole dishes and foil-covered cake pans and bakery boxes, there were three red apples made of pressed wood, one with a smiling pressed-wood worm poking through it: remnants of a back-to-school promotion from Holtzman's shoe store.

In the living room, Dan Lynch was describing another funeral: the church full, the aisles full, the vestibule full, even the steps leading out into the street. It had rained that day, too, but the crowd at the cemetery was so thick that their umbrellas had made a solid canopy. And even if you weren't standing under it, you were so well flanked by other people that only the top of your head and your shoulders could get wet. And out of the crowd, in one silent moment as the coffin was lowered into the grave, Billy Sheehy's dad, all unrehearsed, began to sing. "Danny Boy," of course. A lovely tenor that almost sounded like a record being played, what with the raindrops on all the umbrellas. It nearly killed everybody, it was such a moment. And Dan Lynch had said to Dennis when it was over, both of them teenagers then, "Your father would have loved this." But Dennis pointed across the road to another, smaller group of mourners who were just leaving another grave. "My father would be wondering why we hadn't invited them over," he said.

Out in the street, a passerby had asked Dan Lynch's own mother if it was a politician they had buried—there were so many people. "My mother told him yes, but the best kind of politician, because he never ran for anything. He'd go out of his way to shake your hand, to see how you were doing. He would give you the shirt off his back if that's what you said you needed, but he wasn't running for anything and never had, so he was the best kind of politician." He nodded to put a fine point on it. "That's what she said. I'll never forget it. I thought that was very good."

"He was actually a streetcar conductor," Kate said to the couple from next door. "Over in Brooklyn." She was wealthy enough to be proud of the fact—to use it as a marker of how far she had brought her own branch of the family—while the couple themselves (two more Irish Americans, the man florid, the woman plump) seemed to indicate by their quick nods of approval and their generous "aahhs" that they themselves might have lied about it, said he was a supervisor with the Transit Authority, at least—add a promotion to his history even if he hadn't had one in life, what harm?

"He met Sheila on that trolley," Kate said, and to the neighbor couple: "Dennis's mother, our Aunt Sheila. There was a story that all the passengers on the trolley applauded when she first spoke to him."

"I remember," Dan Lynch said.

"She must have been all of seventeen or eighteen when she married him," Kate said.

"And he was well past forty," Rosemary added.

The two Legion of Mary ladies had come to stand beside her in the dining-room doorway. "It often happened that way in those days," the taller one said. It seemed to amount to a dispensation. "You know, the girls so young and the men middle-aged." She was gray-faced and confident. Even as she leaned casually against the wide doorframe she seemed ready to take over.

Mac was tapping another broken walnut shell into his thick palm. "So there's still hope for you, Danny boy," he said. "You may turn up with some sweet young thing on your arm even yet."

But Dan Lynch held up a hand. "I'm long past that possibility," he said, and laughed and blushed, and then quickly retrieved the teacup and saucer that were about to leave his knee.

Rosemary was turning away from us, into the darkened dining room behind her. "I think my Michael wants to follow in your footsteps, Danny," she said, calling as she went to the sideboard where the Waterford decanter and surrounding glasses were nearly obscured behind a dozen framed photographs. "I told him just the other day that his father and I are off to Florida in two more years." She came back into the living-room light, a picture in her hand. "So if he wants to wait until he's fifty to have children, he's going to miss out on two first-class babysitters."

Mac selected another walnut from the blue porcelain bowl. "He shouldn't be in any hurry," he said, looking over the tops of his glasses. "There's still time for all that."

"He's thirty-two years old!" Rosemary cried: it was the echo of an ongoing argument. "That's hardly too soon."

Her husband, putting pressure on the silver nutcracker, would not meet her eye.

She turned to the Legion ladies, handing them the framed photograph. "This is Uncle Dan and Aunt Sheila," she said pleasantly. "On their wedding day."

The ladies looked and nodded and handed it to Dan Lynch to pass on to the neighbor couple. He paused to look at it, too, although among my father's relatives, the photo was as familiar as a crucifix or the portrait of the Sacred Heart, and as consistently displayed.

"He was a lovely man," Dan Lynch said as he passed the picture on.

There followed a pause that threatened to get awkward, all of us smiling slightly and looking at the floor. "And where did she meet her second husband?" the neighbor woman said softly into it.

Mac winked at her own husband. "These dames can't get enough of this stuff, can they?" he said.

And the man smiled and nodded. "Romance," he said, rolling his eyes.

Mac broke another walnut shell.

"Well, it's interesting," the neighbor lady objected, slapping her husband's knee, smiling.

"You have to talk about *something*," Rosemary said, not.

"In the shoe store." Kate spoke like an adult among bickering adolescents. "In Jamaica, the one where Billy used to work."

"Ah," the woman said, nodding. "Jamaica Avenue. It's Baker's now. Not that you'd want to go there now."

"Not if you're white," her husband said, and got Mac to agree with him.

"She met him during the war," Kate went on, keeping her nose above any onrush of working-class bigotry, "when she went in there looking for shoes."

"Same place Maeve met Billy," Rosemary added.

"There was a shrewd one," Dan Lynch said to the men. "That Holtzman." He counted off on his fingers, "A German," as if compiling a list of grievances, "owned his

own shop, a big brick house in Jamaica, another out on
Long Island, a third place down in Fort Lauderdale. He
bought the Long Island house during the Depression,
from some poor fool who thought Three Mile Harbor out
there was going to be the next Coney Island. Holtzman
paid practically nothing for it. Paid for it right out of his
billfold, Billy said. Standing in the driveway of the place.
Signed the deed on the hood of his car. Shrewd."

"Dennis has it now," Rosemary explained. "It's a nice
little place."

"Dennis and Billy were the ones who fixed it up,"
Kate reminded them. "Right after the war."

In Maeve's own living room, on her brocade chairs and
sofa, under the warm light of her lamps, no one who
thought it would dare say, "Eva." Although Kate could
not resist mentioning that Billy had never gone back out
there, over the years. Except for that once, when he returned from Ireland. Back in 1975. She'd had a postcard
from him.

"Maeve did, too," Rosemary said. She said Maeve had
a postcard upstairs, stuck in the corner of her mirror, from
that trip as well. A picture of Home Sweet Home in East
Hampton. She turned to the neighbor couple. "The house
from the old song," she said. Billy had written something
very sweet on the back. Beautiful wife or lovely girl. She
couldn't remember the exact words now—it might have
been something from one of his poems—but Maeve had
kept the postcard and had shown it to her the other day,
Tuesday, after they'd gotten word from Dennis that Billy
was gone.

"Holtzman was another old bachelor," Kate said, cutting in. "He must have been near sixty when Sheila married him. And he hadn't been married before."

"That we know of." Dan Lynch smiled wickedly. "Billy said once that he wouldn't be surprised to learn that Holtzman had a flock of wives buried in the basement."

"No," Rosemary said, fighting the tears that the mention of Tuesday had brought. "Billy liked Mr. Holtzman. He always got along with him."

"Dennis didn't," Kate said.

Mac examined the last three walnuts in the dish. The lamplight showed the pale scalp beneath his thinning, graying hair. "Holtzman didn't marry Billy's mother," he said.

From the kitchen came the sound of the back door opening. Shortchange scurrying inside, my father's voice speaking to her, saying, "Hold on there, girl" and "Good dog." The ring of the leash. Water running in the sink and the dog bowl being placed on the linoleum.

"How did we ever get onto poor Mr. Holtzman?" Kate asked, and Dan Lynch said, "I was talking about Uncle Daniel—if ever there were two men more opposite."

We heard the clink of the cookie jar where the dog biscuits were kept and my father calling, "Here, girl."

"Well, they both married Aunt Sheila," Rosemary said, but Dan Lynch waved his hand: a meaningless connection.

"And they're all in heaven together," Kate said with a laugh. "There's that."

"I wouldn't be so sure," Dan Lynch murmured, winking at me. "You know what Our Lord said about a rich man getting into heaven." I saw him throw a glance at Kate, who deflected it nicely by leaning to reach for a shelled walnut and placing it elegantly on her tongue.

Rosemary turned to the Legion of Mary pair beside her to say, "I've often wondered how it works in heaven when there's a second marriage. I know it sounds silly, but you have to wonder—you know, who comes first."

"The first marriage is the binding one," the tall lady said with an easy expertise. Mac said, "Ha!" to his wife. "See that, you're stuck," just as Shortchange, in a post-walk ecstasy, came wriggling through the dining room and into the living room, all cool wet fur and wagging tail and snorting black nose. My father came in behind her, half a dog biscuit still in his hand, just as Maeve appeared in the other doorway, the one that opened onto the dim hall and the stairs. She wore a pale housecoat and was in stocking feet. She had her hand to her throat.

"Oh, Dennis," she said, squinting toward him as the dog made a quick circuit of the room, greeting everyone. She put her fingertips to the back of Dan Lynch's chair. "It's you."

With the excitement the dog brought in with her—the neighbor lady grabbed the arms of her chair and lifted her feet as Shortchange sniffed her ankles (Nice dog, nice dog), and Mac held out a walnut and Kate leaned down to say with puckered lips, "Hello, sweetheart"—it seemed to take a minute for us all to hear what Maeve had said.

She said, "I thought it was Billy, coming in from a walk."

Dan Lynch struggled to his feet, awkwardly balancing his teacup, finally placing it on the coffee table, on top of the pile of walnuts, and all the while saying, "Have a seat, Maeve. Please, have a seat."

Shortchange wiggled toward her as she sat down, and Maeve lightly touched the dog's wet fur. "I thought it was Billy," Maeve said to my father. "You sounded so much like him."

A kind of pain swept my father's face. He was standing just outside the living-room doorway, still flushed from the walk, his shoulders still vaguely patterned with raindrops, his coat still holding a whiff of the green spring. "I'm sorry," he said.

Maeve shook her head, her hand now on her heart. "I thought it was Billy," she said a third time. Even the bit of lipstick she'd worn earlier in the day was gone and her simple housecoat was colorless, white and beige. She seemed as plain as a blank page.

She looked around the room, her eyes weak. "I was just getting up," she said. "I hadn't put the light on yet." Now she put her fingertips to her forehead and lowered her eyes. "I thought Billy was down here with the dog."

Beside me, the next-door-neighbor lady clucked her tongue and said, "Awww," with the sound of exaggerated sympathy you might offer a child. The Legion of Mary ladies both put their hands to their mouths. And then Maeve began to weep.

Clearly, this was the moment our presence here was meant to deflect. The moment we'd been waiting for, hoping against, staying around to have a drink and eat up all the food. But we were momentarily stunned by its arrival, unsure of what to do.

Maeve lowered her face into her own raised hand, the

fingers splayed now from forehead to chin (the plain pearl ring), and let out a long, tremulous sigh that was meant perhaps to give her her composure but instead caught in her throat and formed another kind of sigh, terrible and unbidden. "I thought he was here," she said through it. "I thought he was right downstairs."

We stared for a few seconds and then suddenly—as if we had all been caught in that stilled interval between the first thunderclap and the first pelting drops of rain—we began to scurry, moving as though there were windows to close, laundry to be pulled in from the line.

Kate and Rosemary were immediately beside Maeve's chair, Kate with a hand on her shoulder, Rosemary patting her knee. The two Legion ladies hurried back to the kitchen, one to boil water, one to fetch a box of tissues. My father grabbed Shortchange by the collar and dragged her out of the room. The lady from next door stood, which seemed a cue for the rest of the men to scatter, as they did, heading for the kitchen just as my father came back through the dining room, where he paused by the side-board to pour a glass of sherry from the Waterford decanter.

He stepped forward, holding the crystal sherry glass in two hands, but Rosemary waved it away. "She's already had quite a bit," she whispered. Kate reached out and took the glass from him anyway.

"I thought he was down here with the dog," Maeve was saying. "I thought it hadn't happened, after all. It was a dream. He was down here, just coming in." Her voice twisted a little, nearly vanished. "I thought I'd go down and put the kettle on."

Rosemary said, "There now," kindly enough, but
meaning, too, enough of that. "There now."

Her sister leaned forward with the glass of sherry.
"Take a little sip, Maeve," she said.

But Maeve raised her eyes to the two sisters, looking
from one to the other, maybe looking for some trace of
their brother's face, maybe only hoping for understanding.
And then she looked beyond them to my father. "He's
gone," she said to him alone. "Our Billy."

My father nodded. His eyes were dark and he held his
lips together so tightly he might have been breaking the
news all over again. "He is" was all he said, because even
as he said it Maeve put her fingers to her lips and whispered, "I'm going to be sick."

Swiftly the neighbor lady grabbed the blue porcelain
bowl, turned out the remaining walnuts, and handed it to
Rosemary, who held it under Maeve's downy chin. "It's
all right," she told her, shooting a deadly glance at her
sister: there was the smell of sherry. "It's all right, dear."

"Poor girl," the neighbor lady said. The taller Legion
lady had returned with the tissue box and was now pulling
out tissues, one after the other, as if she were doling out
an endless line of rope. She handed them one after the
other to Kate, who was holding them beneath the bowl,
piling them into Maeve's lap.

My father modestly stepped away.

An aluminum pot was produced from the kitchen, but
Maeve, as Rosemary said, had nothing but the sherry in
her stomach—hadn't eaten a bite since Tuesday—and so
the sickness quickly passed. When it was over, Maeve sat
back against the chair, her hands full of tissues, her face

and throat blotched with red but deathly white underneath. "I'm so sorry," she said with her eyes closed. "I'm
so ashamed."

Amid the women's cooing, the two sisters convinced
her to stand and go upstairs to rinse her face and change
her clothes, to make herself feel better. Maeve nodded,
apologizing, coming back to herself, it seemed. Kate took
her by the hand.

When the two of them were gone, we moved around
the living room, sweeping up walnut shells and collecting
teacups, straightening doilies and cushions. We could hear
the men talking softly in the kitchen.

"The colored people have an expression," the shorter
Legion lady began to say. " 'No one's called home who
isn't ready.' "

"She should have eaten something," the other said.

"It's good for her to cry," the neighbor lady told us.
"Not to hold it all back. And what a shock for her, to think
she heard him coming in like that."

The shorter one paused. She was stout, high-breasted
like a wren. Wrenlike, she wore a beige sweater with a
maroon-and-brown harlequin pattern across the front and
brown stretch pants and tiny beige shoes. "I saw my husband three times after he died," she said softly. She held
an empty teacup and saucer before her, in both hands. It
made her look like a woman singing an aria. "In dreams,
I mean. The first time he told me about that expression
the colored people have. I'd never heard it before. The
second time he was sitting right next to me, in church.
There were lots of flowers and we were talking about how
pretty they were. There was a huge snowstorm the day

before his funeral"—turning to me to explain—"this was
back in '78. And we hadn't had too many flowers there. It
had bothered me a lot. That he hadn't had more flowers.
But the dream put my mind at ease." She paused. There
was a threat of tears in her voice. "The third time he just
squeezed my hand and walked away." She took a deep
breath, bending to pick up a crumpled napkin. "And that
was it," she said. "I never have been able to dream his
face again. I dream about him, but he's always in the next
room, or he's got his back to me, or he's just gone out or
is just about to come in. I never see him. There were those
three times in the beginning and then no more."

Solemnly, authoritatively, sweeping a tissue over the
surface of the coffee table, the taller Legion lady nodded
and said, "I believe it's always three."

Rosemary agreed. "That's what they say."

There was a knock at the front door—three short raps
that might have come from beneath a conjurer's table—
and when my father opened it, we heard his soft voice
saying, "Monsignor." A single look went around the
women in the room. You could feel the subject changing.
Rosemary leaned over and turned on another light.

The priest came into the living room just as the other
three men came through the dining room to meet him.
He shook hands all around. He was a heavy, scrubbed-
looking man whose throat seemed to strain against his
white collar just as his shoulders and broad chest seemed
to strain against his black jacket and shirtfront. Even his
shiny scalp looked taut against his skull. And yet, for all
this, there was an air of tremendous ease about him as he
shook hands all around like a politician (although he never

ran for anything), making eye contact, Glad to see you, his palm warm and dry and encompassing. The taller Legion lady went to brew him his cup of tea and I was dispatched by my father to go upstairs and let Maeve know.

The stairs were carpeted, the same pale gray pile as in the living room. There was a wrought-iron rail, open to the hallway halfway up and then closed off by a wall. On the landing there was a round table draped with a pale blue cloth and covered with Hummel children, some of whom had black veins running across their legs and shoulders and through their necks, clearly places where they had been broken and then carefully repaired. Above this table was an oil portrait of the Christ Child that to the uninitiated would seem to be a portrait of a beautiful and dark-skinned prepubescent girl. A framed, cross-stitched copy of the Irish blessing and another of the prayer of St. Francis on the wall between the two bedrooms. The bathroom door at the head of the stairs was closed and I could hear water running behind it.

I glanced into Maeve's bedroom. Kate was sitting on the edge of the bed, on a lovely ice-blue satin quilt that still bore the mark of where Maeve must have been napping when she heard Billy coming in. She held a life-sized baby doll in her lap, cradling it.

"Monsignor's here," I said, and Kate looked up. "Good," she said. She lifted the doll. It was dressed in a white crocheted sweater and cap and a long, yellowing christening gown. A tiny blue medal on a scrap of pale blue ribbon was pinned to its collar. "This was Maeve's," she said. "This gown. She was christened in it."

She turned to place the doll where it belonged, in the

center of the bed, between their two pillows. "Get this," Kate said, rearranging the doll's gown. "Maeve was just telling me that at the luncheon today Ted Lynch went on about an order of nuns that takes widows. He said he'd give her the name of the Mother House if she was interested." Kate rolled her eyes, blue eyes like Billy's. They seemed remarkably quick under the weight of her expensive eyeshadow. Her mouth had Billy's wry thinness. "Can you imagine?" she said. "An hour after a woman buries her husband, he's talking about her entering a convent? Can you imagine the gall?"

I shook my head. I had no trouble imagining it. "What did Maeve think?" I asked.

Kate waved her hand. Some of the makeup had settled into the creases around her eyes, the lines that framed her mouth. "Oh, you know Maeve, she told him she'd think about it." She reached out to smooth the christening dress over the doll's tiny booties. "It's the idea of being alone now, of course, that's getting to her, but I said, 'Come on, when did Ted Lynch become this rabid Catholic?' " She glanced toward the door, lowered her voice. "It's one of the problems with these ex-alcoholics," she said. "They still have to be rabid about something."

She picked up the doll again. She seemed incapable of leaving it alone. "They should have had children," she said suddenly. "Billy and Maeve. They were both so fond of children."

Behind her, the closet door was opened, showing the empty arms and shoulders of Billy's suits and shirts, his shoes lined up on the floor. There were two windows in the far wall, both of them draped with pale blue chintz over white sheers. On the dresser between them was a photograph of Maeve and Billy coming down the aisle on their wedding day—Billy looking off to the side, acknowledging someone in a pew, it seemed, Maeve with her head down, her own smile nearly hidden. There was another, old-fashioned photograph of a pretty young woman in a high lace collar, Maeve's mother, surely, and another framed snapshot—in pre-Kodachrome color, the tones slightly off—of Maeve's redheaded father looking startled, immobile, in one of the living-room chairs. Billy's postcard from Long Island was stuck into the lower-left-hand corner of the mirror—Home Sweet Home.

"Not that it would have changed what happened, but it would be something for Maeve, now," Kate was saying. "To have a few children around." She smoothed the doll's gown, brushed at the bonnet, cradling it with what seemed half her attention, an old habit of motherhood. "You can't help but wonder—what's she got now?"

We heard the bathroom door opening at the end of the hall. "As if I should talk," Kate whispered. And then she put the doll back on the pillow. She said she'd tell Maeve the Monsignor was here.

DOWNSTAIRS, THE PRIEST HAD everyone in the living room laughing softly, teacups and saucers on their knees. The coffee table now held a plate of Dan Lynch's bakery cookies and another of small tea sandwiches, some ham and some cheese. Although he sat in one corner of the couch, legs crossed casually, thighs straining against the black fabric of his pants, elbow up over the plastic-covered armrest, the Monsignor was the center of everyone's attention. He had been recalling Billy. A Holy Name Society meeting and the speaker going on for so long about the significance of the Pascal feast that Billy had leaned over and whispered into the Monsignor's ear that the hind leg of the Lamb of God with a little mint jelly sounded good to him.

When Maeve descended the stairs a few minutes later, her sister-in-law behind her like a handmaiden, everyone stood as if for a meeting of dignitaries. Maeve put both her hands out for the priest and the priest stepped toward her easily, confidently, like an expert, a pro, like a slugger going to the plate or a surgeon to the operating table, a renowned attorney rising for his closing arguments. We all felt it, felt the tremendous sense of relief that we finally had among us someone who knew what he was doing.

She wore brown slacks and a white sweater now, but nice ones, only a step down from her funeral dress. Not ready yet, perhaps, to put on her everyday clothes, to let Billy's death begin to be something less than an occasion.

"How are you, Maeve, my dear?" the priest said, taking her hands (she still clutched a tissue in one of them) with perfect gentleness and sympathy and an understanding that was bolstered—you saw it in his physical ease, his lingering smile—by his utter faith that death was not what we believed it to be tonight, not at all. He apologized for not having made it to the funeral this morning, he'd been called to the hospital (another soul rising, he implied), but she had been in his prayers all day long. "How are you, then?" he said, and once again Maeve put a tissue to her eyes and began to cry.

This time, none of us stirred. We simply stood, watching, as he put his arm around her shoulder and led her to the couch and sat beside her, his large hand covering both her own. Slowly, we all took our seats. It occurred to me that we were like a defeated bucket brigade, our wet and empty buckets dangling from our arms as we watched the fire chief drown a blaze that only minutes before we had merely splashed at.

"I thought I heard him coming in," she said. "Earlier this evening." And he nodded, expert in these matters, letting her speak, tell him what she'd felt, lying down in their darkened room, drifting off a bit, hearing the back door open and the dog coming in and the sound of his voice, and getting up and coming down here as if their lives were merely going on. And then realizing that he was gone. "Gone, Father," she said. The terror of it struck her then. His life was over. Hers was not.

The priest nodded as she spoke. Everything in his face and his manner said he knew. He knew what she said, wanted to say, would say next. He had sat like this, his manner said, with so many other widows, so many times before. When he finally replied it was with an authority that superseded all our experience of Billy, superseded even Maeve's, my father's, his sisters' long years. He was like a physician carrying reports to a waiting family, suddenly more expert than any of them about the dying man. More expert, everything in the priest's gracious manner seemed to say, because only he understood that death was nothing that it seemed to be, to us, tonight.

"Not over, Maeve," he said softly, scolding her, but fondly, gently. "We are not abandoned, Maeve," he said. "You know that."

She bowed her head. Her tears, free-falling now, struck her lap, the back of his hand.

"Billy's life goes on, in Christ."

With her head still down, she said again, "I thought I heard him coming in."

The priest nodded politely. "I understand," he said.

"I thought he was here," she repeated.

He pursed his lips, biding his time, it seemed. "It was another shock," he said. "But think of the joy he's found today, Maeve," he added softly, smiling. "The old reprobate. Think of the peace. Gone to his rest, Maeve," he said, "with the hope of rising again. The promise of rising again, Maeve, in the fulfillment of time. Think of that, if you can."

Maeve lifted her head, but did not raise her eyes. You could see in the stubborn set of her jaw that it was not a figurative life that she wanted for Billy at this moment but a literal one, his literal presence, coming in with the dog as she dozed, opening the cookie jar where they kept the dog biscuits, hanging the chain on the hook by the back door. Their life together, even as it was, simply going on. It was the same literal presence the Legion lady had spoken of earlier, the literal presence, even in a dream, that contained the actual sound of his voice in her ear ("The colored people have an expression . . .") and the actual weight of him beside her, admiring the flowers, putting her mind at ease. She wanted the real pressure of his hand against hers.

"It's a terrible thing, Father," Maeve said softly, her chin raised, her eyes cast down. "To come this far in life only to find that nothing you've felt has made any difference."

A sigh, quickly stifled, seemed to come from the women in the room. The priest raised his hand as if to quiet them.

"Listen to me," he said patiently, "listen now." He waited until she had raised her eyes, her expression showing him, showing us all, that she would not be convinced. "We could all tell ourselves tonight that we didn't do enough, Maeve. I had the thought myself when Dennis called me the other day and told me Billy was gone, and how they found him. I thought, Dear Lord, what could I have done? We could all of us say today that if we loved him it was a poor sort of love, or else his life wouldn't have ended as it did. But you know, if I said it to you, Maeve, if I said that I failed him, or if Dennis said it, or Father Jim, or Danny or Rose or Kate, if any one of Billy's friends said it, you'd be the first to tell us it wasn't true. And you'd mean it. And you'd be right. Billy succumbed to an illness we couldn't cure in time. It wasn't a failure of our affections, it was a triumph of the disease. That's the very thing you would tell any one of us and it's the thing you have to believe yourself. Of course, it mattered. Everything you felt, everything you did for Billy mattered, regardless of how it turned out." He bent his head a little to catch her downcast eyes. "I'm not kidding you about this, Maeve," he said. "I'm not making this up." He gripped both her hands in his, lifted them slightly. "You must believe this," he whispered.

She did not return his gaze. "I suppose I do," she said.

Rosemary stood in the doorway beside her husband, their shoulders nearly touching, their faces, both of them, drawn, as if they were accepting a reprimand. Kate sat in the chair beside the neighbor lady with her head bent, studying her polished nails, her diamond anniversary ring. The neighbor lady's husband had put his hand on her shoulder and was admiring, as were the two Legion ladies, admiring the man at his good work while Dan Lynch searched his pockets and then pulled out a large hand-kerchief and wiped both his eyes with it. He refolded the thing in some complex and elaborate pattern that reduced it to the size of a playing card and then wiped his eyes with it again. I turned to glance at my father, who stood just behind me, and saw some trace of the same look he had worn in the car today: that old annoyance, nearly triv-ialized by time. Or perhaps something troublesome, nearly healed. It was either the near-triumph of faith or the nearly liberating letting go of it. He looked down at me and nodded, as if I should attend to what the Monsignor was saying, as if his own experience, or age, excused him from the discourse, but I should attend.

Abruptly, before Maeve could say another word, the priest asked us all to say a Rosary with him, understanding (of course) that there was only so much more that could be said, that the repetitiveness of the prayers, the hushed drone of repeated, and by its numbing repetition, nearly wordless, supplication, was the only antidote, tonight, for Maeve's hopelessness. Rosemary began to get to her knees and he told her, good-naturedly, that he wasn't in-tending to kneel and would feel far more comfortable if she would simply get herself a chair. Chairs were carried in from the dining room and a kind of circle formed, al-though this was not the sort of Catholic gathering where anyone would think to join hands.

I T WAS THE SPRING of 1950 when Billy first came to
Sunday supper—the old man issuing the invitation
and Maeve in her nervousness dropping the whole
bowl of steamed spinach onto the kitchen floor just as they
were all about to sit down at the dining-room table. She
scooped it back into the serving bowl—what else was
there to do, there were only boiled potatoes and mashed
turnips without it?—fighting with the dog all the while
(Lucky was his name, her father would never be without
a dog in the house, a mix-breed terrier always underfoot
and mad for butter), unable to keep the animal's quick
tongue from the spoon and the bowl and the spinach itself.

She put the bowl out on the table, the spinach still
steaming, and watched Billy and her father help themselves and never said a word about it until years, absolutely years, later when she was serving Billy a bowl of
boiled spinach with his dinner and suddenly couldn't help

but laugh, and confess, and get Billy laughing about it, too. One night over dinner, not so very long ago. Billy sober because it was midday (they had liked having their Sunday dinner around three or four and then just a sandwich or something at around seven) and clean-shaven because he had gone to Mass with her that morning, and although he was only a week or two out of the VA and the fall he'd taken that had put him there, that time, was still evident from the fading yellow bruise on his forehead, although his face had grown thicker over the years, especially around the eyes and the chin, and his skin had begun to scale and peel and wear raw at his waistline and his wrists; although there was more silence between them, in those days, than talk, and she held in her memory, by then, a thousand and one moments she would never recount, things he had said to her, terrible things he had done, ways she had seen him (toothless, incoherent, half-clothed, bloodied, soiled, weeping) that she couldn't begin to tell, because even just putting it into words would kill her—a time, for instance (she will say it just this once), right before he went back to AA in '72, maybe the very thing that got him back to the meetings again, when she came down to the kitchen in the middle of the night and asked him to get himself to bed; she could see he was about to pass out and hoped he'd get himself up the stairs first. She leaned down to him at the table and said *Billy* into his ear (she knew enough to be firm with him, she knew that much), *Billy* (louder), and when he didn't budge, she turned away from him and started toward the stairs. "Dennis won't come, you know," she said from the hallway, talking to herself, as far as she was concerned.

"He's got enough on his mind with Claire, he won't come even if you call him, Billy. Even Dennis has had enough of you. Even Dennis has troubles of his own." And the next thing she knew he had her by the throat. He was so much taller than she, and by then he had grown so heavy. His glasses were off. His face—well, it might have been a total stranger that had broken into the house. "Billy, you'll kill me," she'd said, clawing at his hand. And then he was weeping at her feet. And then he was unconscious on the floor and she had to call the couple next door because Dennis in those days had troubles of his own.

There was a rill of deep laughter from the men in the living room, but the women in the kitchen were silent.

Although, Maeve said softly, they'd had such a good laugh over the story of the spilled spinach that afternoon, a Sunday not long ago, that she saw again, for a minute (Oh, you know how it is), how handsome he was. Saw again those good looks that she had from the first been so taken with. She remembered again what it had done to her, to her nerves, to her beating heart, to have had Billy Lynch there, the boy from the shoe store, in the flesh, at her own table that first evening her father invited him to dinner.

"He was a handsome man," Bridie from the neighborhood said quietly.

In Maeve's kitchen, in Bayside, the day fading, the Monsignor gone off to make another call, and the women bustling about, putting together from the disparate supply of casseroles and cakes a nice little buffet, Maeve leaned over her milkless cup of weak tea and, smiling, said in her soft and patient voice that it wasn't until he was leaving their house that night, until he was right to the door with his coat on and his hat in his hands, that he asked her if she would like to go to the movies with him on Saturday. Naturally, she said she would, thinking of course, all the while—you know how it is—What will I wear? She had her best dress on, as it was, a gray wool with a slash of black velvet in the skirt.

When she went back into the living room, her dad was already asleep in his chair, and you know it was him she blamed, then, for the slight weave she had noticed in Billy's walk as he left their door and headed down the hallway toward the stairs that night—her father and his Jameson's saved for special occasions, such as visits from countrymen like yourself . . . So there was no one for her to tell, because she knew if she told him while she was pulling off his shoes and his pants, pouring him into his bed, it would be as good as talking to the wall. So she was nearly bursting with the news the next morning. But when she finally told him that Billy Lynch had asked her to the movies for Saturday night, her father merely sniffed and stirred his coffee and said, "No doubt he feels obliged." He said Billy had once been engaged, you know, just a few short years ago, to an Irish girl who died.

Rosemary quickly turned from the stove and said to us over her shoulder, "Oh, aren't men cruel?"

But Bridie from the old neighborhood, who had arrived with her famous pound cake just as the Rosary was concluded, smiled kindly at Maeve and said, "I'm sure your dad meant no harm."

Maeve seemed inclined to leave the subject open to discussion. She had thought, she said, to buy herself something new for Saturday, but after her father said that she decided, Why bother? Any old skirt and sweater would probably do. They saw *All About Eve* and stopped at Horn & Hardart. She lit a candle in church that Sunday morning, but she didn't hold out much hope. And yet—the power of prayer—a week or two later, she was at the store and he asked her out again. And then her father asked him to dinner again, and soon they were seeing each other quite regularly. But she knew for certain that she and Billy were an item when they went over to Dennis and Claire's place for dinner one night—they'd only been married themselves a year or so—a nice little apartment off Prospect Park. Their first child ("your brother Danny") was just a few months old and Billy had held the sleeping infant against his chest throughout the meal, so that he had to eat with one hand. So that he had to ask her to lean over and help him cut his steak, which she did, of course, feeling him watching her. Even her father had to admit there was something more than obligation between them after that, Irish girl or no.

"For want of a shoe," the little Legion lady said softly. Everyone turned to her. "How does it go?" She touched the harlequin pattern across her breast. "For want of a shoe the horse was lost, for want of a horse, the rider was lost . . . How's it go?"

There was a moment of puzzled silence.

"For want of a rider," Bridie said helpfully, "the battle was lost . . ."

The rest of us hadn't stopped frowning.

"I mean, for Maeve," the Legion lady finally said, holding out her hand, and while we were all more or less convinced that she did not mean to say that for Maeve the battle, the kingdom was lost—although it might well be said—none of us had yet gotten her true meaning. "For Maeve it was just the opposite," she explained. "For want of a shoe, a boyfriend was found . . ."

The laughter was sudden and brief, crumbs shaken out of a dish towel. "Oh, I see," someone said. "Well, that's true."

Smiling, nodding, getting it (this is good for her, this kind of conversation—you could see all the women thinking it—this is just the kind of thing she needs), Maeve touched her teacup, the tea surely cold now, and said, leaning forward, "I'll tell you what I did."

We all smiled at her.

"I threw my father's shoe down the incinerator." Some color had returned to her cheek or, perhaps, was just returning as she spoke. "Not once but twice. If you can believe it. I said, 'Now, Dad, I don't know what's happened to the mate of your good shoes but we'd better get down to Holtzman's on Saturday or you'll have nothing to wear to church Sunday morning.' "

"Why in the world?" Kate asked. She had just returned from setting out the good silver on the dining-room table.

"Just to go in there," Bridie cried. "Just to have an excuse to go into the shoe store."

Maeve nodded. "Just to see Billy." Another bout of teariness passed briefly over her face—it was like the shadow of a small cloud moving over the earth—but was quickly gone. "I did it once, early on, before Billy and I had ever exchanged more than a few words, and then I did it again after our first date, because it had been a few

months since poor Dad had come home minus a shoe—
which he truly did often enough—and I got a little impatient. So I tossed another one down the incinerator, and
good Lord, wouldn't you know it, we came back from
Holtzman's that afternoon and there was Dad's shoe
propped on the banister in the foyer. The super must have
found it. It was still pretty new, so he must have thought
it had fallen into the incinerator by accident and he put it
out there for someone to claim it. I was certain my father
would turn right around and take the new pair back to
Billy, but when I said, 'Dad, your shoe,' he looked at me
and said, 'It isn't,' very indignant. He wouldn't even look
at it. He just marched up the stairs as if he didn't see it,
refusing to admit anything. Here it was resurrected and
he wouldn't have any part of it. The thing sat there for a
good week or two and then disappeared altogether."

All the women were chuckling now, thinking of it, and
how bright-eyed Maeve had become, telling the tale, and
all without a drop of sherry in her bloodstream.

This was good for her. Good memories. And even if
she'd given fate a push or two, wasn't it finally Billy's good
luck that she'd shown up there, in the shoe store like that,
so wild about him, so ready to give him her heart that
surely it was a compensation of some sort for what he had
lost, for the Irish girl. You could see Kate and Rosemary
thinking it, the question answered: Maeve had known all
along about the Irish girl, and still she had given Billy her
heart. What was it the postcard had said? Lovely wife?

"Wasn't I terrible, though?" she asked us. "Throwing
his shoes away like that?"

"You were determined," the neighbor lady said.

"The things we do when we're young," Rosemary said, shaking her head.

"When we're in love," the taller Legion lady added, although it was a leap even I couldn't make to imagine this gaunt and opinionated holy old woman as a girl in love.

"I told Ted Lynch about it," Maeve continued, "years ago, when he said the best thing I could do for Billy was to leave him. I told him how I'd thrown away those shoes. I wanted him to understand what I'd gone through to get him."

The women all nodded. Even a plain girl with that kind of determination would be compensation enough for the beautiful Eva.

Suddenly Bridie, who was folding paper napkins, said softly, well, since we were telling tales, she'd tell one herself: Oh, what a crush she'd had on Billy Lynch when she was young. How many hours she had spent at her window waiting for him to walk by. Even up until the time she was dating Tim Schmidt, even after, she would have dropped anyone she knew to take up with Billy Lynch. "Except for Jim, of course." Jim was her husband.

"Oh, Bridie," Rosemary said, waving a crocheted pot holder. "Tell us something we don't already know."

"Really?" Bridie said softly, "You're kidding," but Kate had opened the casserole dish brought by the Indian couple and sniffed it and frowned as if to say not as bad as she expected. She held it under the tall Legion lady's nose. "Should we warm this up a bit?" she asked, and the tall Legion lady gave it the same kind of nasal inspection. "Sure," she said.

"It's some kind of chicken with rice," Kate said to Maeve, holding it under her nose as well. "I was afraid it would be something spicy."

"Oh no," Maeve said. "Lili's a wonderful cook." She turned to the neighbor lady. "They're fine people, aren't they?" And the lady agreed. "I have wonderful neighbors," Maeve said to us all. "I've been fortunate in that."

There was a moment of silent assent, and then the neighbor lady, sitting beside her at the small kitchen table, just under the particle-board apples, reached across and patted Maeve's hand. Maeve covered the lady's with her own.

"Monday night," Maeve said, and then corrected herself, "no, Tuesday morning, I called Dorothy here. When? one, two in the morning?"

"It was about two-twenty," Dorothy said softly.

"I didn't know," Maeve said. "I hadn't slept. There was a wind. Spring weather coming in is what Dorothy said. But it pulled at the windows. I usually dozed, waiting for Billy to come in. I usually said a Rosary and dozed, but not that night. I called Dorothy at about two in the morning. My hands were shaking, honestly, shaking like a leaf, and I asked her if she'd throw a coat on and come over."

"She didn't sound like herself," Dorothy told us. "She was frightened."

"And you said you were frightened, too, when you came in. Weren't you?"

Dorothy nodded. "Just crossing our driveways," she said. "There was something weird about the night. The wind and the warmish air."

"No doubt it was the hour, too," Kate said, being reasonable, it seemed.

"It was everything together," Dorothy said.

"We sat right here until when . . . seven or so?"

"Till John called."

"Till her husband called, at about seven. And then I walked her back across. It was raining by then, wasn't it, Dorothy? All that wind and then a cloudy morning anyway. Of course, Billy hadn't come in. John offered to call around for me. Even said he'd take the morning off to drive around a bit, but I didn't want him to trouble. It wasn't like it hadn't happened before, Billy not coming in."

"You said you'd let the police know," Dorothy said, and to the rest of us, "John made her promise to do that much. And to call Dennis. John said, Now, Maeve, Billy's a very sick man. He offered to call the VA himself, see if he was there. 'He's a very sick man,' John said."

"I said I'd call," Maeve told us. "I intended to. But when I got back to the house I did a few things first. I took a little bath. I washed out a few things."

"Billy's good shirt," Dorothy said.

Maeve nodded. "Billy's good white shirt."

"When she told me she'd washed out his good white shirt," Dorothy said to the rest of us, "I knew she knew. She knew he was gone. She'd known it all through the night."

"And then the hospital called," Maeve said. "About nine or so. And I called Dennis at Edison to ask if he could go down there. It was because he hadn't been admitted, see. They found him on the street, so somebody had to identify him." She looked at me. "Your poor father had to do it."

Kate said, "Everything's ready," and we all moved into the dining room, where the men were already waiting. Two or three of the women immediately began to urge Maeve to eat something. Maybe some of that nice chicken-and-rice thing, not too spicy. Maybe some of this ham. They followed her around the lace-covered table in the brightly lit dining room. Something substantial now, they said. Something easy on the stomach, too. Bridie's pound cake, of course. A pound of butter, the way it ought to be made. Old-fashioned ingredients being the best, when you came right down to it, because in the old days you really had to be of some substantial weight, women especially, in order to survive. Such as pioneer women in those covered wagons, or our own mothers making the crossing, although our mother was not a big woman and lived to eighty-three and Dennis's mother was just a wisp, too, and Uncle Ted's wife Aunty M. J.—the Lynch men apparently going for the smaller girls and Rosemary's daughter Jill with her tiny waist and you (me), too, although I see what little portions you've put on that plate, good for you, looking at you who would think you'd had two children, you must exercise, Kate does too, you should see the setup she's got in her basement, Jack La Lanne's, and so your husband's home with the little ones?—it'll be good for him, let him see what it's like with kids all day, right? men never understand until you ask them to do it and then they say, Well, the kids only act like this with me, it has to be much easier when *you're* with them, isn't that the truth? They're really thinking, You can't possibly put up with this day after day, can you? But it was so sweet of you to be here like this. Kevin and Daniel came in last night for the wake, but the girls are both up in New England, you know—both lawyers, have I told you? did you see the flowers they sent? They were fond of Billy, both of them. I know your father appreciates it, your being here with him. He and Billy were so close, like brothers, really—neither one of them having a brother of his own. And Dennis having to go down to the VA to identify Billy like that. What would Maeve have done, over the years, without your father to call on. He was the image of his own father in that, of Uncle Daniel. Always there for whoever needed him—what was it that you called him, Dan? A politician? Well, I don't know about that, but he did everything for my parents when they first came over. I'd call him a saint and I'm not just saying that. Not a good-looking man, your father was lucky to take after his mother's side of his family, but goodness poured out of him. I've never known anyone else quite like him. You would think he'd been put on this earth just to give the rest of us a hand, to give us some relief—isn't that just what a saint is? I remember people laughing, whenever I think of him, and I was sixteen when he died. Wherever he went he got people laughing, like Billy in a way, I suppose. Billy without his trouble. Your poor father losing his own dad at eighteen and his mother and his wife within a few years of one another and now Billy, too. I'm sure he's glad you came in. And tomorrow you'll go out to the Island with him? Good. Your husband will manage fine, don't worry about that. All young mothers think their kids can't survive without them, don't they? Didn't you?

Soon enough you'll see. Next thing you know, they're all grown up and gone from home—isn't it the truth. Next thing you know, your house is empty again. Look at us, Bridie, Rose, Dorothy, Kate, how many kids altogether? Fifteen, good Lord, sixteen, sixteen kids altogether and not one of them left at home, right? Thank God for that, but see what I'm saying, see how fast it goes? But Kate's not going home tonight. No sense in her making that long drive back to Rye in the dark. Give Maeve some company, the first night and all. What's it doing outside? Can you see? It's been raining since Tuesday, hasn't it? Rain on a funeral day is supposed to mean a soul going straight to heaven. Did anyone bring the dog in? We should be going so Maeve can get some rest. Has she eaten a bite? Has she eaten anything? Her color's coming back anyway. It was just the sherry on an empty stomach. And the exhaustion, too, the poor girl. She'll be fine. Time heals and it's been a long haul. In many ways this will be a relief. God forgive me for saying so, she'll have some peace now.

While Rosemary and the Legion ladies cleaned up in the kitchen, Dorothy took Maeve's hands and asked her to please remember she was there, she and John were there, right next door, any time of the day or night, as always. "Thank you," Maeve said softly, "thank you, dear," but in a way that seemed to indicate that she, too, was aware of how little need she would have, now, of aid and assistance in the middle of the night.

"Even if it's just a bad dream," Dorothy said.

She glanced at her husband. "Even if it's just a strange noise or something you need right away from the store. An antacid or something. Just call us. Anything." She glanced at her husband again. "Even if you're just feeling lonely," she said, and then burst into blubbery tears—as much for herself, it seemed, and her own possible, probable long nights of widowhood as for Maeve's. The stocky husband she had just imagined into his grave put his fingers to her elbow and said, "Now, Mama," and Dorothy found a crumpled tissue in her pocket and waved it across her face. "I promised myself I wouldn't do this," she gasped.

But Maeve was smiling indulgently. She looked tired. The skin seemed to have thinned across her cheekbones, beneath her neck, and yet she seemed, too, to have found another source of strength, or composure, some last well of it that would see her through the final ceremonies of the day. "It's all right," she said. She briefly took the woman into her arms. "It's all right," she said again as they drew apart.

"He was a fine person," Dorothy was saying through her tears. "Without the drink. He was a sweet soul sober, Maeve. One of the best. Talking to him was like listening to poetry, wasn't it, John? Even when he was drinking, he was worth listening to. A smart man in his way. A sensitive man, Maeve, when you think about it. Maybe too sensitive for this world, if you know what I mean. A man with his fine feelings. The Lord made him as he was. There was no one to blame. You had your good years with him and that's what counts, doesn't it? Remember what you told us tonight about the spinach. And throwing away those shoes. Think of things like that."

Her husband was slowly drawing her out of the room,

nodding goodbyes to everyone he passed. "Maeve's tired now," he told his wife. "Let Maeve get her rest."

"He was a sweet man," Dorothy was saying, on into the hallway. "If he hadn't taken to drink. What a shame he ever took a drink."

When they had gone, the Legion ladies stepped out of the kitchen, drying their hands on dish towels and slipping into their coats. They told Maeve what she had in the way of food in the kitchen. They'd be by first thing in the morning, they said, and no sooner were they out the door (bustling, in their plastic rain hats and short canvas raincoats, their caution in going sideways down the three wet brick steps the only physical indication of their age) than Mac turned to us all and asked, "Don't any of these holy women have homes and husbands of their own?"

Dan Lynch said, "Apparently not."

Bridie said, "Ah, but I do," putting her purse over her plump and freckled arm and taking her coat from the settee in the hallway, which had begun to fill up with the odor of the wet night and the residual perfumes of the women's headscarves and spring jackets. "And my lady who looks after him will be charging me time and a half because I told her I'd only be here an hour or so," she looked at her watch, "And now it's been three."

"How is Jim?" Mac said soberly. Bridie waved a hand as if to show him there was no need for such solemnity. "He's doing all right, thank you," she said. "He doesn't always know me, that's the hard part. But as long as I can keep him home and keep him happy—things could be worse. He's more or less in his own little world." She shrugged. "Sometimes I envy him." She leaned to kiss Maeve, and then Rosemary and Kate. "God bless," she said to each of them, and then turning to us all: "I'm not going to make a speech. That was Billy's forte. The hard part's going to be going to the mailbox every day without hoping there's a note from him." To which everyone agreed, drawing in a breath as they nodded, as if they had not yet taken this into account but should have, would have, sooner or later. Bridie kissed me and my father and Mac, and with a "You, too, Danny," Dan Lynch.

"You'll be all right driving home?" my father said with his hand on her back.

"I'm fine." She shook her thick ring of keys. "I've got my siren and my Mace. I'm armed and ready. And it's not that late." My father said he would walk her to her car at least.

"She's a riot," Rosemary said when Bridie was gone, clearly meaning something else.

"She's had a hard row to hoe," Kate said, directing her sister toward it. "Her girl with the drugs and Jim with Alzheimer's. And those babies she lost."

"And Tim Schmidt," Rosemary said, "in the war."

"She's a marvel," Maeve said, and Kate touched her shoulder and told her, "You, too, my girl."

Maeve laughed a little. "A marvel of what?" she said. Her shoulders seemed boneless.

"Of endurance," Kate said.

"Of patience," Rosemary added. "And loyalty."

Maeve smiled, dipping her head. It was clear that it pleased her, to have this much recognized and acknowledged. Her endurance, her patience, her long suffering.

That same determination that had once made her throw her father's good shoes down the incinerator had made her a marvel at this, at being Billy's wife.

As Maeve took her leave of us herself, she paused on the stairs, her hand on the simple railing, and said to my father, "Thank you, especially, Dennis. I know how hard this has been for you." (Dan Lynch smiling sympathetically beside him, reserving his own tearful What about me? for another time, tomorrow night at Quinlan's, perhaps, with his cronies and a drink.) My father nodded. "Call if you need me," he said, repeating Dorothy's mistake, forgetting, as she had, that the mad nights were over.

For a moment the familiar weight struck me: I wondered how much lonelier my father's nights would be now, uninterrupted by crisis.

Billy's sisters, handmaidens still, followed her up the stairs, and a few minutes later Rosemary came down again to put her own coat on and gather up her husband. When Kate came down in her stocking feet to lock the door behind us, we followed Mac and Rosemary out. Dan Lynch, his jacket collar turned up and his feelings hurt by Maeve's last remark, began to walk to the bus stop in the light rain, under the orange streetlights, carrying the plastic grocery bag Rosemary had pressed on him, a supper or two's worth of leftovers. But my father called him back and said, almost impatiently, that he would of course drive him home. What did he think?

In the car, Dan straightened his collar and quickly recovered his good humor by asking us, Wasn't the Monsignor something? Wasn't he incredible? The embodiment of every good thing about the priesthood. He said he was certain there were plenty of fine rabbis and ministers, but there was something about a priest, a good priest, that those others couldn't match. A holiness. A closeness to God. "Don't you feel it the minute he walks into a room?" My father admitted he did. Dan twisted in his seat to see me. I admitted I did, too.

Well satisfied, he said, "It's a life lived on another plane, you see. A life that's all God, nothing else." He paused, but there was something false about the way he did, something theatrical. It seemed clear that everything he was about to say was well formed in his mind, well memorized, perhaps, a speech he had already worked out in every detail, that had, until now, lacked only an audience. "Think about it," he said. "A rabbi or a minister closes up his church or synagogue after a service and goes home to dinner with his wife and kids. He pays his bills," tapping his index finger on the car's dashboard, beating out the rhythm of an imaginary day, "does the grocery shopping, tosses a ball with his son, right? What's to distinguish him from anybody else, with any other kind of job? But a priest can take off his collar, play a round of golf, go to a ball game—he's still always different. It's a consecrated life, see, not just a consecrated profession. I mean, take the Pope, for instance, even non-Catholics are excited to meet him, aren't they? They know he's something special. Holy." He shook his head. "Now they're talking about changing things, but I hope they never do. It would be a mistake. We'll lose that, Dennis. The Church will lose the very thing that makes its priests a cut above."

I wondered if he meant celibacy.

"You're right," my father was saying. "Absolutely."

"I don't mean it isn't a sacrifice." I supposed he did. "It's a tremendous sacrifice. We had a young fellow, just out of the seminary, come to our parish a few years back, nice as could be, but he didn't last. He couldn't take it. Eventually he left and got himself married. So I know it's a sacrifice. But get rid of it and the priests will become just like everyone, wait and see. You'll do as well to confess to your barber."

My father was nodding, smiling, wondering, no doubt, as I was, about Dan Lynch's own single state. "Sure," he said.

"You can't have both eyes on heaven when there's a wife and a mortgage and new shoes for the kiddies to buy. It only stands to reason you can't."

"You're right," my father said. "I didn't."

"It only stands to reason," Dan Lynch said again. And then he turned a little, toward my father, lowered his voice just a bit, not enough to keep me from hearing him but to acknowledge, perhaps, that the company was mixed. "But I tell you, it gets my goat to hear the way people talk about it. It gets to me. You know, you can give up anything else these days, give up all kinds of foods to stay healthy, you know, salt, eggs. Or maybe give up sleep so you can be out jogging down the street at 6 a.m. You can give up an old wife for a new one, or a home life so you can run around the world like Henry Kissinger—oh sure, give up anything like that and it's just fine, it's just the ticket. But let the talk turn to Catholic priests and everybody's smiling behind their hands. Snickering. They're all out to make it something perverted. A man enters so fully into his faith that it changes the very fabric of his life, the very fabric, Dennis, do you see what I'm saying, and this society can't tolerate it. They want to see it as something bad. Our Lord's okay as a story, you know, Christmas, Easter, something to talk about on a Sunday morning, but take it to heart, take Him to heart, have your belief change the very fabric of your life and oh ho"—he held his palm out toward the dashboard, shook it—"that's going too far for them. They've got to look for the dirt in it, not the glory. They say, It's an unnatural thing, giving that up, a man can't give *that* up, not for the sake of what's really only a pretty story."

"No one says that about the Pope," my father said, goading him, I thought.

"No, not about the Pope," Dan Lynch said, ever earnest. "Not in the papers, anyway. They're careful about that. He's a celebrity, after all. And he's a robust man. He skis, you know."

"Yes," my father said.

"But they'll say it readily enough about any ordinary priest, won't they? They can sense the holiness, but they don't understand it, so the first thing they want to do is mess it up a bit, kick some dirt on it, throw some sand on the fire. Sure, it's a great relief and comfort to the rest of us to find out no one's any better than we are, right? A man like the Monsignor walks into a room, and you know, it threatens some people."

"Sure," my father said, a touch of weariness in it. He'd had enough of Dan Lynch, I could tell.

Sensing this, not quite taking offense, Dan Lynch crossed his arms in front of his chest and settled farther into his seat. He turned to look out the window, the wet dark streets lit by orange phosphorus. You could see by the way he turned back to my father, and paused, and looked, that he had struck on the thought some seconds before he said it. "Billy had something of that air about him, didn't he?" he asked softly. "That holiness, when he walked into a room. Don't you think?"

"Something of it," my father said, and then: "Look at this." There was an empty parking space right in front of Dan's building. "That's luck," he said as he pulled into it.

Dan Lynch reached down to gather up his plastic bag. He was flustered for a few seconds by his search for the door handle and then again by the unfastening of his seat belt, but when he was fully prepared for his leave-taking, he paused and said with a sigh, "It's the hardest night for Maeve, isn't it? The first night with Billy in his grave." He turned to the window. "It might as well rain." Beside us, his apartment building, pre-war Queens, six stories, dark brick, without cupola or awning or ornamentation of any kind, seemed as forlorn and hopeless as a penitentiary.

Dan Lynch cleared his throat. "Would you come in for a nightcap?" he asked. Without hesitation, my father turned off the engine and reached behind his seat for the club for the steering wheel.

"You don't mind?" he whispered to me as we followed Dan Lynch across the sidewalk and up the barren path. "No," I said, my father's daughter, and stood beside him as we watched Dan Lynch let himself into his apartment building with his own key.

I N MY BOOK of Irish names," Dan Lynch said, "Maeve means 'the intoxicating one.' "

My father nodded. "There's an irony," he said.

"And Eva," Dan went on. "Eva, I suppose, would be some form of Eve. The first woman."

My father nodded again, slowly, his lips drawn a bit as if Dan Lynch had made a good point. As if in response to a good point, my father said, "There you go."

They both sipped their drinks—two fingers of Scotch in stubby glasses, plenty of ice. Serving them, Dan had poured three and then seemed taken aback when my father lifted the first and handed it to me. It might have been an aging bachelor's surprise to think that a woman—especially one he had known as a child—would accept anything stronger than sherry ("Would you rather a ginger ale?" he'd said), but it left me with the feeling that the glass had been meant for someone else. For Billy, perhaps. That I was sipping Billy's drink.

Dan Lynch's living room was dim—dim enough to make the double set of rain-spattered windows seem bright. The furniture was ancient: leather-topped desk where he had poured our drinks; claw-footed chairs, broad couch. Some of them his own mother's pieces, he said. Threadbare Oriental. There were neat stacks of *National Geographic* and *Time* and *U.S. News and World Report* piled against the bowed legs of every end table, and the tables themselves were piled with books, histories and biographies, from the Queensborough Public Library mostly. Winston Churchill and the Desert Fox, the War in the Pacific, D-Day, Guadalcanal, the *Enola Gay*, F. D. R., and Truman. There was a rattan magazine rack crowded with two weeks' worth of precisely folded newspapers. Today's *Daily News* as well as a *St. Anthony Messenger*—a cover story about celibacy and the priesthood—were on the coffee table between us.

There was the odor, especially when we'd first entered, of aftershave and the soap he had used in the shower he must have taken between the funeral lunch and the visit to Maeve's, but it was giving way now, as we sat, to the various scents—curry, onion, garlic—of some immigrant neighbor's late supper.

"Not to make too much of such things," Dan continued, seeming to believe suddenly that my father and I might do just that. "It's only something that occurred to me today, when Kate brought up that girl's name again: Eve—Eva. And when I got home, I looked up Maeve."

My father nodded again, shrugged a little as well, as if

to say he would be careful. He would not make too much of such things.

"It's just that on a day like this," Dan Lynch said, "you find yourself looking at everything. In a new light, if you know what I mean. You want to make some sense of it all."

"It's true," my father said.

Both men sat silently for a moment, cautious, it seemed, weighing words. Neither one of them would want to appear to be trying to say something profound—that was for the priest, of course—and both equally feared growing sentimental. And yet something needed to be said, on a night like this. There was the splatter of rain— like fingertips tapping against the windowpanes. The Scotch was mellow but with a bite. Each sip raised a kind of veil that was both a warmth across the cheeks and a welling in the eyes. A way of seeing, perhaps. Perhaps the very thing that Billy would have found so appealing, had the drink been his.

Not to make too much of such things.

"I never did meet her," Dan said. "That Irish girl. She was long gone back home by the time I was discharged. She was always just a story to me. You and Billy out there on Long Island that summer while I'm still getting eaten alive in the Pacific. Insect-proof fatigues, they told us." He smiled. "What a time that was." He turned to me. "Those A-bombs saved the lives of a lot of GIs, you know. Killed a lot of Japanese, sure. A lot of innocent people, too. But don't let the liberals kid you, none of them ever walked through a jungle sniffing for Japs. That's what we did, you know, sniffed for them. See if you could smell cigarette smoke or, you know, defecation. That's how you'd know they were there. You couldn't see anything but lousy jungle. Those bombs kept an awful lot of GIs from dying in those jungles, you know. Those bombs let a lot of young guys go home in one piece."

I nodded. I recalled that Dan Lynch had once been known as a great letter writer, too, although his were always addressed to the editors of *Time* and *Newsweek*, the presidents of networks. I recalled that he was especially vigilant about slurs against Irish Americans and had once received a personally signed apology from Danny Kaye for a sketch he had done on TV about a drunken leprechaun. A one-man Irish-American anti-defamation league, my grandmother had called Dan Lynch at the time, out on Long Island that last summer when he'd come out for the day and brought the letter along. The rest of the Irish, she'd said, hear a slur against them and instead of being insulted get all guilty thinking that it's true. Kick a Jew in New York, she'd said, and one in Tel Aviv says "Ouch." But kick any Irishman and the rest of them shut their mouths and cover their backsides, thinking they're more deserving. Hadn't Danny Lynch, after all (when you got to the bottom of it), brought the letter in which Danny Kaye admitted all Irishmen were not drunks down to Quinlan's? hadn't he spread it out on the bar?

Dan shifted in his seat, recrossed his legs. "I remember meeting Maeve, though," he went on. "I remember the first time Billy brought her into Quinlan's. It was a Sunday afternoon. They'd been over to one of those tea dances they used to have at the K. of C. This must have been in the early fifties. There was a real downpour and any number of people from the dance were coming in."

I sipped Billy's drink. Another Queens rain, then: the raindrops themselves flashing black and silver in the air, darkening the sidewalk and the gray street and raising the smoky, dirty odor of wet asphalt and wet steel, the darkness of the afternoon making the neon lights in the various small storefronts, drugstore and Chinese restaurant and Quinlan's Bar and Grill, seem brighter than usual, even romantic, making the streets under and around the elevated seem a city unto themselves rather than the mere runoff—as they had always seemed to be to me—from Manhattan's surplus. Billy and Maeve, still younger-looking than anyone would remember them, hurrying along.

"I remember I saw Billy heading toward the bar with this girl in front of him, and my first thought was that she was someone he'd met out on the street or just inside the door. I thought maybe she was a stranger who needed to find a telephone and he was just helping her out. You weren't used to seeing Billy with a girl. It took me a few minutes to get it straight: that he'd actually taken her to the dance, picked her up at her house and brought her the orchid she was wearing. I must have seemed pretty thick, but it came as a surprise to me. You weren't used to it in those days. Not with Billy. You were pretty sure he was a fellow who'd stay single."

Just as Billy must have been sure of it himself by then, five, six years since his summer on Long Island. And yet here was Maeve's very real elbow against his palm, yielding to his slightest pressure. Let me introduce you to my cousin. Here was another girl speaking into his ear—she'd just have a ginger ale, thank you—her breath mingled with the scent of the hothouse orchid on her shoulder, the one he'd brought her. Her face would seem dim in the new light of the crowded barroom, he would be aware of its downy paleness, her plain blue eyes. Thank you, Billy—maybe a little tremor as she lifted the glass and put it to her lips, a tremor of self-consciousness as she lifted her eyes to him over its rim.

Dan Lynch leaned forward a bit, cupping the stubby glass in both hands. "She was no beauty, was she? Maeve. A plain girl. I was going with Carol Wilson then, you know. Butch Wilson's sister, do you remember her?"

My father said he did. There was a beauty.

Dan sniffed a little. Her mouth was a bit too wide, he said. Not the brightest light either. He glanced at me as if to say there was a tale to tell, if it was just my father here alone. I suspected it would be a tale my father already knew.

"But Maeve seemed to be a good-enough sort," Dan Lynch said. "It didn't take much to see that she was wild about Billy. I don't know what Billy thought of her at that point, but she sure thought he was something."

Touching his own glass to hers in the bar where the crowd, just like the other couples at the tea dance that afternoon, was growing younger than them both. Time was passing. The christenings were beginning to outnumber the weddings among his family and his friends, the children born since the war, the nieces and nephews and cousins once removed becoming toddlers now, schoolchildren, startling him with their weight, their language, their blossoming lives. He touched her glass and sipped his whiskey and felt the watery veil cover his eyes. What could he have thought of Maeve, after the Irish girl, after that other future, the brightest of them, had shattered in his hand: Here was safety, here was compensation, here was yet another life, the one that had been waiting for him all along, even while he'd been busy imagining his life with Eva. "Pale brows, still hands and dim hair"—he would have found the lines in Yeats. "I had a beautiful friend / And dreamed that the old despair / Would end in love in the end—"

"When they finally decided to get married, I have to say it was another surprise to me. I never thought it had gotten to that point. Billy never even said that he was thinking of marriage. But I think maybe he was superstitious by then. I think he was afraid to say much to anyone about his plans. After what happened before."

"Could be," my father said.

Dan Lynch nodded and said, "I'm sure it's true."

Or did he think, leaning down to her pale face, the lipstick nearly gone from her dry lips, that here was the will to live, or the will to procreate, or simply the will to be joined to another, rising up in him again, all unbidden. Here was the familiar longing for peace, for sense, for happiness of some sort or another showing itself again in the form of this mild woman. Here it was, bidding him to go on, make plans, wed—weakening his resolve. His resolve to be true to his first intentions.

"All Billy says to me is 'Would you be my best man?' and I said, 'Sure. Who's the bride?' " Dan Lynch laughed, remembering. "I suppose he would have asked you if Claire hadn't been expecting."

He said it somewhat slyly and then seemed pleased when my father told him, "I don't think so. You were the man for the job."

Dan nodded to agree. "He showed me the ring. Just a plain pearl, not a diamond this time, which I suppose was more superstition still." He doubled his chin, looking into his drink. "I remember the way she shored up her old man, coming down the aisle."

My father smiled, nodding, showing that he remembered it, too.

"She did the same for Billy, when the time came. Maneuvered him when he couldn't maneuver himself."

"She was good at it," my father said.

Dan Lynch thought for a moment. A bit of wind picked up some raindrops and hit them against the glass, like pebbles thrown by a persistent suitor. "It was me who told Billy not to stay in the apartment with the two of them," Dan said softly, going on. "After he and Maeve were married. I knew he had some money saved. Working for Holtzman and all. I said, Buy yourself your own house and move Maeve and her old dad into it—or else you'll always be a visitor in their place. We were sitting in the back, at those little tables Quinlan had back there for a while, with the little lamps that had those scorched shades. Billy said Quinlan had gotten the whole set of them, along with the new waitress, at a fire sale somewhere. June was her name, the waitress. I took her out a few times. She did seem a little singed." He raised his eyebrows toward my father, shook his head again: another tale unfit for mixed company. "I said to Billy," he went on, "Tell yourself this is a way of the Irish girl giving something back to you. You took the job with Holtzman because of her, now use what money you've made at it to start out with Maeve. I don't know, maybe I was wrong to bring her up, the Irish girl, I mean. Billy never mentioned her himself." He shrugged. "But that's what I said. And Billy took my advice. He took my advice that time anyway."

Holtzman's money providing yet another down payment, then, this time for the house in Bayside. A narrow pale-brick house on a street lined with a dozen others, a small house with three high brick steps and a wrought-iron railing and a long white driveway that led to a narrow yard. They gave her old father his own room upstairs, moving into it the same bed and dresser and nightstand he had once purchased for his own young bride. The old black police scanner placed over the doily that covered the nightstand mumbling and squawking through most hours of the day that Maeve would spend cleaning and shopping and chatting with the neighbors while Billy was at Con Ed five days a week and Holtzman's Thursday nights and Saturdays, and even the two weeks of his summer vacation, since he would not go out there again.

("You and Maeve come out some weekend," Dennis would say when they met each other on the street or in the lobby or in the elevator at Edison, or when Billy and Maeve came by for supper or had Dennis and Claire over to their place. "Come mid-week," Dennis would offer. "Take a couple of vacation days. We'll be there with the children the first two weeks in July, you and Maeve come on out. Bring the old man, we'll make room."

But Billy would say no, shaking his head. "Thank you, Dennis, but no," he'd say softly. "I won't go out there." No need to ask him why.)

Dan Lynch said, "The real fly in the ointment as far as I could see was her old man. A drunk, pure and simple. And Billy so full of sympathy for him from the first, the way he'd lost his wife and a child and all. Billy thought it was reason enough for the man to drink. Reason enough for no one to deny him his whiskey, even though it was killing him." To me: "You only had to take one look at Maeve's old man to know that the drink was killing him." To my father: "Remember how he was, in his old slippers, the skin all mottled. That nose. Three sheets to the wind by four in the afternoon." He shook his head, shivered a little. "Maeve looking after him day after day. Not the best company for a newly married couple."

And yet Maeve's ordinary days alone with her father in the Bayside house could not have been much different from what they had been back in the apartment, before Billy, so much of the day, now as then, being predicated upon the dog. Her father coming into the kitchen to let the dog out in the morning and then pushing himself out of the living-room chair and into his clothes to take him for his first walk of the day; giving the animal his treat and putting the paper and the can of beer aside to give Trixie or Teddy or Joker a good scratch on the belly or to examine whatever it was that the dog was scratching at himself. Pouring the dog food at five o'clock and cutting up the chicken liver and gizzards that he would scatter on top while Maeve went upstairs to change her dress and comb her hair for Billy's return.

When she came down again, the old man would be in his easy chair in the living room, the dog licking his chops at his feet. He'd look up at her, noting the changes, the lipstick and the touch of rouge. Surely he loved his daughter. Surely he would have said if asked that he wanted to see her happy. But he also had some stake himself in believing in the immutability of first affections, of promises made to the dead. No doubt he waged a kind of battle with himself before he said (no model of self-control), "Does Billy ever mention that other girl, the Irish one?" or "Did you know she was a redhead?"

Glancing in the mirror in the tiny powder room, Maeve might well have thought, Why bother?

By seven her old man might have already polished off a six-pack or fortified himself with more than one glass of Scotch, and Billy might have stopped off at Quinlan's after work, or had his lunch at some city bar-and-grill, but nevertheless, early on at least, there would be the ritual of a cocktail hour before Maeve served the chops or the cutlets or the casserole, the three of them raising their glasses, Good luck, Good luck, before they sat down—in the kitchen during the winter, at the lace-covered dining-room table come summer—the drink moving them along toward another closing of another day and Billy doing most of the talking, since he was the one who had been out working, collecting anecdotes and jokes and running into old friends in the dark and sparkling places where he took his leisure. Watching Maeve and her father watching him, you would be hard-pressed to tell what it was that gave them the most pleasure: Billy himself expending all this charm on just the two of them or their own satisfaction that one of them had managed to procure this entertainment for the other. You would be hard-pressed to tell, watching Billy at the head of the table, before his little family, talking and talking, making them laugh, the disappointment that lingered at his heart's core, disappointment and disbelief, disbelief that the faith he had sworn to an unrealized future should be so simply, so easily betrayed. "She looked into my heart one day / And saw your image was there / She has gone weeping away."

Then there would be the ten o'clock walk—the old man slipping a can or two into the kangaroo pockets of his coat, Billy going along for the fresh air and then—as the old man's legs gave out—going by himself, a cold beer can cupped behind his hand.

Walking through the neighborhood together, Billy and his father-in-law would have had little interest stirred by the lights in other living-room windows or the sound of other voices, shouts of an argument, the sobbing of a child, since all their talk ended up being about the past, about a time in the old man's life when he was a robust and redheaded young cop, the father of two little girls, when the city was what it used to be and the woman who made his life what it was still walked the earth. Billy adding his own recollections of what had once been but was no more. Billy sympathizing and telling him so.

Her father's physical decline, the slowing circulation, the water retention, the falls with their attendant concussions and sprains, the collapsed lung, the seeping capillaries, would have provided Maeve with enough to occupy her mind, consulting doctors now as she had once gone to the nuns, who went to the priest, getting the doctors, as the priest had done, to warn and reprimand him. Red-headed and fair-skinned, Maeve's father wore his dissipation boldly, blatantly, the same way, my father now said to Dan Lynch, he wore his heart on his sleeve.

But Billy called him Mr. Kehoe and took on the task of getting him up the stairs at night and into his bed. Maeve would be listening from their own bedroom with its Blessed Mother colors and the stiff-limbed baby doll that was either a stubborn hanging on to childishness or a balm for her inability to bear a child; a reassuring glance at the past or compensation for what had not been provided by the future. On the dresser before her, the wedding photo taken only minutes after they had made their vows. This will not change. Listening still as Billy made his way back downstairs again to pour himself another drink and lift the phone from the wall, or (Maeve still listening) lift his car keys and head out the door.

The drinking, down at Quinlan's, on his walks with her father, downstairs in the kitchen after she had gone to bed, would have been for her as much a part of Billy's personality as his slow smile, his multitude of cousins and friends, the letters and postcards that seemed to appear beneath his hand, to flow from his fingertips, in a nearly unbidden act of prestidigitation. It was just Billy's way: this need to keep in touch, to keep talking, to be called by name when he entered the crowded barroom, slapped on the back, Glad to see you, have a seat. The drink a warmth across the cheeks, a watery veil that only brought into relief the gleam on the bar, the light in the mirror, the sparkle of a bottle, silver-topped, amber-filled, as it was plucked from its spot among the rows and rows of bright, silver-topped bottles and poured out again. The telltale aftertaste in the back of his throat that could only mean the one drink would have to be followed by another as the talk and the laughter turned, spiraled, not into the heart of his loneliness—he would not mention her now that he was a married man, he was that loyal—but toward the world where that loneliness existed, the world where change and cruelty, separation and loss, pity and sorrow refused to be forgotten, or forgiven, the world seen as it should be seen, through a veil of tears, where Uncle Daniel's life could be examined, or Bridie's troubles, his mother's loneliness and his father-in-law's grief, where the passing of time, the cruelty of war, the failure of hope, the death of the young could be discussed and examined (a young President, over the years, the young sons of cousins and of neighbors and friends, young children right over here in Kew Gardens, taken from their beds). A world where love (more difficult still) could be spoken of by a hand on the shoulder, a fresh drink placed on the bar, Good to see you, through welling tears, real ones now, Ah, Billy, it's always good to see you. Dark, sparkling, sprinkled with moments when the sound and smell and sight of the place, the taste at the back of his throat, transported him, however briefly, to a summer night long ago when he was young and life was all promise and she was there to turn to, to drink in, this was also the world where his faith met him, became actual, no longer as mere promise or possibility but as inevitable and true. No less than the cathedrals and churches and synagogues scattered throughout the city that had once sustained and amazed him, now the various bars he stopped into, for lunch, after

work, between calls for Con Ed, and most evenings as the
day came to a close, reminded him that what he sought,
what he longed for, was universal and constant. Quinlan's
was the best of them, sure, but each bar he went into
offered the same familiar light and scent, the same company, the same talk. And in each of them, the force of his
faith, of his Church, a force he could only glimpse briefly
while sober—maybe for a second or two after Communion
when he knelt and bowed his head, or for that brief instant
when he pushed aside the heavy curtain and stepped into
the dark confessional, or in the first rising scent of the
incense at Benediction—became clear and steady and as
fully true as the vivid past or the as-yet-unseen but inevitable future. A true redemption—it was a favorite word
of his, after a few, Dan Lynch and my father agreed, a
favorite topic—a redemption that was not merely a pretty
story grown up around a good man but a fact that changed
the very fiber of the day, the moment. Drunk, when Billy
turned his eyes to heaven, heaven was there. (Dan Lynch
himself had seen it in Billy's eyes, he said again, years
before, August 15, Feast of the Assumption, when they'd
hightailed it over to Mass.) Heaven was there, utterly necessary, utterly sensible, the only possible reconciliation of
the way he must live day by day and the certainty he'd
felt that life meant something greater. The only redemption, the only compensation for the disappointment, the
cruelty and pain that plagued the living, for love itself,
because when he turned his eyes to heaven, heaven was
there and Eva was in it.

Waiting up for him, Maeve would say a Rosary and

think of the Bing Crosby song, counting her blessings instead of sheep: money was no problem and the house and
yard more than she'd ever dreamed of; he never missed a
day of work at either job and even in his cups never raised
a hand toward her (not for years, anyway), hardly raised
his voice, and never failed to give her his arm when they
went out. He was kind to her father. He was a handsome
man. And although the hour might be late and he might
not make it up the stairs on his own, although she might
have to call Dennis to help her get him in from the lawn
or up off the floor, still he came home every night, eventually, managing always—it might have been planned—
to stay conscious until he had at least stopped the car
somewhere near the driveway or the curb.

She could manage his legs if Dennis could just get him
under the arms. She could place herself between his
knees, her elbows locked beneath his calves, her hips
bearing whatever weight she could not bear on her forearms and maneuver him up the stairs, the landing the
trickiest part, the little round table with the Hummel children being upset more than once (my father muttering,
on his way back down again, "Couldn't you find another
spot for that, Maeve?" telling my mother the next morning, reminding Dan Lynch now, of "her damn figurines").
She would be breathless by the time she got him to the
bed, the backs of her legs black-and-blue from where his
heels might have caught her, her arms weary, rubbed pink
by the rough gabardine of his pant legs. Together they
would undress him as well as they could, Maeve being the
more adept, having cared so long for her old father. Dennis

suspecting sometimes that Billy's determined uncon-
sciousness was willful, even planned, a door he had sought
and had stepped through and pulled closed behind him.

His body remained thin, the same long, thin legs and
hairless chest, the same pale skin, chalk-white except for
the raw patches of psoriasis and the nearly theatrically
ruddy cheeks, so he looked for all the world in that moment before Maeve pulled the sheet up over him like
some broken martyr, a tortured and heaven-bound saint.
Billy Lynch in the flesh, in her own home.

Calmly, she would go downstairs and put the kettle on.
A little sliver of cake with that, Dennis? Dennis sitting
down with her in the tiny kitchen at all hours of the night
to give her some company, to discuss a cure (AA, a drying-
out hospital, a pill he'd read about that makes it impossible to hold down a drink), to let the hot liquid soothe
the grief in his throat that told him that Billy, just like her
old father, was determined to die on them. And that
Maeve was determined to hang on to any kind of life at
all as long as Billy was in it. The appearance of sobriety
alone good enough. Good enough.

"From the very beginning," Dan Lynch went on,
"Billy didn't buy the AA bit, even for the old man. He
didn't buy this getting up and admitting that each and
every one of them, every drunk, is exactly the same. He
didn't buy this trying to freeze people out in order to
make them quit, either. 'Billy's got to hit rock bottom
before he'll quit,' Ted Lynch told me." He shook his
head. "Jesus," he said softly, "nice sentiment. But look
what Billy did: Billy sat with the old man and poured him
his drinks and listened to his tale of woe because he knew

that's what the old man needed. He sympathized." Dan paused, squinted into his drink. "I only wish we'd had sense enough to do the same for Billy," he said. "Maybe then he wouldn't have died out on the street the way he did."

My father said, "He didn't die on the street. He died in the hospital."

"Found on the street, then," Dan Lynch said, but it was clear that in his every telling of it in the future it would remain died in the street. "Found on the street like some bum instead of dying in his bed like Maeve's father did, because Billy had had the sense to feed him his whiskey at home and let him talk." Dan looked into his drink. "I tell you, Dennis, I've got some guilt about it all tonight. I think we should have done the same for Billy. Never mind this trying to trick him into staying sober, forcing him into it. You telling him he couldn't come over to the house to see the kids and me convincing Quinlan not to serve him. Jesus, there was a humiliation for the poor guy. And then Ted siccing his AA buddies on him like storm troopers. There's no drunk like a reformed drunk, Billy said. He made a joke out of it, sure, but they drove him crazy, puffing away on their cigarettes and glassy-eyed from all the coffee they guzzled at those meetings. They hounded him. And then Father Jim—who had a problem himself, you know—dragging him over to Ireland. His sisters wagging their fingers at him, the two husbands, too, although you can't tell me Peter Sullivan isn't in the same boat. And Maeve and her novenas. What were we thinking?" He looked up at my father. "We should have sat him here"—he pointed to the empty space of couch beside him—"and fed him his whiskey and let him talk. There was a pain in him that only alcohol eased. Who were we to tell him to give up the drink and live with the pain?"

My father held out his hand, palm up, a gesture that for me recalled and encompassed my life's entire experience of him, a plea for reasonableness. "That's not what we told him, Dan," he said.

"Essentially, it is," Dan Lynch answered. Stubborn.

"It's not," my father said. "He might have lived another twenty years if we'd gotten him to quit."

"He might not have wanted to," Dan Lynch said.

They were silent again, each one looking into opposite corners of the room, once more weighing words. I sensed that they both understood that this was not an argument either of them was up to pursuing or, for that matter, winning. Dan Lynch would not want to prove, finally, that they should have stood by, ready to pour, while Billy drank himself to death. My father would not want to hear Dan Lynch concede that Billy—their Billy, with his letters and his jokes, his loyalty and his broken heart—could have been cured of his affliction by rote, set back into his life by the simple application of some formula meant for everyone else. I moved the ice around in Billy's drink. Give the man that much credit.

Dan Lynch said, "You know, Billy never mentioned her again after he married Maeve." He lifted an eyebrow. "At least not to me," he added. "In all the nights we met and had a drink or two together, you know, before things got bad with him, you never heard him say a word about that girl, despite all he'd said about her before he met Maeve."

But my father sipped his drink, admitted nothing.

Dan Lynch sat back abruptly. "His sisters asked me today, Did Maeve know anything about her, the Irish girl? I told them I couldn't say." He seemed a little sheepish, as if he were reluctant to part with his authority—he, after all, had been the best man. "I said she must have known something."

My father shrugged. "Her old man had told her something. Billy had told him, early on."

"Much?" Dan asked, one smooth eyebrow still raised. With his bald head cocked and the stubby glass in his fist he looked like a cartoon prizefighter.

"As much as there was to know, I suppose," my father said.

"She can't have liked it."

My father smiled. "Claire was engaged once, too, remember. To one of those fellows who might not have come home if we hadn't dropped the bomb. I can't say it ever bothered either of us."

"But Billy didn't give up the girl. She was taken from him," Dan said. "That would make a big difference to a woman."

My father shrugged, lifted his drink. I wondered for a moment if he would say, Eva never died. Turn up the lights in Dan Lynch's little place and let the irony flood the room. It was only a lie. If you're looking for sense, Dan, you're not going to find it here. But what he said was "We're talking ancient history, Danny. Billy gave

Maeve enough to think about day after day. She wouldn't have to go back that far to find something to fret over."

They were silent again, their glasses nearly empty. I drank from mine and listened to the rain, to a distant siren somewhere, to a few shouted words from down in the street, Spanish, Farsi. The two men looked into their drinks, ignoring it all, concentrating, it seemed to me, concentrating on conjuring something that they both understood would be fleeting, momentary, something that would be glimpsed only briefly if they managed to glimpse it at all. A way to make sense. Or else a way to tell the story that would make them believe it was sensible.

"Were they happy?" Dan said finally. "Billy and Maeve. Do you think? Were they ever close?" He would not look either of us in the eye, as if the question had embarrassed him.

"She put up with him," my father said, knowing it wasn't an answer.

"She chose to," Dan Lynch said. Now he raised his head. "She chose him, and as far as I can see he fit her to a T. Her old man all over again. Someone to maneuver, to shore up. An alcoholic with a shadow across his heart. An alcoholic because he had a shadow across his heart, the way I see it." He shook his head, squinting into the dim room. "I don't begrudge her her tears, of course, but I wonder, too. Would she have known what to do with a sober man, with the full force of the affection of a sober man who'd never loved another?"

Now it was my father's turn to lower his eyes. "Who can say?" he asked.

"I don't think so," Dan Lynch said, sitting back, a

definitive nod. "I don't think she would have known, Dennis. I don't think Billy just as himself, without the girl there first, this Eva, I don't think Maeve would have found him so easy to maneuver. He'd had half the life taken out of him when that girl died and that could well have been just the thing that made him right for Maeve. Sure," he said—he raised his hand from his thigh and then placed it back down again—"sure, she put up with him all these years, but in other ways Billy asked very little of her. I'm certain he asked very little of her." He glanced quickly at me, trying to recall, it seemed, whether I was twenty-eight or twelve. "There were no children," he said. He nearly whispered it, as if the fact had been a secret. "And Billy loved children."

My father shook his head impatiently. He seemed annoyed. It might have been his natural disinclination to wholeheartedly agree with Dan Lynch about anything. It might have been his reluctance to consider the possibility that the lie he'd told Billy all those years ago was not merely the cause of thirty years of pointless grief but the very thing that had made Billy's life with Maeve possible, and fruitless.

"Billy wanted too much," my father said finally. He leaned to put his glass on the coffee table, on top of the *St. Anthony Messenger*. It was both a way to dismiss the conversation and to show he was ready to take his leave. "He had some strange thoughts about the world, Danny, you know he did. About the way the world should be. You wouldn't have tolerated it in most other people. You would have said, 'Oh come on now.' "

He stood. I stood, too, Billy's drink still in my hand.

My father's voice said he was at the end of his patience. His voice said, "Let's get to the bottom of things."

"Maeve made the same mistake we all did, Dan. She not only put up with him, she hoped he was right, in all his strange notions. She hoped the world would somehow turn out to be just the way he believed it to be. She hoped somehow that he'd turn out to be right in the end, with all his hanging on to the past. All his loyalty to the dead. Even if it meant she'd have no life of her own." He swatted the air.

"Billy didn't need someone to pour him his drinks, he needed someone to tell him that living isn't poetry. It isn't prayer. To tell him and convince him. And none of us could do it, Danny, because every one of us thought that as long as Billy believed it was, as long as he kept himself believing it, then maybe it could still be true. Jesus Christ, Danny," he said, and then stopped. In the silence that followed, I fully expected him to say, *It was a lie.* It was a lie and Billy knew it.

Dan Lynch sat in his seat, the empty glass on his tattersall knee, his piles of books and magazines, his mother's own pieces. He looked at my father, his mouth closed, his eyes surprised and maybe a little hurt, but forgiving him already for this outburst, because, you know (he would tell them down at Quinlan's), it was hard on Dennis, having to identify Billy and all, it had been a hard week all around.

My father would not tell Dan Lynch the truth. I knew simply by looking from one to the other that he would never tell Dan Lynch the truth. It was, after all, yet another sweet romance to preserve.

"Jesus Christ," my father said again, but softly now, that old, fading annoyance on his face. "Sometimes the less said the better, do you know what I mean?"

Dan nodded, clearly disappointed to have the conversation pulled out from under him like this (I had the sense that he'd have liked to talk all night), but forgiving my father already.

"Sure," he said. "Let's put it to rest for tonight. Billy's ears must be burning."

My father smiled. "Gone but not forgotten," he said.

H E'D LEFT THE FLUSHING OFFICE at midmorning, driving in the rain to the VA hospital, where the girl at the information desk had said, "You're welcome, Officer," after she'd given him directions to the morgue. "Have a nice day, Detective," she'd called out when he left (the ordeal, at long last, over). She was smiling, he said, but with an edge to it. A young woman, Hispanic of some sort. No doubt with a boyfriend on Rikers Island.

That morning Maeve's neighborhood was sodden with the rain, the shingles and roofs a shade darker, surely, than they would have been in dry weather. Silver puddles in every pothole. A small river flowing along the crumbling curb. There were cardboard bunny rabbits and Easter eggs hung in storm windows here and there, marking the homes where children lived, or visited. Dorothy, the neighbor lady, was already over. Maeve was on the phone, and one of Billy's white shirts was already washed out and on a hanger, dripping dry into the kitchen sink. The undertaker's number was already written out, and the number for the rectory. She'd had nights enough, he supposed, to rehearse her every step should the worst occur, so that now that it had finally happened, it was all, for Maeve, part of an old routine. "She knew," Dorothy whispered, as if knowing, in Billy's case, required any prescience.

Sitting at her kitchen table, Dennis devised a list, writing on the back of an empty, windowed envelope, of the friends and relations he would call himself, and then copied it over again so Maeve would know they'd been taken care of. He called Kate and Rosemary from the phone in the kitchen. And half a dozen Lynch cousins. He brought Billy's best blue suit to the dry cleaners on the corner. And then there seemed for the moment nothing else for him to do but to go back to work.

It was shock that Billy had actually died of, not the cirrhosis, although the cirrhosis was certainly far advanced. Shock, as Dennis understood it, from his stomach being filled up with blood. He'd been found collapsed on the street, in Flushing, just off Main Street. Leaving some two-bit gin mill with his car keys in his hand—*still* in his hand when they found him, although his wallet was gone. It was a patrol car that found him (we're moving, Officer), not dead yet but dying. Dead three hours after they got him to the emergency room, one of the nurses there finally recognizing him and able to give him a name. Not Billy— Dennis's first thought when he saw him. A colored man, thank God.

When he left Maeve's, he took a minute to swing by

Bridie's; it wasn't much out of the way. Standing at the top of her narrow stoop, he saw the curtain that covered the door glass move and had to shout through the wood. Bridie was out at the grocery store—it was the lady who sometimes took care of Jim and she had strict instructions not to let anybody in. He said that she should tell Bridie he'd call her later, he would not stand there in the rain, shouting the news. But of course by the time he called her, Bridie was able to say, "Oh, Dennis, I heard. I called Maeve. I had a feeling that was why you'd stopped by." When in truth he had stopped by mostly to see the shock on Bridie's face when he told her Billy was gone, the disbelief. Standing over Billy in that cold room (and soon enough the fat colored man they had shown him was transformed, by the familiar curve of his hairline, the shape of an ear, the smooth lips, into Billy himself), he had felt his hands form into fists and had turned to the young attendant to say, furiously, "Isn't this a damnable thing?" But how could the poor man respond? No doubt he saw such things every day—the husks of every kind of life carted out and carted away. Details like who he was, how he died, how the dusting of psoriasis on his bare leg recalled a bit of sea salt that had been there once, long ago, irrelevant now, barely interesting. What could the poor man say? Dennis had gone to Bridie's house in the hope of seeing in Bridie's eyes the acknowledgment, the shock— untempered by any premonition—that this was Billy they were talking about, Billy who had collapsed on the street (you could see the mark of the sidewalk on his dark cheek, one of those freckled bruises Dennis had last seen on his children's knees), Billy whose life had ended this way. Billy Lynch. Googenheimer. Our Billy who had left us in this terrible and willful way.

Dennis had a call to make in St. Alban's, a Baptist church with a string of adjectives before its name: First Ethiopian Pentecostal Afro-Asian whatever whatever—so much exclusivity that you might expect the door of the chapel to be no bigger than a needle's eye. The pastor was the intellectual sort. A tall and handsome black man in his early thirties. Full of himself and his calling, his eyes always falling on a spot three or four inches above Dennis's head, his own head always drawn back a bit as he spoke, as if racism were a scent Dennis gave off. (As if it never occurred to the man that most of Dennis's customers these days, for years now, since he'd left Irving Place for the office in Queens, were colored.) And Dennis, to tell the truth, busy recalling all the while they spoke one of Billy's stories, about walking down a street in New York with his mother's sister, who was just off the boat, and a colored man passing them by, and then, minutes later, another, who was walking briskly. Billy's aunt had looked over her shoulder at the second man as he went by and then leaned to Billy, a boy then, and said, "He'll have to walk faster than that if he's going to catch up with his friend."

The pastor wanted to run a new separate line in for the nursery school and up the amperage in the sacristy (did they call it that?) and choir loft for a new sound system and music synthesizer. There was no urgency for the first, but the second "optimally" should be completed by the beginning of May, which was an anniversary of some sort. Dennis said his usual—The best we can—and dropped another "Reverend" into the conversation to show that he respected the man and his diplomas and his good work despite the fact that he himself was white and authentically Christian (i.e., Roman Catholic) and old enough to be this particular reverend's father.

He was surprised when the man walked him all the way to the door of the little church, thinking that perhaps he had, with his calculated deference, won him over. The rain was still coming down in sheets. The gray day still the one in which Billy Lynch had died. Dennis put on his hat and turned to shake the minister's hand and instantly felt the corner of a neatly folded bill prick his palm. "First week of May," the reverend said. "It's really a must." Now, finally, he brought his dark eyes down to Dennis's. He smiled, but not kindly, more as if (if you can picture it) he had looked into Dennis's shallow soul, had heard every "Damn nigger" he had ever breathed—over the newspaper, at the wheel of his car—as if he knew the narrow, ordinary, and ineffectual course of his life, of Billy's life, of the life of everyone like him. The superior smile of someone ennobled by true suffering, justifiable rage. Someone whose pain amounted to something. Whose love saved lives. Dennis nodded. He found himself searching for a joke to make, as if a joke might prove he was more than the sum of the things the man was sure he knew about him. "Dig we must," he said. But the S.O.B. had already turned away.

Standing on the sidewalk beside his car, Dennis unfolded the bill. A ten. There you go, Billy. And then dropped it on the sidewalk for some kid to find.

HERE'S THE THING, he said (we were on our way home, in the dark, in the now steady, heavy rain): Back in the sixties, when it was still Dig We Must, when it looked for certain that he'd be promoted to manager, a nearly twenty-year-old letter was produced from his personnel file. A letter from a Mr. Jacob R. Leibowitz, Jake—from whom, by then, he had bought four layette sets and maybe twenty pairs of footed pajamas, good wool Sunday coats, and at least a half dozen birthday blouses for your mother. The letter said that three weeks ago money was exchanged between him and a certain young man in your employ, a certain Mr. Lynch, with the understanding that as a result of said payment service would be provided in a timely manner, and yet service had only this morning been restored.

Dennis supposed he hadn't been called up on the carpet for it back then because he had plenty of friends in Personnel in those days—Mary Casey was there and his cousin Mal, Uncle Jim's son—but with the possibility of the promotion, the powers that be took a second look and found the letter that Jake had written in 1946 and so passed him over.

"We're passing you over this time," they said, apologizing, but there was little doubt in his mind then that it was for good.

That evening he took the subway home as usual, picked up the car as usual at Lefferts Boulevard, and drove the rest of the way to Rosedale. The kids were crowded into the kitchen, as usual, their mother at the stove frying fish, the dog underfoot. Homework and baths and prayers, not to mention the back of his hand to one or the other of them, and then the evening paper and a smoke before he's winding the clock again. Claire said, Oh, don't let it bother you, but there was the extra money as well as the boost it might have given his ego, and there were four college tuitions to think of. Not to mention the mark the letter left on his good name, his honesty, and the taint it might give to his friendship with Jake, whom you really couldn't blame in the long run because he had written the letter when Dennis was a stranger to him and the bitter taste of all he'd been through in the war was still on his tongue.

"How much was it?" Claire asked.

"Ten dollars," Dennis said.

"Cheapskate," Claire said, making a joke of it. "He could have given you twenty."

And then the phone ringing into his dreams at 2, 3 a.m., that godawful hour. Claire not even bothering to open her eyes for it. He stumbled out into the hallway where the phone was, the only light coming from the dim lamps left burning all night in the children's two rooms. Billy's thick voice, in mid-sentence, it seemed, no doubt because Dennis himself had not yet come fully awake in order to catch the first few words, but giving him then, at 2 or 3 a.m., in the darkness, the impression that his cousin had been talking all along, all through the day and night, his steady stream of words an undercurrent to every moment of their existence.

He was thinking, Billy said, about the life she didn't have. Of all that had been denied her.

Dennis listened first for some sound in the background, some indication of where he was calling from. There was only silence.

Nights in a husband's arms, children, the movement of the seasons. The changes, melancholy or not, that came with age, with having a good span of years to look back on.

"Where are you, Billy?" Dennis said.

Billy said he was thinking about what a brief life it had been. The brevity of it couldn't have struck them then, they were young enough themselves, but now, as they themselves grew older, didn't it become clear that it was only a handful of years that she'd been given, only a blink to call her lifetime. Wasn't it something that as they themselves grew older, the cruelty of it, the unfairness, became more pronounced, more clear?

"Are you at home?" Dennis asked.

Billy said he was, but Dennis was only sure it was true when he heard the dog moving around on the kitchen floor—this one would have been Trixie—scratching her neck and jiggling her collar.

"And where's the old man?" Dennis asked.

"In bed," Billy answered impatiently. Out cold, was how Dennis thought of it.

His own loss of her was one thing, Billy said. He'd long ago stopped thinking of himself in that regard. He'd had life enough himself, hadn't he? Here he was, a married man with a house of his own and two jobs and friends enough. His life had gone on, hadn't it? But he wasn't thinking of himself, you see. Tonight he was thinking only of her, of all she'd been cheated of.

"Go to bed, Billy," Dennis said.

Tonight the cruelty of it struck him. A girl so young, her childhood behind her, her life—marriage, motherhood—just about to begin. Was she born just to live these brief years and die? Was everything she'd felt and thought so utterly meaningless to her Maker? Where was the sense in it? There was no sense in it.

"Close up the bottle now, Billy," Dennis said. "Go upstairs to your wife."

There was a silence. Dennis was familiar enough with these phone calls to know that it could mean Billy had simply put the phone down to reach for another drink or had passed out or, if he was far enough along, had simply forgotten what it was he was saying. He might even have broken the connection. Dennis waited; he heard the muffled ticking of the clock, saw in the dimness the familiar shape of Claire's hip and shoulder under the dark blanket, felt his children's breath on the warm close air of the small house, in the middle of the night. There was the pull of indigestion in his gut, the same indigestion that had plagued him since early this morning, when he'd been called in and told that a letter had been found in his personnel file, written some time ago but troubling still . . .

"We have to rail against it," Billy said hoarsely.

"Go to bed, Billy."

"The injustice of it," Billy said. "The way she was cheated."

Dennis heard the sound of Billy's glass hitting the mouthpiece, the heavy swallow. He could almost smell the stuff on his breath.

"We can't be bribed into silence because we've lived long ourselves. We have to remember what she was deprived of."

"I'm not going to stay on the line with you, Bill," Dennis said patiently, although he well knew that as soon as he hung up Billy would be dialing someone else, Danny or Ted or one of his priests, keeping them up to all hours as well. "We both have to be at work tomorrow, Billy, that's all you need to remember. You're expected at work. You'll be sick as a dog if you don't close up the bottle now and go to bed."

"Death is a terrible thing," Billy said.

"Death comes to us all," Dennis told him. "But 7 a.m. will come sooner."

"Our Lord knew it," Billy went on. "Our Lord knew it was terrible. Why would He have shed His own blood if death wasn't terrible?" There was another pause, another sip of whiskey. "You know what makes a mockery of the Crucifixion?" Billy said. "You know what makes it pointless? Anyone saying that death is just an ordinary thing, an ordinary part of life. It happens, you reconcile yourself, you go on. Anyone saying that is saying Our Lord's coming was to no avail."

Dennis heard the click of the glass again. "I'm not staying on," he said.

"What do we need the Redemption for?" Billy asked him. "If death isn't terrible. If we're reconciled? Why do we need heaven or hell? It makes no difference. If death doesn't trouble us, the injustice of it, then we don't need heaven or hell, do we? It might as well be a lie."

If ever Dennis had the chance and the inclination to say, "Billy, it was a lie," he had it now. But it was 3 a.m. and the indigestion was scratching at the back of his throat. And there was work tomorrow, when he would have to go back to his usual desk and his usual routine, loudmouthed McCauley with the Orange Crush–colored hair moving on to management, that single spark of small ambition that had ever flared in him extinguished now. Wife children house now the extent of his success.

"It's why I won't go back out to the Island," Billy said. His voice had lost some of its fierceness: even he, in his cups, knew this was covered territory.

"Jesus," Dennis whispered, to show Billy he knew it, too.

"I won't be placated by that beauty," Billy said. "I'll do that much for her."

"Go to bed, Billy," Dennis said.

There was another silence. "Is it still the same, Dennis?" he asked, his voice tinged with nostalgia. "Holtzman's place? East Hampton? Three Mile Harbor?"

"It's still the same."

"Are you going out there again this summer?"

"Who knows? She's talking about renting it out."

"I won't go there," Billy said.

"None of us will if she rents it."

"I won't see it again."

"She thinks it's a waste of money, keeping it empty all year. Now that Holtzman's gone."

"I'll do that much for her, Dennis. I'll stay away. She never went back and neither will I."

Dennis paused, trying to convey by his silence, as best he could, the end of his patience. "Close up the bottle now, Billy," he said softly. "You'll be dead yourself if you keep up this drinking."

He heard more silence in return. Another deep swallow. And then: "Are the children asleep, Dennis?"

"Of course," Dennis said.

"God bless them, they're a handful, aren't they?"

Resigned, wide-awake now, Dennis sank into the chair by the old phone table, pulling at the leg of his pajamas as he did, as if he had a crease to preserve. He glanced into his sons' room and saw the shadows strewn across the floor, sneakers and clothes, books and toys. "Some days," he said. He crossed his bare ankles before him, tucked his free hand under his elbow, settling in.

"No broken bones this week?" Billy was chuckling.

"Not this week," Dennis said.

"God bless them," Billy said again.

And another long pause. Another drink taken. Dennis considered telling him a funny little something one of them had said when Billy began to speak again, his voice growing heavier. "It's a pact with the devil," he said. "To be reconciled. Our Lord spilling His every drop of blood on the cross to show us death is terrible, a terrible injustice, and all the while we're telling ourselves that it's not so bad, after all. You get over it. You get used to it. Life is lovely despite the fact of a young woman dying, her children all unborn. Life's still good. What's beautiful stays beautiful. Life goes on pleasantly enough no matter who dies."

"It does," Dennis said wearily, although it struck him on this day, at this hour, that it was, for him, another lie.

"What's that?" Billy said. He was far into it now.

"I said it does," Dennis told him, raising his voice. Claire stirred, pulling the blanket up over her shoulder with a shadowy hand. "Life goes on, Billy," he said.

Billy whispered, "I won't let it."

"We don't have much say in the matter," Dennis said, but Billy was already off the line.

He sat for a few minutes in the dark hallway, a cold draft blowing across his bare feet. He wondered if Maeve would be calling in another hour or two. If he went back to bed would he go back to sleep. He thought of his father, the first and foremost (in those days) of the people he loved who had died. The very thought itself a prayer to the man in heaven, which he had surely earned, if only by dint of the flattery he had poured on God and every detail of His creation for the sixty-odd years he had lived. Or, if God required such things, by dint of the terrible pain he'd endured at the end. Even in compensation for the fact that for all the love he'd poured out for friends and family for all the years that he lived, he was never, let's face it, loved sufficiently in return. Not by the one being whose love he most sought, anyway.

He thought of his father, as he did so often in those days when his father was first and foremost of those he missed, the very thought of him a prayer of sorts (one that said, I'm weary, Dad, and discouraged; I've lost all sense of delight), although truth be told, it struck him that night, at that lonely hour, that his father in death was no more present to him, no more real, no more vivid than Eva was to Billy, in her just-over-the-Atlantic afterlife, pumping gas on the convent road in Clonmel.

Who can trace such things, he said, but it was perhaps the first tremor of the devastation that would strike him, knock him off his feet, in the weeks and months after my mother died. Billy's thirty years of misdirected prayer, Billy's tenacious, life-changing belief. His own lie.

FOR ONE OF MY MOTHER'S birthdays, my father wrapped a box of fifty matchbooks in bright tissue paper and then inscribed the card: *For a mate who is matchless*. It drew a great laugh at the dinner table that night, amid the remains of the sugary, elaborately iced cake, the already-opened birthday blouse from Jake's, and served as catalyst—at least as I recall it—for a discussion about which of them would remarry should anything "happen" to the other, which I suppose would have to place this particular birthday in a time when anything "happening" was such a remote possibility that speculation about it was benign and even pleasurable, a kind of flirtation. When a birthday gift of fifty matchbooks and a carton of cigarettes to go with them held no omen.

Coyly, my mother devised a list. There was a young widower down the street, and the son of the man who owned the delicatessen she shopped in—a good-looking

Italian kid, she said, maybe twenty-five. There was the guy she'd taken driving lessons from when they'd first moved out to Rosedale, married, she thought, but she could still look him up. She could look up Bob O'Brien, her old flame, her old fiancé, the one my father stole her away from while he was still in the Navy, off cleaning up the Pacific. And his brother Ken, who'd had a crush on her all along and never did marry himself, as far as she knew. She could go on, she said, grinning, the cigarette held beside her ear, the thick sweet icing still on her plate. The possibilities were endless. She still had some of the old charm.

"Should I go on?" she said, and my father bowed his head, laughing. "No," he said. "Don't go on."

"And what would you do?" she asked him. "Look up Irish Mary?"

My father shook his head, although we had heard him say, often enough, when my mother had run up a big bill at Gertz or A&S, or had forgotten to buy dessert or had dismissed him with a wave of her hand, I should have married Irish Mary.

"There'd be no one else for me," he said seriously. "I couldn't marry again. You could. You should. But there'd be no one else for me."

In the arc of an unremarkable life, a life whose triumphs are small and personal, whose trials are ordinary enough, as tempered in their pain as in their resolution of pain, the claim of exclusivity in love requires both a certain kind of courage and a good dose of delusion. Irish Mary, Eva's sister, would have been happy enough to accept my father's ring, I suppose, had Eva not chosen to stay in Ireland and marry Tom. My mother's first fiancé would have married her gladly if he hadn't been kept too long overseas by the Navy, if my father hadn't beaten him home, on points, a full year before. It might have been Cody or John in the car with your father, that day on Long Island. I might have been gone. Those of us who claim exclusivity in love do so with a liar's courage: there are a hundred opportunities, thousands over the years, for a sense of falsehood to seep in, for all that we imagine as inevitable to become arbitrary, for our history together to reveal itself as only a matter of chance and happenstance, nothing irrepeatable, or irreplaceable, the circumstantial mingling of just one of the so many million with just one more.

In the weeks and months after my mother died my father grew silent about her, never mentioning her name and drawing his head back just a little every time anyone else did. My brothers and I noticed this about him and, without ever discussing it ourselves, simply let him be. We had all seen his reaction at the graveside when my mother's sister, who read entire books about such things and in church prayed loudly, her eyes closed and her hands raised to the altar, leaned into him and said, "You can cry, Dennis. Big boys do cry." He had smiled a little, looking over her head and wearing the pained, polite expression the early Christians might have worn as the Romans lit the kindling at their feet. Without ever discussing it, my brothers and I agreed we would not torture our father with our advice or our concern or with any well-meaning injunctions for him to tell us what he was feeling.

We would let him be. He could not talk about her, fine. He could not sit through Mass without her, fine.

I was then in my senior year at the Mary Louis Academy. During my mother's last hospitalization, my father had begun driving me there most mornings, stopping first at the hospital so we could say hello and then taking me to school before he went on to Con Ed, to put in an hour or two—face time—before he went back to the hospital again. He continued to drive me to school after she was gone, a convenience for me, an easy-enough detour for him. There was a morning radio show he liked, a father-and-son team, the father having been in broadcasting since before the war, the son clearly being groomed to take over alone when the time came. They cracked corny jokes and recited odd news items between traffic reports and weather updates and easy-listening ballads, and their soft and amicable banter gave us reason enough to say little to each other throughout the ride.

When I got out, I would slam the door and then lean down to wave goodbye through the car window. He would give a little salute and then drive on, his profile, in the last second I could catch it, tense and determined, leaning into the day, it seemed to me, heading toward what must be done and who must be attended to now that the passionate attention he had turned so exclusively to my mother in the past year of her dying was over and she was gone. Unable, he told me on the night of Billy's funeral, when we lingered for a few more minutes in the living room of the Rosedale house before he went up to his bed in the room that used to be their own and I went to the one that used to be mine, utterly unable, he said, to convince himself that the attention he had given her in that last year, the closeness they had felt, the assurance that they had achieved something exclusive, something redemptive in the endurance of their love, had been any more than another well-intentioned deception, another construction, as unbelievable, when you came right down to it, as the spontaneity of a love song in some Broadway musical, the supposedly heartfelt supplication of a well-rehearsed hymn, the bearing any one of Billy's poems about life and death and love and misery had on the actual way any of us lived from day to day.

He could not convince himself then, he said, in those days and months after her death, that heaven was any more than a well-intentioned deception meant to ease our own sense of foolishness, to ease pain. Despite his own years of vigilant Catholicism, despite his own mother's deathbed conversion, despite the promises he and my mother had exchanged, he could no longer see death as anything other than the void that met a used-up body, a spent mind. Not a mere moment over which you could sail, buoyed by love, by faith, but the abyss toward which you stumbled inevitably, part of the crowd. Put out a hand, if you like, to help someone along, surround yourself, if you like, with people who love you, who owe you, whose lives you've changed, but don't expect it to make a difference. It will make no difference; eventually, one after the other, every one of you will fall.

"And now?" I asked him, both of us standing, not sitting, aware that there had been enough talking today. "Do you still feel that way now?" Aware, too, that we were edging close to it, to that embarrassing profundity he and Dan had feared, to that point at which too much had been said, but amazed, I suppose much as my father had once been amazed when his mother told him to get Billy to go out there, he's avoided it for too long—amazed at this kind of conversation, at this stage of the game. A conversation, it occurred to me, that Billy's life had spurred for us as much it had once spurred it for my father and his dying mother.

My father's eyes were a deep brown. He smiled a little, shaking his head. "Oh no," he said. "Not now."

How lonely they all seemed to me that night, my father's family and friends, lonely souls every one of them, despite husbands and children and cousins and friends, all their hopes, in the end, their pairings and procreation and their keeping in touch, keeping track, futile in the end, failing in the end to keep them from seeing that nothing they felt, in the end, has made any difference.

"It was only a brief loss of faith," he said. "It happens. They say it's not uncommon." And then he turned to climb the stairs on the night of the day Billy Lynch was placed in his grave. "I believe everything now," he said, his back to me. "Again."

Of course there was no way of telling if he lied.

S O BILLY RENTED a car and drove down to see her. The pledge taken, the last drink the one he'd had with Father Ryan on the flight over to Shannon. (Father Jim raising the tiny bottle and smacking his lips and telling Billy, "Dear Lord, if this isn't the blind leading the blind," setting the tone, so to speak, for their journey, whose seriousness of purpose—Father Jim was saying in his way—did not have to deprive it of its good humor.) The car was rented in the priest's name and the license Billy carried was the priest's as well, since his own had once again been suspended. So it was Father this and Father that at the rent-a-car office, despite the wedding band that he hadn't bothered to remove, couldn't remove if he tried, the way his hands were. A married priest, then.

Not, as Danny Lynch would say, to make too much of such things.

He'd planned, just as Kate suspected, to visit her grave.

He foresaw a grassy plot and a granite stone engraved with her name, and the dates, the last not merely marking the end of her life but the end of his youth and that glorious and astounding possibility that he had once inhabited. He foresaw his own pale fingers, which trembled anyway, tracing the carved numbers and words. He thought of "Danny Boy" (he was in Ireland, after all, and the clouds were low over the fields he was passing, they were casting their shadows on the green and melancholy hills all around him), even hummed it as he drove—"Ye'll come and find the place where I am lying/And kneel and say an Ave there for me"—which in turn brought him thoughts of Uncle Daniel, and of Billy Sheehy's dad singing out all unrehearsed at the side of his grave. A moment that might have killed them all. The pain of it no less than the beauty. In his own prayer he would say he had not returned to the house on Long Island either, and never would: such was his sympathy and his outrage, both of them as keen as ever, regardless of the time gone by.

But first, he thought, he would go to her family. Mother or father if they still lived, Mary certainly, or one of the three younger sisters who would remember him no doubt as the boy, their sister's fiancé, who had sent them the American shoes. He knew her address by heart, of course, he'd written it out two or three times a year every year since Eva passed away, sending them a card at Christmas and always a line or two in late September, brief notes that said he was thinking of them, remembering Eva, giving Mary his best regards. Never more than a line or two, so he would never be forced to say that he had married, bought a house, carried on. Never really expecting a reply from the old folks and only briefly hurt that Mary hadn't been in touch with him. But Dennis was tied up with that part of it, he knew, her feelings for him, because even though she went straight home when Eva died, she could not have expected another girl—Claire Donavan—to take up Dennis's affections so soon. She could not have helped but feel jilted.

Driving the narrow wrong-sided roads between Dublin and Clonmel—parched, shaky, chilled to the bone by the dampness and the cold although the car's tiny heater was turned up full blast—he knew he would have to go to her family first and at some point tell them that he had a wife at home, a house, despite the number of times, over the years, he had written them to say Eva was in his heart and his mind and his memory still. He'd taken a wife and bought a house and for a good many years had kept fairly steady at the same two jobs he'd had then—one of them the very job he'd first taken simply to bring her back over.

No children, he'd say when they asked him. He'd say, A bit of a problem with the drink.

Clonmel was bigger than he'd imagined it and, as with so many of these Irish cities, not nearly as quaint. He might have been thrilled, or comforted, by the thought that this had been a place well familiar to her, that she'd once strolled these streets as a child, as a young woman, on the day before she left for her first appointment in Chicago—the beginning of her journey toward him—and the day she returned from New York, his diamond on her finger, but he had sense enough to know that the place was not the same city it would have seemed to her then, just before the war and just after it. He passed what looked like a Kentucky Fried Chicken shop, for instance. There was a shabby sense of change, of the modern, all about the place, that had little to do with the backward, quiet little city she had once described for him. He sensed that her ghost would have been as much a stranger here as he was.

And yet it was surely some sense of her ghost that made his heart beat heavily in his chest when, according to his map, not far from where he should be, he pulled into a gas station just outside town, off to the side so he would not block the pumps, and climbed awkwardly out of the tiny Fiesta to ask for directions. The attendant was a man about his own age, in the ubiquitous Irish cap and a filthy pair of mechanic's overalls. Billy and Father Jim had already shared a joke about how every set of directions given in Ireland begins "Go down to the church . . ." and no doubt that was the line he was fully expecting (delivered in its usual thick, nearly incomprehensible, mumbling brogue) when he asked the man how he could find the Kavanaugh place on Boylston Road. But instead the man squinted one eye and said, "An American cousin?" It seemed to Billy to be the beginning of a declarative sentence somehow cut short by a question mark.

"I beg your pardon?" he said politely.

The man pushed back his cap, a deeply lined face, the lines drawn deeper with grime. Bad teeth. A once-good-looking face, perhaps. "Are you an American cousin?" he said.

Billy said no, he was only an old friend.

The man looked him up and down a bit, not unpleasantly, and then looked beyond him to a car that was just pulling in. The car beeped and the driver called, "Tommy!" and the man asked Billy if he'd mind stepping into the tea shop here, his wife would be inside, at the counter, and she'd be happy to draw a little map for him. It wasn't far.

But there was no one at the counter and only a single woman at a table in the corner, a blue-and-white cup before her, the newspaper in front of her face, a white plastic shopping bag at her feet. The place was small, it seemed to have been meant for another purpose—maybe as a place to sell windshield wipers and spare cans of oil, or as a waiting room for the garage next door. The windows were high and narrow and each covered with handmade curtains, blue-and-white cotton gingham. The walls were false stucco, perhaps aiming for a cottage effect, but the floor was pale linoleum, the tables and countertop a beige Formica. There were a plastic rose and a plastic fern in a white milk-glass vase on each table, and a Waterford vase filled with real flowers, tall and weedy things that nevertheless gave a nice effect, beside the register. Altogether, there was something hasty and false about the place—and this was not hindsight, he felt it immediately—as if it had been quickly rearranged to hide its true purpose. As if the woman, casually lifting her cup, intent on *The Irish Times*, had only seconds before been at the window, looking out for him.

He said, "I beg your pardon," and the woman quickly lowered her newspaper, as if she feared she'd been rude. Irish face number four: sharp chin, ruddy cheeks, good long nose, and too many teeth. Not unlike Helen O'Mara at home. He recalled one of Uncle Daniel's little ditties that ended "So I said, Mrs. Clemmon, you'd make a better lemon than you would a big red rose."

"The gentleman outside said I should ask in here for directions to Boylston Road," he told her. "The Kavanaugh place. He said I should ask his wife."

"Let me get her for you," the woman said, standing, smiling enough to show an impressive overbite. "Are you an American cousin?" she asked him over her shoulder as she headed behind the counter.

"No," he said. "Although I'm beginning to think I should be."

She laughed as if she got his meaning. "Well, the Kavanaughs have three of them, three of the girls who've gone over to the States. That's why I asked. Let me just get Eva for you."

She passed through the door behind the counter; he could see a small white enamel stove, a big stainless-steel kettle on top of it, a dishrag tied to its door handle. A shelf with some boxes of wholemeal biscuits, some tins of Earl Grey. A white enamel sink. He heard her say Eva again, and then a door opening, perhaps the back door to the place, and louder now, she cried "Eva!" out the door, into the wind.

For a moment, before the woman returned, he thought it mere coincidence. He thought it was, by some strange convergence of fact and fate, a sign of sorts, from her—no nothing so elaborate as her face in a glass, her actual voice in his ear as he slept, the kinds of signs he had imagined and hoped for so desperately in those first few months and years after her death, but a sign nonetheless, a mild comfort: to have pulled in here, to have been directed inside, to have asked the one woman who went off to fetch the wife whose name, it so happened, was also Eva. To hear on this day of all days, in this place, her name called out. It was a sign that said, You were right to come here, I am with you still.

And then the woman returned with Eva herself coming in behind her, the bouquet of ragged wildflowers only briefly blocking her face.

You could have counted on one hand the seconds it took for the two of them to know each other. Later, sitting with a cup of tea, Eva said for her it was the stoop of his shoulders, and of course those blue eyes. For him (and he, let's face it, had further to come, thirty years of distorted memory to cross), there was no single thing, certainly nothing physical, not at first, since she was so much heavier now, and the pale shade of her dyed hair no longer matched her mahogany eyes. He simply knew, after that initial tumble into disbelief, he simply knew this was Eva standing before him.

Well, what a lot of knots there were to untangle. He held out his hand at first, the homely lady still standing there, grinning between them. Held out his hand and said, "Billy Lynch," and Eva, drying her hands on her apron like some Brigadoon colleen, said, "Billy Lynch, I know it's you." Although the blush on her cheeks when she came in from the wind didn't fade inside the shop. She introduced her friend, Bessie Gordon, and called Billy the boy from New York—like a character listed in a *Playbill*.

"Oh sure," Bessie said, as if she was quite familiar with the entire cast. "The shoes," she said, nodding. The plot as well. "And all those little notes. I've always said I admired you for keeping up." She elbowed her friend. "And her scared to death to ever send a reply. I'm the one that was always telling her she was terrible not to reply."

Eva's blush grew darker and deeper; she was blushing to her roots. "Oh, Bessie's full of advice for everyone," she said in her old, laughing way. "I'm thinking of setting her up in a booth."

She offered him a cup of tea and scooted back around the counter to get it. She said she had some nice scones to go with it, or a ham roll, or some crackers and cheese, and when Billy refused all, she took a small chocolate bar from a pile by the register and slipped it onto his saucer. Bessie carried the cup for him to her own table while Eva poured tea for a group of workmen who had just pushed through the door, bringing the smell of dirt and tar and the damp outdoors in with them. Eva knew every one of them by name. And on their heels two mothers, one with a toddler on her hip—she knew them both as well. And then three elderly women, one with a canvas bag decorated with a cactus and the words *Flagstaff, Arizona*.

"The teatime rush," Bessie said—she made it sound like ruse. "No doubt it'll give Eva a chance to collect her thoughts before she has to speak to you. She's got a guilty conscience, you know. She's carried it for years." She looked at Billy, making sure he understood. Her eyes were a dishwater-gray, the skin around her nose full of scars from old blemishes and open pores. "About the money, we all know the story, the money you sent her to come back to the States. She swore any number of times she was sending it all back to you, but then there'd be another fuel crisis or Tom would get laid up or one of the children.

And then she made up her mind to have this shop." She paused, studying him. It was apparent that her day had taken a delicious turn. "She's been guilty about it, though," she went on, leaning toward him. "Every one of us knew it. And your writing to her folks like that only made it worse. Her dad used to say you were calling in her loan." She drilled her bony fingers along the top of her cold cup. "Honestly, you'd only have to say a single word to her and she'd pay you right back today, straight out of the till."

"I've never even thought about the money," Billy said. He was watching Eva, nearing sixty, matronly waist and breast, lean across the counter to chuck the chubby toddler under his chin. "She's welcome to the money."

Bessie Gordon drew her head back, eyeing him. He noticed that there was a wedding ring on her finger; who'd ever believe it, a woman so ugly—a lid for every pot, as his mother used to say. She closed her lips over her mess of teeth and then pulled them into a kind of smile, sympathetic, even pleasant. This was the face, chosen above a lifetime of other faces, some husband sought his solace in. "That's what I always thought, somehow," she told him. "That's just how I imagined you to be."

There was a small bell ringing somewhere, a far-off, fairy-wing, chinging sound that he gradually saw was the plastic rose knocking against the milk-glass vase, both of them set moving by the way his hand was trembling on the table. Bessie saw it, too, and bit her lip, all sympathy. No doubt she knew the true cause and would add that—a drinking problem—to the tale of Eva Kavanaugh's boy from New York.

He flexed the hand on the table. It was pale, bloated enough to strain against Maeve's ring. "A touch of Parkinson's," he told her, since he could not stop the tremor.

She nodded. "What a shame." And then added, "My mother had it, too." So that Billy had to wonder who was kidding whom.

When Eva finally came to the table, a cup for herself, a teapot to warm his, Bessie volunteered to take the counter for a while so they could chat undisturbed. She held out an icy hand. "It was a pleasure to meet you, Mr. Lynch," she said, and gave Eva a look that told her, at least to Billy's eyes, that here was a man better than she knew.

"Is this a holiday for you?" Eva asked brightly. It seemed to be the question she had decided on while she poured her customers their tea.

He said it was.

"With your family?"

He said he was with some priests. It was a kind of retreat.

"Lovely," she said. Her hair had been lightened to a honey blond and no longer matched her dark eyes, although the eyes themselves had stayed true. Her skin was rough and lined, a new downward turn to her lips, a second chin. She was back from the dead for him, there was that, but there was also half a lifetime of mistaken belief. He told her he was married, with a house, still with Con Ed, and he'd stayed at the shoe store until Mr. Holtzman sold it just before he died in '64.

She had four children, all of them grown now, two with babies of their own. One of them moved to the States, to

Boston, with an American husband, one in London with the BBC. Two helping out here.

It wasn't only her being alive that took some getting used to, it was that she had lived, it was how she had lived.

She suddenly sat forward. It was a terrible thing she'd done, she said, leaving it to her sister to tell him she was marrying Tom, never sending him back his money. She couldn't imagine what he must think of her. She couldn't imagine what had possessed her back then. "What must you think of me?" she said again, lowering her eyes and catching him trying to steady the cup, spilling tea onto the saucer, darkening the red wrapper of the candy bar. He put it down, put his hands on his lap. He knew he'd stop at the first place he came to once he left here, get himself something to quench this thirst. "It was a long time ago," he said.

She said she would write him a check right now, would he let her? She would honestly like to, it had been on her conscience for so long.

But he said no, no. If it was a pub he first came to, well then, so be it. He could get himself a Coke at least.

She had her head bowed. She no longer wore a clean part. "I'm sorry, Billy," she said. "I've wanted to tell you so. It was cruel. It's just that I was afraid it would never happen, Tom getting this business going, us getting a place of our own. You know how it is when you're young, you're afraid your life will never get started. I got your money in my hands and I went a little mad."

"Dennis told me you died," Billy said easily. It was all part of a story now, and as story, it was nothing any of them had truly lived. He suspected there was a good joke in it, too, if he turned the tale around a bit, found the right way to look at it. He could see himself in Quinlan's, his glass to his heart, and Danny Lynch with his face gone red and his shoulders shaking the way they did when you really got him going.

Eva nodded. "We'd figured as much from your letters. Mary told me that's what he said he might do."

Billy nodded, too. "Did he?" He smiled a little. He couldn't risk another try at the cup although his throat was parched. "Like something out of *Romeo and Juliet*, hey?" He might even order a single shot, just one, to steady himself for the drive to Shannon. Because the oath he'd taken was part of a story, too, when you came right down to it. Nothing, when you came right down to it, was unbreakable, unchangeable, under threat of eternal damnation. Who was kidding whom?

"Well, we're both still here," Eva said.

"There's the pity of it," he told her, feigning a brogue to make her smile. One shot for the road and maybe a beer at the airport before he met up with Father Jim. A single glass of stout. Even Father Jim might excuse him, pledge or no, if he knew what he'd been through this afternoon. If he could begin to appreciate this soaking sense of foolishness.

She said she'd known him immediately, as soon as she came through the door: the stoop of his shoulders, those blue eyes. She knew him as if no time had passed at all since the days they had spent on Long Island.

Sitting back from the table, his hands still in his lap, he said he'd be going out there again himself, to visit Dennis in Holtzman's little place, as soon as he returned to

New York. He said he did so enjoy it out there, loveliest place on earth.

"How is Dennis?" she asked, and he told her. He said, "And Mary?"

Something came into her face then, something that had not been there before, during those days they had spent on Long Island, anger and determination and disgust, an old bitterness—something the span of years had taught her. Mary, she said, pulling herself up as if to keep her nose above it. Mary she doesn't hear from. Not since back then, if you want to know the truth. Not since Mary stopped hearing from Dennis. Since he broke off with her. Mary wrote to her at one point back then to say that Dennis might even tell Billy she had died rather than let him know she had merely been cruel. You're as good as dead to me, too, Mary wrote. You've ruined everything for me. "If you can imagine," Eva said, with that new bitterness in her face, in her voice, coming in strong and familiar and true, "a sister saying such a thing to her own flesh and blood. As if it was all my fault Dennis wanted no more to do with her. I wrote back to her and said Dennis was only doing what any decent man would do. It wasn't me who told her to be so loose and free with him." Her skin was dry now, lined, hinting at the dust it would, in another two or three decades, become. In truth this time. It was awkward, Billy thought, more awkwardness, to hear these angry words, these girlish concerns, on the lips of a plump old grandmother who long ago should have attained wisdom enough to dismiss this spleen. An old woman who should have wisdom enough to know that passion gone cold, gone way beyond its prime, was a pathetic thing. "She stopped writing me after that. My younger sister sees her in New York on occasion. She went to college, City College—the Mr. and Mrs. helped her out—and she ended up taking a job as a teacher, somewhere near a city named Binghamton. Never married—" with some satisfaction.

"And you're not in touch?" Billy asked.

She shook her head. He might have said, until now, that time had not much changed her. "I'm as good as dead to her," she said haughtily. "And she to me, I might add."


AT HOLTZMAN'S PLACE, in the two webbed lawn chairs they had set up on the sparse grass of the front lawn because the low steps where they had sat for so many nights when they were young were now too hard on their aging backs and sent pins and needles into their legs, Billy leaned forward, three sheets to the wind, and told Dennis that bitterness, then, was all that was left to it. Two old sisters locked in a silent transatlantic feud because of words exchanged about some boys they knew, thirty years ago—because one (you might say) had given too much and the other had given too little. That was it—all that remained of their lovely idyll in this lovely place. Faith inspired by anger outstripping any inspired by affection. There it was. There was the way it had ended. Nothing but bitterness, truth be told. Or pettiness at best.

What was it the poet said? More substance in our enmities than in our love.

My father shook his head. He leaned forward himself, his forearms on his knees. "You've been done more harm than good by your poetry," he said.

He knew he should send him packing. But Billy had refilled the flask in his pocket from the bottle he'd carried in his case and he was too far gone to be put back on the train. Not that Dennis had the strength now to do it. In the morning he'd send him off with a lecture he could already hear himself deliver, the one about killing yourself and maybe killing someone else as well. Think of Maeve. Think of Rosemary and Kate. Think of poor Father Jim and the trouble he took for you. Think of your friends, Billy. Think of me. He'd never said it before and would surely never say it again, but just this once he might tell him, Think of me, Billy. Without Claire, without even faith or fancy enough left to send her my thoughts, never mind my prayers. Put aside your nonsense, Billy, put aside the past and think of those who really love you, who've loved you all along. Every one of us living proof, Billy, that it's a powerless thing, this loving one another, nothing like what you had imagined. Except in the way it persists.

"I'm sorry, Billy" was what he said instead, shaking his head. "If it's an apology you're after, I'm sorry. I should have told you the truth long ago. But so much time passed. I suppose I began to think that it no longer mattered."

Billy sat erect, bleary-eyed, incurable. And yet still there lingered—was my father only imagining it?—that old longing to admire in Billy's blue eyes, Billy's own persistent love. "It was quite a thing to pull off, over all these years," he said softly.

Dennis agreed.

"Quite a story to tell."

My father nodded, leaning forward, the sparse grass at his feet still sun-warmed although the day was changing, approaching evening. The whiff of tar from the heated black road fading enough now to let the sweetness of the scented air once again come through. Air that was the very memory of that time itself, all those years ago. That was now the very scent of longing.

"Was it difficult?" Billy said with his thin smile.

"Only at first," my father told him. "After a while I suppose I believed it myself."

Billy nodded. "Mary never married," he said again, handing him something.

"And she was a pretty girl, too," my father said, refusing it. "Just goes to show you. You can never tell."

I approached from the road and only caught their attention when I had crossed the gravel driveway.

My father looked up, Billy turned a bit in his chair. I began talking right away, so I would not have to look into Billy's wet eyes, into my father's dark and troubled ones.

I met Matt West, I said, Mr. West's oldest son, the kid in the car this morning. Down at the beach, I said, not wanting to conjure the wide car, the lingering scent of marijuana. I was going to go out with him at seven, if the two of them didn't mind. Maybe a movie or something. I hoped they didn't mind.

My father sat back. "Billy's just here for the evening," he said severely. "It's not a good night to make other plans."

But Billy waved a hand, as my mother might have done. "Go," he said, and to my father: "Let her go. Why in the world would she want to spend an evening with a couple of old geezers?" He gestured toward the lawn and the road, the lengthening shadows and the still-blue sky. "On a night like this," he said, "a summer night in this lovely place." He looked at me, barely able to go on. "Go," he said, the tears welling, ready to spill. "Have a lovely night, dear, with your boy. Go."

THAT WAS THE NIGHT we discovered where our childhoods merged: on a summer evening, one of the last, I suppose, we had spent with my grandmother at the Long Island place. My brothers and I were playing a netless game of badminton in one corner of the yard, while my mother and father and grandmother sat in a semicircle of webbed lawn chairs in another. Fragrant late-summer evening, the sky streaked with brightness, pink and purple and gold, a touch of the bay in the cooling air that was itself touched with the very first hint of fall. There was a pitcher of martinis on an aluminum snack tray before them, a cracked plate of clams on the half shell beside it, each one dotted with a bit of red cocktail sauce, decorated with a slice of lemon. All they knew of heaven.

We could see the driveway from where we played, and so it must have been our slowing down and turning to look that first alerted my grandmother to her visitor, or maybe the sound of the wheels against the gravel. He got out of the car with the index card in his hand and seemed about to show it to us, as if to ask for directions, before he noticed that there were adults on the premises as well. My father getting out of his chair to meet him; my grandmother, knowing more, right behind. She overtook my father just as Mr. West was removing his cap and immediately directed him back around to the front of the house. We heard their voices inside through the screen in the kitchen windows and then again in the back bedroom. She seemed to be doing most of the talking. Her voice had grown huskier in her old age, still a redhead's voice although, spurning hair dye as she had spurned all self-deception, she had let her hair go white. My mother looked to my father and my father shrugged. They exchanged a few words. He stood to top off their drinks. When my grandmother came back around the corner of the house, she had a number of ten-dollar bills in her hand and Mr. West had already once again started his engine.

He drove back to your house in Amagansett, where the long, loud argument that for you was your parents' marriage began again. He came in while you and your brothers were at the dinner table with your mother—something with catsup, you said, as you remembered it; as you remembered it, every meal of your childhood smelled of catsup (and then ducked your head to laugh, or because you had made me laugh). Your mother turned her back to him, this was the routine, and neither you nor your brothers were fooled by the icy silence—in a moment, you knew, it would crack. Your father went banging into the walkup attic, came banging down again with two suitcases, went banging into their bedroom. When he came through the kitchen again with the first suitcase, your mother asked, "What's this?" coolly, and he said, "I'm leaving." Oh sure, she mouthed to you and your brothers, who instantly wanted neither to take her side nor to believe him.

She turned her back again when he returned, but when he came through the kitchen with the second suitcase, she sprang from her chair and followed him, through the kitchen door, down the steps, across the side lawn to the car.

There may be families, you said, who would lower their voices in the open air (mine, for instance, I told you, who at about this same time on that same night were listening quietly over our grilled round steaks to my grandmother's explanation regarding the sensibility of renting out the place all year, fond memories notwithstanding), but yours wasn't one of them. They were at each other a good ten minutes out on the side lawn, and then your father swung into the kitchen again, your mother right behind, trying to catch him by the back of his shirt. Both of them, with their eyes so bright and their jaws so set, with everything about them, you said, tunneled into their anger, unaware of, it seemed, blind to the three boys still at the table, over the remnants of another catsup dinner. Back into the bedroom. *You* was the operative word in these arguments, you said. *You* flung like a spitball. *You* peeled off and flung back again. Me? *You!* If they had only been able to decide which one of them was you they might have known for certain and at last which one of them to blame. They might have resolved something. (Ducking your head again to smile. I liked your mouth, your dark eyes, the leather bracelet on your slim wrist.)

Your father spent the night, perhaps the next dozen of them, on his boat, because it was September at least—at least school had started again—before he actually brought you and your brothers to the little house he had rented.

You hated it, of course, the musty rooms and the blood-red shingles and the sense that whatever latent capacity your father had to become a stranger was now realized as he moved around the tiny kitchen, opening cabinets and drawers and mumbling, Now, where does she keep . . . frying eggs and bacon and serving them to you on faded china plates that were not his, not your mother's, that my mother had picked up, as a matter of fact, at the Opportunity Shop in East Hampton for a dollar or two (the remnant of another upheaval in yet another household) another summer years ago. You hated the little house because it was proof positive, or so it had seemed to you then, that your parents' marriage was over, that the days of the five of you living together were over. That the anger and the shouting would never, as you had always believed, somehow resolve itself into love again, peace. Don't even think about it, you told Cody and John. Don't even hope.

You slept in the room with the particle-board Buster Brown and Tighe on the wall. My room, I said, that's where I always stay—"We've already slept in the same bed, then," you said, smiling, cutting all kinds of corners. Our amazement was at what we hadn't known until now, the parallels in our past no more delightful than what we were beginning to suspect our futures would contain, had contained for us all along, though we hadn't known.

This was the lesson it taught you, you said—we were already on our way, clothes falling off, as they did in those days, the sound of the ocean somewhere above us, the humid night, the same stars, our own summer idyll—this was your particular take on your particular broken home: that in the absence of love, the evaporation, the disinte-

gration, the tossing out of the equation of love, came
peace. This was your particular take: you had one or the
other, paid for one with the other.

I agreed. It was, in those days, the way we all spoke
about love: world-wise, open-eyed, without illusion. Lying, of course. Because what we truly believed at that moment—would believe on and off again for the rest of our
lives—was that the whole history of Holtzman's little
house—from its bankrupt builder to my grandmother's
greed to your parents' bitter marriage—was, on this night,
with our own meeting, redeemed.

IN THE MORNING, at the breakfast table, Billy was blood-
shot but too skillful a drinker to seem hung over. He had
showered and shaved with an electric razor and his hair
was wet, combed back. The open collar of his pale blue
shirt showed the aging throat, the blotched skin of his
neck. Nothing in his face or in his manner indicated that
he had heard a word of the talking-to my father had given
him, in his room, before Billy, or I for that matter (listening to my father's voice coming from behind the wall
where Buster Brown and Tighe were still hung), had even
gotten out of bed. Killing himself and lying to everyone,
and what about the trouble Father Jim went to, and what
about AA again; it worked for Ted and for Mary Casey
and for Uncle Jim, why not? Why not?

Billy's black satchel was already by the front door when
he came into the kitchen. Seeing it there, he said, "Here's
your hat, what's your hurry?"

My father was at the stove, frying eggs. He turned,

smiling, and for a moment I thought he might relent. But he was as adept as his cousin was at keeping himself from what he most enjoyed. "There's an 11:17 train," he said.

At the table, Billy took a spoonful of coffee and lost half of it as it made its shaky way to his mouth, dabbling his plate and his lap and the front of his shirt. He swiped at himself with his napkin and then removed a small pack of postcards and a fountain pen from his breast pocket. He put both on the table beside his plate.

"Another thing about Ireland," he said. "We're all over there. All our faces." To me: "I saw your dad driving a Guinness truck in Dublin. And his dad was moving a herd of sheep across the road up in the northwest."

He uncapped the pen and held it in one hand, but then put it down again when it was clear his trembling fingers could not manage it yet.

"I saw my mother," he went on. "Good Lord, I saw my mother in nearly every shop I went into, usually behind the counter. And my father's face was on one of the priests who said Mass at the retreat house."

He lifted the cards, shuffled through them. The duck pond. Home Sweet Home. The Maidstone Club. A sunset on the beach at Amagansett.

"Everybody," he was saying. "You and Danny and Claire. Both my sisters. Mac rented us a car at the airport. Ted Lynch was right behind us at a hurling match, and I'm sorry to say, Dennis, that he was pie-eyed for sure." He winked at me. "Easy does it, my foot," he said.

My father was smiling, an old habit. He couldn't help but get a kick out of Billy, even Billy hung over, lying to everyone, Billy incurable.

Billy placed the cards on the table again, white side up. He took another spoonful of coffee, steadier now than with the last.

"I didn't see anyone who resembled Kate's Peter, though," he said. "Which only proves what I've always said about that black-Irish bit being a lie. Sulinowsky turned to Sullivan, if you ask me."

He lifted the pen, turned the card over again to look at the photograph. Home Sweet Home. "Maeve, of course," he said. "And her father. Her father's face was a dime a dozen over there. Uncle Jim. Bridie Shea as a girl again." He began to write, slowly, carefully keeping control. "Wouldn't that be a gift for poor Bridie, to be a girl again? Sitting up there in her mother's window the way she used to. Not a care in the world. I told Father Jim that it was like a taste of the hereafter, going over there. I must have seen some version of every Irishman I know."

"What about yourself?" my father said. "Anyone look like you?"

Billy looked up from his postcard. He had written a single line across, two spindly words, as far as I could see.

"Oh sure," he said. "I was this young fellow in Clonmel. A regular legend around the gas station." My father laughed a little and Billy looked at me. "Get your father to tell you the tale," he said, although of course I never did, not then, my own future coming at me as it was. And I was too busy trying to make out what was written on the card under his hand. *Beautiful friend*, it looked like, just the two words.

And then I saw him address the card to Maeve.

THE LONG ISLAND HOUSE was squat, rectangular, red-shingled, and green-roofed, the shingles rough to the touch but sparkling in sunlight, flecked with mica. There were two windows in front, trimmed in deep green, a door between them, also green. Three wooden steps painted to match the door, the paint well peeled now, mostly showing bare board.

The lawn, in April, was pale green, the blades of grass wet and thin, newborn. Even the low weeds that edged the property seemed freshly sprouted, as did the tangle of honeysuckle vine that covered the wire fence along the side and that would, in summer, be tangled itself with the hum of bees. The gravel driveway was scattered with puddles. The road out front was still black from all the rain that had guaranteed Billy's swift ascent into heaven, but it was drying out now, a no-longer-solid brushstroke that by noon would have feathered back into dust along its edges. A road that on the hottest days gave off the same sharp odor it had had the moment it was spread. And swimming heat waves, of course, earth agitating air.

The suburban homes and sandy cottages were mostly silent, lights on in only one or two of them: another Saturday morning gained. The crescent of bay beach was deserted, the rocks and shells collected at its edges, the dark wash of lapping water running over them and back again.

The lot across the street was still empty and still contained at its heart the remains of a crumbling foundation for a house that was never built, so well grown over by now that even in April the property was all fledgling weeds and dried stalks and last year's leaves.

This had always been the view from the front steps of the Long Island house: the pale green lot, the tree line, the blue sky that in certain kinds of sunlight seemed to be reflecting the mirror flashes of sunlight off the bay.

There was a screen door at the top of the steps, patched, as all screen doors in summer homes seem to be patched, against wire-cutting mosquitoes with a two-inch square of mesh—upper-right-hand corner of the top screen (always). A heavy green door behind it.

The door opened onto a narrow room, a breath of mildew, of ocean dampness. A small rag rug at the door, another larger one under the heavy coffee table. Three damp *Reader's Digest*s on top, and a blue-and-white schedule for the Long Island Railroad, East Hampton station. A wood-framed couch with tweed cushions worn white along the edges. A dark rocker, a plaid wingback. A table and lamp beside it, the base of the lamp a shellacked coil of rope. An old Cinzano ashtray, an ancient, useless pack of matches from Jungle Pete's. A wrought-iron floor lamp. There was a trace of last summer's sand on the wood floor, under the couch. A trace of dust in every corner. Charcoal along the baseboards meant to discourage mildew.

At the other end of the room, and open to it, the kitchen with its heavy Formica table and red countertops and domed refrigerator. The sink was against the back wall, under a long row of narrow windows hung high enough to block the view for all dishwashers 5'2" and under. A back-yard door beside the sink that contained the only curtained window in the house, all others being covered by yellowed shades. Another door beside the refrigerator that led to a narrow corridor that led to the three bedrooms. The only bath at the end of these, chipped white porcelain fixtures, the sink wobbly on steel mosquito legs, the cracked gray linoleum.

Across the hall, the largest bedroom by an inch or two and the brightest due to a second window was painted yellow and decorated with eight wooden shoe-store daisies tacked by my grandmother in an unfathomable constellation across the far wall. A tall dresser with a long bureau scarf. A night table with a milk-glass lamp, a magazine opened and folded back to show a white page filled with black print, unrelieved by photographs, a pair of reading glasses placed over the page, placed there the night before because it was too late to finish and there were too many words and it was all about how much the citizenry loved the President, who was just an actor when you got right down to it, an actor reading them his lines.

On the double bed, dark mahogany headboard, no footboard, white chenille spread folded back, thin floral sheets washed pale, my father opened his eyes to the same room he had gone to sleep in. The same room he had gone to sleep in: then the shadowy circle of the milk-glass lamp, now sun-shot early morning, ebb and flow of it as the breeze sucked in the bottom of the yellow shade and then let it go again (a child in a swing) to snap back against the sash. The very sound that had awakened him. Distant ringing of the buoys in the bay (Oh, but she's a girl). Scent of new grass and of ocean, of mildew, of the Long Island house, of eastern Long Island. I am still here.

He swung his feet out of the bed and sat for a moment. Nothing changed but the light, the magazine on the table, eyeglasses there, clothes in the chair, daisies, dresser, Dopp kit on the bureau because his daughter was here with him and liked to keep her makeup bag on the back of the toilet.

It was there when he made his way across the hall, pale pink and blue, plump. He nudged it gently when he lifted the lid.

Back in the room he raised the shade up above the open window so the snap of it wouldn't wake her—and then heard the same sound, faint but persistent, coming from the shade and window in her room next door. They had both kept the windows open all night, then, despite the cold air. There was still mist on the gray grass, mist all along the vine-covered fence. There was no place in the world he'd rather wake to.

He stood for a moment between the dresser and the bed and offered himself as some elemental part of under-standing: the same room he had gone to sleep in, consciousness dropped and then picked up again, only the light changed. The return of day.

In the kitchen, he put the kettle on. Cut oranges and squeezed them under his palm on an old-fashioned glass juicer. The very one, in fact, his mother had used when he was young, in the apartment in Woodside. The very one, washed up on this shore somehow after what he imagined had been a long, newspaper-wrapped odyssey, box-bound, from that tiny kitchen in Queens to the basement of Holtzman's house in Jamaica (years passing there, light in the narrow basement window and then darkness, light again, a thousand times over while he himself returned from overseas, met Mary, met Claire, married, had children) until someone—himself? Holtzman? his mother?—hoisted the box marked *Kitchen Things* and brought it out here to the Long Island house, where it dropped out of his sight for years and then returned again as something he shared with Mr. West while he was still "my mother's tenant" and not yet "my daughter's father-in-law" and then found himself on this morning in April, the second morning with Billy in his grave, surprised and even delighted by the thing, by the things that ride out time.

He poured the juice into two short, thick glasses, washed and dried his hands. He pulled open the back door—frame sticking, curtain swinging—on a stage the whole wall would have moved with it. He stepped out onto the narrow back porch, where the brushstrokes in the dark green paint were his own, and Billy's. Marvelous sweet spring air of eastern Long Island. New grass and sweet blossom and tang of sea salt. In the bright green of the pale trees, high up, narrow shafts of yellow sunlight, theatrical as well. The sound-track birdsong: gulls and sparrows and distant crows.

He did a few calisthenics. His arms winter pale, the fine hairs on them mostly gray, certainly grayer than Claire had ever seen them. By sundown his arms will have turned a ruddy brown, what with the work he had planned, clippers and scythe and scraping some paint. He touched his waist, his shoulder, raised his hands above his head, looking for all the world like a man giving praise. The return of day.

Inside, the plumbing was moaning and clunking, the sound of water rushing through the walls as if the place had been framed in pipes, not lumber. His daughter in the shower.

He took the breakfast tray from under the counter, placed cups and saucers on it, bowls, cereal, sugar, spoons, a carton of milk, a jar of jam. He toasted four slices of bread and poured water into the teapot just as she came into the kitchen, barefoot, sweatpants and an old T-shirt, her hair wet and smelling of shampoo.

"Good morning, Glory," he said, and she said, "Good morning," the towel draped around her shoulders. She had already been out for a run, she said, down to the beach and back, and he realized that the shade he'd heard had been snapping in an empty room. Tomorrow they'd drive back to Rosedale. Tomorrow evening she'd fly home.

He lifted the tray and she walked ahead of him through the living room. She once more unlocked the green door, pulled it open, sunlight and birdsong transforming a long

shaft of the damp, dark room. She stepped outside, holding the screen open for him.

He said, "Thank you, ma'am," and then caught the
door with his elbow to let her go first. She went to the
bottom step and then turned to take the tray from him,
but he said, "I've got it," and let the screen door close
behind him as he stepped down and turned to place the
tray carefully, crockery rattling, on the top step. He sat
beside it. She sat below him, at his feet, shaking out her
hair, running her fingers through it, and wafting a shampoo
that was some false yet strenuous version of the scent of
the spring air. He lifted the teacup and poured for her.
She reached back.

"Thank you," she said.

"You're most welcome."

She sipped from the cup. The breeze that had woken
him had grown weaker in the sun, but something of the
cold dawn still lingered. One did not dare say to a grown
daughter, a married woman with children of her own, Are
you warm enough? Do you need a sweater? Wouldn't you
rather wear shoes?

He said, "You'll have to give the in-laws a call while
you're here."

I said yes, I had already told them I'd stop by.

"There's a happy pair," my father said, meaning Mr.
West and his wife, united again now that their three boys
had grown, and flown. Nesting again, as you yourself had
said, in the Amagansett house, nesting among the ruins.
What was more tenacious, you'd said, than the desire to
be connected, especially in old age, more tenacious than
fact, than memory. Your parents would turn away, wide-

eyed, whenever you or your brothers said, But you hated
... They'd only needed space, they would tell you, turning our own words against us. They'd only gone through
a rough patch in their marriage that had, unlucky for you
boys, more or less corresponded to your childhoods...

Sitting on the steps of the Long Island house, Billy
two days in his grave, my father and I discussed what the
little house needed to have done to get it in shape for
summer, for his retirement next year, when he would put
the Rosedale house on the market and live out here permanently. Another overhaul, long overdue. Insulation,
plumbing, heating, paint. Redoing and then supplement-
ing all that work he and Billy had done years ago. New
furniture. A real garden, once he was out here permanently, plenty of visitors, too, what with a good six months
to schedule them, April through September at least,
maybe October, too. My three brothers and their families
would each take a turn, and he hoped I'd come in from
the coast with the children. Take at least a week or two.

My father sat on the step above me, the step he would
begin to scrape and sand that very afternoon, and looking
toward the blue sky above the bay and the crescent beach
behind the treeline, he described for me all the ways he
would spend his time in this lovely place, still old Holtzman's place when you came right down to it, his surprise
inheritance from a mother who hadn't put much stock in
elaborate emotion but nevertheless had married twice and
loved him and had said at the end, having scattered Holtzman's money to the charitable winds, Bring Billy out
there, with his wife, because when you got right down to
it, there were all kinds of things in her heart and in her

mind that we never knew. There was, for instance, her capacity to believe. There was as well her capacity to be deceived, since you can't have one without the other, each one side of the other.

He'd have the Quinns out, my father said, Mickey will be retiring soon, too, and all the various Lynches, sure, Danny, too, and Bridie when she needed a break in a beautiful place from taking care of poor Jim. He'd have the Caseys out and both sets of our Rosedale neighbors, my mother's sister Louise with her family, although she drove him crazy. And, he said, he'd ask Maeve.

I looked at him over my shoulder. I'd been thinking, as he counted off the names, how clear it was that Billy's was missing from the list, although Billy over the years would not come, and I thought then that my father mentioned her name just for that, for Billy's sake. He said, Maeve's never been out this way, as far as I know. She should see it. She would enjoy it.

I nodded. Sure, I said. I could imagine her, I supposed, getting off the train at the East Hampton station, tentative and slow, her hand on the rail beside the steps (the plain pearl ring) for much longer than was necessary, lingering there until the conductor offered her his own hand to help her down. (Dorothy or maybe Bridie behind her, since it would not do for her to come out here all alone.) A simple dress, or a pant suit for traveling, her round face and her short hair. My father would take her bag, take her for lunch across the street, take her on the usual tour past the beautiful houses (cottages, he'd say) that neither one of them would have ever thought to own, or even to enter, but would be content, as we'd all been content, to merely

pass by and admire. Billy's idea of heaven, he'd tell her—
the idea itself sufficient alone.

Early evening in the lawn chairs on the sparse lawn, a
cocktail, then dinner in town, or maybe something on the
grill. The far bedroom, for privacy's sake, with the bed
turned down. Fresh, worn towels from the Rosedale house
on the dresser for her. A laugh over the smiling pressed-
wood seahorse on the wall—another decoration from
Holtzman's store.

Holtzman with his literal wealth the one in the long
run who had changed the lives of them all ("Even my
daughter," he would say. "She met Matt out here, you
know.") Figurative wealth changing nothing, in the long
run, except maybe the stories that were told.

"If it comes to a choice between love and money," my
father would tell Maeve, repeating an old joke, "take
money."

And then bringing her back to the station on Sunday
afternoon, after Mass and a bit of breakfast. The gorgeous
people on the platform with her, most of them young, all
of them transformed by a weekend in the sun, fruit and
wildflowers in their arms.

Maeve would be working by then, two years, three
years, after Billy's death. A little job Ted Lynch found for
her with the archdiocese once she'd convinced him that
whatever inclination she'd had to enter a convent had disappeared long ago. The sweet Indian couple meeting her
at the Bayside station and driving her home to the narrow
house where she now lived alone with the dog; peacefully,
she would have to say. Where she would begin to wonder,
no doubt, when Dennis would invite her out again, be-

cause it was so lovely out there and because Billy had so loved the place, regardless of how vigorously and for how long he had deprived himself of it. He had, after all, deprived himself of much that he loved best, poor man.

Hoping he would invite her out again, because when she and Dennis sat at the table last night with a piece of toast and a cup of tea, the dead were there with them, just outside the circle of light. Billy and Claire, not forgotten, no less mourned, but silent, for now, in dreams their faces always turned away, so that the course of other lives, the lives of those they'd loved, could be completed, could go on.

Surely just as the Irish girl, whom Billy had loved when he was young, just back from the war, had eventually turned her face away.

No less remembered, no less mourned. My father would say it himself in another six or seven years' time, as we sat together on these steps again and I watched our children playing croquet on the lawn (wondering, counting, how many more years would such summers continue, my father alive, our children still children, how many more were enough). No less loved now as then, my father would say, breaking the news, but still life goes on. Some relief is required. Some compensation.

I would look at him over my shoulder. Was it penance, I'd want to ask him, was it compensation for an old and well-intentioned lie, for the life it had deprived her of? Or was it merely taking care, more taking care? A hand held out once again to whoever happened to be nearby.

I couldn't ask, of course. And it was impossible to say. His capacity for sympathy was no less than Billy's for self-

denial. Their faith, both of them—all of them, I suppose—
was no less keen than their suspicion that in the end they
might be proven wrong. And their certainty that they
would continue to believe anyway.

They were married in March of 1991, my father and
Maeve. At the little church in East Hampton, Most Holy
Trinity now, no longer St. Philomena's—the poor woman
having been tossed out of the canon of saints in the mid-
sixties because some doubt had arisen about whether or
not she had actually lived. As if, in that wide-ranging anthology of stories that was the lives of the saints—that
was, as well, my father's faith and Billy's and some part
of my own—what was actual, as opposed to what was
imagined, as opposed to what was believed, made, when
you got right down to it, any difference at all.

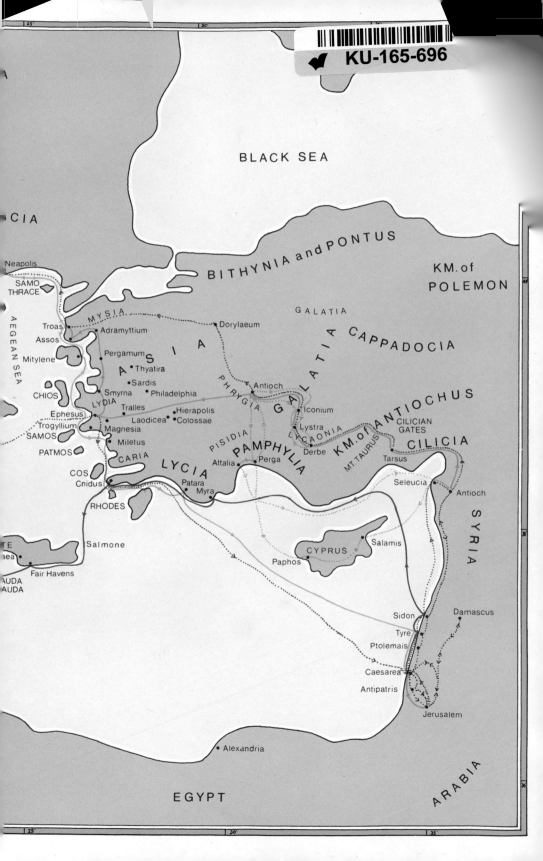

BLACK SEA

BITHYNIA and PONTUS

KM. of
POLEMON

GALATIA

CAPPADOCIA

Neapolis

SAMO
THRACE

MYSIA

Dorylaeum

Troas

Assos

Adramyttium

AEGEAN SEA

Mitylene

Pergamum

A S I A

Thyatira

Sardis

Antioch

PHRYGIA

G A L A T I A

KM. of ANTIOCHUS

Iconium

CILICIAN
GATES

Smyrna

Philadelphia

CHIOS

LYDIA

Tralles

Ephesus

Hierapolis

Laodicea

Colossae

Lystra

LYCAONIA

Trogyllium

Magnesia

SAMOS

Miletus

PISIDIA

Derbe

MT. TAURUS

CILICIA

PATMOS

CARIA

LYCIA

PAMPHYLIA

Tarsus

COS

Attalia

Perga

Cnidus

Patara

Seleucia

Myra

Antioch

RHODES

S Y R I A

Salmone

CYPRUS

Salamis

aea

Paphos

AUDA

Fair Havens

AUDA

Sidon

Damascus

Tyre

Ptolemais

Caesarea

Antipatris

Jerusalem

Alexandria

EGYPT

ARABIA

CIA

Dad

All our love

John, Sally

Rachel & Jonathan

x x x x

Christmas 1977

PAUL: APOSTLE OF THE FR

# PAUL:

## Apostle of the
## Free Spirit

*"Where the Spirit of the Lord is, there the heart is free"*
(2 Corinthians 3: 17, Basic English Version)

## F. F. BRUCE

Exeter

The Paternoster Press

ISBN: 0 85364 209 5

AUSTRALIA
*Emu Book Agencies Pty. Ltd.,
63 Berry St., Granville, 2142, N.S.W.*

SOUTH AFRICA:
*Oxford University Press,
P.O. Box 1141, Cape Town*


**British Library Cataloguing in Publication Data**

Bruce, Frederick Fyvie
   Paul: apostle of the free spirit.
   1.  Bible.  New Testament.  Epistles of
  Paul – Commentaries
   I. Title
   225.9'24      BS2650.3

   ISBN 0–85364–209–5

*Typeset by Input Typesetting Ltd
and Printed in Great Britain for The Paternoster Press,
Paternoster House, 3 Mount Radford Crescent, Exeter, Devon
by Butler and Tanner Ltd, Frome*

# Contents

# List of Illustrations

ACKNOWLEDGEMENTS: The Author and Publishers are grateful to the following for help in supplying illustrations:
*Abbazia delle Tre Fontane, facing pp 449, 464; Barnaby's Picture Library, facing pp 97, 352: Colin Hemer, facing pp 129, 256, 257; Pieterse Davison International, facing p 465; Bastian VanElderen, facing pp 96, 128, 288, 289; Pontifical Commission of Sacred Archaeology, facing pp 353, 384.*

# Preface

THIS WORK IS DESIGNED TO GIVE A CONTINUOUS PRESENTATION of material which has been delivered in lectures or published piecemeal in written articles over many years.

When I entered on my present appointment in the University of Manchester in 1959, one of the lecture-courses already prescribed in the syllabus for the Honours School of Biblical Studies was entitled "The Missionary Career of Paul in its Historical Setting". My lectures for this specially congenial course have provided the nucleus of the following chapters. I had not previously been a stranger to Paul's life and thought, but in the past eighteen years I have devoted more time and attention to this field of study than to any other. I have not attempted to expound Paul's teaching systematically but rather to treat its main themes in their historical context, as Paul himself had occasion to develop them in his letters.

Year by year since I came to Manchester I have given a public lecture in the John Rylands Library (since 1972 the John Rylands University Library of Manchester). Most of these have dealt with some aspect of Pauline studies. They have subsequently been published in the Library's *Bulletin*. The substance of eight of them is reproduced in the following pages: "St. Paul in Rome, 1", *BJRL*, March 1964 (Chapters 4, 31 and 32), "St. Paul in Rome, 2", Autumn 1965 (Chapter 34), "St. Paul in Rome, 3", Spring 1966 (Chapter 35), "St. Paul in Rome, 4", Spring 1967 (Chapter 36), "St. Paul in Rome, 5", Spring 1968 (Chapter 37), "Paul and the Historical Jesus", Spring 1974 (Chapter 11), "Paul and the Law of Moses", Spring 1975 (Chapter 18), "Christ and Spirit in Paul", Spring 1977 (Chapter 12). For permission to reproduce these in revised or adapted form I am indebted to Dr. F. W. Ratcliffe (University Librarian and Director) and Dr. Frank Taylor (Principal Keeper and Editor of the *Bulletin*).

Acknowledgment is also made to the Editor of *The Expository Times* for permission to reproduce in Chapter 22 an expanded version of my paper "Paul and the Athenians" which appeared in that journal for October 1976.

A specially grateful expression of indebtedness must be made to my secretary, Miss Margaret Hogg, who with her customary diligence and cheerfulness has typed the whole work and given valuable help with proof-reading and with the compilation of the index. Her beautiful and accurate typescript has made the printer's task incomparably easier than it would have been if he had been faced with the problem of deciphering my manuscript – a problem which she has tackled with confidence and success.

1977                                                                    F.F.B

# Abbreviations

| | |
|---|---|
| *AJA* | *American Journal of Archaeology* |
| *Ant.* | *Antiquities* (Josephus) |
| AV | Authorized (King James) Version |
| *BC* | *The Beginnings of Christianity*, ed. F. J. Foakes Jackson and K. Lake (London, 1920–33) |
| *BGU* | *Berliner Griechische Urkunden* |
| *BJ* | *De Bello Iudaico (Jewish War)* (Josephus) |
| *BJRL* | *Bulletin of the John Rylands (University) Library*, Manchester |
| *BZNW* | *Beiträge zur Zeitschrift für die neutestamentliche Wissenschaft* |
| CD | Book of the Covenant of Damascus (= Zadokite Work) |
| *GIG* | *Corpus Inscriptionum Graecarum* |
| *CIL* | *Corpus Inscriptionum Latinarum* |
| *CSEL* | *Corpus Scriptorum Ecclesiasticorum Latinorum* |
| *DACL* | *Dictionnaire d'Archéologie chrétienne et de Liturgie* |
| *EQ* | *The Evangelical Quarterly* |
| E.T. | English Translation |
| *Ev. Th.* | *Evangelische Theologie* |
| *HDB* | *Hastings' Dictionary of the Bible* (5 volumes) |
| *Hist. Eccl.* | *Historia Ecclesiastica* (Eusebius) |
| *HJP* | *History of the Jewish People in the Age of Jesus Christ*, E.T. (E. Schürer) |
| *ibid.* | *ibidem* ("in the same place") |
| ICC | International Critical Commentary |
| *IGRR* | *Inscriptiones Graecae ad Res Romanas Pertinentes* |
| *JBL* | *Journal of Biblical Literature* |
| *JRS* | *Journal of Roman Studies* |
| *JTS* | *Journal of Theological Studies* |
| *loc. cit.* | *loco citato* ("at the place cited") |
| LXX | Septuagint (pre-Christian Greek version of Old Testament) |
| *MAMA* | *Monumenta Asiae Minoris Antiqua* |
| MT | Massoretic Text |
| *Nat. Hist.* | *Naturalis Historia* (Pliny the Elder) |
| NEB | New English Bible |
| n.s. | new series |
| *NTS* | *New Testament Studies* |
| *OGIS* | *Orientis Graeci Inscriptiones Selectae* (ed. W. Dittenberger) |

| | |
|---|---|
| *op. cit.* | *opus citatum* ("the work cited") |
| Q | Qumran |
| 1QH | *Hodayot* (Hymns of Thanksgiving) from Qumran Cave 1 |
| 1QIs$^a$ | Complete scroll of Isaiah from Qumran Cave 1 |
| 1QIs$^b$ | Incomplete scroll of Isaiah from Qumran Cave 1 |
| 1QM | *Milḥamah* (War scroll) from Qumran Cave 1 |
| 1QpHab | *Pesher* (commentary) on Habakkuk from Qumran Cave 1 |
| 1QS | *Serek* (Rule of the Community) from Qumran Cave 1 |
| 4QpNah | *Pesher* (commentary) on Nahum from Qumran Cave 4 |
| *QDAP* | *Quarterly of the Department of Antiquities of Palestine* |
| *RE* | *Realencyclopädie für die klassische Altertumswissenschaft* (A. F. von Pauly and G. Wissowa) |
| *RHPR* | *Revue d'Histoire et de Philosophie Religieuses* |
| RSV | Revised Standard Version |
| *s.v.* | *sub voce* ("under the word") |
| TB | Babylonian Talmud |
| *TDNT* | *Theological Dictionary of the New Testament*, i–ix (1964–74), E.T. of *TWNT* (*Theologisches Wörterbuch zum Neuen Testament*), i–ix (1933–74), ed. G. Kittel and G. Friedrich |
| TJ | Jerusalem (Palestinian) Talmud |
| *ZAW* | *Zeitschrift für die alttestamentliche Wissenschaft* |
| *ZDPV* | *Zeitschrift des Deutschen Palästina-Vereins* |
| *ZNW* | *Zeitschrift für die neutestamentliche Wissenschaft* |
| *ZTK* | *Zeitschrift für Theologie und Kirche* |

# Introduction

NO EXCUSE IS OFFERED FOR THE PUBLICATION OF YET ANOTHER book on Paul save the excuse offered by the second-century author of the *Acts of Paul*: it was written *amore Pauli*, for love of Paul. For half a century and more I have been a student and teacher of ancient literature, and to no other writer of antiquity have I devoted so much time and attention as to Paul. Nor can I think of any other writer, ancient or modern, whose study is so richly rewarding as his. This is due to several aspects of his many-faceted character: the attractive warmth of his personality, his intellectual stature, the exhilarating release effected by his gospel of redeeming grace, the dynamism with which he propagated that gospel throughout the world, devoting himself single mindedly to fulfilling the commission entrusted to him on the Damascus road ("this one thing I do") and labouring more abundantly than all his fellow-apostles – "yet not I, but the grace of God which was with me". My purpose in writing this book, then, is to share with others something of the rich reward which I myself have reaped from the study of Paul.

## 1. Paul the letter-writer

Of all the New Testament authors, Paul is the one who has stamped his own personality most unmistakably on his writings. It is especially for this reason that he has his secure place among the great letter-writers in world literature – not because he composed his letters with a careful eye to stylistic propriety and the approving verdict of a wider public than those for whom they were primarily intended, but because they express so spontaneously and therefore so eloquently his mind and his message. "He is certainly one of the great figures in Greek literature", said Gilbert Murray;[1] and a greater Hellinist even than Murray, Ulrich von Wilamowitz-Moellendorff, described him as "a classic of Hellenism". Paul, he said, did not directly take over any of the elements of Greek education, yet he not only writes Greek but thinks Greek; without realizing it, he serves as the executor of Alexander the Great's testament by carrying the gospel to the Greeks.

1. G. G. A. Murray, *Four Stages of Greek Religion* (New York, 1912), p. 146.

15

At last, at last, once again someone speaks in Greek out of a fresh inward experience of life. That experience is his faith, which makes him sure of his hope. His glowing love embraces all mankind: to bring them salvation he joyfully sacrifices his own life, yet the fresh life of the soul springs up wherever he goes. He writes his letters as a substitute for his personal activity. This epistolary style is Paul, Paul himself and no other.[2]

No mean tribute from a Hellenist of Hellenists to one who claimed to be a Hebrew of Hebrews!

Paul's letters are our primary source for his life and work; they are, indeed, a primary source for our knowledge of the beginnings of Christianity, for they are the earliest datable Christian documents, the most important of them having been written between eighteen and thirty years after the death of Jesus. Some writers have no doubt used the letter-form to conceal their true thoughts; Paul's transparent honesty was incompatible with any such artificiality. He tries, where necessary, to be diplomatic, whether he is writing to his own converts or to people personally unknown to him; but even so he wears his heart on his sleeve.

This spontaneity was no doubt facilitated by Paul's practice of dictating his letters instead of writing them out himself. As he dictates, he sees in his mind's eye those whom he is addressing and speaks as he would if he were face to face with them. Even if he made use of amanuenses, the style is his own, especially in the "capital epistles" (a designation conveniently used for the letters to the Galatians, Corinthians and Romans). Where the amanuensis was one of his close associates, like Timothy or Luke, some greater stylistic discretion may have been allowed to him. But when Paul warmed to his theme, it can have been no easy task for any one to write down at his dictation. If his amanuenses followed the customary procedure, they would take down what Paul dictated with a stylus on wax tablets, possibly using some system of shorthand, and then transcribe the text in longhand on to a papyrus sheet or roll.

Because of the self-evident spontaneity of Paul's letters, any account of him which is irreconcilable with their evidence must be suspect. From the first century we have one account of Paul composed (it appears) in complete independence of his letters; that is the account given in the Acts of the Apostles (a work which was designed as the second part of a history of Christian origins whose first part we know as the Gospel of Luke). This is our principal secondary source for the life and work of Paul, and the present work is based on the conviction (for which arguments have been set out elsewhere)[3] that it is a source of high historical value. The

2. U. von Wilamowitz-Moellendorff, *Die griechische Literatur des Altertums = Die Kultur der Gegenwart*, ed. P. Hinneberg, i, 8 (Berlin/Leipzig, [3]1912), p. 232.

differences between the portrait of Paul drawn in his undisputed letters and that drawn in Acts are such differences as might be expected between a man's self-portrait and the portrait painted of him by someone else for whom he sat either consciously or (as in this instance) unconsciously. The Paul of Acts is the historical Paul as he was seen and depicted by a sympathetic and accurate but independent observer, whose narrative provides a convincing framework for the major epistles at least and may be used with confidence to supplement Paul's own evidence.[4]

## 2. Paul and the expansion of Christianity

It is, however, not only as a man of letters but perhaps even more as a man of action that Paul has made his mark on world history. Consider, for example, two historical phenomena which would be surprising if they were not so familiar.

First, Christianity arose as a movement within the Jewish community, not in the lands of the dispersion but in the land of Israel. Its Founder was a Jew, and so were his disciples, who in the years following his departure from them proclaimed only to Jews the good news with which he entrusted them. Yet in little more than a generation after his death Christianity was recognized by the authorities of the Roman Empire as a predominantly Gentile cult, and to this day there are parts of the world where the antithesis Jew/Christian is simply another way of stating the antithesis Jew/Gentile.

Second, Christianity arose in south-western Asia, among people whose vernacular was Aramaic. Yet its foundation documents have come down to us in Greek, the language in which they were originally written; and over many centuries now it has been regarded, for better or worse, as a predominantly European religion.

Both of these phenomena, which in fact are but two aspects of one and the same phenomenon, are due principally to the energy with which Paul, a Jew by birth and upbringing, spread the gospel of Christ in the Gentile world from Syria to Italy, if not indeed to Spain, during the thirty years or so which followed his conversion to Christianity about A.D. 33. The energy with which he undertook

---

3. Cf. F. F. Bruce, *The Acts of the Apostles* (London, [2]1952), pp. 15ff. *et passim*.

4. The last two sentences are amplified in F. F. Bruce, "Is the Paul of Acts the Real Paul?" *BJRL* 58 (1975–76), pp. 282–305. Two important essays which should be mentioned are P. Vielhauer, "On the 'Paulinism' of Acts", E. T. in *Studies in Luke-Acts: Essays in Honor of Paul Schubert*, ed. L. E. Keck and J. L. Martyn (Nashville/New York, 1966), pp. 33–50 (a study which defends quite different conclusions on the subject from mine), and C. K. Barrett, "Acts and the Pauline Corpus", *Expository Times* 88 (1976–77), pp. 2–5 (a study which whets the reader's appetite for the major work on Acts which Professor Barrett is preparing for the International Critical Commentary).

and accomplished his commission may be illustrated by one phase
of his apostolic ministry – the decade between A.D. 47 and 57. Here
is Roland Allen's summary:

> In little more than ten years St. Paul established the Church in
> four provinces of the Empire, Galatia, Macedonia, Achaia and
> Asia. Before A.D. 47 there were no Churches in these provinces;
> in A.D. 57 St. Paul could speak as if his work there was done,
> and could plan extensive tours into the far West without anxiety
> lest the Churches which he had founded might perish in his
> absence for want of his guidance and support.[5]

His confidence was justified: they did not perish, but grew and
prospered.

Paul was not the only preacher of Christianity in the Gentile
world of that day – there were some who preached it in sympathy
with him and others who did so in rivalry to him [6] – but he
outstripped all others as a pioneer missionary and planter of
churches, and nothing can detract from his achievement as the
Gentiles' apostle *par excellence*.

### 3. Paul the preacher of free grace

But Paul's pre-eminent contribution to the world has been his
presentation of the good news of free grace – as he himself would
have put it (rightly), his re-presentation of the good news explicit in
Jesus' teaching and embodied in his life and work. The free grace of
God which Paul proclaimed is free grace in more senses than one –
free in the sense that it is sovereign and unfettered, free in the sense
that it is held forth to men and women for their acceptance by faith
alone, and free in the sense that it is the source and principle of
their liberation from all kinds of inward and spiritual bondage, including the bondage of legalism and the bondage of moral anarchy.

The God whose grace Paul proclaimed is the God who alone
does great wonders. He creates the universe from nothing; he calls
the dead to life; he justifies the ungodly. This third is the greatest
wonder of all: creation and resurrection are consistent with the
power of the living and life-giving God, but the justifying of the ungodly is *prima facie* a contradiction of his character as the righteous
God, the Judge of all the earth, who by his own declaration "will

---

5. R. Allen, *Missionary Methods: St. Paul's or Ours?* (London, 1927), p. 3.

6. C. K. Barrett ("Acts and the Pauline Corpus", pp. 4 f.) discerns at least two
Christian missions in the Graeco-Roman world of the time in addition to Paul's: one
led by Peter and one which ran back to Stephen and his fellow-Hellenists. Acts he
regards as a monument of the process by which the three came to terms with one
another after the deaths of their founders and the events of A.D. 70.

not justify the ungodly" (Exodus 23: 7). Yet such is the quality of divine grace that in the very act of extending it to the undeserving God demonstrates "that he himself is righteous and that he justifies the one who has faith in Jesus" (Romans 3: 26).

Paul's understanding of God is completely in line with Jesus' teaching. The God who, in one parable after another, freely forgives the sinner or welcomes the returning prodigal does not exercise the quality of mercy at the expense of his righteousness: he remains the self-consistent God whose very self-consistency is the reason sinners "are not consumed" (Malachi 3: 6) or, in the words of another Old Testament prophet, "he does not retain his anger for ever because he delights in steadfast love" (Micah 7: 18).

But grace is manifested not only in God's acceptance of sinners but in the transformation of those thus accepted into the likeness of Christ. The words of Thomas Erskine have frequently been quoted to the effect that, "in the New Testament, religion is grace, and ethics is gratitude".[7] If this dictum were turned into Greek, one word, *charis*, would serve as the equivalent of both "grace" and "gratitude"; for the gratitude which divine grace calls forth from its recipient is also the expression of that grace imparted and maintained by the Holy Spirit, through whom the love of God is poured out into the hearts of believers. Jesus had cited the two commandments enjoining love to God and love to one's neighbour as those on which "all the law and the prophets depend" (Matthew 22: 40); so for Paul the free activity of this divine love in the lives of those redeemed by grace represented "the fulfilling of the law" (Romans 13: 10). Therefore, he insisted, the gospel of free grace did not annul the essential law of God, but rather established it (Romans 3: 31).

Love is a more potent incentive to doing the will of God than legal regulations and fear of judgment could ever be. This at least was grasped by that strange second-century Christian Marcion, whose devotion to Paul's teaching was not matched by his understanding of it. Marcion cut the gospel off from its past and its future, denying the Christian relevance of the Old Testament and of coming judgment. Paul, for his part, did not jettison the Old Testament (as we call it): for him its writings constituted the holy scriptures (Romans 1: 2), the only holy scriptures he knew. He called them "the law and the prophets" (Romans 3: 21) and described them as "the oracles of God" (Romans 3: 2). They found their fulfilment and had their meaning made plain in Christ; when people read them without using this key to unlock their significance, "a veil lies over their minds" (2 Corinthians 3: 15). Paul attached the greater value to them because they bore witness to the message of

7. T. Erskine, *Letters* (Edinburgh, 1877), p. 16.

justification by faith in Christ: the gospel which in them was "preached beforehand to Abraham" (Galatians 3: 8) was the gospel which Paul was commissioned to proclaim; it was no recent invention.

Neither did Paul repudiate the idea of coming judgment. In a moral universe divine retribution must be reckoned with; "else how could God judge the world?" (Romans 3: 6). But Marcion was unrealistically radical as Paul was not. Let it be counted to him for righteousness, nevertheless, that he grasped Paul's message of salvation by grace – grasped it as many more "orthodox" Christians of his century did not.

Tertullian, for example, writing his treatise *Against Marcion* after Marcion's death, challenges him dramatically to say why he did not abandon himself to an extravaganza of sin since he did not believe that the God and Father whom Jesus revealed would judge mankind.[8] "Your only answer", says Tertullian, apostrophizing Marcion, "is *Absit, absit* ('Far from it, far from it')" – and on such an answer he pours scorn. But at this very point Tertullian shows that it is he, and not Marcion, who is out of tune with Paul. The Latin *absit* which Tertullian puts into Marcion's mouth appears to be the equivalent of the Greek *mē genoito* ("God forbid" in older English versions of the New Testament), which Marcion, whose language was Greek, probably used.

But if Marcion repelled such a challenge as Tertullian's with *mē genoito*, he was using these words in precisely the sense in which Paul used them when replying to the question: "What then? Are we to sin because we are not under law but under grace? Far from it!" (Romans 6: 15). Marcion, like Paul, realized that for one who through faith had received the new life (which was nothing less than Christ's risen life shared by him with the believer) to go on in sin was a moral contradiction in terms: "How can we, who died to sin, still live in it?" (Romans 6: 2). Paul, unlike Marcion, knew that he must one day give an account of his stewardship to the Lord who commissioned him; but it was not the prospect of his appearance before the tribunal of Christ that deterred him from sin. He who had formerly attained the standard of righteousness prescribed by the Mosaic commandments could not be content with a lower standard now that he was "under law to Christ" (1 Corinthians 9: 21). Rather, since it was no longer he that lived but Christ that lived in him, the perfection of Christ was the goal to which he now pressed forward. Tertullian may have known this; perhaps he was simply trying to score a debating point against Marcion. Even so, he was inviting the retort: "And is *your* only reason for abstaining from sin your fear of the wrath to come?"

---

8. Tertullian, *Against Marcion* i. 27.

Marcion probably, and Paul certainly, knew the love of Christ to be the all-compelling power in life. Where love is the compelling power, there is no sense of strain or conflict or bondage in doing what is right: the man or woman who is compelled by Jesus' love and empowered by his Spirit does the will of God from the heart. For (as Paul could say from experience) "where the Spirit of the Lord is, there the heart is free" (2 Corinthians 3: 17).

# CHAPTER 1

# The Rise of Rome

## 1. Rome through eastern eyes

IN THESE DAYS OF WORLD SUPER-POWERS IT IS NOT EASY TO ENVISAGE how a single city could have acquired an adequate power-base to extend its authority over a wide area and establish a large empire. Yet in world history many cities have in their day become imperial states. There were several at various times in the Euphrates-Tigris valley: the best known of these was Babylon, which in the eighteenth century B.C. achieved this kind of power under the great Hammurabi and later, in the sixth century B.C., dominated not only its Mesopotamian neighbours but the lands to the west as far as the Mediterranean and the Egyptian frontier. The Mediterranean Sea itself has witnessed the rise and fall of a succession of imperial cities. In the fifth century B.C. the Athenian Empire held sway not only over the Aegean Sea but over a large area of the Eastern Mediterranean and as far west as Sicily, while for three centuries Carthage – itself a colony of the Phoenician city-state of Tyre – controlled the Western Mediterranean until her rival, Rome, compelled her to relinquish all her overseas dominions after defeating her in the Second Punic War at the end of the third century B.C. During the Christian era the city of Venice was able to "hold the gorgeous East in fee" from Crusading times until the seventeenth century.

But of all the cities which have dominated the Mediterranean lands none has exercised such an abiding influence on them, and on others far removed from the Mediterranean, as Rome. Rome's swift rise to power made a deep impression on men's minds in antiquity. A Greek politician named Polybius, who was taken to Rome as a hostage in 167 B.C. and had the good fortune to win the friendship of Scipio Aemilianus, the leading Roman general of his day, wrote a historical work (still of exceptional value, in so far as it survives) in order to trace the steps by which the city of Rome, in a period of fifty-three years (221–168 B.C.), became mistress of the Mediterranean world – a thing unique in history.[1] Less accurate, but informative because of its vivid reflection of the idealized image of

1. Polybius, *History* i. 1. He then carried the story down to 146 B.C.

Rome current in the Near East towards 100 B.C., is the picture given in 1 Maccabees 8: 1–16, where we are told how Judas Maccabaeus, seeking what support he could find in his struggle against the Seleucids, sent an embassy to Rome:

Now Judas heard of the fame of the Romans, that they were . . . well-disposed toward all who made an alliance with them, and that they were very strong. Men told him of their wars and of the brave deeds which they were doing among the Gauls, how they had defeated them and forced them to pay tribute, and what they had done in the land of Spain to get control of the silver and gold mines there, and how they had gained control of the whole region by their planning and patience, even though the place was far distant from them. They also subdued the kings who came against them from the ends of the earth, until they crushed them and inflicted great disaster upon them; the rest paid them tribute every year. Philip,[2] and Perseus[3] king of the Macedonians, and the others who rose up against them, they crushed in battle and conquered. They also defeated Antiochus the Great, king of Asia,[4] who went to fight against them with a hundred and twenty elephants and with cavalry and chariots and a very large army. He was crushed by them; they took him alive and decreed that he and those who should reign after him should pay a heavy tribute and give hostages and surrender some of their best provinces, the country of India and Media and Lydia. These they took from him and gave to Eumenes the king [of Pergamum]. The Greeks planned to come and destroy them, but this became known to them, and they sent a general against the Greeks and attacked them. Many of them were wounded and fell, and the Romans took captive their wives and children; they plundered them, conquered the land, tore down their strongholds, and enslaved them to this day.[5] The remaining kingdoms and islands, as many as ever opposed them, they destroyed and enslaved; but with their friends and those who rely on them they have kept friendship. They have subdued kings far and near, and as many as have heard of their fame have feared them. Those whom they wish to help and to make kings, they make kings, and those whom they wish they depose; and they have been greatly exalted. Yet for all this not one of them has put on a crown or worn purple as a mark of pride, but they have built for themselves a senate chamber, and every day three hundred and twenty senators[6] constantly deliberate concerning the people, to govern them well. They trust one man each year to rule over them and to control all their land; they all heed the one man, and there is no envy or jealousy among them.

2. Philip V of Macedonia, defeated at the battle of Cynoscephalae in 197 B.C.
3. Perseus, defeated at the battle of Pydna in 168 B.C.
4. Antiochus III, Seleucid king, defeated at the battle of Magnesia in 190/189 B.C.
5. The reference to the crushing of the revolt of the Achaian League and devastation of Corinth in 146 B.C. shows that this account of Roman power, while ostensibly set in the period preceding Judas's death (160 B.C.), carries the story down well beyond that.
6. The nominal strength of the Roman senate in the second century B.C. was 300.

This account has many detailed inaccuracies, the most astonishing of which is the statement at the end that they entrust supreme power to one man each year: in fact, to prevent the concentration of power in one man's hands they elected two collegiate chief magistrates (consuls) year by year, each of whom had the right of veto over the other's proceedings. Nevertheless, it does give us a fair idea of what was thought of the Romans in Western Asia at the time; experience of their oppressiveness at close quarters gave currency to a much less favourable picture after two or three decades.[7]

## 2. From hill-settlements to world empire

Rome was originally a group of pastoral and agricultural hill-settlements in the Latin plain, on the left bank of the Tiber. At an early stage in her history she fell under Etruscan control, but after a generation or two succeeded in shaking off this yoke. The Etruscans retired to the right bank of the Tiber. Rome's career of world conquest began with her crossing of the Tiber to besiege and storm the Etruscan city of Veii (c. 400 B.C.). From that time on Rome became first the mistress of Latium and then of Italy. Intervention in a Sicilian quarrel in 264 B.C. brought her into conflict with the Carthaginians, who had substantial commercial interests in Sicily. The result was the two Punic Wars (264–241 and 218–202 B.C.), in the second of which Rome came within an ace of annihilation; but after the decisive defeat of Hannibal at Zama, in North Africa, she emerged as undisputed mistress of the Western Mediterranean.

Rome was to have no respite after her exhausting struggle against Hannibal and his forces: the Second Punic War was scarcely over when she found herself engaged in war with Macedonia, one of the states which inherited part of Alexander's empire. In 195 B.C. she restored to the city-states of Greece the freedom which they had lost to Philip, Alexander's father, nearly a century and a half before: this restored freedom, indeed, was strictly limited, as Rome constituted herself the protector of the liberated cities. But no other power could intervene in their affairs with impunity: when the Seleucid kingdom (another of the succession states to Alex-

7. This may be seen just before and after the Roman conquest of Judaea (63 B.C.) by the description of the *Kittim* in the Qumran commentary on Habakkuk (1QpHab 2, l. 4–6, l. 12) and reactions to their arrogance and impiety in the Psalms of Solomon (2: 20–32; 17: 8–15). The former passage may reflect the anti-Roman propaganda of Mithridates VI of Pontus, of which a sample is preserved in a letter of his (c. 69 B.C.) to Arsaces XII, king of Parthia (Sallust, *History*, fragment iv. 69. 1–23). See F. F. Bruce, *New Testament History* (London,[2] 1971), pp. 9–12, and "The Romans through Jewish Eyes" in *Mélanges offerts à M. Simon*, ed. M. Philonenko (Strasbourg, 1977).

ander's empire) attempted to do so in 192 B.C., it was not only repulsed but invaded by the Roman legionaries, and found itself incurably crippled and impoverished. Rome lost no opportunity of encouraging opposition to Seleucid interests, whether in Ptolemaic Egypt (yet another of the succession states) or among the Jewish insurgents led by Judas Maccabaeus and his brothers (from 168 B.C. onwards).

These moves led to Rome's increasing involvement in the Near East. In 133 B.C. the last king of Pergamum, an ally of Rome, died and bequeathed his territory (the western part of Asia Minor) to the Roman senate and people. The bequest was accepted, and the territory became the Roman province of Asia. Roman rule was not universally popular, and in 88 B.C. an anti-Roman rising was fomented in the province by Mithridates VI, king of Pontus (on the Black Sea coast of Asia Minor), who himself cherished imperial ambitions in that area. The result was a war between Rome and Pontus which dragged on for a quarter of a century; when, at the end of that period, Roman arms triumphed under the generalship of Pompey, Pompey was faced with the task of reconstructing the whole political order of Western Asia. He occupied Judaea in 63 B.C., having given Syria the status of a Roman province in the preceding year.

For thirty years and more after Pompey's settlement the Roman world was torn between rival aspirants to supreme power, but the naval victory of Actium (31 B.C.), which meant the downfall of Cleopatra, the last sovereign of Ptolemaic Egypt, with her Roman ally Antony, left Octavian, adopted son and political heir of Julius Caesar, master of the Roman world. With consummate statesmanship Octavian, who in 27 B.C. assumed the style Augustus, preserved the republican framework of the Roman state but concentrated the reality of power in his own hands. In Rome he was content with the title *princeps*, first citizen of the republic; but in the eastern provinces he and his successors were recognized for what they were in fact – the heirs to the dominion of Alexander and the dynasties among which his empire was partitioned – kings of kings, like the great oriental potentates of old.

Under the control of Rome, then – first of the original Rome and then, from the fourth century onwards, of the New Rome established at Constantinople – the peoples of the Near East continued to live until the Arab conquest of the seventh century.

# CHAPTER 2

# The Jews under Foreign Rule

## 1. From Cyrus to Vespasian

CYRUS, THE FOUNDER OF THE PERSIAN EMPIRE (559–529 B.C.), AND his successors were the most enlightened imperialists the ancient world had seen up to their day. They saw the wisdom of keeping their subject-nations contented. Instead of deporting them forcibly to distant regions in order to break their will or capacity to rebel, as the Assyrians and Babylonians had done, they allowed them to live in their homelands (unless they themselves preferred to live elsewhere). Instead of compelling them to worship the gods of the master-race, they encouraged them to practise their ancestral religion and even on occasion extended financial aid to this end. There is evidence for this policy in Egypt (which they conquered in 525 B.C.) and among the Greek settlements of Western Asia Minor as well as in their dealings with the exiles from Judaea whom they authorized to return to their native territory from which they had been uprooted by the Babylonians. There were two levels of administration of the province of Judaea under the Persians. The Persian king was represented by a governor, who might be a Jew himself (as Nehemiah was) or a non-Jew. The governor was responsible for safeguarding the imperial interests, like the maintenance of security and the collection of tribute. But the internal administration of Judaea was in the hands of the high priest – always a member of the family of Zadok. Judaea under the Persians comprised a limited area centred on Jerusalem; it was organized as a temple-state, and Jerusalem itself was given the status of a holy city.[1] There were other temple-states similarly constituted within the Persian Empire, and they preserved this constitution when the Persian supremacy was superseded by that of the Greeks and Macedonians after the conquests of Alexander the Great (336–323 B.C.). When Alexander's empire was broken up after his death, Judaea found itself subject first to the dynasty of the Ptolemies, ruling from Alexandria, and then (after 198 B.C.) to that of the Seleucids, ruling from Antioch in Syria. But Jerusalem and Judaea retained their sacral constitution, apart from intervals when attempts were made

1. See F. F. Bruce, *Israel and the Nations* (Exeter, ² 1969), pp. 97 ff.

26

to abolish or modify it, until the outbreak of the Jewish revolt against Rome in A.D. 66.

The most notable attempt to abolish the sacral constitution of Jerusalem and Judaea was made by the Seleucid king Antiochus IV (175–164 B.C.) who, largely for reasons of external security, tried to assimilate his Jewish subjects in culture and religion to the Hellenistic way of life followed throughout his dominions. Judaea lay on the frontier between his kingdom and Egypt, and this became a sensitive frontier after the Romans assumed the rôle of protectors of Egypt against Seleucid ambitions in 168 B.C. Antiochus's policy was ill-advised and ended in failure. The Jews, under Judas Maccabaeus and his brothers, put up a resistance which led to their regaining religious freedom in 164 B.C. and, twenty-two years later (thanks largely to civil strife within the Seleucid kingdom), to the gaining of political independence. For nearly eighty years Judaea was ruled by the native Hasmonaean dynasty of priest-kings.

When Judaea fell under Roman control in 63 B.C., the Hasmonaean kingship was abolished but the sanctity of Jerusalem was preserved. For a time the Romans preferred to control Judaea indirectly through Jewish rulers – in particular, through Herod the Great (37–4 B.C.), who violated its temple constitution more ruthlessly than did any Gentile overlord, with the exception of Antiochus IV. But when, in A.D. 6, Judaea was made a Roman province, it was given the same kind of two-tier administration as it had enjoyed under Persian and Graeco-Macedonian rule. The Roman Emperor appointed a provincial governor, called a prefect or procurator, who was responsible for maintaining peace and order and for ensuring the efficient collection of the "tribute to Caesar". But the internal affairs of the Jews in Judaea were administered by the high priest together with a council of seventy elders (the Sanhedrin) over which he presided *ex officio*. The high priest and his colleagues naturally recognized that supreme power was wielded by Rome, and made it their business to maintain reasonably good relations with the governor. This was no easy task at times, because of the inexperience or insensitivity of some of the governors. Yet, as a last resort, the high priest and his colleagues had channels of communication with Rome, so that they could go over the governor's head and lodge a complaint which might lead to his being severely reprimanded or even dismissed from office. One of the best examples of this interplay between the two seats of authority in the province is the action and reaction between the chief priests and Pontius Pilate in the gospel records of the trial of Jesus.

Despite the fact that their internal interests were in the hands of their own religious establishment, many of the Jews of Judaea found Roman rule irksome. For one thing, they had to endure double taxation: tribute to Caesar had to be paid over and above their temple dues (which included considerably more than the tithe, or ten per cent. income tax).[2] The chief priests and leading members of the Sanhedrin were wealthy, to a point where they had insufficient appreciation of the economic stress under which their poorer fellow-countrymen lived; they knew, moreover, that the continued enjoyment of their wealth depended on the maintenance of the existing order. Their consequent *modus vivendi* with the occupying power did nothing to endear them to the common people.

Some of the provinces of the empire assimilated Roman civilization so thoroughly that their inhabitants came to think of themselves as Romans, and their descendants to this day speak a language which has developed from "vulgar Latin".[3] The Jews of Judaea were perhaps the least assimilable of all Rome's subject-nations. This was due to their unique and exclusive religion, the practice of which was guaranteed to them by imperial decrees, as it had been safeguarded by earlier imperial overlords. Under these earlier Gentile rulers, it had never been suggested that the Jews' payment of tribute to them was in some way offensive to the God whom they worshipped. In so far as this payment of tribute to foreigners was given a religious significance, it tended to be interpreted as a token of Yahweh's displeasure with his people: if he allowed foreigners to rule over them, the payment of tribute to those foreigners was an act of submission to divine judgment. But when Judaea became a Roman province in A.D. 6 and its population incurred liability to pay tribute direct to the emperor, a new doctrine was voiced – that for the people of Israel, living in the holy land, to acknowledge a pagan ruler by paying him tribute was to be guilty of high treason against the God of their fathers, Israel's true king. The principal teacher of this new doctrine was Judas the Galilaean, who at that time led a rising against the Roman government of the new province.[4] The rising was put down, but the teaching lived on, and became a dominant feature of the policy of the Zealots. The party of the Zealots, which made no distinction between what we should call politics and religion, became active from about A.D. 44 onwards, and although it did not initiate the revolt against Rome of A.D. 66, it soon took over the leadership of the ensuing war.[5]

The insurgents continued throughout the war to hope against hope. They had taken up the struggle in vindication of the crown

2. Cf. F. C. Grant, *The Economic Background of the Gospels* (Oxford, 1926), pp. 87 ff.

3. The "Romance" languages of France, the Iberian Peninsula, Italy, parts of Switzerland, and Romania.

4. Josephus, *BJ* ii. 118; *Ant.* xviii. 4 ff.

5. Cf. M. Hengel, *Die Zeloten* (Leiden, 1961).

rights of Israel's God: he could not let them down. They relied upon an ancient oracle – perhaps a combination of oracles – which they understood to be due for fulfilment just then, according to which world dominion was to pass from the Gentiles into Jewish hands.[6] An initial victory over much superior Roman forces imbued them with the confidence that the successes of Judas Maccabaeus (who, with his associates, had been similarly activated by zeal for God) would be repeated in their experience. The internecine fighting throughout the empire, and in Rome itself, which marked the "year of the four emperors" (A.D. 69).[7] made them think that Gentile imperialism, embodied in the Roman state, was undergoing its death-throes. But in the event it was the Jewish commonwealth, in the form which it had taken since the return from the Babylonian exile six centuries before, that collapsed. The temple in Jerusalem was burned, the city was sacked and laid in ruins, its sacred status was abolished, the chief-priestly establishment was no more, the sacrificial order was at an end. The annual half-shekel which adult Jews throughout the world had hitherto paid for the maintenance of the temple, under the protection of the Roman authorities, had henceforth to be paid into a special fund – the *fiscus Iudaicus* – for the support of the temple of Jupiter on the Capitoline hill in Rome.

But even in Judaea the situation of the Jews might have been worse. Permission was obtained for the institution of a new Sanhedrin of scholars for the codification of religious law, and indeed Jewish religious life flourished all the better for the disappearance of the temple and its ritual.

## 2. *The Jews of the dispersion*

Then as now, however, there were many more Jews living outside Judaea than within its frontiers, and (apart from the business of the *fiscus Iudaicus* after A.D. 70) those Jews of the dispersion suffered no disabilities in relation to Roman law as a result of the war. There were anti-Jewish riots and pogroms in a number of cities in Syria and Egypt, but that was another matter. In fact, a succession of edicts issued by the highest authorities had secured to Jews throughout the Roman Empire quite exceptional privileges, and these were not rescinded.

6. Probably a combination of the "sceptre" oracles of Genesis 49: 10 and Numbers 24: 17 chronologically interpreted in the light of the seventy heptads outlined in Daniel 9: 24–27. See Josephus, *BJ* vi. 312 f.; Tacitus, *History*, v. 13; Suetonius, *Vespasian*, 4.

7. A.D. 69 witnessed the fall of Nero's successor Galba, the rise and fall of Otho and Vitellius, and the accession of Vespasian.

The history of the Jewish dispersion can be traced back to the beginning of the sixth century B.C. At that time we have ample evidence of Jewish settlements in Egypt[8] and a hint of others in Asia Minor as far west as Sardis, capital of the kingdom of Lydia (the Sepharad of Obadiah 20). A large number of the exiles in Babylonia settled in their new home and did not avail themselves of permission to return to Judaea. Under Persian rule they were to be found in all the territories of the Persian Empire, even on the shore of the Caspian Sea;[9] and Alexander's conquests enabled them to spread even farther afield. There was a Jewish population in Alexandria from its foundation in 331 B.C.; by the first century A.D. Jews formed a majority in two out of the city's five wards. About 300 B.C. the first Ptolemy settled a body of Jews in Cyrenaica to help ensure the loyalty of that province.[11] A century later, the Seleucid king Antiochus III, with a similar purpose, moved many Jews into Phrygia and Lydia, and after he wrested Judaea and Coelesyria from the Ptolemies he encouraged Jewish settlement in Antioch, his capital, and other cities of his kingdom.[12] In Rome itself there was a Jewish colony even before the incorporation of Judaea into the empire in 63 B.C., and it was greatly augmented in the years that followed. It is estimated that by the beginning of the first century A.D. there were between 40,000 and 60,000 Jews in Rome – about as many, probably, as in Jerusalem itself.[14] The discovery and examination of six Jewish catacombs in Rome has greatly increased our knowledge of Jewish life in the city. The Jews of Rome appear to have been concentrated on the right bank of the Tiber (Trastevere), where most of the eleven synagogues attested by inscriptions were probably situated.[15]

The extent of the Jewish dispersion in the apostolic age is indicated in Luke's catalogue of the "Jews, devout men" who were present in Jerusalem for the feast of Pentecost in A.D. 30, from the

---

8. Cf. Jeremiah 44: 1; a Jewish community settled by Psammetichus II (594–588 B.C.) to guard his southern frontier at Syene (Aswan) and Elephantine survived there till c. 400 B.C. and has left a substantial Aramaic archive; cf. A. E. Cowley, *Aramaic Papyri of the Fifth Century B.C.* (Oxford, 1923); E. G. Kraeling, *The Brooklyn Museum Aramaic Papyri* (Oxford, 1953).

9. Jerome's edition of Eusebius's *Chronicle* preserves the tradition of a settlement of Jews in Hyrcania by Artaxerxes III of Persia (359–338 B.C.).

10. Philo, *Flaccus*, 55; cf. Josephus, *BJ* ii. 495.

11. Josephus, *Apion*, ii. 44.

12. Josephus, *Ant.* xii. 149 ff. Much earlier, the founder of the Seleucid dynasty, Seleucus I (312–281 B.C.), conferred citizen rights on all Jews resident in the cities which he founded, especially in Antioch (Josephus, *Ant.* xii. 119).

13. Cf. H. J. Leon, *The Jews of Ancient Rome* (Philadelphia, 1960), pp. 135 f.

14. Cf. J. Jeremias, *Jerusalem in the Time of Jesus*, E.T. (London, 1969), p. 83; "Die Einwohnerzahl Jerusalems zur Zeit Jesu", *ZDPV* 66 (1943), pp. 24–31.

15. Cf. H. J. Leon, *The Jews of Ancient Rome*, pp. 46 ff. See p. 380 below.

"Parthians and Medes and Elamites and residents of Mesopotamia" in the east to the "visitors from Rome, both Jews and proselytes" in the west (Acts 2: 5–11).[16]

16. Cf. B. M. Metzger, "Ancient Astrological Geography and Acts 2: 9–11", in *Apostolic History and the Gospel*, ed. W. W. Gasque and R. P. Martin (Exeter, 1970), pp. 123 ff. For a comprehensive account, see M. Grant, *The Jews in the Roman World* (London, 1973).

# CHAPTER 3

# "Of No Mean City"

## 1. The province of Cilicia

WHEN PAUL WAS ARRESTED DURING HIS LAST VISIT TO Jerusalem (A.D. 57) and brought before the military tribune who commanded the auxiliary cohort in the Antonia fortress, the tribune imagined that he was an Egyptian agitator who had recently attempted some kind of coup in the neighbourhood of the city. Realizing his error when he heard Paul speaking idiomatic Greek, he asked who he was and received the reply, "I am a Jew, from Tarsus in Cilicia, a citizen of no mean city" (Acts 21: 39).

Cilicia, the territory bordering the Mediterranean in South-East Asia Minor, comprised two quite different areas. There was the fertile plain in the east called Cilicia Pedias, between the Taurus range and the sea; the trade route from Syria to Asia Minor ran through it, crossing Mount Amanus by the Syrian Gates and crossing the Taurus range by the Cilician Gates into Central Asia Minor. To the west of that lay the rugged coastland of Cilicia Tracheia (Rough Cilicia), where the Taurus range comes down to the sea.

In Hittite records the Cilician territory is called Kizzuwatna; it was linked by treaty to the Hittite Empire and was later incorporated in it until the downfall of that empire *c.* 1200 B.C. In the *Iliad* the Cilicians are mentioned as allies of the Trojans: Hector's wife Andromache was a Cilician princess.[1] In the ninth century B.C. Cilicia fell under the control of the Assyrians, who called it Hilakku (probably the "Helech" of Ezekiel 27: 11). From the early sixth century B.C. Cilicia was ruled by a succession of native kings bearing the dynastic title Syennesis; they continued to rule under the overlordship of the Persian Empire until *c.* 400 B.C., when they were replaced by satraps.[2] In 333 B.C. Cilicia became part of the empire of Alexander, who won his decisive battle of Issus there in

---

1. Homer, *Iliad* vi. 397, 415. At that time (*c.* 1200 B.C.) the Cilicians apparently resided in N.W. Asia Minor; the extension of their name to the historical Cilicia resulted from their eastward penetration of the peninsula along with other Indo-European speaking groups.

2. The satraps minted silver staters with the divine title *Ba'al Tarz* ("lord of Tarsus") on the obverse.

that year.[3] After his death it was controlled by the Seleucids, although for a time the possession of part of the coast of Cilicia Tracheia was contested by the Ptolemies. When the Romans forced Antiochus III to give up most of his territory in Asia Minor (188 B.C.), Eastern Cilicia remained part of the Seleucid Empire for several decades more, but the breakdown of Seleucid control in the second half of the second century B.C. and the consequent exploitation of Cilicia Tracheia as a base for robbers and pirates led the Romans to take an increasingly direct part in the concerns of that area. Part of Western Cilicia became a Roman province in 102 B.C., and after Pompey's brilliant victory over the pirates in 67 B.C. the whole of Cilicia was reduced to provincial status, with Tarsus as its capital. From about 25 B.C. Eastern Cilicia (including Tarsus) was united administratively with Syria, which had become a Roman province under Pompey in 64 B.C. Western Cilicia was allotted to a succession of client kings. When the last of these kings abdicated in A.D. 72, Eastern Cilicia was detached from Syria and united with Western Cilicia to form the province of Cilicia. For the whole of Paul's lifetime, however, the area of Cilicia in which his native city stood was part of the united province of Syria-Cilicia, a situation implied in Paul's statement that some three years after his conversion, following a brief visit to Jerusalem, he "went into the regions of Syria and Cilicia" (Galatians 1: 21).

## 2. The city of Tarsus

Tarsus, the principal city of the fertile plain of East Cilicia, stood on the river Cydnus, about ten miles from its mouth, and some thirty miles south of the Cilician Gates (on the road between the modern towns of Mersin and Adana). It was a fortified city and important trade entrepôt before 2000 B.C. In the second millennium B.C. it is mentioned in Hittite records as a leading city of Kizzuwatna. It was destroyed during the incursions of the Sea Peoples c. 1200 B.C. and some time later was settled anew by Greeks. It was captured by the Assyrian king Shalmaneser III in 833 B.C. and again by Sennacherib in 698 B.C. Under the Persians it was the capital of the client kingdom, and later of the satrapy, of Cilicia. It began to issue its own coinage in the fifth century B.C. In 401 B.C. Cyrus the Younger, with the Ten Thousand, spent twenty days in the city on his way east to claim the Persian crown, and exchanged gifts with King Syennesis, whose palace was in Tarsus.[4]

Alexander the Great saved the city from being fired by the retreating Persians in 333 B.C. Under his Seleucid successors it

---

3. It was this victory over Persian forces that opened up the road to Syria before him.

4. Xenophon, *Anabasis*, i. 2. 23.

assumed the name of Antioch-on-the-Cydnus, a name which appears on its new coin issue in the reign of Antiochus IV (from 171 B.C. onwards). This new coin issue seems to coincide with a reorganization of the city's constitution, which conferred on it a greater degree of municipal autonomy.[5] In 83 B.C. it fell into the power of Tigranes I, king of Armenia, the ally and son-in-law of Mithridates VI, but passed into Roman hands as a result of Pompey's victories, and became the capital of the province of Cilicia, while it retained its autonomy as a free city (67 B.C.). Cicero took up residence in the city during his proconsulship of Cilicia in 51–50 B.C. When Julius Caesar visited the city in 47 B.C. it adopted the name Iuliopolis in his honour. After Caesar's death and the defeat of the anti-Caesarian party at Philippi in 42 B.C., Tarsus enjoyed the favour of Antony, who controlled Rome's eastern provinces. It was there in 41 B.C. that the celebrated meeting between Antony and Cleopatra took place, when she was rowed up the Cydnus in the guise of Aphrodite:

> From the barge
> A strange invisible perfume hits the sense
> Of the adjacent wharfs. The city cast
> Her people out upon her; and Antony,
> Enthroned i' the market-place, did sit alone,
> Whistling to the air; which, but for vacancy,
> Had gone to gaze on Cleopatra too,
> And made a gap in nature.[6]

When Augustus ruled the whole Roman world, Tarsus enjoyed further privileges, including exemption from imperial taxation. In the later part of Antony's domination of the Near East, and for some years after, Tarsus had suffered under the maladministration of a nominee of his named Boethus. Augustus entrusted the administration of the city to one of its most illustrious sons, Athenodorus the Stoic, who had been his own tutor. When Athenodorus returned to Tarsus, he expelled Boethus and his associates, and reformed the civic administration. It may have been at this time that a property qualification of 500 drachmae was fixed for admission to the roll of citizens.[7] Athenodorus and his successor, Nestor the Academic (tutor of Marcellus, the nephew of Augustus), also exercised great cultural influence in Tarsus.

According to the geographer Strabo, writing probably in the early years of the first century A.D., the people of Tarsus were avid in the pursuit of culture. They applied themselves to the study of

5. A sequel to the revolt mentioned in 2 Maccabees 4:30.
6. Shakespeare, *Antony and Cleopatra*, Act 2, Scene 2 (his description is based on Plutarch, *Life of Antony*, 26).
7. Dio Chrysostom, *Oration* 34. 23.

philosophy, the liberal arts and "the whole round of learning in general" – the whole "encyclopaedia" – so much so that Tarsus in this respect at least surpassed even Athens and Alexandria, whose schools were frequented more by visitors than by their own citizens. Tarsus, in short, was what we might call a university city. Yet people did not come from other places to study in its schools: the students of Tarsus were natives of the city, who frequently left it to complete their education elsewhere and rarely returned to it.[8] Athenodorus was one of those who left it, but in later years he did return.

A less flattering picture of Tarsus than Strabo's is given by Philostratus in his *Life of Apollonius* (the Neopythagorean sage). According to Philostratus, Apollonius, who was born early in the Christian era at Tyana in Cappodocia, went to Tarsus at the age of fourteen to study under the rhetorician Euthydemus. He was much attached to his teacher, but was dismayed to find the general atmosphere of Tarsus not at all conducive to study, for the people were addicted to luxury, levity and insolence, and "paid more attention to their fine linen than the Athenians paid to wisdom". So he left Tarsus for a more congenial environment.[9]

This account should not be taken too seriously, however; in this work Philostratus was a romancer rather than a serious biographer and, writing about A.D. 200, he was probably influenced by Dio Chrysostom, who in two orations delivered early in the second century A.D. had castigated the Tarsians for their lack of moral earnestness.[10]

The prosperity of Tarsus was based on the fertile plain in which it stood. Linen woven in Tarsus from the flax which grew in the plain is repeatedly mentioned by ancient authors (like Philostratus). Reference is made also by Roman writers to a local material called *cilicium*, woven from goat's hair, from which were made coverings designed to give protection against cold and wet.

When Paul claimed to be "a citizen of no mean city", he plainly had good cause to describe Tarsus thus. If his words mean (as they appear to do) that his name appeared on the roll of citizens of Tarsus, this would indicate that he was born into a family which possessed the citizenship. The property qualification for citizenship, laid down perhaps by Athenodorus, has been mentioned already. Dio Chrysostom implies that by organizing itself thus as a timocracy, Tarsus debarred linen-workers and other tradespeople from citizenship, but there seems to be no reason why some tradespeople might not have qualified for it on the strength of

8. Strabo, *Geography* xiv. 5. 12 ff. (673 ff.).
9. Philostratus, *Life of Apollonius*, i. 7; cf. vi. 34.
10. Dio Chrysostom, *Orations* 33; 34.

their property. Paul is said by Luke to have been a "tent-maker" (*skēnopoios*), by which we may understand that he was engaged in the manufacture of wares from the local *cilicium*, but he appears to have belonged to a well-to-do family.

Questions about his Tarsian citizenship have arisen more from his being a Jew than from his being a tent-maker. The citizen body, as in other cities of the Greek type, was presumably organized in tribes or *phylai*. Since the common life of the tribe or *phylē* involved religious ceremonies which would have been offensive to Jews, it has been suggested that the Jewish citizens of Tarsus were enrolled in a tribe of their own, solemnized by ceremonies of the Jewish religion. This may indeed have been so, although we have no explicit evidence to this effect. In many Gentile cities Jewish settlers lived as resident aliens, but in some, such as Alexandria, Cyrene, Syrian Antioch, Ephesus and Sardis, they enjoyed citizen rights, and they could well have done so as a distinct group in Tarsus. [11]

11. Cf. E. Schürer, *s.v.* "Diaspora", *HDB* v, p. 105; W. M. Ramsay, *The Cities of St. Paul* (London, 1907), pp. 176 ff.; H. J. Cadbury, *The Book of Acts in History* (New York, 1955), pp. 32 ff.; A. D. Nock, "*Isopoliteia* and the Jews", *Essays on Religion and the Ancient World* (Oxford, 1972), pp. 960 ff. With Paul's status in Tarsus may be compared that of "Marcus Aurelius Alexander, also called Asaph, of the people of the Jews" at Hierapolis in Phrygia, where his epitaph (in Greek) has survived from the second century A.D. He was apparently a citizen of Hierapolis, and he was self-evidently a Roman citizen (cf. *Corpus Inscriptionum Iudaicarum*, ed. J.-B. Frey, iii [Rome, 1952], no. 776).

# CHAPTER 4

# "This Man is a Roman Citizen"

## 1. Citizen rights

I N TARSUS, THEN, PROBABLY IN THE FIRST DECADE OF THE CHRISTIAN era, Paul was born. The privilege of Tarsian birth and civic status was, however, outweighed by the fact that he was born a Roman citizen.

The same military tribune in Jerusalem to whom Paul introduced himself as a Jew of Tarsus was surprised to be informed later that Paul was also a Roman citizen. "Tell me", he said to Paul, "are you a Roman citizen?" When Paul said "Yes", the tribune answered, "I bought this citizenship for a large sum".[1] "But I", said Paul, "was *born* a citizen" (Acts 22: 27 f.).

If he was born a Roman citizen, his father must have been a Roman citizen before him. Roman citizenship was originally confined to freeborn natives of the city of Rome, but as Roman control of Italy and the Mediterranean lands extended, the citizenship was conferred on a number of other people who were not Roman by birth, including certain select provincials.[2]

But how did a Jewish family of Tarsus acquire this exceptional distinction? The members of this family, by all accounts, were not assimilationist Jews who compromised with Gentile ways: this much is implied by Paul's claim to be "a Hebrew born of Hebrews" (Philippians 3: 5). We just do not know how it obtained Roman citizenship. Cilicia fell within the sphere of command of more than one Roman general in the first century B.C. – Pompey and Antony, for example – and the grant of citizenship to approved individuals was included in the overall authority (*imperium*) conferred on those generals by law. Presumably Paul's father, grandfather or even great-grandfather had rendered some outstanding service to the Roman cause. It has been suggested, for example, that a firm of tent-makers could have been very useful to a fighting proconsul.[3]

1. The tribune, Claudius Lysias, probably acquired his citizenship during the principate of Claudius (A.D. 41–54) when, according to Dio Cassius (*History* lx. 17. 5 f.), citizenship was open to purchase. Technically the citizenship itself was not for sale; the money went to the various intermediaries who could arrange for a man's name to be put on the list of candidates for enfranchisement. See p. 351.
2. See A. N. Sherwin-White, *The Roman Citizenship* (Oxford,[2] 1973).
3. E.g. by Sir William Calder in a letter to the author (February 18, 1953).

But no certain evidence is available. One thing is certain, however: among the citizens and other residents of Tarsus the few Roman citizens, whether Greeks or Jews by birth, would constitute a social élite.

As a Roman citizen, Paul had three names – forename (*praenomen*), family name (*nomen gentile*) and additional name (*cognomen*). Of these we know only his *cognomen*, Paullus. If we knew his *nomen gentile*, we might have some clue to the circumstances of the family's acquisition of the citizenship, since new citizens commonly assumed their patrons' family name – but we are given no hint of it. His *cognomen* Paullus may have been chosen because of its assonance with his Jewish name Saul (Heb. *Sha'ul*), which in the Greek New Testament is sometimes spelt *Saoul* but more frequently *Saulos*, the latter form rhyming with Greek *Paulos*.

If the circumstances in which Paul's family acquired Roman citizenship are obscure, many other questions relating to his citizenship are hardly less so. On more than one occasion, for example – at Philippi and, some years later, at Jerusalem – he appealed to his rights as a Roman citizen. The former occasion was when he protested at having been summarily beaten with rods by the lictors who attended the chief magistrates of Philippi (a Roman colony), without being given a proper trial (Acts 16: 37).[4] On the latter occasion he invoked his rights in order to be spared a scourging (much more murderous than a beating with rods) to which the military tribune already referred to was about to have him subjected in an effort to discover why his presence and movements in the temple precincts had provoked a riotous outburst among the Jerusalem populace.[5] Paul voiced his protest to the centurion in charge of the men detailed to carry out the scourging, and the centurion in alarm went to the military tribune: "What are you about to do?" he said. "This man is a Roman citizen" (Acts 22: 26). Hence the interchange between the tribune and Paul quoted at the beginning of this chapter.

Wherever he went throughout the Roman Empire, a Roman citizen was entitled to all the rights and privileges which Roman law provided, in addition to being liable to all the civic duties which Roman law imposed. A citizen's rights and privileges were laid down in a long succession of enactments – most recently the Julian Law on the public use of force (*lex Iulia de ui publica*)[6] – going back traditionally to the Valerian Law (*lex Valeria*) passed at the incep-

4. See p. 221.
5. See p. 351.
6. Since this was a Julian law, it was sponsored either by Julius Caesar or by his adopted son Octavian (Augustus). A. H. M. Jones gives reasons for dating it in the principate of Augustus, after 23 B.C. (*Studies in Roman Government and Law* [Oxford, 1960], pp. 97 f.; cf. A. N. Sherwin-White, *Roman Society and Roman Law in the New Testament* [Oxford, 1963], pp. 57 f.). See p. 363.

tion of the Republic (509 B.C.). These rights and privileges included a fair public trial for a citizen accused of any crime, exemption from certain ignominious forms of punishment, and protection against summary execution. To none of these privileges could a non-citizen subject of Rome lay legal claim.

## 2. Citizen registration

But when a man claimed his citizen rights – when he said *ciuis Romanus sum* ("I am a Roman citizen"), or its equivalent in Greek – how did he prove his claim? In the absence of any provision for verification on the spot, it must have been tempting for a man in a tight corner to make the claim even when he had no title to it, and hope to get away with it. Certainly it was a capital offence to claim falsely to be a Roman citizen, but how was the official before whom the claim was made to know whether the claim was true or not?

A new citizen might have a duly witnessed copy of his certificate of citizenship; auxiliary soldiers received such a document when they were enfranchised, and civilians may have been given something of the same sort.[7] But Paul was not a new citizen. He might, however, produce a diptych, a pair of folding tablets, containing a certified copy of his birth registration. Each legitimately born child of a Roman citizen had to be registered within (it appears) thirty days of his birth. If he lived in the provinces, his father, or some duly appointed agent, made a declaration (*professio*) before the provincial governor (*praeses prouinciae*) at the public record-office (*tabularium publicum*). In the course of his *professio* the father or his agent declared that the child was a Roman citizen; the *professio* was entered in the register of declarations (*album professionum*), and the father or agent would receive a copy, properly certified by witnesses. This certificate recorded the *professio* in the third person, in indirect speech, and it would include the words: *ciuem Romanum esse professus est* ("he [the father or agent] declared him [the child] to be a Roman citizen"). It may have been customary for a Roman citizen who was constantly on the move to carry this certificate around with him.[8] If so, we can envisage Paul as producing it when he had to claim his citizen rights. But could another copy have been readily procured if the original one was lost? If Paul carried his around, the chances of his losing it were considerable – for instance, on the occasion when he spent a night and a day adrift at sea (2 Corinthians 11: 25). On the other hand it may have been more usual to keep these certificates in the family

7. Cf. Sherwin-White, *Roman Society* . . . , pp. 146 f.
8. Cf. F. Schulz, "Roman Registers of Births and Birth-Certificates", *JRS* 32 (1942), pp. 78 ff.; 33 (1943), pp. 55 ff.

archives; we cannot be sure.[9] There is a further point to consider: this registration of Roman citizens at birth was apparently enacted by two fairly recent laws – the *lex Aelia Sentia* of A.D. 4 and the *lex Papia Poppaea* of A.D. 9. If Paul was born even a year or two before the earlier of these enactments, would he necessarily have been registered in this way? The fact that such questions can be asked but not answered emphasizes how limited our knowledge is.

Paul's most momentous invoking of his privileges as a Roman citizen came at a late stage of his career, when he found himself on trial before the procurator of Judaea and "appealed to Caesar" – i.e. appealed to have his case transferred from the provincial court to the supreme tribunal in Rome (Acts 25: 10 f.). The details and implications of this appeal will engage our attention in due course.[10]

9. Cf. Sherwin-White, *Roman Society* . . . , p. 149.
10. See pp. 363f.

# CHAPTER 5

# "A Hebrew Born of Hebrews"

## 1. Paul's Jewish heritage

MORE IMPORTANT BY FAR IN PAUL'S OWN EYES THAN HIS Tarsian birthplace and his Roman citizenship, and more important by far for our understanding of him, was his Jewish heritage. When, from a Christian perspective, he looks back on the natural advantages in which at one time he had taken pride, he begins: "circumcised the eighth day, of the people of Israel, of the tribe of Benjamin, a Hebrew born of Hebrews; as to the law a Pharisee . . ." (Philippians 3: 6).

Here, to the statement that he came "of the people of Israel" – i.e. that he was a Jew by birth – he adds further details indicating more particularly what kind of Jew he was.

First, he belonged to the tribe of Benjamin (a claim repeated in Romans 11: 1). The tribal territory of Benjamin originally lay immediately to the north of the much larger area of Judah: Jerusalem, although formally allocated to Benjamin, actually formed an enclave between the two. When the united monarchy was disrupted after Solomon's death, Benjamin was drawn by the gravitational pull of Judah and Jerusalem into the southern kingdom. The people of Benjamin naturally tended to lose their tribal identity, but some at least did not allow it to be obliterated, and even after the return from exile there were re-settlements both in Jerusalem and in the adjacent Judaean territory of people who continued to be known distinctively as "the children of Benjamin" (Nehemiah 11: 7–9, 31–36). It was probably from some of these that Paul's family traced its descent.

His parents' choice of Saul as his Jewish name may be associated with their tribal connexion. The most outstanding Benjaminite in Hebrew history was Saul, the first king of Israel. If this consideration weighed with Paul's parents, it is possible to recognize an "undesigned coincidence" [1] in the fact that it is only from Acts that we know that his Jewish name was Saul, while it is only from his letters that we know that he belonged to the tribe of Benjamin. Early Christian writers loved to trace in Paul's activity as a persecutor

1. The expression is derived from J. J. Blunt's *Undesigned Coincidences in the Writings of the Old and New Testaments* (London, 1847).

41

of the infant church the fulfilment of words in the patriarch Jacob's blessing of his sons: "Benjamin is a ravenous wolf . . ." (Genesis 49: 27)[2] – but this ingenious fancy has nothing to do with sober exegesis.

In the second place, he describes himself as "a Hebrew born of Hebrews". In Paul's writings, as certainly in Luke's, "Hebrew" is probably a more specialized term than "Israelite" or "Jew". On another occasion, in a reference to visitors to Corinth who tried to undermine his position in the eyes of his converts there, he says, "Are they Hebrews? So am I" – and the context suggests that "Hebrews" has a more restricted sense than "Israelites" or "descendants of Abraham" (2 Corinthians 11: 25). In Acts 6: 1 "Hebrews" is used in contradistinction to "Hellenists", although both Hebrews and Hellenists were Jews (in this instance, Jewish disciples of Jesus, members of the primitive Jerusalem church). The distinction was probably linguistic and cultural: the Hebrews, in that case, attended synagogues where the service was conducted in Hebrew and used Aramaic as their normal mode of speech, while the Hellenists spoke Greek and attended synagogues where the scriptures were read and the prayers recited in that language. Many of the Hellenists in Jerusalem would have roots in the lands of the dispersion, like the Cyrenians, Alexandrians, and people from Cilicia and Asia who attended the synagogue mentioned in Acts 6: 9.[3] In the dispersion throughout the Graeco-Roman world, on the other hand, the Hellenists would be the majority of resident Jews while the Hebrews would be recent immigrants from Palestine or members of families which made a special point of preserving their Palestinian ways. We know from inscriptions in Rome and Corinth that each of these cities contained a "synagogue of (the) Hebrews":[4] such a designation may point to a meeting-place for Palestinian (and probably Aramaic-speaking) Jews, over against others used by Greek-speaking Jews. Paul's contemporary, Philo of Alexandria, himself a Hellenistic Jew, employs the word "Hebrews" to denote those who speak Hebrew [5] (and in Jewish Greek literature of the first century A.D., including the New Testament writings, "Hebrew" in a linguistic sense is broad enough to embrace Aramaic).

A Jew born in a Greek-speaking city like Tarsus would naturally be expected to be a Hellenist. Paul might be called a Hellenist in that Greek was manifestly no foreign language to him, but the

2. E.g. Hippolytus, *On the Blessing of Jacob*, at Genesis 49: 27.
3. It is not certain whether the reference here is to one or more synagogues, but more probably it is to one, attended by Jewish "freedmen" from the places mentioned. See p. 67.
4. *CIG* iv. 9909 (Rome); B. Powell, "Greek Inscriptions from Corinth", *AJA* series 2, 7 (1903), pp. 60 f., no. 40 (Corinth).

designation on which he insists is not Hellenist but Hebrew. Moreover, this insistence is not based on his upbringing and education in Jerusalem: the phrase "a Hebrew born of Hebrews" indicates that his parents were Hebrews before him. It is difficult to know how much credence to give to Jerome's statement that Paul's family came originally from Gischala in Galilee.[6] According to the record of Acts, he could address a Jerusalem audience in Aramaic (Acts 21: 40; 22: 2) and from the fact that the heavenly voice on the Damascus road addressed him in Aramaic – "in the Hebrew language" (Acts 26: 14) – it is a fair inference that this was his mother tongue.

It appears, then, that while Paul was born into a Jewish family which enjoyed citizen rights in a Greek-speaking city, Aramaic and not Greek was the language spoken in the home and perhaps also in the synagogue which they attended. Unlike many Jews resident in Anatolia, this family was strictly observant of the Jewish way of life and maintained its links with the home country. Paul would have been given little opportunity of imbibing the culture of Tarsus during his boyhood: indeed, his parents made sure of an orthodox upbringing for him by arranging for him to spend his formative years in Jerusalem.

According to the most probable punctuation of Acts 22: 3, the exordium of his Aramaic address to a crowd of hostile Jews in the outer court of the Jerusalem temple, he was (a) "a Jew, born at Tarsus in Cilicia", but (b) "brought up in this city" (Jerusalem) and (c) "educated at the feet of Gamaliel according to the strict manner of the law of our fathers, being zealous for God . . .".[7] The last part of this account is in essential agreement with his more general statement in Galatians 1: 14: "I advanced in Judaism beyond many of my own age among my people, so extremely zealous was I for the traditions of our fathers". He would have entered the school of Gamaliel at some point in his 'teens, but his parents saw to it that even his earlier boyhood was spent under wholesome influences in Jerusalem.

Thirdly, by his own account, Paul was "as to the law a Pharisee". This account is consistent with his statement reported in Acts 22: 3 that he was "educated at the feet of Gamaliel", who was the leading Pharisee of his day, and with his declaration before the younger Agrippa: "according to the strictest party of our religion I

5. Philo, On Dreams, ii. 250; Abraham, 28.
6. Jerome, De uiris illustribus, 5.
7. This is implied by the punctuation of Acts 22: 3 in the Nestle-Aland Novum Testamentum Graece (Stuttgart, [25]1963) and in the editions of the Greek New Testament published by the British and Foreign Bible Society (London, [2]1958) and the United Bible Societies (London and New York, [3]1976). See W. C. van Unnik, Tarsus or Jerusalem: The City of Paul's Youth, E. T. (London, 1962).

have lived as a Pharisee" (Acts 26: 5). Even more emphatic is his claim before the Sanhedrin to be "a Pharisee, a son of Pharisees" (Acts 23: 6). The natural sense of this is that his father or remoter ancestors were associated with the Pharisees; it is just possible, thought less probable, that "a son of Pharisees" means "a pupil of Pharisees".

## 2. *The Pharisees*

Who, then, were the Pharisees? They first appear by name about the middle of the second century B.C. In his account of the governorship of Jonathan (160–143 B.C.), brother and successor to Judas Maccabaeus, Josephus says that about this time there were three schools of thought among the Jews, the Pharisees, Sadducees and Essenes, and that while the Essenes were strict predestinarians and the Sadducees insisted that all things happened in accordance with men's free will, the Pharisees occupied a middle position in which room was afforded for both divine predestination and human choice.[8] These in fact were probably not the most important points in which the three groups differed one from another, but Josephus was prone to speak of Jewish religious parties as if they were Greek philosophical schools, and drew attention to those features in which he thought Greek and Roman readers would be interested.

Later on he says that Jonathan's nephew, John Hyrcanus, who ruled Judaea for about thirty years (134–104 B.C.), was at first a disciple of the Pharisees, but that he took offence at the blunt outspokenness of one of their number and broke with them, allying himself instead with their rivals, the Sadducees.[9] The Pharisees thus formed a kind of opposition party for several decades, and suffered harsh repression, especially at the hands of Alexander Jannaeus (103–76 B.C.).[10]

Josephus does not trace the spiritual ancestry of the Pharisees, but it is very probable that they arose within the ranks of the *ḥᵃsîdîm* or "godly people", who are referred to in the books of Maccabees as "Hasidaeans" (1 Maccabees 2: 42; 7: 14; 2 Maccabees 14: 6). The origin of these Hasidaeans is probably to be sought among the godly people in Judaea who, some decades after the return from exile, banded themselves together in order to encourage one another in the study and practice of the sacred law in the midst of what they saw as moral and religious declension. In the book of Malachi we are told that "those who feared Yahweh spoke to one another; Yahweh heeded and heard them, and a book of remembrance was

8. Josephus, *Ant.* xiii. 171 f.
9. Josephus, *Ant.* xiii. 288–296.
10. Josephus, *BJ* i. 88 ff.; *Ant.* xiii. 372 ff.; TB *Soṭah* 47a; *Qiddušîn* 66a; 4QpNah frag. 4, col. 1, ll. 1 ff.

written before him of those who feared Yahweh and thought on his name. 'They shall be mine', says Yahweh of hosts, 'my special possession on the day when I act, and I will spare them as a man spares his son who serves him' " (Malachi 3: 16 f.). And those whose names were entered in the book of remembrance would not only be spared on that coming day but would be the executors of his judgment on the ungodly: "for you who fear my name the sun of righteousness shall rise, with healing in its wings. . . . And you shall tread down the wicked, for they will be ashes under the soles of your feet, on the day when I act, says Yahweh of hosts" (Malachi 4: 3).

These people's passionate devotion to the law of their God is well illustrated in Psalm 119, the composition of one who has endured hardship and persecution for his loyalty to the divine "testimonies", but continues to find them a light to his path and sweeter than honey to his taste. They deplored the inroads of Hellenistic ways into Jewish life under the Ptolemies and Seleucids, and were despised as antiquated spoil-sports by those of the younger generation, even within the priestly families, who ardently welcomed the new fashion. But when Hellenism showed its unacceptable face, in the action of Antiochus Epiphanes which bade fair to extinguish Jewish religious and national identity, it was the Hasidaeans who showed themselves the truest patriots. Some of them offered passive resistance to the Seleucid forces, and won the crown of martyrdom. Others, and these perhaps the majority, made common cause with the Hasmonaean family – Judas Maccabaeus and his brothers – and their followers when they raised the standard of revolt and initiated guerrilla warfare against the Seleucids.

The guerrilla warfare was more successful than could have been expected. The king and his counsellors realized that their Judaean policy had been ill-advised, and by the end of 164 B.C. they reversed it, permitting the Jews once more to practise their ancestral religion and restoring the temple in Jerusalem to the worship of the God of Israel. Many of the Hasidaeans were disposed to be content with this, since the free practice of their religion was the object of their resistance. They did not immediately break off their alliance with the Hasmonaeans, but they no longer collaborated so enthusiastically in the fight for political independence, especially as this fight increasingly involved the aggrandisement of the Hasmonaean power. When Jonathan accepted the high-priesthood in 152 B.C. by the gift of a pretender to the Seleucid throne, one body of Hasidaeans – that which developed into the community of Qumran – was so outraged by this usurpation of the ancestral dignity of the house of Zadok that it not only refused to acknowledge him as high priest but refused to worship in the temple which was polluted by the illegitimate action of Jonathan himself and his heirs and successors.[11]

When at last political independence was gained, the high-priesthood was confirmed to the Hasmonaean family by the decree of a popular assembly.[12] But many of the Hasidaeans who could not go so far as the intransigent minority which opted out of public life because of its objection to the Hasmonaean assumption of the sacred office were not at all happy about it. When Josephus tells of the breach between the Pharisees and John Hyrcanus, he says that what gave John mortal offence was the suggestion that he should be content with political and military leadership and give up the high-priesthood.

Were the Pharisees, then, Hasidaeans? It appears that they were, or at least that they took their rise within the Hasidaeans' fellowship and should indeed be recognized as their mainstream development. The designation Pharisees is associated with a Hebrew and Aramaic root meaning "separate". The Greek word *Pharisaioi* ("Pharisees") is evidently borrowed from Aramaic *p'rîšayyâ*, "the separated ones". It has been held by some that they received this name because of their separation from the alliance with the Hasmonaeans, but perhaps it has a more general meaning, and denotes their policy of strict separation from everything which might convey moral or ceremonial impurity. Such separation was the negative side of the holiness to which they felt themselves specially called. This is spelled out in a later rabbinical commentary on Leviticus, where the injunction, "You shall therefore be holy, for I the LORD your God am holy" (19: 2), is amplified: "As I am holy, so you also must be holy; as I am separate (Heb. *pārûš*), so you also must be separate (Heb. *p'rûšîm*)".[13]

The Pharisees exercised great care in observing the sabbath law and the food restrictions, thus perpetuating the principles of the Jewish martyrs under Antiochus IV, who endured torture and death rather than commit apostasy in these matters. They scrupulously tithed the produce of the soil – not only grain, wine and oil but garden herbs as well – and refused to eat food that was subject to the tithe unless the tithe had actually been paid on it.[14]

In their study of the law they built up a body of interpretation and application which in due course acquired a validity equal to that of the written law, being treated by a legal fiction as originating with Moses on Sinai along with the written law. The

11. See F. F. Bruce, *Second Thoughts on the Dead Sea Scrolls* (Exeter,[3] 1966), pp. 104 ff., 110 ff.

12. 1 Maccabees 14: 41.

13. *Leviticus Rabba* 24: 4 on Leviticus 19: 2.

14. Cf. Matthew 23: 23; Luke 11: 42; see also F. F. Bruce, *New Testament History* (London,[2] 1971), p. 68, n. 4.

purpose of this oral law – "the tradition of the elders", as it is called in the Gospels (Mark 7: 5) – was to adapt the ancient prescriptions to the changing situations of later days and so guard them from being dismissed as obsolete and impracticable. There were differing schools of interpretation among the Pharisees, but they all agreed on the necessity of applying the written law in terms of the oral law. This distinguished them from their principal theological opponents, the Sadducees, who believed (in theory, at any rate) that the written law should be preserved and applied without modification, no matter how harshly its literal enforcement might bear on people.

We are imperfectly informed about Sadducean theology, because no first-hand account of it has come down to us. What we are told relates only to the points on which they differed from the Pharisees. We learn, for example, that unlike the Pharisees they said that there was "no resurrection, nor angel, nor spirit" (Acts 23: 8). The belief in bodily resurrection, as the Pharisees held it, is attested among the martyrs under Antiochus; it is to be distinguished from the idea (expressed, for example, by Ben Sira) that the most desirable kind of immortality was posterity's remembrance of a good man's virtues, especially when they were reproduced in his descendants.[15] The Sadducees may well have thought this idea more consistent with the earlier scriptures – although some of them were surprised one day in Jerusalem about A.D. 30 to hear a visitor from Galilee deduce the hope of resurrection from the divine utterance which came to Moses from the burning bush.[16] As for the Sadducees' disbelief in angels and demons, what they rejected was probably the concept of opposed hierarchies of good and evil spirits, each hierarchy headed by seven named archangels and arch-demons. They may have recognized an affinity between these Pharisaic beliefs and those of the Zoroastrian religion; indeed, one scholar has suggested that "Pharisee" originally meant "Persianizer" and that it was an uncomplimentary designation invented by the Sadducees for their opponents.[17] This is improbable, but it is conceivable that the Sadducees satirically reinterpreted "Pharisee" as "Persianizer". The Sadducees certainly regarded themselves as maintaining the old-time religion and looked on the Pharisees as dangerous innovators – modernists, in fact.

The Pharisees emerged into a position of influence when Alexander Jannaeus was succeeded by his widow Salome Alexandra;

15. This is the point of the passage beginning "Let us now praise famous men . . ." (Ecclesiasticus 44: 1 ff.), well known from its frequent recital at commemoration services.

16. Mark 12: 18–27. (See pp. 109, 336.)

17. T. W. Manson, "Sadducee and Pharisee", *BJRL* 22 (1938), pp. 153 ff.; *The Servant-Messiah* (Cambridge, 1953), pp. 19 f.

48     PAUL: APOSTLE OF THE FREE SPIRIT

her reign of nine years (76–67 B.C.) was remembered in rabbinical tradition as a miniature golden age. Herod paid them respectful attention in the earlier part of his reign; as late as 17 B.C. he exempted them from an oath of allegiance which he exacted from the rest of his subjects.[18] But soon afterwards he began to resent their recalcitrance, and when in 7 B.C. he imposed a fresh oath of allegiance, to Augustus and himself, he fined those Pharisees – the great majority – who refused to be sworn.[19] When, towards the end of his life, a number of Pharisaic disciples, at the instigation of their teachers, pulled down the great golden eagle which he had placed over the temple gateway, he took an atrocious vengeance on them.[20]

Under the Roman administration the Pharisees were represented in the Sanhedrin; although they were in a minority, Josephus says, yet their influence with the people was such that the chief-priestly and Sadducean majority was obliged to respect their views.[21] Many, perhaps most, of the scribes – the professional expositors of the law and the prophets – were disciples of the Pharisees and gave currency to their interpretations.

The Pharisees organized themselves in local fellowships. Such a fellowship was called a ḥᵃbûrāh; each member of a ḥᵃbûrāh was a ḥābēr to the other members. Josephus, who tells us that from his nineteenth year onwards he regulated his life by the Pharisees' rule, estimates their number at about 6,000.[22]

Because of their meticulous concern for the laws of purity and tithing, they could not associate easily with those, even among their fellow-Jews, who were not so particular in this regard as they themselves were. These latter included the great majority of the Jewish population of Palestine, peasants and artisans, who could not devote so much time or interest to the study of those laws as the Pharisees did. The Pharisees therefore tended to hold aloof from the "people of the land",[23] as they called them, for such people, they were convinced, were incapable of true piety.[24] On the other hand, the Pharisees themselves were criticized as too half-hearted in their pursuit of holiness by the sectarians of Qumran, who pressed their own "separation" to the point of isolation (not to say in-

18. Josephus, *Ant.* xv. 370.
19. Josephus, *Ant.* xvii. 42.
20. Josephus, *Ant.* xvii. 151 ff.
21. Josephus, *Ant.* xviii. 17.
22. Josephus, *Ant.* xvii. 42.
23. The phrase ʿam hāʾareṣ, which in OT times was a collective expression ("people of the land"), became in rabbinical usage the designation of an individual, "one of the people of the land" or "one of the common people" – i.e. an ignoramus (in matters of religion, at least).
24. Hillel is credited with the remark that "no ʿam hāʾareṣ is pious" (*Pirqê Abôt* 2: 6). Cf. the dismissive words of the Jerusalem authorities in John 7: 49: "this crowd, who do not know the law, are accursed".

sulation) and, with Isaiah 30: 10 at the back of their minds, called the Pharisees "seekers after smooth things" or (as the phrase may alternatively be rendered) "givers of smooth interpretations".[25]

Although a certain family likeness no doubt characterized the whole Pharisaic movement, there were wide varieties within the movement – varieties associated partly with diverse schools of interpretation and partly with diverse temperaments and motives. One frequently quoted passage in the Talmud, admittedly of much later date, distinguishes seven types of Pharisee, of which only one, the Pharisee who is a Pharisee for the love of God, receives unqualified commendation.[26]

## 3. Pharisaism in Paul's day

At the beginning of the Christian era there were two leading schools of legal interpretation, founded respectively by Shammai and Hillel. The school of Shammai is traditionally credited with a stricter interpretation than the school of Hillel – stricter not only in the application of individual laws but in the approach to the law in its entirety. Whereas the Shammaites regarded the breach of one law (by action or by omission) as a breach of the law as such, the Hillelite attitude was rather that divine judgment had regard to the preponderance of good or bad in a man's life viewed as a whole.

One of the best known sayings of Hillel was his reply to a man who asked him to summarize the whole law in as few words as possible. "What is hateful to yourself", said Hillel, "do not to another; that is the whole law, all the rest is commentary." [27] This citing of the negative golden rule as an epitome of the law could be interpreted in ways which many Pharisees would have thought dangerous. Even if this was not Hillel's intention, it might have encouraged someone to argue, when faced with one particular commandment of the law, that that commandment was binding only in so far as it prevented a neighbour's suffering ill or promoted his good. This, according to a prevalent view among the rabbis, introduced an illicit subjective criterion; far better that people, when confronted with a commandment of the law, should obey it simply because it was a commandment of the Holy One: theirs not to reason why.[28]

25. Cf. 4 QpNah. frag. 4, col. 1, l. 7; 1 QH 2, ll. 15, 32; CD 1, l. 18.
26. TJ *Berakôt* 9: 7.
27. TB *Shabbat* 31a, although doubt is cast on the historicity of the incident by J. Neusner, *The Rabbinic Traditions about the Pharisees before 70* (Leiden, 1971), i, pp. 338 f. For an earlier instance of the negative golden rule cf. Tobit 4: 15, "What you hate, do not do to any one".
28. Thus Yohanan ben Zakkai, commenting on the purificatory ritual of the red heifer (Numbers 19), remarks that in fact a corpse does not convey spiritual defilement nor does water effect inward cleansing; the ordinance is to be carried out simply because it is a divine command (*Numbers Rabba* 19: 8 on Numbers 19: 2).

What kind of Pharisee was Paul? The question is not easily answered. According to Acts 22: 3, he was educated in the school of Gamaliel, and later tradition makes Gamaliel the successor of Hillel as head of his school, if not indeed his son or grandson.[29] But those earlier traditions which reflect some direct memory of the man and his teaching do not even associate him with the school of Hillel. Instead, they speak of others as belonging to the school of Gamaliel, as though he founded a school of his own.[30]

There is some difficulty in distinguishing traditions about this Gamaliel from those about a later teacher of the same name (Gamaliel II, *c.* A.D. 100), but those traditions which presuppose that the temple is still standing certainly relate to the elder Gamaliel. "When Rabban Gamaliel the elder died," it was said, "the glory of the Torah ceased, and purity and 'separateness' died"[31] – which is almost as much as to say that he was the last of the true Pharisees, since "separateness" (Heb. *p'rîšût*) is a formation from the same root as "Pharisee" and might even be translated "Pharisaism". Among the rulings with which he is credited is one liberalizing the law of remarriage after divorce.[32]

Both in the rabbinic traditions and in the New Testament Gamaliel appears as a member of the Sanhedrin. At an early stage in the life of the Jerusalem church, Luke relates, the apostles were charged before this court with disobeying its previous directive to them not to teach publicly in the name of Jesus. When some members of the court were for taking extreme measures against them, "a Pharisee in the council named Gamaliel, a teacher of the law, held in honour by all the people", reminded his colleagues of other movements in the recent past which had seemed to be dangerous for a short time, but quickly collapsed, and he added (Acts 5: 38 f.):

> So in the present case I tell you, keep away from these men and let them alone. If this plan or undertaking is of men, it will fail; but if it is of God, you will not be able to overthrow them. You might even be found opposing God!

This is certainly sound Pharisaic doctrine. Men might disobey God, but his will would triumph notwithstanding. The will of men was not fettered, but what they willed would be overruled by God

---

29. TB *Shabbat* 15a seems to interpose an otherwise unknown Simeon between Hillel and Gamaliel as leader of the school; the idea of a blood-relationship between them is later still.

30. Cf. J. Neusner, *The Rabbinic Traditions about the Pharisees before 70*, i, pp. 341–376.

31. Mishnah *Soṭah* 9: 15.

32. Mishnah *Giṭṭin* 4: 2.

for the accomplishment of his own purpose.[33] In the words of a later rabbi, Yohanan the sandal-maker, "every assembling together that is for the sake of heaven will in the end be established, but any that is not for the sake of heaven will not in the end be established."[34] That Gamaliel should take the line ascribed to him by Luke is what we might have expected.

But if it was Gamaliel's line, it was certainly not Paul's. In most matters indeed, including, for example, the resurrection hope and the techniques of biblical exegesis, Paul was probably an apt pupil and faithful follower of his teacher.[35] It has indeed been thought that an unnamed pupil of Gamaliel who manifested "impudence in matters of learning" and tried to refute his master was no other than Paul.[36] If this is so (and it is quite uncertain), then the tradition reflects disapproval of Paul's later departure from the rabbinical path; it preserves no reminiscence of Paul's actual behaviour while he sat at Gamaliel's feet. But in one respect Paul did deviate from his master's example: he repudiated the idea that a temporizing policy was the proper one to adopt towards the disciples of Jesus. To his mind, this new movement posed a more deadly threat to all that he had learned to hold dear than Gamaliel seemed able to appreciate. Moreover, Paul's temperament appears to have been quite different from Gamaliel's: as against Gamaliel's statesmanlike patience and tolerance, Paul was characterized, on his own confession, by a superabundance of zeal [37] – which, indeed, he never entirely lost.

Since the cherished object of his zeal was the ancestral traditions – the ancient law of Israel and its interpretation as taught in the school of Gamaliel – we should not be surprised to learn that he was dissatisfied with the Hillelite view that a bare preponderance of good over bad in a man's life was sufficient to win him a favourable verdict on the day of judgment. On this point at least he seems to have inclined rather to the Shammaite view that the law was to be kept in its totality. That this was Paul's attitude is implied at a later date when he tells his converts in Galatia, who were being pressed to adopt certain legal requirements of Judaism, that they need not imagine that, if they chose this way of acceptance with God, they

33. Cf. Josephus, *Ant.* xiii. 172; xviii. 13; cf. the dictum of Aqiba: "Everything is foreseen, but freedom of choice is given" (*Pirqê Abôt* 3: 19).

34. *Pirqê Abôt* 4: 14.

35. Cf. J. Jeremias, "Paulus als Hillelit", in *Neotestamentica et Semitica: Studies in Honour of M. Black*, ed. E. E. Ellis and M. Wilcox (Edinburgh, 1969), pp. 88 ff.; on the other side, K. Haacker, "War Paulus Hillelit?", *Das Institutum Iudaicum der Universität Tübingen*, 1971–72, pp. 106–120.

36. So J. Klausner, *From Jesus to Paul*, E.T. (London, 1944), p. 310, in reference to TB *Shabbat* 30b.

37. Galatians 1: 13 f.; Philippians 3: 6.

could pick and choose among the divine commandments: "I testify
. . . to every man who receives circumcision that he is bound to keep
the whole law" (Galatians 5: 3). Such an attitude to the law determined Paul's hostile assessment of the followers of Jesus and their
teaching.

# CHAPTER 6

# "When the Time had Fully Come"

*1. The expected deliverance*

THE COMING OF THE ROMANS TO JUDAEA AND THE DOWNFALL OF the native Hasmonaean dynasty compelled religious Jews to re-think their situation and try to interpret it with reference to the divine purpose. Some of the Hasmonaeans' supporters had remained content with their regime for the greater part of its duration. Under John Hyrcanus (134–104 B.C.) many of his subjects, believing that they discerned in him a rare combination of the three offices of prophet, priest and king,[1] were disposed to think that with him the messianic age had dawned. True, the great prophets of Israel had foreseen the embodiment of the national hope in a prince of the house of David, but in the earlier years of Hasmonaean rule there was little sign that the house of David had any further part to play in the life of Israel, whereas freedom from the Gentile yoke had been secured under the leadership of a priestly dynasty. Might it not be God's will that the expected Messiah or "anointed one" of the end-time should be a priest of the tribe of Levi rather than a king of the tribe of Judah?[2]

But the military ambition and barbarity of Alexander Jannaeus (103–76 B.C.) alienated the best part of the nation from the Hasmonaean cause, and when, after the death of his widow and successor, Salome Alexandra, in 67 B.C., civil strife broke out between their two sons, Hyrcanus and Aristobulus, even the supporters of the Hasmonaean cause were divided. It was this civil strife that provided the Romans with the opportunity to occupy Judaea.

The religious groups in Judaea, who had suffered under the Hasmonaeans, saw in their dethronement at the hands of the Romans a divine judgment for their general injustice and particularly for their usurpation of dignities that were not legally theirs. If the Qumran community disapproved of their assumption

1. Josephus, *Ant.* xiii. 299 f.
2. While the *Testaments of the Twelve Patriarchs* (1st century B.C. – 1st century A.D.) for the most part assign the kingship to Judah and the priesthood to Levi, the kingship is assigned to Levi in *Testament of Reuben* 6: 7–12 – a reflection, probably, of the Hasmonaean ascendancy.

53

of the high-priesthood, which belonged exclusively to the family of Zadok, and saw in the Romans the executors of divine retribution on them for this offence, another pious group, apparently akin to the Pharisees, reckoned that they were being punished for having "laid waste the throne of David".[3] This latter group has left us as the expression of their aspirations the collection of eighteen poems conventionally called the *Psalms of Solomon*.[4] These poems show clearly – as indeed the Qumran literature testifies in some degree – that the hope attached to the house of David had not been allowed to die out entirely in Israel, and with the collapse of the Hasmonaean dynasty and consequent dissipation of any hope of a messianic priesthood associated with it, the Davidic hope no longer had this rival to contend with.

While the authors of the *Psalms of Solomon*, like the men of Qumran, recognized in the Roman occupation the judgment of God on the Hasmonaeans, they cherished no illusions about the Romans and were not surprised to find them more oppressive and rapacious than the Hasmonaeans at their worst. Pompey's sacrilegious insistence on entering the holy of holies when he stormed the fortified temple area in 63 B.C. was regarded as exceptionally shocking, and when he was assassinated in Egypt fifteen years later it was felt that nemesis had overtaken him at last.[5] But the Romans were foreigners, and would dominate the holy land only so long as God permitted. The day of their expulsion would come – and come by divine action. There were varying views about the identity of the divine agent or agents in their expulsion, but one substantial body of opinion expected the Messiah of David's line to be raised up quite soon for this very purpose. This expectation finds ardent expression in the seventeenth of the *Psalms of Solomon*;[6] it can be recognized also in some of the canticles in Luke's nativity narrative. Thus, when Gabriel visits Mary to announce the birth of her son (Luke 1: 32 f.), he says:

> The Lord God will give him the throne of his father David,
> and he will reign over the house of Jacob for ever,
> and of his kingdom there will be no end.

Similarly Zechariah (father of John the Baptist) celebrates the impending deliverance in his hymn of praise (Luke 1: 68 ff.):

---

3. *Psalms of Solomon* 17: 8.
4. Codex Alexandrinus originally included them as an appendix to the New Testament. They were first composed in Hebrew, but are extant only in Greek, and in a Syriac translation from the Greek.
5. *Psalms of Solomon* 2: 30–32.
6. *Psalms of Solomon* 17: 23 ff.

> Blessed be the Lord God of Israel,
>     for he has visited and redeemed his people,
> and has raised up a horn of salvation for us
>     in the house of his servant David . . .

For Mary the fulfilment of this promise means the scattering of the proud in the imagination of their hearts, the putting down of the mighty from their thrones and the exaltation of "those of low degree" (Luke 1: 51 f.); for Zechariah it similarly means "salvation from our enemies and from the hand of all who hate us" (Luke 1: 71).

When, in 40 B.C., the Romans decided to govern Judaea through a Jewish king, it would have taken exceptional powers of mental penetration to discern messianic traits in Herod. Herod may have cherished messianic pretensions himself, and was possibly encouraged in this by some of his supporters, but the general Jewish attitude to him was hostile. He figures in one apocalyptic work, produced twenty or thirty years after his death under the title *The Assumption of Moses* (because its contents told of Moses' purported farewell charge to Joshua and assumption into heaven), as an "insolent king" – possibly in fulfilment of the picture of the "king" of Daniel 11: 36, who "shall do according to his will" – who wipes out the remnant of the Hasmonaeans and spares neither old nor young in his wicked fury.[7]

## 2. *The expected deliverer*

Towards the end of Herod's reign Jesus was born – Jesus, acclaimed by his first followers as the expected redeemer of Israel. Although Luke's nativity canticles heralded him as the promised prince of the house of David, and the same status is given to him in Christian preaching from early days, he does not appear to have made this claim for himself. He did not repudiate the designation "son of David" when it was given to him by others, but his one recorded reference to the widespread belief that the Messiah would be the son of David sets a question-mark against it.[8] Davidic descent plays no part in John the Baptist's description of the Coming One who was to baptize with the Spirit. Paul, for his part, does quote part of a confessional formula which spoke of Jesus as "descended from David according to the flesh" (Romans 1: 3),[9] but in his own understanding and exposition of the significance of Jesus the Davidic descent plays practically no part.

In what sense, then, was Jesus recognized as the redeemer of

---

7. The Latin version of the *Assumption of Moses* calls him *rex petulans* (6: 2).
8. Mark 12: 35–37.
9. Cf. 2 Timothy 2: 8, perhaps another confessional formula.

Israel? When, in his early thirties, he emerged from the obscurity of his home in Nazareth and began his public ministry, the burden of his preaching was that the kingdom of God had drawn near – that it was already present in measure in his works of mercy and power.[10] When his hearers heard him speak of the kingdom of God, they would naturally think of the divine order which, according to the visions in the book of Daniel, would supersede a succession of pagan world-empires and in which rule would be exercised by the "saints of the Most High" (Daniel 7: 18, 27).

There were others in Israel in the first century A.D. who thought along these lines, and whose conception of the rule of the saints boded ill for those who were not included among the "saints". They could have found inspiration, for example, in the "saints" of Psalm 149: 5–9, with the "high praises of God" in their mouths and two-edged swords in their hands,

> to wreak vengeance on the nations
>     and chastisement on the peoples,
> to bind their kings with chains
>     and their nobles with fetters of iron.

According to Luke, when Jesus shared the passover supper with his apostles the evening before his death, he made it plain that it was they who were to bear rule in the kingdom of which he spoke (Luke 22: 28–30):

> You are those who have continued with me in my trials; as my Father appointed a kingdom for me, so do I appoint for you that you may eat and drink at my table in my kingdom, and sit on thrones judging the twelve tribes of Israel.

But those for whom Jesus appointed this rôle had learned from him how it was to be discharged – not in dominating others but in serving them. In this saying he speaks of the kingdom as "my kingdom", and this brings us to the close relation in his teaching between the kingdom of God and the eschatological figure of "the Son of man".

In Daniel's vision of the new kingdom, it is conferred on "one like a son of man" (a human figure in distinction from the wild beasts which denote the pagan empires); it is in the interpretation of the vision that the "saints of the Most High" appear, forming the counterpart to the "one like a son of man" in the vision itself. Jesus did not make an outright identification of the saints of the Most High with the Son of man; his disciples were the "little flock" to whom the Father was to give the kingdom (Luke 12: 32), but they constituted the "little flock" by virtue of their association with the

10. Cf. Mark 1: 14 f.; Matthew 12: 28/Luke 11: 20.

shepherd – or, to change the metaphor, with the Son of man. When Jesus spoke of the Son of man, he meant "the 'one like a son of man' " to whom was given "dominion and glory and kingdom, that all peoples, nations, and languages should serve him" (Daniel 7: 13 f.). As his ministry advanced, it became increasingly clear that he accepted the mission of the Son of man as something which he was personally called to fulfil.[11] This was a costly calling: as the kingdom of God had to suffer violence before it was inaugurated in power, so the Son of man had to "suffer many things and be treated with contempt"[12] in order to be invested with kingly glory. In this confidence he went to his death: "the Son of man goes as it is written of him" (Mark 14: 21). But his investiture with kingly glory would involve no change of character: then as now he would remain "servant of all", for it is in such self-giving service that true kingly glory consists.[13]

In so far as Jesus acknowledged the title Messiah, it was in these terms that he acknowledged it. When he was brought before the high priest and his colleagues and asked if he was the Messiah, he replied that he was, since that was the term they chose to use, but that he himself chose to speak of himself as the Son of man, who (although standing there deserted and humiliated) would be vindicated by God before their eyes. And in his vindication it would be seen that he was the one in whom God had visited and redeemed his people.[14]

Jesus' preaching of the kingdom of God did not take place in a vacuum. Galilee, where he spent most of his life, was ruled by Herod Antipas, a creature of Rome; Judaea and Samaria were ruled by the prefect Pontius Pilate, directly appointed by the Roman Emperor. The temple establishment in Jerusalem was in the hands of the Sadducean house of Annas; taxes had to be paid for its maintenance in addition to the tribute exacted by Rome. The popular teachers expounded the religious law according to the "tradition of the elders". The message of Jesus was so radical that it challenged all those authorities at once.

He did not challenge the Roman occupation like those who tried to meet force with force. That would have meant accepting the Romans' own conception of power, the only question at issue being who wielded the power. But when he bade the children of the kingdom cultivate righteousness and mercy, poverty and meekness, purity of heart and peace among men, when he taught them to turn

11. Cf. T. W. Manson, *The Teaching of Jesus* (Cambridge, [2] 1935), pp. 211 ff.; A. J. B. Higgins, *Jesus and the Son of Man* (London, 1964); M. D. Hooker, *The Son of Man in Mark* (London, 1967).

12. Mark 9: 12; Luke 17: 25.

13. Mark 10: 43 f.; Luke 22: 25–27.

14. Mark 14: 61 f.

the other cheek and go the second mile and requite their enemies by doing them good, when he insisted that the will of God was fully done in the performance of acts of love,[15] he turned accepted canons upside down and posed a more deadly threat to the basis of imperial power than those who offered it armed resistance. At the same time he set such little store by material wealth that he made no issue of the payment of tribute to Caesar,[16] any more than he did of the payment of the annual half-shekel to the temple.[17] But in the end it was the temple establishment and the Roman prefect between them who were responsible for his death.

As for his attitude to the law, it was in some respects not dissimilar to Hillel's. If Hillel said that everything else in the law was but a commentary on the negative golden rule, Jesus said much the same thing about the rule in its positive formulation: "whatever you wish that men would do to you, do so to them; for this is the law and the prophets" (Matthew 7: 12).[18] To the same effect he singled out from the 613 precepts of the law two positive precepts beginning with the injunction "you shall love" – "you shall love the Lord your God . . ." (Deuteronomy 6: 4) and "you shall love your neighbour as yourself" (Leviticus 19: 18) – as the first and second commandments of the law on which all the others depended (Mark 12: 28–31; cf. Matthew 22: 35–40).[19]

So far Jesus would have commanded considerable agreement among rabbis of the Hillelite school. But in his application of these principles to practical issues he seemed to treat the law with a sovereign freedom which even a Hillelite would have found disturbing.

This was seen with special clarity in his attitude to the sabbath law. The original wording of that law instituted the sabbath as a day of rest, on which no work should be done. "Work" was not defined; presumably it related primarily to the recurring activities of agricultural life: "in ploughing time and in harvest you shall rest" (Exodus 34: 21).[20] From time to time, even within the period of the written law, it was necessary to define "work" more precisely, until by the first century A.D. we have thirty-nine categories of work distinguished, first of all (it appears) in the school of Hillel, all of them prohibited on the sabbath.[21] The school of Shammai had a

15. See the Sermon on the Mount (Matthew 5–7; cf. Luke 6: 17–49), *passim.*
16. Mark 12: 13–17.
17. Matthew 17: 24–27.
18. See p. 49. A positive formulation of the golden rule in Jewish orthodoxy is provided by Maimonides, *Mishneh Torah* 2: *Hilʿkôt Abel* 14: 1.
19. In Luke 10: 27 it is the enquiring lawyer who summarizes the law thus, in response to Jesus' counter-question.
20. This probably meant "*even* in ploughing time and in harvest . . ." rather than "*only* in ploughing time and in harvest . . .".

stricter interpretation, and that in force at Qumran is known to have been stricter still.[22] But Jesus did not trouble himself with definitions of work; rather, he reminded his hearers of the original purpose of the sabbath institution – to promote the relief and well-being of men and women – and insisted that any action (such as healing the sick) which furthered this purpose was done most appropriately on the sabbath.[23]

He laid down the same principle when he was asked for a ruling on the law of divorce. What was the "indecency" or "unseemliness" (Deuteronomy 24: 1) in a man's wife which justified him in divorcing her? The Hillelites interpreted it liberally, of a wide range of defects, the Shammaites interpreted it more narrowly, of pre-marital unchastity, but Jesus, going back behind Moses to the creation narrative, argued from the terms of the institution of marriage that divorce was no part of God's original intention. To the minds of his male hearers, this ruling was so stringent as to be impracticable: "if such is the case of a man with his wife," they replied, "it is not expedient to marry" (Matthew 19: 10). But the effect of his ruling was to correct a social imbalance which worked for the detriment of women, who had little opportunity for initiative or redress in this matter; from their point of view it was a liberal ruling.

Many of Jesus' strictures on the scribes and Pharisees of his day were probably directed at members of the school of Shammai. It was they in particular who could be reproached for "loading men with burdens hard to bear" and doing nothing to relieve them (Luke 11: 46). But the milder Hillelites, too, must often have found him disconcerting.

One specially perplexing feature of Jesus' conduct, in the eyes even of liberal Pharisees, was his readiness to associate with people who did not even attempt to respect the law, whose lives were in scandalous conflict with its basic principles. He did not associate with them as a condescending benefactor performing a pious duty; he gave the impression that he enjoyed their company – indeed, that he chose it by preference, accepting invitations to eat with them and so incurring the reproach of being "a glutton and a wine-bibber, a friend of tax collectors[24] and sinners" (Luke 7: 34). When he was taxed with giving offence to godly people by such behaviour, he defended himself by saying that it was sick people, not healthy ones, who needed a doctor, and that it was sinners that he came to call. Not only so, but he maintained that God himself

21. Mishnah *Shabbat* 7: 1 ff.
22. CD 10, l. 14–11, l. 18.
23. Mark 2: 23–3: 5; Luke 13: 10–17; 14: 1–6.
24. Government tax-collectors were reckoned by definition to be 'ammê hā'areṣ (see p. 48).

acted thus, bestowing his gifts with undistinguishing regard on good and evil alike, even on the ungrateful and selfish. And in parable after parable he drove this lesson home, emphasizing the welcoming grace extended by God to the inadequate and undeserving, the despised and alienated, the insecure and underprivileged. In his teaching and in his example, Jesus' message was one of good news for the outsider.[25] When John the Baptist, imprisoned by Herod Antipas in the Peraean fortress of Machaerus, sent messengers to Jesus to ask if he really was the Coming One whose advent John had announced (Jesus' ministry was so unlike the judgment which John had described the Coming One as executing), Jesus told them to go back and tell John what they had seen and heard while they were with him, but especially to tell him this: "the poor have good news preached to them" (Luke 7: 22).

In these words John was sure to recognize the language of Isaiah 61: 1, where an unnamed speaker claims to have been *anointed* with the Spirit of God for this very purpose: "to bring good news to the poor". Would John acknowledge that Jesus was the one of whom the prophet spoke? If so, he would not feel that Jesus was letting him down by failing to inaugurate "the day of vengeance of our God" forthwith.[26]

It is most probable that Jesus identified this Spirit-anointed speaker of Isaiah 61: 1 with the one whom God introduces earlier in the same book (Isaiah 42: 1) with the words:

Behold my servant, whom I uphold,
  my chosen, in whom my soul delights;
I have put my Spirit upon him . . .

– words echoed by the heavenly voice which came to Jesus at his baptism.[27] This servant is given a mission to discharge both for Israel and for the Gentiles; the fulfilment of the mission involves him in unjust persecution, humiliation and death, but by accepting all this obediently as God's will for him he accomplishes the divine purpose, which coincides with his own dearest desire. This purpose includes the forgiveness of many, whose sins the servant bears. Indeed, much of what Jesus says about the predestined suffering of the Son of man is best understood if in his mind he identified the Son of man with the Isaianic Servant of the Lord: in the light of

25. See p. 105.
26. In his programmatic sermon in the Nazareth synagogue (Luke 4: 16 ff.), Jesus chooses Isaiah 61: 1f. as his text, but ends at the words "to proclaim the acceptable year of the Lord", without continuing the sentence: "and the day of vengeance of our God".
27. Mark 1: 11 ("You are my Son, my beloved; with you I am well pleased"); as those words were spoken, he saw "the Spirit descending on him like a dove" (Mark 1: 10).

what is said of the latter figure one can appreciate all the more the gospel logion that "the Son of man came not to be served by others but to be a servant himself, and to give his life a ransom for many" (Mark 10: 45). This was the spirit in which Jesus accepted death. And it was this spirit to which Paul was to refer in days to come when he spoke of "the mind which was in the Messiah Jesus, who . . . emptied himself, taking the form of a servant" (Philippians 2: 5–7) or described Jesus as being "delivered up for our trespasses" (Romans 4: 25).[28] Before Gamaliel's pupil came to this assessment of the ministry and death of Jesus, a revolution had to take place in his . life and thought. But when it took place, he could sum up the significance of those events in the affirmation that "when the time had fully come, God sent forth his Son . . ." (Galatians 4: 4).

28. See pp. 89 f. with nn. 16, 17.

# CHAPTER 7

# The Beginning of "The Way"

*1. He is risen!*

WHEN, AFTER HIS EXECUTION, THE BODY OF JESUS WAS SAFELY entombed, the chief priests and temple authorities no doubt felt that they could breathe freely. There was now no risk of a popular rising in support of a discredited leader, and as for his closest followers, their inglorious flight when he was arrested made it clear that no more would be heard from them. They would disappear into the welcome obscurity of the occupations which they had so rashly left in order to follow the ill-starred Nazarene. Some members of the establishment who were not devoid of decent feelings would have agreed that it was sad that the Nazarene had ventured into Judaea and become a focus for such dangerous enthusiasm in and around Jerusalem. But such enthusiasm had to be nipped in the bud. If ever the end justified the means, it was then. Perhaps even the coincidence that the Roman penalty of crucifixion, to which Jesus had been sentenced, came within the meaning of the declaration of Deuteronomy 21: 23, that "a hanged man is accursed by God", could be overruled for good: it would discredit the Nazarene and his claims in the eyes of truly religious Jews more effectively than anything else.

Many of the religious Jews, Pharisees and others, who disagreed with the policies of the chief priests and the Roman administration and deplored the manner of Jesus' execution, may nevertheless have experienced their own sense of relief at the removal of such a disturbing presence.

All these calculations were shattered by Jesus' return to life. No one saw him leave the tomb, but on the third day from his death and burial, and for several days after that, he appeared to many of his followers in a manner which left them in no doubt that he was "alive again after his passion" (Acts 1: 3). Twenty-five years after the event Paul could summarize the facts as he had been told them, reminding his converts at Corinth that Christ, having died,

was raised on the third day in accordance with the scriptures, and that he appeared to Cephas [Peter], then to the twelve. Then he appeared to more than five hundred brethren at one time, most of whom are still alive, though some have fallen asleep. Then he appeared to James, then to all the apostles.

This summary (1 Corinthians 15: 4–7) raises one or two interesting critical problems to which Paul himself elsewhere helps to provide a solution.[1] But it is sufficient at the moment to observe the variety of the resurrection appearances – occasionally to individuals, at other times to groups, and once to quite a large number. The followers of Jesus were taken completely by surprise when he appeared to them thus, and the experience made all the difference in life to them. In addition to those who were most closely associated with him during his ministry, members of his family, who had not hitherto been conspicuous in their support of him or approval of his activity, also saw him in resurrection, and were henceforth prominent among his followers.

The resurrection faith, to which the "Easter event" gave birth, was followed by an inflow of new life and new power, in which they quickly recognized the gift of the Holy Spirit with which, as John the Baptist had announced, the Coming One of whom he spoke would baptize his people.[2] Jesus was the Coming One: now, raised and exalted by God, he had poured out the promised gift on his disciples. The immediate effect of this outpouring was an urge to bear public and personal witness that Jesus, the crucified one, had been vindicated by God, and to proclaim forgiveness and the blessings of the new age thus inaugurated for all who yielded their allegiance to him. They soon won an impressively large body of adherents, who formed with them a new religious fellowship in Jerusalem – the fellowship of disciples of Jesus, knit together in unity by the newly imparted Spirit. They followed what they called the Way – the way of faith and life initiated by Jesus. This expression was not unprecedented in Israel: it is found, for example, in the writings of the Qumran community as a designation for that community's faith and life. One scholar, indeed, has argued that it was from the Qumran community that the disciples of Jesus took it over – in the first instance, in Damascus (because it is in a Damascene context that it first appears in a Christian sense).[3] But there is no need to posit such borrowing: it is characteristic of minority groups that abbreviated expressions of this kind become current within them as part of their esoteric vocabulary, and "the way" is a shortened version of "the true way" or "the right way".

1. The information about the appearances to Peter (the leader of the twelve) and James (the brother of Jesus) was probably received by Paul when he visited Jerusalem in the third year after his conversion and met those two men (Galatians 1: 18 f.). See pp. 84 ff.
2. Mark 1: 8 and parallels; John 1: 33.
3. E. Repo, *Der "Weg" als Selbstbezeichnung des Urchristentums* (Helsinki, 1964).

It is convenient to refer to the fellowship as the church of Jerusalem, even if the term "church" is strictly an anachronism when used of the earliest period of its existence. In addition to being called disciples, its members were variously described as the believers, the saints or the poor. Those of them who had landed property sold it and put the proceeds into a common pool, from which a daily distribution was made to the needier members. By the time this common fund was exhausted, other sources of supply began to become available, as the gospel spread farther afield and converts in other provinces were taught to regard it as a privilege to send material aid to the mother church.[4]

Many Pharisees soon recognized that the revived "Jesus movement" was not such a menace to pure religion as they had feared. Jesus' disciples appeared to be much less radical in their attitude to the law and sacred tradition than he himself had been. Their leaders attended the temple services and conducted themselves in general as observant Jews, enjoying popular good will. If they proclaimed Jesus as Messiah, it was at least counted to them for righteousness that the basis of their proclamation was the claim that he had been raised from the dead. Their firm grasp of the doctrine of resurrection was commendable, even if their witness to the resurrection of Jesus was held to be misguided.

For this very emphasis on resurrection, however, they incurred the further disapproval of the Sadducean chief-priesthood, who in any case were gravely shaken by this renewal of public agitation (as they reckoned it) in the name of one who they had hoped would soon be forgotten.[5] The Jesus movement was reaching alarming proportions, and many of them felt that if drastic measures were not taken to suppress it, it would get hopelessly out of hand. On one occasion when the apostles were arrested and brought before the Sanhedrin, charged with disobeying an earlier order of the court to stop preaching and teaching in the name of Jesus, it was the Pharisaic leader Gamaliel, as we have seen, who persuaded his colleagues to regard their offence as a technical one and treat them leniently.[6]

Some Pharisees, indeed, joined the disciples; if they were persuaded by the apostles' witness that Jesus had indeed risen from the dead and was therefore the Messiah, they could add this belief to what they already held, without giving up their essential Pharisaism with its devotion to the law.[7] If the chief priests maintained their implacable opposition to the movement, many of

4. See pp. 151, 319 ff.
5. Acts 4: 1 ff.; see p. 47.
6. See p. 50.
7. Cf. Acts 15: 5.

the ordinary priests, humble in character as in social status, were disposed to join it.[8]

## 2. Primitive christology

At quite an early period in their new corporate existence as companions of the Way, the disciples found themselves assessing the place of Jesus in the unfolding of the divine purpose. With increasing clarity they saw his identity and rôle adumbrated in the ancient scriptures, especially as he himself had taught them how to understand those scriptures. In the apostolic speeches of the early chapters of Acts there are quite a number of interlacing christologies – explanations of the person and work of the crucified and exalted Jesus in terms of biblical prophecy. He was the anointed prince of the house of David; [9] he was the humiliated and vindicated servant of the Lord; [10] he was the promised prophet like Moses.[11] Nor was he identified only with personal figures of prophecy; impersonal images also were pressed into service. He was "the stone which the builders rejected" which, according to Psalm 118: 22, had become the capstone of the pediment.[12]

These christological interpretations of Hebrew prophecy are not to be set down as constructions of the author of Acts; their primitive character is shown by the fact that they are presupposed in several strands of New Testament thought, and seem therefore to lie behind them all. The theme of the rejected stone, for example, was early combined with other "stone" oracles in the Old Testament to produce a composite *testimonium* which is appropriated and variously exploited in the Pauline corpus, in 1 Peter and in the Gospel of Luke.[13]

We must not think that these "christologies" were originally kept separate, as though a Davidic christology, a servant christology, a prophet christology and a "stone" christology stood side by side, each developed independently by one group or school within the new movement. They have been interwoven with each other

---

8. Acts 6: 7. C. Spicq has argued that these converted priests were "Esseno-Christians", former members of the Qumran community ("L'Epître aux Hébreux: Apollos, Jean-Baptiste, les Hellénistes et Qumrân", *Revue de Qumran* 1 [1958–59], pp. 365 ff.).

9. Acts 2: 25–36.

10. Acts 3: 13–26.

11. Acts 3: 22 f.; 7: 37.

12. Acts 4: 11.

13. Such oracles are those relating to the "stone of stumbling" of Isaiah 8: 14, the foundation-stone laid in Zion of Isaiah 28: 16, the stone "cut out by no human hand" of Daniel 2: 34 f., 44 f. For their combination cf. Luke 20: 17 f.; Romans 9: 32 f.; 1 Peter 2: 6–8. See F. F. Bruce, *This is That: The New Testament Development of Some Old Testament Themes* (Exeter, 1968), pp. 65 f., and "The Corner Stone", *Expository Times* 84 (1972–73), pp. 231 ff.

throughout the history of Christian thought, and such evidence as we have indicates that it was so from the beginning.[14]

Even more important, however, than these "christologies" in themselves was the acknowledgment of Jesus as Lord in a sense which implied universal sovereignty. His exaltation pointed to him as the one designated "my lord", to whom the divine oracle of Psalm 110: 1 was addressed: "Yahweh says to my lord, 'Sit at my right hand, till I make your enemies your footstool'." The first impetus to this interpretation of the oracle was provided by Jesus' own allusion to it in his reply to the high priest's question about his identity: "you shall see the Son of man seated at the right hand of the Almighty" (Mark 14: 62). His words had been vindicated in the event, for God had made the crucified Jesus "both Lord and Messiah" (Acts 2: 36).

From early days the concept of Jesus being enthroned at the right hand of God became a commonplace of Christian thought and language: there are few strands of New Testament teaching in which it does not appear. (Then, as now, the expression was understood as a figure of speech for supreme God-given authority.) And when it was asked how he was engaged at the right hand of God, the answer was soon forthcoming: he was engaged in a ministry of intercession. The fourth servant song ends with the statement that the servant "bore the sin of many, and made intercession for transgressors" (Isaiah 53: 12); moreover, Jesus had spoken of the Son of man as exercising such a ministry in the presence of God. "Every one who acknowledges me before men", he had said, "the Son of man also will acknowledge before the angels of God" (Luke 12: 8). So, in what appears to be a quotation of a primitive and widespread Christian confession, Paul speaks of Jesus as the one "who is at the right hand of God, who indeed intercedes for us" (Romans 8: 34). The picture, says H. B. Swete, is not that of "an orante, *standing* ever before the Father with outstretched arms, . . . pleading our cause in the presence of a reluctant God", but that of "a *throned* Priest-King, asking what He will from a Father who always hears and grants His request."[15]

The primitiveness of the ascription to Jesus of the title "Lord" is shown by its currency in the Aramaic form *maran* or *maranā* as well as in the Greek *kyrios*: indeed the Aramaic invocation *maranā-thā* ("Our Lord, come"), used probably in the eucharistic commemoration, antedated the beginnings of Gentile Christianity and

14. M. Hengel argues that the crucial phase of christological development was the first five years after the death and resurrection of Christ ("Christologie und neutestamentliche Chronologie", in *Neues Testament und Geschichte: O. Cullmann zum 70. Geburtstag*, ed. H. Baltensweiler and B. Reicke [Zürich/Tübingen, 1972], pp. 43–67).

15. H. B. Swete, *The Ascended Christ* (London, 1912), p. 95. See pp. 119 f.

made its way (like the liturgical *Amen* and *Hallelujah*) untranslated into the vocabulary of Greek-speaking churches. [16]

The early currency of the invocation *maranā-thā* bears witness to the disciples' lively expectation of Jesus' parousia, his advent in glory, to consummate the kingdom inaugurated by his death and resurrection. One of the most primitive eschatological passages in the New Testament comes in Peter's exhortation to the people of Jerusalem to repent and turn again, so that their sins may be blotted out and "that times of refreshing may come from the presence of the Lord", with the sending of Jesus, their foreordained Messiah, "whom heaven must receive until the time for establishing all that God spoke by the mouth of his holy prophets from of old" (Acts 3: 19–21). Here it is implied that early repentance on the part of the people of Jerusalem (perhaps as representing all Israel) would speed the parousia. This form of the expectation was soon superseded by others, but the expectation itself lived on as a potent hope throughout the apostolic age, not least in the thought of Paul.

## 3. Activity and death of Stephen

It would be strange if Jesus' radical attitude to the law and religious tradition in general had not survived at all among his followers. [17] Survive it did, and remarkably enough (so far as our records provide information), among the Hellenists rather than among the Hebrews.

The Hellenists in the primitive church of Jerusalem soon came to be recognized, by themselves and by the Hebrews, as a distinct group within it, on both economic and theological grounds. We are imperfectly informed about them, but we have some knowledge of two of their early leaders, both exceptionally gifted men – Stephen, outstanding in theological debate, and Philip, active as an evangelist. Stephen attracted attention by his critical attitude to the temple. At a time when the leaders of the church were attending its services daily, he took seriously Jesus' prediction of its downfall, and maintained that such a permanent structure was no part of the divine plan for a pilgrim people. The ideal was rather a movable tent-shrine such as the ancestors of Israel had in the wilderness, not fixed to one specially sacred locality. He further maintained that the coming of Jesus had profoundly changed the status of the Mosaic law.

He appears to have defended these theses vigorously in the Hellenistic "synagogue of the freedmen", as it was called, which was attended by Jews who had come to Jerusalem from Cyrene,

---

16. The eucharistic setting of *maranā-thā* (1 Corinthians 16: 22) is explicit in *Didache* 10: 6. See p. 117 with nn. 11, 12.
17. See p. 57.

Alexandria, Cilicia and Asia.[18] We may wonder whether Paul the Cilician, Hebrew though he was rather than Hellenist, visited this synagogue and heard what Stephen had to say.

The upshot of Stephen's outspoken expression of these radical views was that he was charged before the Sanhedrin with blasphemy – more particularly, blasphemy against the temple. An earlier attempt to procure a conviction against Jesus on this very charge had failed because of conflicting testimony;[19] on this occasion there was no possibility of failure, because Stephen's reply to the charge was a repetition and elaboration of his argument, delivered with something like prophetic fervour. The death-sentence was inevitable, as Stephen knew well. But as he faced the adverse verdict of the court, he invoked the superior advocacy of "the Son of man, standing at the right hand of God" (Acts 7: 56).[20]

When Judaea became a Roman province in A.D. 6, the Jewish administration was deprived of capital jurisdiction, which the prefect reserved to himself.[21] In one area, however, capital jurisdiction was left with the Sanhedrin: that was in cases affecting the sanctity of the temple. Where that sanctity was violated, by word or action, the Jewish authorities were empowered to execute their own law.[22] The penalty for blasphemy was death by stoning,[23] and this penalty was carried out against Stephen.[24]

His trial and execution gave the chief-priestly establishment an opportunity to launch a thorough-going campaign of repression against the church. The general populace of Jerusalem were as much shocked by an attack on the temple as their ancestors had been when Jeremiah delivered one over six centuries before.[25] The apostles still enjoyed popular favour to such a degree that no action against them was possible, but many members of the church, and in particular those who were most nearly associated with Stephen, were compelled to leave Jerusalem and, indeed, the whole area in which the writ of the Sanhedrin ran. Two results of this dispersion were: first, that the gospel was carried by those Hellenists to territories outside Palestine; secondly, that the church of Jerusalem became much more uniformly Hebrew in its composition and outlook. But it is this campaign of repression that first brings Paul into close involvement with primitive Christianity.

18. Acts 6: 9; see p. 42.
19. Mark 14: 57–59.
20. It is not far-fetched to see in Stephen's vision the fulfilment of Jesus' promise in Luke 12: 8 (see p. 66).
21. Josephus *BJ* ii. 117; cf. *Ant.* xviii. 2; John 18: 31.
22. Cf. Josephus, *BJ* vi. 126. See p. 349.
23. Cf. Leviticus 24: 10–16.
24. Acts 7: 58 f.
25. Jeremiah 7: 1–15; 26: 1–6.

# CHAPTER 8

# Persecutor of the Church

## 1. Campaign of repression

**B**Y HIS OWN REPEATED ACCOUNT, PAUL'S FIRST RELATION TO the young Christian movement was that of a persecutor.[1] "I am the least of the apostles", he could say in later days, "unfit to be called an apostle, because I persecuted the church of God" (1 Corinthians 15: 9). "You have heard of my former life in Judaism", he reminds his Galatian converts, "how I persecuted the church of God beyond all measure and tried to destroy it" (Galatians 1: 13). It would be unnecessary to ask where this persecuting activity took place, were it not that some have tried to locate it anywhere but in or around Jerusalem – in Hellenistic communities in and around Damascus, for example.[2] But in those early days, where would one find the church of God if not pre-eminently in Jerusalem? It was "the churches of Christ in Judaea" who heard it said, a few years after his conversion, "Our former persecutor is now preaching the faith he once tried to destroy" (Galatians 1: 23), and while this report may conceivably have been referring to him as the persecutor of Christians in general, it is more natural to understand it of his record as a persecutor of Christians in fairly close touch with the churches of Judaea. The news that he was now preaching the Christian faith came from Syria and Cilicia, but it was not the new converts from those parts who described him as "our former persecutor".

There is nothing in the evidence of Paul's letters on this score which conflicts with the testimony of Acts. According to this testimony, he associated himself with Stephen's accusers, guarding the outer garments of the witnesses as, in conformity with the ancient law, they threw the first stones at his execution.[3] Then he took part enthusiastically in the campaign of repression against the church of Jerusalem, "breathing threats and murder against the disciples of the Lord" (Acts 9: 1), arresting and imprisoning men and women, endeavouring to make them renounce their faith when

1. Cf. A. J. Hultgren, "Paul's Pre-Christian Persecutions of the Church: their Purpose, Locale and Nature", *JBL* 95 (1976), pp. 97–111.
2. Cf. E. Haenchen, *The Acts of the Apostles*, E. T. (Oxford, 1971), pp. 297 ff.
3. Deuteronomy 17: 7.

they were brought before synagogue courts, and pursuing refugees beyond the frontiers of Judaea in an attempt to bring them back to face trial and punishment. Luke's record certainly agrees with Paul's own evidence that he persecuted the church beyond all measure and provides a commentary on his statement that this activity was the measure of his zeal for the law and the ancestral traditions.

An out-and-out zealot for those traditions such as he declares himself to have been would certainly have offered vigorous opposition to any tendency to "change the customs delivered by Moses".[4] Gamaliel might counsel patience and moderation but, as Paul viewed the situation, it was too serious for such temporizing measures. If Stephen saw the logic of the situation more clearly than the apostles, Paul saw it more clearly than Gamaliel. In the eyes of Stephen and Paul alike, the new order and the old were incompatible. If Stephen argued, "The new has come; therefore the old must go", Paul for his part argued, "The old must stay; therefore the new must go". Hence the uncompromising rigour with which he threw himself into the work of repression.

Paul might have agreed that on one conceivable condition the customs delivered by Moses might be changed. It is possible that he had been taught that Messiah, when he came, would change the customs or even abrogate the law. There was an ancient Jewish chronological scheme, probably going back beyond the time of Paul, which divided world history into three ages of two thousand years each – the age of chaos, the age of law (beginning with the revelation to Moses on Sinai) and the messianic age. These three ages would be followed by the eternal sabbath rest.[5] Those who accepted this scheme might well have believed that the validity of the law was but temporary, lasting only to the dawn of the messianic age. If Paul had been brought up to accept it, then no doubt he would have expected the law to be superseded by a new order when Messiah came.

But that Jesus of Nazareth could be the expected Messiah, as his disciples maintained, was out of the question. It is unlikely that the status, career and teaching of Jesus conformed in any way with Paul's conception of the status, career and teaching of the Messiah – but that was not the conclusive argument in Paul's mind. The conclusive argument was simply this: Jesus had been crucified. A

4. Part of the charge laid against Stephen in Acts 6: 14.
5. For this doctrine of the three ages cf. TB *Sanhedrin* 97a; for the eternal sabbath rest cf. also Mishnah, *Tamid* 7: 4. For someone brought up to accept this doctrine, the argument would be valid: "If the 'Days of the Messiah' have commenced, those of the Torah came to their close. On the other hand, if the Law, the Torah, still retained its validity, it was proclaimed thereby that the Messiah had not yet arrived" (L. Baeck, "The Faith of Paul", *Journal of Jewish Studies* 3 [1952], p. 106; cf. H. J. Schoeps, *Paul*, E. T. [London, 1961], pp. 171 ff.). See p. 190.

crucified Messiah was a contradiction in terms. Whether his death by crucifixion was deserved or resulted from a miscarriage of justice was beside the point: the point was that he was crucified, and therefore came within the meaning of the pronouncement in Deuteronomy 21: 23, "a hanged man is accursed by God". True, the pronouncement envisaged the hanging until sundown, on a tree or wooden gibbet, of the dead body of an executed criminal, but as formulated it covered the situation in which someone was hanged up alive.[6] It stood to reason, therefore, that Jesus could not be the Messiah. The Messiah, practically by definition, was uniquely endowed with the divine blessing – "the Spirit of the LORD shall rest upon him" (Isaiah 11: 2) – whereas the divine curse explicitly rested on one who was crucified. A crucified Messiah was worse than a contradiction in terms; the very idea was an outrageous blasphemy. In later years Paul acknowledged that in preaching a crucified Messiah he was preaching something which was "a stumbling block [a *skandalon*] to Jews" (1 Corinthians 1: 23) and showed, by quoting Deuteronomy 21: 23, how necessary it was in his eyes to demonstrate from Scripture why one who (as he had come to realize) was indubitably the Messiah must nevertheless die under "the curse of the law" (Galatians 3: 13).[7] But when he was first confronted by people who publicly affirmed that the crucified Jesus was the Messiah, his course was clear: they were guilty of blasphemy, and should be dealt with accordingly. No heed could be paid to them when they supported their affirmation by the claim that Jesus had come back from the dead and appeared to them. In making this claim they were either deceivers or self-deceived, for none of the arguments which they used for Jesus' messiahship could stand against the one irrefragable argument on the other side: a crucified man could not conceivably be the elect one of God.

The law and the customs, the ancestral traditions, and everything that was of value in Judaism, were imperilled by the disciples' activity and teaching. Here was a malignant growth which called for drastic surgery. The defence of all that made life worth living for Paul was a cause which engaged all the zeal and energy of which he was capable. When the chief priests and their associates launched their attack on the disciples, Paul came forward as their eager lieutenant. Their motives may have been partly political, while his were entirely religious, but their action provided him with the occasion to protect the interests of the law. If the principal

6. "Hanging up alive" is the Hebrew phrase used for crucifixion in 4QpNah frag. 4, ll. 5–8, a passage which well conveys the horror with which this fate was viewed by pious Jews.

7. According to Luke, the phrase "hanging on a gibbet" ( ξύλον, the Greek word used in the LXX of Deuteronomy 21: 22 f.) was used in the primitive apostolic preaching, as though to emphasize how religiously shocking this mode of execution was (Acts 5: 30; 10: 39).

threat to those interests came from Stephen's party, then let that party be attacked and suppressed first of all; but the disciples of Jesus as a whole, however outwardly observant of the law they might be, undermined it by proclaiming their crucified master as Messiah.

## 2. Mission to Damascus

Paul's own narrative implies that his conversion to the faith which he was attempting to wipe out took place at or near Damascus:[8] the narrative of Acts tells us what took him to Damascus. The violence of the persecution drove many of the disciples, especially the Hellenists, out of Judaea, but even so they were not necessarily out of reach of the Sanhedrin. When the Jewish state won independence under the Hasmonaeans, it had powerful patrons in the Romans, who let the countries surrounding Judaea know this and demanded that Judaea should be granted the rights and privileges of a sovereign state, including the right of extradition. Thus, a letter delivered by a Roman ambassador to Ptolemy VIII of Egypt in 142 B.C. concludes with the requirement: "if any pestilent men have fled to you from their country [Judaea], hand them over to Simon the high priest, that he may punish them according to their law" (1 Maccabees 15: 21).[9] Those rights and privileges were confirmed anew to the Jewish people (even though they no longer constituted a sovereign state), and more particularly to the high-priesthood, by Julius Caesar in 47 B.C.[10] Paul in his crusading zeal resolved that the high priest should exercise his right of extradition against the fugitives, and procured from him "letters to the synagogues of Damascus, so that if he found any belonging to the Way, men or women, he might bring them bound to Jerusalem" (Acts 9: 1).

It appears that there was already in Damascus a community of followers of the Way, with whom the fugitives from Judaea could hope to find refuge. These Damascene disciples were not the subjects of the extradition papers which Paul carried; he may not even have been aware of their presence there. It was the refugees whom he had come to apprehend,[11] no doubt hoping that if he could

---

8. Cf. Galatians 1: 17, "I returned to Damascus".

9. The author of the letter is "Lucius, consul of the Romans" (1 Maccabees 15: 16) – presumably L. Caecilius Metellus, consul in 142 B.C. (E. J. Bickermann, review of M. S. Ginsburg, Rome et la Judée, in Gnomon 6 [1930], pp. 358 f.).

10. Josephus, Ant. xiv. 192–195. See S. Safrai and M. Stern (ed.), The Jewish People in the First Century, i (Assen, 1974), p. 456.

11. This is the implication of the adverb ἐκεῖσε, "thither", in Acts 22: 5; "those who were there" are "those who had gone thither".

accomplish this purpose satisfactorily in Damascus, he could repeat the procedure in other foreign cities.[12] But the first disciple of Jesus with whom he had to do in Damascus was a member of this local community, one Ananias, "a devout man according to the law, well spoken of by all the Jews who lived there" (Acts 22: 12).

Until the last moment of his pre-Christian career, then, Paul showed himself to be (in his own words) "as to zeal a persecutor of the church" (Philippians 3: 6).

12. Acts 26: 11, "I persecuted them even to foreign cities".

# CHAPTER 9

# Paul Becomes a Christian

## 1. On the Damascus road

WITH ASTONISHING SUDDENNESS THE PERSECUTOR OF THE church became the apostle of Jesus Christ. He was in mid-course as a zealot for the law, bent on checking a plague which threatened the life of Israel, when, in his own words, he was "apprehended by Christ Jesus" (Philippians 3: 12) and constrained to turn right round and become a champion of the cause which, up to that moment, he had been endeavouring to exterminate, dedicated henceforth to building up what he had been doing his best to demolish.

What caused this revolution? His own repeated explanation is that he saw the once-crucified Jesus now exalted as the risen Lord. "Have I not seen Jesus our Lord?" he asks indignantly when his apostolic credentials are questioned (1 Corinthians 9: 1), referring to the same occasion as that mentioned later in the same letter (1 Corinthians 15: 8) where, after listing earlier appearances of Christ in resurrection, he adds, "Last of all . . . he appeared also to me" (perhaps in the sense, "he let himself be seen by me"). The resurrection appearance granted to him, he insists, was as real as the appearances witnessed by Peter, James and many others on the first Easter and the days immediately following. When, in 2 Corinthians 4: 6, he says that "God . . . has shone in our hearts to give the light of the knowledge of the glory of God in the face of Christ", his language perhaps implies a reminiscence of the same event – more particularly of that great "light from heaven, brighter than the sun" which flashed about him as he and his companions approached Damascus, according to the evidence of Acts (9: 3; 22: 6; 26: 13).

The evidence of Acts corroborates Paul's claim to have seen the risen Christ but also insists time and again that he heard him speak. "The God of our fathers", he is told by Ananias of Damascus, "appointed you to see the Just One and to hear a voice from his mouth" (Acts 22: 14; cf. 9: 17). Whatever variations there are in Luke's three accounts of Paul's conversion, all three agree that about midday, as he was approaching Damascus, he "heard a voice saying to him, 'Saul, Saul, why do you persecute me?' And he said, 'Who are you, Lord?' And he said, 'I am Jesus [of Nazareth], whom you are persecuting' " (9: 4 f.; 22: 7 f.; 26: 14 f.).

Some verbal communication, beyond the heavenly vision in itself, is implied in Paul's statement that "he who had set me apart before I was born, and had called me by his grace, was pleased to reveal his Son in me, *in order that I might preach him among the Gentiles*" (Galatians 1: 15 f.). Objective as the revelation was, it was experienced inwardly as well as outwardly: it was granted, as Paul puts it, not merely "to me" but "in me". He speaks as if the call and commission were part of the one conversion experience.[1]

No single event, apart from the Christ-event itself, has proved so determinant for the course of Christian history as the conversion and commissioning of Paul. For anyone who accepts Paul's own explanation of his Damascus-road experience, it would be difficult to disagree with the observation of an eighteenth-century writer that "the conversion and apostleship of St. Paul alone, duly considered, was of itself a demonstration sufficient to prove Christianity to be a divine revelation".[2]

With no conscious preparation, Paul found himself instantaneously compelled by what he saw and heard to acknowledge that Jesus of Nazareth, the crucified one, was alive after his passion, vindicated and exalted by God, and was now conscripting him into his service. There could be no resistance to this compulsion, no kicking out against this goad[3] which was driving him in the opposite direction to that which he had hitherto been pursuing. He capitulated forthwith to the commands of this new master; a conscript he might be,[4] but henceforth also a devoted and lifelong volunteer.

Attempts to account for Paul's experience in physiological or psychological terms are precarious, and inadequate to boot unless they take adequately into consideration the fact that it involved the intelligent and deliberate surrender of his will to the risen Christ

1. We may compare the experience of Isaiah, who was both cleansed and commissioned in the course of his vision of the glory of Yahweh (Isaiah 6: 1–9a), or of Ezekiel, whose call came in the course of a similar vision (Ezekiel 1: 4–3: 11) – although it was to Israel, not to the nations, that these two prophets were sent. Paul's language also echoes the narrative of the call of Jeremiah, to whom Yahweh said, "before you were born ... I appointed you a prophet to the nations" (Jeremiah 1: 5). See p. 144, n. 37.

2. G. Lyttelton, *Observations on the Conversion and Apostleship of St. Paul* (London, 1747), paragraph 1.

3. Although the known literary analogues of this metaphor (Acts 26: 14) are Greek and Latin, not Semitic, it is the kind of expression that might be found in any agricultural community.

4. Cf. Philippians 3: 12, where "I was apprehended by Christ Jesus" conveys the sense of κατελήμφθην better than the weaker verbs used in some more recent versions.

who had appeared to him – the risen Christ who, from this time on, displaced the law as the centre of Paul's life and thought.

"Blinded with excess of light", Paul was led into Damascus, to the house of one Judas in the "street called Straight" (a name which survives to this day in the Darb al-Mustaqim), where presumably arrangements had been made for him to lodge. There he was visited by Ananias, one of the local disciples of Jesus, who greeted him as a brother and a fellow-disciple. Immediately Paul recovered his sight and was baptized in the name of Jesus. The man who had set out for Damascus to work havoc among the disciples there now found himself welcomed into their fellowship.

## 2. The covenanters of Damascus

Damascus has been claimed to be the oldest continuously inhabited city in the world. It is mentioned in the biblical story of Abraham (Genesis 14: 15; 15: 2), who indeed is said in later (Hellenistic) tradition to have reigned in Damascus.[5] In patriarchal times it was an Amorite centre, but came into the power of the Aramaeans about 1200 B.C. In the period of the Hebrew monarchy it was the capital of an Aramaean kingdom which waged intermittent war with the kingdom of Israel until both were overrun and annexed by the Assyrians in the late eighth century B.C. It was subject successively to the Assyrian, Babylonian, Persian and Graeco-Macedonian empires. Throughout the third century B.C. it lay on the frontier between the Ptolemaic and Seleucid realms, and was claimed by both. When, as a result of their victory at Paneion in 200 B.C., the Seleucids extended their realm south to the Egyptian frontier, Damascus passed decisively into their power.

In the period when the Seleucid empire was rapidly disintegrating, Damascus was seized by the Nabataean king Aretas III (c. 85 B.C.). The Nabataeans were Arabs; their homeland was the territory between the Dead Sea and the Gulf of Aqaba, and Petra was their capital. The Nabataean kingdom was incorporated in the Roman Empire as the province of Arabia in A.D. 106, but in its heyday it was a power to be reckoned with, posing a recurrent threat to the Hasmonaean and Herodian rulers of Palestine. The Nabataeans did not retain Damascus for long. During the Mithridatic wars it was taken from them by Tigranes I of Armenia (72/1 B.C.). He lost it in 66 B.C. to the Romans, in whose control it thereafter remained (apart from the brief Parthian occupation of

5. According to Josephus (Ant. i. 159), Herod's court historian, Nicolaus of Damascus, recorded in the fourth book of his Histories that Abraham (Abramēs) reigned there. A similar statement is quoted from the Latin writer Pompeius Trogus (c. 20 B.C.) in the third-century Epitome of Justin (xxxvi. 2. 3).

Syria in 40–39 B.C.), as one of the cities of the Decapolis,[6] under the general supervision of the governors of Syria. It was from Damascus that Pompey's lieutenant Scaurus set out in 64 B.C. to intervene in the quarrel between the Hasmonaean brothers Hyrcanus II and Aristobulus II, both of whom sought Roman support – which led inevitably to Pompey's occupation of Judaea the following year. In the time of Tiberius the territory assigned to Damascus extended west to border on that of Sidon.

Under the Seleucids Damascus had become largely hellenized. Its tutelary deity was identified with Dionysus, who came to figure in its foundation legend. It was planned on the Hippodamic grid pattern[7] and appears to have had the installations essential to a Hellenistic city: when, for example, Herod the Great presented it with a gymnasium,[8] this was presumably designed to replace an earlier one. Greek may well have been the language most commonly used in Damascus in Paul's time; yet Aramaic would also be heard in its streets – this being the language not only of the desert-dwellers to the east but also (probably) of its Jewish colony. This colony was a sizeable one, even if we do not accept at face value Josephus's estimate that 10,000 or even 18,000 Jews were massacred in Damascus in A.D. 66.[9]

Damascus, which plays a part in Muslim eschatological tradition as the place to which Jesus will descend to destroy Antichrist,[10] may well have figured in this way in a branch of Christian tradition from which the Muslims took over the expectation. Any such Christian tradition would be too late to have first-century relevance; it could, however, have had Jewish antecedents. In some strands of Jewish tradition, too, Damascus or the surrounding territory figures as the place where Gentile dominion will be finally overthrown, and while most of these strands are of late attestation, there is one which dates back to pre-Christian times.[11]

Two imperfect manuscripts of early mediaeval date, discovered towards the end of the nineteenth century in the genizah of the ancient synagogue of Fostat (Old Cairo), were recognized to be copies of a composition provisionally called the *Zadokite Work* or the *Book*

6. The Decapolis comprised about ten federated cities: Damascus, Hippos, Canatha, Raphana, Gadara, Philadelphia (modern Amman), Gerasa, Dion, Pella and Scythopolis (Beth-shan), only the last of which lay west of the Jordan.

7. So called from the town-planner Hippodamus of Miletus (5th century B.C.).

8. Josephus, *BJ* i. 422 (he also built a theatre in Damascus).

9. According to *BJ* ii. 561 the number of those massacred (in the gymnasium) was 10,500; according to *BJ* vii. 368 it was 18,000.

10. Cf. A. J. Wensinck, *A Handbook of Early Muhammadan Tradition* (Leiden, 1927), p. 113.

11. Cf. N. Wieder, *The Judaean Scrolls and Karaism* (London, 1962), pp. 5–14; "The 'Land of Damascus' and Messianic Redemption", *Journal of Jewish Studies* 20 (1969), pp. 86–88.

*of the Covenant of Damascus.*[12] Not until the discovery of the Qumran texts in 1947 and the following years was it realized that this composition came from the same community as those others. Not only did the contents match those of some of the Qumran documents, but additional fragments of the same composition, centuries older than the Cairo manuscripts, were identified among the Qumran finds. The composition was called the *Zadokite Work* because of the place of esteem which it gives to Zadok and his dynasty (the legitimate high-priesthood in Israel); it was called the *Book of the Covenant of Damascus* because it speaks of "those who enter the new covenant in the land of Damascus",[13] presumably the same people referred to as "the repentant of Israel who went out from the land of Judah and sojourned in the land of Damascus" under the leadership of "the expositor of the law".[14] The "land of Damascus" was evidently a district where this covenant community spent some time in the early period of its existence; Damascus also figured in its expectation of the end of the age then current, for another "expositor of the law" was expected to come to Damascus then [15] – in company, it appears, with the Davidic Messiah.[16]

"Damascus" has been held by some scholars to be a code-name for the community's place of exile [17] – a code-name chosen because they interpreted their emigration as the fulfilment of the prophecy of Amos 5: 26 f., quoted in the strange form: "I have exiled the tabernacle of your king and the pedestal of your images from my tent to Damascus".[18] But the form of the quotation – not to speak of its interpretation – is so strange as to suggest that it was adapted to fit the fulfilment: the interpreters, that is to say, sought a text to suit their migration to Damascus and found it in Amos 5: 26 f.[19]

The covenanters regarded the "Teacher of Righteousness" (who was no longer alive) as the first leader and organizer of their community. If Damascus be taken literally, the question arises of the relation of this community to that of Qumran, which also venerated

12. First published by S. Schechter, *Fragments of a Zadokite Work*, i (Cambridge, 1910).

13. CD 6, l. 19; 8, l. 21; cf. 20, l. 12.

14. CD 6, ll. 5–7.

15. CD 7, ll. 18 f.

16. Called "the prince of all the congregation" and equated with the "sceptre" of Numbers 24: 17, as the "star" in that verse is interpreted of the coming "expositor of the law" (CD 7, l. 20). Cf. also J. Daniélou, "L'étoile de Jacob et la mission chrétienne à Damas", *Vigiliae Christianae* 11 (1957), pp. 121–138.

17. E.g. my T. H. Gaster, *The Dead Sea Scriptures* (Garden City, N.Y.,[3] 1977), pp. 5, 27 ff. But a migration to Qumran would scarcely be described as leaving "the land of Judah" for "the land of the north" (CD 5, l. 5; 7, ll. 12–14).

18. CD 7, l. 15.

19. Cf. J. T. Milik, *Ten Years of Discovery in the Wilderness of Judaea* (London, 1959), p. 91.

the Teacher of Righteousness as its first leader and organizer. The means of reconstructing the history of the community are too scanty to make any firm answer possible.[20] Perhaps the community as a whole resided in "the land of Damascus" for some years: at one time the attractive suggestion was made that it resided there during the thirty years or more of its abandonment of the Qumran centre at the end of the first century B.C. (driven thence, perhaps, by the Parthian invasion), but the palaeography of the Qumran fragments of the *Zadokite Work* points to a date several decades earlier. Another possibility is that one branch of the community lived in the land of Damascus for a time while the main body lived at Qumran. The troubles under Alexander Jannaeus might provide an appropriate historical setting, but we do not know. There is serious reason to believe, however, that those who betook themselves to the land of Damascus did so "in order to anticipate there the appearance of the Messiah, or, in general, the inauguration of the messianic drama".[21]

### 3. With the disciples at Damascus

We may wish we knew something about the antecedents of the community of Jesus' disciples at Damascus – that is, if we are right in inferring from Luke's record that such a community had been established there before the arrival of refugees from Judaea after the death of Stephen. Unfortunately, we have no evidence to guide us and are driven to speculate. One scholar has ventured the speculation that the founders of the community were actually members of the holy family, brothers and other relatives of Jesus, and that they settled in the region of Damascus because they expected Jesus to be speedily manifested in glory there.[22] This cannot be disproved – there is no reason why one should wish to disprove it – but equally it cannot be proved. The most that can be said is that the community was probably Galilaean rather than Judaean in its provenance, if only because Galilee (where Jesus had more disciples during his ministry than he had in Judaea) lay so near to Damascus and the other cities of the Decapolis. We know that a generation or two later there were several Jewish-Christian settlements in and around

20. Cf. H. H. Rowley, *The Zadokite Fragments and the Dead Sea Scrolls* (Oxford, 1952); "The History of the Qumran Sect", *BJRL* 49 (1966–67), pp. 203–232.

21. N. Wieder, *The Judaean Scrolls and Karaism*, p. 3.

22. E. Lohmeyer, *Galiläa und Jerusalem* (Göttingen, 1936), pp. 54 ff.; so also H. J. Schoeps, *Theologie und Geschichte des Judenchristentums* (Tübingen, 1949), pp. 270 ff. For a more disciplined and better documented examination of evidence on the expansion of Christianity in the first three to five years of its existence see M. Hengel, "Zwischen Jesus und Paulus", *ZTK* 72 (1975), pp. 172–206.

the Decapolis, but they are scarcely relevant to this much earlier settlement in Damascus.[23]

Still more speculative is the possibility of contact, or even mutual influence, between these disciples in Damascus and the covenanters attested in the *Zadokite Work*; and most speculative of all is the question how far, if at all, Paul's thinking was indebted to these new friends among whom he first enjoyed Christian fellowship. It has been pointed out that the Qumran texts and the Pauline letters share a twofold concept of divine righteousness – the personal righteousness of God and the righteous status which he freely bestows on those who trust in him [24] – but here we should probably recognize a parallel development; Paul's doctrine, as we shall see, was shaped in the light of his own quite exceptional experience of law and grace. The antithesis of flesh and spirit is also common to Paul and Qumran, but this too is distinctively developed by Paul.[25]

It was not to the disciples in Damascus, nor indeed to the disciples anywhere else, that Paul was indebted for the basic elements in his theology. In this regard his own claim about the gospel which he preached may safely be admitted: "I did not receive it from man, nor was I taught it, but it came through a revelation of Jesus Christ" (Galatians 1: 12). It did not come in its fulness all at once, of course, but, as Paul saw it, it was all implicit in the Damascus-road revelation. It was this that put a new perspective on all his previous experience and training. Formerly, all the elements in his life and thought were organized around the central focus of the law. When the revelation of Jesus Christ showed him in a flash the bankruptcy of the law, the law could no longer be the magnet which drew all those elements together in a well-defined pattern. With the removal of the magnet they would have been dispersed and disorganized, had the law not been immediately replaced at the centre by the risen Lord, around whom Paul's life and thought were reorganized to form a new pattern. Inevitably it took time for him to think through all that was involved in this reorganization – in fact, the remainder of his mortal life was insufficient for him fully to explore what he called "the surpassing worth of knowing Christ Jesus my Lord" (Philippians 3: 8). But he could at least declare his new faith in the affirmation "Jesus is the risen Lord" or "Jesus is the Son of God"; indeed, Luke says that he

23. Luke implies, however, that the baptism which Paul underwent at Damascus (Acts 9: 18; 22: 16) was no less valid than if it had been administered in Jerusalem.

24. Cf. H. Braun, *Qumran und das Neue Testament*, ii (Tübingen, 1966), pp. 170 ff.; W. Grundmann, "The Teacher of Righteousness of Qumran and the question of justification by faith in the theology of the Apostle Paul", in *Paul and Qumran*, ed. J. Murphy-O'Connor (London, 1968), pp. 85–114.

25. Cf. W. D. Davies, "Paul and the Dead Sea Scrolls: Flesh and Spirit", in *The Scrolls and the New Testament*, ed. K. Stendahl (London, 1958), pp. 157–182.

quickly declared it in the latter words in the synagogues of Damascus to which he had been accredited by the high priest for a very different purpose.[26] Paul himself says that on receiving the revelation he "did not confer with flesh and blood" but "went away to Arabia and returned again to Damascus" (Galatians 1: 16 f.), so perhaps his preaching in the Damascene synagogues should be dated after he returned from his Arabian journey (of which Luke has nothing to say).

Why did Paul go away to Arabia? A common answer is that he went into the desert to reflect on his new situation, perhaps to commune with God in the vicinity of "Horeb, the mount of God", where Moses and Elijah had communed with him in days gone by.[27] This may indeed have been part of his purpose, but probably his three days of blindness in Damascus had been sufficient for his mind to be reorientated. The implication of his own narrative relates his Arabian visit rather closely to his call to preach Christ among the Gentiles; the point of his reference to it in writing to his Galatian converts is to underline the fact that he began to discharge this call before he went up to Jerusalem to see the apostles there, so that none could say that it was they (or any other authorities on earth) who commissioned him to be the Gentiles' apostle.

By "Arabia" in this context we naturally understand the Nabataean kingdom, which was readily accessible from Damascus. At this time it was ruled by Aretas IV (9 B.C. – A.D. 40). If Paul preached the gospel to the subjects of Aretas, we may wonder where he found a point of contact in their outlook which could dispose them to listen with some interest to his message that the crucified Jesus had been vindicated and exalted by God as universal Lord; but we should not underestimate Paul's resourcefulness and versatility. It certainly appears from a piece of evidence elsewhere in his correspondence that it was not simply a quiet retreat that Paul sought in Arabia. In a later reminiscence he recalls a humiliating experience from his early Christian days: "At Damascus the ethnarch of King Aretas guarded the city of the Damascenes in order to seize me, but I was let down in a basket through a window in the wall, and escaped his hands" (2 Corinthians 11: 32 f.). The "ethnarch of King Aretas" was probably the representative of the king's subjects who were resident in Damascus, just as the Jewish colony in Alexandria appointed an ethnarch to be their representative and spokesman before the civic and imperial authorities there.[28] But why should the Nabataean ethnarch take this hostile action against Paul, if Paul had spent his

26. Acts 9: 20. See pp. 117 f.
27. Cf. Exodus 3: 1; 1 Kings 19: 8.
28. Strabo, quoted by Josephus, *Ant.* xiv. 117; the term ἐθνάρχης here is probably equivalent to γενάρχης in Philo, *Flaccus* 74.

time in Arabia in silent contemplation? If, on the other hand, he
spent his time there in preaching, he could well have stirred up
trouble for himself and attracted the unfriendly attention of the
authorities. Since the Nabataean territory came up almost to the
walls of Damascus, the ethnarch, with an adequate body of his
fellow-nationals to help him, may have watched the city gate from
the outside, so as to arrest Paul if he left the city. By the help of his
friends, however, he left Damascus in such a way as to avoid the
ethnarch's notice.[29] It was probably now, in the third year after he
set out for Damascus on his anti-Christian errand, that he paid his
first visit to Jerusalem since his conversion.

29. Luke represents Paul as compelled to escape because of the hostility of the
Damascene Jews (Acts 9: 23–25).

# CHAPTER 10

# Paul and the Jerusalem Tradition

## 1. Paul goes up to Jerusalem

THE NEWS OF PAUL'S CONVERSION MUST HAVE REACHED Jerusalem long before he himself arrived there. But it was hardly credible. The Ethiopian could more easily change his skin or the leopard its spots than the arch-persecutor become a believer. Might it not be part of a deep-laid plot to gain acceptance within the Christian fellowship so as to deal it a more effective death-blow? The simple-minded and warm-hearted disciples of Damascus might welcome him impulsively as one of themselves, but if he came to Jerusalem it would be best to keep him at arm's length until his *bona fides* could be established beyond any doubt.

According to Luke, it was Barnabas whose good offices brought Paul and the leaders of the Jerusalem church together. Although Paul says nothing of this, it is antecedently probable that someone acted as mediator, and all that we know of Barnabas suggests that he was the very man to act in this way. Barnabas first appears in Luke's narrative as an outstandingly generous contributor to the common fund set up in the primitive Jerusalem church; he is said to have been given this sobriquet by the apostles (in addition to his personal name Joseph) because of his encouraging character.[1] And throughout the apostolic record, Barnabas lived up to this reputation: wherever he found a person or a cause needing to be encouraged, he supplied all the encouragement he could. How he was able to assure himself that Paul's conversion was genuine we are not told, but he was probably in touch with those believing Hellenists who sought refuge in Damascus; he may even have been with them for some time. At any rate his interposition on Paul's behalf in Jerusalem is completely in character. When Paul sorely needed a friend in Damascus, Ananias filled this rôle, and equally now Barnabas befriended him when he stood in similar need in Jerusalem. His old friends would now repudiate him as a renegade, and new friends could be made only with difficulty in the community which he had harried so ruthlessly. Luke's introduction of Barnabas here is too particular for it to be regarded as simply part of his generalizing summary of Paul's present visit to Jerusalem; he

1. Acts 4: 36 f.

83

draws on precise information when he says that "Barnabas took him, and brought him to the apostles" (Acts 9: 27).

Not to all the apostles, indeed: where Luke generalizes, Paul is specific, and makes it plain that he met only two of them. "I went up to Jerusalem to get to know Cephas", he says, "and remained with him fifteen days; but I saw none of the other apostles except James the Lord's brother" (Galatians 1: 18 f.). Then he adds a solemn asseveration of the accuracy of his narrative: "In what I am writing to you, before God, I do not lie!" (Galatians 1: 20). Evidently some variant account of Paul's movements and contacts about this time was circulating among his Galatian friends,[2] and he swears that his own account is the true one.

## 2. Paul meets Peter and James

Cephas – the Aramaic *Kēphā* ("rock" or "stone") equipped with the Greek termination -*s* – is Paul's regular designation for the apostle who is better known to us as Peter (i.e. *Petros*, the Greek equivalent of Aramaic *Kēphā*). The purpose of Paul's going to Jerusalem on this occasion was to make the acquaintance of the leading apostle – and not merely to make his acquaintance but to inquire of him (for this is the force of the verb *historēsai* which he uses).[3] For Peter was a primary informant on matters which it was now important that Paul should know – the details of Jesus' ministry and the "tradition" of teaching which derived from him. There is in some quarters considerable resistance to the idea that Paul was interested in acquiring information of this kind, but even if Paul had no such interest (which is incredible), what would Peter talk about during those fifteen days? Peter could impart to Paul much information of the kind he sought, more indeed than James could, but there was one thing, he insists, which neither Peter nor James did or could impart to him, and that was his apostolic commission, which he had already received direct from the risen Lord on the Damascus road. His object in going up to Jerusalem was to establish bonds of fellowship with the leaders of the mother church and obtain from them information which could be obtained nowhere else.

Whatever else he obtained by way of information, he himself indicates in another place two facts at least which he learned. We

2. O. Linton, "The Third Aspect: A Neglected Point of View", *Studia Theologica* 3 (1949), pp. 79 ff., argues that this variant account is that on which Luke draws in Acts 9: 1–30.

3. Among other discussions of this verb cf. G. D. Kilpatrick, "Galatians 1: 18 ἱστορῆσαι Κηφᾶν " in *New Testament Essays . . . in Memory of T. W. Manson,* ed. A. J. B. Higgins (Manchester, 1959), pp. 144 ff.; W. D. Davies, *The Setting of the Sermon on the Mount* (Cambridge, 1964), pp. 453 ff.

have already quoted the list of Jesus' resurrection appearances of which Paul reminds his Corinthian readers.[4] In that list two individuals are mentioned by name as having seen the risen Christ, and two only: "he appeared to Cephas" and "he appeared to James" (1 Corinthians 15: 5, 7). It is no mere coincidence that these should be the only two apostles whom Paul claims to have seen during his first visit to Jerusalem after his conversion.

The resurrection appearance to Peter is independently attested in Luke 24: 34. The appearance to James reappears, with what are probably legendary embellishments, in the Gospel according to the Hebrews,[5] but the tradition thus embellished is quite probably not derived from Paul.

James, with other members of the family of Jesus, does not appear to have been a follower of his before his death; indeed, the family as a whole appears to have viewed Jesus' public activity with aloofness, not to say hostility. Yet after Jesus' resurrection his mother and brothers are found in association with the apostles and other disciples. The brothers became figures of note in the church at large, and James in particular occupied an increasingly influential position in the church of Jerusalem. If we look for some explanation of their sudden change in attitude towards Jesus, we can find it in the statement that in resurrection he appeared to James.

Peter and James appear to have been the respective leaders of two distinct groups within the primitive church of Jerusalem. The group led by Peter met in the house of Mary, the mother of John Mark: it was to this group that Peter made his way, a few years after this, when he unexpectedly escaped from Herod Agrippa's prison; and when he took his leave of them he said, "Tell this to James and to the brethren" (Acts 12: 17) – meaning presumably the brethren more closely associated with James.

It may be concluded, then, that during Paul's fifteen days with Peter in Jerusalem he called on James and heard his side of the story. If Peter told him how the risen Lord had appeared not only to himself but also to "the twelve" and again to "more than five hundred brethren at one time", James told him how he had appeared not only to him but also to "all the apostles". For Paul, "the apostles" were not restricted to "the twelve"; he counts James

4. See pp. 62 f.
5. According to Jerome (*De uiris illustribus*, 2), the Gospel according to the Hebrews recorded: "Now when the Lord had given his linen garment to the priest's servant, he went to James and appeared to him. For James had sworn that he would eat no bread from that hour when he had drunk the cup of the Lord until he saw him rising from the dead. [And again, a little later:] 'Bring a table and bread', said the Lord; [and immediately it continues:] he took bread and gave thanks and broke it, and thereafter he gave it to James the Just and said to him: 'My brother, eat your bread, because the Son of Man has risen from those who sleep'."

as an apostle, according to the most probable sense of Galatians 1: 19, "I saw none of the other apostles [apart from Cephas] except James the Lord's brother".[6] If the qualification of an apostle was to have been commissioned by the risen Christ, then James apparently had the same claim to the designation as Paul himself had.

This series of resurrection appearances, together with the preceding statements "that Christ died for our sins in accordance with the scriptures, that he was buried, that he was raised on the third day in accordance with the scriptures" (1 Corinthians 15: 3 f.), Paul says he "received" by way of tradition, as in turn he delivered it to his converts.[7] Tradition was a living and growing thing in the first-century church: the tradition which Paul delivered was fuller than what he received, for he was able to amplify the record of appearances of the risen Lord with his personal testimony: "Last of all, as to one untimely born, he appeared also to me" (1 Corinthians 15: 8).[8] This does not exhaust what Paul claims to have received by tradition – the tradition included an account of words and actions of the historical Jesus (pre-eminently his words and actions at the institution of the Lord's Supper) and some guide-lines and principles of Christian conduct [9] – but it has special importance as an outline of early Christian preaching, a kerygmatic outline, to use modern theological jargon. Whatever differences might develop between Paul's preaching and that of the Jerusalem leaders, they were agreed on this: "whether then it was I or they", he says to the Corinthians at the end of this outline: "so we preach and so you believed" (1 Corinthians 15: 11).

## 3. Revelation and tradition

It was almost certainly during these fifteen days in Jerusalem that Paul received this outline. But this raises the question of the relation between his insistence in Galatians 1: 12 that he did not "receive" his gospel from man, since "it came through a revelation

---

6. L. P. Trudinger, "A Note on Galatians i. 19", *Novum Testamentum* 17 (1975), pp. 200 ff., translates ἕτερον δε τῶν ἀποστόλων κτλ as "other than the apostles I saw none except James the Lord's brother" – but this is a dubious way of construing the Greek text.

7. See F. F. Bruce, *Tradition Old and New* (Exeter, 1970), pp. 29 ff.

8. In referring to himself thus as "one untimely born" – an abortion ( ἔκτρωμα ) – Paul may be taking up a term of reproach cast at him for the "unnaturalness" of the resurrection appearance and apostolic commission which he claimed to have received. See A. Fridrichsen, "Paulus abortivus", in *Symbolae philologicae O. A. Danielsson dicatae* (Uppsala, 1932), pp. 79 ff.; G. Björck, "Nochmals Paulus abortivus", *Coniectanea Neotestamentica* 3 (1938), pp. 3 ff.; J. Munck, "Paulus tamquam abortivus" in *New Testament Essays . . . in Memory of T. W. Manson*, ed. A. J. B. Higgins, pp. 180 ff.

9. See pp. 105 ff.

of Jesus Christ", and his statement in 1 Corinthians 15: 3 (and elsewhere) that he did "receive" it. The Greek verb rendered "receive" in both places is *paralambanō*, which implies receiving by tradition, especially when it is accompanied by the correlative verb *paradidōmi*,[10] which implies handing on what one has thus received. Evidently Paul was aware of a sense in which he had not received the gospel by tradition, and a sense in which he had. What, then, was the relation in his mind between the gospel as revelation and the gospel as tradition?

The gospel as revelation was what accomplished his conversion. Others had confessed Jesus as the risen Lord before he did, but it was not their testimony that moved him to make that confession his own. Their testimony moved him rather to oppose them with might and main: it was blasphemy in his ears. The one thing that could have convinced Paul that Jesus was indeed the risen Lord was the Damascus-road revelation: the risen Lord appeared to him in person and introduced himself as Jesus. This was henceforth the heart of his gospel: he owed it to no witness on earth but to that "revelation of Jesus Christ".[11]

Wrapped up in that revelation, as Paul proceeded to unpack it, was much that was distinctive of the gospel as he understood and proclaimed it. His concept of the church as the body of Christ, for example, and of individual Christians as members of that body, may go back to the implication of the risen Lord's complaint: "why do you persecute *me*?" With this was bound up his understanding of Christian existence "in Christ" – an existence in which social, racial and other barriers within the human family were done away with. Among those barriers none was so important in Paul's eyes as that between Jew and Gentile. If before his conversion he looked upon it as one that had to be maintained at all costs, after his conversion he devoted himself to demolishing it, doing in practice what had been done in principle by Christ on the cross.[12] This insight was implicit in his call to preach Christ among the Gentiles, which was contemporaneous with his conversion. As he himself, a Jew by birth, had received new life in Christ through faith, apart from the works of the law, so they, Gentiles by birth, could similarly receive new life in Christ through faith, apart from the works of the law, and thus enjoy an equal status in the redeemed community with himself and other believing Jews. Through Paul's ministry in particular "the mystery hidden for ages and generations" was disclosed in all its fulness – the mystery which, as he told the Colossians,

10. As it is also in 1 Corinthians 11: 23.

11. The genitive "of Jesus Christ" is objective: the reference is to the conversion-experience in which, as he said, God "was pleased to reveal his Son in me" (Galatians 1: 16).

12. Cf. Ephesians 2: 14–16.

was summed up in the message: "Christ in you [in you Gentile believers as well as in Jewish believers], the hope of glory" (Colossians 1: 26 f.). In other words, he viewed himself as chosen by heavenly grace in order that the saving purpose of God, conceived in Christ before all worlds, might be made effective in Christ through his ministry, and might in due course be consummated when everything in the universe was reconciled and united in Christ.

We may say then, in general, that those aspects in Paul's ministry which were distinctively his belong to the gospel as revelation, while those elements which he shared with others (apart from his unmediated recognition of Jesus as the Son of God) belong to the gospel as tradition, and in the first instance, to the information he received in Jerusalem when he went up there to make inquiry of Peter in the third year after his conversion.

We have already considered the account of appearances of the risen Christ which he says that he received – evidently on that occasion. But the series of resurrection appearances is preceded by three clauses which he includes in what he received and then delivered to his converts "as of first importance" – (a) "that Christ died for our sins in accordance with the scriptures", (b) "that he was buried", (c) "that he was raised on the third day in accordance with the scriptures". The fact that each of these three clauses, like the fourth which follows ("and that he appeared . . ."), is introduced by the conjunction "that" indicates that Paul presents them as successive quotations from his source.

(a) *Christ died for our sins in accordance with the scriptures.* Does the whole of this clause belong to the tradition, or does part of it represent Paul's interpretation of the tradition? The words "in accordance with the scriptures" certainly correspond to a primitive emphasis in the gospel story, an emphasis which is recognizable in every area of New Testament teaching – in the non-Pauline letters as clearly as in the Pauline, in the speeches of Acts and in all the strands which have been woven together to produce the material of the four Gospels. The earliest Gospel, for example, introduces itself with prophetic quotations and represents Jesus as submitting to his captors with the words, "Let the scriptures be fulfilled" (Mark 1:2f.; 14: 49). That Christ *died* "in accordance with the scriptures" was part of the early apostolic witness. When Peter, in the temple court at Jerusalem, says with reference to the condemnation of Jesus that "what God foretold by the mouth of all his prophets, that his Christ should suffer, he thus fulfilled" (Acts 3: 18), his words are summarized in Luke's idiom but express a primitive belief. If we ask where in the prophetic oracles it was foretold that the Christ was to suffer, an answer is offered by this same speech, which begins with the announcement that "the God of our fathers glorified his servant

Jesus" who was disowned by his people – an echo of the fourth Isaianic Servant Song, where the Servant who has been "despised and rejected by men" is "exalted and lifted up" by God (Isaiah 52: 13; 53: 3; cf. Acts 3: 13).[13]

But what of the statement that Christ died "for our sins" – could that belong to the tradition which Paul received, especially to the Jerusalem tradition? It is pointed out that if the early speeches in Acts reflect the Jerusalem tradition, the expiatory significance of the death of Christ is not a prominent feature in them; in fact the one speech in Acts where it does find expression is Paul's speech to the elders of the Ephesian church, whom he exhorts "to feed the church of God which he purchased with the blood of his beloved one" (Acts 20: 28).[14]

Now clearly Paul, in writing as he does to the Corinthians, may have reproduced what he received in his own words and with his own emphasis. But his is not the only New Testament tradition to attach expiatory importance to the death of Christ. The writer to the Hebrews portrays Christ as priest and victim in one, who by his self-offering "made purification for sins" (Hebrews 1: 3); the readers of 1 Peter are reminded that they were "ransomed . . . with the precious blood of Christ" (1 Peter 1: 18 f.); the readers of 1 John are assured that "the blood of Jesus . . . cleanses us from all sin" (1 John 1: 7), and the seer of Patmos speaks of Christ as "him who loves us and has freed us from our sins by his blood" (Revelation 1: 5).[15] Above all, the earliest Gospel reports Jesus as telling his disciples that "the Son of man came . . . to give his life a ransom for many" (Mark 10: 45) – a form of words which, in a Jewish context at that time, implies an atonement for their sins, whether or not it echoes the prophet's language about the Servant who "makes himself an offering for sin", thus causing "many to be accounted righteous" (Isaiah 53: 10 f.).[16]

Thus, even if those are right who maintain that Luke presents a *theologia gloriae* rather than a *theologia crucis*, the wide spread of the *theologia crucis* in the New Testament writings indicates that it is not peculiar to Paul but is more probably pre-Pauline, going back in fact to Jesus' own understanding of his death.

13. Cf. T. W. Manson, *The Servant-Messiah* (Cambridge, 1953), pp. 72 ff.; J. Jeremias in W. Zimmerli and J. Jeremias, *The Servant of God*, E.T. (London, 1957), pp. 79 ff.; for a critique of this view see M. D. Hooker, *Jesus and the Servant* (London, 1959).

14. See p. 342, n. 15.

15. In the account of the institution of the holy communion in Matthew 26: 28, the words "this is my covenant blood, which is poured out for many" (cf. Mark 14: 24) are glossed by the explanatory phrase "for the forgiveness of sins".

16. For other possible backgrounds to Mark 10: 45 see C. K. Barrett, "The Background of Mark 10: 45", in *New Testament Essays . . . in Memory of T. W. Manson*, ed. A. J. B. Higgins, pp. 1 ff. See pp. 60 f.

In the early speeches of Acts, however, forgiveness of sins is linked with faith in Christ. "To him", says Peter in the house of Cornelius, "all the prophets bear witness that every one who believes in him receives forgiveness of sins through his name" (Acts 10: 43). If the atoning virtue of his death is not expressly mentioned in such utterances, it is difficult to see how it could be absent from the thought of those who made forgiveness of sins dependent not on repentance in general but specifically on faith in the crucified and exalted Jesus. And when we find Jesus plainly identified with the Isaianic Servant of Yahweh, it is unlikely that those who made this identification did not draw the natural conclusion from the Servant's bearing "the sin of many" when he "poured out his soul to death"[17] (Isaiah 53: 12) – the natural conclusion being that this was what Jesus did.

We cannot, then, too readily assume that the phrase "for our sins" is Paul's epexegetic gloss on the statement that "Christ died" and that it could not have belonged to the tradition which he received.

Some scholars have detected a Semitic (more specifically, an Aramaic) substratum beneath the Greek text of the clause, "Christ died for our sins in accordance with the scriptures".[18] Others doubt this, on the highly improbable ground that the Greek phrase "in accordance with the scriptures" has no Aramaic equivalent. Such questions are precarious and unimportant. In whatever language Paul received the tradition, he delivered it to his converts in Greek, and was under no compulsion, when he did so, to reproduce Aramaic idiom cr anything of the sort.

One element in the debate about a Semitic substratum is the absence of the Greek definite article before the word "Christ".[19] This really proves nothing one way or the other. Much more significant is the use of the designation "Christ", whether with or without the article. It reminds us that the gospel from the beginning proclaimed Jesus as Messiah. If a pagan said "Christ died" – as when Tacitus, for example, says "Christ was executed"[20] he would be making a simple statement of fact, not a theological affirmation for

17. This Hebrew clause is translated into Greek in Philippians 2: 7 f., where Christ is said to have "emptied himself . . . unto death". Whether this passage is pre-Pauline or not, Paul uses it to express his own thought. See p. 131 with n. 25, p. 124 with n. 33.

18. Cf. J. Jeremias, *The Eucharistic Words of Jesus*, E. T. (Oxford, 1955), pp. 129 ff.; B. Klappert, "Zur Frage des Urtextes von 1 Kor. xv. 3–5", *NTS* 13 (1966–67), pp. 168 ff.; for contrary arguments cf. H. Conzelmann, "Zur Analyse der Bekenntnisformel 1 Kor. 15, 3–5", *Ev. Th.* 25 (1965), pp. 1 ff.

19. Cf. J. Jeremias, "Artikelloses Χριστός", ZNW 57 (1966), pp. 211 ff.; "Nochmals: Artikelloses Χριστός", *ZNW* 60 (1969), pp. 215 ff.; to the contrary cf. P. Vielhauer, "Ein Weg zur ntl. Christologie;" *Ev. Th.* 25 (1965), pp. 24 ff., especially pp. 57 f.

20. Tacitus, *Annals* xv. 44. 4.

him "Christ" would be nothing more than an alternative name for Jesus. But for a first-century Jew to say "Christ died" involves an assessment of the person who died, an acknowledgment that Jesus was the Lord's anointed. This first clause in the tradition, then, enshrines three theological propositions: that Jesus was the Messiah, that he died for his people's sins, and that this death of his took place in fulfilment of prophetic scripture.

(b) *Christ . . . was buried.* This second clause may be an appendix to the first ("Christ died . . .") as the fourth clause ("he appeared . . .") is appended to the third ("he was raised . . .").[21] Even so, the fact that the burial is given a clause to itself suggests that it was an independent feature in the tradition. Why should this be so? The fact of burial sometimes receives special mention in order to underline the reality and finality of death. "David both died and was buried", says Peter on the day of Pentecost, "and his tomb is with us to this day" (Acts 2: 29). But more than this is implied in the present context: the burial sets the seal on the death, no doubt, but it also provides the background for the resurrection. The resurrection was the reversal of the death and burial, and Paul's giving the burial separate mention points to the motif of the empty tomb. "What he has to say about the resurrection of Jesus in 1 Cor. 15", wrote S. H. Hooke, "clearly implies that he did not believe that the body of the Lord remained in the grave. The absence, however, of any reference to the fact that the grave was empty, shows that he did not regard it as a proof of the resurrection".[22] The emptiness of the tomb in itself might simply mean that the body had been removed. But if the body had still been there, that would have constituted a refutation of the resurrection claim, no matter how confidently the disciples maintained that the risen Lord had appeared to them. Hence the separate clause: "he was buried".

(c) *Christ . . . was raised on the third day in accordance with the scriptures.* It may be that this third clause makes two distinct statements about the resurrection of Christ: first, that it took place "on the third day", and second, that it took place "in accordance with the scriptures".[23] If this is so, then we are not obliged to find Old Testament scriptures which could point to resurrection on the third day. Such scriptures have indeed been adduced, but their relevance is doubtful. There is the frequently cited passage in Hosea 6: 2, "after two days he will revive us; on the third day he will raise us

21. Cf. E. Schweizer, "Two New Testament Creeds Compared", in *Current Issues in New Testament Interpretation: Essays in honor of O. A. Piper*, ed. W. Klassen and G. F. Snyder (London, 1962), pp. 166 ff.; R. H. Fuller, *The Formation of the Resurrection Narratives* (London, 1972), pp. 9 ff.
22. S. H. Hooke, *The Resurrection of Christ* (London, 1967), p. 114.
23. Cf. B. M. Metzger, "A Suggestion concerning the Meaning of 1 Cor. xv. 4b", *JTS*, n.s. 8 (1957), pp. 118 ff.

up, that we may live before him" – but it is hardly a natural *testimonium* of the Messiah's resurrection. Even less natural as such a *testimonium* is Isaiah's assurance to Hezekiah: "on the third day you shall go up to the house of Yahweh" (2 Kings 20: 5). As for Jonah, he is not said to have emerged from the fish's belly "on the third day", although his remaining there for "three days and three nights" appears as a resurrection *testimonium* in another and non-Pauline context (Matthew 12: 40). The waving of the sheaf of first fruits before God on "the morrow after the sabbath" (Leviticus 23: 9–21) may influence Paul's statement later in the same chapter that "Christ has been raised from the dead, the first fruits of those who have fallen asleep" (1 Corinthians 15: 20); [24] but that is part of Paul's own exposition of the subject, and "the morrow after the sabbath" was not necessarily "the third day" after Passover (although it may have been so in the year of Jesus' death and resurrection).

If the third day be dissociated from the phrase "in accordance with the scriptures", then we are less restricted in identifying those Old Testament passages to which the tradition may have made appeal. If the fourth Servant Song provided a *testimonium* for the death of Christ, it could also have provided a *testimonium* for his resurrection (as it clearly does for his exaltation): the Servant who "was cut off out of the land of the living" is promised that he will "prolong his days" and "see light [25] after the travail of his soul" (Isaiah 53: 8, 10 f.). Then there are other *testimonia* adduced in the speeches of Acts: for example, "thou wilt not abandon my soul to Hades, nor let thy holy one see corruption" (Psalm 16: 10, quoted in Acts 2: 27; 13: 35). This expression of confidence, ascribed to David, is seen in the apostolic preaching to have found its fulfilment in Messiah, the son of David, by whose resurrection God made good to his people "the holy and sure blessings of David" (Acts 13: 34, quoting Isaiah 55: 3). [26] Such *testimonia*, depending for their relevance on the identification of Jesus as the son of David, might be expected to figure in the Jerusalem tradition.

24. Cf. B. W. Bacon, *The Apostolic Message* (New York, 1925), pp. 134 f. The "sabbath" in "the morrow after the sabbath" was understood as the weekly sabbath in the chief-priestly interpretation which regulated the temple calendar, but in the Pharisaic interpretation which has become normative since A.D. 70 this sabbath is the festival day of unleavened bread, so that Pentecost in the orthodox Jewish calendar today need not fall on a Sunday, as it did in the temple calendar. See Mishnah *Menaḥôt* 10: 3; Tosefta *Menaḥôt* 10: 23 (528); TB *Menaḥôt* 65 a.

25. The noun "light" evidently dropped out of the Massoretic text at some stage but it was retained in LXX and is attested by two pre-Christian Hebrew manuscripts found in Qumran Cave 1(1QIs[a] and 1QIs[b]).

26. Paul in his letters rarely adduces Davidic promises as *testimonia* (an instance is Romans 15: 12, where the prophecy about "the root of Jesse" in Isaiah 11: 10 is quoted with reference to the Gentile mission), and never with regard to the resurrection.

The statement that it was "on the third day" that Christ rose is based not on any Old Testament scripture but on historical fact. Such an expression as "after three days" (not to speak of "three days and three nights"), used in predictions of the resurrection before the event (e.g. in Mark 8: 31), might have the general sense of "in a short time"; but after the event we regularly find it dated "on the third day", because it was actually on the third day that the tomb was found empty and Jesus first appeared in resurrection to Peter and others. It was these appearances that certified that he was risen: "The early Christians did not believe in the resurrection of Christ because they could not find his dead body. They believed because they did find a living Christ." [27]

Jerusalem commends itself as the fountain-head of the tradition which Paul says he received. Nothing that he might be told in Damascus or anywhere else could compare in authority with what Peter and James could provide. To the end of his active life, whatever tensions might develop between him and the Jerusalem leaders, Jerusalem remained in Paul's eyes the headquarters of the faith; the church in that city was the mother-church and was to be esteemed as such. It was to the disciples in Jerusalem that the Spirit of Christ was first given after his exaltation, and if Paul received the same Spirit in Damascus, that bound him the more closely to the original Spirit-baptized community. His receiving of the Spirit was one aspect of the revelation which dawned upon him on the Damascus road and during the days immediately following, but in the fellowship of the Spirit he gladly assimilated the tradition delivered to him in Jerusalem by those who were apostles before him.

When all this has been said, however, about the gospel as revelation and the gospel as tradition, it should be added that for Paul the gospel was more than a body of affirmations or factual data. The gospel was also for him, it has been said, "an on-going entity 'in' which one can 'be' or 'stand'" (cf. 1 Corinthians 15: 1), God's powerful agency for the salvation of believers (cf. Romans 1: 16); it was "the field of God's activity as it touches man's life"; [28] it was God's comprehensive plan for the redemption of all creation (cf. Rom. 8: 19–23); it was the Christ-event in its total outreach. Within this gospel's field of force Paul himself stood; to its service he knew himself called and consecrated; [29] in its saving dynamism he participated, and this participation carried its own reward with it (cf. 1 Corinthians 9: 16–23).

---

27. C. T. Craig, *The Beginning of Christianity* (New York, 1943), p. 135.
28. J. H. Schütz, *Paul and the Anatomy of Apostolic Authority* (Cambridge, 1975), pp. 43 ff., 53.
29. He refers to his gospel ministry as a "priestly service" (Romans 15: 16).

## 4. Paul leaves for Syria and Cilicia

When the fifteen days in Jerusalem were up, Paul departed, he says, for "the regions of Syria and Cilicia" (Galatians 1: 21) – that is, for his native territory (the united province of Syria-Cilicia). Luke gives us further details: short as his visit was, Paul's life was threatened by the Hellenists, presumably his old associates who had formerly mounted the attack on Stephen and others and who now regarded their lost leader as a traitor to the cause. Paul did not remain in hiding in Peter's lodging during his visit to Jerusalem. It is in the context of this visit that we should most naturally place his visit to the temple referred to in Acts 22: 17–21, when the risen Lord appeared to him again and confirmed afresh that his vocation was to the Gentiles, not to his fellow-Jews in Jerusalem.[30] Perhaps his return to Jerusalem as a Christian filled Paul with a burning desire to witness to his former companions, but he was assured that he was the last person to whose testimony they would listen. For his own safety, then, his new friends took him down to Caesarea and saw him on board a ship bound for Tarsus (Acts 9: 29 f.).

This detail, like the earlier reference to Barnabas, does not appear to be part of Luke's generalizing summary here. At any rate, when Paul's new friends saw the sail of his ship disappearing beneath the horizon, they probably breathed a sigh of relief and returned to Jerusalem with a sense of relaxation. Paul in his persecuting days had been a thorn in their flesh, but they were to learn that Paul the Christian also could be a disturbing presence, and trouble was liable to break out every time he visited Jerusalem. For the present, however, as Luke says, "the church . . . had peace" (Acts 9: 31).[31]

30. See p. 144.
31. The statement that "the church throughout all Judaea and Galilee and Samaria had peace" (Acts 9: 31) may be little more than a means of transition from the story of Paul's conversion to an account of the evangelization of the Mediterranean seaboard of Palestine; but it is noteworthy as providing the only New Testament reference to the church in Galilee (see p. 79).

# CHAPTER 11

# Paul and the Historical Jesus

THE SPEAKER WHO INTRODUCED HIMSELF ON THE DAMASCUS road as "Jesus, whom you are persecuting", was recognized by Paul as the exalted Son of God, identical nevertheless with that Jesus of Nazareth who had been crucified some three years before. Those to whom Jesus had previously appeared in resurrection had known him well in earlier years: the one whom they henceforth came to acknowledge as risen Lord and Saviour was the one with whom they had been acquainted as the Galilaean teacher. Paul had not been acquainted with Jesus before his crucifixion; he first came to know him as the risen Lord. His perspective on the "historical Jesus" was inevitably different from that of the original disciples. In speaking of the "historical Jesus" we do not try to distinguish, as do some scholars of today, between Jesus as he really was and what can be known of Jesus by the methods of historical science.[1] But it is of interest to discover, as far as possible, the extent of Paul's knowledge of, and interest in, the life and teaching of Jesus of Nazareth.

## 1. Historical allusions

While Paul's apostolic claim was discounted by some on the ground that, unlike the Jerusalem apostles, he had not been a follower of Jesus during his Palestinian ministry, Paul is, notwithstanding, our earliest literary authority for the historical Jesus. He does not tell us much about him, in comparison with what can be learned from the Gospels, but he does tell us a little more than the bare facts that Jesus was born, lived and died. Jesus, he says, was a descendant of Abraham (Galatians 3: 16) and David (Romans 1: 3), who lived under the Jewish law (Galatians 4: 4); he was betrayed, and on the night of his betrayal instituted a memorial meal of bread and wine (1 Corinthians 11: 23–25); he endured death by crucifixion (Galatians 3: 1, etc.), a Roman method of execution, although Jewish authorities shared some degree of responsibility for his death (1 Thessalonians 2: 15); he was buried,

---

1. Cf. J. M. Robinson, *A New Quest of the Historical Jesus* (London, 1959), pp. 26 f.

rose the third day, and was thereafter seen alive on several occasions by eyewitnesses varying in number (from one occasion to
another) between one by himself and five hundred together, the
majority of whom were alive to attest the fact twenty-five years later
(1 Corinthians 15: 4–8).

Paul knows of the apostles of Jesus, of whom Cephas (Peter) and
John are mentioned by name as "pillars" of the Jerusalem church
fifteen to twenty years after his death, and of his brothers, of whom
James is similarly mentioned as a "pillar" (Galatians 2: 9; cf. 1:
19). He knows that many of those apostles and brothers were
married men; Cephas (Peter) is specially named in this regard (1
Corinthians 9: 5), and this provides an incidental point of agreement with the gospel story of Jesus' healing of Peter's mother-
in-law (Mark 1: 30 f.). On occasion he quotes sayings of Jesus, and
at some of these we shall look more closely.

Even where he does not quote actual sayings of Jesus, he shows
himself well acquainted with the substance of many of them. We
have only to compare the ethical section of the Epistle to the
Romans (12: 1–15: 7), where Paul sets out the practical implications of the gospel in the lives of believers, with the Sermon on
the Mount, to see how thoroughly imbued the apostle was with his
Master's teaching. Moreover, there and elsewhere Paul's chief
argument in his ethical instruction is the example of Jesus himself.
And the character of Jesus as Paul understood it is consistent with
the character of Jesus as portrayed in the Gospels. When Paul
speaks of "the meekness and gentleness of Christ" (2 Corinthians
10: 1) we recall the claim of the Matthaean Jesus to be "meek and
lowly in heart" (Matthew 11: 29). The self-denying Jesus of the
Gospels is the one of whom Paul says that "Christ did not please
himself" (Romans 15: 3); and just as the Jesus of the Gospels called
on his followers to deny themselves, so the apostle insists that it is
our duty as followers of Christ "to bear the infirmities of the weak,
and not to please ourselves" (Romans 15: 1). When Paul invites his
Philippian friends to reproduce among among themselves the mind
which was in "Christ Jesus", who took "the form of a slave"
(Philippians 2: 5–7), we may think of him who, according to Luke,
said to his disciples at the Last Supper, "I am among you as the
servant" (Luke 22: 27), and who on the same occasion, according
to John, performed the humble service of washing their feet (John
13: 3 ff.).

In short, what Paul has to say of the life and teaching of the
historical Jesus agrees, so far as it goes, with the outline preserved
elsewhere in the New Testament and particularly in the four
Gospels. Paul is at pains to insist that the gospel which he preaches
rests on the same factual basis as that preached by the other
apostles (1 Corinthians 15: 11) – a claim the more noteworthy

Tarsus: St. Paul's Gate (see p. 32)

Damascus: The Street Called Straight today (see p. 76)

because he was a companion neither of the earthly Jesus nor of the original apostles, and vigorously asserts his independence of the latter (Galatians 1: 11 ff.; 2: 6).

At the same time, there are some of the most familiar facts about Jesus that we could never have learned from Paul's letters: that he habitually taught in parables, that he healed the sick and performed other "signs". From those letters we should know nothing of his baptism and temptation, of his Galilaean ministry, of the turning-point at Caesarea Philippi, of the transfiguration or of the last journey to Jerusalem. While we find clear and repeated references in them to Jesus' crucifixion, we should know nothing from them of the events which led up to it.

## 2. The new perspective

That the Christ-event marked an epoch in the history of salvation is common ground to Paul and the Evangelists. According to Mark, Jesus inaugurated his Galilaean ministry with the announcement: "The appointed time has been fulfilled and the kingdom of God has drawn near" (Mark 1: 15). According to Paul, "when the time had fully come, God sent forth his Son . . . so that we might receive adoption as sons" (Galatians 4: 4 f.). The substance of the two announcements is the same, but there is a change of perspective; Good Friday and Easter Day have intervened, and the original Preacher has become the Preached One.[2] This change of perspective is anticipated in Jesus' own teaching. While the kingdom of God had drawn near in his ministry, it had not been unleashed in its fulness. Until Jesus underwent the "baptism" of his passion, he was conscious of restrictions (Luke 12: 50). With the passion and triumph of the Son of Man, however, those restrictions would be removed and, as he told his hearers on one occasion, some of them would live to see "the kingdom of God come in power" (Mark 9: 1).

For Paul, this coming in power is an accomplished fact. Jesus has been "designated Son of God in power, according to the Spirit of holiness, by the resurrection from the dead" (Romans 1: 4). The divine power which raised Jesus from the dead is now at work in his followers, conveyed to them by his indwelling Spirit; the same indwelling Spirit provides the assurance that the work of renewal, so well begun, will be successfully consummated. Hostile spiritual forces, already disabled, must be destroyed; by the destruction of death, the last of those forces, the coming age of resurrection glory will be achieved (1 Corinthians 15: 25 f.), but its blessings are en-

2. Cf. A. Schweitzer, *The Mysticism of Paul the Apostle*, E.T. (London, 1931), p. 113. In Jesus and Paul we have to distinguish not (as Martin Buber put it in the title of one of his books) *Two Types of Faith*, E.T. (London, 1951) but two *ages* of faith.

joyed here and now through the Spirit by those who have experienced faith-union with Christ (2 Corinthians 5: 5). "Therefore", says Paul, "if any one is in Christ, he is a new creation; the old has passed away, behold, the new has come" (2 Corinthians 5: 17).

This change of perspective, then, can be viewed in two ways. Absolutely, it can be dated in terms of world-history, around A.D. 30; empirically, it takes place whenever a man or woman comes to be "in Christ". And when it takes place thus empirically, one's whole outlook is revolutionized. "Wherefore we henceforth know no one after the flesh: even though we have known Christ after the flesh, yet now we know him so no more" (2 Corinthians 5: 16).

These words have played a crucial part in much discussion of Paul's relation and attitude to Jesus. What is meant by this knowledge of Christ "after the flesh", which for Paul and his fellow-Christians is now a thing of the past?

Few, if any, nowadays take the line followed at the beginning of this century by Johannes Weiss among others. He thought that Paul's language reflected "the impression received by direct personal acquaintance", that Paul had most probably seen and heard Jesus in Jerusalem during Holy Week and that it is this kind of knowledge that Paul was disparaging by contrast with the new knowledge that he had now received "according to the Spirit".[3]

Whether Paul ever did see or hear Jesus before the crucifixion is not the question at issue.[4] The question at issue is whether his language in 2 Corinthians 5: 16 could have any reference to such seeing or hearing, and it is best answered in Rudolf Bultmann's words: "that he even saw Jesus and was impressed by him . . . is to be read out of II Cor. 5: 16 only by fantasy."[5] But Professor Bultmann's own interpretation of the text can be read out of it only if it be first read into it. For him, the knowledge of Christ "after the flesh" which Paul depreciates is much the same thing as an interest in the historical Jesus: "it is illegitimate to go behind the kerygma, using it as a 'source', in order to reconstruct a 'historical Jesus' with his 'messianic consciousness'. . . . That would be merely 'Christ after the flesh', who is no longer".[6]

This point of view is so prevalent, especially in Germany (probably under Bultmann's influence), that nowadays we are

3. J. Weiss, *Paul and Jesus*, E.T. (London, 1909), pp. 47 f.
4. That he did so might be regarded as more probable if we accepted W. C. van Unnik's thesis in *Tarsus or Jerusalem*, E.T. (London, 1962) that Jerusalem was the city of Paul's boyhood and upbringing. See p. 43.
5. R. Bultmann, "Paul", E.T. in *Existence and Faith* (London, 1964), p. 133.
6. R. Bultmann, "The Significance of the Historical Jesus for the Theology of Paul", E.T. in *Faith and Understanding*, i (London, 1966), p. 241. Cf. H. J. Schoeps, *Paul*, E.T. (London, 1961), pp. 57, 72, 79.

familiar with statements like this: "Paul had no interest in the historical Jesus (2 Corinthians 5: 16!)." But the point which is thus made by reference to 2 Corinthians 5: 16, and reinforced by an exclamation mark, however valid it may be in its own way, is not the point that Paul is making here. Still less is Paul concerned to disparage the knowledge of Jesus enjoyed by the twelve because of their companionship with him during the ministry, in comparison with his own present knowledge of the exalted Lord.[7] Whatever differences there might be between himself and the twelve, they, like him, were now "in Christ"; they, like him, now possessed the Spirit, as he could not but agree. The contrast he is making is that between his former attitude to Christ (and to the world in general) and his present attitude to Christ (and to the world in general), now that he is "in Christ". The point is brought out excellently in the New English Bible: "With us therefore worldly standards have ceased to count in our estimate of any man; even if once they counted in our understanding of Christ, they do so now no longer."

But a further question arises. When Paul speaks of his former knowledge of Christ "after the flesh", does he refer to his former conception of the Messiah, which has been radically changed now that he has come to acknowledge the Messiah in Jesus; or does he refer to his former hostility to Jesus of Nazareth and his followers – a hostility which has now been displaced by love?

More probably, he means that his former conception of the Messiah was "worldly" and wrong. Now that he has learned to identify the Messiah with Jesus, crucified and risen, his understanding of the Messiah has been revolutionized. The conception of the Messiah now takes character from the person of Jesus.

This is exactly opposite to the view of William Wrede, according to whom Paul had an antecedent idea of the Messiah as a "supramundane, divine being" which he retained after his conversion. He had no knowledge of, or interest in, the historical Jesus and his authentic message, but was moved by his Damascus road experience to transfer to the Jesus of his vision all the qualities which hitherto belonged to his ideal Messiah.[8] On the contrary, when Paul's Damascus road experience taught him that Jesus was Lord and Messiah, he thenceforth dismissed from his reckoning the "Christ" whom he had previously known "according to the flesh". By the same token, of course, his estimate of the historical Jesus was revolutionized, even if this is not what is uppermost in his mind in 2 Corinthians 5: 16.

7. Cf. S. G. F. Brandon, *Jesus and the Zealots* (Manchester, 1967), p. 183.
8. W. Wrede, *Paul*, E.T. (London, 1907, pp. 147 ff. Wrede here takes sharp issue with J. Wellhausen, A. Harnack and other contemporaries of his who maintained that Paul was the man who understood most truly the essence of Jesus' message.

Since his first encounter with Jesus, like his continued experience of him, impressed on him that Jesus was the risen Lord, this aspect remained primary in his consciousness. Yet the risen Lord, with whom he enjoyed immediate acquaintance, was in his mind identical with the historical Jesus, with whom he had not enjoyed such acquaintance. Hence perhaps his characteristic word-order "Christ Jesus" – the enthroned Christ who is at the same time the crucified Jesus.

### 3. The gospel tradition

It is Paul's immediate acquaintance with the risen Lord, from his conversion onward, that forms the basis of his gospel as direct *revelation*, as he expresses it in Galatians 1: 12. On the other hand, when he elsewhere speaks of his gospel as *tradition*, "received" by him from those who were "in Christ" before him, he speaks of a message which begins with the historical Jesus. Whatever further dimensions may be recognized in the preaching of Christ crucified, which stands in the forefront of the "tradition", his crucifixion roots him firmly in history.

One sample of this "tradition" is the narrative in 1 Corinthians 11: 23–25 of Jesus' institution of the Eucharist "on the night when he was betrayed". Paul here reminds the Corinthian Christians of something which he "delivered" to them when he planted their church five years previously. His narrative goes back ultimately to the same source as the institution narrative of Mark 14: 22–25, although it has come down along a separate line of transmission. Paul's narrative, even in its written form, is about ten years earlier than Mark's; even so, Mark's may preserve some more archaic features. Thus, Jesus' words in Mark 14: 25, "I shall not drink again of the fruit of the vine until that day when I drink it new in the kingdom of God", may be paraphrased or summarized in Paul's own words "until he comes" in 1 Corinthians 11: 26. Again, some features of Paul's narrative, such as the injunction "do this in remembrance of me", are akin to the longer reading of Luke 22: 17–20 – an interesting textual problem with a bearing on eucharistic origins, but hardly essential to our present concern. Paul's version was probably that which was current in the communities where he first enjoyed Christian fellowship. Since it related what "the Lord Jesus" did and said, it was a tradition ultimately "received from the Lord" and accordingly delivered by Paul to his converts. The core of the narrative would have been preserved with but little change because it was constantly repeated in church meetings as often as Christians "ate this bread and drank the cup", together with the passion story as a whole: "you proclaim the Lord's death", says Paul (verse 26).

Not only from its repetition at celebrations of the Lord's Supper did the passion story early acquire firm outlines, but also from its repetition in the proclamation of the gospel. According to Paul, "Jesus Christ was publicly portrayed as crucified" (Galatians 3: 1) when the gospel was preached, and equally on every such occasion Christ was "preached as raised from the dead" (1 Corinthians 15: 12).

That this preaching of Christ crucified and risen belonged to the tradition shared by Paul with the earlier apostles is evident, as has been said already, from his summary of resurrection appearances in 1 Corinthians 15: 3–11.[10] Apart from that, the empty tomb and the resurrection appearances mark the transition from the historical Jesus to the exalted Christ. Paul's gospel as tradition bridges whatever gulf may be felt to separate the one from the other, for it includes both within its scope, and affirms their continuity and identity.

## 4. The teaching of Jesus

One aspect of Paul's dependence on the teaching of Jesus is the relation between the message of Jesus' parables and Paul's doctrine of justification by faith.

That salvation was to be found in Jesus Christ was a proposition to which Paul and his judaizing opponents would equally have subscribed. They might even have agreed that salvation was to be found in him alone. But on what conditions was the salvation found in Christ alone to be secured? This was the crucial question. No doubt Jesus did sit very loose to the traditions of the elders,[11] but when it was a question of the admission of Gentiles to the fellowship of his disciples, could Paul or anyone else adduce a single utterance of his which suggested that circumcision could be dispensed with? (Indeed, when we consider the important part played by the circumcision question in the development of the early church, we may be impressed by the absence from our gospel tradition of any attempt to find a dominical ruling to which one side or the other could have appealed.) Paul might have appealed to the spirit of Jesus' teaching, or (as he did) to the logical implication of the gospel,[12] but people like his opponents would be satisfied with nothing less than *verbatim* chapter-and-verse authority; and this was not forthcoming.

From the perspective of nineteen centuries' distance, despite our

9. See pp. 283 ff. for further consideration of Paul's understanding of the Lord's Supper.
10. See pp. 62 f., 88 ff.
11. Cf. Mark 7: 1–23.
12. Cf. Galatians 3: 2–5; 4: 4–7, etc.

ignorance of many elements in the situation that were well known to the protagonists, we can probably present an objective argument in defence of Paul's claim that the message he preached was the authentic gospel of Christ. It is this: two things on which Paul pre-eminently insisted – that salvation was provided by God's grace and that faith was the means by which men appropriated it – are repeatedly emphasized in the ministry of Jesus, and especially in his parables, regardless of the strata of gospel tradition to which appeal may be made. When we reflect on the almost complete lack of evidence in Paul's letters that he knew the parables of Jesus,[13] we may wonder how Paul managed to discern so unerringly the heart of his Master's message. We may suspect that this discernment was implicit in the "revelation of Jesus Christ" which, according to him, was the essence of his conversion experience.

The response of faith regularly won the approval of Jesus, sometimes his surprised approval, as when it came from a Gentile,[14] and was a sure means of securing his help and blessing; in face of unbelief, on the other hand, he was inhibited from performing works of mercy and power.[15] "Faith as a grain of mustard seed"[16] was what he desired to see, but too often looked for in vain, even in his own disciples.

As regards the teaching of the parables, the point we are making can be illustrated from two, belonging to two quite distinct lines of tradition – Luke's special material and Matthew's special material.

In the Lukan parable of the Prodigal Son (Luke 15: 11–32), the father might very well have adopted other means for the rehabilitation of his younger son than those described (with approval) by Jesus. When the black sheep of the family came home in disgrace, the father, having a father's heart, might well have consented to give him a second chance. Listening to his carefully rehearsed speech, he might have said, "That's all very well, young man; we have heard fine phrases before. If you really mean what you say, you can buckle to and work as you have never worked before, and if you do so, we may let you work your passage. But first you must prove yourself; we can't let by-gones be by-gones as though nothing had happened." Even that would have been generous; it might have done the young man a world of good, and even the elder brother might have been content to let him be put on probation. But for Jesus, and for Paul, divine grace does not operate like that. God does not put repentant sinners on probation to see how they

13. The description of the gospel in Colossians 1: 6 as "bearing fruit and growing" throughout the world has been thought to echo the parable of the four soils (cf. Mark 4: 8).
14. Cf. Matthew 8: 10/Luke 7: 9.
15. Cf. Mark 6: 5/Matthew 13: 58.
16. Matthew 17: 20; Luke 17: 6.

will turn out; he gives them an unrestrained welcome and invests them as his true-born sons. For Jesus, and for Paul, the initiative always rests with the grace of God. He bestows the reconciliation or redemption; men receive it. "Treat me as one of your hired servants", says the prodigal to his father; but the father speaks of him as "this my son". So, says Paul, "through God you are no longer a slave but a son, and if a son then an heir" (Galatians 4: 7).

In the Matthaean parable of the Labourers in the Vineyard (Matthew 20: 1–16), the last-hired workmen did not bargain with their employer about their pay. If a denarius was the fair rate for a day's work, those who worked for the last hour only might have expected a small fraction of that, but they accepted his undertaking to give them "whatever is right" and in the event they received a denarius like the others who had worked all day. The grace of God is not to be parcelled out and adjusted to the varieties of individual merit. There was, as T. W. Manson pointed out, a coin worth one-twelfth of a denarius. "It was called a *pondion*. But there is no such thing as a twelfth part of the love of God." [17]

This is completely in line with Paul's understanding of the gospel. If law is the basis of men's acceptance with God, then the details of personal merit and demerit are of the utmost relevance. But the great blessings of the gospel had come to Paul's Gentile converts, as they knew very well, not by the works of the law but by the response of faith – the faith which works by love. [18] And when we speak in terms of love, we are on a plane where law is not at home.

A comparison of Paul's doctrine of justification by faith with Jesus' proclamation of the kingdom of God has been made by Eberhard Jüngel, in his book *Paulus und Jesus*. [19] It is in the parables of Jesus especially, he insists, that the kingdom of God comes to expression, and the hearers' response to the parables is their response to the kingdom of God. Jesus' parabolic teaching is more than mere teaching; it is a "language-event", a *Sprachereignis*, in the terminology of Jüngel's teacher Ernst Fuchs. [20] That is to say, the parabolic teaching is itself an event confronting the hearer and challenging him to give a positive reply to the demand of the

17. T. W. Manson, *The Sayings of Jesus* (London, [2] 1949), p. 220. It should not be overlooked that a very different emphasis is found in some other parts of the material peculiar to Matthew, which indeed have lent themselves in some commentators' hands to a directly anti-Pauline interpretation, such as the criticism in Matthew 5: 19 of him who "relaxes one of the least of these commandments and teaches men so" (on this too see T. W. Manson, *The Sayings of Jesus*, pp. 25, 154).

18. Galatians 3: 2, 5; 5: 6.

19. E. Jüngel, *Paulus und Jesus* (Tübingen, 1962).

20. Cf. E. Fuchs, *Studies of the Historical Jesus*, E.T. (London, 1964), pp. 125 f.; cf. G. Ebeling's similar formation *Wortgeschehen* ("word event"), *The Nature of Faith*, E.T. (London, 1966), pp. 182 ff.

kingdom of God. With Fuchs, Jüngel sees in the parables Jesus' christological testimony to himself, if only in veiled form. During the ministry, Jesus' action and attitude supplied the parables with a living commentary sufficient to convey their meaning to those who responded in faith; later, the church felt it necessary to supply its own verbal commentary. The eschatological note which sounds in the parables is heard in Paul's teaching about justification by faith. "The law was our custodian until Christ came", says Paul, "that we might be justified by faith. But now that faith has come, we are no longer under a custodian; for in Christ Jesus you are all sons of God, through faith" (Galatians 3: 24–26). In other words, as he says to the Romans, "Christ is the end of the law, that every one who has faith may be justified" (Romans 10: 4).[21] Jüngel relates "the end (telos) of the law" to the fact that in Christ the eschaton has arrived. In the preaching of Jesus and the teaching of Paul he finds the same relation between eschatology and history, the same emphasis on the end of the law, the same demand for faith. The difference lies in the fact that the eschaton which for Jesus lay in the near future was present for Paul.

It would be more accurate to say that, for Paul, the period through which he was living was not yet the absolute eschaton or telos (cf. 1 Corinthians 15: 24) but its threshold – that period "between the times" during which the presence of the Spirit in the people of Christ confirmed to them their status and heritage as sons of God (Galatians 4: 6): "through the Spirit, by faith, we wait for the hope of righteousness" (Galatians 5: 5). But already, with the coming of Christ and the completion of his redemptive work, the age of law had come to an end for the people of God.

When Paul calls Christ "the end of the law" he is expressing a theological insight. But this insight was based on sound historical fact: many of Paul's fellow-Pharisees who engaged in debate with Jesus during his ministry must have felt that, on a practical level, his conduct and teaching involved "the end of the law" – not only because of his rejection of their oral traditions but because of the sovereignty with which he treated such elements of the written law as the sabbath institution and food regulations. True, as we have seen, he does not appear to have made any pronouncement on the circumcision question. But when we consider how he related the law as a whole to the basic requirements of love to God and love to one's neighbour, and insisted on the paramountcy of heart-devotion, "truth in the inward parts", righteousness, mercy and faith,[22] the conclusion is inescapable that he would not have included circumcision among the weightier matters of the law. If no word of his

21. See pp. 190 ff.
22. Matthew 23: 23; cf. Luke 11: 42.

on the subject has survived (apart from the incidental *ad hominem* argument in the course of a sabbath debate in John 7: 22 f.), it is simply because the issue did not arise in the situation of his ministry. When, later, it did arise in the situation of the Gentile mission, it is difficult to deny that Paul's position was in keeping with Jesus' general attitude to the externalities of religion.

Paul, like Jesus, shocked the guardians of Israel's law by his insistence on treating the law as a means to an end and not as an end in itself, by his refusal to let pious people seek security before God in their own piety, by his breaking down of barriers in the name of the God who "justifies the ungodly" (Romans 4: 5) and by his proclamation of a message of good news for the outsider. In all this Paul saw more clearly than most of his Christian contemporaries into the inwardness of Jesus' teaching.

## 5. Incidental contacts

But there are more incidental passages in Paul's letters which link up with sayings of Jesus recorded here and there in the Gospels.

In 1904 Arnold Resch thought he could detect allusions to 925 such sayings in nine of the Pauline letters along with 133 in Ephesians and 100 in the Pastorals.[23] At the other extreme we have Rudolf Bultmann maintaining that "the teaching of the historical Jesus plays no role, or practically none, in Paul" ("and", he adds, "John").[24] A few dominical utterances, he concedes, may be echoed in Paul's hortatory sections,[25] and he recognizes two such utterances in regulations for church life (1 Corinthians 7: 10 f.; 9: 14). Moreover:

> The tradition of the Jerusalem Church is at least in substance behind the "word of the Lord" on the parousia and resurrection in 1 Thess. 4: 15–17, though it is not certain whether Paul is here quoting a traditionally transmitted saying or whether he is appealing to a revelation accorded to him by the exalted Lord.[26]

23. A. Resch, *Der Paulinismus und die Logia Jesu = Texte und Untersuchungen* 27 (Leipzig, 1904). He also identified 64 sayings of Jesus in the Pauline speeches in Acts, but credibility is strained to the limit by his claim to find allusions in the letters of Paul to dozens of otherwise unrecorded sayings of Jesus. We can all relate the "faith that removes mountains" in 1 Corinthians 13: 2 to Mark 11: 23 or Matthew 17: 20, but incidental expressions so unambiguously dominical are rare.
24. R. Bultmann, *Theology of the New Testament*, E.T., i (London, 1952), p. 35.
25. E.g. Romans 12: 14 (Matthew 5: 44); 13: 9 f. (Mark 12: 31); 16: 19 (Matthew 10: 16); 1 Corinthians 13: 2 (Mark 11: 23) (*Theology of the New Testament*, i, p. 188).
26. *Theology of the New Testament*, i. pp. 188 f.

Here we must share Professor Bultmann's hesitation. But the two citations of Jesus' teaching in Pauline regulations for church life will repay further attention.

(a) *Divorce and remarriage.* In answering the Corinthians' questions about marriage, Paul cites Jesus' ruling on divorce as binding on his followers. "To the married I say, not I but the Lord, that the wife should not separate from her husband (but if she does, let her remain single or else be reconciled to her husband) – and that the husband should not divorce his wife" (1 Corinthians 7: 10 f.).

While this is not a *verbatim* quotation, its relation to Mark 10: 2 ff. is fairly plain. When Jesus was asked if it was permissible for a man to divorce his wife for any cause, he appealed back from the implied permission of Deuteronomy 24: 1–4 to the Genesis record of the creation of man and the institution of marriage (Genesis 1: 27; 2: 24) and concluded: "What therefore God has joined together, let not man put asunder".[27] But what Paul echoes is the more explicit reply given later by Jesus when the disciples asked him for a fuller explanation: "Whoever divorces his wife and marries another, commits adultery against her; and if she divorces her husband and marries another, *she* commits adultery" (Mark 10: 11 f.).

We need not stay to consider whether the words about the wife's initiating divorce proceedings are a later addition made in the light of the circumstances of the Gentile mission or refer (as I suspect) to the case of Herodias, so topical a scandal at the time of Jesus' Galilaean ministry.[28] It is noteworthy that Paul (in the Lord's name) forbids the wife to separate from her husband before he forbids the husband to divorce his wife. Perhaps this sequence was dictated by the way in which the Corinthians framed their question at this point. "Should a Christian wife separate from her husband?" No, she should not; she should continue to live with him as his wife. "But what if she has already separated from him?" Then let her remain celibate or else be reconciled to her husband. Perhaps she separated from her husband because she acquired a distaste for married life – or at least for married life with him. But if she finds the consequent abstention irksome, it is out of the question for her to marry someone else; let her go back to her husband. Having dealt with that aspect of the question which may have been uppermost in the minds of his correspondents, Paul repeats the substantive clause in Jesus' ruling: the husband must not divorce his wife.[29]

(b) *The labourer deserves his wages.* The Corinthian Christians

27. Gk. χωρίζειν , the same verb as is used in the passive in 1 Corinthians 7: 10, "she should not separate ( χωρισθῆναι )."
28. Cf. F. F. Bruce, *New Testament History* (London, [2] 1971), pp. 26 f.
29. See pp. 267 f.

could not understand why Paul refused to accept financial support from them when, as they knew, he accepted it from other churches. One reason for his policy was that he suspected that, if he accepted money from the church in Corinth, his opponents there would seize the opportunity to accuse him of mercenary motives. But he could not win: since he determined to give them no such opportunity, they argued that his unwillingness to accept money proved that he was none too confident of his apostolic status, and did not feel himself entitled to the privilege which Peter and his colleagues, together with the brothers of Jesus, enjoyed, of living at the expense of those for whose spiritual well-being they cared. He replies that he is indeed an apostle in the fullest sense – the existence of the Corinthian church is proof enough of that – and that he certainly has the right of living at his converts' expense, but chooses to exercise his liberty by not availing himself of that right. That it is indeed a right he argues on the basis of natural and divine law, but pre-eminently on the ground that none less than "the Lord commanded that those who proclaim the gospel should get their living by the gospel" (1 Corinthians 9: 14). This "command" appears in our gospel tradition in the Matthaean commission to the twelve (Matthew 10: 10), "the labourer deserves his food", and in the Lukan commission to the seventy (Luke 10: 7), "the labourer deserves his wages." [30] Of these two forms, it is the latter that comes closer in sense to the "command" that Paul mentions. It is nowhere suggested that he would refuse to eat *food* in the home of one of his Corinthian friends. It was not food but *wages*, monetary payment, that he declined.

In a recent and valuable study, Dr. David Dungan discusses at some length why Paul, in quoting this "command" of the Lord, nevertheless deliberately disobeys it. He concludes that Paul either "initially turned this regulation into a permission" of which he was free to avail himself or not, or else "simply inherited this alteration ready-made". Either way, "this alteration is based on the realization that this regulation was no longer appropriate in every case". [31] It should rather be said that the "regulation" from the outset had the nature of a "permission". Paul had been brought up to believe that the teaching of the Torah should not be made a means of livelihood or personal aggrandisement. "He who makes a worldly use of the crown of the Torah will waste away", said Hillel; [32] and

30. Matthew's "food" is τροφή, while Luke's "wages" is μισθός. The injunction of Luke 10: 7 is quoted *verbatim* in a similar context in 1 Timothy 5: 18.

31. D. L. Dungan, *The Sayings of Jesus in the Churches of Paul* (Oxford, 1971), p. 32.

32. *Pirqê Abôt* 1: 13; 4: 7. (The latter passage quotes also the similar dictum of R. Zadok: "make not of the Torah a crown wherewith to magnify thyself or a spade wherewith to dig". From the two sayings the inference is drawn:

so Paul, whether he was a Hillelite or not, was by manual occupation a tent-maker. But he claimed for others the right which he chose to forgo for himself: "Let him who is taught the word share all good things with him who teaches" (Galatians 6: 6).

It should further be noted that Hillel's dictum comes quite close to an injunction of Jesus included in his commission to the twelve, according to the Matthaean account: "You received without pay; give without pay" (Matthew 10: 8).[33] If Paul had known this injunction, he might have quoted it to justify his personal policy. Even in his dealings with other churches, he found it embarrassing to accept and acknowledge personal gifts of money.

(c) *Eat what is set before you.* One of the questions raised in the Corinthians' letter to Paul concerned the eating of the flesh of animals which had been consecrated to pagan divinities. A Christian with conscientious scruples about such food could bar it from his own house, but what was he to do when he was eating out? Naturally, no direct answer to this question would be expected in the teaching of Jesus; it was one which could arise only in a Gentile environment. Paul's answer is: "If one of the unbelievers invites you to a dinner and you are disposed to go, *eat whatever is set before you* without raising any question on the ground of conscience" (1 Corinthians 10: 27).

But even here we have an echo of words of Jesus. In his instructions to the seventy disciples in Luke 10: 8, Jesus says: "Whenever you enter a town and they receive you, *eat what is set before you.*"[34] No such injunction appears in Jesus' commission to the twelve, in any of the three accounts of it, whereas in the commission to the seventy the injunction appears twice, albeit in different terms (cf. Luke 10: 7: "remain in the same house, eating and drinking what they provide"). The mission to the twelve was restricted to Israel, explicitly so in Matthew 10: 5 f. and by implication in Mark 6: 7–11 and Luke 9: 1–5. But the mission of the seventy, which is peculiar to Luke, has often been thought to adumbrate the wider Gentile mission which he records in his second volume. Whereas twelve was the number of the tribes of Israel, seventy was in Jewish tradition the number of the nations of the world.[35]

---

"whosoever derives a profit for himself from the words of the Torah is helping on his own destruction".)

33. This makes it quite clear that τροφή in Matthew 10: 10 means "food" and excludes money.

34. Gk. ἐσθίετε τὰ παρατιθέμενα ὑμῖν, which closely resembles πᾶν τὸ παρατιθέμενον ὑμῖν ἐσθίετε of 1 Corinthians 10: 27.

35. Cf. A. R. C. Leaney, *A Commentary on the Gospel according to St. Luke* (London, 1958), p. 176. Of course, if we adopt the variant reading "seventy-two", a different symbolism is indicated. Cf. B. M. Metzger, "Seventy or Seventy-two Disciples?" in *Historical and Literary Studies, Pagan, Jewish and Christian* (Leiden/Grand Rapids, 1968), pp. 67 ff.

If Paul here is quoting from Jesus' instructions to the seventy, he is generalizing from a particular occasion to a recurring situation. And that he is indeed quoting from those instructions – or at least from the tradition of Jesus' commissions to his disciples – is rendered the more probable by his appeal, which we have already considered, to that same tradition in defence of the principle that the preacher of the gospel is entitled to get his living by the gospel.

(d) *Tribute to whom tribute is due.* Jesus' ruling on the subject of divorce, at which we have already looked, was given as an answer to a question which (according to Mark 10: 2) was put to him "in order to test him". The same evangelist records another question which was later put to him with a similar motive: "they sent to him some of the Pharisees and some of the Herodians, to entrap him in his talk; and they came and said to him, 'Teacher, . . . is it lawful to pay tribute to Caesar, or not?' " (Mark 12: 13 f.).

Paul deals with the payment of tribute in the debatable paragraph Romans 13: 1–7, but here he does not invoke the Lord's authority as he does with regard to divorce, or support for missionaries. Besides, whereas Jesus' answer to the question about the tribute money draws a distinction between rendering to Caesar what is Caesar's and rendering to God what is God's, Paul sees in the rendering of Caesar's dues to Caesar one form of rendering to God what is due to God, for the secular authorities are God's servants, and resistance to them involves resistance to God. Therefore, he says, "render to all of them their dues, tribute to whom tribute is due . . ." (Romans 13: 7).

Even if Paul makes no reference to Jesus' words here, may he have had them at the back of his mind? It is possible to understand his "render to all of them their dues" as a generalization of Jesus' answer in Mark 12: 17: "Render to Caesar what is Caesar's and to God what is God's".[36] But if Paul's words are a generalization of Jesus' answer, the generalization goes much farther here than with regard to other words of Jesus to which attention has been paid in this chapter. It was one thing to answer the question implied behind Romans 13: 1–7: "Should Christians in Rome and the Empire generally, subjects of Caesar, render obedience and tribute to him and to his subordinate officials?" Paul's answer is "Yes, because Caesar and his subordinates exercise authority by divine appointment, and they perform God's service when they maintain law and order, protecting the law-abiding and executing judgment against criminals." It was quite another thing to answer the implications of the question put to Jesus in Jerusalem, against the background of the rising of Judas the Galilaean in A.D. 6 and the insurgent movement which perpetuated his ideals. Judas and his followers main-

---

36. In Mark 12: 17 and Romans 13: 7 alike "render" is ἀπόδοτε ("give back").

tained that it was high treason against the God of Israel for his people in his land to acknowledge the sovereignty of a pagan ruler by
paying him tribute. Jesus' questioners hoped to impale him on the
horns of a dilemma; no such dilemma confronted Paul. To Paul the
issue was clear, and his apostolic experience had given him
repeated opportunities of appreciating the benefits of Roman rule.
He was not so simple-minded as to imagine that the imperial
authorities could never contravene the ordinance of God and issue
decrees to which Christians would be bound to refuse compliance,
although he does not raise that issue here. But even here he makes
it plain that the duty of obedience to the secular powers is a temporary one, lasting only to the end of the present "night"; in the
"day" which is "at hand" a new order will be introduced in which
"the saints will judge the world" (Romans 13: 12; 1 Corinthians
6: 2).

## 6. The law of Christ

Paul could have been taught in the school of Gamaliel that the
whole law was comprehended in the law of love to one's neighbour;
we recall how in an earlier generation Hillel summarized the whole
law in the injunction: "Do not to another what is hateful to
yourself."[37] But when Paul speaks of the bearing of one another's
burdens as the fulfilment of "the law of Christ" (Galatians 6: 2), we
may reasonably infer that he knew how Christ had applied the
commandment of Leviticus 19: 18: "you shall love your neighbour
as yourself". Moreover, the injunction "bear one another's
burdens" seems to be a generalizing expansion of the words immediately preceding it: "If a man is overtaken in a trespass, you
who are spiritual should restore him in a spirit of gentleness"
(Galatians 6: 1). This is remarkably reminiscent of words of Jesus
occurring in a series of community rules preserved by the First
Evangelist only: "If your brother sins,[38] go and tell him his fault,
between you and him alone; if he listens to you, you have gained
your brother" (Matthew 18: 15).

Further features of "the law of Christ" may be discerned in
Romans 12: 9–21, with its injunctions to sincere and practical love,
so close in spirit (as has been said already) to the Sermon on the
Mount. Mutual love, sympathy and esteem within the believing
brotherhood are to be expected, but this section enjoins love and
forgiveness towards those outside the brotherhood, not least
towards its enemies and persecutors. "Bless those who persecute
you; bless and do not curse them" (Romans 12: 14) echoes Luke 6:

37. TB *Shabbat* 31a. See p. 49.
38. The words "against you" ( εἰς σέ ) should probably be omitted after "sins"
( ἁμαρτήσῃ ), as in NEB.

28: "bless those who curse you; pray for those who abuse you". So Paul, speaking elsewhere of his own practice, can say: "When reviled, we bless; when persecuted, we endure; when slandered, we try to conciliate" (1 Corinthians 4: 12 f.).

"Repay no one evil for evil" (Romans 12: 17) breathes the same spirit as Matthew 5: 44 and Luke 6: 27: "Love your enemies, do good to those who hate you." So does the quotation from Proverbs 25: 21 f. in Romans 12: 20, where it is probably significant that Paul leaves out the last clause of the original. "If your enemy is hungry", he says, "feed him; if he is thirsty, give him drink; for by so doing you will heap burning coals on his head" – but he does not add "and the Lord will reward you". Perhaps the figure of the "burning coals" originally suggested intensified retribution, but in this new context it receives a nobler significance: Treat your enemy kindly, for this may make him ashamed of his hostile conduct and lead to his repentance. In other words, the best way to get rid of an enemy is to turn him into a friend and so "overcome evil with good" (Romans 12: 21).

The theme is resumed in Romans 13: 8–10, after Paul's words about the duty of Christians to the civil authorities. After saying, with reference to the authorities, "Render to all of them their dues, . . . honour to whom honour is due" (Romans 13: 7), he goes on, more generally: "Let the only debt you owe anyone be the debt of neighbourly love; the man who has discharged this debt has fulfilled the law" (Romans 13: 8). This is supported by the quotation of Leviticus 19: 18 ("You shall love your neighbour as yourself") as the sum of all the commandments – and this places Paul squarely within the tradition of Jesus. For Jesus set this commandment next to that of Deuteronomy 6: 5 ("You shall love the LORD your God . . .") and said: "On these two commandments depend all the law and the prophets" (Matthew 22: 37–40; cf. Mark 12: 28–34). Paul quotes the second great commandment here and not the first because the immediate question concerns a Christian's duty to his neighbour. The commandments in the second table of the decalogue, most of which are quoted in Romans 13: 9, forbid the harming of one's neighbour in any way; since love never harms another, "love is the fulfilling of the law" (Romans 13: 10).

When in the next paragraph (Romans 13: 11–14) Paul speaks of Christian life in days of crisis, he once more echoes the teaching of Jesus. When Jesus told his disciples of the critical events preceding the coming of the Son of Man, he said: "when these things begin to take place, look up and raise your heads, because your redemption is drawing near" (Luke 21: 28). Those who hoped "to stand before the Son of Man" must therefore be vigilant (Luke 21: 36). "It is high time now", says Paul, "for you to wake from sleep; for salvation is nearer to us now than when we first believed" (Romans 13:

11). To Paul, at the beginning of A.D. 57, it was plain how the crucial events of the next decade or so were casting their shadow before. Their course and outcome could not be foreseen in detail, but Jesus' words, "he who endures to the end will be saved" (Mark 13: 13), were to verify themselves in the experience of his people who passed through these crises. With the trial comes the way of deliverance (1 Corinthians 10: 13). Meanwhile the sons of light must live in readiness for the coming day, renouncing all the "works of darkness" (Romans 13: 12).

In another place where Paul deals with the same subject, he tells his readers that, since they are sons of light, the day of the Lord, which comes "like a thief in the night", will not take them by surprise (1 Thessalonians 5: 2–5). This too takes up a note of Jesus' teaching: "if the householder had known at what hour the thief was coming, he would have been awake and would not have left his house to be broken into. You also must be ready; for the Son of Man is coming at an hour you do not expect" (Luke 12: 39 f.).[39]

Paul's exhortation in Romans 13 concludes with the command in verse 14 to "put on the Lord Jesus Christ". This expresses more directly what he speaks of elsewhere as putting on "the new man" (Colossians 3: 10; Ephesians 4: 24).[40] The Christian graces – making up the "armour of light" which he tells his friends to wear instead of gratifying unregenerate desires (Romans 13: 12) – are the graces which he knew to have been displayed in harmonious perfection in Jesus. While Paul did not know the written Gospels as we have them, his tradition ascribed the same ethical qualities to Jesus as are portrayed in the Gospels,[41] and he commends those qualities, one by one or comprehensively, as an example for his converts and others to follow.

---

39. Cf. Matthew 24: 43 f.; Revelation 3: 3; 16: 15 (also 2 Peter 3: 10).

40. "Put on" may have been one of several captions under which the sections of a primitive baptismal catechesis were summed up; cf. Galatians 3: 27 ("as many of you as were baptized into Christ have put on Christ"); also Colossians 3: 12.

41. According to R. Bultmann (*Theology of the New Testament*, i, p. 188), "when he refers to Christ as an example, he is thinking not of the historical but of the pre-existent Jesus". This is true of two of the Pauline texts he quotes in support, where Christ's self-denial in becoming man is the subject (Philippians 2: 5 ff.; 2 Corinthians 8: 9), but not of the third (Romans 15: 3), where his enduring of reproach for God's sake during his life on earth is in view, nor yet of those others mentioned above, where many of the virtues recommended to Christians would not have been relevant to the pre-existent Christ.

# CHAPTER 12

# Paul and the Exalted Christ

I F, AS HAS BEEN SAID ABOVE, "THE EMPTY TOMB AND THE resurrection appearances mark the transition from the historical Jesus to the exalted Christ",[1] it is implied that the exalted Christ is continuous and personally identical with the historical Jesus. This continuity and personal identity were maintained by Paul. While, however, the historical Jesus was known to him only by hearsay and tradition, he claimed a direct and profound personal acquaintance with the exalted Christ.

## 1. The glory of that light

Paul makes little attempt to describe the form in which the exalted Christ appeared to him on the Damascus road, perhaps because words were inadequate for the purpose. Radiant light is the outstanding feature of the appearance as Paul recalls it. When, for example, he speaks of the ministry of the new covenant with which he was then entrusted, he contrasts it with the inferior ministry committed to Moses by setting over against the fading glory reflected on Moses' face the unfading glory associated with the gospel.[2] He describes the dawn of faith as "seeing the light of the gospel of the glory (*doxa*) of Christ, who is the image (*eikōn*) of God" – "for", he goes on, "it is the God who said, 'Let light shine out of darkness', who has shone in our hearts to give the light of the knowledge of the glory of God in the face of Christ" (2 Corinthians 4: 4, 6). As the old creation was inaugurated by the shining of light to dispel the darkness which lay "upon the face of the deep" (Genesis 1: 2 f.), so the new creation was inaugurated by the shining of light to dispel the blindness of unbelief; and Paul's choice of this figure was probably dictated by his own experience. We recall the reference in Acts 9: 3 to the "light from heaven" which "flashed about him" on the Damascus road; in the parallel account of the experience in Acts 22: 11 Paul himself says that he could not see "because of the glory of that light", and in all three records of the incident in Acts it is made fairly clear that in that light the risen Christ appeared to him (9: 17; 22: 14; 26: 16).

1. See p. 101.
2. 2 Corinthians 3: 7–16; see pp. 200 f; 275.

113

While Paul had no doubt about the personal identity of the earthly Jesus and the heavenly Christ, he equally had no doubt that the heavenly Christ's mode of existence was different from that of the earthly Jesus. When he affirms that "flesh and blood cannot inherit the kingdom of God" (1 Corinthians 15: 50) – i.e. the resurrection order – he makes it plain that this is as true of the Lord as of his people. The earthly Jesus was a man of woman born who endured a real death; but the risen Christ, while still man, was now vested with heavenly humanity, a different order of humanity from that of this present life. "The first man was from the earth, a man of dust; the second man is from heaven" (1 Corinthians 15: 47). While the creation narrative of Genesis 2: 7 tells how "the first man, Adam, became a living soul", the character of the new creation is disclosed in the affirmation that "the last Adam became a life-giving spirit" (1 Corinthians 15: 45). The risen Christ, for Paul, exists no longer in a body of flesh and blood but in a "spiritual body" (1 Corinthians 15: 44).

Those who, even while living on earth in mortal bodies, are by faith united to the risen Christ have something of this new order of existence communicated to them. This is a different kind of personal union from those which bind human beings together in their present life. The closest personal union in this life is that between man and woman, described in the words of the creation narrative as their becoming "one flesh" (Genesis 2: 24) – "but", says Paul, "he who is united to the Lord becomes one spirit with him" (1 Corinthians 6: 17). It is difficult to dissociate "one spirit" in this sense from the "one Spirit" in whom all the people of Christ are united into one body with him, just as it is difficult to dissociate the "life-giving spirit" that Jesus became in resurrection from the Spirit of life that indwells his people. To this we shall return.

If even while in mortal body a believer in Christ becomes "one spirit" with him, this unity is to become more fully experienced in resurrection. For the "spiritual body" worn by the risen Lord is the prototype for his people, who are to share his resurrection and have their present bodies of humiliation transmuted into the likeness of his body of glory (Philippians 3: 21). "As we have borne the image of the man of dust", says Paul, "we shall also bear the image of the man of heaven" (1 Corinthians 15: 49). It was as the "man of heaven" that Jesus appeared to Paul on the Damascus road, we gather, vested with his body of glory; but when Paul attempts to describe what he saw, the only vocabulary he can use is that of light.

Paul looked forward to the parousia of Christ, his manifestation in glory; but the appearance of Christ at his parousia would be of the same character as his appearance on the Damascus road, except that it would not be a momentary flash but a more enduring experience, and that it would be accompanied by the instantaneous glorification of his people – whether by the resurrection of those who had died or the transformation of those still alive. The revelation of the Son of God would be attended by the simultaneous "revelation of the sons of God" (Romans 8: 19), a prospect also described as their liberation from bondage to decay and futility, their adoption as sons, the redemption of their bodies (Romans 8: 20–23). This is the climax of their salvation, the consummation of God's eternal purpose of grace towards them.

"In this hope", says Paul, "we were saved. . . . But if we hope for what we do not see, we wait for it with patience" (Romans 8: 24 f.). The subject-matter of this chapter relates to the present period of hope – the interval between the past event of Christ's death and resurrection and the future event of his parousia.

## 2. The exalted Lord

Paul may well have been brought up to think of the days of the Messiah as an interval separating this age from the age to come, the resurrection age.[3] But whether he had entertained the belief in such an interval before his conversion or not, the logic of the Christ-event imposed it on him now. Only, the days of the Messiah were not characterized by Messiah's reigning from an earthly throne, like the throne of his father David, but by his reigning from the right hand of God. The oracle of Psalm 110: 1, "Sit at my right hand, till I make your enemies your footstool", is one of the most primitive Christian *testimonia*. If, as was widely held, this oracle was addressed to the Messiah,[4] then, since in the eyes of his followers Jesus was the Messiah, the oracle was fulfilled in him.

Paul does not often use the expression about the right hand of God; when he does so, it is probably because it had already become familiar to Christians when they confessed their faith in the Christ "who died, . . . who was raised from the dead, who is at the right hand of God, . . ." – as Paul puts it in Romans 8: 34, apparently quoting such a confession of faith. (That is the only place where the expression occurs in his "capital" epistles; it appears also in Colossians 3: 1 and Ephesians 1: 20.) Like his fellow-Jews, he knew "the right hand of God" to be a metaphor denoting supreme authority, but he may have preferred to use it sparingly lest some of his Gentile hearers or readers should imagine that it had physical or local significance. It is, of course, difficult to think or speak of exaltation or supremacy without the use of spatial imagery. Christian astrophysicists who recite the historic creeds are not charged with inconsistency for employing the terminology of the three-decker

3. See pp. 70, 190.
4. Cf. Mark 12: 35–37.

universe; this terminology provides serviceable metaphors for the expression of transcendence, or of communication in both directions between God and man. Even in the first century such terminology was recognized by many thinking people as metaphorical, and among those thinking people Paul is entitled to be included.

Instead of referring to Christ as being seated at God's right hand, Paul speaks of him as "highly exalted",[5] endowed with "the name which is above every name" (Philippians 2: 9).[6] The "name which is above every name" is the designation "Lord". It is the divine purpose, says Paul (or the source which he quotes), that "every tongue should confess that Jesus Christ is Lord" (Philippians 2: 11). The Greek noun he uses is *kyrios*, which because of the Septuagint usage lent itself happily to this exalted connotation. In the Septuagint it is used not only to render such a Hebrew word as *'ādôn* ("lord") but also to render the ineffable name of the God of Israel – the name which we commonly reproduce as Yahweh. Thus the Septuagint of Psalm 110: 1 uses *kyrios* twice – "The *kyrios* said to my *kyrios*" – just as most of our English versions use "Lord": "The LORD said to my lord". But the Hebrew text means "Yahweh's oracle to my lord (*'ādôn*)". The person addressed by the psalmist as "my lord" was probably the Davidic king, so that the later messianic interpretation was not inappropriate.[7] But in the Septuagint the person addressed in the oracle is designated by the same word as Yahweh himself: in that sense he shares "the name which is above every name".

The wording of Philippians 2: 10 f. is based on Isaiah 45: 23, where Yahweh swears by himself: "To me every knee shall bow, every tongue shall swear".[8] Here, however, it is in Jesus' name that every knee shall bow, and it is Jesus' lordship that every tongue shall confess. Nor is this by any means the only instance in the New Testament where an Old Testament passage containing *kyrios* as the equivalent of Yahweh is applied to Jesus.[9] In any case, the title Lord in the highest sense that it can bear belongs distinctively to the risen and exalted Jesus, and not for Paul only. Luke's testimony is to the same effect: his account of Peter's address in Jerusalem at

5. Perhaps the compound verb *ὑπερύψωσεν* echoes *ὑψωθήσεται* ("shall be exalted"), used of the Servant of Yahweh in the Greek version of Isaiah 52: 13 (cf. Ephesians 1: 20–22).

6. The passage Philippians 2: 6–11 may be pre-Pauline, but Paul makes it his own. See p. 131 with n. 25.

7. Cf. A. R. Johnson, *Sacral Kingship in Ancient Israel* (Cardiff, 1955), pp. 120 ff.; H. Ringgren, *The Messiah in the Old Testament* (London, 1956), pp. 13 ff.

8. Quoted by Paul in Romans 14: 11 with the appended comment: "So each of us shall give account of himself to God" (i.e. before his judgment seat).

9. Another example is 1 Peter 3: 15, where Isaiah 8: 13, "Yahweh of hosts (LXX *κύριον αὐτόν*), him you shall sanctify", is adapted in the form: "sanctify Christ as Lord in your hearts".

the first Christian Pentecost ends with the quotation of Psalm 110: 1 and the peroration based on it, calling on all the house of Israel to know assuredly that God has made the crucified Jesus "both Lord and Christ" (Acts 2: 34–36).

To Paul, however (and to other early Christians), the acknowledgment of Jesus as Lord in the highest sense which that title can bear was far from being the result of a linguistic accident; it was far, too, from being but an *ex officio* designation of the Messiah. It was the most adequate term for expressing what he (and his fellow-believers) had come to understand and appreciate of Jesus' person and achievement and his present decisive rôle in the out-working of God's purpose of blessing for the universe. [10]

If it be asked if this use of the title "Lord" goes back to the earliest Aramaic-speaking phase of the church's life, the answer is Yes. The Aramaic equivalent of Greek *kyrios* is *mar*, as in the invocation *maranā-thā* ("Our Lord, come"), which found its way untranslated into the vocabulary of Greek-speaking Christians (1 Corinthians 16: 22) – more particularly, into the eucharistic liturgy (*Didache* 10: 6). [11] That *mar* could be used (as *kyrios* was) to denote the God of Israel is shown by the targum on Job from Cave 11 at Qumran, where the form *mārē* appears as an equivalent of Shaddai, and in the Aramaic fragments of 1 Enoch from Cave 4, where *maranā* (9: 4) and the emphatic state *maryā* (10: 9) are used with reference to God. [12]

The title "Son of God" is also given to Jesus in a distinctive sense in resurrection: he was "designated Son of God in power, according to the Spirit of holiness, by his resurrection from the dead" (Romans 1: 4). In Paul's thought, of course, he did not *begin* to be Son of God at the resurrection: speaking of his coming into the world Paul says that "God sent forth his son, born of a woman" (Galatians 4: 4). But during his earthly life he was the Son of God, comparatively speaking, "in weakness"; [13] as the risen Lord he is the Son of God "in power". [14]

---

10. Cf. F. F. Bruce, "Jesus is Lord", in *Soli Deo Gloria: New Testament Studies in Honor of William Childs Robinson*, ed. J. McD. Richards (Richmond, Va., 1968), pp. 23–36, and *Paul and Jesus* (Grand Rapids, 1974), pp. 81–91.

11. Cf. H. Lietzmann, *Mass and Lord's Supper*, E.T. (Leiden, 1953 ff.), p. 193; C. F. D. Moule, "A Reconsideration of the Context of *Maranatha*", *NTS* 6 (1959–60), 307 ff. See pp. 66 f.

12. Cf. M. Black, "The Christological Use of the Old Testament in the New Testament", *NTS* 18 (1971–2), 10; "The Maranatha Invocation", in *Christ and Spirit in the New Testament: Studies in Honour of C. F. D. Moule*, ed. B. Lindars and S. S. Smalley (Cambridge, 1973), pp. 189 ff.; and see now most recently *The Books of Enoch: Aramaic Fragments of Qumran Cave 4*, ed. J. T. Milik (Oxford, 1976), pp. 171, 175. The form *maryā* corresponds to ὁ κύριος in (Greek) 1 Enoch 10: 9.

13. Cf. 2 Corinthians 13: 4a.

14. There is a close connexion between his being "designated Son of God in

Like the title "Lord", "Son of God" was also confirmed by an oracular *testimonium* – by Psalm 2: 7, where Yahweh addresses his anointed one in the words: "You are my Son; today I have begotten you". [15] But (like the title Lord "Son of God" is for Paul much more than a designation which Jesus, as Messiah, bears *ex officio*; [16] it expresses the unique personal relation which Jesus bore to God, as indeed it appears to have done for Jesus himself. [17]

Luke seems to recognize the special place that the designation of Jesus as Son of God had in Paul's ministry, for whereas he makes other preachers of the apostolic message in its early days proclaim Jesus as Lord and Messiah, he sums up Paul's earliest public testimony to Jesus in the words, "He is the Son of God" (Acts 9: 20). Perhaps the language in which Paul himself describes his call and commission, "God . . . was pleased to reveal his Son in me, that I might proclaim him among the Gentiles" (Galatians 1: 15 f.), implies that an appreciation of Jesus as the Son of God was inherent in his conversion experience.

Although Paul makes infrequent use of the metaphor "the right hand of God", he takes the oracle of Psalm 110: 1 seriously as a messianic *testimonium*, and in fact in 1 Corinthians 15: 24–28 he gives a fuller exposition of it than does any other New Testament writer. "Sit at my right hand", ran the oracle, "till I make your enemies your footstool" – and Paul undertakes to identify these enemies. They are not flesh-and-blood enemies; they are "principalities and powers", forces in the universe which work against the purpose of God and the well-being of man. It is to forces of this order that Paul has referred earlier in 1 Corinthians as the "rulers of this age" who, in ignorance of the hidden wisdom decreed by God from ages past for his people's glory, "crucified the Lord of glory" (1 Corinthians 2: 6–8). Pontius Pilate and others may have played their historic part in this, but without realizing it they were agents of those hostile forces in the spiritual realm. Now, thanks to

power" and the coming of the kingdom of God "in power" in Mark 9: 1. During Jesus' earthly ministry the Kingdom of God was subject to limitations (cf. Luke 12: 50). See p. 141.

15. Like the oracle of Psalm 110: 1, this one also probably had its original life-setting in the enthronement of a Davidic king. The clause "You are my Son" is part of the utterance of the heavenly voice to Jesus at his baptism in Mark 1: 11 (cf. John 1: 34, "I have seen and have borne witness that this is the Son of God"); in the Western text of the parallel in Luke 3: 22 the heavenly voice repeats the full wording: "you are my Son; today I have begotten you".

16. Cf. A. D. Nock, " 'Son of God' in Pauline and Hellenistic Thought", in his *Essays on Religion and the Ancient World*, ed. Z. Stewart, ii (Oxford, 1972), pp. 928–939; M. Hengel, *The Son of God: The Origin of Christology and the History of Jewish-Hellenistic Religion*, E.T. (London, 1976).

17. Cf. the Q-logion Matthew 11: 27/Luke 10: 22; but Jesus' use of *Abba* is evidence enough. See pp. 208 f.

the victory of the cross and the reign of the risen Lord, those forces are being progressively destroyed. The last and most intractable of those forces is death, which is to be destroyed at the final resurrection of which the resurrection of Christ is the first instalment.

"Sit at my right hand", said the oracle, "till I make your enemies your footstool" – so, says Paul, "Christ must reign till God has put all his enemies under his feet" (1 Corinthians 15: 25). But when all those enemies are subjugated, including death itself, then the reign of Christ is merged in the eternal reign of God. The reign of Christ, "the age of the Messiah", is thus an intermediate phase between the present age and the endless age to come, or from certain points of view it may be regarded as the overlapping of the two, a phase in which the present age is not fully ended and the age to come has not been fully established.

A further word must be interjected here about those principalities and powers. A close examination of what Paul has to say about them shows that, to his way of thinking, they are largely those elemental forces that dominate the minds of men and women and are powerful so long as men and women believe in them and render them allegiance. But when their minds are liberated by faith in the crucified and risen Christ, then the bondage imposed by those forces is broken, their power is dissolved and they are revealed as the "weak and beggarly" nonentities that they are in themselves. To mention two of the most potent, the strength of sin and the fear of death could bind men and women's lives in an iron grip, but those who enjoyed the liberation effected by Christ knew that sin had no more dominion over them and that even death, in advance of the coming resurrection, could be greeted as pure gain. The destruction of the principalities and powers may be expressed in figurative language, but the reality is the enjoyment of inward release and freedom experienced by the believer.[18]

In the passage already quoted from Romans 8: 34, where Paul seems to echo a primitive confession of faith in "Christ Jesus who died, yes, who was raised from the dead, who is at the right hand of God", he continues with the clause: "who indeed intercedes for us". The reigning Christ, that is to say, is not passively waiting for the Father to fulfil his promise to make his enemies his footstool; he is actively engaged on his people's behalf. The confessional words are placed by Paul in a forensic context, in imitation of a recurring Old Testament motif [19]: he begins with the challenge, "Who shall bring any charge against God's elect?" and affirms that no one will

18. See pp. 182 f., 412 ff.; cf. also F. F. Bruce, "Galatian Problems, 3. The 'Other' Gospel", *BJRL* 53 (1970–1), pp. 266–70. For the characterization of those elemental powers as "weak and beggarly" see Galatians 4: 9.
19. Cf. the challenge of the Servant of Yahweh in Isaiah 50: 8 f.

dare to fill the rôle of the Old Testament *saṭān* [20] and attempt to prosecute them in the heavenly court because God himself is their justifier and the Christ who died and rose is present as counsel for their defence.

The ascription of an intercessory ministry to the ascended Christ may be based on Isaiah 53: 12, where the humiliated and vindicated Servant of the Lord is said to have "made intercession for the transgressors"; [21] it is not peculiar to Paul among the New Testament theologians, for in 1 John 2: 1 "Jesus Christ the righteous" is presented as his people's "advocate with the Father", while the theme is elaborated by the writer to the Hebrews in his portrayal of Jesus as the enthroned high priest, who "is able for all time to save those who draw near to God through him, since he always lives to make intercession for them" (Hebrews 7: 25). [22]

In other words, Christ's active concern for his people is not exhausted by his death on their behalf; in his new order of existence he is still their friend and helper, supplying spiritual sustenance to meet their varied need.

## 3. *The Lord and the Spirit*

But when Paul deals with this supplying of the present spiritual need of the people of Christ, he does so for the most part in terms of the activity of the Spirit, to the point where much that he says about the ministry of the ascended Christ can be paralleled by what he says about the ministry of the Spirit. The love, for example, which the Spirit pours out into the hearts of believers (Romans 5: 5) is no abstraction; it is described in 1 Corinthians 13 in almost personal terms, as though the character of Christ were being portrayed. Similarly, in 2 Corinthians 3: 18 the Spirit's function in the lives of believers is to transform them progressively into the image of Christ, "from one degree of glory to another; for this comes from the Lord who is the Spirit".

This phrase, "the Lord who is the Spirit", is based on a midrashic interpretation which Paul has just been giving of the narrative in Exodus 34: 29–35. Moses, his countenance shining from his confrontation with the divine glory, wore a veil to conceal the radiance from his fellow-Israelites, but removed it when he "went in before the LORD". Paul takes this to mean that each time

20. Cf. the abortive attempt to prosecute Joshua the high priest in the heavenly court in Zechariah 3: 1–5.

21. This intercession is obscured in LXX, but the Targum of Jonathan introduces the theme elsewhere in the fourth Servant Song, e.g. at Isaiah 53: 4, 11 ("for their trespasses he will make entreaty"), 12 ("he will make entreaty for many trespasses"). See p. 66.

22. Cf. E. G. Rupp, "The Finished Work of Christ in Word and Sacrament", in *The Finality of Christ*, ed. D. Kilpatrick (Nashville/New York, 1966), pp. 175 ff.

Moses went into the presence of God he was "re-charged" with the divine glory, and veiled his face when he went out so that the Israelites should not see that this glory was a fading one which required repeated renewal. The fading glory on Moses' face is contrasted, as we have seen, with the unfading "glory of God in the face of Christ" (2 Corinthians 4: 6), by way of pointing the contrast between the inferior glory of the law, introduced for a limited period and destined to pass away, and the surpassing glory of the gospel, "the dispensation of the Spirit" (2 Corinthians 3: 8).

But even in the Exodus narrative Paul sees the gospel age adumbrated: as Moses removed the veil from his face when he "went in before the LORD" (Exodus 34: 34), so, "when a man turns to the Lord, the veil is removed. Now [Paul adds] the Lord is the Spirit, and where the Spirit of the Lord is, there is freedom" (2 Corinthians 3: 16 f.).[23] That is to say, "the LORD" in the Exodus narrative corresponds to the Spirit in this new order, and where the Spirit of the Lord is, there is freedom of access to the divine presence "with unveiled face".[24] Access to God in the dispensation of law, he implies, was difficult and hedged about with restrictions and inhibitions; access to God in the dispensation of the Spirit is free and unreserved.

The statement, "the Lord is the Spirit", has been taken to assert an identity between Christ as Lord and the Spirit of God, but this is probably not Paul's intention. The statement is rather Paul's interpretation of Moses' entering the divine presence, or his adaptation of Moses' experience to that of the believer under the new covenant. What the Lord was to Moses, the Spirit is to the believer; yet in saying "the Lord is the Spirit" and in his later reference to "the Lord who is the Spirit" – literally "the Lord the Spirit" – Paul suggests, not indeed the identity, but certainly the close association that exists between the ascended Christ and the Spirit in the believer. His language, in the circumspect words of George Smeaton, a nineteenth-century Scottish theologian, "shows how fully he apprehended their joint mission, and how emphatically he intimates that Christ is never to be conceived of apart from the Spirit, nor the Spirit conceived of apart from Him".[25] In our own day Ernst Käsemann is more forthright, if less circumspect, and

23. Cf. J. D. G. Dunn, "2 Corinthians iii. 17 – 'the Lord is the Spirit' ", *JTS* n.s. 21 (1970), 309 ff.; C. F. D. Moule, "2 Cor. 3: 18 b, *Kathaper apo kuriou pneumatos*", in *Neues Testament und Geschichte, Oscar Cullmann zum 70. Geburtstag*, ed. H. Baltensweiler and B. Reicke (Zürich/Tübingen, 1972), pp. 231 ff.

24. Cf. Paul's use of παρρησία in 2 Corinthians 3: 12; see W. C. van Unnik, "The Christian's Freedom of Speech", *BJRL* 44 (1961–2), pp. 466 ff., and "With Unveiled Face", *Novum Testamentum* 6 (1963), pp. 153 ff.

25. G. Smeaton, *The Doctrine of the Holy Spirit* (Edinburgh, 1882), p. 57.

describes the Spirit as "the earthly *praesentia* of the exalted Lord".[26]

But this is Professor Käsemann's comment not on "the Lord who is the Spirit" but on a statement to which we have already alluded: that Jesus in resurrection became "a life-giving Spirit" (1 Corinthians 15: 45). And whatever may be said of "the Lord is the Spirit", *prima facie* an identity of the risen Christ with the Spirit would seem to be affirmed in the clause: "the last Adam became a life-giving Spirit". Elsewhere Paul knows of only one life-giving Spirit, and that is "the Spirit of life in Christ Jesus" (Romans 8: 2), the Spirit whose indwelling power quickens mortal bodies (Romans 8: 11), the Spirit whose life-giving property is set in contrast with the death-dealing effect of the law (2 Corinthians 3: 6), the Spirit through whom the believer's inner being is renewed from day to day even while the outer being disintegrates (2 Corinthians 4: 16), the Spirit whose presence within is the guarantee of the believer's investiture with a heavenly and imperishable body (2 Corinthians 5: 5).

True, in using the phrase "life-giving spirit" of the last Adam, Paul may be moved by the desire to find an appropriately balancing phrase to the "living soul" predicated of the first Adam in Genesis 2: 7. But the phrase chosen to describe the last Adam is particularly suitable in view of two crucial articles of faith which Paul repeatedly emphasizes: (i) that Christ, by his resurrection from the dead, is the first-fruits of the resurrection harvest in which all his people will share, and (ii) that the Spirit has been given to his people here and now as the pledge and first instalment of their eventual participation in their Master's resurrection life and glory. Here and now "he who is united to the Lord becomes one Spirit with him" (1 Corinthians 6: 17). This is another balancing phrase, chosen by Paul as a counterpoise to the "one flesh" which man and woman become in marital union (Genesis 2: 24), but it is not chosen for stylistic reasons only. It expresses a recurring theme in Pauline thought: "he who is united to the Lord" by faith derives from him eternal life now and the hope of glory to come; but since it is through the Spirit that the life and hope are mediated, "he who is united to the Lord becomes one Spirit with him" – and with all those who are similarly united to him.

## 4. The image of God

Paul, as we have seen, associates "the light of the gospel of the glory of Christ" with the fact that Christ is "the image of God". If the former phrase recalls his Damascus road experience, what about the latter phrase? Was there something about the

26. E. Käsemann, *Religion in Geschichte und Gegenwart*³, ii (Tübingen, 1958), col. 1274 (*s.v.* "Geist").

appearance of the risen Christ which instantaneously impressed him as being the image of God? Did he, for example, see "a likeness as it were of a human form" as Ezekiel did when he saw "the likeness of the glory of the LORD" (Ezekiel 1: 26, 28) and recognize that it was Jesus by the words which he heard him speak? We cannot be sure; it is difficult to know what meaning the expression "the image of God" would have had for Paul. Yet when he speaks of seeing "the light of the knowledge of the glory of God in the face of Christ" he uses language which practically amounts to seeing in Christ the image of God.[27]

Paul is not the only New Testament writer to present Christ in these terms: the Fourth Evangelist records the progressive revelation of God in the ministry of the incarnate Word, until it finds its climax on the cross; and the writer to the Hebrews speaks of the Son of God as "the effulgence of his glory and the very stamp of his being" (Hebrews 1: 3). But it is in Paul that the presentation of Christ as the image of God is worked out most fully and consistently, with its corollary of the increasing transformation of the people of Christ into that same image by the power of the indwelling Spirit,[28] until nothing remains of the earthly image in those who finally display the image of the heavenly man.[29]

Man, according to the Old Testament, was made in God's image (Genesis 1: 26 f.) and for his glory (Isaiah 43: 7): in the order of creation he is, as Paul says, "the image and glory of God" (1 Corinthians 11: 7).[30] It is difficult to dissociate Paul's portrayal of the risen Christ as the second man, the last Adam, from his view of Christ as the image of God and the revealer of his glory. What the first man was, imperfectly, in the old creation, Christ is, perfectly, in the new creation – the resurrection order.

It is tempting to go farther and relate another aspect of Paul's christology to this appreciation of Christ as the image of God. In the Alexandrian book of Wisdom, which was evidently known to Paul, wisdom is not only personified but described as the "image" (*eikōn*) of God's goodness.[31]

27. The foundation of Paul's appreciation of Christ as the image of God in his conversion experience is receiving close attention from one of my research students, Mr. Seyoon Kim, whose studies on the bearing of the Damascus-road Christophany on Paul's gospel have provided a welcome stimulus to my thought on this and related subjects.

28. 2 Corinthians 3: 18 (see p. 210); cf. Galatians 4: 19.

29. 1 Corinthians 15: 49.

30. Paul says this of the ἀνήρ, the male, although in Genesis 1: 26 f. it is said of ἄνθρωπος , mankind. But he read Genesis 1: 26 ff. in the light of 2: 18 ff., and concluded that it was first in the form of the male that mankind was created to bear the image of God: "male and female he created them" being taken to mean "first male and later female".

31. Wisdom 7: 26, where wisdom is also described as "a reflection ( ἀπαύγασμα ,

124 PAUL: APOSTLE OF THE FREE SPIRIT

One thing is certain: that Paul, in common with some of his fellow-theologians among the New Testament writers, identified Christ with the wisdom of God and ascribed to him certain activities which are predicated of personified wisdom in the wisdom literature of the Old Testament. When, for example, Paul speaks of the "one Lord, Jesus Christ, through whom are all things and through whom we exist" (1 Corinthians 8: 6), or describes him as "the image of the invisible God" in that "all things were created through him and for him" (Colossians 1: 15 f.), this identification of Christ with divine wisdom underlies such statements, just as it underlies the affirmation of John 1: 4 that "all things were made through him" (i.e. the incarnate Word) and that of Hebrews 1: 2 that the Son of God is the one "through whom also he made the worlds".[32] But here it is not particularly the *risen* Christ that is in view: it is the eternal Christ, whose entry into the world of mankind was no involuntary experience but a deliberate act of condescension: "being in the form of God, . . . he emptied himself and took the form of a servant" (Philippians 2: 6 f.);[33] "though he was rich, yet for your sake he became poor" (2 Corinthians 8: 9).

If this aspect of Paul's christology is not related to his vision of Christ as the image of God, then it is difficult to relate it to Paul's subsequent personal experience of Christ. Before his conversion he probably identified divine wisdom with the Torah, the "desirable instrument"[34] by which God made the world, if not the goal for which he made it.[35] After his conversion the centrality of the Torah in Paul's thought and life was displaced by the centrality of Christ, and this might suggest the transference to Christ of properties and activities previously ascribed to the Torah. But this is less likely: Christ displaced the Torah in Paul's scheme of things, but, far from being its equivalent, he was for Paul "the end of the law" (Romans 10: 4).[36] But he was not the end of divine wisdom; he was its very embodiment.

It is probably significant, however, that the pre-existent Christ is

---

cf. Hebrews 1: 3, where the Son is the ἀπαύγασμα of God's glory) of eternal light, a spotless mirror of the working of God" (with ἔσοπτρον, "mirror", cf. κατοπτριζόμενοι, "beholding", "reflecting", in 2 Corinthians 3: 18 and δι' ἐσόπτρου, "in a mirror", in 1 Corinthians 13: 12).

32. Cf. Revelation 3: 14, where Christ speaks as "the Amen, . . . the beginning of God's creation" – an echo of Proverbs 8: 22, 30 where Wisdom speaks as "the beginning of his way", his 'āmôn ("master workman") at the creation.

33. The wording echoes that of Isaiah 52: 13–53: 12, but in another Greek rendering than that of the Septuagint (where the servant is παῖς, not δοῦλος as here): ἐκένωσεν ἑαυτὸν . . . εἰς θάνατον reflects "he poured out his soul to death" (Isaiah 53: 12). See p. 131 with n. 25, p. 90 with n. 17.

34. Cf. Rabbi Aqiba in *Pirqê Abôt* iii. 19.

35. Cf. Rabbi Banna'ah in *Genesis Rabba* 1: 4 (on Genesis 1:1).

36. See pp. 104, 190 ff.

not associated by Paul with the Spirit as the risen Christ is: for Paul, the Spirit is distinctively the herald and sign of the new age, coming into his purview first of all in relation to Christ's being "designated Son of God in power according to the Spirit of holiness by his resurrection from the dead" (Romans 1: 4). Why the phrase "Spirit of holiness" should be used here rather than Paul's more usual "Holy Spirit" is a matter for inquiry, but it is a literal translation of the Hebrew construction for "holy spirit" [37] and so cannot be distinguished in meaning from "the Spirit of him who raised Jesus from the dead", whose residence in the lives of the people of Christ is the pledge of their resurrection too (Romans 8: 11). The Spirit of Christ, as Albert Schweitzer put it, "is the life-principle of His Messianic personality"; [38] it is the living Christ himself who is his people's hope of glory and it is in him that the hope is to be realized: "When Christ who is our life appears", says Paul, "then you also will appear with him in glory" (Colossians 3: 4). When the people of Christ in resurrection share fully in the image of their exalted Lord, the Spirit's present ministry has been fulfilled. But the Spirit who fulfils this present ministry is the Spirit that came upon Jesus before he came upon his followers: for Paul, in other words, the exalted Lord whose risen life and powers are conveyed to his people by the indwelling Spirit is identical and continuous with him who lived among men as a servant, the crucified one, the historical Jesus.

---

37. Heb. *rûah haqqōdeš*.
38. A. Schweitzer, *The Mysticism of Paul the Apostle*, E.T. (London, 1931), p. 165.

# CHAPTER 13

# Paul and the Hellenistic Mission

## 1. Paul returns to the Greek world

WITH HIS RETURN TO "THE REGIONS OF SYRIA AND CILICIA" Paul was irrevocably committed to the Hellenistic world. He had been sent or brought to Jerusalem in his youth by his parents in order to be immunized against the infection of the Hellenistic world – that "place of evil waters" (as the sage Abtalyon called it a generation or more before the birth of Paul), which brought death to those who drank from them and caused the name of God to be profaned.[1] Now he had come back to this ill-omened territory to claim it and its inhabitants for his new master.

Judaea, and even Jerusalem, formed part of the Hellenistic world.[2] Greek was spoken alongside Aramaic (and possibly Hebrew) in the holy city itself[3] and, as we have seen, Hellenistic Jews had their synagogues there in which the scriptures were read and worship was conducted in Greek. The pagan influences of Hellenism were kept at bay from the circle in which Paul received his education, but even the sages knew Greek and were capable of giving their pupils prophylactic courses in Greek language and culture. Simeon the son of Gamaliel is said to have had many pupils who studied "the wisdom of the Greeks" alongside as many others who studied the Torah,[4] and it need not be doubted that Gamaliel the elder also had such pupils. It is quite probable that Paul acquired the rudiments of Greek learning in Gamaliel's school. But from his return to Tarsus throughout the rest of his active life he was exposed to the Greek way of life in one city after another, for he no longer led a cloistered existence, but lived for the most part as a

1. *Pirqê Abôt* 1:11.
2. Cf. I. H. Marshall, "Palestinian and Hellenistic Christianity: Some Critical Comments", *NTS* 19 (1972–73), pp. 271–287.
3. Cf. J. N. Sevenster, *Do you know Greek?* (Leiden, 1968). On the possibility that Hebrew was spoken cf. M. H. Segal, *A Grammar of Mishnaic Hebrew* (Oxford, 1927), pp. 14–19; T. W. Manson, *The Teaching of Jesus* (Cambridge,[2] 1935), pp. 46 ff.
4. TB *Soṭah* 49b. Both Gamaliel I and Gamaliel II had a son called Simeon. The rabbis called Gamaliel are not always clearly distinguished, and the reference here may be to the son of Gamaliel II (c. A.D. 140) but this would not affect the probable practice of Gamaliel I.

Gentile among Gentiles in order to win Gentiles for the gospel.[5]
The knowledge of Greek literature and thought that his letters
attest was part of the common stock of educated people in the
Hellenistic world of that day; it bespeaks no formal instruction
received from Greek teachers. The direction of his faith and life was
by now too firmly fixed – first by his Jewish upbringing and then by
his submission to Jesus as Lord – for Hellenism to exercise a
decisive influence on his mind. We can recognize in his writings
concepts and expressions, drawn especially from popular Stoicism,
which were in the air at the time and which he freely pressed into
service in a Christian context; [6] but while he preached the gospel to
the Hellenes, it was no hellenized gospel that he preached. His
proclamation of deliverance and life through Christ crucified
brought his gospel into basic conflict with accepted standards of
Hellenistic value and gave it the quality of "folly" which it had in
the eyes of those of his hearers who made their assessments by what
Paul called "the wisdom of the world" (1 Corinthians 1: 20 ff.).

For about ten years from his arrival back in Tarsus only the scan-
tiest information has been preserved about Paul's movements and
experiences. He himself makes it clear that he spent those years in
evangelization: this was the period during which the Judaean
churches heard reports of how their former persecutor was "now
preaching the faith he once tried to destroy" (Galatians 1: 23).[7] If,
by his own account (Galatians 1: 22), he was personally unknown
to those churches – from which the church of Jerusalem cannot be
excluded – that was because his former persecution had been
directed more particularly against the Hellenistic disciples, few of
whom now remained in Judaea.

It is possible that during these years he endured some of the
hardships which he later lists in 2 Corinthians 11: 22–27 as credentials of his apostolic commission. When, for example, he speaks of
having on five occasions "received at the hands of the Jews the forty
lashes less one"[8] – none of these occasions being mentioned
elsewhere either by himself or by Luke – they must be assigned to a
stage in his Christian career when he still submitted to synagogue
discipline. Presumably he could have claimed exemption from this
discipline on the ground of his Roman citizenship, but that would

5. Cf. his own account of the matter in 1 Corinthians 9: 19–23.
6. Cf. M. Pohlenz, *Paulus und die Stoa* (Darmstadt, 1964). Paul's possible indebtedness (especially in 2 Corinthians 10–13) to an older philosophical method is
discussed by H. D. Betz, *Der Apostel Paulus und die sokratische Tradition* (Tübingen,
1972).
7. See p. 69.
8. The maximum number of lashes prescribed by the written law was forty
(Deuteronomy 25: 3); on the principle of "setting a hedge around the law" to prevent its accidental transgression, it was traditionally restricted to thirty-nine
(Mishnah *Makkôt* 3: 10–15).

have meant in effect the denial of his Jewishness and the renunciation of his regular policy of using the synagogue as his preliminary base of operation. So long as he made a practice of visiting the synagogue as an observant Jew in each new city to which he came, he was obliged to accept its discipline, until he finally withdrew from it. It may well be that some of his experiences of the thirty-nine lashes belong to this Cilician phase of his life. Whether more of the "countless beatings"[9] and other instances of harsh treatment to which he refers in the same context can also be located in this phase it is not possible to say with any certainty.

## 2. Jewish missionary enterprise

There is evidence of considerable proselytizing activity among the Gentiles in the earlier part of the first century A.D.[10] "Love your fellow-creatures", said Hillel, "and draw them near to the Torah."[11] The conversion to Judaism of the ruling house of Adiabene, east of the Tigris, about A.D. 40, is the most conspicuous instance of proselytization known to us from this period, and illustrates the missionary activity of Jews whose business made them travel from time to time in foreign parts.[12] Among the groups from the dispersion listed by Luke as being present in Jerusalem for the festival of Pentecost in A.D. 30 were "visitors from Rome, both Jews and proselytes" (Acts 2: 10). One of the seven leaders of the Hellenistic section in the primitive church of Jerusalem was "Nicolaus, a proselyte of Antioch" (Acts 6: 5).[13] Philip, another of the Hellenistic leaders, baptized an Ethiopian proselyte or God-fearer who was travelling home from a pilgrimage to Jerusalem and sent him "on his way rejoicing" (Acts 8: 27–39), while Peter about the same time baptized the God-fearer Cornelius, a Roman centurion stationed in Caesarea, together with his household.[14] God-fearers were Gentiles who attached themselves in varying degrees to the Jewish worship and way of life without as yet becoming full proselytes. To become a full proselyte, a member by conversion of the Jewish religious community, a male Gentile was normally required to submit to circumcision, in addition to undergoing a ceremonial bath ("proselyte baptism"), offering a

9. These include the five occasions just mentioned and three beatings with rods – presumably at the hands of Roman authorities, like that at Philippi (Acts 16: 22 f.); see p. 221.
10. Caution on this is urged by J. Munck, *Paul and the Salvation of Mankind*, E. T. (London, 1959), pp. 264 ff.; cf. also A. D. Nock, *Essays on Religion and the Ancient World*, ii (Oxford, 1972), p. 929.
11. *Pirqê Abôt* 1: 12.
12. Josephus, *Ant.* xx. 17 ff.
13. See p. 67.
14. Acts 10: 47 f.

Jerusalem and the Temple area today, seen from the Mount of Olives (see p. 144)

Athens: A bronze tablet at foot of Areopagus recording Paul's speech (see p. 238)

sacrifice and undertaking to keep the law of Moses.[15] For this reason it was easier for Gentile women to become proselytes: the three last requirements sufficed for them. But proselytes and God-fearers, especially God-fearers, were present in large enough numbers throughout the provinces of the Roman Empire to provide a nucleus for the churches which Paul planted in one city after another.

The presence of those proselytes and God-fearers throughout the provinces was the product of Jewish religious witness and missionary activity among the Gentiles. Those Jews who shared in this activity took seriously Israel's mission, promulgated through the prophet of consolation, to be Yahweh's witnesses in the world and declare his praise among the nations (Isaiah 43: 10–12, 21). It has been suggested by some that Paul himself, before his conversion, had conceived a desire to take a leading part in this activity, to bring Gentiles into obedience to the law.[16] This cannot be proved. But if there is any truth in the suggestion, then it would serve as a background for his new vocation to proclaim Christ among the Gentiles – the law being displaced in his plan of missionary campaign, as it was in his personal life, by the crucified and exalted Jesus.

## 3. The gospel comes to Syrian Antioch

Paul was far from being the only Christian missionary in Syria and Cilicia during those years. The Hellenistic disciples who had shaken the dust of Jerusalem and Judaea from their feet, considering perhaps that the severe persecution they had undergone after Stephen's death would bring on the city and region divine retribution which nothing could avert, settled in the surrounding territories and began to propagate their faith there.[17] If a high estimation of the holiness of Jerusalem had earlier brought them from their original homes to settle there, their disillusionment was all the greater when the holy city drove them out. If, as they now found, pagan or semi-pagan environments would provide them with greater freedom to serve God and maintain their witness to his saving act in Christ, the place of such environments in the divine

15. Cf. H. H. Rowley, "Jewish Proselyte Baptism and the Baptism of John", in *From Moses to Qumran* (London, 1963), pp. 211–235; T. F. Torrance, "Proselyte Baptism", *NTS* 1 (1954–55), pp. 150–154.

16. "We have to give serious consideration to the possibility that, before he became a Christian, the 'Hillelite' Paul was committed to the Jewish mission" (M. Hengel, "Die Ursprünge der christlichen Mission", *NTS* 18 [1971–72], p. 23. Cf. H. J. Schoeps, *Paul* (London, 1961), pp. 219 ff. This may be the background to Paul's words in Galatians 5: 11, "if I . . . *still* preach circumcision".

17. Cf. M. Hengel, "Zwischen Jesus und Paulus", *ZTK* 72 (1975), pp. 196 f.

scheme must be reappraised. Philip, one of Stephen's colleagues in the Jerusalem church, who seems to have taken over the Hellenistic leadership after Stephen's death, initiated a remarkably successful Christian mission in a Samaritan city, and then took up residence in the largely Gentile city of Caesarea Maritima.[18] Other Hellenistic fugitives travelled farther afield – some, quite probably, to Alexandria and Cyrene, from which a number of them had originally come, and others, of whom Luke tells us more particularly, to Phoenicia and Syria, as far north as Antioch.

Antioch on the Orontes (modern Antakya in the Hatay province of Turkey), standing at the foot of Mount Silpius, some eighteen miles upstream from its seaport Seleucia Pieria, was founded in 300 B.C. by Seleucus Nicator, first ruler of the Seleucid dynasty, and named by him after his father Antiochus. As the capital of the Seleucid empire it rapidly became a city of importance, and when Syria became a Roman province in 64 B.C. Antioch was the seat of administration and residence of the imperial legate.[19] It remained the provincial capital when Eastern Cilicia was united with Syria in 25 B.C. It was at this time the third largest city in the Roman world, planned on the grid pattern, surpassed in population only by Rome and Alexandria. Julius Caesar, Augustus and Tiberius enlarged and adorned it, while Herod the Great contributed colonnades on both sides of the main street and paved the street itself with polished stone.[20] It was a centre of commerce as well as a political capital; the products of Syria passed through it on their way to the rest of the Mediterranean lands. Since it was near the frontier between the settled Graeco-Roman world and the Orient, it was more cosmopolitan than most Hellenistic cities.

Jews formed part of the population of Antioch from its foundation onward, even before Judaea itself was governed from Antioch (as it was during the first half of the second century B.C.). In 145 B.C. the city had experience of Jews in another rôle than that of settlers and merchants, for Demetrius II, involved in civil war with a rival contender for the Seleucid throne, whose forces occupied most of Antioch, enlisted the support of three thousand soldiers from the army of Jonathan the Hasmonaean, who showed their skill in urban fighting and, after working considerable and perhaps unnecessary destruction, helped to regain control of the city for the

18. Acts 8: 5–40.
19. Cf. B. M. Metzger, "Antioch-on-the-Orontes", *Biblical Archaeologist* 11 (1948), pp. 70–88; G. W. Elderkin, R. Stillwell, F. O. Waage, D. B. Waage, *Antioch-on-the-Orontes*, I–IV/2 (Princeton and Oxford, 1934–52); G. Downey, *A History of Antioch in Syria from Seleucus to the Arab Conquest* (Princeton, 1961) and *Ancient Antioch* (Princeton, 1963).
20. Cf. Josephus, *Ant.* xvi. 148.

king.[21] By the beginning of the Christian era, proselytes to Judaism are said (by Josephus) to have been specially abundant in Antioch;[22] one of them, Nicolaus, became in turn a convert to the faith of Jesus and is listed, as was mentioned above, among the Hellenistic leaders in the church of Jerusalem.[23]

To this city of Antioch, then, came a number of Hellenistic refugees from Jerusalem, including (Luke tells us) some men whose original homes were in Cyprus and Cyrene.[24] The refugees were active propagandists for their faith, although for the most part they confined their propaganda to their fellow-Hellenists – Greek-speaking Jews – but when these men of Cyprus and Cyrene came to Antioch, they conceived the idea of letting the local Greeks, pagans though they were, share in their good news. Large numbers of those Greeks hailed the good news as something which exactly met their need. In their great city there would have been many competing cults and mystery religions which held out the promise of salvation from the power of evil or from a sense of estrangement in an unfriendly world. When the visitors told their good news of salvation through Christ, the terms in which they spoke would not be entirely unfamiliar to their hearers; but there was something about the Christ whom they proclaimed as saviour which was peculiarly attractive and not paralleled in any of the lords or saviours celebrated in those other cults. Perhaps they spoke of him as one who existed in the form of God before he came to earth as man, who as man accepted humiliation and death, and was accordingly exalted by God above all creation and endowed with the title "Lord" (*kyrios*) in the highest sense which it was capable of bearing. This possibility hangs on the view that the hymn in honour of Christ which Paul incorporates in Philippians 2: 5–11, widely believed to be pre-Pauline,[25] was current as early as the Hellenistic mission in Syrian Antioch. The hymn in any case harks back to the fourth Ser-

---

21. 1 Maccabees 11: 41–51.

22. Josephus, *BJ* vii. 45.

23. Acts 6: 5 (see p. 128).

24. Acts 11: 20.

25. Cf. E. Lohmeyer, *Kyrios Jesus: Eine Untersuchung zu Phil. 2, 5–11* (Heidelberg, 1928, [2]1961); E. Käsemann, "A Critical Analysis of Philippians 2: 5–11" (1950), E.T. in *Journal for Theology and Church* 5 (1968), pp. 45–88; D. Georgi, "Der vorpaulinische Hymnus Phil. 2, 6–11", in *Zeit und Geschichte: Dankesgabe an R. Bultmann*, ed. E. Dinkler (Tübingen, 1964), pp. 263–293; R. P. Martin, *Carmen Christi: Philippians ii. 5–11 in Recent Interpretation and in the Setting of Early Christian Worship* (Cambridge, 1967); I. H. Marshall, "The Christ-Hymn in Philippians 2: 5–11", *Tyndale Bulletin* 19 (1968), pp. 104–127; C. F. D. Moule, "Further Reflexions on Philippians 2: 5–11", in *Apostolic History and the Gospel*, ed. W. W. Gasque and R. P. Martin (Exeter, 1970), pp. 264–276; M. D. Hooker, "Philippians 2: 6–11", in *Jesus und Paulus: Festschrift für W. G. Kümmel*, ed. E. E. Ellis and E. Grässer (Göttingen, 1975), pp. 151–164; O. Hofius, *Der Christushymnus Philipper 2, 6–11* (Tübingen, 1976).

vant Song which, as had been said already,[26] gave rise to an important strand of christological thinking in the early Jerusalem church.

It is natural that the designation "Christian" should first have been given to the followers of Jesus in Antioch, and by Gentiles. As the Herodians in the Gospels were adherents of Herod,[27] so the Christians (christianoi) were adherents of Christ (such forms consisting of the stem of a personal name followed by an originally Latin suffix, -ianus). Greek-speaking Jews at that date would not have referred to Jesus as Christ, for that was still a title (christos, the "anointed" one, corresponding to the Semitic messiah);[28] to refer to him thus would have been to acknowledge him as Messiah. But in Gentile ears Christ was simply an alternative name for Jesus; it had no such associations for them as it had for Jews. Christos sounded exactly like a fairly common slave-name, Chrēstos (Latin Chrestus), and among Greeks and Romans there was considerable confusion between the two spellings,[29] as also between christianoi and chrēstianoi. Even in Acts 11: 26, where it is mentioned that "in Antioch the disciples were for the first time called Christians", a few Greek witnesses to the text (including the first hand in Codex Sinaiticus) exhibit the spelling chrēstianous (accusative plural) instead of christianous. The latter is certainly what Luke wrote, but the former may well represent what some of the Antiochenes thought they were saying.

The leaders of the Jerusalem church at this stage appear to have exercised a general supervision or, indeed, control over the spread of the gospel into adjacent territories. For example, when Philip's recent preaching in a Samaritan city won a large number of converts there,[30] Peter and John came from Jerusalem and welcomed these new converts into the messianic fellowship.[31] A similar situation faced them now, when news came to Jerusalem of the revolutionary extension of the gospel among the Gentiles of Antioch. Who could tell what wild syncretism, so congenial to Antioch, might not develop from it if proper direction were not given? A delegate was accordingly sent to Antioch to see what was going on. The results might have been disastrous if the wrong type of delegate had been chosen; fortunately, the man who was sent was Barnabas, the "encourager".[32] No doubt the forward movement at

26. See pp. 65 f., 89.
27. Cf. Mark 3: 6; 12: 13.
28. Hebrew māšîaḥ, Aramaic (emphatic state) mᵉšîḥâ, verbal adjectives of māšaḥ, mᵉšaḥ ("anoint").
29. Cf. Suetonius, Life of Claudius 25. 4 (impulsore Chresto); see p. 381.
30. See p. 130.
31. The two apostles laid their hands on the Samaritan converts, so that they received the Holy Spirit (Acts 8: 17).

Antioch presented features which some members of the church of Jerusalem would have found deeply disturbing, but Barnabas found much cause for satisfaction. "When he came and saw the grace of God, he was glad", says Luke (Acts 11: 23), so he settled down at Antioch and gave the Hellenistic missionaries and their converts the sympathetic encouragement and wise guidance that they needed. Before long, a large and growing church was established in Antioch – a church which, with the rapid progress of the gospel among the Greek population, was bound very quickly to have more members of Gentile birth than of Jewish birth.

In this situation, Barnabas began to feel the need of a colleague to share the responsibility of supervising the life and activity of this new church, and his mind turned to Paul. He knew of Paul's vocation to the evangelizing of Gentiles, and perhaps heard reports from time to time of what Paul had been doing in this regard in Cilicia. All that he knew of Paul convinced him that there was no man more suitable to join him in his work at Antioch, so he journeyed to Tarsus to find him, and persuaded him to return to Antioch with him. If we say that Paul was thus (about A.D. 45) brought back into the main stream of Christian action, Paul would not necessarily have agreed; wherever he was would have been the main stream in his eyes at any particular time. But he was brought into the main stream of *recorded* Christian action (so far as records are extant), for it is now that he reappears in Luke's narrative, after his departure for Tarsus at the end of his brief visit with Peter in Jerusalem. The evangelization of Antioch and the path of Christian advance from that city would be of special interest to Luke if, as tradition asserts, he was himself an Antiochene by birth.[33]

32. See p. 83.

33. The earliest reference to Luke's being a native of Syrian Antioch comes at the beginning of the anti-Marcionite prologue to the Gospel of Luke, late in the second century. Eusebius (*Hist. Eccl.* iii. 4) and Jerome (*De uiris illustribus*, 7) repeat this testimony. The tradition is attested in one form of the Western text, where Acts 11: 28 appears as a "we" passage: the prophecy of Agabus to the Antiochene church (see p. 150) is introduced by the words, "and when we were gathered together, one of them, named Agabus, spoke . . .". J. Smith, in the light of this tradition, sees significance in the fact that of the seven Hellenistic almoners appointed in the church of Jerusalem (see p. 128) only one has his place of origin mentioned – "Nicolaus, a proselyte of Antioch" (Acts 6: 5); he notes, by way of analogy, that out of eight accounts of Napoleon's Russian Campaign in 1812 – three by Frenchmen, three by Englishmen and two by Scots – only the two Scots writers mention that the Russian general Barclay de Tolly was of Scots descent (*The Voyage and Shipwreck of St. Paul* [London,[4] 1880], p. 4).

# CHAPTER 14

# Man of Vision and Man of Action

## 1. A strange experience

TOWARDS THE END OF THE LARGELY UNCHRONICLED INTERVAL between Paul's return to Tarsus and his call to Antioch he had a strange experience which left its mark on him for the rest of his life. He gives some account of it in 2 Corinthians 12: 2–10, where he says that it happened fourteen years before the time of writing. Since the time of writing was about A.D. 56, the date of the experience would have been A.D. 42 or 43. The experience belongs to the category which is commonly designated ecstatic, but it is difficult to come to a definite conclusion about its nature because Paul himself describes it in such vague terms. What he says is that "whether in the body or out of the body" – a question to which he can give no answer – he found himself rapt to the extraterrestrial realm variously called "paradise" and "the third heaven"[1] and there heard things impossible and impermissible to put into words.

This type of experience, described in this kind of language, is not unparalleled in Paul's world. We have a literary parallel in the account of Enoch's bodily transportation into the celestial realms and his return to earth (1 Enoch 12: 1 ff.; cf. 71: 1 ff.). But whereas we are told quite particularly what Enoch saw and heard, Paul gives no such details: what he heard was incommunicable. In his account of the experience itself he stands outside it and relates it as if it had happened to a third party – to "a man in Christ" whom he once knew or, even more vaguely, to "So-and-so". Only when the normal mode of existence has been resumed and he describes the sequel does he continue the narrative in the first person singular.

As a parallel from real life rather than apocalyptic literature we

---

1. "Paradise" ( παράδεισος ) was a word of Persian origin, used in the Septuagint (Genesis 2: 8 ff.) of the primaeval Eden and in later Jewish usage of the Eden above. Whether Paul thought of "the third heaven" as the highest heaven or not – the idea of seven heavens was commonest at the time (cf. *Testament of Levi* 2: 7 ff.; *Ascension of Isaiah* 6: 13; 7: 13 ff.; TB *Ḥagigah* 12b) – this was evidently the heaven in which he located paradise. According to Luke 23: 43 paradise was the abode of bliss after death; in Revelation 2: 7 it is the eschatological Eden.

have the story of four rabbis – Ben Azzai, Ben Zoma, Elisha ben Abuyah and Aqiba (all of whom flourished in the earlier part of the second century A.D. and so were two generations younger than Paul) – who entered Paradise. Ben Azzai looked and died, Ben Zoma looked and went mad, Elisha ben Abuyah became an apostate. Only Aqiba survived the experience unscathed.[2] What exactly is meant by their entry into Paradise is a matter of debate, but some mystical experience is probable in their case as in Paul's. The point of the story is that such an experience is perilous and liable to leave its mark indelibly on one who undergoes it.

Paul did not escape from this experience of his unscathed, but because of the spirit in which he accepted its disagreeable consequences, they became a blessing to him instead of a curse (verses 7–10):

> To keep me from being too elated by the abundance of revelations, I was given a splinter in the flesh, a messenger of Satan, to harass me, to keep me from being too elated. Three times I besought the Lord about this, that it should leave me; but he said to me, "My grace is sufficient for you, for my power is made perfect in weakness." I will all the more gladly boast of my weaknesses, that the power of Christ may rest upon me. For the sake of Christ, then, I am content with weaknesses, insults, hardships, persecutions, and calamities; for when I am weak, then I am strong.

The sequel to Paul's mystical experience was a distressing, indeed humiliating, physical ailment which he feared at first might be a handicap to his effective ministry but which in fact, by giving his self-esteem a knock-out blow and keeping him constantly dependent on the divine enabling, proved to be a help, not a handicap. Many guesses have been made about the identity of this "splinter in the flesh"; their very variety proves the impossibility of a certain diagnosis. One favourite guess has been epilepsy – a guess which, if substantiated, would put Paul into the company of such men of action as Julius Caesar and Napoleon – but it is no more than a guess.[3] Whatever it was, it was probably the "bodily ailment" from

2. TB *Ḥagigah* 14b–15b. This experience appears to have been an early instance of *merkābāh* ("chariot") mysticism, in which contemplative techniques were employed with a view to attaining the vision of the chariot-throne of God described in Ezekiel 1 and 10. See G. Scholem, *Jewish Gnosticism, Merkabah Mysticism and Talmudic Tradition* (New York, [2] 1965), pp. 14–19; J. W. Bowker, " 'Merkabah' Visions and the Visions of Paul", *Journal of Semitic Studies* 16 (1971), pp. 157–173.

3. Cf. W. Wrede, *Paul*, E.T. (London, 1907), pp. 22 ff. Other guesses are ophthalmia (e.g. J. T. Brown, "St. Paul's Thorn in the Flesh", in *Horae Subsecivae*, ed. J. Brown [Edinburgh, 1858]), Malta fever (e.g. W. M. Alexander, "St. Paul's Infirmity", *Expository Times* 15 [1903–4], pp. 469 ff., 545 ff.), malaria (e.g. W. M. Ramsay, *St. Paul the Traveller and the Roman Citizen* (London, [14] 1920), pp. 94 ff.;

which he suffered when he first visited the Galatians – an ailment
which was a "trial" to them as well as to him and which might have
been expected to repel them or make them spit in aversion, whereas
on the contrary they welcomed him "as an angel of God"
(Galatians 4: 13 f.). His thrice-repeated prayer for the removal of
the ailment was answered, not by his deliverance from it, but by his
receiving the necessary grace to bear it – not simply to live with it
but to be thankful for it. If his ministry was so effective despite this
physical weakness, then the transcendent power was manifestly
God's, not his own.[4] Infirmities like this were welcomed, together
with the other hardships which were part of the apostolic lot, if they
were the condition on which the power of the risen Christ operated
through him. They constantly reminded him not so much of his
own inadequacy as of the total adequacy of Christ, in whom, when
he was personally most weak, he knew himself to be most strong.

## 2. Paul's "mysticism"

Such a record as this very naturally raises the question whether
or not Paul can be described as a mystic. That he can be so described has been believed and affirmed by some students of the man and
his writings whose names carry exceptional weight in the
theological world. We have only to think of such titles as Albert
Schweitzer's *The Mysticism of Paul the Apostle*[5] or Johannes
Schneider's *Die Passionsmystik des Paulus*[6] – the wording of the latter
title being borrowed from Adolf Deissmann, who used it of Paul's
interpretation of Christian existence in terms of dying and rising
with Christ. For Deissmann, *Mystik* ("mysticism") was a term
applicable "to every religious tendency that discovers the way to
God through inner experience without the mediation of
reasoning".[7]

A more positive definition was offered by Evelyn Underhill, for
whom mysticism was "the name of that organic process which involves the perfect consummation of the Love of God: the achievement here and now of the immortal heritage of men".[8] This

neurasthenia (e.g. H. Lietzmann, *The Beginnings of the Christian Church*, E.T. [Lon-
don,[2] 1949], p. 113), an impediment in his speech (cf. 2 Corinthians 10: 10). Some
are perhaps less improbable than others, but they are all equally guesses.

4. 2 Corinthians 4: 7.

5. English translation by W. Montgomery (London, 1931) of *Die Mystik des
Apostels Paulus* (Tübingen, 1930).

6. Leipzig, 1929.

7. A. Deissmann, *Paul: A Study in Social and Religious History*, E.T. (London,
1926), p. 149.

8. E. Underhill, *Mysticism* (London,[12] 1930), p. 81 (where she defines it
alternatively as "the art of establishing . . . conscious relation with the Absolute").
Rufus M. Jones described "mysticism, in its normal aspect" as "a type of religion

definition may cover Paul's religious experience, if we bear in mind that for him the love of God was mediated and indeed embodied "in Christ Jesus our Lord" (Romans 8:39). [9]

According to Albert Schweitzer, Paul's mysticism is unique because, in spite of its high intellectual level, it does not take the form of direct union with God but rather of union with Christ. "In Paul", he says, "there is no God-mysticism; only a Christ-mysticism by means of which man comes into relation to God. . . . This 'being-in-Christ' is the prime enigma of the Pauline teaching: once grasped it gives the clue to the whole". [10]

When Schweitzer says that there is no "God-mysticism" in Paul, he concludes that Paul could not have used with approval the quotation from Epimenides which in Acts 17: 28 he is said to have recited in his speech before the Athenian Areopagus: "In him we live and move and have our being". [11] On this two things should be said. First, the so-called mysticism of the Pauline epistles belongs to the new creation, the order of redemption; in the Areopagitica it is man's relation to God in the order of the old creation that is in view. Second, whatever was the force of the preposition "in" intended by Epimenides, Luke represents Paul as quoting his words to prove that God is the creator of all men and that they accordingly are his offspring. This is not really a form of "God-mysticism" and in any case does not conflict with Paul's statement that in the order of redemption, or, as he puts it, "in Christ Jesus", believers are "all sons of God through faith" (Galatians 3: 26). Moreover, the locution "in God" is not foreign to the Pauline vocabulary: we recall the twofold mention of "the church of the Thessalonians in God the Father and the Lord Jesus Christ" (1 Thessalonians 1: 1; 2 Thessalonians 1: 1) and the reference in Ephesians 3: 9 to "the mystery hidden for ages in God who created all things" – although this last reference cannot be understood in terms of "God-mysticism"; it means something like "in the mind (or purpose) of God". [12]

But such phrases as "in Christ Jesus" (quoted above) or "in Christ" or "in the Lord" are characteristic of Paul, and it is the concept which they express that is often in view (as with Schweitzer) when people speak of "Pauline mysticism".

---

which is characterized by an immediate consciousness of personal relationship with a Divine Being" (*Studies in Mystical Religion* [London, 1909], p. xviii). Cf. also R. C. Zaehner, *Mysticism, Sacred and Profane* (Oxford, 1957); D. Knowles, *What is Mysticism?* (London, 1967); G. Parrinder, *Mysticism in the World's Religions* (London, 1976).

9. See R. C. Tannehill's definition quoted below (p. 147).

10. *The Mysticism of Paul the Apostle*, p. 3.

11. See p. 245.

12. Still less can "we rejoice in God" in Rom. 5: 11 be understood in a mystical sense.

If these expressions have a mystical significance, then they signify a communal or corporate mysticism. There is little enough in Paul's writings that savours of "the flight of the alone to the Alone".[13] Even when he introduces the strange personal experience described in 2 Corinthians 12: 2–10 by saying that it happened to "a man in Christ", he uses a phrase which is applicable to all other Christians and binds him together with them.

The corporate significance of "in Christ" and similar phrases is brought out well by the New English Bible, which occasionally uses such terms as "incorporate" and "concorporate" to express it. In other words, "in Christ" and similar expressions convey the same thought as Paul elsewhere conveys by speaking of Christians as fellow-members of the body of Christ – a mode of thought which he develops along fresh and influential lines of his own – although one may be doubtful about the propriety of describing it in terms of the "mystical" body of Christ.

The body of Christ (the believing community as a whole), together with its members one by one, is vitalized by the life of the risen Christ and energized by his Spirit. Incorporation into this body is effected by personal faith in Christ, sacramentally sealed in baptism and sustained by the eucharist.[14] For Paul, baptism symbolizes the believer's dying and rising with Christ: "the man we once were" (Romans 6: 6) has died in his death and the "new man", bearing the Christ-likeness, has come alive in his resurrection. The external washing in water has an inward and spiritual counterpart: "in one Spirit we were all baptized into one body, whether we were Jews or Greeks, slaves or freemen; and we were all watered with one Spirit" (1 Corinthians 12: 13).[15]

It is plain, however, that for Paul dying and rising with Christ was not only a matter of sacramental theology or church doctrine but of personal experience. He thought of his entry into Christian life in these terms: "I have been crucified with Christ", he writes to the Galatian churches, and adds: "it is no longer I who live, but Christ who lives in me; and the life I now live in the flesh I live by faith in the Son of God, who loved me and gave himself up for me" (Galatians 2: 20). This personal appropriation of the love manifested to mankind in the self-sacrifice of Christ was as real as his awareness of personal faith-union with Christ and of that faith-union as the source of his Christian life. With even greater intensity he describes himself in his apostolic service as "always carrying about in the body the dying of Jesus, so that the life of Jesus may also be manifested in our bodies. For [he adds] while we live we are always being given up to death for Jesus' sake, so that

13. Plotinus, *Ennead* vi. 9. 11 ( φυγὴ μόνου πρὸς μόνον ).
14. 1 Corinthians 10: 16 f.; 11: 20–34a. See pp. 280 ff.
15. See p. 210.

the life of Jesus may be manifested in our mortal flesh" (2 Corinthians 4: 10 f.).

### 3. Sharing the messianic sufferings

When Paul thought of himself in particular as "a man in Christ", a member of his body, it was more often than not to take seriously his special responsibility towards fellow-members of the same body. The sufferings of the Messiah (a feature of rabbinical expectation) were, in Paul's view, the sufferings to be borne by the Messiah. Jesus accordingly had suffered on earth, enduring death by crucifixion to procure his people's liberation from spiritual bondage. In his present exaltation he was, naturally, immune from such sufferings as he had endured on earth; yet (as Paul had learned on the Damascus road) [16] he still counted as his own the sufferings endured by his people for his sake. According to Luke's record, the risen Lord said of the newly-converted Paul, "I will show him how much he must suffer for the sake of my name" (Acts 9: 16), and Paul's own account confirms the magnitude and variety of hardships which he experienced in the course of his apostolic ministry. He did not resent these things; "we rejoice in our sufferings", he said (Romans 5: 3), not only because of their character-building power but also because he was thus able to realize his ambition of sharing Christ's sufferings, "becoming like him in his death, that if possible I may attain the resurrection from the dead" (Philippians 3: 11).

Nor was his motive in gladly accepting this share in the sufferings of Christ purely self-regarding. He seems to have held that the more of these sufferings he personally absorbed, the less would remain for his fellow-Christians to endure. "I rejoice in my sufferings for your sake", he writes to the Colossians, "and in my flesh I complete what is lacking in Christ's afflictions for the sake of his body, that is, the church" (Colossians 1: 24). [17] To the same effect he tells his friends in Corinth that "if we are afflicted, it is for your comfort and salvation" (2 Corinthians 1: 6). As Jesus had offered up to God as an atonement "for many" the injuries inflicted on him, so Paul accepted his injuries and trials the more readily in the hope that thus his converts and other fellow-believers would be spared the

16. The implication of the words "why do you persecute me?" cannot readily be paralleled elsewhere in Luke's writings, but they are completely in tune with Pauline theology.

17. Among recent studies of this passage see R. Yates, "A Note on Colossians 1: 24", *EQ* 42 (1970), pp. 88 ff.; L. P. Trudinger, "A Further Brief Notice on Colossians 1: 24", *EQ* 45 (1973), pp. 36 ff.; R. J. Bauckham, "Colossians 1: 24 Again: The Apocalyptic Motif", *EQ* 47 (1975), pp. 167 ff.

like. "So, then", he says, "death is at work in us [that is, 'in me'], but life in you" (2 Corinthians 4: 12).

### 4. Life in the Spirit

The bestowal of the Spirit of God, or the Holy Spirit, in the New Testament is primarily an eschatological phenomenon in the sense that it is presented as the fulfilment of Old Testament promises associating this bestowal with the age of renewal. Ezekiel, for example, during the exile, declares that when God restores his people's fortunes, he will give them a new spirit, his own spirit, so that, cleansed from their moral and religious defilement, they may thenceforth do his will from the heart (Ezekiel 11: 16-20; 36: 24–27). A post-exilic oracle announces that in the days of restoration God will pour out his spirit on "all flesh" (Joel 2: 28 f.). The context suggests that "all flesh" refers in the first instance to Israel, although its ultimate range may be wider. The context further indicates that the chief effect of this outpouring of Yahweh's spirit will be an unprecedented exercise of the gift of prophecy, even by slaves and slave-girls, not to mention freemen and freewomen.

Not long before the dawn of the Christian era, we find this expectation taken up in the Qumran community. Part of the community's preparation for the new age was its provision of a "foundation" for the spirit of holiness (or holy spirit). The community is pictured as a living temple, in which the lay members constitute the outer compartment, the holy place, while the priestly members constitute the inner shrine, the holy of holies. This living temple seems to be envisaged as a dwelling-place for the spirit of holiness, where the offering of obedient lives and praising lips is an acceptable substitute for the animal sacrifices of the old order.[18]

Not only so, but in the community the spirit of holiness is the fount of knowledge. The spirit that formerly spoke through the prophets, God's "anointed ones" by whom he taught his people,[19] is now available to dwell not only within the community as a whole but also within individual members, making known to them, and especially to their leaders, the interpretation of the prophets' words and the way in which God's hidden purpose was about to be accomplished at the impending end-time. "I, as instructor", runs one of the *Hymns of Thanksgiving*, "have come to know thee, O God, by the spirit which thou hast placed within me, and by thy holy spirit I have listened faithfully to thy wonderful secret counsel."[20]

18. 1 QS col. 9, ll. 4 f., alluding to Hosea 14: 2 (cf. Hebrews 13: 14).
19. In some places in the Qumran texts (e.g. 1 QM col. 11, ll. 7 f.; CD 2, l. 12; 6, l. 1) the prophets are called God's "anointed ones", in accordance with the precedent set in Psalm 105: 15.
20. 1 QH col. 12, ll. 11 ff.

In the gospel narrative Jesus receives the Holy Spirit at his baptism[21] as the necessary endowment for his messianic ministry which involved baptizing others with the same Spirit.[22] There are hints in the Synoptic tradition that Jesus knew that he was operating under limitations during his Palestinian ministry,[23] and these become more explicit in the upper-room discourses of the Fourth Gospel, where Jesus' departure means the coming of the Spirit and the empowering of his followers to accomplish greater works then he himself had done.[24] We are thus prepared for something like Luke's account of the descent of the Spirit at the first Christian Pentecost, accompanied by the signs of the new age on a greater scale than had been seen during Jesus' ministry.[25]

This general understanding of the presence and power of the Spirit is presupposed in Paul. For him, the Spirit has come: his indwelling presence is experienced by the people of Christ both corporately and individually: the church and the individual believer may equally be spoken of as a temple of the Holy Spirit.[26] And this concept is no mere *theologoumenon*; it is something which is experienced intensely and makes an immense difference to present existence. The Spirit pours the love of God into the hearts of believers[27] and brings them increasingly into conformity with the character of Christ. "Where the Spirit of the Lord is", says Paul, "there is freedom. And we all, with unveiled face, beholding the glory of the Lord, are being changed into his image from one degree of glory to another; for this comes from the Lord who is the Spirit" (2 Corinthians 3: 17b, 18). What this "image" amounts to in practical experience is spelt out in the ninefold "fruit of the Spirit" in Galatians 5: 22 f. – "love, joy, peace, patience, kindness, goodness, faithfulness, gentleness, self-control". These were the qualities which marked the historical Jesus, and Paul desires to see them reproduced in his converts – and, of course, in himself. Some of those qualities, he knew, did not come to him naturally. He was too fond of portraying the Christian life as a strenuous exercise – a race

21. Mark 1: 9 f.; cf. John 1: 32.

22. To John the Baptist's prophecy that the Coming One would baptize "with the Holy Spirit" the words "and fire" are added in Matthew 3: 11/Luke 3: 16; cf. the action of wind and fire in the metaphor of Matthew 3: 12/Luke 3: 17.

23. Cf. Luke 12: 50, where Jesus speaks of being under constraint until he has accomplished his "baptism".

24. Cf. John 14: 12; 16: 7.

25. Whatever be the primary reference of Mark 9: 1, it may be said that the first Christian Pentecost saw "the kingdom of God come in power": in that one day Jesus acquired many more followers than had attached themselves to him during his earthly ministry. For the "signs" of the early apostolic age cf. Acts 2: 43; 5: 12; Galatians 3: 5; Hebrews 2: 4, etc.

26. 1 Corinthians 3: 16 f.; 6: 19.

27. Romans 5: 5.

to be run, a battle to be fought (especially against himself) [28] – for us to suppose that victory came to him "sudden, in a minute". [29]

The tension could not be completely resolved so long as he lived at once in the present age (temporally) and in the age to come (spiritually) – that is, so long as he lived on earth in mortal body. But he found the secret of victory in the liberating "law of the Spirit of life in Christ Jesus" (Romans 8: 2). The central principle of this "law of the Spirit" is the love of God in Christ – first descending vertically and implanted in the heart by the Spirit and then flowing out into the lives of others. The canticle of love in 1 Corinthians 13 is an eloquent celebration of this truth.

### 5. Fellowship and "mysteries"

Despite what has been said about "corporate mysticism" in Paul's thought, it is probably true that the mystic, as commonly conceived, tends to be self-sufficient in his religious life, or at least can well be self-sufficient when circumstances require. He may be gregarious and friendly; he may attach high importance to life in society, but he does not depend on it for his religious sustenance. Paul insisted on the common life in the body of Christ, in which the members were interrelated and interdependent, each making a personal contribution to the good of the others and of the whole; [30] yet, when necessity so dictated, he could maintain his spiritual existence apart from external aids, human or material. "I have learned the secret of being content (autarkēs)", he says, "in whatever state of life I am" (Philippians 4: 11). Yet this autarkeia is not Stoic self-sufficiency: it is so complete a dependence on the Christ who lives within him that all else is, by comparison, expendable: "I can do all things", he adds, "in him who strengthens me" (Philippians 4: 13). At the same time he makes it plain that the well-being of his friends meant much for his personal sense of well-being: it is life itself for him to know that his Thessalonian converts "stand fast in the Lord" (1 Thessalonians 3: 8); "you are in my heart", he tells the Corinthian Christians, "to die together and to live together" (2 Corinthians 7: 3). He looked forward with special joy to the day of Christ because he hoped then to present his converts to the Lord who commissioned him as the visible evidence of his discharge of his trust: "For what is our hope or joy or crown of exultation before our Lord Jesus at his parousia? Is it not you?" (1 Thessalonians 2: 19). [31]

28. 1 Corinthians 9: 24–27.
29. F. W. H. Myers, *Saint Paul* (London, 1867), stanza 15; cf. Philippians 3: 12–14.
30. 1 Corinthians 12: 14 ff.; Romans 12: 4 f.
31. Cf. Philippians 2: 14–16.

Phenomena such as glossolalia, to which Paul makes special reference in one of his letters, are not necessarily bound up with mysticism: the one may exist without the other. When Paul says that the person speaking with tongues "utters mysteries in the spirit", he does not mean that he is communicating special revelations: in fact, he is not communicating anything, "for no one understands him" (1 Corinthians 14: 2). This last clause, indeed, is another way of saying that he "utters mysteries". Paul himself can practise glossolalia, but we should never have guessed it had he not, in dealing with this and similar phenomena in Corinth, divulged the fact; and he divulges it in order to play it down.[32] Clearly he regarded it as an exercise of little value or importance. To his way of thinking, it is the source and content of an utterance that are important, not the bare fact of its being an "inspired" utterance. He knew that the phenomenon could be paralleled in paganism: hence it was necessary to understand what was being uttered.[33]

When he himself, on the other hand, imparts "mysteries" – new revelations – he does so in intelligible language. How he received those mysteries is not so clear. It was not by simple reflection on the problems of Christian faith and life: when he gives the results of such reflection he does not claim to be imparting a mystery. Thus he can say, when introducing new teaching about the coming resurrection, "Lo! I tell you a mystery" (1 Corinthians 15: 51) – the "mystery" or revelation being that at the resurrection not only will the dead be raised immortal but the living will exchange perishable for imperishable bodies to cope with the environment of a new order. But when he goes on to think of the state of the individual (of himself, more particularly) between death and resurrection, he expresses his own conviction – "we know" (2 Corinthians 5: 1, 6) – arising from a confrontation with what had seemed to be certain and imminent death, but he has no revelation, no "mystery", to impart.[34]

His "mysteries", which he treats as direct communications from the risen Lord through the Spirit, may have been given to him in the course of visionary or ecstatic experiences; but we cannot be sure, since he does not tell us. In the one experience of this kind which he does relate in some detail, the words which he heard were, as we have seen, incommunicable. The "mysteries" which he was granted were not private experiences for his own spiritual enrichment; they were revelations of the divine purpose and its fulfilment to be imparted for the upbuilding and healthy functioning of the whole Christian fellowship.

32. 1 Corinthians 14: 18.
33. Cf. 1 Corinthians 12: 2 f.
34. See p. 311.

## 6. The evidence of Acts

If we turn from Paul's letters to the evidence of Acts, it confirms in general the impression made by the letters. "Visions and revelations of the Lord" (to quote Paul's words in 2 Corinthians 12: 1) are not lacking in Luke's account of Paul's career. In his letters Paul refers repeatedly to his conversion experience, the central feature of which was the appearing of the risen Lord, but he gives a minimum of narrative detail. The narrative of Acts gives three fuller and more graphic accounts of his experience,[35] differing in some details but essentially in agreement, which certainly mention the fact of Paul's *seeing* the risen Lord but lay chief stress on the call which he received to be his witness and herald.

Attempts have been made to explain the physiological features of the conversion story in Acts, but they are even less successful than attempts so to explain his ecstatic rapture to the third heaven and the ensuing "splinter in the flesh". If Luke's threefold account of the event can be accommodated within our definition of mysticism, then Paul's conversion might be called a mystical experience, provided that such a description does not call into question the objective reality of the vision which he saw and the voice which he heard.

When Paul revisited Jerusalem after his conversion, his call to evangelize the Gentiles was reaffirmed in another vision of the risen Lord. "I was praying in the temple," he says (Acts 22: 17 ff.), "and fell into a trance, in which I saw him saying to me, 'Make haste, get out of Jerusalem without delay, because they will not accept your testimony about me.' 'Lord', said I, 'they know that I was the one who, in synagogue after synagogue, used to imprison and flog those who believed on you. They know that when your witness Stephen shed his blood I stood by approving and guarded his executioners' clothes.'[36] 'Begone', said he, 'I will send you far away to the Gentiles'."[37] Again, the kind of experience here described by the Paul of Acts is by no means out of keeping with the impression gained from his letters. Both seeing and hearing are implied, as they are in the incident at a critical juncture in his ministry at Corinth, when

35. Acts 9: 1–19; 22: 3–16; 26: 4–18 (the first of these is related in the third person, the second and third in the first person, on Paul's own lips).

36. He seems to mean: They know how hostile I was to you and your people; they will therefore understand that my change of heart must have been the result of the most convincing proof, and so they will take my testimony seriously.

37. See p. 94. According to Acts 9: 15 his commission had originally been to Jews as well as Gentiles (cf. Acts 26: 17, 20). On the relation of the Acts record to Paul's testimony in Galatians 1: 16 see O. Betz, "Die Vision des Paulus im Tempel von Jerusalem", in *Verborum Veritas, Festschrift für G. Stählin*, ed. O. Böcher and K. Haacker (Wuppertal, 1970), pp. 113–123; he concludes that Luke's account was composed on the pattern of Isaiah's temple vision (Isaiah 6: 1 ff.).

"the Lord said to Paul in a vision by night: 'Do not be afraid: speak
and let no one silence you. I am with you: no one will harm you by
any attack. I have a multitude of people in this city' " (Acts
18: 9 f.).

Similarly, when he was placed in protective custody during his
last and most perilous visit to Jerusalem, "the Lord stood by him
and said, 'Take courage; as you have borne witness to me in
Jerusalem, you must bear witness in Rome also' " (Acts 23: 11). It
was not the Lord himself, but (as Paul puts it) "the messenger of
the God to whom I belong and whom I serve" that stood by him
during the last night of his adventurous voyage from Asia to Malta
and said, "Have no fear, Paul. You must stand before Caesar, and
see, God has spared for your sake the lives of all your ship's company" (Acts 27: 23 f.).

The perspective of Acts does not expose as some of Paul's letters
do the deeper inner springs of his spiritual life, but provides some
hint of them from the viewpoint of an associate and admirer whose
own pattern of religious experience may have been different from
Paul's – the "once-born" pattern, perhaps, as against the "twice-
born" pattern, in the special sense in which those terms were used
by F. W. Newman and William James.[38] Yet Luke's perspective is
not inconsistent with the self-portrait in Paul's own writings.

## 7. Vision and apostleship

Paul's Christian life, then, began with an experience in which the
risen Lord appeared to him and spoke to him, and its subsequent
course was marked by further experiences of a similar kind,
attested both by himself and by Luke.

While to others the "visionary" inception of Paul's Christian
career might throw doubt on the validity of his claim to be an apostle, to Paul it was the basis of that claim. There was no difference in
his eyes, apart from the lapse of time, between the risen Lord's
appearance to him and his earlier appearances to the original
apostles. He could and did appeal to the remarkable achievement
of his Gentile mission, to the record of what Christ had accomplished through him, as *confirmation* of his apostolic claim,[39] but
that was an *ad hominem* argument: in his own consciousness it was
the personal call of the risen Christ that made him an apostle.[40] We
may wonder if he would have begun to entertain doubts on this
point if his missionary endeavours had been unsuccessful, but that

38. F. W. Newman, *The Soul: its Sorrows and its Aspirations* (London, ᵌ 1852), pp.
89 ff.; W. James, *The Varieties of Religious Experience* (London, 1902), pp. 80 ff., 166
ff.
39. Romans 15: 18; cf. 1 Corinthians 15: 10.
40. 1 Corinthians 9: 1; 15: 8 f.

is a hypothetical question. Paul, it seems, never had occasion to suspect that he might have been "seduced", as Jeremiah did when his message proved so consistently unacceptable to his people, although Paul's call is recorded in terms reminiscent of Jeremiah's call to his prophetic ministry.[41] When Paul says that God had set him apart for his life's work, to preach Christ among the nations, "before I was born" (Galatians 1: 15) – he echoes, as we have seen, the inaugural oracle to Jeremiah. And when his apostolic credentials were challenged, he might well have said, as Jeremiah said in a similar situation, "in truth the LORD sent me . . . to speak all these words" (Jeremiah 26: 15).

Even more impressive is the parallel with the language of Isaiah 49: 1–6, where the Servant of Yahweh summons the coastlands and distant peoples to hear him as he proclaims:

> Yahweh called me from the womb,
>    from the body of my mother he named my name . . .
> And now says Yahweh,
>    who formed me from the womb to be his servant . . .
> "It is too light a thing that you should be my servant
>    to raise up the tribes of Jacob
>    and to restore the preserved of Israel;
> I will give you as a light *to the nations*
>    that my salvation may reach to the end of the earth."

It is not by chance that in Acts 13: 47 Paul and Barnabas, in the synagogue of Pisidian Antioch, quote this last couplet as their authority for turning to the Gentiles with the gospel.[42] As for Paul, others might undertake that part of the Servant's vocation which had to do with Israel; he knew himself called to fulfil that part of it which involved the carrying of God's saving light among the Gentiles, near and far.

It was with the assurance of his divine commission, then, that Paul embarked upon his programme and carried it out stage by stage to Central Asia Minor, to the Aegean world, to Illyricum and then on to Rome and (in intention at least) to Spain. Many others were engaged in Gentile evangelization, but none with the overall strategic planning conceived in Paul's mind and so largely executed by his dynamic energy. This energy was the fruit of his conviction that he was a figure of eschatological significance, a key agent in the progress of salvation history, a chosen instrument in the Lord's hands to bring Gentiles into the obedience of faith as a necessary preparation for the ultimate salvation of all Israel and the consummation of God's redeeming purpose for the world. If this convic-

41. See p. 75.
42. See p. 167.

tion, and the experience which gave birth to it, can be called mysticism, then it is mysticism of a very exceptional order.

Perhaps R. C. Tannehill has the answer. Defining mysticism as "the doctrine that the individual can come into immediate contact with God through subjective experiences which differ essentially from the experiences of daily life", he adds: "By this definition Paul may be spoken of as, among other things, a 'mystic' (cf. his visions, II Cor. 12: 1–4), but he does not have a mystical theology." [43] This last point is well taken: Paul's theology was not based on experiences which might be described as mystical: it is based on Jesus, the fulfiller of God's promise and purpose of salvation; Jesus, the crucified and exalted Lord; Jesus, the divine wisdom, in whom God creates, maintains and brings to consummation everything that exists; Jesus, who here and now lives within his people by his Spirit. To the exposition of this theology not only prophetic scripture but also rabbinical exegesis and primitive Christian tradition make their contributions, but the whole is fused into a new compound in the alembic of Paul's passionate embracing of "the all-surpassing knowledge of Christ Jesus my Lord" (Philippians 3: 8). And this knowledge did not encourage contemplative quietism; it constituted an insistent call to lifelong action.

43. R. C. Tannehill, *Dying and Rising with Christ* (Berlin, 1967), p. 4, n. 7.

# CHAPTER 15

# Conference in Jerusalem

## 1. Leaders in Antioch

THE CHRISTIAN COMMUNITY IN SYRIAN ANTIOCH QUICKLY became a metropolitan church rivalling in size the church of Jerusalem. If the church of Jerusalem was the mother-church of Christians in general, the church of Antioch was the mother-church of Gentile Christians in particular.

The little we know about the leaders of the church of Antioch suggests that they were men of interesting antecedents and relationships and makes us wish we knew more about them. As it is, we can at best make intelligent guesses. In addition to Barnabas and Paul, Luke names three leaders at Antioch, and associates all five together as "prophets and teachers" (Acts 13: 1). The three were Symeon surnamed Niger, Lucius of Cyrene and Manaen, sometime companion of Herod the tetrarch.

As for Symeon, his Latin sobriquet Niger ("black") could imply an African origin for him as well as for his colleague Lucius. The New Testament record knows of an African of this name – Simon (the hellenized form of Symeon) of Cyrene, whose services were commandeered to carry the cross of Jesus to the place of execution. When Mark the evangelist relates this incident, he identifies Simon of Cyrene for his readers of the next generation, primarily in Rome, as "the father of Alexander and Rufus" (Mark 15: 21). We know of one Rufus in the Christian community of Rome about A.D. 57 – that "Rufus, eminent in the Lord", to whom Paul sends greetings by name in Romans 16: 13. This presupposes indeed that the greetings of Romans 16 are intended for Rome and not (as many hold) for Ephesus; [1] but if Paul's friend Rufus did live in Rome the coincidence of his name with that of one of the sons of Simon of Cyrene may be more than a *mere* coincidence. Then what significance lies in the fact that Paul sends greetings not only to Rufus but also to "his mother and mine"? The implication is that there was a time when the mother of Rufus had proved herself a mother to Paul. A writer of historical fiction might picture Paul as lodging, during his years in Antioch, in the home of Simon of

---

1. See pp. 385 ff.

148

Cyrene *alias* Symeon surnamed Niger and as being mothered by his host's wife.[2] But one who is not setting out to write fiction must be content with noting possibilities and beware of going beyond the evidence, tantalizingly scanty as it is.

Whatever may have been the provenance of Symeon surnamed Niger, Lucius of Cyrene has his clearly indicated, and it is not out-running the evidence to think of him as one of the men of Cyprus and Cyrene who started Gentile evangelization in Antioch. The name Lucius appears in one other place in the New Testament – in Romans 16: 21, where Paul sends greetings to his readers from one Lucius, whom he includes among his "kinsmen", which may mean fellow-Christians of Jewish birth. This Lucius may be identical with our Lucius of Cyrene; there is no means of being sure. He is probably not identical with Paul's companion Luke (Lucas), "the beloved disciple", as he is called in Colossians 4: 14, and the traditional author of the Third Gospel and Acts. Luke probably belonged to Antioch, and his name could well be a by-form of Lucius,[3] but the context in which he is mentioned in Colossians 4: 14 suggests that he was a Gentile Christian, not a Jewish Christian.[4] Nevertheless, the identification of Lucius of Cyrene with Luke the evangelist is found at quite an early date [5] and has been defended by scholars in more recent times.[6]

It is thought-provoking to find that one of the leaders of the Antiochene church had been a companion of Herod Antipas, tetrarch of Galilee and Peraea from 4 B.C. to his deposition in A.D. 39. The word that Luke uses for Manaen's relationship to Herod Antipas (*syntrophos*) is attested in the sense of "intimate friend" or "courtier",[7] but the version of 1611 may well be right in saying that he "had been brought up with Herod the tetrarch". Antipas was the youngest son of Herod the Great, and Manaen could have been the son of a family known to the king who was chosen to come to

2. A reviewer with some concern for verisimilitude might ask if a dark-skinned man was likely to have a red-headed son (for the name Rufus was no doubt as appropriately bestowed as the designation Niger); but the fiction-writer could readily explain that Rufus's mother was auburn.

3. Cf. W. M. Ramsay, *The Bearing of Recent Discovery on the Trustworthiness of the New Testament* (London, 1915), pp. 374 ff.

4. In Colossians 4: 10 f. Paul sends greetings from three companions whom he calls "the only men of the circumcision among my fellow-workers for the kingdom of God". It is a natural inference that the three other companions whose greetings he sends immediately afterwards (verses 12–14) – Epaphras, Luke and Demas – were not of Jewish birth.

5. Ephrem Syrus (4th century A.D.), in his commentary on Acts adds "and Luke the Cyrenean" after "Mark" in Acts 12: 25, with a comment that "these were both evangelists".

6. Cf. H. J. Cadbury, "Lucius of Cyrene", in *BC* i, 5 (London, 1933), pp. 489 ff.

7. Cf. J. H. Moulton and G. Milligan, *The Vocabulary of the Greek Testament* (Edinburgh, 1930), p. 615.

the palace and be brought up with the prince, as his playmate and schoolmate, and occasionally, it may be, as whipping-boy. If we try to identify the family to which Manaen belonged, conjecture must come in (as with Symeon surnamed Niger) to take the place of evidence. Manaen is a Greek spelling of the Hebrew name Menahem. One conjecture which has been ventilated is that he was the grandson of an Essene named Menahem, who was honoured by Herod the Great for having predicted his rise to royal estate.[8] However that may be, if the author of Luke-Acts was a member of the church of Antioch at that time, the fact that a former associate of Herod Antipas now occupied a position of influence in that church may point to one possible source from which he could have derived some of his special information about the Herods and their entourage.

## 2. Famine in Judaea

For all the differences between the church of Jerusalem and the church of Antioch, they recognized their common bond and there was considerable coming and going between the two. On one occasion a deputation of prophets from the Jerusalem church visited Antioch. One of them, Agabus by name, possessed by the spirit of prophecy, foretold that there would be great scarcity throughout the Roman world. "This took place", Luke adds, "in the days of Claudius" (Acts 11: 28), and in fact we have the testimony of Suetonius that the principate of Claudius (A.D. 41–54) was marked by a succession of droughts and poor harvests.[9] One of the resultant famines was specially severe in Judaea; it was on this occasion – in the procuratorships of Cuspius Fadus and his successor Tiberius Julius Alexander (c. A.D. 46) – that Helena, queen-mother of Adiabene and a proselyte to Judaism, bought grain in Egypt and figs in Cyprus for the relief of her co-religionists in Judaea, while her son, King Izates, sent money to the Jewish authorities in Jerusalem for distribution among the poor.[10] It was probably about the same time that the church of Antioch sent to the leaders of the Jerusalem church a sum of money which they had been collecting ever since they heard the prophecy of Agabus. Their brethren in Jerusalem, they knew, would not be able to afford the high cost of food in famine conditions without such Christian aid. The conveying of the money was entrusted to Barnabas and Paul.[11]

8. Cf. Josephus, *Ant.* xv. 373–378.
9. Suetonius, *Life of Claudius* 18. 2.
10. Cf. Josephus, *Ant.* iii. 320 f., xx. 51–53, 101. It may have been while visiting Jerusalem in connexion with her famine relief that Helena undertook a Nazirite vow (Mishnah *Nazir* 3: 6).
11. Acts 11: 27–30.

In later years the organizing of financial relief from Gentile Christians to the Jerusalem church was a major concern of Paul's;[12] it may well be that he had played a leading part in organizing this gift in Antioch. This may be the point of a remark he makes when he reports a special request made to Barnabas and himself by the leaders of the Jerusalem church.

## 3. Interview with the Jerusalem leaders

This report comes at the end of an account which Paul gives in Galatians 2: 1–10 of an occasion when he and Barnabas went up to Jerusalem from Antioch. The occasion may be the same as the famine-relief visit mentioned by Luke; we cannot be sure. The implication of Paul's account is that this was the second visit which he paid to Jerusalem after his conversion. The first was that which he paid "after three years" to spend a fortnight with Peter (Galatians 1: 18); this one took place "after fourteen years" (Galatians 2: 1). Fourteen years from the earlier visit or fourteen years from his conversion? Once more we cannot be sure; the construction of the phrase "after fourteen years" is different from that of the phrase "after three years", but it is not clear what significance, if any, lies in the difference of construction.[13] One thing emerges clearly from Paul's narrative: he is leaving out no material phase of his relations with the Jerusalem leaders, and it is unlikely that he had paid another visit to Jerusalem between the two expressly described and dated in the letter to the Galatians. He was concerned to argue that at no point between his conversion and the writing of the letter had the Jerusalem leaders conferred on him any authority which he did not possess already by direct commission of the risen Christ. Had he omitted from his retrospect an intervening visit, somebody would have been sure to spot the omission and draw unfavourable conclusions from it. After the fourteen years, he says (Galatians 2: 1 f.):

> I went up again to Jerusalem with Barnabas, taking Titus along with me. I went up by revelation; and I laid before them (but privately before the men of repute) the gospel which I preach among the Gentiles, lest somehow I should be running or had run in vain.

When Paul speaks of going up to Jerusalem "by revelation" it is improbable that he has the prophecy of Agabus in mind. The Paul of Acts was not over-responsive to other people's revelations which

12. See pp. 319 ff.
13. In Galatians 1: 18 Paul says "after ($\mu\varepsilon\tau\acute{a}$) three years"; in 2: 1 he says "in the course of ($\delta\iota\acute{a}$) fourteen years". For a recent discussion see J. A. T. Robinson, *Redating the New Testament* (London, 1976), pp. 36 ff.

affected himself,[14] and the Paul of the epistles – not least the Paul of this epistle – is so constantly aware of his unmediated authorization by Christ that it is natural to conclude that, when he did anything by revelation, the revelation was personally received. Whether this visit had any other purpose than to meet the leaders of the Jerusalem church he does not say; he does say that he and Barnabas had a private conference with those leaders – the "men of repute",[15] as he calls them, who turn out to have been James the Lord's brother with Peter and John. At this conference he set before them the gospel as he was accustomed to preach it to Gentiles, and the reason which he gives for doing so gives us pause: it was, he says, "lest somehow I should be running or had run in vain". There is nothing surprising in the athletic metaphor: this is not the only place where Paul describes his apostolic service as a race to be run.[16] But there is certainly cause for surprise in the implication of his statement that, failing the recognition by the Jerusalem authorities that the gospel he preached was the authentic gospel, his apostolic service would have been, and would continue to be, fruitless. It is certainly not implied that, if this recognition had been withheld, Paul would have changed his mind about the gospel he preached or changed his method of presenting it. A gospel received by direct revelation is not to be modified out of deference to any human authority. What Paul was concerned about was not the validity of his gospel but its practicability. His commission was not derived from Jerusalem, but it could not be effectively discharged except in fellowship with Jerusalem. A cleavage between his Gentile mission and the mother-church in Jerusalem would be disastrous for the progress of the gospel: the cause of Christ would be divided, and all the devotion with which Paul had thus far prosecuted his apostolate to the Gentiles, and hoped to go on prosecuting it, would be frustrated.

## 4. Demarcation of mission fields

As it was, however, everything seemed to turn out well at the conference. The Jerusalem leaders recognized not only that Paul's

14. Not even when Agabus was the channel of revelation (cf. Acts 21: 10–14).

15. Gk. *οἱ δοκοῦντες* . Three times in this context Paul uses this form (the present participle of *δοκεῖν*, "seem") to denote the leaders of the Jerusalem church. In itself this use has no nuance of disparagement or sarcasm, either here or in verse 9 ("men of repute as pillars"). But in verse 6, where Paul speaks of them as "men of some repute" and adds "what they were makes no difference to me; God has no favourites", he is at least reacting vigorously against those who reckoned his apostolic authority dubious by comparison with that of the Jerusalem leaders (perhaps because of their association with the historical Jesus).

16. Cf. Philippians 2: 16; also 1 Corinthians 9: 24–27, with 1 Timothy 6: 12; 2 Timothy 4: 7 f.

gospel was the authentic gospel, but also that his vocation, unlike theirs, was to preach it to the Gentiles. The men of repute, he says (Galatians 2: 6–9):

added nothing to me. On the contrary, they saw that I had been entrusted with the gospel to the uncircumcised, just as Peter had been entrusted with the gospel to the circumcised (for he who worked through Peter for the mission to the circumcised worked through me also for the Gentiles). So, when they perceived the grace that was given to me, James and Cephas and John, the men of repute as pillars, gave to me and Barnabas the right hand of fellowship, that we should go to the Gentiles and they to the circumcised.

The Jerusalem leaders were reputed to be "pillars" – pillars, perhaps, in the new temple of living stones which Jesus spoke of founding, a distinction which was not confined to their status in the church of Jerusalem, but betokened a claim to special recognition wherever the name of Christ was confessed.[17] The order in which Paul names them suggests that James had now attained a position of primacy, in Jerusalem at least, in which he was beginning to overshadow the Twelve themselves. No longer is he mentioned almost incidentally alongside Peter, as in Paul's account of his earlier visit to Jerusalem.[18]

Paul does not commit himself to acceptance of their status as "pillars". He affirms, however, that they "added nothing" to him – neither to the subject-matter of his gospel nor to his authority to preach it. What was settled at the conference, he says, was an amicable demarcation of the two mission-fields. But there is one exceptional feature of usage in his account of this agreement. Whereas he regularly refers to the prince of the apostles by his Aramaic name Cephas, its Greek equivalent Peter (*Petros*) appears twice in this account, and then "Cephas" takes over again. The most probable explanation (though by no means the certain explanation) of this feature is that the passage containing the form "Peter" is an extract from a more or less official record of the conference, the reference to Paul being changed to the first personal pronoun singular so as to integrate the quotation into the construction of its context.[19] If this explanation be accepted, we have first Paul's adapted quotation:

17. Cf. C. K. Barrett, "Paul and the 'Pillar' Apostles", in *Studia Paulina in honorem J. de Zwaan*, ed. J. N. Sevenster and W. C. van Unnik (Haarlem, 1953), pp. 1 ff. Perhaps four "pillars" were originally recognized, but one (James the son of Zebedee) had been removed by martyrdom (Acts 12: 12).
18. Galatians 1: 18 f.; see p. 84.
19. Cf. O. Cullmann, *Peter: Disciple-Apostle-Martyr*, E.T. (London, 1953), p. 18,

they saw that I had been entrusted with the gospel to the uncircumcised, just as *Peter* had been entrusted with the gospel to the circumcised (for he who worked through *Peter* for the mission to the circumcised worked through me also for the Gentiles) –

and then his repetition and continuation of the same situation in his
own words:

when they perceived the grace that was given to me, James and *Cephas*
and John, the men of repute as pillars, gave to me and Barnabas the
right hand of fellowship, that we should go to the Gentiles and they to
the circumcised.

The difference in Peter's name is not the only difference between
the two passages. In the former Paul and Peter are set over against
each other; in the latter it is not Paul only, but Paul and Barnabas,
whose call to evangelize the Gentiles is acknowledged, and it is not
Peter only, but James, Cephas and John, who are to discharge an
apostleship to Jews. One suggestion in this regard is that the extract represents the situation at the time of the conference, while
Paul's re-wording which follows, and indeed his general language
about the "men of repute", reflects the situation as it had developed
in the interval between the conference and the writing of the
letter.[20] In the event not Peter in particular, but the triumvirate as a
whole, undertook the responsibility for directing and executing the
mission to Jews, with James becoming more and more *primus inter
pares* and issuing directives which even Peter felt bound to obey.[21]

It is possible that the agreement about the demarcation of the
two mission-fields concealed one or two unobserved ambiguities
which did not come to light until a later date, when they caused
some tension between Paul and Jerusalem.

First, were the terms of the demarcation sufficiently clear? Was it
to be interpreted geographically or communally? Either way, it
must have been difficult to define the boundaries of the two mission-fields. Jews and Gentiles were to be found in practically every
city in the eastern Mediterranean world. It was almost certainly
not envisaged that the Jerusalem leaders should be debarred from
evangelizing the Jews of (say) Ephesus or Corinth or Rome. But
since the churches planted in due course in those cities comprised
both Jewish and Gentile converts, some dovetailing or overlapping

---

and *TDNT* vi (Grand Rapids, 1968), *s.v.* Πέτρος, p. 100, n. 6; E. Dinkler, "Der
Brief an die Galater", in *Verkündigung und Forschung*, 1953–55, pp. 182 f. J. Munck
curiously inclined to the opposite view: "Perhaps we should rather say that vv. 7 f.
are Paul's formulation, while v. 9 . . . is a citation of the argument" (*Paul and the
Salvation of Mankind*, E.T. [London, 1959], p. 62, n. 2).
   20. Cf. G. Klein, "Galater 2, 6–9 und die Geschichte der Jerusalemer
Urgemeinde", in *Rekonstruktion und Interpretation* (München, 1969), pp. 107 ff.
   21. Cf. Galatians 2: 12 (see pp. 175 ff.).

of the two spheres of missionary action was inevitable. Again, it was probably not envisaged that Paul should be debarred from visiting synagogues in Gentile cities. According to the narrative of Acts, it was in synagogues that he regularly found the nucleus of his churches – mainly among the God-fearing Gentiles who habitually attended the services of worship there. But this could constitute a fruitful source of misunderstanding, unless entire mutual confidence was maintained between the two parties to the agreement.

Next, misunderstanding could arise from Paul's own account of the conference. Some, on hearing it, might well say to him, "So you did receive the recognition of the Jerusalem leaders!" To this his reply would probably have been: "I did not receive their recognition as though my commission was previously defective without it; they recognized that I had already been called to this ministry, but they did not in any sense confer on me the right to exercise it." Paul and Barnabas had been energetically engaged for several years in Gentile evangelization, but whereas Barnabas undertook this work in Antioch as commissioner of the Jerusalem church, Paul had been engaged in it long before Barnabas brought him to Antioch as his colleague in the work there. The nature of the recognition which Paul received at this conference in Jerusalem could easily have been misunderstood or misrepresented by any one who was unable or disinclined to distinguish between various forms of recognition. Perhaps the Jerusalem leaders would not have given precisely the same account of the matter as Paul does. In our more sophisticated days we are familiar with the device of calculated ambiguity in ecclesiastical as in other agreements; but such ambiguity as inhered in the Jerusalem agreement was probably not deliberate but inadvertent. Even so, we may see as our narrative progresses the kind of misunderstanding to which it could lead.

It has just been suggested that Paul would have seen a distinction between Barnabas's commission and his own. Nevertheless, he nowhere says anything that could imply a depreciation of Barnabas's commission alongside his. His concern was to assert the authentic and unmediated character of his own apostleship; for the rest, he uses the designation "apostles" in a fairly wide sense – a wider sense, certainly, than Luke gives it.[22] He does not explicitly

22. The debate about the New Testament apostleship has come a long way since K. H. Rengstorf's epoch-making article ἀπόστολος in *TWNT* i (Stuttgart, 1933) – E.T. in *TDNT* i (Grand Rapids, 1964), pp. 407–447. For a judicious assessment of the state of the question cf. R. Schnackenburg, "Apostles before and during Paul's Time", in *Apostolic History and the Gospel*, ed. W. W. Gasque and R. P. Martin (Exeter, 1970), pp. 287–303; see also W. Schneemelcher and others, "Apostle and Apostolic", etc., in *New Testament Apocrypha*, E.T., ed. E. Hennecke, W. Schneemelcher and R. McL. Wilson (London, 1965), pp. 25–87; J. A. Kirk, "Apostleship since Rengstorf: Towards a Synthesis", *NTS* 21 (1974–75), pp. 249–264.

call Barnabas an apostle, but he does so by implication in a passage where he is stoutly defending his own apostleship and sets Barnabas and himself on one side over against "the other apostles and the brethren of the Lord and Cephas" on the other (1 Corinthians 9: 5 f.). Luke, for his part, reserves the designation "apostle" almost exclusively for the Twelve: the one occasion on which he uses it of Paul is the exception that proves the rule, for there he speaks of "the apostles Barnabas and Paul" (Acts 14: 14) in a context which suggests that he viewed them as apostles in the sense of commissioners from the church of Antioch – which indeed they were on the occasion referred to (cf. Acts 13: 3). To be sure, when Paul in his letters argues for the validity of his apostleship by an appeal to his achievements, the record of Acts provides abundant independent confirmation of his argument; [23] nevertheless, Luke nowhere gives him the title "apostle" in the sense in which Paul claims it for himself – which reminds us that the choice of a word is less important than the meaning attached to it.

## 5. "Remember the poor"

We return to the Jerusalem conference. Paul ends his account of it by mentioning one condition which the three "men of repute" pressed on Barnabas and himself (Galatians 2: 10):

> only they would have us remember the poor, which very thing I was eager to do.

There are two verbs in this sentence. The former, "remember", is present subjunctive in Greek and may suggest continued action; the latter, "was eager", is aorist indicative, which in appropriate contexts (of which this is perhaps one) can be rendered by the pluperfect in English. [24]

> "Only", said they, "please continue to remember the poor"; and in fact I had made a special point of attending to this very matter.

If this rendering gives the right emphasis, then the leaders' request that Paul and Barnabas should continue to remember "the

23. Tertullian ridicules the Marcionites for their recognition of Paul as the only true apostle of Jesus Christ at the same time as they disowned the one independent witness to his apostolic credentials: "Let me say here to those who reject the *Acts of the Apostles*: 'It is of primary necessity that you show us who this Paul was, what he was before he was an apostle, and how he became an apostle" – so very great is the use which they make of him in respect of other questions" (*De praescriptione haereticorum*, 23).

24. Cf. C. W. Emmet, "The Case for the Tradition", in *BC* i, 2 (London, 1922), p. 279.

poor" is illuminated by Luke's account of the carrying by these two of the famine relief which the Antiochene church provided for their brethren in Jerusalem in time of famine. The phrase "the poor" may denote the poorer members of the Jerusalem church; it might, on the other hand, be a designation for that church as a whole.[25] In later times there was a body of Jewish Christians, claiming to represent the church of Jerusalem in dispersion, which was called the Ebionites; this is derived from Hebrew *hā'ebyōnîm*, "the poor", which could well underlie the Greek phrase used in Galatians 2: 10, especially if, as seems probable, Paul is echoing the language of the Jerusalem leaders.[26] How seriously Paul continued to "remember the poor" will be shown in the sequel. But even here there was a possibility of misunderstanding: what Paul regarded as a voluntary gesture of Christian charity and fellowship was perhaps viewed by the mother-church as a tribute due from her daughter-churches among the Gentiles.[27]

## 6. The circumcision issue

One issue which might have been expected to arise at the conference has not been mentioned yet. That is the issue of the circumcision of Gentile converts, which soon became the subject of an animated debate. Did it arise on this occasion? The answer to this question is not clear. Paul does make a reference to it, but while his Galatian readers, who knew something of the background of his reference, no doubt grasped his meaning, his modern readers find it more difficult to do so. This is partly because we know less of the background than his first readers did, partly because his construction is fractured and partly because there is a variant reading which changes the sense by omitting a material "not".[28]

Immediately after telling how he laid his gospel before the Jerusalem leaders, lest he "should be running or had run in vain", Paul goes on (Galatians 2: 3–5):

> But even Titus, who was with me, was not compelled to be circumcised, though he was a Greek. But because of false brethren secretly brought in, who slipped in to spy out our freedom which we have in Christ

25. Cf. K. Holl, "Der Kirchenbegriff des Paulus in seinem Verhältnis zu dem der Urgemeinde", in *Gesammelte Aufsätze* ii (Tübingen, 1928), pp. 44 ff., especially pp. 58 ff.

26. At an earlier date the men of Qumran called themselves "the poor" (*hā'ebyōnîm*) and in more recent times there have been separatist Christian groups which described themselves by such terms as "the poor of the flock" (cf. Zechariah 11: 7, 11, although there the word in the Massoretic text is not *'ebyōnîm*).

27. So K. Holl, *loc. cit.*

28. The Western text of Galatians 2: 5 omits οὐδέ before πρὸς ὥραν and thus makes Paul say the exact opposite of what he most probably meant.

Jesus, that they might bring us into bondage – to them we did not yield submission even for a moment, that the truth of the gospel might be preserved for you.

Then he goes back to the "men of repute" and affirms that they "added nothing" to him.

Titus, a Greek Christian, who accompanied him from Antioch to Jerusalem on this occasion, was "not compelled to be circumcised". To us, though probably not to Paul's first readers (who knew whether Titus had been circumcised or not), this statement is ambiguous. It may mean (i) that Titus was not circumcised or (ii) that Titus *was* circumcised, not by compulsion, but voluntarily, or perhaps by a temporary concession on Paul's part – on the principle, presumably, of *reculer pour mieux sauter*. The editors of the Western text of the Pauline corpus appear to have understood it the latter way, for they make Paul say, "to them [to the false brethren] we yielded submission for a moment, that the truth of the gospel might be preserved for you". How the circumcision of a Gentile convert could have been imagined by any one, especially by Paul, to help towards preserving the gospel of free grace for other Gentile converts, is something which passes all understanding. F. C. Burkitt might ask, "who can doubt that it was the knife which really did circumcise Titus that has cut the syntax of Galatians ii. 3–5 to pieces?" [29] – but to this question, as to many others beginning with the rhetorical "who can doubt . . .?" an effective answer is "I can"; and so, it is evident, can many exegetes who have dealt with the passage. "If he was circumcised", T. W. Manson comments on Burkitt's argument, "the fact would be well advertised in Galatia by Paul's opponents, and the involved and stumbling verbiage of these verses would be worse than useless as camouflage for that nasty fact." [30]

The last-named scholar has pointed the way to a more satisfactory understanding of the abrupt reference to the false brethren: it is a parenthesis, referring to a later development, and introduced here because Paul is reminded of this subsequent occasion by his reference to Titus. [31] At the time of the Jerusalem conference, he says, so far was the circumcision question from presenting any

29. F. C. Burkitt, *Christian Beginnings* (London, 1924), p. 118; so also S. C. Neill, *Jesus Through Many Eyes* (London, 1976), pp. 55 f.

30. T. W. Manson, *Studies in the Gospels and Epistles* (Manchester, 1962), pp. 175 f.

31. Cf. T. W. Manson, *ibid.*; the parenthesis, he suggests, comprises verses 4 and 5. B. Orchard, "A New Solution of the Galatians Problem", *BJRL* 28 (1944), pp. 154 ff., adopts a similar interpretation, but includes verse 3 in the parenthesis. Cf. his "The Ellipsis between Galatians 2,3 and 2,4", *Biblica* 54 (1973), pp. 469–481, and "Once Again the Ellipsis between Galatians 2,3 and 2,4", *Biblica* 57 (1976), pp. 254 f.

difficulty that although Titus, a Greek, was in Jerusalem with Barnabas and himself, no pressure was brought to bear to have him circumcised. The circumcision issue, he adds in a parenthesis which lacks a principal clause, became acute at a later date on account of "false brethren" who infiltrated the Gentile churches and tried to impose a yoke of legal bondage in place of the Christian freedom which they enjoyed. This later development may be linked with Luke's statement in Acts 15: 1, that "some men came down from Judaea [to Antioch], and were teaching the brethren, 'Unless you are circumcised according to the custom of Moses, you cannot be saved'."[32] It was to those infiltrators that Paul refused to concede an inch, so as not to prejudice his converts' gospel liberty. Having concluded his parenthesis on this note, he returns to the point where he had left off and continues to tell what happened at the Jerusalem conference.

That the question of circumcising Titus or any other Gentile convert was not raised during this visit is quite consistent with the evidence of Acts. The Gentile mission in Antioch had been proceeding for some years before visitors from Judaea tried to insist on the circumcision of the converts. Similarly, when Cornelius, the Roman centurion of Caesarea, and his household believed the gospel and received the Spirit, they were baptized, but no one seems to have suggested that they should be circumcised. Although Peter, on returning to Jerusalem, had to defend his visit to them, his fellow-apostles, when they accepted his defence, did not say, "Well, it is all right provided they accept circumcision." [33] In Acts as in Galatians the question of circumcising Gentile converts did not arise until later. When it did arise, those who raised it were steadfastly resisted by Paul and others who, with him, could not allow the truth of the gospel to be compromised by an infusion of legalism. But if it did not arise at the conference described in Galatians 2: 1–10, that conference cannot be identified with the Council of Jerusalem described in Acts 15: 6–29, for on the latter occasion circumcision was the main issue under debate. The conference of Galatians 2: 1–10 may well have coincided in that case with the famine-relief visit of Acts 11: 30, although this cannot be positively affirmed. Before circumcision became a burning issue, the Gentile mission had a further advance to record.

32. See p. 175.
33. Cf. Acts 10: 34–11: 18.

# CHAPTER 16

# Church Extension in Cyprus and Asia Minor

## 1. Barnabas and Paul in Cyprus

THE ANTIOCHENE MINISTRY OF BARNABAS AND PAUL WAS NOT confined to the city or church of Antioch. Antioch had a vast hinterland, which might be as ripe for evangelization as Antioch itself was. The missionaries who first brought the gospel to Antioch had preached it in Syria and Phoenicia on the way there: Paul had preached it in Cilicia before Barnabas brought him to Antioch. But beyond Cilicia there was the main land-mass of Asia Minor, through which ran the road to Ephesus and the west. And west-by-south-west from Antioch, some 90 miles (150 kilometres) out in the Mediterranean, at its nearest point, lay the island of Cyprus. The men of Cyprus who had taken part in the evangelization of Antioch did not neglect their native island, but there was in Antioch one man of Cyprus who was set on evangelizing it more systematically, and that was Barnabas. Paul, for his part, may already have seen in his mind's eye the possibilities which Asia Minor presented for gospel penetration and expansion, and the time was to come when he and Barnabas would part company, Barnabas devoting himself to his native Cyprus and Paul to Asia Minor and the lands farther west.

To begin with, however, they undertook their project of missionary outreach together. Luke tells how the leaders of the church of Antioch were directed by the Holy Spirit – presumably through a prophetic utterance – to release Barnabas and Paul for this further ministry to which they had been called. The two men went down to the port of Seleucia and set sail for Cyprus with the blessing of the church and its leaders.[1] The church regarded them as its representatives and commissioners; it was their home base, and to it in due course they returned to report "all that God had done with them" (Acts 14: 27).

When they set out, they took as their attendant Barnabas's young cousin, John Mark of Jerusalem. The house of John Mark's mother Mary was the meeting-place of one group in the Jerusalem

---

1. Acts 13: 1 ff.

160

church – the group which was led by Peter.[2] Barnabas and Paul took John Mark back to Antioch at the end of their famine-relief visit to Jerusalem: Barnabas in particular discerned in him qualities which could be developed and profitably exercised in the Christian mission.

Cyprus was settled in antiquity by Phoenicians and Greeks: from one of the Phoenician settlements, Kition (modern Larnaka) on its south-eastern shore, it derived the name Kittim by which it was known to the Hebrews. Since the sixth century B.C. it had been controlled by the Persians and the Ptolemies, among others. The Romans annexed it in 58 B.C. and two years later added it to the province of Cilicia. After various changes it became a separate imperial province, governed by a *legatus pro praetore*, in 27 B.C., but five years later Augustus handed it over to the jurisdiction of the Roman senate, and from that date it was, like other senatorial provinces, administered by a proconsul. At the time of Barnabas and Paul's visit the proconsul was Sergius Paullus, member of a noble Roman family with a record of public service over several generations. We know, for example, of one Lucius Sergius Paullus who was a curator of the Tiber in the principate of Claudius;[3] we know of another of the same name (probably his son) who occupied an important office in Galatia (perhaps the governorship of that province) a generation later,[4] and of yet another of the same name who was consul at Rome about A.D. 150 and again in 168.[5] It has been widely supposed that the proconsul of Cyprus could have been identical with the first of these,[6] but he is more probably to be identified with the Quintus Sergius Paullus whose name has been deciphered in fragmentary form on a Greek inscription from Kythraia in North Cyprus.[7]

The missionary party landed at Salamis, a Greek settlement on the east coast, founded in the sixth century B.C. and for long the principal city of Cyprus. Like most other Cypriot cities, it had a Jewish community. Barnabas and Paul visited the synagogues of

2. Cf. Acts 12: 12.
3. *CIL* vi. 31545.
4. He is named on a Latin inscription found by W. M. Ramsay and J. G. C. Anderson at Pisidian Antioch in 1912; see Ramsay, *The Bearing of Recent Discovery on the Trustworthiness of the New Testament* (London, 1915), pp. 150–152.
5. In *CIL* vi. 253 he is named as *consul suffectus* along with Torquatus Asprenas on the former occasion. He is mentioned twice by Galen (*De anatomicis administrationibus* i. 2; *De praenotione* 2).
6. E.g. by E. Groag, in Pauly-Wissowa *RE*, *s.v.* "Sergius", No. 34, and (tentatively) by K. Lake, in *BC* i, 5, p. 458.
7. *IGRR* iii. 935; the name of his official position is missing but he is said to have held it under Claudius. Another inscription (*IGRR* iii. 930), from Soli on the north coast of Cyprus, mentions a proconsul named Paullus as holding office, perhaps, in the tenth year (? of Claudius); cf. T. B. Mitford, *Annual of the British School at Athens* 42 (1947), pp. 201–206.

Salamis and preached the gospel in them, with unrecorded results. The preaching of the gospel in synagogues would be largely a matter of expounding the scripture lessons in terms of their Christian fulfilment.

From Salamis they made their way by the road which ran along the southern shore of the island, until they arrived at New Paphos, the provincial seat of government. (New Paphos was a Greek settlement; Old Paphos, originally a Phoenician settlement, lay about seven miles or twelve kilometres to the south-east. Old Paphos was a traditional centre of the cult of Aphrodite, who was hence referred to as "the Paphian".) [8] Here they were summoned before Sergius Paullus, who presumably wished to satisfy himself that their activity presented no threat to public order. In several parts of the empire around this time unrest was being stirred up in Jewish communities by travelling agitators.[9] Evidently the proconsul was satisfied on this score; indeed, he was quite favourably impressed by the missionaries and their message, despite the attempts of a Jewish member of his entourage to dissuade him from paying them serious attention.[10] (Luke describes this Jew as a "false prophet", which might simply refer to his speaking against the gospel, but the fact that he goes on to call him a *magos* suggests that he had a reputation for some form of esoteric wisdom.)[11]

## 2. The gospel comes to Phrygia

From Cyprus the missionary party sailed north-by-north-west to the mainland of Asia Minor, to the port of Side, perhaps, or Attaleia (modern Antalya) farther west, and made their way to the city of Perga, about six miles inland, situated on the coastal road from Ephesus to Tarsus. It was the chief city of Pamphylia (the territory between the Taurus range and the Mediterranean), which at this time was joined with Lycia on its western frontier to form a united Roman province. There were Jewish settlements in Pamphylia, so some evangelistic activity in Perga may be implied in Luke's mention of the place, but the only incident he records is

8. Mainly by the poets but also in a considerable number of inscriptions. She was also called Kypris ("the Cyprian"). Her cult at Paphos was probably Phoenician in origin: Herodotus (*History* i. 105) derives it from Ascalon, Pausanias (*Description of Greece* i. 14. 6) from Assyria.

9. Cf. Acts 17: 6 f.; see p. 225.

10. "The proconsul believed", says Luke, ". . . for he was astonished at the teaching of the Lord" (Acts 13: 12).

11. Possibly Luke intends ὁ μάγος to be the equivalent of the false prophet's name Elymas, which may have been a Semitic word cognate with Arabic *ʿalīm* ("wise", "learned"). See further A. D. Nock, "Paul and the Magus", in *BC* i, 5, pp. 164 ff.

John Mark's departure here from his two senior companions and his return to Jerusalem. The reason for his departure and return is not stated, but perhaps he had not reckoned on the more extended journey into the highlands of the province of Galatia on which Paul and Barnabas were about to embark.

The Roman province of Galatia covered a large area in the heart of Asia Minor. It derived its name from the former kingdom of Galatia, founded by the Galatians or Gauls who in the third century B.C. invaded the peninsula and settled in territory which had formerly belonged to Phrygia. In due course the Galatian kings became allies of Rome. When in 25 B.C. the last of these kings, Amyntas, fell in battle against raiders from the northern Taurus, Augustus reorganized the kingdom as an imperial province, in which he incorporated a good deal of territory to the south which had never belonged ethnically to Galatia – the regions of Eastern Phrygia, Pisidia, Isaurica and Western Lycaonia. The principal cities of the former kingdom of Galatia lay in the northern part of the Roman province: Pessinus to the west, Tavium to the east, and between them Ancyra (modern Ankara), the capital of the kingdom and then of the province, as it is today of the Turkish Republic. Whether or not Paul ever visited those northern cities we have no means of knowing for certain: we have abundant evidence for his interest in cities of South Galatia – that is, of that part of the Roman province which Augustus added to the realm of King Amyntas when he took it over.

It was to one of these cities, Pisidian Antioch, that Paul and Barnabas came after travelling north from Perga for 100 miles and more. Pisidian Antioch is referred to more precisely by Strabo as "Antioch near Pisidia"; it was actually situated in the region of Phrygia, over the border from Pisidia. The ancient kingdom of Phrygia was now divided between the Roman provinces of Asia and Galatia: it was in Galatic Phrygia (as we may call it in distinction from Asian Phrygia) that Pisidian Antioch lay. It lies near modern Yalvaç, on a plateau some 3600 feet high. Sir William Ramsay conjectured that Paul had caught malaria in Pamphylia and sought to recuperate in this highland region: he linked this conjecture with Paul's reminder to his Galatian converts that it was "because of a bodily ailment" that he first came to them with the gospel (Galatians 4: 13).[12] This can be neither proved nor disproved.

As its name indicates, Pisidian Antioch was a Seleucid foundation (early third century B.C.), although the site was inhabited long before Seleucid times. The position was well chosen by the Seleucids to serve as a border fortress, and the same strategic advantages probably moved Augustus in 6 B.C. to give the city the

---

12. *St. Paul the Traveller*, pp. 94 ff.; see p. 135.

status of a Roman colony, under the new designation Colonia Caesarea. Army veterans were settled there among the local population, the city became the military centre for the surrounding territory, new roads were built leading deep into Pisidia for the more effective romanization of that region. The name Pisidian Antioch reflected the rôle marked out for the city by Roman imperial policy.

A Roman colony was a settlement of Roman citizens, designed to safeguard and promote Roman interests in an environment of non-Roman inhabitants (incolae). The administration of a Roman colony was modelled on that of Rome itself, with two annually appointed collegiate magistrates at its head. Epigraphic evidence in and around Pisidian Antioch shows that one of the principal Roman families of the colony bore the name Caristanius Fronto. One member of this family, about a quarter of a century after the time with which we are here concerned, married a Roman lady called Sergia Paulla, possibly a daughter of that Lucius Sergius Paullus who held a responsible post in the provincial administration.[13]

As in other Phrygian cities, there was in Pisidian Antioch a considerable Jewish community, dating from the reign of Antiochus III (223–187 B.C.).[14] In accordance with their practice in cities where there were Jewish communities, Barnabas and Paul visited the synagogue of Pisidian Antioch on the first sabbath after their arrival in that city, and were invited by the governing body of the synagogue to address a "word of exhortation" or homily to the worshippers after the reading of the first and second lessons.[15] At this point Luke ascribes to Paul the outline of a homily, which probably summarizes the way in which the gospel was presented to a synagogue congregation, comprising Jews and God-fearing Gentiles, against the familiar background of the history of Israel. Paul, perhaps in allusion to the contents of the scripture lessons for the day, reminds his hearers of the mighty acts of God in the Old Testament

13. Cf. G. L. Cheesman, "The Family of the Caristanii at Antioch in Pisidia", *JRS* 3 (1913), pp. 253 ff., especially pp. 261–265. W. M. Ramsay, eking out the limited epigraphic evidence with a generous supply of imagination, argued that Sergia Paulla was a Christian, having inherited the faith from her supposed ancestor the proconsul of Cyprus (*The Bearing of Recent Discovery on the Trustworthiness of the New Testament*, pp. 152 ff.) – an argument consisting, as K. Lake put it, of "marvellously ingenious, but not very convincing combinations" (*BC* i, 5, p. 458).

14. Pisidian Antioch was probably one of the "fortresses and most important places" in Phrygia where Jews were settled by Antiochus III (Josephus, *Ant.* xii. 149).

15. "Word of exhortation" ( λόγος παρακλήσεως ) is the expression used by the writer to the Hebrews (13: 22) to describe his "epistle" – a written homily. The first lesson was taken from the Law, the second from the Prophets (see F. F. Bruce, *New Testament History* [London, ² 1971], pp. 136 f.).

narrative from the Exodus to the reign of David, after which he goes on: "Of this man's posterity God has brought to Israel a Saviour, Jesus, as he promised" (Acts 13: 23). In this retrospect, though it begins with Moses and the Exodus, there is no mention of the law: it is the fulfilment of promise that is emphasized – even if here it is not the promise made to Abraham (as in Galatians 3: 6–18) but to David. The link between David and Jesus is mentioned by Paul in the preamble of his letter to the Romans, where Jesus is said to have been "descended from David according to the flesh" (Romans 1: 3).[16] After proceeding straight from David to Jesus, Paul enlarges on the climax of salvation-history – the preparatory witness of John the Baptist, the mighty acts of God in Christ, crowned by his resurrection, in fulfilment of psalm and prophecy.

It may be said that there is not much difference between what Paul says in Pisidian Antioch and what Peter is reported to have said in Jerusalem on the first Christian Pentecost. This is so, but perhaps there actually was but little difference in substance between the Petrine and Pauline presentations of the gospel to Jewish audiences. If Paul, faced with a synagogue congregation in the dispersion, did not speak as Luke makes him speak at Pisidian Antioch, then let us be told how he did speak. True, there is less "theology of the cross" in the account of Jesus' death in this speech than might be expected from Paul, whether he was addressing Jews or Gentiles. And when the Paul of Acts tells how the risen Christ "appeared to those who came up with him from Galilee to Jerusalem, who are now his witnesses to the people" (Acts 13: 31), the historical Paul would certainly have added, and (we may be sure) did add, "Last of all . . . he appeared also to me" (cf. 1 Corinthians 15: 8). But a Pauline touch is introduced at the end of the homily. Where other preachers in Acts proclaim that "forgiveness of sins" is available through Jesus (cf. Acts 2: 38; 10: 43), Paul at Pisidian Antioch not only says that "through this man forgiveness of sins is proclaimed to you", but adds that "by him every one that believes is *justified* from all things, from which you could not be justified by Moses' law" (Acts 13: 38 f.). From these words as they stand, indeed, the full Pauline doctrine of justification by faith could not be deduced,[17] but the words are quite in line with Paul's teaching in Romans 3: 20–26, that God "justifies him who has faith in Jesus" whereas "no human being will be justified in his sight by works of the law". The language of Acts 13: 39 need

16. These words are widely thought to have been quoted by Paul from a current confession of faith. This, "though it is hardly as certain as it is sometimes assumed to be, seems highly probable" (C. E. B. Cranfield, *The Epistle to the Romans*, ICC, i [Edinburgh, 1975], p. 57).

17. RSV and NEB render "freed", not "justified". But Luke probably intended the word to be understood in its Pauline sense.

not be construed to mean that faith in Christ takes over responsibility for a man's salvation when Moses' law has done all that it
can and can do no more – a most un-Pauline sentiment, to be sure,
but probably a non-Lukan one too.[18]

The God-fearers in the congregation were specially attracted by
Paul's message, and spread the news abroad among their
fellow-Gentiles. The result was that a week later there were more
Gentiles than Jews present at the synagogue service. The leaders of
the Jewish community were displeased and visited their displeasure
on the two missionaries. But many of the Gentiles accepted the
salvation through faith in Christ which the missionaries proclaimed
and formed a Christian group in separation from the synagogue –
the first of the churches of Galatia.

From Pisidian Antioch the missionaries moved on to Iconium
(modern Konya), nearly ninety miles (about 150 kilometres) east-
by-south-east, then as now an important road-junction. Xenophon
(c. 400 B.C.) knew it as "the last city of Phrygia" [19] and into the
second and third centuries A.D. its inhabitants considered
themselves Phrygians,[20] but it lay at the western end of the
Lycaonian Plain, so near to the frontier between the regions of
Phrygia and Lycaonia that several Greek and Roman writers of this
period refer to it (inaccurately) as a city of Lycaonia.[21] The
Emperor Claudius had recently permitted the city to use his own
name as an honorific prefix, so it was called for a time
Claudiconium (we may compare the use of "King's" as a prefix or
"Regis" as a suffix with some English place-names).

The missionaries' experience in Iconium appears to have been
almost a carbon copy of that in Pisidian Antioch, except that they
were able to stay longer in Iconium than in the other city. At last a
riot of such intensity was stirred up against them that they had to
leave Iconium and cross the regional border into Lycaonia, but
not before a distinct Christian community had been established
there as earlier in Pisidian Antioch. The memory of Paul in particular impressed itself on the people of Iconium: Iconium, a century later, is the centre of the fictitious adventures recounted in the
Acts of Paul and Thekla.[22]

18. Cf. B. W. Bacon, The Story of St. Paul (London, 1905), p. 103.

19. Xenophon, Anabasis i. 2. 19.

20. In the second-century Acts of Justin (ch. 4) one of the Christians accused at
Rome along with Justin Martyr, a slave named Hierax, says that he was "dragged
away from Iconium of Phrygia".

21. E.g. Cicero, Ad Familiares xv. 4. 2, and Pliny, Nat. Hist. v. 95, but on the
latter see W. M. Ramsay, "The 'Galatia' of St. Paul and the 'Galatic territory' of
Acts", in Studia Biblica et Ecclesiastica iv (Oxford, 1896), pp. 15 ff., especially pp.
46–55.

22. The best-known episode in the second-century Acts of Paul (see p. 467).

## 3. Problems of Gentile evangelization

At the conference which Barnabas and Paul attended with the Jerusalem leaders it was probably no part of the agreement that the two missionaries to the Gentiles should abstain from visiting synagogues in the cities to which they came. But it may not have been envisaged on either side that events would turn out as they did in Pisidian Antioch and Iconium, so that it would be necessary to detach Gentile God-fearers from the synagogues which they attended and form them into separate congregations.

Certainly many more Gentiles than Jews were converted to Christianity under Paul's preaching, but if he regularly made the synagogue his first base of operations, more Jews than Gentiles would probably hear the gospel from him at the outset, in one city after another. He himself takes it for granted that the gospel is to be presented "to the Jew first" (Romans 1: 16). Was there not the possibility that in some synagogue the whole congregation would respond positively to his preaching? Would the Jerusalem leaders not have regarded this as a breach of the agreement, in spirit at least? (Two or three years later the synagogue congregation at Beroea in Macedonia gave him a favourable hearing, but it is implied that this was an exceptional occurrence.) Paul might have said that, if only the Jews accepted the gospel themselves, it would be for them to evangelize the neighbouring Gentiles; but in fact he knew that the direct evangelization of Gentiles was his prime vocation. According to Luke, he and Barnabas claimed at Pisidian Antioch that in this respect they were discharging the commission laid by Yahweh on his Servant (Isaiah 49: 6):

I have set you to be a light for the Gentiles,
    that you may bring salvation to the uttermost parts of the earth.

As for Luke's report of the hostile response of the Jewish leaders in Pisidian Antioch and Iconium, it is consistent with Paul's own account of those Jews who "drove us out, and displease God and oppose all men by hindering us from speaking to the Gentiles that they may be saved" (1 Thessalonians 2: 15 f.).[23]

Conscious as he was of his call to be the Gentiles' apostle, Paul looked on the God-fearers who were in the habit of attending synagogue services as a providentially prepared bridgehead into the wider Gentile world. By listening to the reading and exposition of the scriptures those Gentiles learned to worship the "living and

23. For an argument that the paragraph 1 Thessalonians 2: 13–16 is an anti-Jewish interpolation cf. H. Boers, "The Form-Critical Study of Paul's Letters: 1 Thessalonians as a Case Study", *NTS* 22 (1975–76), pp. 145–153. Such an argument is difficult to establish in the absence of supporting textual evidence.

true God" and became familiar in some sense with the hope of
Israel. But they were told that they could not participate in this
hope, or share the privileges of the people of God, unless they were
prepared to become proselytes to Judaism – an issue to which, no
doubt, their Jewish friends confidently looked forward. Now,
however, these Gentiles were assured by Paul that the hope of
Israel had been fulfilled by Jesus, and that through faith in him
they could receive the saving grace of God on equal terms with
Jewish believers, and become members of the new messianic
fellowship of the people of God in which the religious distinction
between Jew and Gentile was obliterated. It was as natural for
God-fearing Gentiles to embrace the blessings of the gospel on
these terms as it was for Jews to decline them on these terms. Only
by visiting the synagogue could Paul establish contact with these
God-fearers, but the almost inevitable result of his policy was a
breach with the synagogue. It was probably impossible for one who
concentrated on Gentile evangelization to be at the same time an
effective missionary to Jews; hence the division of mission-fields
agreed upon at the Jerusalem conference was a wise decision.

Paul came to accept this situation, but he did not find this acceptance easy. While he knew himself to be apostle to the Gentiles by
divine vocation, yet the salvation of his own kith and kin was
specially close to his heart. As he put it later, in his epistle to the
Romans, if their salvation could be bought at the cost of his own, he
would willingly pay the price – willingly be "accursed and cut off
from Christ" for their sake (Romans 9: 3). In time, however, he
found reassurance in the hope that his very activity in Gentile
evangelization might serve indirectly to expedite the salvation of his
fellow-Jews. There came to his mind a passage in the Song of
Moses where God says to his rebellious people, "I will make you
jealous of those who are not a nation" (Deuteronomy 32: 21), and
he interpreted it in the light of the new gospel situation. "Those
who are not a nation" [24] were Gentiles. When, through Paul's own
ministry, Gentiles were availing themselves in ever-increasing
numbers of the blessings brought to mankind by Israel's Messiah –
blessings which fulfilled the promises made to Israel's ancestors
and were applicable, in the natural course of events, "to the Jew
first" – this spectacle would stir the Jews to jealousy. It would
suddenly dawn upon them that they had a prior claim to those
blessings which Gentiles were so eagerly enjoying, and they would
assert their own right to a share in them. The ingathering of the
Gentiles would thus lead, in the unfolding of the divine purpose, to
the salvation of Israel, and Paul learned to "magnify his ministry"

24. Hebrew *lō' 'am*, which was readily associated in the mind of a biblical expositor like Paul with *lō' 'ammî* ("Not my people") of Hosea 1: 9 (cf. Romans 9: 25
f.). See pp. 333 ff.

because of this more remote sequel over and above its immediate effect in producing among other nations "the obedience of faith" (Romans 10: 19; 11: 13–27; 16: 26).

## 4. Cities of Lycaonia

The first city of Lycaonia to which Barnabas and Paul came was Lystra, now the mound of Zordula, near Hatunsarai, about 18 miles (30 kilometres) south-by-south-west from Iconium.[25] Like Pisidian Antioch, Lystra was made a Roman colony by Augustus; the two colonies were linked by a military road which did not pass through Iconium and although they were separated by 100 miles they appear to have maintained cordial relations with each other.

There were some Jewish residents in Lystra, with whom the missionaries had dealings – Timothy, for example, the son of a Jewish mother and a Greek father, seems to have been one of their converts during this visit [26] – but the one incident recorded by Luke brings Barnabas and Paul into direct contact with pagan Lycaonians, not the Roman citizens of the colony but the indigenous *incolae*. These latter, impressed by Paul's healing of a congenitally lame man, concluded that their city was being favoured with a visit by two gods in human form: "Barnabas they called Zeus, and Paul, because he was the chief speaker, they called Hermes" (Acts 14: 12). The conjoint worship of these two deities, or of their Anatolian counterparts, is variously attested in legend and inscription for that part of Asia Minor.[27] The local priest of Zeus Propolis – Zeus whose temple stood facing the city gate – initiated appropriate sacrificial rites in honour of the two visitors. For a time they did not realize what was afoot, because everyone was speaking Lycaonian – a language which they did not understand (though they may have recognized that it was different from the Phrygian speech which they had left behind in Iconium). But when the truth of the situa-

---

25. The identification was made by J. R. S. Sterrett in 1885, on the strength of a Latin inscription found there (*CIL* iii. 6786), naming the place as *Col(onia) Iul(ia) Felix Gemina Lustra*. Cf. W. M. Ramsay, *Historical Geography of Asia Minor* (London, 1890), p. 332.

26. Cf. Acts 16: 1 f.

27. The best-known attestation in legend is the story of Philemon and Baucis, who received a visit from these two gods *incognito* (Ovid, *Metamorphoses* viii. 626 ff.). There is inscriptional evidence of their joint worship around Lystra, e.g. at Sedasa, where some men with Lycaonian names dedicated to Zeus a statue of Hermes together with a sun-dial *c*. A.D. 250 (W. M. Calder, "A Cult of the Homonades", *Classical Review* 24 [1910], pp. 77 ff.), and at another spot in the same neighbourhood, where a stone altar was dedicated to the "hearer of prayer" ('Επ-ήκοος), presumably Zeus, and to Hermes (*MAMA* viii [Manchester, 1962], No. 1). Cf. also W. M. Calder, "Zeus and Hermes at Lystra", *Expositor*, series 7, 10 (1910), pp. 1 ff., and "The Priest of Zeus at Lystra", *ibid.*, pp. 148 ff.

tion dawned on them, they were horrified and (addressing the people in Greek) urgently begged them to desist (Acts 14: 14–17):

> Men, what is this you are doing? We are only human beings, with the same nature as yourselves, but we have come to bring you good news. Turn away from this futile worship; seek the living God. He is the God who made heaven, earth and sea with all that is in them. In the ages that are past he has allowed all nations to follow their own ways; yet he has not left you without any clue to his being and character: he sends you rain from heaven and seasons of fruitfulness, and satisfies you with food and joy.

If Luke, in his account of the synagogue service at Pisidian Antioch, has given us a sample presentation of the gospel to Jews and God-fearers, here he has given us, in still more summary form, a sample of the approach to untutored pagans (later he gives a sample of the approach to "tutored" pagans when he brings Paul to Athens).[28]

Barnabas and Paul's protest to the men of Lystra takes them up in the midst of their religious practice and points them to a worthier form of worship – the worship of the living God, who created the universe and makes provision for man's need. The terms in which God is presented as Creator had been used for generations in Jewish testimony to pagans: "I am a Hebrew", said the prophet Jonah to the storm-tossed mariners; "and I fear the LORD, the God of heaven, who made the sea and the dry land" (Jonah 1: 9). "He gives food to all flesh", said the psalmist, "for his steadfast love endures for ever" (Psalm 136: 25).

No attempt was made on this occasion, as later by Paul at Athens,[29] to identify the Creator with Zeus: the Zeus who was worshipped at Lystra was too anthropomorphically conceived to provide the link with monotheism that the Zeus of Stoic poets and philosophers provided. Zeus and Hermes alike had to be displaced by the God who made heaven and earth and sent seasonal rain and harvests year by year.

In the summary given by Luke no expressly Christian note is struck, but preparation is made for the gospel by the statement that God "in the ages that are past" had allowed all nations to follow their own ways – that is, their own religious ways. Now, it is implied, a change has taken place – the change accomplished by the saving work of Christ. What is only implied in this summary is stated plainly in Paul's later speech at Athens, as it is also stated plainly and at greater length in his letter to the Romans, where God, who had given the Gentile world over to the consequences of

28. Acts 17: 22 ff.; see pp. 238 ff.
29. In the poetical quotations in Acts 17: 28.

its idolatry,[30] is shown to have provided by the self-offering of Christ a new way of approach to himself in which Gentiles as well as Jews might enjoy the forgiveness of sins previously committed in the time of God's forbearance together with the righteous status open to all who had faith in Jesus.[31]

If some of Barnabas and Paul's converts at Lystra had been involved in the attempt to pay divine honours to the two missionaries it could have been said of them, as was said later of Paul's Gentile converts in Thessalonica, that they "turned to God from idols to serve a living and true God" (1 Thessalonians 1: 9).

For all the enthusiasm with which they were greeted at first, Barnabas and Paul found public opinion at Lystra turning against them. Apart from those who believed the good news they brought, the people who had tried to offer them sacrifice must have been offended when their worship was refused. Accordingly, when Lystra was visited by some of the people who had stirred up trouble for the missionaries in Pisidian Antioch and Iconium, it was not difficult for them to exploit this sense of grievance. In the ensuing riot Paul in particular was badly knocked about: when, years later, he says to his friends in Corinth, "once I was stoned" (2 Corinthians 11: 25), this was the occasion he had in mind. He must have been knocked unconscious, for those who stoned him "dragged him out of the city, supposing that he was dead" (Acts 14: 19). But as the new converts gathered round to see what could be done for him, consciousness returned and he went back into the city with them. Whatever his physical disabilities were, Paul had an extraordinarily tough and resilient constitution and remarkable staying-power: "often knocked down but never knocked out" (as his words in 2 Corinthians 4: 9 have been paraphrased). When he speaks of bearing on his body "the marks of Jesus" – the *stigmata* which indicated who his master was, just as slaves sometimes had their owner's name branded in their flesh (Galatians 6: 17) – it is very probable that he includes among them the indelible scars resulting from his ill-treatment at Lystra.

Next day Barnabas and he set out for Derbe, situated on the mound of Kerti Hüyük, about 60 miles south-east of Lystra, or else (as some think) at Devri Şehri, about two and a half miles south-east of Kerti Hüyük.[32] According to the lexicographer

30. Romans 1: 18 ff.
31. Romans 3: 21–26.
32. See M. H. Ballance, "The Site of Derbe: A New Inscription", *Anatolian Studies* 7 (1957), pp. 147–151; "Derbe and Faustinopolis", *Anatolian Studies* 14 (1964), pp. 139 f. In the former paper he argued for Kerti Hüyük; in the latter for Devri Şehri. But in view of conflicting evidence on the provenance of the inscription on which the latter identification is based, "Kerti Hüyük cannot be so quickly eliminated as the site of ancient Derbe" (B. Van Elderen, "Some Archaeological

Stephanus of Byzantium, the name of Derbe was derived from the Lycaonian word for "juniper". Like Iconium, Derbe had the name of Claudius as an honorific prefix: well into the second century at least it was known as Claudioderbe. It lay near – perhaps even beyond[33] – the frontier between the Roman province of Galatia and the client kingdom of Commagene (governed by Rome's ally Antiochus IV from A.D. 41 to 72), a frontier which cut the old territory of Lycaonia in two. This was the farthest stage of Barnabas and Paul's present journey: having preached in Derbe and made some converts there they retraced their steps, visiting and encouraging the members of the newly-planted churches of Lystra, Iconium and Pisidian Antioch. Luke's statement that they now "appointed elders" in those churches (Acts 14: 23) has been questioned, as presupposing a stage of church administration more characteristic of the Pastoral Epistles.[34] Luke may use the terminology of the Pastoral Epistles, but if Paul, some years later, could tell the Thessalonian church to give due respect to its "leaders and counsellors" (1 Thessalonians 5: 12 f.) and indicate to the Corinthian church which of its members were worthy of recognition because of their "special service to the people of God" (1 Corinthians 16: 15–18), there is no reason why Barnabas and he should not have taken appropriate action at this earlier date in respect of those who had begun to develop the qualities of leadership in the young churches of South Galatia. In addition to giving them what help was necessary in this regard, they urged them to stand firm in their new-found faith and not to be dismayed by hardship and persecution, for these were inseparable from Christian existence in this age: "through many tribulations we must enter the kingdom of God" (Acts 14: 22).

They then continued their journey to the coast, back through Perga to Attaleia, where they took ship for the mouth of the Orontes, and so returned to Syrian Antioch. Thanks to their enterprise since they had set out, the church of Syrian Antioch was now a mother-church in her own right, with several flourishing daughter-churches, mainly Gentile in composition like herself.

Observations on Paul's First Missionary Journey", in *Apostolic History and the Gospel*, ed. W. W. Gasque and R. P. Martin [Exeter, 1970], pp. 156–161).

33. Possibly beyond, according to G. Ogg, "Derbe", *NTS* 9 (1962–63), pp. 367–370; B. Van Elderen, *loc. cit.*, pp. 159 f.

34. Cf. E. Haenchen, *The Acts of the Apostles*, E.T. (Oxford, 1971), p. 436.

# CHAPTER 17

# The Gentile Problem

*1. Repercussions in Jerusalem*

NEWS OF THE EXPANSION OF GENTILE CHRISTIANITY NATURALLY brought pleasure to the church of Antioch, but it was received with mixed feelings in Jerusalem. It was good, certainly, that so many Gentiles had come to acknowledge Jesus as Lord. But when the Jerusalem leaders had shaken hands with Barnabas and Paul, they had scarcely envisaged such a rapid influx of Gentile believers. Hitherto they had tried to maintain some measure of control over the extending Christian mission, but this was henceforth going to prove more and more difficult. It does not appear that they were specifically consulted about Barnabas and Paul's recent mission to Cyprus and South Galatia.[1] Any concern which they felt about this should not be put down merely to a desire to keep the reins of power in their own hands. There was an important question of principle at stake, as they saw it: with such an increase in the number of Gentile Christians, to a point where they must soon outnumber Jewish Christians (if they had not done so already), how were the church's ethical standards to be safeguarded? Jews in general had no great opinion of Gentile morality,[2] and the church's ethical standards were based on the peculiarly demanding requirements of Jesus. Jesus may have relaxed various non-ethical prescriptions of Jewish tradition, such as those relating to food restrictions and sabbath observance, but he sharpened the ethical prescriptions, carrying them back beyond overt speech and action to the hidden motives and emotions of the heart,[3] and insisting on "the weightier matters of the law, justice and mercy and faith" (Matthew 23: 23). His disciples were taught to practise a righteousness exceeding "that of the scribes and Pharisees" (Matthew 5: 20) – no easy matter. But it was evident

1. T. W. Manson, *Studies in the Gospels and Epistles* (Manchester, 1962), pp. 176 f., suggests that this was the purpose of Barnabas and Paul's Jerusalem visit of Galatians 2: 1–10.

2. Paul's indictment of paganism in Romans 1: 18 ff. is a commonplace in Jewish literature of the period; cf. Wisdom 13: 1 ff. (especially 14: 12); *Letter of Aristeas*, 134–138.

3. Cf. Matthew 5: 21 ff.

that Gentiles would have a hard task to bring their practice, especially in relations between the sexes, up to the ordinary Jewish level, let alone that of the scribes and Pharisees. What could be done to protect Christian standards?

It was all very well for Barnabas and Paul to forge ahead with Gentile evangelization, but meanwhile the Jerusalem leaders had to discharge their own responsibility to commend the gospel to their fellow-Jews. The discharge of this responsibility would not be rendered any easier by reports that large numbers of Gentiles were entering the new fellowship on what must have seemed to be very easy terms. The whole issue of the approach to Gentiles was a delicate one in the Jerusalem situation. During the brief reign of Herod Agrippa as king of the Jews there had been a short but sharp campaign against at least one section of the Jerusalem church, in which the apostles, far from being unmolested as they had been in the earlier persecution which followed Stephen's death, were now the principal targets of attack. James the son of Zebedee had been executed and Peter would have shared his fate had he not escaped from prison and gone into hiding.[4] This attack on the apostles was not unconnected with the recent first steps in Gentile evangelization, such as Peter's visit to Cornelius in Caesarea [5] – first steps which, cautious though they were, apparently lost the apostles much of the public goodwill which they had formerly enjoyed in Jerusalem.

Herod Agrippa's attack came to an end with his sudden death in A.D. 44, but fresh trouble for the church sprang up from another quarter. Judaea reverted to the control of Roman procurators, under whom during the next eight years there was a succession of militant actions led by men who might be generally described as Zealots, even if they did not all adopt this designation. Josephus, less politely, calls them brigands or impostors.[6] Most important of these insurgent leaders were two sons of Judas the Galilaean, James and Simon by name, who were caught and crucified by Tiberius Julius Alexander (procurator c. 46–48).[7] Such insurgents were not only fiercely anti-Roman; they showed hostility also to those Jews whom they suspected of collaborating with the Romans.[8] Those principally guilty in this last respect were members of the chief-

4. Acts 12: 1 ff.
5. Acts 10: 1–11: 18.
6. While Zealots as such are first mentioned by Josephus when he so describes the extremists among the insurgents in Jerusalem in the winter of A.D. 66–67 (*BJ* ii. 651), he makes it plain that they are the same people to whom he refers pejoratively as "bandits" (λῃσταί) from the rising of Judas the Galilaean in A.D. 6 onwards (*Ant.* xviii. 8).
7. Josephus, *Ant.* xx. 102.
8. Josephus, *BJ* ii. 254 ff.; *Ant.* xx. 186 f.

priestly establishment, but even a pious body of humble Jews, like the Jerusalem church, would incur their disfavour if they, or their associates elsewhere, were thought to be building bridges to the Gentile world.

On religious and political grounds alike, then, the Gentile mission was bound to pose problems for the Jerusalem church and its leaders. Some members of the church suggested a simple solution: Gentile converts to Christianity should comply with the same requirements as Gentile converts to Judaism – they should be circumcised (if they were men) and undertake to keep the law of Moses. This would not only limit the intake of Gentiles into the church; it would ensure that those who did enter it would have to observe an acceptable ethical standard. Even the Zealots could have no valid argument against the admission of Gentiles on these terms. If this suggestion were adopted, however, it would have a disconcerting effect on the large number of Gentiles who had already been admitted to Christian fellowship without any such requirements – in Caesarea, Antioch, and places farther afield. Nevertheless, the suggestion commended itself to many, and some were disposed to insist on it, especially those who had links with the Pharisees. How far they could count on the support of the leadership of the Jerusalem church is uncertain: the apostles had already compromised themselves in the eyes of such rigorists, but they may have hoped for the approval of James the Just, who was respected by all the people for his piety and self-denial.[9]

## 2. Confrontation at Antioch

Some of these people visited Antioch and tried to impose their line on the Gentile Christians there: "Unless you are circumcised according to the custom of Moses, you cannot be saved" (Acts 15: 1). This may well be the situation to which Paul refers when he speaks about the "false brethren" who infiltrated the Gentile-Christian fellowship "to spy out our freedom which we have in Christ Jesus, that they might bring us into bondage" (Galatians 2: 4). This, too, provides a setting in which we can place the incident which Paul recounts in Galatians 2: 11–14:

When Cephas came to Antioch I opposed him to his face, because he stood condemned. For before certain men came from James, he ate with the Gentiles; but when they came he drew back and separated himself, through fear of the circumcision party. The rest of the Jews who were there joined in this play-acting; matters went so far that even Barnabas was carried away into joining their play-acting. But when I saw that they were deviating from the straight path of gospel truth, I

9. Cf. Josephus, *Ant.* xx. 200.

said to Cephas in front of them all, "If you, Jew as you are, live in the
Gentile and not the Jewish way, how is that you try to compel the
Gentiles to live like Jews?"

The picture that Paul here gives of Peter's habitual practice agrees
with the picture that Luke gives in Acts. From his vision on the flat
roof of Simon the tanner's house in Joppa and from his experience
with Cornelius and his household at Caesarea Peter had learned
that he "should not call any one common or unclean" (Acts 10:
28). Having broken decisively with his former practice and eaten
with Gentiles at Caesarea, he continued to eat with Gentiles
thereafter as opportunity offered. So, when he visited Syrian Antioch some time, probably, after Barnabas and Paul's return from
Asia Minor, he had no difficulty in enjoying table fellowship with
Gentile Christians there. This was as true of ordinary social meals
as of the special meal of bread and wine which Christians took as
the memorial of their Lord and as a sign of their joint participation
in him; in fact, no practical distinction could be made between the
two, since the memorial bread and wine were normally taken in the
context of a social meal. It is Peter's habitual practice that gives
point to Paul's charge of "play-acting" (*hypokrisis*) against him
when he withdrew from table fellowship with Gentile Christians
and ate with Jewish Christians only. Had Paul been confronted
with a convinced Judaizer, an advocate of the circumcision of Gentile converts, he would have rebuked him too, but in different
terms: he would not have charged him with "play-acting", for such
a man, even if his conduct amounted to "perverting the gospel of
Christ" (Galatians 1: 7), would be acting in accordance with his
true convictions. But Peter was no judaizer; in the company of Gentile Christians he was quite happy to live like a Gentile himself.
Why, then, did he suddenly charge his course?

This question could be answered more adequately if Peter's own
account of the incident had been preserved alongside Paul's, and
more particularly if we knew exactly the part played by "certain
men" who "came from James". These are not identified by Paul
with the "false brethren" whose infiltration he deplores; they
appear rather to have been commissioned by James to deliver a personal message to Peter. One variant reading, indeed, refers in the
singular to "a certain person" who "came from James".[10] The
message conveyed to Peter could have been to the effect that news
of his free and easy intercourse with Gentiles at Antioch had come
to Jerusalem and was causing scandal to many good brethren

---

10. Gk. τινα for τινας . D. W. B. Robinson, "The Circumcision of Titus and
Paul's 'Liberty' ", *Australian Biblical Review* 12 (1964), pp. 40 f., takes τινα as
neuter plural — "certain things" — and suggests that the reference may be to the
contents of the Jerusalem decree of Acts 15: 28 f, (see p. 184).

there, besides hampering the mission in which James and others were engaged among their Jewish neighbours.[11] The reported conduct of the prince of the apostles was being exploited by unsympathetic scribes and Pharisees to the detriment of the Christian cause in Judaea, and might even provoke violent reprisals from those militants who condemned fraternization with non-Jews as treasonable.[12]

It is not difficult to appreciate Peter's dilemma, or to see how he could have defended his change of course. Though he could not emulate Paul's versatility, he too was endeavouring to be "all things to all men" for the gospel's sake.[13] For him, as for Paul, the interests of the gospel were paramount, and if the interests of the gospel in Judaea were being prejudiced by his way of life in Antioch, he was prepared to alter that way of life. In his eyes, as in Paul's, there was nothing in the non-ethical realm, such as food, which should be regarded as inherently "unclean", but he might have decided, as Paul was to put it at a later date, "not to eat meat or drink wine or do anything that makes your brother stumble" (Romans 14: 13–21). A major Jewish objection to eating with Gentiles was that, in doing so, one would almost certainly infringe the Jewish food-laws.[14] If, then, Peter's practice in Antioch was a stumbling-block to members of the Jerusalem church whose consciences were scrupulous and unemancipated, he might well think it right to discontinue it for their sakes.

Paul, for his part, was equally concerned on this occasion to safeguard the interests of the gospel and to avoid putting a stumbling-block in the path of his fellow-Christians. The aspect of the gospel that meant most to him was the Gentile mission, and the fellow-Christians whose interests he had most at heart were Gentile Christians. Whatever Peter's motives were, Paul would have regarded them as negligible in comparison with the progress of the Gentile mission and the wellbeing of Gentile Christians. Even worse, if possible, than Peter's action in itself was the effect of his example on other Jewish Christians, and when even Barnabas – the last man of whom it might have been expected – was persuaded to join in withdrawing from table-fellowship with Gentiles, what must the Gentile Christians have thought? They could draw only one

11. Cf. T. W. Manson, *Studies in the Gospels and Epistles*, pp. 179–181. It is indeed possible (but unlikely) that what was said to Peter to make him desist from table-fellowship with Gentiles was additional to James's message.

12. Cf. R. Jewett, "The Agitators and the Galatian Congregation", *NTS* 17 (1970-71), pp. 198 ff.

13. 1 Corinthians 9: 22 f. So Tertullian: "since Paul made himself all things to all men so that he might gain them all, Peter too may well have had this in mind in acting somewhat differently from what he taught" (*Against Marcion* iv. 3.3).

14. Worse still, there was the risk of eating food that had been presented in sacrifice to pagan divinities (see pp. 185 f, 270 ff.).

conclusion: so long as they remained uncircumcised, they were at best second-class citizens in the new community. In that case they might either repudiate the message which (despite what Paul said) consigned them to second-class status in comparison with their fellow-believers of Jewish birth, or they might decide that (despite what Paul said) their best policy was to go the whole way of the proselyte and accept circumcision, since only so could they become first-class citizens. If they took the latter course, this would be what Paul meant when he said that Peter was trying "to compel the Gentiles to live like Jews". Either way, the good which had apparently been achieved at the Jerusalem conference would be undone; the truth of the gospel would be hopelessly compromised. In Christ, Paul believed and affirmed, there was "neither Jew nor Greek" (Galatians 3: 28), whatever distinctions might persist in the world at large. The middle wall of partition between them had been demolished by the work of Christ; Paul would not stand idly by and see it rebuilt, whether as a religious or as a social barrier. The only logical reason for preserving it as a social barrier would be its continuing validity as a religious barrier, and to recognize such a continuing validity, even if it were only in outward behaviour, would be to nullify the grace of God. If God's redeeming grace was to be received by faith, and not by conformity with the law of Moses, then it was available on equal terms to Jew and Gentile, and to make a distinction in practice between Jewish and Gentile believers, as Peter and the others were doing, was in practice to deny the gospel.

What the immediate outcome of this confrontation between Paul and Peter was cannot be known with certainty. Perhaps the Galatian Christians, to whom Paul relates the incident, were aware of the sequel; perhaps the situation was still fluid when Paul wrote. Such information as we can glean about Peter after this does not suggest that he persisted for long in this charade of "separate tables". Peter was more conservative than Paul, no doubt, but since at heart he was in basic agreement with Paul he probably resumed his more liberal course when the awkward situation at Antioch was a thing of the past. At any rate, Paul here does not say how Peter responded to his rebuke, for his account of the rebuke merges into a more general comment on the principles involved, for the benefit of his Galatian readers.

## 3. The letter to the Galatians

Since there is no document in the New Testament more indisputably Paul's than the letter to the Galatians, it is strange that there is no unanimity on its date, or even on the identity of "the churches of Galatia" to which it is addressed. If there is no unanimity, the reason must be that the evidence is not unambiguous. It was evidently written by Paul to warn his Galatian converts against certain "trouble-makers" [15] who were urging upon them a line of teaching and course of action which, as he saw the situation, threatened to undermine the gospel which he had brought to them and which they had accepted. But even on the character and policy of these "trouble-makers" there is disagreement.

The view adopted here – provisionally, not dogmatically – is that the letter was written shortly after the confrontation at Antioch, to the churches recently planted by Barnabas and Paul in cities of South Galatia, and that the "trouble-makers" were visitors to those churches who were insisting, as others of the same outlook did at Antioch, that it was necessary for Gentile converts to be circumcised. That circumcision was a major plank in their religious platform is plain even on a superficial reading of the letter. Along with circumcision, the Galatian Christians were beginning to adopt other Jewish customs, such as the observance of holy days. It is a natural conclusion, then, that the "trouble-makers" were judaizers, and this indeed has been the general opinion. In more recent times the opinion has been expressed by some scholars that the "trouble-makers" were inculcating a form of gnosticism. [16] This is a term which is capable of a wide range of meaning. Strictly it denotes a lop-sided and over-intellectualized development of Christian teaching which is well attested in the second century, but in so far as first-century anticipations of it can be traced, they may be described as incipient gnosticism. Such incipient gnosticism is presupposed (and deprecated) in 1 Corinthians [17] and Colossians. [18] It may be that the "trouble-makers" in Galatia told their hearers that they were imparting to them the true knowledge (gnōsis) of God: this might be the point of Paul's remark in Galatians 4: 9, "now that you have come to know God, or rather to be known by God". But the incipient gnosticism which has been discerned in this letter is much more likely to have arisen in the minds of modern interpreters from a misunderstanding of some of Paul's arguments in it than to be part of the propaganda of the "trouble-makers." [19]

15. Galatians 1: 7; 5: 12.
16. Cf. W. Schmithals, *Paul and the Gnostics*, E.T. (Nashville/New York, 1972), pp. 13 ff. See also the earlier studies by W. Lütgert, *Gesetz und Geist* (Gütersloh, 1919), and J. H. Ropes, *The Singular Problem of the Epistle to the Galatians* (Harvard Theological Studies, 14 [1929]), and a judicious survey by R. McL. Wilson, "Gnostics – in Galatia?" in *Studia Evangelica* iv, ed. F. L. Cross = *Texte und Untersuchungen* 102 (Berlin, 1968), pp. 358–367.
17. See p. 261.
18. See pp. 408 ff.
19. See R. McL. Wilson, "Gnostics – in Galatia?" p. 361, in criticism of Schmithals.

If the "trouble-makers" were judaizers – or even if they were gnostics – the first response to their teaching would have been, "But this is not what we were taught!" Such a response would have provoked the question: "Who taught you?" If they replied, "Barnabas and Paul", then they would be told that the authority of Jerusalem was superior to Barnabas and Paul's – in fact, that Barnabas and Paul had no authority apart from that conferred on them by the leaders of the Jerusalem church.

Paul, says Luke, was recognized as "the chief speaker" by the men of Lystra (Acts 14: 12), and they probably shared this recognition with the men and women in other South Galatian cities. It is probable that the "trouble-makers" saw that it was Paul's authority in particular that had to be diminished in the eyes of the Galatian Christians. If so, they showed wisdom, even if they did not know of Barnabas's recent action in Syrian Antioch. In any case, it is Paul's own authority that he defends in his letter because, whatever might be said of the source of Barnabas's authority, Paul claimed to have received his, without human mediation, from the risen Christ.

Paul devotes a good part of the letter to an autobiographical outline, in which his main point seems to be to prove that at no time between his conversion and the date of writing the letter had the Jerusalem leaders an opportunity of conferring any authority on him: rather, they recognized the authority which he already possessed and by virtue of which he had been energetically discharging an apostolic ministry for several years. This presupposes that the "trouble-makers" maintained that his authority *was* derived from Jerusalem and therefore dependent on Jerusalem. But, if they were judaizers, could they maintain that Paul had derived his gospel from Jerusalem and yet find fault with a gospel so derived? Does not their criticism of the gospel which, as they insisted, Paul received from the Jerusalem leaders, imply that they rejected the authority of the Jerusalem leaders – that, consequently, they were not judaizers but more probably gnostics?

Not necessarily. Their argument may well have run along these lines: "Paul has no authority of his own, no gospel of his own, apart from what he has received from Jerusalem. But he has not given you the whole Jerusalem gospel. The Jerusalem believers, with their leaders, revere the law of Moses; every man among them has been circumcised. Of course they did not receive circumcision when they accepted Jesus as the Messiah, because they were circumcised already. But you were uncircumcised when you believed the gospel; if you are to be on the same footing as the Jerusalem Christians and to be acknowledged by them as fellow-heirs of salvation, fellow-members of the people of God, you must be circumcised too. If Paul told you otherwise, he had no authority to do so. His gospel is all right so far as it goes, but it is defective: be ruled by us, and have the deficiencies made good at once".

Paul's position on the circumcision question was clearcut because he had thought it through; the Jerusalem leaders had not as yet had any occasion to think it through, and so their position was not so clearcut. The conversion of Cornelius, and even the in-gathering of Gentile believers at Antioch, had been treated by them on an *ad hoc* basis. When, as a result of the current agitation, they were compelled to think it through, they reached the same conclusion as Paul, in so far as they came to agree that circumcision was not to be imposed on Gentile Christians. As Paul saw the new situation introduced by the coming of Christ, circumcision was no longer of any account. A man might be circumcised or uncircumcised: it made no difference in his relation to God.[20] What Paul did oppose was the idea that, by submitting to circumcision as a religious obligation, a man could acquire merit in God's sight. Similarly, the observance of certain days or of various food restrictions was neither here nor there, unless it was thought that such observance was necessary to win divine approval. These were features of the old order of law, which had been superseded by the new order of grace. Once Paul had relied on these and other forms of legal obedience for his justification before God: now he had found a more excellent way. But if, as those people maintained, "justification were through the law, then Christ died to no purpose" (Galatians 2: 21); in fact, if the law were still in force, as the way of justification, then the age of the Messiah had not yet dawned, and so Jesus could not be the Messiah.[21] No wonder that Paul pronounced an anathema on the bearer of a message which led to this conclusion. Such a message was no gospel, whatever it might be called; it was a travesty of the true gospel.

Moreover, if justification came through the law, then it must be through the whole law. Let no one imagine that the requirements of the law could be satisfied by such a token performance as circumcision. If a man had himself circumcised as a religious obligation, the obligation which he undertook thereby involved the keeping of the law in its entirety. Paul knew from his own experience what that meant: the Galatian Christians had not begun to appreciate it, and even the visitors who were pressing circumcision on them were far from keeping the whole law in any serious sense. One could not pick and choose among the ordinances of the law; it was all or nothing. The law pronounced an explicit curse on all who failed to keep it in its entirety.[22] The gospel showed how men and women

20. Galatians 5: 6; 6: 15; cf. 1 Corinthians 7: 19 (see p. 215, n. 14).
21. See pp. 70, 115, 190.
22. Deuteronomy 27: 26, quoted in Galatians 3: 10.

could be redeemed from that curse by faith in Christ, who by the manner of his death absorbed the curse in his own person. [23]

Again, no one should be misled by the idea that the law, by virtue of its antiquity, had a greater claim to veneration than a message so recent as the gospel. The gospel was the fulfilment of God's promise to Abraham, which antedated the law by centuries. Abraham, whose faith in God was counted to him for righteousness, was the prototype of all who were justified by faith. [24] The law was a parenthetical dispensation, introduced to serve a temporary purpose, but now rendered obsolete by the coming of Christ, the true offspring of Abraham, in whom the promises and their fulfilment were embodied.

The Galatians did not realize what a retrograde step they were being encouraged to take: a step back from freedom to bondage, from maturity to infancy, from the status of sons to the status of servants. They had come of age in Christ: why should they want to revert to the apron-string stage? The beginning of their Christian life had been attended by manifestations of the presence and power of the Spirit: were they now to seek the perfection of Christian life in ordinances of an outmoded regime, related not to the Spirit but to the flesh?

But the majority of the Galatian Christians were converts from paganism, who had never lived under the Jewish law; how could their submission to the yoke of the law be described as a reversion to their former state? The answer to this question reveals perhaps more sharply than anything else how radical was Paul's reorientation to the law which had once been the centre of his devotion. By putting themselves under the law the Galatians would be subjecting themselves to the same *stoicheia* or "elements" under which they had formerly lived as pagans. So Paul, counting himself in along with his converts from paganism, says, "when we were infants" (that is, before we had attained the age of spiritual majority through faith in Christ), "we were slaves to the *stoicheia* of the universe"; but how, he asks (now that they have attained the age of spiritual majority), "how can you turn back again to the weak and beggarly *stoicheia*, whose slaves you want to be once more?" (Galatians 4: 3, 9). Then he immediately gives an example of what he means: "you observe days, and months, and seasons, and years" (Galatians 4: 10). If the observance of such special occasions by way of religious obligation was a form of servitude to the *stoicheia*, then the *stoicheia* are best identified with the planetary bodies by which the calendar was regulated. According to the creation narrative, the heavenly luminaries were ordained not only to give

23. "A hanged man is accursed by God" (Deuteronomy 21: 23, quoted in Galatians 3: 13).
24. Genesis 15: 6, quoted in Galatians 3: 6.

light on earth but also to be "for signs and for seasons and for days and years" (Genesis 1: 14). Pagan religion to a large extent deified the heavenly luminaries; Judaism regarded them as instruments serving their Creator's will. But those who felt themselves compelled to pay special veneration to a calendar regulated by those luminaries were in effect giving them the same status as the pagans did – treating them as elemental powers. Elemental powers indeed they were so long as they dominated men's minds, together with other forces which had the same effect, like the weight of outworn tradition or the pressure of current opinion, but those whose minds were emancipated by the gospel from their domination knew all such influences to be in themselves "weak and beggarly", unable to exercise control where their control was not admitted. But why should people who had experienced the emancipating grace of the gospel submit to those elemental powers all over again? To consent to such bondage afresh was to fall from grace, to cut oneself off from Christ and his liberating gospel. "For freedom Christ has set us free; stand fast therefore, and do not submit again to a yoke of slavery" (Galatians 5: 1).

As regularly in the Gentile mission-field, it was necessary to deal with some converts from paganism who misinterpreted gospel freedom to mean licence to do whatever they chose, to indulge their old propensities unchecked. There is an occasional word of admonition for them too in this letter, but it has the nature of an aside: "you were called to freedom, brethren; only do not use your freedom as an opportunity for the flesh" (Galatians 5: 13). The burden of the letter, however, is the warning against exchanging Christian freedom for legal bondage: that was the main danger at this time in the churches of Galatia. Paul pours out his urgent and affectionate concern for his new-born children in the faith, his hot indignation against those who were upsetting them and leading them astray, and at times his bewilderment at the ease with which they allowed themselves to be hoodwinked. He was one of those men of powerful intelligence who find it difficult to understand how others cannot see a logical argument as clearly as they can themselves, especially when they can be presumed to share the same premises – premises which, in this case, the Galatians had learned from Paul himself. "Who has cast a spell on you?" he asks in his perplexity (Galatians 3: 1).[25]

## 4. The apostolic decree

We do not know what immediate effect the letter had in the churches of Galatia. But the agitation caused in the church of

---

25. Cf. Rosemary Haughton, *The Liberated Heart* (London, 1975), pp. 100 f.

Syrian Antioch by the insistence of the circumcision party led that church to send a deputation to Jerusalem to have the issue settled, if possible, once for all. The apostles who were present in the city together with James and his fellow-elders of the Jerusalem church held a meeting – commonly referred to as the Council of Jerusalem – to consider the question and reach a decision. The Council of Jerusalem, as described by Luke in Acts 15: 6–29, was not an inter-church meeting, despite the presence of the delegates from Antioch; it was a meeting of the leaders of the Jerusalem church. No one could have foretold with confidence the outcome of the meeting. The circumcision of Gentile converts was vigorously advocated by some members of the church. But thanks to Peter's advocacy of the line he had defended when he was questioned about his visit to Cornelius and to James's judicious summing-up, the Jerusalem leaders confirmed their previous practice and gave that confirmation official expression in a written document addressed to the church of Antioch and her daughter-churches in Syria and Cilicia, often called the apostolic decree: circumcision was not to be required of Gentile converts.

> It has seemed good to the Holy Spirit and to us to lay upon you no greater burden than these necessary things: that you abstain from what has been sacrificed to idols and from blood and from what is strangled and from fornication. If you keep yourselves from these, you will do well. Farewell.[26]

The decision against imposing circumcision on Gentile Christians must have given great satisfaction to the church of Antioch, and not least to Paul. He was not likely to change his practice or policy whichever way the verdict went, but his work would have been rendered immeasurably more difficult if Jerusalem had gone on record as insisting on circumcision. No longer would it be possible for "trouble-makers" to visit his churches and claim that the circumcision of Gentile believers was the official policy in the church of Jerusalem.[27] That question was now closed. In fact, an argument for the early dating of Paul's letter to the Galatians, which has been followed here, is that if the Council of Jerusalem, as reported by Luke, had already taken place, Paul could hardly have refrained from mentioning its decision on the main issue with which the letter is concerned. True, he was not disposed to invoke the authority of the Jerusalem church, but a bare statement of

26. Acts 15: 28 f.
27. Paul's warning against the "mutilation" party in Philippians 3: 2 and his insistence in Colossians 2: 11 on the inward and spiritual character of true circumcision do not imply pressure on Gentile Christians by members of the Jerusalem church.

historical fact would have been an effective argument for the cause which he was defending.

Although the apostolic decree did not impose circumcision, it did lay down certain requirements for Gentile converts to observe. These requirements may have been intended to facilitate social intercourse between Jewish and Gentile Christians. Some Gentile practices were specially offensive to Jews, and if these practices were given up, Jewish Christians would feel that an obstacle in the way of table-fellowship and the like with their Gentile brethren had been removed. Three of the requirements have the nature of food-restrictions;[28] the fourth – abstention from fornication – is apparently ethical. While the collocation of ethical and non-ethical requirements may seem strange to us, it would not necessarily have seemed so to Jewish Christians; they were familiar with the juxtaposition of such (to us) disparate requirements in the law.

Perhaps, however, fornication in the decree does not mean general sexual laxity but has a more technical sense. The most elementary teaching given to converts from paganism almost certainly made it clear that fornication and similar practices were incompatible with the Christian way. Even so, the Jerusalem leaders may have felt that no harm would be done by underlining this in the decree. But fornication could bear a more technical sense of marital union within the prohibited degrees of consanguinity or affinity laid down in the Hebrew "law of holiness" (Leviticus 18: 6–18).[29] There are one or two other places in the New Testament where fornication may have this technical sense – e.g. the concession "except on the ground of fornication" added in the Matthaean version of Jesus' prohibition of divorce for his followers (Matthew 5: 32; 19: 9). There may have been some unions which did not flout Gentile convention but would have been scandalous in Jewish eyes.

As for the food-restrictions, these resolve themselves into two: Gentile Christians were to abstain from eating the flesh of animals which had been sacrificed to pagan divinities and flesh from which the blood had not been completely drained (the phrase "and from what is strangled", which is missing in some authorities for the text, simply denotes one form of flesh with the blood still in it). Eating with blood was absolutely tabu for Jews: it is expressly forbidden in Leviticus 17: 10–14 and even earlier, in the command-

---

28. Abstention from eating (*a*) things sacrificed to idols, (*b*) the flesh of strangled animals, (*c*) flesh with blood in it. The second of these is one instance of the third. In the Western text of Acts 15: 20, 29 (cf. 21: 25), these three are reduced to two, idolatry and blood (probably in the sense of bloodshed); with the ban on fornication they constitute a threefold ethical prohibition.

29. The corresponding Hebrew word, *zᵉnût*, is so used in CD 4, ll. 17, 20 ff. (of polygamy and, more particularly, of intermarriage between uncle and niece).

ments enjoined on Noah and his family (Genesis 9: 4).[30] People who had been brought up in the Jewish way of life could not be expected to accept such food at Gentile tables. To eat the flesh of animals which had been sacrificed in pagan temples was regarded as participation (however remotely) in idolatry: this also must be avoided. If a Jewish Christian suspected that the meat set before him in a Gentile house, or the meat shared with a Gentile Christian at a fellowship meal or love-feast, had come from such a tainted source, it would be impossible to sit with him at a common table. Many Gentile Christians were perfectly willing to make practical concessions of this kind: indeed, over wide areas of the Christian world the terms of the apostolic decree were observed for many centuries as essential to the Christian way of life.[31]

What of Paul? Where the principles of the gospel were not at stake he was the most conciliatory of men. He repeatedly urged Christians with robust consciences to be specially considerate of their fellow-Christians whose consciences were less emancipated than their own, even to the point of curbing their personal freedom in the interests of Christian charity, and he was careful to show them a good example in this regard.

He was familiar with an argument, voiced at times by his own Gentile converts, that since sexual activity belonged entirely to the sphere of the body, it was as morally and religiously neutral as food to truly "spiritual" men.[32] But he disagreed completely. Anything which involved personal relations, especially at such a deep level as sexual union, was of the utmost moral and religious importance, and of quite a different order from food. Where fornication was concerned, Paul's own teaching was at one with that of the apostolic decree. People who persisted in this kind of practice must not be tolerated in the church, whether fornication was understood as ordinary commerce with harlots or in the more technical sense, as with the man in the church of Corinth some years later who was openly cohabiting with his father's wife – a breach of the permitted limits of affinity which flouted even pagan convention (1 Corinthians 5: 1).

30. The commandments of Gen. 9: 1–7 were held in rabbinical teaching to be binding on all Noah's descendants, Gentiles as well as Jews. But, according to the oldest form of this teaching, six of these seven "Noachian decrees" had already been enjoined on Adam: only the seventh, the ban on eating flesh with the blood in it (Genesis 9: 4) was given for the first time to Noah (*Deuteronomy Rabba* 2: 25 on Deuteronomy 4: 41; TB *Sanhedrin* 59b). See p. 195 with n. 19.

31. They are regarded as obligatory in the letters to the seven churches of Asia (Revelation 2: 14, 20), and were held to be binding in the churches of the Rhone valley in A.D. 177 (Eusebius, *Hist. Eccl.* v. 1. 26) and by Tertullian in Carthage a decade or so later (*Apology*, 9). In the late ninth century Alfred the Great incorporated them in his English law-code.

Where food laws were concerned, Paul's conscience was completely emancipated. He knew from the teaching of Jesus that no species of food was religiously impure or contaminated in itself; [33] any such impurity or contamination attaching to it had its origin not in the food but in the human mind. But he was anxious not to upset those who were more scrupulous in this respect than he himself was. He would happily accept the food restrictions specified in the apostolic decree if this would facilitate fellowship between Christians, and recommend their acceptance to others on the same ground. But such acceptance must be voluntary, not compulsory, and it must be intelligent, based on the dictates of Christian charity and not on the idea that there was something wrong and impermissible *per se* about certain kinds of food. It is noteworthy that when, in later years, he was asked to give a ruling on this matter, he appealed to first principles and never to the apostolic decree.

The dictates of Christian charity, on which Paul bases his ruling, are summed up by him as "the law of Christ", in fulfilment of which his people should, among other things, "bear one another's burdens" (Galatians 6: 2). When he warns some members of the Galatian churches not to exploit their Christian freedom "as an opportunity for the flesh", this is the corrective which he applies to such licence: "but through love be servants of one another" (Galatians 5: 13). The "law of Christ" is a repromulgation of the injunction of Leviticus 19: 18, "You shall love your neighbour as yourself" (Galatians 5: 14). [34] But when "law" is used in this way, it cannot be understood "legally": the law of love is incapable of being imposed or enforced by external authority. Rather, it is the spontaneous principle of thought and action in a life controlled by the Spirit of Christ; it is willingly accepted and practised. Paul was persuaded that the freedom of the Spirit was a more powerful incentive to the good life than all the ordinances or decrees in the world.

32. 1 Corinthians 6: 13 (see p. 261).
33. Romans 14: 14.
34. Cf. Mark 12: 31 (see p. 58).

# CHAPTER 18

# "What the Law could not do"

*1. Paul's experience of the law*

PAUL'S DAMASCUS-ROAD EXPERIENCE, IN A SENSE, CONTAINED within itself the totality of his apostolic message. But that totality was, naturally, not grasped by him in all its detail immediately. Further "revelations of the Lord" brought home to him the fuller significance of that initial crisis when God "was pleased to reveal his Son" in Paul; his increasing knowledge of Christ enabled him to appreciate more and more that "wisdom of God in a mystery", foreordained before the ages for his people's glory and now at length disclosed in the gospel (1 Corinthians 2: 7). The Damascus-road revelation coincided with his call to preach Christ among the Gentiles, but not until he was fully launched on his career of Gentile evangelization could he understand what this call entailed. His contretemps with Peter and Barnabas at Antioch and his involvement in the Galatian controversy taught him much that he could not otherwise have learned. The essence of his gospel was not affected by these experiences, but his comprehension of it was enriched, as was his appreciation of the ways in which it was to be effectively presented and defended. Justification by faith, so vigorously asserted in the letter to the Galatians, was implicit in his conversion, but now it became in his hands a fighting doctrine – not only a principle *for* which to contend but a weapon *with* which to contend.

Speaking of his Christian standing by contrast with his earlier situation, he describes himself as "not having a righteousness of my own, based on law, but that which is through faith in Christ, the righteousness from God which depends on faith" (Philippians 3: 9). His exchanging his former quest for a righteous status in God's sight through keeping the law for the way of acceptance made available in the gospel suggests that he found his former quest inadequate. But its inadequacy was realized in an instantaneous flash, not by a process of growing disillusionment.

To keep the whole law was no easy task, but it was not impossible. The rich man who assured Jesus that he had kept all the commandments of the decalogue from his youth [1] was no hypocrite, and no more was Paul when, looking back on his earlier life from the

---

1. Mark 10: 20 and parallels.

perspective of twenty to thirty years' Christian experience, he says that "as to righteousness under the law" he was "blameless" (Philippians 3: 6).

The law was God's law; it was the revelation of his will. To keep the law was to do the will of God. To be born under the law was an immense privilege. Unlike Gentiles, who lacked this privilege, a Jew who was "instructed in the law" could know God's will "and approve what is excellent"; he was qualified to be "a guide to the blind, a light to those who are in darkness, a corrector of the foolish, a teacher of children" (Romans 2: 18–20). The words are Paul's, and he spoke from experience. Yet at the time when he wrote he had embraced another way. No longer did he rely upon the law and boast of his relation to God as one who had been born a Jew; no longer did he make his aim the attainment of that righteousness before God which was based on keeping the law. He had found a new way of righteousness, based on faith in Christ.[2] Allegiance to a person had displaced devotion to a code – which was, indeed, not merely a code but more a way of life.

There were many disciples of Jesus in the early church who thought it quite possible – and indeed eminently desirable – to combine faith in Christ with the pursuit of righteousness through keeping the law, but Paul regarded this attitude as an impossible compromise. No one had kept the law with greater devotion than Paul, and the law, far from securing his righteousness before God, actually led him into sin. It was his devotion to the law that made him such a zealous persecutor of the church: his persecuting zeal was but one aspect of his zeal for the law. He persecuted the church with a good conscience: right up to the moment of his confrontation with the risen Christ no shadow of doubt appears to have entered his mind that what he was doing brought pleasure to God. But with the revelation on the Damascus road came the recognition that Jesus was the Messiah; the crucified Jesus was the risen Lord. Then the followers of Jesus had been right after all, and Paul had been terribly wrong. Instead of pursuing the path of righteousness, as he thought, he had been persistently, albeit unwittingly, committing the sin of sins – attacking the witnesses of the Messiah and, through them, attacking the Messiah himself. But he had relied on the law! Given the law and Paul's passionate resolution to keep it, what other course could he have followed? His disillusionment with the law when he understood where his devotion to it had led him is reflected in his words: "I through the law died to the law, that I might live to God" (Galatians 2: 19).[3] When it is pointed out that

2. Philippians 3: 9.

3. It would be a mistake, however, to see here only the reflection of Paul's personal experience: see the exposition of the context in R. C. Tannehill, *Dying and Rising with Christ* (Berlin, 1967), pp. 55 ff.

Paul's attitude to the law is so completely out of step with the general rabbinic attitude as to be unique, we cannot but agree; but his experience was unique.

## 2. Christ the end of the law

It is plain that Paul believed and taught that the law had been in a major sense abrogated by Christ. "Christ is the end of the law", he wrote, "that every one who has faith may be justified" (Romans 10:4). The age of law, which was never designed to be other than a parenthesis in God's dealings with mankind (Galatians 3: 19; Romans 5: 20a), had been superseded by the new age, which might be variously called "the age of Christ", with reference to Christ's reigning at the right hand of God (1 Corinthians 15: 25, quoting Psalm 110: 1), or "the age of the Spirit", with reference to the Spirit's presence with the people of Christ on earth as the pledge of their eternal inheritance in the resurrection life (Romans 8: 10 f.). Was it purely the impact of the Damascus-road event that forced this conclusion on Paul, or had he been in some degree prepared for it in his earlier training?

There are some scholars who have argued for such a preparation. In particular, Rabbi Leo Baeck maintained in an influential essay that Paul had been brought up to accept a doctrine of three epochs of world-history which implied that the reign of law would come to an end with the dawn of the messianic age.[4]

The doctrine of the three epochs is said to be a teaching of the school of Elijah – an expression which, according to W. Bacher, has a similar meaning in relation to *haggadah* to that of "a commandment of Moses from Sinai" in relation to *halakhah* – both expressions denote great antiquity.[5] The doctrine, in that case, was current long before Paul's time.

But in fact we cannot be sure if Paul had been brought up to accept this doctrine. If he had, then the logic of the situation was plain: the epoch of the Messiah had set in, and therefore the epoch of the law was past. But even if he had not, his personal situation involved a logic of its own: Jesus was shown to be the Messiah, and he had accomplished for Paul and in Paul something beyond what the law had accomplished. Whereas the law had led him, all unconsciously, along a path contrary to God's will, his new faith in Jesus as Messiah and Lord brought him consciously into a state of righteousness before God and peace with God. His former zeal for God had been an unenlightened zeal. So long as he was ignorant of

---

4. L. Baeck, "The Faith of Paul", *Journal of Jewish Studies* 3 (1952), pp. 93 ff.; see p. 70 with n. 5.

5. L. Baeck, "The Faith of Paul", pp. 105 f., quoting W. Bacher, *Tradition und Tradenten* (Frankfurt, 1914), pp. 25 ff., 233 f.

the "righteousness that comes from God" and sought to establish his own, he could not submit to God's way of setting men right with himself. But now, as he learned, "Christ is the end of the law, that every one who has faith may be justified" (Romans 10: 2–4).

The affirmation that "Christ is the end of the law" has been variously understood. The word "end" (*telos*) can mean "goal" or "terminus", and here it probably means both. Christ, for Paul, was the goal of the law in the sense that the law was a temporary provision introduced by God until the coming of Abraham's offspring in whom the promise made to Abraham was consummated; the law, in other words, "was our custodian until Christ came, that we might be justified by faith" (Galatians 3: 19, 24). But Christ was also, for that reason, the terminus of the law: if, as Paul says, the law was a temporary provision, the coming of Christ meant that the period of its validity was now at an end.

Some of Paul's interpreters have tried to modify the starkness of this statement; others have tried to sharpen it, or at least to extend its scope. To be sure, if Jewish Christians continued to observe various customs prescribed by the law as part of their inherited way of life, Paul raised no objection: he himself conformed to those customs from time to time when he judged it appropriate to do so.[6] But what he is concerned with in his statement that "Christ is the end of the law" is the place of law in man's approach to God; the *prima facie* meaning of the statement is: now that Christ has come there is no more place for law in man's approach to God. To the thinking of many, this is a hard saying, which lies open to the charge of antinomianism – a charge which Paul met and rebutted in his own day.

The traditional Lutheran doctrine of the threefold use of the law envisages it (i) as a means of preservation, (ii) as a summons to repentance, (iii) as guidance for the church.[8] In so far as the first use involves the administration of law by magistrates for the restraint of evil and the maintenance of good order, this is not an aspect of the gospel; what Paul has to say about this subject may be seen in Romans 13: 1–7. The second use is recognized by Paul as a fact of experience – "through law comes knowledge of sin" (Romans 3: 20) – but not, it appears, as an aid to gospel preaching. It may be held, as a principle of pastoral theology, that confrontation with the law is a salutary means of leading the sinner to

6. Cf. 1 Corinthians 9: 20; Acts 16: 3; 21: 20-26.
7. Cf. Romans 3: 8; 6: 1 ff.
8. Cf. *Formula of Concord* (1576), article 6, in P. Schaff, *The Creeds of Christendom*, iii; *The Evangelical Protestant Churches* (New York, 1878), pp. 130–135. Luther himself, in contrast to his followers, taught only two uses of the law: the *usus theologicus* (sometimes called the *usus spiritualis*) and the *usus politicus* (sometimes called the *usus civilis*). (For this information about Luther I am indebted to Professor James Atkinson.)

acknowledge his inability and cast himself on the mercy of God. But there is no evidence that Paul ever used the law in this way in his apostolic preaching. His hearers, whether Jews or Gentiles, were in bondage, as he saw it, and his message was one of liberation. In fact, when he urges his Gentile converts in the churches of Galatia not to "submit again to a yoke of slavery" (Galatians 5: 1), he implies that by placing themselves under the yoke of the law they would be reverting to the same kind of bondage as they had endured in their pagan past. It appears, indeed, that the angels through whom the law was ordained (Galatians 3: 19) [9] are equated with the "elemental spirits of the world" (Galatians 4: 3, 8) which impose their yoke on the minds of men outside of Christ, whether they be Jews or Gentiles.[10]

As for the third use of the law, Paul's thoughts on the guidance of the church may sometimes be expressed by means of the term "law", but when he speaks of "the law of the Spirit" or "the law of Christ" he uses "law" in a non-legal sense.[11]

In the Reformed tradition derived from Geneva, it has frequently been said that, while the man in Christ is not under law as a means of salvation, he remains under it as a rule of life.[12] In its own right, this distinction may be cogently maintained as a principle of Christian theology and ethics, but it should not be imagined that it has Pauline authority. According to Paul, the believer is *not* under law as a rule of life – unless one thinks of the law of love, and that is a completely different kind of law, fulfilled not by obedience to a code but by the outworking of an inward power. When Paul says, "sin will have no dominion over you, since you are not under law but under grace" (Romans 6: 14), it is the on-going course of Christian life that he has in view, not simply the initial justification by faith – as is plain from the point of the antinomian retort which Paul immediately quotes: "What then? Are we to sin because we are not under law but under grace?" (Romans 6: 15).

Again, it is sometimes said that Christ is the end of the ceremonial law (including not only the sacrificial cultus but circumcision and the observance of the sacred calendar) but not of the moral law.[13] Once more, this is a perfectly valid, and to some extent an obvious, theological and ethical distinction; but it has no

9. For these angelic intermediaries in the giving of the law see Acts 7: 53; Hebrews 2: 2; cf. also Jubilees 1: 29; *Mekhilta* (tractate *Baḥōdeš* 5) on Exodus 20: 18; *Sifre* 102 on Numbers 12: 5; *Pesiqta Rabbati* 21. More general mediation or intercession is ascribed to angels in Philo, *On Dreams* i, 141 ff.; *Testament of Dan* 6: 2.

10. Cf. Colossians 2: 8, 20; see pp. 182 f., 413 ff.

11. See pp. 187, 201 f.

12. Cf. J. Calvin, *Institutio Christianae Religionis* (Edinburgh, 1874 [1559]), ii. 7. 12–15.

13. Cf. Calvin, *Institutio* ii. 7. 17.

place in Pauline exegesis. It has to be read into Paul, for it is not a distinction that Paul himself makes.

As for the sharpening of Paul's assertion that Christ is the end of the law, we may think of Karl Barth's insistence that Christ is the end of *religion* [14] (which may be accepted or refused according to our understanding of the amorphous word "religion"), or of Ernst Fuchs's paraphrase "Christ the end of *history*" – by which he means that Christ, as the *eschaton* in person, achieves for faith the cessation of history (including especially salvation-history) and the beginning of real life.[15] But this is the expression of an existentialist interpretation of the gospel which, however well founded it may be, goes beyond what Paul meant.[16]

## 3. Man under the law

We have quoted Romans 6: 14: "sin will have no dominion over you, since you are not under law but under grace." The implication of these words is as astounding for traditional theological ethics today as in the first century. To be under law – not only the law of Moses but the law of God – means to be under the dominion of sin. To be under grace – the grace of God brought near in Christ – is to be liberated simultaneously from the rule of law and the dominion of sin. So Paul had proved in his own life.

The close association in Paul's mind between sin and the law is illustrated by the parallel analogies of the slave-market (Romans 6: 12–23) and the marriage bond (Romans 7: 1–6). In the former analogy a slave is bound to obey his master; but if the slave dies, or passes by purchase into the ownership of another master, the will of his former master is no longer binding on him. In the latter analogy a woman is bound by law to her husband so long as he lives; but when he dies she is no longer so bound and can legally marry another husband. The second master in the former analogy, like the new husband in the latter analogy, is Christ; but in the former analogy the old master is sin (personified), whereas in the latter

14. K. Barth, *The Epistle to the Romans*, E.T. (Oxford, 1933), pp. 37 ("the perception which moves outwards from God cannot have free course until the arrogance of religion be done away"), 238 ("But religion must die. In God we are rid of it"), 374: "All human religion is directed towards an *end* beyond itself (3: 21); and that *end* is Christ". Barth, however, insists elsewhere that τέλος in Romans 10: 4 means "the 'aim', the contents, the substance, the sum total of the Law, its meaning and at the same time the way to its fulfilment"; he compares Matthew 5: 17 (*A Shorter Commentary on Romans*, E.T. [London, 1959], p. 126).

15. E. Fuchs, "Christus das Ende der Geschichte", *Evangelische Theologie* 8 (1948/9), pp. 447 ff. = *Gesammelte Aufsätze* ii (Tübingen, 1960), pp. 79 ff.; cf. his *Studies of the Historical Jesus*, E.T. (London, 1964), pp. 40, 176 ff.; R. Bultmann, *History and Eschatology* (Edinburgh, 1957), p. 43 ("history has reached its end, since Christ is the end of the law"). See pp. 245 f., 335.

16. Cf. O. Cullmann, *Salvation in History*, E.T. (London, 1967), pp. 40–63.

analogy the old husband is the law (also personified). One and the same transition liberates the soul from slavery to sin and from the yoke of the law. No wonder that Paul goes on to picture an objector as asking if "the law is sin" (Romans 7: 7). Paul cannot agree: the law is God's law; every one of its commandments is "holy and just and good" (Romans 7: 12). Yet we can see how the objector thinks he is carrying Paul's argument to its logical conclusion. According to Paul, the law not only brings sin to light; it forbids sin, indeed, but it stimulates the very thing it forbids. In fact, says Paul, "the power of sin is the law" (1 Corinthians 15: 56).

The analogy of the marriage bond in Romans 7: 1–6 is followed by one of the most controversial exegetical problems in the Pauline corpus. In Romans 7: 7–25 Paul describes the bearing of the law on the life of a man, or on the life of man generically, and uses the first person singular throughout. This use of the first person singular makes the passage ostensibly autobiographical, but is it really autobiographical? Does Paul use "I" dramatically in order to make the experience of the man described more vivid, or does he use "I" representatively, portraying the experience of mankind in terms of his own experience? The latter view was favoured by T. W. Manson: "We may call it autobiography if we like, but here Paul's autobiography is the biography of Everyman." [17]

The passage falls into two sections: (a) verses 7–13, in which the first-personal experience is related in the past tense; (b) verses 14–25, which it is related in the present tense.

It is more particularly in the former of these two sections that Paul's autobiography is the biography of Everyman. "Everyman" in this sense is equivalent to the Old Testament "Adam", and Paul, in effect, is re-telling the Genesis fall story in the first person singular. "I was once alive apart from the law", he says, "but when the commandment came, sin sprang to life and I died. . . . Sin, finding opportunity in the commandment, beguiled me and by it killed me" (Romans 7: 9, 11). Adam and his wife lived a carefree life until they were tested by the commandment banning the fruit of the tree of knowledge: that very commandment, brought to their remembrance by the tempter, directed their attention to the forbidden fruit and made it so irresistibly attractive that they ate it. Sin, which is personified in Paul's account, is given the concrete form of the serpent in the Genesis narrative: as Eve complains "the serpent beguiled me" (Genesis 3: 13), so Paul says "sin beguiled me". The sentence pronounced in advance on the taking of the forbidden fruit was death – "in the day that you eat of it you shall die" (Genesis 2: 17) – and Paul says that he "died" when sin sprang to

17. T. W. Manson, in *Peake's Commentary on the Bible*, ed. M. Black and H. H. Rowley (London and Edinburgh, [2] 1962), p. 945.

life: "sin . . . killed me". Again, the particular form of sin that Paul specifies in this section is covetousness – "sin, finding opportunity in the commandment, wrought in me all kinds of covetousness" (Romans 7: 8), the "commandment" in question being the last commandment of the decalogue: "Thou shalt not covet" (Exodus 20: 17; Deuteronomy 5: 21). Although the prohibition of the forbidden fruit in the fall narrative is not part of the law of Moses, it could well be regarded as an anticipatory instance of the commandment against covetousness. And it could be argued that covetousness is the quintessential sin.

To a large degree, moreover, the fall narrative in Paul's eyes presents in encapsulated form the experience of mankind before and after the promulgation of the law of Moses, as he expounds that experience in Romans 5: 12–21.[18] Although men were sinful by nature before the law was promulgated, says Paul, sin was not accounted to them in the absence of any law: *nulla poena sine lege* (there is no penalty apart from an explicit law, i.e. one can be punished only for the breach of an explicit law). The introduction of law not only brought with it the recognition of sin and the incitement to sin but also accountability for sin and consequent liability to the death-penalty passed on sin. "When the commandment came, sin sprang to life and I died" (Romans 7: 9). Even apart from the law sinful man needed the grace of God, but it took the law to render him aware of that need.

In Romans 7: 7–13, then, Paul repeats in terms of individual experience both the fall narrative and the more general history of mankind before the law and under the law. To understand him, we must forget all that we know of law-codes in the ancient Near East antedating the Exodus; all the pre-Mosaic history accessible to Paul was contained in Genesis and the earlier part of Exodus. Before the time of Moses there was no law in the sense that no law is recorded in scripture. (If we bear in mind the place occupied in rabbinical thinking by the Noachian regulations of Genesis 9: 1–7, which were held to be binding on Gentiles as well as Jews, we may ask what part they played in Paul's scheme of things; from the fact that nowhere in his extant writings is there any reference to them, as indeed there is none to Noah himself, we may conclude that they played little or no part.) [19]

But what element of purely personal reminiscence enters into Paul's account in Romans 7: 7–13? Does he recall what happened when, in his early teens, he became conscious of his personal obligation to keep the law? Is there any personal significance in the

18. Cf. also M. D. Hooker, "Adam in Romans i", *NTS* 6 (1959–60), pp. 297 ff.
19. Cf. C. K. Barrett, *From First Adam to Last* (London, 1962), pp. 23–26. In Paul's eyes the ungodliness of the pagan world consisted in disobedience to the *creation* ordinances (Romans 1: 18 ff.). See p. 186, n. 30.

fact that the one commandment of the decalogue which he cites to illustrate his argument is that which forbids not an outward act or word but an inward attitude or appetite – covetousness? Even if an affirmative answer is to be given to these questions, we have no other record of Paul's early development which would give us anything approaching certainty. His emphatic assertions that throughout his pre-Christian career he maintained without fault the standard of righteousness demanded by the law [20] lead us to conclude that, whatever his first reaction may have been to the realization of his duty to keep the whole law, he quickly learned to live with that duty and preserve a blameless conscience before God.

This last consideration excludes one popular interpretation of Romans 7: 14–25, where Paul moves from the past into the present tense – the interpretation which envisages Paul as being increasingly uneasy in conscience as his persecuting career went on. This section is often quoted as one of the classic descriptions in world literature of the divided mind [21] – the mind of the man who finds himself impelled by a power greater than his own, the power of what Paul calls indwelling sin, to do not the good that he approves and wants to do but the evil that he hates and does not want to do. This is indeed a picture of man under the law, acknowledging that the law's requirements are good but deploring the powerlessness of the law to ensure that its requirements are translated into action. But it is not a picture of Paul's conscious mind while he himself lived under the law. There is no hint that Paul, before his conversion, was the victim of such an inward conflict as he describes here; on the contrary, all the evidence is against it. It may be that Augustine and Luther's discovery that Paul spoke so directly to their condition led to the assumption that, before his conversion, he must have endured the same kind of spiritual disturbance as they endured before theirs, [22] and to the ascribing to Paul of the "introspective conscience of the West", as Professor Krister Stendahl has put it. [23] If Paul's conversion was preceded by a period of subconscious incubation, this has left no trace in our surviving records. The goads against which, as he was told on the Damascus road, it was fruitless for him to kick (Acts 26: 14) were not the prickings of an uneasy

20. Cf. Philippians 3: 6; also Acts 23: 1.

21. Parallels have been adduced from Greek and Latin literature (e.g. Euripides, *Medea* 1078–80; Ovid, *Metamorphoses* vii. 20 f.; *Amores* iii. 4. 17; Horace, *Epistles* i. 8. 11; Epictetus, *Enchiridion* ii. 26. 4), but however similar their wording may be, none of them means exactly what Paul does.

22. Luther's interior conflict was spiritual, while Augustine's was moral, but Paul seems to have been troubled in neither respect before his conversion.

23. K. Stendahl, "The Apostle Paul and the Introspective Conscience of the West", *Harvard Theological Review* 56 (1963), pp. 199 ff. See also the critique of Stendahl in E. Käsemann, *Perspectives on Paul*, E.T. (London, 1969), pp. 60 ff., and Stendahl's reply in *Paul among Jews and Gentiles* (Philadelphia, 1976), pp. 129 ff.

conscience over his persecuting energy but the new forces which were now driving him in the opposite direction to that which he had followed until then. For Paul, in the words of E. K. Lee, "the true meaning of sin was not discovered at the feet of Gamaliel but at the foot of the cross".[24]

In my inmost being, says Paul (whether speaking personally or symbolically), I approve of the law of God – indeed, I delight in it, like the psalmist who sings "Oh, how I love thy law!" (Psalm 119: 97) – "but", he adds, "I see in my members another law at war with the law of my mind and making me captive to the law of sin which dwells in my members" (Romans 7: 23). In this sentence the word "law" is used three times. The first two occurrences denote two opposed principles which wage war within Paul, comparable (we may say) to the evil and good inclination in Jewish anthropology. But what is "the law of sin" to which the former principle makes him captive? Perhaps it is the domination or dictate of sin, which in the previous chapter (as we have seen) is personified as a slave-master; this is rendered the more probable by the language in which Paul sums up the contents of Romans 7: 14 ff.: "So then, I of myself serve the law of God with my mind, but with my flesh I serve the law of sin" (verse 25b). There the law of sin and the law of God are set in sharp contrast.

And yet it may be asked if there is not a sense in which "the law of sin" could be an aspect of the law of God. Earlier in chapter 7 Paul has spoken of the way of freedom from law, and he returns to this in 8: 2: "the law of the Spirit of life in Christ Jesus has set you free from the law of sin and death". Can the law of God, which is by definition holy, be described as "the law of sin and death"? Yes, in so far as it stimulates sin and passes sentence of death on the sinner. As Paul has said in an earlier letter, "the written code kills, but the Spirit gives life" (2 Corinthians 3: 6). What is this but the antithesis of Romans 8: 2 between "the Spirit of life in Christ Jesus" and "the law of sin and death"? If Paul speaks of "the *law* of the Spirit of life in Christ Jesus", he does so as much for the sake of the verbal antithesis with "the law of sin and death" as for anything else: the *law* of the Spirit is the Spirit's vitalizing principle or power.

What Paul is doing in Romans 7: 7–25, in so far as his description is truly autobiographical,[25] is voicing a Christian perspective

24. E. K. Lee, *A Study in Romans* (London, 1962), p. 27.
25. The psychological-autobiographical interpretation of Romans 7: 7–25 received a heavy (though not mortal) blow from W. G. Kümmel, *Römer 7 und die Bekehrung des Paulus* (Leipzig, 1929), to the point where it has been spoken of as "now relegated to the museum of exegetical absurdities" (P. Démann, "Moïse et la loi dans la pensée de saint Paul", in *Moïse, l'homme de l'alliance* [Paris, 1954], p. 229). Kümmel treats the "I" as symbolical, referring to the condition of all Jews under the law.

on his existence under the law, both in the earlier section where he uses the past tense and in the later section where he uses the present tense. Maurice Goguel is probably right in discerning in the exclamation of the later section, "Wretched man that I am!" (Romans 7: 24a),[26] no "abstract argument but the echo of the personal experience of an anguished soul" and also in assigning the experience of this section to the period immediately following Paul's conversion.[27] We can readily believe that a man of Paul's imperious zeal found it no easy matter to win the victory over a hasty tongue, a premature judgement, a resentment at the encroachment of others on the sphere of his own service. These things were not specifically forbidden by the law; it was by the standard of Christ that their sinfulness was revealed to Paul. He can entreat his friends "by the meekness and gentleness of Christ" (2 Corinthians 10: 1), but these qualities did not come to him naturally. The man who knew the importance of self-discipline, "lest after preaching to others I myself should be disqualified" (1 Corinthians 9: 27), the man who pressed on to gain "the prize of the upward call of God in Christ Jesus" (Philippians 3: 14), knew that that "immortal garland" was to be run for "not without dust and heat".[28] But the victory which eluded him who sought it under the law or by his own strength was quickly won when he learned to rely on the aid of the Spirit.

The tension which finds expression in Romans 7: 14–25 is the tension necessarily set up when one lives "between the times" – in two aeons simultaneously.[29] How can one who exists temporally in "the present evil age" nevertheless enjoy deliverance from it and live here and now the life of the age to come? By the aid of the indwelling Spirit, who not only makes effective in the believer the saving benefits of Christ's passion but also secures to him in advance the blessings of the age to come.

## 4. Liberation from the law

It is, then, "the law of the Spirit of life in Christ Jesus" that liberates a man from "the law of sin and death" (Romans 8: 2). "For", Paul continues, God has done what the law could not do, because of the powerlessness of the human nature on which it

26. In the following words, "Who will deliver me from this body of death?" (verse 24b), the "body of death" is human nature in its frailty, existing κατὰ σάρκα.

27. M. Goguel, *The Birth of Christianity*, E.T. (London, 1953), pp. 213 f.; cf. C. H. Dodd, *The Epistle of Paul to the Romans* (London, 1932), p. 107 ("A man is not moved like that by an ideal construction").

28. J. Milton, *Areopagitica* (1644).

29. Cf. A. Nygren, *Commentary on Romans*, E.T. (London, 1952), pp. 291 ff.

operated; he has sent his Son to accomplish a work as man and for man that could not otherwise have been accomplished, "in order that the just requirement of the law might be fulfilled in us, who walk not according to the flesh but according to the Spirit" (Romans 8: 3 f.). The law belongs to the old age, the age of man's spiritual powerlessness (which is expressed by Paul's characteristic use of the noun "flesh"); the Spirit is the earnest of the new age, in which man, liberated from the bondage which is inevitable under the old age, can "do the will of God from the heart" (Ephesians 6: 6)[30] or, as Paul expresses it elsewhere, produce "the fruit of the Spirit" (Galatians 5: 22 f.).

The transition from the old age to the new – from the weakness of the "flesh" to the power of the Spirit – is brought about by the coming of Christ. The ineffectiveness of the law was due to the inadequacy of the "flesh" – weak human nature – to keep it. But in this human nature, "in the likeness of sinful flesh" (Romans 8: 3), the Son of God entered our world. He came as true man of woman born, he lived "under law" (Galatians 4: 4), but triumphed where others failed. Not only did he himself do the will of God from the heart (thus embodying the new covenant) but on behalf of others he endured the curse pronounced by the law on law-breakers (by accepting the form of death which, according to the law, incurred the divine curse) [31] and thus redeemed from that curse whose who were under law, so that they might through faith receive the promised Spirit and adoption as sons in the family of God (Galatians 3: 10–14; 4: 4–6).

Thus by Christ's incarnation and his offering himself for the sin of others, God (says Paul) "condemned sin in the flesh" (Romans 8: 3) – condemned it in human nature as a whole – and inaugurated the new age of spiritual freedom, the age, we may say, of the new covenant.

For in Romans 8: 1–4 Paul echoes the sense, if not the very language, of the new covenant oracle of Jeremiah 31: 31–34. In that oracle there is no substantial difference in content between the law which Israel failed to keep under the old covenant and the law which God undertakes hereafter to place within his people, writing it "upon their hearts". The difference lies between their once knowing the law as an external code and their knowing it henceforth as an inward principle. So for Paul there was no substantial difference in content between the "just requirement of the law" which cannot

30. To live "according to the flesh" means for Paul to live "under law" (i.e. in the old aeon of bondage); to live "according to the Spirit" means to live "under grace" (i.e. in the new aeon of freedom).
31. Deuteronomy 21: 23.

be kept by those who live "according to the flesh" and the just requirement fulfilled in those who live "according to the Spirit". The difference lay in the fact that a new inward power was now imparted, enabling the believer to fulfil what he could not fulfil before. The will of God had not changed; but whereas formerly it was recorded on tablets of stone it was now engraved on human hearts, and inward impulsion accomplished what external compulsion could not. So far as the written requirements of the law were concerned, Paul in his pre-Christian days had kept them punctiliously, but his keeping them all did not add up to doing the will of God from the heart. For the sum of the commandments was love, and this was something which became possible to him only when the divine love was poured into his heart by the Spirit (Romans 5: 5). The reference to the Spirit should remind us that Paul's teaching here points to the fulfilment not only of Jeremiah's "new covenant" oracle but also of the companion oracles in Ezekiel 11: 19 f. and 36: 25–27, where God promises to implant within his people a new heart and a new spirit.

It is to this new heart, "a heart of flesh" (Ezekiel 11: 19; 36: 26), that Paul refers when he says that the message of the new age is written "with the Spirit of the living God, not on tablets of stone but on tablets which are hearts of flesh" (2 Corinthians 3: 3). A written law-code was an inadequate vehicle for communicating the will of God; the will of God was given that form only for a temporary purpose – to make quite clear to man the inability and sinfulness to which he was prone in the flesh – that is, in his creaturely weakness. Doing the will of God is not a matter of conformity to outward rules but of giving expression to inward love, such as the Spirit begets. Hence, says Paul, "the written code kills, but the Spirit gives life" (2 Corinthians 3: 6). The written code kills, because it declares the will of God without imparting the power to do it, and pronounces the death-sentence on those who break it. The Spirit gives life, and with the life he imparts the inward power as well as the desire to do the will of God.

Because it is the promulgation of God's will, the law is "holy and just and good" (Romans 7: 12); because of its effect on man, it might even be described as "the law of sin and death" (Romans 8: 2). But the Spirit is holy in both respects – both as being the Spirit of God and as creating holiness in man. It is the Spirit who renews the minds of the people of God so that they not only approve but do his will – everything, that is, which is "good and acceptable and perfect" (Romans 12: 2). The holiness which the Spirit creates is nothing less than transformation into the likeness of Christ, who is the image of God; and this cannot be effected by external constraint: "where the Spirit of the Lord is, there is freedom" (2 Corinthians 3: 17 f.). The purpose of the law, that men should be holy as God is holy (Leviticus 11: 44 f., etc.), is thus (according to Paul) realized in the gospel.

This may be what Paul means in Romans 3: 31 where, after presenting God's way of justifying sinners, Jews and Gentiles alike, on the same principle of faith, he asks "Do we then overthrow the law by this faith?" and answers his own question: "By no means! On the contrary, we uphold the law." In the immediate context, in which Paul goes on to expound the narrative of Abraham's faith which was reckoned to him for righteousness (Romans 4: 1–25), [32] it might appear that the law which is upheld by the gospel of justification by faith is the Torah in the wider sense – the Pentateuch, and more particularly the Genesis account of Abraham. That is so, but Paul goes on farther to show that the law in its stricter sense, as the embodiment of God's will, is upheld and fulfilled more adequately in the age of faith than was possible "before faith came", when law kept the people of God "under restraint" (Galatians 3: 23). Only in an atmosphere of spiritual liberty can God's will be properly obeyed and his law upheld.

## 5. The law of love

If the law of the Spirit is the law of love, then it is identical with what Paul elsewhere calls "the law of Christ" – "Bear one another's burdens, and so fulfil the law of Christ" (Galatians 6: 2). By "the law of Christ" he may mean "the law which Christ exemplified" or "the law which Christ laid down" when he said that the whole law and prophets depended on the twin commandments of love to God and love to one's neighbour (Matthew 22: 40). [33] This reinterpretation of the law is echoed by Paul when he says that "the whole law is fulfilled in one word: 'You shall love your neighbour as yourself' " (Galatians 5: 14) or that "love does no wrong to a neighbour; therefore love is the fulfilling of the law" (Romans 13: 10).

But the law of love is a different kind of law entirely from that which Paul describes as a yoke of slavery. Love is generated by an inner spontaneity and cannot be enforced by penal sanctions. Reference was made above to the "third use" of the law in Lutheran tradition – its use to provide guidance for the church. [34] So far as Paul is concerned, guidance for the church is provided by the law of love, not by the "law of commandments and ordinances" (Ephesians 2: 15). In his letters he himself lays down guidelines for his converts and others, often couched in the imperative mood, but

32. Genesis 15: 6.
33. See pp. 19, 58, 337.
34. See p. 192.

these guidelines mostly concern personal relations. Food sacrificed to idols, for instance, is ethically and religiously indifferent; what does matter in this or in any other activity is the effect of my conduct and example on others. If I ignore their true interests, he says, then I am "no longer walking in love" (Romans 14: 15). The same principle may be discerned in his instructions about such diverse matters as sexual life or behaviour in church.[35]

This insistence on the law of love, instead of prudential rules and regulations, was felt by many of Paul's Christian contemporaries to come unrealistically near to encouraging moral indifferentism; and many Christians since his day have shared their sentiments. But, unlike Paul's contemporary critics, Christian moralists since Paul's day have tended to hold that, in insisting on prudential rules and regulations, they are following the implications of his teaching, if not his express judgements. But we should appreciate that Paul conforms no more to the conventions of religious people today than he conformed to the conventions of religious people around A.D. 50; it is best to let Paul be Paul. And when we do that, we shall recognize in him the supreme libertarian, the great herald of Christian freedom, insisting that man in Christ has reached his spiritual majority and must no longer be confined to the leading-strings of infancy but enjoy the birthright of the freeborn sons of God. Here if anywhere Luther entered into the mind of Paul: "A Christian man is a most free lord of all, subject to none. A Christian man is a most dutiful servant of all, subject to all." [36] "Subject to none" in respect of his liberty; "subject to all" in respect of his charity. This, for Paul, is the law of Christ because this was the way of Christ. And in this way, for Paul, the divine purpose underlying Moses' law is vindicated and accomplished.[37]

35. Cf. 1 Corinthians 6: 12–20; 11: 17–22.
36. M. Luther, *Tractatus de libertate christiana* (1520), in *Luthers Werke* (Weimar edition), 7 (1897), p. 49.
37. See also T. W. Manson, "Jesus, Paul and the Law", in *Judaism and Christianity*, iii: *Law and Religion*, ed. E. I. J. Rosenthal (London, 1938), pp. 125 ff.; C. F. D. Moule, "Obligation in the Ethic of Paul", in *Christian History and Interpretation: Studies presented to John Knox*, ed. W. R. Farmer, C. F. D. Moule, R. R. Niebuhr (Cambridge, 1967), pp. 389 ff.; E. P. Sanders, "Patterns of Religion in Paul and Rabbinic Judaism: A Holistic Method of Comparison", *Harvard Theological Review* 66 (1973), pp. 455 ff.; D. P. Fuller, "Paul and 'The Works of the Law' ", *Westminster Theological Journal* 38 (1975–76), pp. 28 ff.

# CHAPTER 19

# Flesh and Spirit

## 1. Flesh

FOR PAUL, TO BE "UNDER LAW" IS ONE WAY OF BEING "IN THE flesh". His use of the term "flesh" (*sarx*) plays such a central part in his theology that it calls for careful examination. The background of his terminology is provided by the Old Testament, although the Old Testament usage is extended along lines peculiarly his own.

In the Old Testament "flesh" is the basic material of human and animal life. Apart from occurrences of the word in the sense of animal life in general (as in Genesis 6: 19) [1] or the meat of animals which may or may not be eaten (as in Exodus 12: 8), men are categorized as "flesh" in contrast to "the gods, whose dwelling is not with flesh" (Daniel 2: 11). When God imposes a limit on the duration of human life, he says, "My spirit shall not abide in man for ever, for he is flesh" [2] (Genesis 6: 3). Man, in fact, is animated flesh: "all flesh" means "all mankind" (except in a few places where it has the wider sense of "all animal life"). "Flesh" may denote human nature in its weakness and mortality: "he remembered that they were but flesh" (Psalm 78: 39). It can be used of the human body, as when a man is directed to "wash his flesh in water" (e.g. Leviticus 14: 9), or of the man himself in a more general sense, as in Psalm 63: 1, where "my flesh faints for thee" stands in synonymous parallelism with the preceding clause, "my soul thirsts for thee" – here both "my soul (Heb. *nefeš*)" and "my flesh (Heb. *bāśār*)" are little more than alternative ways of saying "I".

We turn, then, to Paul's usage against this Old Testament background.

First, he uses "flesh" in the ordinary sense of "bodily flesh", as in Romans 2: 28, of literal circumcision (cf. Genesis 17: 11), by con-

1. Where a male and a female "of every living thing of all flesh" were to be taken by Noah into the ark; so also in Genesis 7: 15 f. Apart from these, "all flesh died" (Genesis 7: 21).
2. This is the probable meaning (cf. NEB: "he for his part is mortal flesh"); less likely is the suggestion in RV margin: "in their going astray they are flesh" (Hebrew *bᵉšaggām hû' bāśār*).

203

trast with spiritual circumcision, the circumcision "of the heart",[3] or in 2 Corinthians 12: 7, where he describes his physical affliction as his "thorn (splinter) in the flesh" (cf. Galatians 4: 13).[4] More generally, when he speaks in Galatians 2: 20 of "the life I now live in the flesh", he means "in mortal body".

Next, he uses "flesh" in the sense of natural human descent or relationship, as when Christ is said to be David's descendant or a member of the race of Israel "according to the flesh" (Romans 1: 3; 9: 5), when Abraham is called "our forefather according to the flesh" (Romans 4: 1) and his biological descendants are called "the children of the flesh" as against "the children of the promise" (Romans 9: 8; cf. Galatians 3: 7; 4: 23 ff.), or when the Jews are referred to as Paul's "kinsmen according to the flesh" (Romans 9: 3) or simply his "flesh" (Romans 11: 14).[5]

In the third place, he uses "flesh" in the sense of "mankind", as in Galatians 2: 16 and Romans 3: 20, "no flesh shall be justified by works of the law", or 1 Corinthians 1: 29, "so that no flesh might boast in the presence of God". Sometimes he expresses the same idea by the phrase "flesh and blood", as in Galatians 1: 16, "I did not confer with flesh and blood" (i.e. with any human being).[6]

But most distinctively, he uses "flesh" in the sense of "human nature", in the following ways:

(a) *Weak human nature.* In Romans 6: 19 Paul explains himself by means of an analogy from everyday life "because of the weakness of your flesh" (i.e. your natural understanding). In Romans 8: 3 he speaks of the law as unable to produce righteousness because it was "weakened by the flesh" (i.e. by the frail human nature with which it had to work). He speaks of an occasion when, because of his anxiety over his friends at Corinth, his "flesh (*sarx*) had no rest" (2 Corinthians 7: 5); he refers to the same experience in 2 Corinthians 2: 13 by saying "I had no rest for my spirit (*pneuma*)" – a remarkable instance of the practically synonymous usage of two nouns which are normally antithetical in his writings (and not in Paul's writings only, as is indicated by the familiar antithesis of Mark 14: 38, "the spirit indeed is willing, but the flesh is weak").

(b) *The human nature of Christ.* The humanity of Christ is shared by him with all mankind. But ours is "sinful flesh", because sin has established a bridgehead in our life by means of which it dominates the human situation. Christ came in real flesh – he lived and died in a "body of flesh" (Colossians 1: 22)[7] – but he did not come in "sinful flesh", because sin gained no foothold in his life; he is said

3. Cf. Deuteronomy 10: 16; 30: 6; Jeremiah 4: 4; Philippians 3: 3.
4. See p. 135.
5. Cf. 2 Samuel 5: 1.
6. See p. 81.
7. Cf. Colossians 2: 11; the Hebrew equivalent occurs in 1 Qp Hab. 9, 1. 2.

therefore to have come "in the *likeness* of sinful flesh",[8] so that, when he presented his life as a sin-offering, God thus "condemned sin in the flesh" (Romans 8: 3) – passed the death-sentence on it by virtue of the sinless humanity of Christ.

(c) *Unregenerate humanity.* Paul at times denotes the sinful propensity which belongs to his heritage "in Adam"[9] as "my flesh". In "my flesh" in this sense nothing good resides; with it, he says (perhaps speaking representatively) "I serve the law of sin" (Romans 7: 18, 25).[10] Its surviving influence can be traced even in the regenerate: the Corinthian Christians, for example, are addressed as "men of the flesh", despite their having received the Spirit, because they are still prone to jealousy and strife and judge men according to the standards of worldly wisdom (1 Corinthians 3: 1–4). The "works of the flesh", listed in Galatians 5: 19–21 in contrast to the "fruit of the Spirit", include not only sensual vices like fornication and drunkenness but mental attitudes like jealousy, anger and party spirit. "Those who belong to Christ Jesus", however, "have crucified the flesh with its passions and desires" (Galatians 5: 24) – a statement similar to that of Romans 6: 6, "our old man (NEB 'the man we once were') was crucified with him [Christ], so that the sinful body [the sin-dominated nature that was ours 'in Adam'] might be destroyed".[11] That the "flesh" was crucified with Christ and can yet be a menace to the believer is one aspect of a paradox that recurs repeatedly in Paul's writings. Believers are said to have "put off the old man" and "put on the new man" (Colossians 3: 9 f.), while elsewhere they are exhorted to do just that – to "put off the old man" and "put on the new man" (Ephesians 4: 22, 24). The "old man" is what they once were "in Adam", the embodiment of unregenerate humanity; the "new man" is what they now are "in Christ", the embodiment of the new humanity. Therefore to "put on the new man" is to "put on Christ": if Paul can say that all who were baptized into Christ "have put on Christ" (Galatians 3: 27), he can also urge such people to "put on the Lord Jesus Christ" (Romans 13: 14) and thus be in practice what they already are by the call of God.

Though "my flesh" (as Paul thus puts it) is still a reality to the believer, he is no longer "in the flesh" in this sense. To be "in the flesh" in this sense is to be unregenerate, to be still "in Adam", in a

8. Literally, "in likeness of flesh of sin"; cf. A. Nygren, *Commentary on Romans*, E.T. (London, 1952), pp. 313 ff.; C. E. B. Cranfield, *The Epistle to the Romans*, ICC, i (Edinburgh, 1975), pp. 379 ff. See p. 199.

9. See p. 329.

10. See p. 197.

11. Cf., however, R. H. Gundry, *"Sōma" in Biblical Theology* (Cambridge, 1976), p. 39; he distinguishes "the body of sin" from the "flesh" in that the former "is the body which sin, or the flesh, dominates". Its destruction, he says, is its "future dissolution" and replacement by the resurrection body (*ibid.*, pp. 57 f.).

state in which one "cannot please God" (Romans 8: 8). Believers were formerly "in the flesh" (Romans 7: 5), but now they are "not in the flesh, but in the Spirit", if the Spirit of God really dwells within them – and if he does not, they have no title (according to Paul) to be called the people of Christ (Romans 8: 9).

Since, then, believers are no longer "in the flesh" but "in the Spirit", they should no longer live "according to the flesh" but "according to the Spirit" (Romans 8: 4 f., 12 f.). They have exchanged their unregenerate outlook ("the mind of the flesh") for that which is proper to the children of God ("the mind of the Spirit"); it is their duty henceforth to "make no provision for the flesh, to gratify its desires" (Romans 8: 5–7; 13: 14).

The "flesh" is subject to the law of sin and death and so is under sentence of death: "if you live according to the flesh, you will die" (Romans 8: 13); "for he who sows to his own flesh will from the flesh reap corruption" (Galatians 6: 8). Sin, of any kind, is a "work of the flesh", and results in death.

Sometimes the word "body" is used in place of "flesh". What are called "the works of the flesh" in Galatians 5: 19 are called "the deeds of the body" in Romans 8: 13.[12] So also "the body of sin" (Romans 6: 6) is a near-synonym of "sinful flesh" (literally "flesh of sin") in Romans 8: 3. We may compare "this body of death" in Romans 7: 24, from which deliverance is so earnestly sought.[13] On the other hand, the "body" of Romans 8: 10, which is "dead because of sin", is simply the mortal body of flesh and blood, which at the resurrection is to be replaced by the "spiritual body" (1 Corinthians 15: 44).[14] "Body" for Paul is an altogether nobler word than "flesh". When he says that "the body is . . . for the Lord, and the Lord for the body", calls the believer's body "a temple of the Holy Spirit", and urges his Corinthian converts to "glorify God" in their "body" (1 Corinthians 6: 13, 19, 20), it would be inconsistent with his usage to replace "body" by "flesh", just as he speaks of the redemption of the body (as in Romans 8: 23) and not of the resurrection of the flesh. The flesh, in the distinctive Pauline sense, is doomed to die; the body is destined for immortality.

## 2. Spirit

In the Old Testament, as in the New, "spirit" is the antithesis of "flesh". "The Egyptians are men, and not God; and their horses

12. "The deeds of the body have their immediate source in the *sōma*, but their ultimate source in the *sarx*, which dominates the *sōma* and is thereby indistinguishable from it" (R. H. Gundry, *op. cit.*, p. 39).

13. "But here the body of death is not 'flesh' in the sense of sin itself; it is the physical body destined to die because within its members dwells the law of sin and death" (Gundry, *op. cit.*, p. 40).

14. Cf. Gundry, *op. cit.*, pp. 43–45.

are flesh, and not spirit" (Isaiah 31: 3). God, by implication, is Spirit (cf. John 4: 24); not only so, but the Spirit of God energizes men and imparts to them physical power, mental skill or spiritual insight (expressed pre-eminently in prophetic utterance) that they would not otherwise have. So, in Paul, the antithesis to "flesh" is "spirit" – not so much the human spirit as the Spirit of God. [15]

The Old Testament prophets foretold a coming age which would be marked in a special way by the activity of the Spirit of God. Two strands of this expectation are specially important. In one, the activity of the Spirit is associated with a coming figure – variously depicted as the ideal ruler of David's line (Isaiah 11: 1 ff.) and as the humble and self-sacrificing Servant of the Lord (Isaiah 42: 1 ff.) – who would be anointed with the Spirit in order to discharge a ministry of mercy and judgment for Israel and the nations. In the other, the promise is given that in days to come the same Spirit will be poured out on "all flesh", so that the gift of prophetic utterance will no longer be confined to a chosen few but will be widespread (Joel 2: 28 f.). [16]

These two strands of expectation are brought together in the New Testament with the beginning of Jesus' public ministry. The Spirit came upon him in power at his baptism, so that he could identify himself with the speaker of Isaiah 61: 1 f.: "The Spirit of the Lord is upon me, because he has anointed me to preach good news to the poor . . ." (Luke 4: 18 f.). At the same time, John the Baptist pointed to him as the Coming One who would baptize with the Holy Spirit (Mark 1: 8; John 1: 32–34). Jesus, then, receives a special endowment of the Spirit of God and in turn imparts this Spirit to others.

When and how this impartation of the Spirit to others would be effected might be a matter of debate, but two of the Evangelists unambiguously view it as dependent on the passion and triumph of Jesus. "As yet the Spirit had not been given", [17] says the Fourth Evangelist, referring to Jesus' ministry in Jerusalem, "because Jesus was not yet glorified" (John 7: 39), while the author of Luke-Acts, in one of the most remarkable "undesigned coincidences" of the New Testament, narrates the outpouring of the Spirit by the exalted Jesus on the first Christian Pentecost, together with the sequel to that outpouring, in a manner which practically documents the detailed fulfilment of the promise of the Spirit given by Jesus in the upper-room discourse of John 14–16. [18]

15. In 2 Corinthians 7: 1, "let us cleanse ourselves from every defilement of flesh and spirit", it is the human spirit that is meant.

16. See pp. 55, 60, 428 ff.

17. Literally "Spirit was not yet". Cf. John 16: 7 (one of Jesus' upper-room promises about the Paraclete): "if I go, I will send him to you".

18. Acts 2: 1 ff.; cf. W. F. Lofthouse, "The Holy Spirit in the Acts and the Fourth Gospel", *Expository Times* 52 (1940–41), pp. 334–336.

The picture given in Acts of the presence and activity of the Spirit is probably true to the general experience of the primitive church, or at least to that major segment of it which had links with the original community of believers in Jerusalem. The Spirit enables the disciples to bear witness and proclaim the gospel with convicting effect and to perform signs and wonders in the name of Jesus; [19] he speaks through prophets in the church; [20] when the apostles and their colleagues reach a common mind, his is the primary authority invoked in its promulgation; [21] it is he who directs the course of missionary activity. [22]

This picture is assumed throughout the Pauline letters, but further and distinctive emphases are added. If in the upper-room discourses of the Fourth Gospel the Spirit is to recall to the disciples' minds the teaching of Jesus and makes its meaning plain to them, as well as to lead them into all the truth and show them things to come, [23] in Paul he communicates the life and power of the risen Christ to his people. For Paul, as for Luke and John, the age which follows the departure of Jesus in visible form from earth is the age of the Spirit, but for Paul the age of the Spirit supersedes the age of law. The law means bondage, while the Spirit brings freedom; "the written code kills, but the Spirit gives life" (2 Corinthians 3: 6).

Thanks to the coming of the Spirit, the people of God, who were formerly in their infancy, restrained by the leading-strings of the law, have now come of age. "If you are led by the Spirit", says Paul, "you are not under law" (Galatians 5: 18), for the leading of the Spirit is not a restraining, but a liberating, force: "all who are led by the Spirit of God are sons of God" (Romans 8: 14). He is therefore called "the Spirit of sonship" (Romans 8: 15), the Spirit who enables them to claim and enjoy their status as full-grown sons of God, in anticipation of that fully manifested "adoption as sons" which will be theirs on the day of resurrection – that "revealing of the sons of God" for which the created universe eagerly waits. On that day, says Paul, creation will be "set free from its bondage to decay and obtain the glorious liberty of the children of God" (Romans 8: 21); but the children of God themselves exult in that liberty here and now by the power of the indwelling Spirit. By the power of that same Spirit they can address God confidently and spontaneously as Father: "when we cry 'Abba! Father!' it is the Spirit himself bearing witness with our spirit that we are children of God" (Romans 8: 15 f.). It is, in fact, one and the same Spirit who

19. Acts 2: 43; 4: 8, 31; 5: 32 (cf. John 15: 26 f.), etc.
20. Acts 11: 28; 13: 1 f.; 20: 23; 21: 4, 10 f.
21. Acts 15: 28.
22. Acts 13: 4; 16: 6–10.
23. John 14: 26; 16: 12–15.

enables believers to call God "Father" and to call Jesus "Lord" (cf. 1 Corinthians 12: 3). But "Abba" was the distinctive word for "Father" that Jesus had used (cf. Mark 14: 36); that Christians – even Greek-speaking Christians – should take over this Semitic form and use it in their devotions is a token that the Spirit whom God has sent into their hearts is not only "the Spirit of sonship" but "the Spirit of his Son" (Galatians 4: 6), the Spirit that indwelt and empowered Jesus himself.

To be "in the Spirit" is for Paul the opposite of being "in the flesh". All believers, according to him, are "in the Spirit": "you are not in the flesh, you are in the Spirit", he tells the Roman Christians, "if the Spirit of Christ really dwells in you. Any one who has not the Spirit of Christ does not belong to him" (Romans 8: 9). The two following sentences begin with the conditional clauses, "But if Christ is in you . . ." (Romans 8: 10) and "If the Spirit of him who raised Jesus from the dead dwells in you . . ." (Romans 8: 11). It appears, then, that there is no difference between the indwelling of the Spirit and the indwelling of the risen Christ, so far as the believer's experience is concerned, although this does not mean that Paul identified the risen Christ and the Spirit outright. There is a dynamic equivalence between them,[24] but they are nevertheless distinguished. The Spirit conveys the resurrection life of Christ to believers (which may be a further reason for his being called the Spirit of Christ), and in doing so he conveys the assurance that they in their turn will rise in the likeness of Christ's resurrection – the assurance that "he who raised Christ Jesus from the dead will give life to your mortal bodies also through his Spirit which dwells in you" (Romans 8: 11). This is one of the most distinctive Pauline insights regarding the Spirit: it is because of this that he describes the Spirit as the "first fruits" of the resurrection life (Romans 8: 23), the "seal" and "guarantee" – the *arrhabōn* or initial down-payment – of the heritage of glory into which they will then be ushered (2 Corinthians 1: 22; 5: 5; Ephesians 1: 13 f.).[25] The Spirit not only makes the benefits of Christ's saving work effective in them, but also enables them to appropriate and enjoy in advance the benefits of the age to come.

For the present, then, they live in hope, but theirs is a living and

24. Cf. 1 Corinthians 15: 45, "the last Adam [i.e. Christ in resurrection] became a life-giving spirit" (with E. Käsemann's comment, quoted above, p. 122 with n. 26).

25. The practically interchangeable force of "seal" and "guarantee" (Gk. ἀρραβών ) as used of the Spirit is specially evident in 2 Corinthians 1: 22 and Ephesians 1: 13 f. Gk. ἀρραβών is derived from a Phoenician mercantile term, which appears in Hebrew as 'ērābôn. It may be nothing more than a coincidence, but it is noteworthy that on the first occasion where 'ērābôn occurs in the Hebrew Bible, meaning the "pledge" or "guarantee" of repayment of a debt, the debtor's "seal" (Heb. ḥōtām) was an important part of the pledge (Genesis 38: 18, 25).

certain hope because it rests in the living Christ, dwelling within them as their personal "hope of glory" (Colossians 1: 27), and is sustained by the power of the Spirit. The Spirit at the same time aids their prayers, interpreting their deepest, even inarticulate, aspirations and presenting them to God in an intercessory ministry.[26] He co-operates in everything for good with those who love God,[27] enabling them to live as befits the children of God and liberating them from the law of sin and death which dominates the children of "this age".[28]

The Spirit is the sanctifying agency in the lives of believers: he wages perpetual warfare against the flesh, but he is more powerful than the flesh, and can put the flesh progressively out of action in those lives which are yielded to his control. It is by "the Lord who is the Spirit" that believers, "with unveiled face, beholding the glory of the Lord, are being changed into his likeness from one degree of glory to another" (2 Corinthians 3: 17).[29] This reproduction of the image of Christ in the lives of his people is the Spirit's most congenial ministry, and forms a preparation for that day when Christ, their true life, will be manifested, and they too "will be manifested with him in glory" (Colossians 3: 4), wearing in its perfection "the image of the man of heaven" (1 Corinthians 15: 49).

Nor is the Spirit's ministry confined to believers' individual lives: in uniting them to Christ, he unites them one to another. Paul's conception of the church as the body of Christ is inseparably bound up with his doctrine of the Spirit: "in one Spirit we were all baptized into one body – Jews or Greeks, slaves or free – and all were watered by one Spirit" (1 Corinthians 12: 13). In the narrative of Acts John the Baptist's promise that the Coming One would baptize with the Holy Spirit is viewed as fulfilled on the day of Pentecost; indeed, the authority of the risen Christ is cited for this (Acts 1: 5; 11: 16). The "togetherness" of the church from Pentecost onwards is emphasized in the narrative of Acts (cf. 2: 44; 4: 32) in a manner which may be thought to pave the way for Paul's teaching, but it is Paul who gives distinctive expression to the idea of all believers, whatever their race or social status, united in a common life as fellow-members of a body, with the Spirit as the source and principle of its corporate existence and its bond of unity, each member discharging for the good of the whole that function with which the energizing Spirit has endowed it. "To each is given the manifestation of the Spirit for the common good" (1 Corinthians 12: 7).[30] But the prime function of the indwelling Spirit in the

26. Romans 8: 26 f.
27. Romans 8: 28; see p. 332, no. 22.
28. Romans 8: 2.
29. See p. 120.
30. Cf. Romans 12: 4–8. Occasionally Paul expresses this corporate unity in

believing community, as in the individual believer, is for Paul the reproduction of the Christ-likeness in his people, until the whole body corporate attains "the measure of the stature of the fulness of Christ" (Ephesians 4: 13).[31]

terms not of a body but of a temple; cf. 1 Corinthians 3: 16 ("you are God's temple and God's Spirit dwells in you"). While the image of the body seems to be original with him, that of the temple had earlier antecedents: the Qumran community, for example, looked on itself as a living temple in which the general membership constituted the holy place and the inner council the holy of holies (1QS 8, ll. 5 f.). (Paul also uses the temple image for the individual believer, as in 1 Corinthians 6: 19, "your body is a temple of the Holy Spirit within you").

31. A wealth of exegetical material is presented in E. Schweizer's *TDNT* articles πνεῦμα (vi [1968], pp. 332–455), σάρξ and σῶμα (vii [1971], pp. 98–151, 1024–1094). See also A. Sand, *Der Begriff "Sarx" in den paulinischen Hauptbriefen* (Regensburg, 1967); M. E. Isaacs, *The Concept of Spirit* (London, 1967). A specially sympathetic exposition of Paul's doctrine of the Spirit is presented by J. D. G. Dunn, *Jesus and the Spirit* (London, 1975), pp. 97–114, 199–342.

## CHAPTER 20

# Antioch to Philippi

*1. Paul and Silas set out for Asia Minor*

NEXT TIME PAUL SET OUT FROM ANTIOCH FOR ASIA MINOR IT WAS
with another companion than Barnabas. According to
Luke's account, there was some word of their going together
to revisit the churches which they had jointly planted on their
previous journey, but this plan foundered on their inability to agree
whether John Mark should accompany them this time or not. Paul
felt that Mark had let them down on the former occasion when he
left them at Perga and returned home; Barnabas thought that he
should be given another chance. When they could not agree, they
parted company: Barnabas took Mark and went back to Cyprus.[1]
In the event, this was probably the best thing that could have
happened: Mark developed unsuspected qualities of character and
usefulness under his relative's encouragement, and Paul himself at
a later stage was to voice his appreciation of Mark's presence and
help.[2]

But even if there had not been this disagreement, it is doubtful if
Paul and Barnabas would have been as happy in each other's company as they had once been. The old mutual confidence must have
been damaged on the occasion when, as Paul says, "even Barnabas" followed Peter's example in withdrawing from the society of
Gentile Christians at Antioch.[3] Henceforth relations between the
two men could not be the same as before: "never glad confident
morning again". When Paul has occasion to refer to Barnabas after
this, he does so with the warmth of old affection,[4] but a change had
set in nevertheless.

In place of Barnabas, Paul chose a new fellow-traveller – Silas or
Silvanus, a member of the Jerusalem church. He first appears in the
record as one of the two messengers sent by the Jerusalem leaders
to carry the letter containing the apostolic decree to Antioch.[5] This
in itself might suggest that he was likely to be *persona grata* to Gen-

1. Acts 15: 36–39.
2. Colossians 4: 10; cf. Philemon 24; 2 Timothy 4: 11.
3. Galatians 2: 13.
4. Cf. 1 Corinthians 9: 6.
5. Acts 15: 22, 32 f.

tile Christians. Paul had opportunity to take stock of him and to judge that he would prove a kindred spirit. There might indeed be diplomatic advantages in having as his companion a Jerusalem Christian: if any one hoped to put Paul on the spot by asking what was said or done at Jerusalem, here was a man from Jerusalem to give an answer based on first-hand information. Moreover, if Silas was, as the narrative of Acts implies, a Roman citizen like Paul,[6] Paul would not find himself in an embarrassing situation where he could claim for himself civic privileges in which his companion could not share. Silas's two alternative names, Silas and Silvanus, might bear the same relation to each other as Saul and Paul – the former being the Jewish family name, the latter the Roman *cognomen*.[7]

The two men set out, then, with the blessing of the Antiochene church, first travelling north, perhaps through Syrian Alexandria (modern Iskanderun), and then turning west into Cilicia, probably along the road which led through Mopsuestia, Adana and Tarsus. How many of the cities through which they passed had been evangelized by this time is unknown, but such communities of Christians as they found were given copies of the Jerusalem letter. The letter was addressed to the Gentile brethren throughout Syria and Cilicia as well as in Antioch, and Silas was named in it as one of the messengers appointed to deliver it.[8] Evidently he continued to discharge this responsibility until Paul and he left Cilicia.[9] From Tarsus they turned north and crossed the Taurus range by the Cilician Gates; when they had passed through these they were out of Cilicia and into Cappadocia. Turning west they followed a Roman road which brought them into the territory of Rome's ally, King Antiochus, and so to Derbe, the most easterly point reached by Paul and Barnabas when they traversed South Galatia from the opposite direction.[10]

## 2. *Timothy joins the missionary party*

In Derbe and Lystra Paul was able to greet friends and converts, and in Lystra he renewed acquaintance with a young man whose career was thenceforth to be interwoven with his own. This was

6. Cf. Acts 16: 37.
7. Cf. 1 Thessalonians 1: 1; 2 Thessalonians 1: 1; 2 Corinthians 1: 19.
8. Acts 15: 27.
9. It is implied in Acts 16: 4 that the contents of the letter were communicated to South Galatian churches also, but see A. S. Geyser, "Paul, the Apostolic Decree and the Liberals in Corinth", in *Studia Paulina in Honorem J. de Zwaan*, ed. J. N. Sevenster and W. C. van Unnik (Haarlem, 1953), pp. 124 ff., where a case is argued for the deletion of that verse.
10. See pp. 171 f.

Timothy, son of a mixed marriage. His mother was a Jewess, who had brought him up in the Jewish faith; [11] but his father was a Greek, and so Timothy had never been circumcised. Timothy had probably become a Christian when Barnabas and Paul visited Lystra, and now older Christians from Iconium as well as Lystra spoke enthusiastically of his spiritual development and promise. A young man of such qualities and gifts would make an admirable apprentice to Paul if he was minded to give up whatever other ambitions he had and join Paul in his apostolic ministry. Timothy was plainly so attracted by Paul that he counted the world well lost for the sake of accompanying such a man as his aide-de-camp. There are hints in the Pastoral Epistles of prophetic utterances which clearly marked out this course as the divine will for Timothy and which were confirmed by a special spiritual endowment received by him at the same time. [12]

There is ample evidence that Paul wholeheartedly appreciated the selfless devotion with which Timothy supported and served him for the rest of the older man's life. Here is how he speaks of him some year later when he proposes to send him as his representative to the church of Philippi (Philippians 2: 19–22):

> I have no one like him, who will be genuinely anxious for your welfare. They all look after their own interests, not those of Jesus Christ. But Timothy's worth you know, how as a son with a father he has served with me in the gospel.

Paul knew that Timothy was naturally diffident by temperament: when he sends him, for example, as his representative to the more turbulent church of Corinth, he has to ask his friends there not to underestimate him but to put him at his ease and see that he is not intimidated (1 Corinthians 16: 10 f.). But he had the utmost confidence in entrusting him with responsible and delicate missions: Timothy, he knew, would not misrepresent him.

But in order that Timothy might serve him most effectively in these ways Paul decided that he should be circumcised. Luke's statement that Paul "took him and circumcised him because of the Jews" of Lystra and its neighbourhood, "for they all knew that his father was a Greek" (Acts 16: 3), is cryptic enough, but not so incredible as has sometimes been thought. [13] Such an action on the part of the writer to the Galatians is surprising indeed (no matter what view be taken of the date of the letter), but there is no point in

11. Her name is given as Eunice in 2 Timothy 1: 5.
12. Cf. 1 Timothy 4: 14; 2 Timothy 1: 6.
13. Luke's statement about Timothy's circumcision, coming as it does after his account of the Jerusalem decree in Acts 15: 22–29, is astonishing indeed – so much so that he is unlikely to have made it without very good authority.

ascribing to Paul a consistency which his own acquaintances were far from seeing in him. Timothy was not a Gentile Christian in the sense in which Titus was. By birth, as the son of a Jewish mother, and by religious upbringing Timothy was a Jew in all respects save the admittedly material one of circumcision. To the Gentiles around he was probably a Jew, but he could not be so in the eyes of the Jews unless he received circumcision. In the social setting of that place and time he was neither the one nor the other, and Paul resolved to regularize his position by circumcising him. He was now legitimized in Jewish eyes and shared Paul's own status as a Jewish Christian. Whether Paul was wise or not in his action could be determined only by a more detailed knowledge of the circumstances than is available, but the action was not inconsistent with Paul's own principles. Even in writing to the Galatians he insists twice over that neither circumcision nor uncircumcision matters in itself (5: 6; 6: 15); [14] it is only when circumcision is undertaken as a legal obligation that a man "is bound to keep the whole law" (5: 3). In this same letter, too, it is implied that Paul was charged with not always maintaining the rigid line on circumcision which he adopted with the Galatians. What does he mean by his rhetorical question, "But if I, brethren, still preach circumcision, why am I still persecuted?" (5: 11), if not that some people told the Galatians that he was not always so opposed to circumcision as he was with them? [15]

As frequently when Paul's actions and motives are under consideration, it is necessary to distinguish a higher and a lower consistency. Paul's higher consistency appears in his defence and promotion of the law-free gospel, for the sake of which many lower consistencies might be ignored. If one so thoroughly emancipated from legalism as Paul wishes for certain proper purposes to perform a ritual act which in itself is ethically indifferent, he will perform it, not by compulsion but freely. If expediency suggests that someone who is a Jew in every respect but circumcision (presumably because his Greek father would not allow it when he was an infant) be circumcised for his greater usefulness in the gospel, Paul will circumcise him; in such a situation circumcision is nothing but a minor surgical operation performed for a practical purpose. It is

14. Cf. 1 Corinthians 7: 19 ("neither circumcision counts for anything nor uncircumcision, but keeping the commandments of God"), where J. W. Drane (with doubtful cogency) sees in the "but" clause an instance of Paul's more positive attitude to the principle of law in 1 Corinthians than in Galatians (*Paul: Libertine or Legalist?* [London, 1975], p. 65). What Paul means here is that being circumcised or uncircumcised is irrelevant to the doing of God's will.

15. This may have reference to Paul's missionary enterprise in his pre-Christian days, when he would naturally have insisted on the circumcision of proselytes from paganism (see p. 129).

natural that many people in Paul's day did not appreciate the difference between doing such things voluntarily and doing them by way of religious duty, and accordingly charged Paul with inconsistency.[16] But there is a right as well as a wrong way of being "all things to all men", to use Paul's own expression (1 Corinthians 9: 22).[17]

If we have been right about the date and destination of the letter to the Galatians, then the churches of Lystra and Iconium, which were specially interested in Timothy, had received that letter only a few months before. What would they make of Paul's circumcising Timothy so soon after writing to them as he had done on that subject? That the circumcision was kept secret from them is incredible on every count. Perhaps Paul's action was not only performed "because of the Jews that were in those places", as Luke says (Acts 16: 3), but also served as an object-lesson for the Gentile Christians in those places of the difference between circumcision as an act of legal obedience, undertaken by people like themselves who were under no such obligation, and circumcision as a practical and religiously neutral expedient adopted in a most exceptional case. If so, would they have taken the lesson to heart?

### 3. The call to Macedonia

Paul's plan had been, after visiting his converts in South Galatia, to follow the westward road to Ephesus. Perhaps he had already thought of this city as a base from which the great province of Asia could be evangelized. But this plan was not to be put into effect yet. According to Luke, by the time he and his two companions (Silas and Timothy) "went through the Phrygian and Galatic region", they had already "been forbidden by the Holy Spirit to speak the word in Asia" (Acts 16: 6). This language implies that a prophetic utterance – perhaps one of those heard at Lystra [18] – had given this negative guidance without indicating positively where they were to turn. One possible course was to turn north and go to Bithynia, the province in the north-west of Asia Minor, in which lay the cities of Nicaea and Nicomedia.

If the negative guidance was granted at Lystra, they had to go on to Iconium in any case. If by this time they thought of Bithynia they could either cut out Pisidian Antioch and take the road into the northern part of Phrygia Paroreios (the territory lying north and

16. Cf. R. W. Emerson: "A foolish consistency is the hobgoblin of little minds, adored by little statesmen and philosophers and divines" ("Essay on Self-Reliance", in *Essays, Lectures and Orations* [London, 1848], p. 30). See also F. J. Foakes-Jackson, *Life of St. Paul* (London, 1927), p. 15.

17. Cf. H. Chadwick, "All Things to all Men", *NTS* 1 (1954–55), pp. 261 ff.

18. See p. 214.

south of the mountain range of Sultan Dağ) or they could go on to Pisidian Antioch (which, for the sake of the church recently planted there, they probably did) and reach northern Phrygia Paroreios from there by crossing Sultan Dağ. One way or the other, they would arrive at Philomelium (modern Akşehir).

But what does Luke mean by "the Phrygian and Galatic region" – a phrase which seems to mean "the region which is both Phrygian and Galatic"? Almost certainly he means the part of Phrygia which belonged to the Roman province of Galatia, the region in which Iconium and Pisidian Antioch lay [19] – Phrygia Galatica, as it might be called (although there is no direct evidence that this was its official designation).[20] Any other interpretation of the phrase is fraught with difficulties, especially an interpretation which envisages a visit on this occasion to one or more of the cities of ethnic Galatia, in the north of the province (Pessinus, Ancyra and Tavium).

Leaving Philomelium for the north-west, they would pass at once into the Asian part of Phrygia and arrive in due course at the important road-junction of Dorylaeum. To the north lay the frontier of the province of Bithynia; to the west lay Mysia, the north-westerly territory of the province of Asia. But when they made to cross into Bithynia, "the Spirit of Jesus did not allow them" (Acts 16: 7). This may point to another prophetic utterance, but the slight change in wording from the previous occasion may point to another kind of monition – an inward sense of inhibition, perhaps. There was only one way to go now: since they could not take the north road into Bithynia, they turned west, skirted the territory of Mysia, and reached the Aegean coast at the port of Alexandria Troas (modern Kestambol).[21]

Alexandria Troas stood on the site of the earlier Greek city of Sigeia. It was founded (with the name Antigonia Troas) by Alexander's successor Antigonus and, after him (with the name Alexandria Troas), by Lysimachus, king of Thrace (c. 300 B.C.), and it had the status of a free city. In the New Testament it is called simply Troas, which is also the name of the surrounding district of the Troad (the district called after the ancient city of Troy). Julius

19. Cf. W. M. Calder, "The Boundary of Galatic Phrygia", *MAMA* vii (Manchester, 1956), pp. ix ff.

20. See F. F. Bruce, "Galatian Problems: 2. North or South Galatians?" *BJRL* 52 (1969–70), pp. 246–258. An analogy to the postulated Phrygia Galatica is Pontus Galaticus, specified (as distinct from Pontus Polemonicus) in *CIL* iii. 6818 as one of the regions over which the legate of Galatia exercised control.

21. From Eski Istanbul (Old Istanbul). Cf. C. J. Hemer, "Alexandria Troas", *Tyndale Bulletin* 26 (1975), pp. 79–112, where it is pointed out that "Troas was a nodal point on what became a sophisticated system of international routes" (p. 91). See also W. Leaf, *Strabo on the Troad* (Cambridge, 1923), p. 238; J. M. Cook, *The Troad* (Oxford, 1973), pp. 16 ff.

Caesar, it is said, toyed with the idea of making it his imperial capital[22] – an idea taken up three and a half centuries later by Constantine who, however, decided in favour of a city on the European side of the narrow seas which here divide Europe from Asia. Augustus showed his appreciation of the importance of Troas by establishing a Roman colony there.

Some years later there was a church in Troas: [23] whether it was founded at this time or on a subsequent occasion is uncertain. But when Paul and his two friends arrived here, two things happened: they were joined by a fourth companion, and at last positive guidance about their next move was granted.

The fourth companion was the author of Acts – or, if fine distinctions are to be made, the author of the travel-diary incorporated in the narrative of Acts.[24] His joining the others is indicated in the most unobtrusive manner – by a sudden switch from the third person to the first person plural, from "they" to "we". There are three sections of Acts in which the story is told in the first person plural and, interestingly enough, each of the three is largely concerned with a journey by sea.[25]

The positive guidance came to Paul in the form of a night vision. "A man of Macedonia stood beseeching him: 'Come over to Macedonia and help us'" (Acts 16: 9). No need to inquire, as some writers have done, how Paul knew that the man was a Macedonian: his invitation, "Come over to Macedonia", was enough. Paul related his vision to the others, and "immediately", says the narrator, "we at once set about getting a passage to Macedonia, concluding that God had called us to bring them the good news" (Acts 16: 10).

### 4. The gospel comes to Philippi

The first passage they could get for Macedonia took them in a couple of days to Neapolis (modern Kavalla), the seaport of Philippi: the ship put in for one night at the mountainous island of Samothrace. Plainly they had a favourable wind; some of them made the same voyage in the reverse direction seven or eight years later and it took five days.[26]

22. Cf. Suetonius, *Life of Julius Caesar* 79. 3 (the "Alexandria" there mentioned along with "Ilium" [Troy] is naturally Alexandria Troas).
23. Cf. Acts 20: 5–12.
24. One and the same person, in my judgment; contrast C. K. Barrett: "On any showing it is unlikely that Luke (by which name I intend the author of the complete work) knew Paul personally" ("Acts and the Pauline Corpus", *Expository Times* 88 [1976–77], p. 4).
25. Acts 16: 10–17; 20: 5–21: 18; 27: 1–28: 16. Each of the three ends with a statement in which Paul is distinguished from the narrator and the rest of his companions.
26. Acts 20: 6 (see p. 340).

At Neapolis the Via Egnatia, the great Roman military road which linked the Adriatic with the Aegean and the Bosporus, met the sea. Following this road for about ten miles (16 kilometres) in a north-westerly direction, they came to Philippi. Philippi bore the name of Philip II of Macedonia (father of Alexander the Great), who established it in 356 B.C. on the site of the earlier settlement of Krenides. Luke describes it as "a city of the first district of Macedonia"[27] (with reference to the division of Macedonia into four districts in 167 B.C. by its Roman conqueror Lucius Aemilius Paullus); he adds that it was a Roman colony (Acts 16: 12). Although several cities mentioned in the New Testament were in fact Roman colonies, Philippi is the only one which is explicitly called a colony by and New Testament writer; Luke apparently had a special interest in Philippi.[28] It became a Roman colony in 42 B.C., after the battle of Philippi in which Antony and Octavian (later Augustus), the political heirs of Julius Caesar, defeated the party led by Caesar's chief assassins, Brutus and Cassius. The victors settled a number of their veteran soldiers here, and called the new colony Colonia Victrix Philippensium. Twelve years later Octavian (who had by this time disposed of his former ally and subsequent rival Antony) settled a number of Antony's followers in Philippi, and renamed the colony after himself: Colonia Iulia Philippensis (in which the title Augusta was inserted when he was designated Augustus in 27 B.C.).

There does not appear to have been a synagogue in Philippi, presumably because there was no Jewish community worth speaking of. A properly constituted synagogue requires a *minyān* or quorum of ten male Jews.[29] But outside the city walls, by the river Gangites, there was an unofficial place of worship where a number of women – God-fearers and possibly some Jewesses – met on sabbaths and holy days to recite the appointed synagogue prayers and thanksgivings.[30] The four missionaries found this meeting-place

27. This text survives only in a few Latin codices and a couple of mediaeval European versions based on the Latin. It postulates πρώτης (agreeing with μερ-ίδος , "district", "division") in place of the majority reading πρώτη (agreeing with πόλις , "city"). So, rightly, E. Haenchen, *The Acts of the Apostles*, E.T. (Oxford, 1971), p. 494; also, more tentatively, H. Conzelmann, *Die Apostelgeschichte* (Tübingen, 1963), p. 91.

28. The first "we" section of Acts ends in Philippi (16: 17), the second begins there (20: 6). A simple-minded inference would be that the narrator spent the intervening period in Philippi, and was possibly entrusted with the Philippian Christians' contribution to the relief fund for the Jerusalem church (see p. 339).

29. Cf. Rabbi Halafta in *Pirqê Abôt* 3: 7. A similar practice obtained in the Qumran community (1 QS 6, l. 3) and among the Essenes (Josephus, *BJ* ii. 146).

30. The Byzantine reading ἐνομίζετο προσευχὴ εἶναι (cf. AV: "where prayer was wont to be made") may well be original as against the readings of the early codices, which apparently represent attempts to mend a primitive corruption.

one sabbath morning soon after their arrival in Philippi, and sat down and talked to the women, imparting the good news which they brought. The leader of these women was Lydia, a God-fearer from the city of Thyatira in the province of Asia, who was an agent for the sale of the purple dye, derived from molluscs of the Murex genus, for which her native region was famed as early as Homer's day.[31] Since there was a Jewish colony in Thyatira, it was probably there that she had become a God-fearer. As she listened to the gospel, she was convinced of its truth and was baptized, together with her household.[32] Thereupon she insisted that the missionaries should be her guests for the remainder of their stay in Philippi.

This may prompt one to ask how the missionaries normally supported themselves when hospitality such as Lydia's was not forthcoming. So far as Paul is concerned, the answer is not in doubt: he supported himself, and his companions where necessary, by his "tent-making".[33] Many rabbis practised a trade so as to be able to impart their teaching without charge.[34] Paul scrupulously maintained this tradition as a Christian preacher, partly as a matter of principle, partly by way of example to his converts, and partly to avoid giving his critics any opportunity to say that his motives were mercenary. When, however, hospitality was spontaneously offered, as by Lydia on this occasion, he gladly accepted it: it would have been ungracious to refuse.

Luke's account of their stay at Philippi illustrates some aspects of the life of a Roman colony in the Greek world, with its citizens so proud of being Romans and their two collegiate magistrates rejoicing in the honorary designation of "praetors"[35] and attended, as were the two consuls in Rome itself, by the lictors. The lictors bore as their badge of office the bundles (*fasces*) of rods and axes which denoted the authority of the magistrates whom they served.[36] The two Philippian praetors and their lictors make an appearance in the incident of the fortune-telling slave-girl. This girl told fortunes by the aid of a "pythonic spirit", a pale imitation, we may suppose, of the spirit that possessed the Pythian prophetess at Delphi so that

31. Cf. Homer, *Iliad* iv. 141 f., "as when some Maeonian [Lydian] or Carian woman dyes ivory with purple". "Lydia" means "the Lydian woman"; it may not have been her original name.

32. Probably not merely her "nuclear" family (it is unknown whether she was married or not) but her *familia*, including slaves and other dependants as well as kinsfolk.

33. See p. 291.

34. See p. 107 with n. 32.

35. Their official title was *duo uiri* ("duumvirs" or "two men") but, like the duumvirs of the colony of Capua, they "wished to be called praetors" (Cicero, *De lege agraria*, ii. 93).

36. In Greek the lictors are called ῥαβδοῦχοι , "rod-bearers" (as in Acts 16: 35).

she became for the time being the mouthpiece of Apollo.[37] The spirit that enabled the Philippian slave-girl to tell fortunes was exorcized by Paul when she persisted in shouting unsolicited testimonials after him and his companions through the streets of the city. Her owners were naturally incensed at this violation of property rights and accused Paul and Silas before the praetors of being itinerant Jews who were troubling this Roman city with their unwelcome and indeed illegal propaganda.[38] Paul and Silas were not only the leaders of the missionary party but were full Jews and perhaps looked it (Luke was a Gentile and Timothy a half-Gentile); they were thus natural targets for anti-Semitic resentment. Without staying to inquire into the grounds of the accusation, the praetors ordered the two men to be soundly beaten (with the lictors' rods) and locked up overnight – they would be expelled from Philippi next day. But when the lictors arrived at the town jail in the morning to take custody of them and expel them, they were met with a protest – a protest which may have been made the day before but, if so, went unheard or unheeded in the public excitement. "We are Roman citizens", said Paul and Silas; "we have been beaten publicly without being granted a trial".[39] Ordinary provincials might be treated summarily, but Roman citizens had their legal rights and could appeal to higher authority if those rights were infringed. The praetors had to come in person and apologize to them, but. even so they requested them to move on: the responsibility of protecting two unpopular Roman citizens was more than they felt able to bear.

Paul and Silas, with Timothy, moved on, but by the time they did so they had gathered a promising young church together in Philippi. The last converts they made before leaving the place were the town jailer and his family. Luke seems to have been left behind in Philippi; he disappears from the narrative of Acts at this point and reappears at Philippi some years later.[40] If the letter to the Philippians (or at any rate the relevant part of it) was written during this interval,[41] Luke may well be the unnamed "true yokefellow" whom Paul asks to help Euodia and Syntyche "to agree in the Lord", for these two women, he says, "have laboured

37. Her soothsaying appears to have been a form of ventriloquism, except that the ventriloquist (ἐγγαστρίμυθος) was normally in conscious control of his utterances, whereas the Philippian slave-girl was not.

38. The proselytizing of Roman citizens, even if not formally forbidden, was officially discouraged; it was, nevertheless, widely practised. See A. D. Mornigliano, *Claudius the Emperor and his Achievement* (Oxford, 1934), pp. 29 ff.; A. N. Sherwin-White, *Roman Society and Roman Law in the New Testament* (Oxford, 1963), pp. 78 ff.

39. Acts 16: 36.

40. That is, if Luke is the narrator of the "we" sections (see p. 218).

41. See pp. 299, 390.

PAUL: APOSTLE OF THE FREE SPIRIT

side by side with me in the gospel together with Clement and the rest of my fellow-workers" (Philippians 4: 2 f.). Euodia, Syntyche and Clement are but names to us, but it is plain that Paul set a high value on the friendship and activity of many of his converts in Philippi.

They, for their part, maintained a warm affection for their apostle, and showed it by sending him personal gifts from time to time. Paul was not too happy about accepting such gifts from his converts, but the generosity of his Philippian friends was so unanimous and spontaneous that he could do no other than accept their gifts in the spirit in which they were given and view them as the outward expression of their faith and love, and thus not only a donation to himself but an acceptable offering to God.[42]

42. Cf. Philippians 4: 10 ff.

# CHAPTER 21

# Christianity in Thessalonica

## 1. Philippi to Thessalonica

FROM PHILIPPI PAUL, SILAS AND TIMOTHY JOURNEYED west-by-south-west along the Via Egnatia, through Amphipolis on the Strymon (capital of the first district of Macedonia) and Apollonia, and arrived at Thessalonica, about 90 miles (150 kilometres) distant from Philippi.

The city and port of Thessalonica stood near the earlier city of Therme, which gave its name to the Thermaic Gulf (now the Gulf of Thessaloniki) on the west side of the Chalcidice peninsula. It was founded about 315 B.C. by Cassander, king of Macedonia, who named it after his wife Thessalonica, daughter of Philip II and half-sister of Alexander the Great. Its original residents were the former inhabitants of Therme and some twenty-five other towns or villages in the area, whom Cassander forcibly settled in his new foundation. When the Romans divided Macedonia into four districts in 167 B.C., Thessalonica became the capital of the second district; when they made Macedonia a province in 146 B.C., Thessalonica became the seat of provincial administration. From 42 B.C. it enjoyed the status of a free city, governed by its own politarchs. (This title appears to have been peculiar to the chief magistrates of Macedonian cities; it appears nowhere in Greek literature apart from Acts 17: 6, where it is used of the chief magistrates of Thessalonica, but it is amply attested in inscriptions belonging to our period for Thessalonica itself and other Macedonian cities.) [1] The Via Egnatia ran through the city from N.W. to S.E., and part of the thoroughfare which follows its line bears the same name today.

In the largest city of Macedonia there was naturally a Jewish colony with its synagogue. To the synagogue, then, Paul and his two companions made their way, and for three successive sabbaths Paul expounded the scriptures to the congregation, arguing that they had found their fulfilment in Jesus. Some members of the congregation believed: Jason, who became host to the three missionaries while they were in Thessalonica, was probably one of

---

1. Cf. E. D. Burton, "The Politarchs", *American Journal of Theology* 2 (1898), pp. 598 ff.

224 PAUL: APOSTLE OF THE FREE SPIRIT

these. (Jason was, of course, a good Greek name, but it was commonly adopted in the Hellenistic period by Jews whose Hebrew name was Joshua or Jeshua.) [2] Aristarchus was evidently another, [3] and Secundus may have been a third. [4] There were several God-fearers also among those who adhered to Paul; these included the wives of some of the principal citizens of Thessalonica. [5]

When they were no longer welcome in the synagogue, the missionaries continued their evangelistic activity among the pagans of Thessalonica, and by the time they left the city the Christian community which they had gathered appears to have comprised, in the main, former pagans. This is the inference most readily drawn from the words addressed to them not long afterwards in 1 Thessalonians 1: 9, "you turned to God from idols to serve a living and true God".

But, as the weeks went on, the missionaries found themselves involved in trouble. The principal citizens might have tolerated their wives' attendance at synagogue: such attendance, in fact, was at this time quite fashionable among ladies of good family in many cities of the Roman Empire, not least in Rome itself. But they would look quite differently on their wives' association with a very odd collection of enthusiasts who (as it seemed to them) were hypnotized by these strangers who had come to their city from goodness knew where and who (they might be sure) meant no good. It was their wealth that they were after, if not something more discreditable still. That such things were being said is plain from Paul's apologia in 1 Thessalonians 2: 3–12, where he appeals to his converts' personal memory of his colleagues and himself as evidence that their preaching did not spring "from error or uncleanness" and was not used craftily "as a cloak for greed". On the contrary, he says, "we worked night and day, that we might not burden any of you, while we preached to you the gospel of God"; and he calls them to witness that their behaviour among them was "holy and righteous and blameless" – calculated, indeed, to present to them an example of the Christian way of life.

## 2. The charge of subversion

The synagogue authorities, for their part, would resent the withdrawal from their services of men and women of repute, and it was not difficult to translate their resentment into action by direc-

2. Cf., at an earlier period, Jason the son of Simon II and last Zadokite high priest in Jerusalem (c. 174–171 B.C.).

3. Cf. Acts 19: 29; 20: 4; 27: 2; Colossians 4: 10 (where it is made plain that he was a Jewish Christian).

4. Cf. Acts 20: 4.

5. The Western text of Acts 17:4 specifically includes among the converts "not a few of the wives of the leading men".

ting the suspicion of the magistrates against the visitors. With the aid of a gang of idlers around the city marketplace or *agora*, they fomented a riot. The rioters hoped to lay hands on the visitors and drag them to court but, unable to find them, they contented themselves with doing so to Jason, the visitors' host, and some other converts. The charge which they pressed against them was extremely serious – much more serious, indeed, than is suggested by its traditional rendering in the King James Version: "These that have turned the world upside down are come hither also" (Acts 17: 6). These words have been worn quite smooth by frequent repetition; they have been used as a text by preachers (more especially, perhaps, younger preachers) who have applied them to themselves. But the words imply subversive or seditious activity: "these men who have upset the civilized world have now arrived here, and Jason has harboured them. Their practices are clean contrary to Caesar's decrees: they are proclaiming a rival emperor,[6] Jesus."

The charge must be set in the context of widespread unrest in the Jewish communities throughout the Roman Empire. Jewish freedom-fighters[7] were particularly active in Judaea itself during the principate of Claudius, and their activity could not be contained within the frontiers of their native province. A militant messianism was working like a ferment among Jews of the dispersion, and the custodians of law and order in the imperial provinces and cities were not likely to draw a distinction between it and the "messianism" of Paul and his colleagues. In Rome itself there had been trouble of this kind quite recently, so much so that Claudius had expelled the Jewish community from the capital.[8] At the beginning of his principate he had sent a severe letter to the citizens of Alexandria where, a short time before, there were fierce and sanguinary riots between the Greek and Jewish communities. In a passage specially intended for the Jewish community, he gave this admonition:

> Do not bring in or invite Jews who sail to Alexandria from Syria or down the Nile from other parts of Egypt. If you do, this will make me very suspicious, and I will punish them severely for fomenting a general plague throughout the whole world.[9]

6. The same Greek word βασιλεύς does duty for both king (Latin *rex*) and emperor (Latin *imperator*); since it is over against Caesar that Jesus is set here, "a rival emperor" is the sense (as in John 19: 15 where, in answer to Pilate's sarcastic question "Shall I crucify your βασιλεύς ?" the chief priests say "We have no βασιλεύς but Caesar").

7. This term is used because it is currently an acceptable euphemism for people more bluntly described as "terrorists".

8. Cf. Acts 18: 2; see pp. 235, 381.

9. Cf. H. I. Bell (ed.), *Jews and Christians in Egypt* (London, 1924), pp. 1 ff., for *editio princeps*.

The immigrant Jews to whom he refers were probably being invited by the Jews of Alexandria to join them so as to augment their strength in the event of further attacks by their Greek neighbours. But "Syria" would include Judaea, and some of the illegal immigrants could have been militant messianists such as disturbed the imperial peace elsewhere; this would account for Claudius's language about "a general plague throughout the whole world" (and it so happens that the Greek term for "world" in the copy of the emperor's letter is the same term, *oikoumenē*, as is used in the charge against Paul and his friends in Acts 17: 6).

Paul himself was careful to inculcate respect for imperial law and order, but it could not be denied that, more often than not, his coming to any city was a prelude to rioting and, in particular, that the Jesus whom he proclaimed as sovereign lord had been executed by sentence of a Roman court on a charge of claiming to be king of the Jews. The wording of the charge pressed against him before the Thessalonian politarchs was skilfully thought out.

As for Caesar's decrees, which he and his companions were alleged to be flouting, these might be understood in a general and comprehensive sense, or (more convincingly) with reference to certain specific decrees.[10] The *dēmos* or civic body of Thessalonica, before which the rioters had hoped to drag Paul and his associates, together with the politarchs, before whom they voiced their complaint, may well have taken an oath, as other cities in various parts of the empire are known to have done, binding themselves to obedience to the emperor: such an oath would empower them, and even require them, to take up such a charge as was now being made. Moreover, in Paul's preaching in Thessalonica there was apparently a markedly predictive element. His Thessalonian converts, who turned to worship the living and true God, learned also, he says, "to wait for his Son from heaven . . ., Jesus, our deliverer from the wrath to come" (1 Thessalonians 1: 10), and it appears that he taught them in addition something about the way in which world events would unfold up to the parousia of Jesus.[11] Now, prediction was an exercise of which one emperor after another disapproved: prediction could too easily be used as a political weapon. Augustus, in A.D. 11, had issued a decree forbidding it;[12] this decree was reinforced on pain of death by Tiberius in A.D. 16.[13] Paul's prediction was centred on the one whom he was accused of putting forward as a rival to the emperor in Rome.

10. Cf. E. A. Judge, "The Decrees of Caesar at Thessalonica", *Reformed Theological Review* 30 (1971), pp. 1–7.
11. See pp. 231 ff.
12. Dio Cassius, *History* lvi. 25. 5 f.
13. *Ibid.* lvii. 15. 8.

### 3. Paul's hasty departure

It says much for the sanity of the politarchs that they did not panic when they heard these serious charges. They decided that the heat could be taken out of the situation if they made Jason and his companions go bail for the missionaries' good behaviour – more particularly, for Paul's – and this involved his prompt quiet departure from Thessalonica. He left reluctantly, but his hands were tied by the action of his friends, who indeed had little option in the matter. The church which he and his colleagues had just begun to establish required further guidance and teaching for its consolidation, he felt, and he wondered how it would fare in the aftermath of the riot and his enforced departure. That its members would be exposed to some persecution was certain. One can well imagine what the leading citizens would say to their wives who had attached themselves to this new group: "A fine lot these Jewish propagandists are! They come here and entice you to leave the synagogue and follow them, but the moment trouble arises, off they go and leave their dupes to face the music!" Paul knew very well that his converts would be exposed to this sort of ridicule, and in some instances to worse than ridicule, and he made one or two attempts to return to Thessalonica and strengthen them, but these attempts were abortive: "Satan hindered us", he says (1 Thessalonians 2: 18).

If we ask how it could be known which hindrances, like those on the road to Troas, were tokens of divine guidance and which, like the present ones, were evidence of Satanic frustration, the apostolic answer would probably be that those which turned out to further the progress of the gospel and the wellbeing of the churches belonged to the former category and those which worked to the detriment of those causes belonged to the latter. Sometimes, indeed, a visitation of Satan could be recognized – in retrospect, at least – as a means employed or overruled for the furtherance of the divine purpose, as with Paul's "splinter in the flesh" which followed his ecstatic transportation to paradise.[14] But whether the satanic hindrance on this occasion was an illness,[15] or a continuation of the political circumstances which had made him leave Thessalonica, he does not seem to have discerned any divine overruling here – not, at any rate, at the time of writing the letter in which those words occur, the letter which has come down to us as 1 Thessalonians.

14. Cf. 2 Corinthians 12: 7 (see p. 135).
15. Cf. T. W. Manson, *Studies in the Gospels and Epistles* (Manchester, 1962), p. 271.

## 4. The Thessalonian correspondence

There are two letters in the New Testament addressed to "the church of the Thessalonians in God our Father and the Lord Jesus Christ"; the relation between the two is not easy to determine. There is a considerable community of subject-matter between the two, but for the most part the treatment of the common themes is fuller in 1 Thessalonians. Apart from one near-apocalyptic paragraph (2 Thessalonians 2: 1–12),[16] 2 Thessalonians has seemed to many readers to be a pale echo of 1 Thessalonians, and there has therefore been a tendency, especially among German scholars, to dismiss it as unauthentic – but it is difficult to see what purpose any one could have had in view in composing it. Other suggestions have been that 1 Thessalonians was written to Gentile Christians in Thessalonica and 2 Thessalonians to Jewish Christians,[17] or that the superscription of both letters, naming "Paul, Silvanus and Timothy" as joint-authors,[18] indicates that more than one of them shared in the correspondence. There is really nothing in the two letters which points to diversity of destination, and the idea that a church planted by Paul comprised separate Jewish and Gentile sections is antecedently improbable. "I adjure you by the Lord", says the writer of 1 Thessalonians (5: 27), "that this letter be read to all the brethren" – evidently, then, it was intended for the whole church. And the "I" which forms the grammatical subject of this direction cannot well be distinguished from "I Paul" of 1 Thessalonians 2: 18; when the assurance of 2 Thessalonians 3: 17, "I Paul write this greeting with my own hand", is also taken into consideration, the natural conclusion is that, whoever acted as scribe, Paul took personal responsibility for the contents of both letters.

Another possibility is that 2 Thessalonians is the earlier of the two.[19] Their traditional sequence implies nothing about relative dating: the arrangement of letters in the Pauline corpus is based mainly on descending order of length. One argument in favour of treating 2 Thessalonians as the earlier letter is that its recipients are described (1: 4 f.) as actually enduring persecution for their faith, whereas in 1 Thessalonians 1: 6 and 2: 14 such persecution is mentioned in the past tense.

16. See p. 231.
17. Cf. K. Lake, *The Earlier Epistles of St. Paul* (London, [2] 1914), pp. 83 ff., following A. Harnack, "Das Problem des zweiten Thessalonicherbriefs", *Sitzungsberichte der königlichen preussischen Akademie der Wissenschaften*, 1910, pp. 562 f.
18. Cf. F. C. Burkitt, *Christian Beginnings* (London, 1924), pp. 128 ff.
19. Cf. J. Weiss, *Earliest Christianity*, E.T. i (New York, 1959), pp. 289 ff.; T. W. Manson, *Studies in the Gospels and Epistles*, pp. 268 ff.; R. G. Gregson, "A Solution to the Problems of the Thessalonian Epistles", *Evangelical Quarterly* 38 (1966) pp. 76 ff.

Paul's Thessalonian friends got him safely away by night to Beroea, a city about 60 miles west-by-south-west of Thessalonica; from there he was escorted to Athens. In Athens he was rejoined by Silas and Timothy, whom he immediately sent back to Macedonia – Timothy to Thessalonica and Silas, perhaps, to Philippi. By the time they returned to him, he had moved on from Athens to Corinth.[20] If Timothy was given 2 Thessalonians to deliver to the church at Thessalonica, then 1 Thessalonians was written in response to the news which he brought back to Paul in Corinth, answering questions which the Thessalonians had raised during Timothy's visit, possibly including some which were prompted by the letter which they had received from Timothy's hands.

The news which Timothy brought from Thessalonica greatly relieved and cheered Paul. Far from being discouraged or disillusioned by recent events, the new Christians in Thessalonica had begun to propagate the gospel on their own initiative, "so that", as Paul tells them in the letter which he wrote from Corinth on hearing Timothy's report, "you became an example to all the believers in Macedonia and Achaia" (1 Thessalonians 1: 7). They had had to put up with various degrees of persecution – some petty, some severe – but this had not damped their enthusiasm: "not only has the word of the Lord sounded forth from you in Macedonia and Achaia, but your faith in God has gone forth everywhere, so that we need not say anything" (1 Thessalonians 1: 8).

Even so, Timothy's report indicated that there were some matters on which they required more explicit teaching than Paul had been able to give them before his hasty departure. They had to be reminded of the importance of sexual purity and the inviolability of the marriage bond – a lesson which converts from Greek paganism frequently had difficulty in learning.[21] The eschatological excitement which had infected even Gentile believers was producing excesses, such as a disinclination to carry on with their daily work; why trouble about such matters if the present order of things was about to be wound up? Paul had to refer them to his own example and urge them to do their own work and earn their own living; otherwise they would become spongers and forfeit the respect of outsiders.[22]

His unfinished instruction about the parousia gave rise to another concern. Some of their number had died already: would they be denied the blessings to be enjoyed by those still living at the parousia? No, says Paul; far from being at a disadvantage, they will

20. Cf. 1 Thessalonians 3: 1 f., 6; Acts 17: 14 f.; 18: 5. A useful suggestion about the relation between the two accounts is made by K. Lake, *The Earlier Epistles of St. Paul*, p. 74.

21. Cf. 1 Thessalonians 4: 3–8.

22. Cf. 1 Thessalonians 4: 9–12; 2 Thessalonians 3: 6–12.

have precedence, for when the parousia trumpet sounds, "the dead in Christ will rise first" (1 Thessalonians 4: 16).[23] The expectation of the parousia should not be an excuse for idleness but for vigilance and sobriety, for "the day of the Lord", he says (echoing a word of Jesus), "will come like a thief in the night" (1 Thessalonians 5: 2).[24]

## 5. The day of the Lord and the man of lawlessness

The near-apocalyptic paragraph in 2 Thessalonians 2: 1–12, to which reference has already been made, says on the other hand that the day of the Lord will be heralded by certain signs. This has been thought to involve a contradiction so sharp as to rule out the probability that both passages come from one author.[25] But it is noteworthy that the same apparent contradiction is found in gospel reports of Jesus' teaching about the coming of the Son of Man. Whereas in Luke 17: 22–37 [26] it will come as suddenly as a lightning-flash, like the flood in Noah's day or the storm of fire and brimstone which overwhelmed Sodom and its sister-cities, in Mark 13: 5–32 it will be preceded by the worldwide proclamation of the gospel and a time of unprecedented tribulation. Yet the latter passage is followed by a call to keep awake and be on the look-out, "for you do not know when the time will come" (Mark 13: 33–37), and the former passage ends with the proverb, "Where the body is, there the eagles will be gathered together" (Luke 17: 37) [27] – which is as much as to say that where there is a situation ripe for judgment, there the judgment will fall. Presumably those whose spiritual eyes and ears were open would recognize that such a situation was present and be prepared for the ensuing judgment. The fact is that in the earliest ascertainable forms of the gospel tradition these two strands – suddenness calling for vigilance and the significance of antecedent events – are interwoven, so that one need not be surprised if they are similarly interwoven in Paul's teaching.

23. See pp. 305 f.

24. See p. 112 with n. 39. It is uncertain whether the "word of the Lord" to which Paul appeals was spoken by the historical Jesus or by a prophet in his name; see p. 105 with n. 26.

25. So, first, J. E. C. Schmidt in a succession of works: *Philologisch-exegetische Clavis über das Neue Testament*, i. 2 (Giessen, 1798); *Bibliothek für Kritik und Exegese des Neuen Testaments* (Hadamar, 1801), pp. 385 f.; *Einleitung in das Neue Testament* (Giessen, 1804), pp. 256 f.

26. Possibly a "Q" passage, conflated with its Markan counterpart (Mark 13: 5–37) in Matthew 24: 4–44.

27. Cf. Matthew 24: 28. If the saying is proverbial, a reference to vultures would be expected; they may have been replaced by eagles here in allusion to the Roman legionary standards (*aquilae*). When the temple area in Jerusalem was stormed in A.D. 70, the victorious Romans set up their standards in the sacred area opposite the east gate and offered sacrifice to them (Josephus, *BJ* vi. 316).

If 2 Thessalonians was written before 1 Thessalonians, then the statement that the day of the Lord would not come until certain events had taken place might have stimulated the Thessalonian Christians' concern about the lot of those of their number who died before it came. On the other hand, if 1 Thessalonians was written first, it might have unintentionally provided ammunition for those who argued that, with the coming day so imminent, there was no point in planning or working in the short interval before it came, so that, to cope with this unhealthy argument, Paul might well have said, "The parousia is imminent indeed, but not so imminent as all that: certain things must happen first" (2 Thessalonians 2: 3–7):

> That day will not come, unless the rebellion comes first, with the revelation of the man of lawlessness, the son of perdition, who opposes and exalts himself against every so-called god or object of worship, so that he takes his seat in the temple of God, proclaiming himself to be God. Don't you remember that, when I was still with you, I told you this? And now you know what is restraining him, so that he may be revealed in his proper time. For the mystery of lawlessness is already at work: only he who now restrains it will do so until he is out of the way. And then the lawless one will be revealed, but the Lord Jesus will slay him with the breath of his mouth and destroy him by the manifestation of his parousia.

Few passages in the New Testament can boast such a variety of interpretations as this; yet in the historical context its general sense is fairly clear. The verbal imagery is that of the Antichrist expectation.[28] Behind the figure of Antichrist, the end-time opponent of God and his people, stands the primaeval dragon of chaos,[29] but in Hellenistic times this figure had assumed more personal lineaments with the attempt of Antiochus Epiphanes to abolish the worship of the true God and replace it by that of the pagan deity of whom he himself was acclaimed as the earthly manifestation. In the visions of Daniel, Antiochus is the king who is to "exalt himself and magnify himself above every god" (Daniel 11: 36), while the pagan apparatus which he instals in the temple is called, by a mocking pun, the "abomination of desolation" (Daniel 11: 31, etc.).[30] After

---

28. The word $\dot{a}\nu\tau\dot{i}\chi\rho\iota\sigma\tau\sigma\varsigma$ occurs in the New Testament only in the Johannine epistles (1 John 2: 18, 22; 4: 3; 2 John 7), but the idea was quite familiar. Cf. F. F. Bruce, *The Epistles of John* (London, 1970), pp. 64 ff.

29. Compare the apocalyptic seven-headed dragon (Revelation 12: 3 ff.) and his agent, the seven-headed beast, i.e. the Roman Empire (Revelation 11: 7; 13: 1 ff.; 17: 3 ff.).

30. Cf. 1 Maccabees 1: 54. Olympian Zeus, whose cult was established in the Jerusalem temple towards the end of 167 B.C., was equated with the Syrian deity *Ba'al Shamen* ("lord of heaven"; *Ba'al Shamaim* in Hebrew), whose name was parodied by the Jews as *šiqqûṣ m'šomēm* ("the desolating abomination"). Cf. E. Nestle, "Zu Daniel, 2: Der Greuel der Verwüstung", *ZAW* 4 (1884), p. 248.

three years' profanation, the temple was cleansed and restored to its original function; but the character and action of Antiochus provided a precedent for an expected Antichrist of the future.

In A.D. 40 it looked for a short time as if this expected Antichrist had shown his hand. The Emperor Gaius, who took his divinity very seriously, was stung by what he regarded as insulting conduct on the part of the Jews of Jamnia (in western Palestine) to an altar set up in his honour by their Greek neighbours, and gave orders that his statue should be set up in the Jerusalem temple. The legate of Syria was instructed to see that it was done, and to lead two legions to Jerusalem in case there was a revolt. Judaea and the Jewish world in general were thrown into consternation: this was the end, and the Jews steeled themselves to resist the outrageous decree to the death.[31]

The Jewish Christians were as deeply concerned as all their Jewish brethren. Some of them called to mind certain words of Jesus which appeared to them to have been spoken with direct reference to this crisis. Speaking of trouble in days to come which would herald the destruction of the temple and desolation of Jerusalem, Jesus warned his followers in Judaea to "flee to the mountains" when they saw "the abomination of desolation standing where he ought not" (Mark 13: 14).[32] (That the "abomination", though expressed in Greek by a noun in the neuter gender, is to be construed as personal may be inferred from the anomalous masculine form of the participle "standing" which qualifies it.) [33] It may well be that at this time these words of Jesus, together with some others of like import, were circulated as a broadsheet among the faithful to prepare them for the impending catastrophe. If so, this broadsheet was subsequently incorporated in the Gospel of Mark.

In the event, the crisis under Gaius proved not to be the fulfilment of Jesus' prophecy: the decree was countermanded at the last moment. Thirty more years were to pass before the desolation engulfed Jerusalem and its temple. But the crisis made a deep impression on the thinking of the early church, and the prophecy of Jesus supplied a form of words which can be recognized in Christian documents of the following decades, including the passage quoted above from 2 Thessalonians. The crisis had sharpened es-

31. Cf. Philo, *Embassy to Gaius* 203 ff.; Josephus, *BJ* ii. 184 ff.; *Ant.* xviii. 261 ff.

32. It is uncertain if this should be related to the oracle mentioned by Eusebius which the members of the church of Jerusalem received before the outbreak of war in A.D. 66, bidding them leave the doomed capital and settle in the Peraean city of Pella (*Hist. Eccl.* iii. 5. 3); departure for Pella is scarcely the same thing as "fleeing to the mountains". Eusebius may owe his account to the second-century writer Ariston of Pella.

33. βδέλυγμα (neuter) qualified by ἑστηκότα (masculine).

chatological expectation among Jews and Christians alike, and made its contribution to the militant messianism which manifested itself in those years in many Jewish communities around the Mediterranean.

The day will come, says Paul, when another potentate will actually do what Gaius planned to do: he will not merely erect his image but occupy a throne personally in the temple, claiming to be the manifestation of the supreme God and exacting divine honours exceeding those paid to any other deity. Great numbers will be hypnotized into giving him the worship he demands, but when he is at the height of his power he will be brought down and destroyed by the parousia of Christ. This will fulfil an ancient word of prophecy about the Messiah: "with the breath of his lips he shall slay the wicked" (Isaiah 11: 4).

## 6. The restraining power

This sinister being, called Antichrist by other writers, is designated by Paul "the man of lawlessness" because he is the embodiment of lawlessness or anarchy. The "mystery" or hidden power of anarchy had not yet revealed itself in its full malignity. It was already at work beneath the surface, erupting from time to time, as in those forces at Thessalonica which had combined (but fruitlessly, as the event proved) to thwart the progress of the gospel. At present, however, it was checked by a restrainer; but one day this restraint would be removed, and then "the man of lawlessness" would make his début.

Paul writes as though he expected his readers to understand what he had in mind: he had told them something of this while he was still with them. But to later readers his words have presented an enigma, and even today there is no agreement on their meaning, especially on the identity of the restraining power. One influential view, proposed in the first place by Oscar Cullmann, is that the restraining power was Paul's own apostolic ministry, which (ex hypothesi) had to be completed before the parousia and attendant events took place.[34] But if this were so, why should Paul be so allusive, instead of speaking plainly? It is much more probable that the restraint was exercised by imperial law and order, embodied in the emperor – "he who now restrains". Paul had already begun to appreciate the protection afforded to the gospel by the organization

34. O. Cullmann, "Le caractère eschatologique du devoir missionnaire et de la conscience apostolique de saint Paul", RHPR 16 (1936), pp. 210 ff.; cf. J. Munck, Paul and the Salvation of Mankind, E.T. (London, 1959), pp. 36 ff. Munck linked this interpretation with his exegesis of Romans 11: 13–27; the cessation of Paul's missionary activity would be followed by the rise of Antichrist, whose lordship would be ended by Christ's appearing as "Deliverer from Zion".

and administration of the Roman Empire, curbing the hostile forces of anarchy. If this is the true interpretation of his words, it is easy to understand his allusiveness. If he had spoken explicitly about the coming removal of the imperial power, or of the emperor himself, and the letter had fallen into the wrong hands, the consequences for Paul and his friends alike could have been serious. Such language would have seemed to confirm the charge brought against him before the Thessalonian politarchs, of contravening the decrees of Caesar and proclaiming a rival emperor.

The near-apocalyptic imagery of this and other passages in Paul's Thessalonian correspondence is not characteristic of the main body of his writing. In his later letters he deals from time to time with the same topics – resurrection, coming glory, and the subjection of all other authority beneath the dominion of Christ – but he deals with them in other terms.[35] Since the Thessalonian letters are among the earliest, if not absolutely the earliest, of his extant writings,[36] this may suggest that he came increasingly to feel that apocalyptic imagery was not the most adequate vehicle for expressing the Christian hope.

As for the restraining effect of the imperial order, beneficial as this was for the cause of the gospel, Gaius's brief spell of madness ten years before had shown what could happen when an emperor took his divinity too seriously: what had happened before could happen again, and indeed would happen again – more decisively and effectively than under Gaius. It is not necessary to think that Paul was thinking specifically of Claudius, although some have (most implausibly) envisaged a concealed play on words between that emperor's name and the idea of restraint (via such Latin verbs as *claudere*, "to close", and *claudicare*, "to limp").[37] Still less is it necessary to connect the removal of restraint with Claudius's stepson and eventual successor, Nero (who at this time was only thirteen or fourteen years old). Paul was thinking much more of his own experience of Roman justice: it was on the strength of this experience that he could describe the imperial authorities several years later, when Nero had already been emperor for over two years, as "ministers of God" (Romans 13: 6), and it was on the strength of this same experience that, two or three years after that, he appealed to have his case transferred from the jurisdiction of the governor of Judaea to the emperor's tribunal in Rome.[38]

---

35. Cf. in particular 1 Corinthians 15: 24–28; Romans 8: 17–25.

36. His letter to the Galatians may be earlier; see p. 179.

37. F. W. Farrar goes as far as caution allows: "Whether there is any allusion to his [Claudius's] name in the word κατέχω ["restrain"] I am not prepared to say" (*Life and Work of St. Paul*, ii [London, 1879], p. 584).

38. Acts 25: 11; see p. 363.

# CHAPTER 22

# Paul and the Athenians

## 1. Visit to Beroea

PAUL HAD FOLLOWED THE VIA EGNATIA FROM PHILIPPI TO Thessalonica, and he might have continued to follow it from Thessalonica westward. It was to Macedonia that he had been called, and the Via Egnatia ran on through Macedonia to its Adriatic terminus at Dyrrhachium. Instead, Paul left the main road and made for Beroea, which lay some distance south of it. It is perhaps with reference to its being off the Via Egnatia that Cicero describes Beroea as *oppidum deuium*, "an out-of-the-way town".[1]

Perhaps Paul had little choice in the matter: it was to Beroea that his Thessalonian friends sent him and Silas. But an interesting suggestion has been made to the effect that when Paul first set out with his companions to travel from east to west along the Via Egnatia he had conceived the plan of following it to Dyrrhachium and then crossing the Adriatic to Italy, and so to Rome.[2] We know from his letter to the Roman Christians, written six or seven years after this, that he had often intended to visit them, but had been prevented thus far (Romans 1: 13; 15: 22 f.). If this was one of those occasions, what prevented him? Possibly he was unwilling to go to Rome until the stigma of the charge of subversion at Thessalonica had faded; but he could have had a more conclusive reason for changing his plan if news reached him about this time of Claudius's edict expelling the Jewish community from Rome (c. A.D. 49). This would have deprived him of his natural base of operations in Rome. On the other hand, Claudius's edict was indirectly to prove a personal boon to him a month or two later, when he came to Corinth and found there two of those recently expelled from Rome, who promptly became his firm and lifelong friends.[3]

---

1. Cicero, *In Pisonem* 89. It was the first city to surrender to the Romans after their victory at Pydna in 168 B.C.
2. Cf. A. Harnack, *The Mission and Expansion of Christianity*, E.T., i (London, 1908), pp. 74 f.; H. J. Cadbury, *The Book of Acts in History* (New York, 1955), pp. 60 f.; G. Bornkamm, *Paul*, E.T. (London, 1971), pp. 51 ff.; E. A. Judge and G. S. R. Thomas, "The Origin of the Church at Rome", *Reformed Theological Review* 25 (1966), p. 90.
3. Acts 18: 2; see p. 250.

Since he found himself in Beroea, however, he availed himself of the opportunities for witness which were afforded here. There was a Jewish synagogue in Beroea, so he and Silas visited it and communicated the gospel to the congregation as they had done at Thessalonica. The Beroean Jews gave them a courteous and unprejudiced hearing: "they received the word with all eagerness", says Luke, "examining the scriptures daily to see if these things were so" (Acts 17: 11). The result was that several converts were won at Beroea, special mention being made here, as at Thessalonica, of "not a few Greek women of high standing" (Acts 17: 12). One at least of the Beroean converts is known to us by name – Sopater, the son of Pyrrhus, who appears to have accompanied Paul and others to Jerusalem seven years later as a delegate from the Beroean church (Acts 20: 4). If he is identical (as is probable) with Sosipater of Romans 16: 21, he was a Jewish convert, since Paul there calls him one of his "kinsmen".

But those who had stirred up trouble for Paul in Thessalonica, hearing of his presence in Beroea, came and stirred up similar trouble there. Plainly it was best that Paul should leave Macedonia until the agitation in the province died down, so his Beroean friends got him down to the coast and accompanied him (presumably by sea) to Athens, which lay in the province of Achaia. Between Beroea and Athens lay the region of Thessaly, but the Beroean Christians judged (as the Western text of Acts 17: 15 says fairly explicitly) that Thessaly would not be safe for Paul and did not leave him until they had brought him to Athens.[4] Then they returned, bearing instructions from Paul to Silas and Timothy about rejoining him.

## 2. Paul in Athens

Luke's vivid account of Paul's stay in Athens, for all the accuracy of its local colour, has for a variety of reasons been assessed sceptically by several students of his writings. Happily, we have Paul's assurance that he did spend some time in Athens, and that for part of that time he was on his own: he tells the Christians of Thessalonica how he sent Timothy back to visit and help them, while he himself was "willing to be left behind at Athens alone" (1 Thessalonians 3: 1). From all that we know of Paul, we can be certain that in Athens, as elsewhere, he allowed no opportunity for apostolic witness to pass him by. Luke describes some opportunities which he seized, and goes into considerable detail about one of them.

No city in the Hellenic world could match Athens for those

4. "He by-passed Thessaly, for he was forbidden to preach the word to them" (cf. Acts 16: 6–8). Thessaly formed part of the province of Macedonia.

qualities which Greeks counted most glorious. Athens, the cradle of democracy, attained the foremost place among the city-states of Greece early in the fifth century B.C., because of the leading part she played in resisting the Persian invasions. For the next half-century she controlled a powerful and wealthy maritime empire, and after her defeat by the Spartans and their allies in the Peloponnesian War (431–404 B.C.) was not long in regaining much of her earlier influence. In the fourth century she again took the lead in resisting Macedonian aggression, and even after Philip's victory at Chaeronea (338 B.C.) was generously treated by him and allowed to retain much of her ancient liberty, which she enjoyed until the Roman conquest of Greece in 146 B.C. The Romans, too, in consideration of the city's glorious past, permitted her to carry on her own institutions as a free and allied city within the empire. The sculpture, literature and oratory of Athens in the fifth and fourth centuries B.C. have never been surpassed; in philosophy, too, she took the leading place, being the native city of Socrates and Plato and the adopted home of Aristotle, Epicurus and Zeno:

> Athens the eye of Greece, Mother of Arts
> And Eloquence, native to famous wits
> Or hospitable, in her sweet recess,
> City or Suburban, studious walks and shades;
> See there the Olive Grove of Academe,
> Plato's retirement, where the Attic Bird
> Trills her thick-warbl'd notes the summer long,
> There flowrie hill Hymettus with the sound
> Of Bees industrious murmur oft invites
> To studious musing; there Ilissus rouls
> His whispering stream; within the walls then view
> The schools of antient Sages; his who bred
> Great Alexander to subdue the world,
> Lyceum there, and painted Stoa next: . . .
> To sage Philosophy next lend thine ear,
> From Heaven descended to the low-rooft house
> Of Socrates, see there his Tenement,
> Whom well inspir'd the Oracle pronounc'd
> Wisest of men; from whose mouth issu'd forth
> Mellifluous streams that water'd all the schools
> Of Academics old and new, with those
> Sirnam'd Peripatetics, and the Sect
> Epicurean, and the Stoic severe.[5]

The persistence of the cultural influence of Athens in the Hellenistic age is further to be seen in the fact that it was the Attic dialect of Greek, spoken at first over a very restricted area as com-

5. John Milton, *Paradise Regained* iv. 240 ff.

pared with Ionic and Doric, that formed the main basis of the *Koinē*.

Luke pictures Paul as viewing the temples, altars and images of Athens through the eyes of one brought up in the spirit of Jewish monotheism and the aniconic principles of the second commandment of the decalogue. "What pagans sacrifice", Paul maintained, "they offer to demons and not to God" (1 Corinthians 10: 20), and those who "exchanged the glory of the immortal God for images resembling mortal man" or anything else "exchanged the truth of God for a lie" because they "worshipped and served the creature rather than the Creator" (Romans 1: 23, 25). In the *agora* at the foot of the Acropolis, where the citizens of Athens met to exchange the latest news, there was no lack of men ready to enter into debate with him about the nature of the divine being. Some of those professed attachment to the Stoic or Epicurean schools of philosophy, but none of them could come to terms with this strange visitor, so passionately in earnest as he talked about Jesus, "designated Son of God in power . . . by his resurrection from the dead" (as Paul puts it in Romans 1: 4). To some he appeared to be a retailer of scraps of second-hand learning (a *spermologos*, as they said, using an Athenian slang term); [6] to others he appeared to be commending foreign divinities, and so rendered himself amenable to the jurisdiction of the court of the Areopagus.

This body, the most venerable of Athenian institutions, going back into the mists of legendary antiquity, had at one time discharged the functions of a senate. With the growth of democracy in Athens, its earlier powers were greatly reduced, but it retained considerable prestige and continued to exercise responsibility in the realm of religion, morals and homicide. It derived its name from the fact that its original meeting-place was on the Areopagus, the hill west of the Acropolis; in Roman times, however, it held most of its meetings in the Royal Portico (the *stoa basileios*) in the *agora*.

### 3. The Areopagus speech

Before this court, then, Paul was brought and invited to expound his teaching. It is uncertain whether we are intended to envisage him as addressing it in the Royal Portico or on the Areopagus itself. The latter is the traditional view: the visitor to Athens today can see the text of Paul's address to the court inscribed on bronze at the foot of the ascent to the hill.

> Men of Athens, I see that in all respects you are very religious. As I was walking through your city and observing your objects of worship I

---

6. It was used of Aeschines as a term of abuse by Demosthenes, *De corona* 127. NEB renders it "charlatan", which is more accurate than the traditional "babbler".

found an altar bearing the inscription: "To an Unknown God". I here-
by declare to you the nature of what you worship as unknown.

The God who made the world and everything that is in it is Lord of
heaven and earth and does not dwell in temples made by human hands.
It is not because he is in need of anything that he accepts service at
men's hands, for it is he who gives to all men life and breath and everything else. He has made every race of men from one stock, to occupy the
whole face of the earth, and he has ordained the allotted periods and
the frontiers of their habitable territory. His purpose was that they
should seek God, so as to touch him and find him – though indeed he is
not far from each one of us. "For in him we live and move and have
our being", as in fact some of your poets have said – "for we are also his
offspring". Since then we are God's offspring we ought not to think that
the divinity is like an object of gold or silver or stone, engraved by
human art and design.

God has overlooked the period of your ignorance, but now he commands men that all of them everywhere should repent, because he has
set a day on which he will judge the world in righteousness by a man
whom he has appointed, and of this he has provided a pledge to all by
raising him from the dead.[7]

Some of the motifs of this speech have appeared earlier in the
short summary of Barnabas and Paul's protest to the people of
Lystra who were preparing to pay them divine honours,[8] but the
*Areopagitica* is fuller, more detailed and adapted to the intellectual
climate of Athens. At Athens, as formerly at Lystra, the Paul of
Acts does not expressly quote Old Testament prophecies which
would be quite unknown to his audience: such direct quotations as
his speech contains are from Greek poets. But he does not argue
from "first principles" of the kind that formed the basis of various
systems of Greek philosophy; his exposition and defence of his
message are founded on the biblical revelation and they echo the
thought, and at times the very language, of the Old Testament
writings. Like the biblical revelation itself, his speech begins with
God the creator of all, continues with God the sustainer of all, and
concludes with God the judge of all.

### 4. The knowledge of the unknown God

He finds his text, his point of contact, in an altar-dedication
which illustrated the intense religiosity of the Athenians – a quality
which impressed many other visitors to their city in antiquity. The
dedication read: *Agnōstō Theō* ("To an Unknown God"). Other
writers tell us that altars to unknown gods were to be seen at
Athens:[9] if it is pointed out that no other speaks of an altar "to an

7. Acts 17: 22–31.
8. Acts 14: 15–17; see p. 170.
9. Pausanias, *Description of Greece* i. 1. 4; Philostratus, *Life of Apollonius* vi. 3. 5.

unknown god" (in the singular), it may suffice to say that two or more dedications "to an unknown god" might be summarily referred to as "altars to unknown gods" (in the plural).

Various tales were told to account for such anonymous dedications: according to one tale, they were set up by the direction of Epimenides, a wise man of Crete, one of the poets quoted in the course of the speech.[10] Whatever may have been the original circumstances or intention of the inscription which Paul took as his text, he interprets it as a confession of ignorance regarding the divine nature, and says that the purpose of his coming is to dispel that ignorance.

He proceeds, then, to instruct them in the doctrine of God. First, God has created the universe with all that it contains; he is Lord of heaven and earth. This is the very language of biblical revelation: God Most High is "maker of heaven and earth" (Genesis 14: 19, 23); "the earth is the LORD's and the fulness thereof" (Psalm 24: 1). No concessions are allowed to Hellenistic paganism; no distinction is made between the Supreme Being and a "demiurge" or master-workman who fashioned the world because the Supreme Being was too pure to come into polluting contact with the material order.

Second, God does not inhabit shrines which human hands have built. Stephen's defence makes this point to the Sanhedrin with reference to the Jerusalem temple, built for the worship of the living God; much more could Paul see fit to impress it on the Areopagus in full view of the magnificent temples which crowned the Acropolis, dedicated to gods that were no gods. The higher paganism, indeed, acknowledged that no material structure could accommodate the divine nature: "What house fashioned by builders", asked Euripides, "could contain the form divine within enclosing walls?"[11] But the affinities of Paul's language are biblical and not classical.

Third, God requires nothing from those whom he has created. Here, too, parallels to Paul's argument can be adduced from classical Greek literature: Plato's *Euthyphro* comes to mind. But Paul stands right within the prophetic tradition. The prophets and psalmists in their day had to refute the idea that the God of Israel was in some degree dependent on his people and their gifts: his people were completely dependent on him. Thus in Psalm 50: 9–12 he declines their sacrifices in these terms:

I will accept no bull from your house,
    nor he-goat from your folds.
For every beast of the forest is mine,

10. Diogenes Laertius, *Lives of Philosophers* i. 110.
11. Euripides, fragment 968.

the cattle on a thousand hills.
I know all the birds of the air,
  and all that moves in the field is mine.
If I were hungry, I would not tell you,
  for the world and all that is in it is mine.

This is precisely Paul's emphasis when he declares that, if God accepts service from men, it is not because he cannot do without it.[12] Far from their supplying any need of his, it is he who supplies every need of theirs.

## 5. *The doctrine of man*

Since the creator of all things in general is the creator of the human race in particular, Paul moves on from the doctrine of God to the doctrine of man.

First, man is one. The Greeks might take pride in their natural superiority to barbarians; the Athenians might boast that, unlike their fellow-Greeks, they were autochthonous, sprung from the soil of their Attic homeland. But Paul affirms that mankind is one in origin, all created by God and all descended from a common ancestor. Before God, all human beings meet on one level.

Second, man's earthly abode and the course of the seasons have been designed for his wellbeing. This too is a biblical insight. The earth, according to Genesis 1, was formed and furnished to be man's home before man was introduced as its occupant. Moreover, part of the forming and furnishing of man's home on earth consisted in the provision of habitable zones to serve as living space for mankind and in the regulation of "allotted periods". The former provision is implied in Deuteronomy 32: 8:

When the Most High gave to the nations their inheritance,
  when he separated the sons of men,
He fixed the bounds of the peoples
  according to the number of the sons of God.

The "allotted periods" are to be identified either with the sequence of seed-time and harvest (as in the speech at Lystra) or with the epochs of human history (as in the visions of Daniel).

Third, God's purpose in making these arrangements was that men might seek and find him − a desire all the more natural because they are his offspring and he aids them in the attainment of his desire by his nearness to them. It is here that the terminology of the speech shows closest Hellenistic affinities, but to a different

12. The NEB rendering of Acts 17: 25 is unsurpassed in conveying the precise force of the words: "It is not because he lacks anything that he accepts service at men's hands . . .".

audience Paul could have expressed the same thought by saying that man is God's creature, made in his image. To his Athenian audience he establishes his point by two quotations from Greek poets which set forth men's relation to the Supreme Being.

The first quotation is based on the fourth line of a quatrain attributed to Epimenides the Cretan, in which his fellow-islanders are denounced for their impiety in claiming that the tomb of Zeus could be seen in Crete:

> They fashioned a tomb for thee, O holy and high one –
> The Cretans, always liars, evil beasts, idle bellies!
> But thou art not dead: thou livest and abidest for ever,
> *For in thee we live and move and have our being.*[13]

The second comes from the poem on *Natural Phenomena* by Paul's fellow-Cilician Aratus, a poet deeply influenced by Stoicism. This poem opens with a celebration of Zeus – Zeus the Supreme Being of Stoic philosophy rather than Zeus the head of the Greek mythological pantheon:

> Let us begin with Zeus: never, O men, let us
> leave him unmentioned. Full of Zeus are all the ways
> and all the meeting-places of men; the sea and the
> harbours are full of him. It is with Zeus that
> every one of us in every way has to do,
> *for we are also his offspring.*[14]

It is not suggested that even the Paul of Acts (let alone the Paul whom we know from his letters) envisaged God in terms of the Zeus of Stoic pantheism, but if men whom his hearers recognized as authorities had used language which could corroborate his argument, he would quote their words, giving them a biblical sense as he did so. Paul's concern was to impress on his hearers the responsibility of all men, as God's creatures into whom he has breathed the breath of life, to give him the honour which is his due. And this honour is not given when the divine nature is depicted in material forms. Again we hear the echo of Hebrew prophecy and psalmody when pagan idolatry is under review (Psalm 115: 4):

> Their idols are silver and gold,
>      the work of men's hands . . .

Finally, a call to repentance is issued. Their ignorance of the

---

13. Preserved in Syriac translation by Isho'dad of Merv; cf. *Horae Semiticae* x, ed. M. D. Gibson (Cambridge, 1913), p. 40 (Syriac). The second line of the quatrain is quoted in Titus 1: 12.

14. Aratus, *Phainomena* 1–5; cf. Cleanthes, *Hymn to Zeus* 4.

divine nature was culpable, but God had mercifully overlooked it. As the people of Lystra were told that God had hitherto "allowed all the nations to follow their own ways", with the implication that now a fresh beginning had come about, so the members of the Areopagus are told that the recent resurrection of Christ is the pledge that by his agency God is about to "judge the world in righteousness" – a further echo of the Hebrew psalmists, who announce that God "will judge the world in righteousness and the peoples in equity" (Psalm 98: 9). The "man whom he has appointed" to execute this judgment is readily identified with the "one like a son of man" who, in Daniel 7: 13 f., is seen receiving world-wide authority from the Ancient of Days, and therefore with the one to whom, according to John 5: 27, the Father has given "authority to execute judgment, because he is Son of man".

## 6. The Paulinism of the Areopagus speech

There are many features in this speech which have caused it to be marked down quite confidently as non-Pauline. H. J. Cadbury remarked that "the classicists are among the most inclined to plead for the historicity of the scene of Paul at Athens" [15] – Areopagus address and all. Outstanding among such classicists was Eduard Meyer, who not only professed his inability to understand "how any one has found it possible to explain this scene as an invention"[16] but even claimed to have persuaded Eduard Norden to concede at least the possibility that Luke reproduced the genuine content of Paul's speech.[17] Norden had argued against its authenticity in his Agnostos Theos (1913), a work based on an exceptionally penetrating analysis of the speech: the Attic flavour of the passage betokened, to his mind, a literary construction made with the aid of an external model. And a more illustrious classicist than Norden or Meyer, the great Wilamowitz, had concluded that the religious sentiment of the Areopagitica was not that of the real Paul, who (unlike the composer of the speech) did not directly take over any of the elements of Greek education.[18]

But it is theologians rather than classicists who have, one after another, most categorically denied any association of the Areopagitica with the Paul of the letters. Here, says one, the Pauline emphasis on being "in Christ" by grace is replaced by a pagan

---

15. BC i, 5, p. 406.
16. E. Meyer, Ursprung und Anfänge des Christentums, iii (Stuttgart/Berlin, 1923), p. 105.
17. Meyer, op. cit., p. 96.
18. U. von Wilamowitz-Moellendorff, Die griechische Literatur des Altertums (Berlin/Leipzig, ³ 1912), p. 232.

emphasis on being "in God" by nature.[19] Instead of setting forth
the Pauline gospel, says another, the speech anticipates the
rationalism of the second-century apologists, in its attempt to establish the true knowledge of God by an appeal to Greek poets and
thinkers.[20] Its message, says a third, is set in a context not merely of
salvation-history but of world-history, which is even more
un-Pauline.[21] According to a fourth, the "word of the cross" is tactfully omitted, because it was known to be "folly to Gentiles" [22] (cf.
1 Corinthians 1: 23).

Yet it is not too difficult to envisage the author of the first three
chapters of Paul's letter to the Romans making several of the points
which are central to the *Areopagitica*.[23] The differences in emphasis
can be appreciated if it is remembered that the letter was written to
Christians while the speech was delivered to pagans. In the letter
Paul insists that the knowledge of God, his "everlasting power and
divinity", is available from his works in creation, to the point where
men are "without excuse, for although they knew God they did not
honour him as God or give thanks to him, but they became futile in
their thinking and their senseless minds were darkened" (Romans
1: 19–21). Nevertheless God in his forbearance had passed over
these and other sins previously committed, but now that he had
manifested his way of righteousness "through faith in Jesus Christ
for all who believe" a new responsibility rested upon those to whom
the gospel came (Romans 3: 21–26). If in the speech God's purpose
in making himself known to men was that they might "touch him
and find him", in Romans 2: 4 his forbearance and kindness are
designed to lead them to repentance. Jesus Christ, through faith in
whom the divine pardon and gift of righteousness were obtainable
by men, was at the same time the one through whom, on a coming
day, according to Paul's gospel, God would "judge the secrets of
men" (Romans 2: 16).

Take the author of those words and bring him to Athens: invite
him to expound his teaching not to fellow-believers but to cultured
pagans. Remember that he has now for several years been a
successful evangelist in the pagan world – a fact which, despite his
own modest disclaimer in 1 Corinthians 2: 2–5, implies considerable persuasiveness in speech and approach, including the

19. A. Schweitzer, *The Mysticism of Paul the Apostle*, E.T. (London, 1931), pp. 6
ff.

20. M. Dibelius, *Studies in the Acts of the Apostles*, E.T. (London, 1956), pp. 26 ff.

21. H. Conzelmann, "The Address of Paul on the Areopagus", in *Studies in
Luke-Acts*, ed. L. E. Keck and J. L. Martyn (Nashville/New York, 1966), pp. 217 ff.

22. P. Vielhauer, "On the 'Paulinism' of Acts", in *Studies in Luke-Acts*, ed. Keck
and Martyn, pp. 36 f.

23. For a more positive appraisal cf. B. Gärtner, *The Areopagus Speech and Natural
Revelation* (Uppsala, 1955).

ability to find and exploit an initial area of common ground with his hearers, apart from which any attempt at communication would be fruitless. How will he address himself to such an audience? He will certainly try not to alienate them in his first sentence or two. It is underestimating Paul's versatility, his capacity for being "all things to all men", to think that he could not have presented the essence of Romans 1–3 to pagans along the lines of Acts 17: 22–31. True, Luke did not hear Paul address the court of the Areopagus, but he knew how Paul was accustomed to present his *praeparatio evangelica* to such an audience, and endeavoured, following the example of Thucydides, "to give the general sense of what was actually said".[24]

If it be borne in mind that this is Luke's summary of a speech which may in any case have been more *praeparatio* than *evangelium*, then some of the objections to its substantial authenticity may not appear to be insuperable. As has been said already, the quotation "In him we live and move and have our being" does not imply a "God-mysticism";[25] it is adduced simply to confirm that God is the author and sustainer of our life. The thought of being "in Christ" by grace would have been meaningless to pagans. Epimenides and Aratus are not invoked as authorities in their own right; certain things which they said, however, can be understood as pointing to the knowledge of God. But the knowledge of God presented in the speech is not rationalistically conceived or established; it is the knowledge of God taught by Hebrew prophets and sages. It is rooted in the fear of God; it belongs to the same order as truth, goodness and covenant-love; for lack of it men and women perish; in the coming day of God it will fill the earth "as the waters cover the sea" (Isaiah 11: 9). The "delicately suited allusions" to Stoic and Epicurean tenets which have been discerned in the speech,[26] like the quotations from pagan poets, have their place as points of contact with the audience, but they do not commit the speaker to acquiescence in the realm of ideas to which they originally belong. Unlike some later Christian apologists, the Paul of Acts does not cease to be fundamentally biblical in his approach to the Greeks, even when his biblical emphasis might seem to diminish his chances of success.

The salvation-history of the *Areopagitica* finds its climax in Christ, as does the salvation-history of the Pauline letters.[27] The

24. Thucydides, *History* i. 22. 1.
25. See p. 137.
26. J. H. Moulton and W. F. Howard, *Grammar of New Testament Greek*, ii (Edinburgh, 1929), p. 8, n. 3.
27. On Pauline salvation-history (*Heilsgeschichte*) see J. Munck, *Paul and the Salvation of Mankind*, E.T. (London, 1959); O. Cullmann, *Salvation in History*, E.T. (London, 1967), pp. 248 ff.; E. Käsemann, *Perspectives on Paul*, E.T. (London 1971), pp. 60 ff.

salvation-history of the letters is naturally more detailed and comprehensive: the outline in Romans 1: 18 ff. of the progressive working of divine retribution against human sin forms the backcloth to the unfolding of divine grace in the gospel; the gospel itself was preached in advance to Abraham and foreshadowed by the prophets, and was fulfilled in Christ. To the "*now* God commands" of the speech corresponds the "*now* is the acceptable time" of 2 Corinthians 6: 2. As for world-history, it plays no greater part here than it plays in Paul's letters: in both the life of humanity moves forward between the poles of creation and judgment. "In the beginning, God" is matched by "in the end, God".

True, "the word of the cross" is absent from the speech. This could be as much because the speech is more *praeparatio* than *evangelium* as because Luke's *theologia gloriae* has taken precedence over Paul's *theologia crucis*. The former possibility used to be linked with Paul's confessed decision, when he moved on from Athens to Corinth, to "know nothing" among the Corinthians "except Jesus Christ and him crucified" (1 Corinthians 2: 2), as though he realized that his tactics in Athens were unwise. But Paul by this time was no novice in Gentile evangelization, experimenting with this approach and that to discover which was most effective. It is probable that Paul's decision at Corinth was based on his assessment of the situation there.

## 7. *The resurrection of the dead*

There is nothing, however, to commend the suggestion that "the word of the cross" was tactfully omitted from the *Areopagitica* because it was known to be folly to Gentiles: any mention of the cross could not have appeared more foolish to these particular Gentiles than did the note on which the speech concluded – the resurrection of the dead. God, it is stated, has confirmed the certainty of the coming day of judgment by raising from the dead the man through whom that judgment will be delivered.

If the speech be treated realistically, some of the hearers could be pictured as asking to be told more about this man – to be told, in particular, what there was about him that occasioned his being raised from the dead. If it is viewed stylistically, then it is seen to end with a fitting peroration. But the content of the peroration was totally uncongenial to the majority of the hearers. If Paul had spoken of the immortality of the soul, he would have commanded the assent of most of his hearers except the Epicureans, but the idea of resurrection was absurd. When the Athenian tragedian Aeschylus, half a millennium before, described the institution of that very court of the Areopagus by Athene, the city's patron deity, he had made the god Apollo say:

When the dust has soaked up a man's blood,
Once he is dead, there is no resurrection [28]

– and the word for resurrection there (*anastasis*) is the word which
Paul used. To what purpose did this man come to Athens with his
talk of resurrection when every Athenian knew, on the highest
authority, that there could be no such thing?

Outright ridicule and polite dismissal were the main responses to
Paul's exposition of the knowledge of God. One member of the
court of the Areopagus is said to have believed his message –
Dionysius, who shares with the apostle the honour of having a
street named after him in present-day Athens, and who about A.D.
500 provided a pseudonym for the author of a literary corpus of
Neoplatonism and mystical theology. Among the few others who
adhered to Paul at Athens special mention is made of a woman called Damaris, of whom nothing more is known. Of those who were
persuaded to positive action by the Areopagus speech it might be
said, as was said of his Thessalonian converts, that they "turned to
God from idols to serve a living and true God, and to wait for his
Son from heaven, whom he raised from the dead, Jesus, our
deliverer from the wrath to come" (1 Thessalonians 1: 9 f.). There
is as little explicit mention of the *theologia crucis* in these words of
Paul as there is in the Areopagus speech, but it would be precarious
to infer that Paul was silent about the cross at Thessalonica. But we
hear of no church in Athens in the apostolic age, and when Paul
speaks of the "firstfruits of Achaia" it is to a family in Corinth that
he refers (1 Corinthians 16: 15). [29]

28. Aeschylus, *Eumenides* 647 f.
29. A sober study of the whole Athenian episode has been published by T. D.
Barnes, "An Apostle on Trial", *JTS*, n.s. 20 (1969), pp. 407–419.

# CHAPTER 23

# The Church of God at Corinth

*1. Paul comes to Corinth*

PAUL TRAVELLED FROM ATHENS TO CORINTH IN A MOOD OF dejection. It had probably been no part of his programme when he crossed the sea to Macedonia to turn south into the province of Achaia. But he had been driven from one Macedonian city after another, and it seemed that, for the time being, there was no place for him in that province, despite his previous assurance that God had called him to evangelize it. True, his preaching in Macedonia had not been fruitless: he had left small groups of converts behind him in Philippi, Thessalonica and Beroea. But his mind was full of misgivings about their well-being. No violence had been offered to him in Athens, but the polite amusement which had greeted his witness there was perhaps more difficult to take than violence: violence at least showed that some impact was being made. So far as positive response to his preaching was concerned, Athens had been much less encouraging than the cities of Macedonia. So he arrived in Corinth, as he says, "in weakness and in much fear and trembling" (1 Corinthians 2: 3). There was no reason to suppose that Corinth would prove less troublesome than the cities of Macedonia. Any traveller in the Aegean world of those days must have known of Corinth's reputation; this city would provide uncongenial soil indeed for the good seed of the gospel. In the event, Paul spent eighteen months at Corinth – a longer time than he had spent in any city since he parted company with Barnabas in Syrian Antioch – and, by the time he left, there was a large and vigorous, though volatile, church there. Luke tells how, shortly after Paul's arrival in Corinth, he had a vision one night in which the Lord said to him, "Do not be afraid: speak, and do not be silent. I am with you, and no one shall harm you by any attack; I have many people in this city" (Acts 18: 9 f.). Paul was reassured, and the promise was fulfilled: he came to recognize that, while Corinth had not figured on his own programme, it had a prominent place in the Lord's programme for him. His time in Corinth, and his experiences with the Corinthian church during the years which followed his departure from Corinth, did much to deepen his human sympathy and to promote his pastoral maturity.

248

## 2. Corinth

Corinth was an ancient city of Greece; its name, at least, antedates the coming of the Dorian Greeks early in the first millennium B.C.[1] It was situated on the Isthmus of Corinth, where it commanded the land-routes between Central Greece and the Peloponnese and, through its harbours at Lechaeum on the west of the Isthmus and Cenchreae on the east, early became an entrepôt for Mediterranean trade. It was built on the north side of the Acrocorinthus, which rises 1900 feet (nearly 600 metres) above the plain and served the Corinthians as their citadel. The citadel had an inexhaustible water supply in the upper fountain of Peirene; the lower fountain of the same name served the requirements of the city itself.[2]

Thanks to its commercial advantages, Corinth enjoyed great prosperity in classical Greek times. It enjoyed a reputation for luxury and its name became proverbial for sexual laxity.[3] It was a centre of the worship of Aphrodite, whose temple crowned the Acrocorinthus. Her cult-statue was attired in the armour of the war-god Ares, with his helmet for a foot-rest and his shield for a mirror. At the foot of the citadel stood the temple of Melicertes, patron of seafarers; his name is a hellenized form of Melkart, the principal deity of Tyre. The Isthmian Games, over which Corinth presided, and in which all the Greek city-states participated, were held every two years;[4] at them the sea-god Poseidon was specially honoured. Corinth paid respect, in Paul's words, to "many 'gods' and many 'lords' " (1 Corinthians 8: 5).

Corinth survived many crises in Greek history, but suffered disaster in 146 B.C. By way of reprisal for the leading part it had played in the revolt of the Achaian League against the overlordship of Rome, a Roman army led by Lucius Mummius razed the city to the ground, sold its population into slavery and confiscated its territory to the Roman state. Little of the Greek city remains visible today; the main exception is the Doric temple of Apollo, dating back to the sixth century B.C.

1. The -nth- sound-group is generally recognized as a pre-Greek formation. On the history and archaeology of Corinth see J. G. O'Neill, *Ancient Corinth* (Oxford, 1930); O. Broneer, "Corinth: Center of St. Paul's Missionary Work in Greece", *Biblical Archaeologist* 14 (1951), pp. 78–96.

2. Corinth first appears in Greek literature in Homer (*Iliad* ii. 570, xiii. 664, and under the name Ephyre, vi. 152); the *name* (though perhaps in reference to another place) has been identified in a Mycenaean text from Pylos.

3. The verb κορινθιάζεσθαι , lit. "to play the Corinthian", was current from the fifth century B.C. in the sense of practising fornication.

4. According to one strand of tradition, the Isthmian Games were founded in honour of Melicertes (Thrasyllus, according to Clement of Alexandria, *Stromateis* i. 137. 1).

The site lay derelict for a century; the city was re-founded in 44 B.C. by Julius Caesar as a Roman colony, under the name *Laus Iulia Corinthiensis*. In addition to having its own colonial administration, it was from 27 B.C. onwards the seat of government of the Roman province of Achaia.

Roman Corinth quickly regained the prosperity of its predecessor. At the narrowest part of the Isthmus a sort of railroad of wooden logs, called a *diolkos* by the Greeks, was constructed: on this smaller ships were dragged across the three and a half miles (about six kilometres) between the Corinthian Gulf on the west and the Saronic Gulf on the east. With the old prosperity, the old reputation for sexual laxity returned. The temple of Aphrodite was staffed by a thousand female slaves, who are said to have made the place a tourist attraction and enhanced its prosperity.[5] This background helps to explain the frequency of the admonitions against unchastity in Paul's Corinthian correspondence.

As Corinth was a Roman colony, its citizens were Romans, probably freedmen from Italy, but the population was greatly augmented by Greeks and Levantines, the latter including a considerable Jewish community. The museum on the site of Roman Corinth contains part of a stone lintel inscribed in Greek, "Synagogue of the Hebrews".[6] While the style of the lettering points to a date rather later than the apostolic age, the synagogue to which it belonged perhaps stood on the site of the synagogue which Paul visited soon after his arrival in Corinth.

## 3. Priscilla and Aquila

In accordance with his regular practice, Paul maintained himself in Corinth by his own manual labour, and he found employment with a tent-making firm owned by a Jew, originally from Pontus, named Aquila, and his wife Priscilla. The couple had been until recently resident in Rome, which was possibly Priscilla's birthplace,[7] but had been compelled to leave that city because of Claudius's edict expelling the Jewish colony from Rome.[8] They appear to have been a well-to-do couple, and their tent-making business may have had branches in several centres, with a manager in charge of the branches in those places where they themselves were not actually resident. They were thus able to move back and

5. Cf. Strabo, *Geography* viii. 6. 20–23; Pausanias, *Description of Greece* ii. 1. 1–5. 2.

6. Cf. B. Powell, "Greek Inscriptions from Corinth", *American Journal of Archaeology*, series 2, 7 (1903), pp. 60 f., No. 40; A. Deissmann, *Light from the Ancient East*, E.T. (London, [2] 1927), p. 16.

7. She was probably associated in some way with the *gens Prisca*. While Luke gives her the more familiar name Priscilla, Paul refers to her more formally as Prisca (e.g. in 1 Corinthians 16: 19).

8. See pp. 235, 381.

forth easily between Rome, Corinth and Ephesus. After their initial meeting in Corinth, Paul had no more loyal friends or helpers than Priscilla and Aquila, "to whom", as he put it some years later, "not only I but also all the churches of the Gentiles give thanks" (Romans 16: 4): [9] their services to the Christian cause evidently far exceeded their personal services to Paul. They are always mentioned together, and more often than not Priscilla is named before her husband; [10] this may suggest that she was the more impressive personality of the two. In none of Paul's references to them is there any hint that they were converts of his: all the indications are that they were Christians before they met him, and that accordingly they were Christians while they lived in Rome – which may throw light on Suetonius's statement that the Jews were expelled by Claudius because of their constant rioting "at the instigation of Chrestus". [11]

## 4. First Corinthian converts

In Corinth, as in the cities which he had previously visited, Paul attended the sabbath services in the synagogue for several weeks and made it his first base of operations. As his custom was, he argued that Jesus was the fulfiller of Hebrew prophecy and, according to the Western text of Acts 18: 4, "inserted the name of the Lord Jesus" at appropriate points in the scripture readings. [12] A number of Jews and God-fearing Gentiles were persuaded by his preaching; the former included a ruler of the synagogue named Crispus [13] and the latter included the owner of a house next door to the synagogue, whom Luke calls Titius Justus. [14] If, as is probable, he is identical with the Corinthian Christian described by Paul as "Gaius, who is host to me and to the whole church" (Romans 16: 23), then his full name Gaius Titius Justus marks him out as a Roman citizen. [15] Paul singles out Crispus and Gaius, together with one Stephanas and his family, "the firstfruits of Achaia", as the only ones of his Corinthian converts whom he baptized

9. See p. 298.

10. Both by Luke (Acts 18: 18, 26) and by Paul (Romans 16: 3; cf. 2 Timothy 4: 19). The Western reviser of Acts reverses the order in 18: 26, and this is not the only place where he appears to play down the prominence of women in the narrative.

11. Suetonius, *Life of Claudius* 25. 4.

12. Making it plain that it was to him that the scriptures in question pointed. We may compare the insertion of "Messiah" at appropriate points in the Isaianic Servant Songs (Isaiah 42: 1; 52: 13) and elsewhere (43: 10) in the Targum of Jonathan on the Prophets.

13. Acts 18: 8; 1 Corinthians 1: 15.

14. Acts 18: 7.

15. Cf. E. J. Goodspeed, "Gaius Titius Justus", *JBL* 69 (1950), pp. 382 f.

personally.[16] This would confirm that they were his first converts in
Corinth. After a few weeks Silas and Timothy joined him, having
completed their commissions in Macedonia, and they were able to
relieve him of part of his burden, including the baptism of converts.
They probably brought Paul a gift from some of his Macedonian
friends, which made it possible for him to discontinue tent-making
for a time and give himself entirely to preaching and teaching.[17]

But the time came in Corinth as elsewhere when the Jewish
authorities decided that they had had enough of him, and allowed
him the use of the synagogue no longer. Conveniently for Paul, his
friend and convert Titius Justus put his house at his disposal so that
he might carry on the work which he had started in the nearby synagogue. This house apparently became not only Paul's headquarters but also the first meeting-place of the Corinthian church.
Here Paul continued to proclaim salvation through Christ crucified, and the number of his converts grew rapidly; they now included
not only Jews and God-fearers but an increasing proportion of
pagans.

Among the converts from paganism we should probably include
Erastus of Corinth. The name Erastus appears in reference to
Paul's circle of friends and helpers once in Acts (19: 22) and twice
in the Pauline corpus (Romans 16: 23; 2 Timothy 4: 20), but it is
not at all certain that the same man is meant on all three occasions.
The Corinthian Erastus, however, is mentioned in Romans 16: 23
alongside Paul's host Gaius (Titius Justus) as sending his greetings
to the people addressed, and he is described as "city
treasurer"(Greek *oikonomos*, equivalent to Latin *arcarius*). On April
15, 1929, archaeologists based on the American School at Athens
uncovered in Old Corinth a slab bearing a Latin inscription which
should probably be rendered: "Erastus, in consideration of his
aedileship, laid this pavement at his own expense."[18] When the
pavement was repaired about A.D. 150, the inscribed slab was
removed from its original position. It may have been first laid
during the second half of the first century. The possibility – some
would say the probability – must be recognized that the Erastus of
the inscription is identical with Paul's Corinthian friend; if so, his
service as city treasurer (the post which he was occupying at the
beginning of A.D. 57) proved so satisfactory that some twenty years
later he was promoted to the dignity of aedile (curator of public
works) and marked his promotion by donating to the city the
pavement of which the inscribed slab formed part.[19]

16. 1 Corinthians 1: 15 f.; cf. 16: 15.
17. Acts 18: 5; cf. 2 Corinthians 11: 9.
18. Reported by T. L. Shear in *AJA*, series 2, 33 (1929), pp. 325 f.
19. Cf. H. J. Cadbury, "Erastus of Corinth", *JBL* 50 (1931), pp. 42–58; P. N.
Harrison, "Erastus and his Pavement", in *Paulines and Pastorals* (London, 1964),
pp. 100–105. The inscription runs: ERASTVS. PRO. AED. S. P. STRAVIT.

Paul's insistence on "knowing nothing" among the Corinthians "except Jesus Christ and him crucified" (1 Corinthians 2: 2) had some regard to the intellectual climate of the city. As he came to know something of the Corinthians' reverence for current wisdom, he stressed that element in the gospel for which current wisdom could have no place: what more abject spectacle of folly and helplessness could be imagined than a crucified man? A crucified deliverer was to Greeks an absurd contradiction in terms, just as to Jews a crucified Messiah was a piece of scandalous blasphemy. But as Paul persisted in preaching Jesus as the crucified Saviour and sin-bearer, the unexpected happened: pagans, as well as Jews and God-fearers, believed the message and found their lives transformed by a new, liberating power, which broke the stranglehold of selfishness and vice and purified them from within. The message of Christ crucified had thus accomplished something which no body of Greek philosophic teaching could have done for them.

## 5. Gallio's "judgment"

An attempt was made to stir up trouble for Paul at Corinth, similar to the attempts made in Thessalonica and Beroea, but less successful in the event.

In July of A.D. 51 (less probably, twelve months later),[20] Lucius Junius Gallio came to Corinth to take up his appointment as proconsul of Achaia. Gallio (originally named Marcus Annaeus Novatus) belonged to a well-known Roman family of Spanish origin: he was a son of Marcus Annaeus Seneca, a distinguished professor of rhetoric, and a younger brother of Lucius Annaeus Seneca, Stoic philosopher and at this time tutor to the future Emperor Nero. His change of family name is due to his having been adopted as heir by his father's friend Lucius Junius Gallio.[21]

Not long after Gallio's arrival in Corinth, some members of the

20. The evidence for the date of Gallio's proconsulship of Achaia is provided by an inscription recording a rescript of Claudius to the people of Delphi (W. Dittenberger, *Sylloge Inscriptionum Graecarum* ii[3], 801; E. M. Smallwood, *Documents illustrating the Principates of Gaius, Claudius and Nero* [Cambridge, 1967], p. 105, no. 376), which mentions Gallio as holding that office in the period of Claudius's 26th acclamation as *imperator* – a period known from other inscriptions (*CIL* iii. 476; vi. 1256) to have covered the first seven months of A.D. 52. Proconsuls entered on their tour of duty on July 1. Unless, then, the rescript belongs to the very end of the period in question (in which case Gallio could have entered on his proconsulship on July 1, A.D. 52), Gallio arrived in his province on or about July 1, A.D. 51.

21. Gallio does not appear to have retained his proconsulship long: soon afterwards we find him going on a cruise to throw off a fever (Seneca, *Epistulae morales* 104, 1). Later we find him taking another voyage from Rome to Egypt, after his consulship (55 or 56), because of threatened phthisis (Pliny, *Nat. Hist.* xxxi. 33). In A.D. 65, with his brother Mela, he fell victim to Nero's malice soon after the enforced suicide of their brother Seneca (Dio Cassius, *History* lxii. 25. 3).

local Jewish community charged Paul before him with propagating an illegal religion. It is not said if the charge hinted at political implications in Paul's preaching; perhaps he was simply accused of introducing a cult of which Roman law took no cognizance.[22] In any case, Gallio quickly decided that there was nothing in this charge which called for action on his part. The accused man was as self-evidently Jewish as his prosecutors were: this was a quarrel over the interpretation of disputed points in Jewish law and theology. Crime and threats to the imperial peace fell within his jurisdiction, but he had no mind to arbitrate in a Jewish religious controversy. Accordingly, without waiting to hear the defence which Paul had prepared, he bade them begone from his tribunal.[23] (The stone platform which may well have served as Gallio's tribunal is still to be seen in Old Corinth.) The Corinthian bystanders, pleased at seeing a snub administered to the leaders of the Jewish community, seized the opportunity to assault the ruler of the synagogue, Sosthenes by name, before the tribunal, while Gallio turned a blind eye.[24] (If this Sosthenes is the Sosthenes whom Paul associates with himself in the superscription of 1 Corinthians, then he too, like his former colleague Crispus, became a Christian.)

Gallio's refusal to take up the charge [25] against Paul may have constituted an important negative precedent. Certainly, if he had taken up the charge and found Paul guilty of the alleged offence, such an adverse ruling by an influential governor would have been followed as a precedent by magistrates elsewhere in the Roman Empire, and Paul's apostolic work would have been seriously handicapped. Gallio's was no merely local and municipal authority, like that of the Philippian praetors or the Thessalonian politarchs. As it was, his inaction in the matter was tantamount to a ruling that what Paul was preaching was a form of Judaism, an association sanctioned by Roman law. The time was fast approaching, thanks mainly to Paul's own activity as apostle to the Gentiles, when it would no longer be possible for any Roman magistrate to

22. Cf. S. Applebaum in *The Jewish People in the First Century*, ed. S. Safrai and M. Stern, i (Assen, 1974), p. 460, for Judaism as a "permitted" association. If Paul and his followers could be dissociated from Judaism in the eyes of Roman law, their fellowship and activity would *ipso facto* become "illicit".

23. The βῆμα of Acts 18: 12; the word is used of Pilate's tribunal at Jerusalem from which the death sentence was pronounced on Jesus (John 19: 13) and again of the tribunal of Festus at Caesarea (Acts 25: 6), which Paul recognized as "Caesar's tribunal" (Acts 25: 10).

24. This is the point of Acts 18: 17, "Gallio paid no attention to this" (RSV); it is made explicit in the Western text, "Gallio pretended not to see".

25. The verb ἀνέχεσθαι in Acts 18: 14 (RSV "I should have reason to bear with you") has this sense in a judicial context (see W. Bauer, W. F. Arndt, F. W. Gingrich, *A Greek-English Lexicon of the New Testament* [Cambridge, 1957], p. 65).

regard Christianity as a form of Judaism; but for the present Paul was able to prosecute his ministry in Corinth and elsewhere without molestation from Caesar's representatives.

## 6. *Paul leaves Corinth*

In the spring of (probably) A.D. 52 he left Corinth with his friends Priscilla and Aquila, and crossed the Aegean to Ephesus. He visited the synagogue in Ephesus, and the Jews there were so interested in what he had to say that they expressed a desire to hear more, but he excused himself because of a pressing engagement in Jerusalem. According to the Western text of Acts 18: 21, he had to be in Jerusalem for the approaching festival – either Passover or Pentecost. His Jerusalem engagement may have had to do with a Nazirite vow which he had undertaken in Corinth – probably in response to the promise of protection which he had received from the Lord in a night-vision. As he left Corinth, he discharged part of his vow by cutting his hair short before embarking at the harbour of Cenchreae,[26] but the completion of the vow required a visit to the temple in Jerusalem. He therefore left Priscilla and Aquila in Ephesus and set sail from there to Caesarea in Palestine. He fulfilled his obligation in Jerusalem and paid his respects to the mother church; then he went north to Syrian Antioch, renewing acquaintance with his old friends there, before he returned to Ephesus.

## 7. *Apollos and his "school"*

Meanwhile another visiting Jew came to the Ephesian synagogue and took an active part in the exposition of the scriptures; like Paul, he too taught that the scriptures had been fulfilled by Jesus. Priscilla and Aquila listened to him with great interest; they approved of all that he said, but became aware of certain deficiencies (as it seemed to them) in his knowledge of the gospel. He had an accurate acquaintance with the story of Jesus, but knew nothing of baptism in Jesus' name: the only baptism known to him was that introduced by John the Baptist (and possibly still administered by some of John's disciples). Accordingly, Priscilla and Aquila invited him to their home in Ephesus, and there they "expounded to him the way of God more accurately" (Acts 18: 26).

This visitor was Apollos, a Jew of Alexandria in Egypt. Luke applies to him the adjective *logios*, which meant "learned" or "cultured" in classical Greek, but acquired the sense of "eloquent" in Hellenistic and later Greek; the latter sense is probably what Luke intends, but the former need not be excluded. He is also described by Luke as "well versed in the scriptures", which

26. Acts 18: 18. See p. 348.

suggests not only a mastery of the text but a facility in exposition.

According to the Western text of Acts 18: 25, Apollos (who in this text receives his unabridged name Apollonius) had received his instruction in the way of the Lord in his *patris*, his home city (Alexandria). This implies that Christianity had reached Alexandria by about A.D. 50, and this is highly probable, no matter what evidence was available to the Western editor when he made this addition.[27] Whether or not Apollos's expository skill, over and above his ability to find the fulfilment of the scriptures in Jesus, indicates his competence in the allegorical method used by Philo, the great Jewish philosopher of Alexandria (who had died probably a year or two before the appearance of Apollos in our record), we have no means of knowing. It is not at all unlikely, but must not be taken for granted.

How was it, we may ask, that, for all his accurate knowledge of the story of Jesus, he was acquainted with no baptism but John's? To this it can only be said that the gospel had reached him (whether in Alexandria or elsewhere) by a different road from that traced in the main narrative of Acts and presupposed in the letters of Paul – by a road, that is to say, which did not start in Jerusalem. There were groups of believers in Jesus in various parts of Palestine (even in Samaria),[28] and some of these may have engaged in missionary activity without having experienced the pentecostal event which attended the inception of the church of Jerusalem. It is certain that Alexandrian Christianity, whatever the date and circumstances of its inception may have been, was for some generations regarded as defective by the standards of Jerusalem (in the apostolic age) and Rome (in post-apostolic times).[29] Further speculation is fruitless, but the more accurate instruction which Apollos received from Priscilla and Aquila would have included something about baptism in the name of Jesus, with its corollary (of which they themselves had learned from Paul) of incorporation by the Spirit into the new community.

Apollos seems to have been one of the travelling Jewish merchants of whom some others receive mention in the Near Eastern history of this period for combining a readiness to give religious instruction with whatever other business took them from place to place.[30] When he had completed his business in Ephesus

27. If it reached Cyrene early (see p. 131), it must have reached Alexandria earlier still.

28. See Acts 8: 5–25.

29. Cf. W. Bauer, *Orthodoxy and Heresy in Earliest Christianity*, E.T. (Philadelphia, 1971), pp. 44 ff.; A. A. T. Ehrhardt, *The Framework of the New Testament Stories* (Manchester, 1964), pp. 174 ff.; F. F. Bruce, *The 'Secret' Gospel of Mark* (London, 1974), pp. 13 ff.

30. Like Ananias and Eleazar who played leading parts in the conversion to Judaism of King Izates of Adiabene (Josephus, *Ant.* xx. 34–48).

Athens: The Acropolis (see p. 240)

Corinth: Gallio's *bema* (see p. 254)

he crossed the Aegean to Corinth, armed with a letter of introduction from his new friends in Ephesus to the "disciples" in Corinth.
Luke's statement that it was to the "disciples" in Corinth that this
letter was addressed points to the church in Corinth rather than the
synagogue: however, Apollos appears to have visited the synagogue
on his own initiative and argued, as Paul had done, that the
Messiah foretold in the scriptures was to be identified with Jesus –
though his exegetical method may have been different from Paul's.

At any rate, he proved to be a tower of strength to the Christian
cause in Corinth, and many members of the Corinthian church
were greatly impressed by his gifts – some going so far as to regard
themselves as his disciples. Evidently there was a quality about his
ministry that made it more appealing to them than Paul's.
Apollos's eloquence may have been contrasted with what Paul
acknowledged to be his own "contemptible" delivery (2
Corinthians 10: 10), or conceivably his imaginative allegorization
may have been preferred to Paul's deliberate eschewing of "lofty
words or wisdom" (1 Corinthians 2: 1).

Others, out of a sense of loyalty to Paul, felt that they should
emphasize his unique claim, as founder of their church, to be their
teacher; so, over against the self-styled school of Apollos there
emerged another group whose watchword was "I belong to
Paul".[31] There does not appear to have been any difference of principle between the Paul party and the Apollos party: when Paul
refers to the subject, he simply regards it as deplorable that such
party-spirit should exist at all. "What then is Apollos? What is
Paul? Servants through whom you believed, as the Lord assigned to
each. I planted the seed, Apollos watered it, but it was God who
made it grow" (1 Corinthians 3: 5 f.). In his references to Apollos
Paul shows no trace of reserve: every mention he makes of him is
marked by friendliness and confidence. Apollos's teaching evidently commanded Paul's approval. Towards the end of 1 Corinthians
(written from Ephesus in the spring of A.D. 55) he says, among
other personal notes: "As for our brother Apollos, I strongly urged
him to visit you with the other brethren, but it was plainly not
God's will for him to come now; he will come when he has opportunity" (16: 12). The details of this postponed visit are quite
obscure to us (in fact, we cannot be sure if it was God's will or
Apollos's own will that stood in the way of his visiting Corinth just
then),[32] but some recent contact between Paul and Apollos in
Ephesus is implied. Perhaps Apollos had left Corinth in embarrass-

31. Cf. 1 Corinthians 1: 12; 3: 4.
32. It is not expressly stated whose will is in question; among Greek-speaking
Jews "the will" was a way of referring to the will of God (as in Romans 2: 18).
Perhaps Apollos himself was quite unwilling to go back to Corinth, in spite of
Paul's urgency.

ment at being set up as a party leader there in potential rivalry to Paul. Paul was not too happy about some Christian visitors who went to Corinth and tried to amplify the teaching he had given to his converts there, but he plainly had no misgivings about a visit by Apollos.

## 8. News from "Chloe's people"

Paul first learned about the development of the "school" of Apollos, and the rival "school" which claimed himself as patron, from some Corinthian visitors to Ephesus to whom he refers as "Chloe's people" (1 Corinthians 1: 11) – members of a well-to-do household or house-church, presumably.[33] They told him of yet another group which invoked the name of Peter (whom Paul, as usual, calls Cephas). Had Peter paid a visit to Corinth in Paul's absence? This is possible: Peter seems, from about A.D. 50 onwards, to have embarked on a more widespread ministry than hitherto, concentrating probably (in accordance with the Jerusalem leaders' agreement with Paul and Barnabas) on Jewish communities in various centres.[34] If he visited the synagogue in Corinth, he would no doubt also have greeted the church there, which included converts from Judaism as well as from paganism. We have already remarked on the impossibility of maintaining a clear line of demarcation between the Jewish and the Gentile mission-fields, and on the opportunities of misunderstanding which were liable to arise between the two parties to the agreement. Apollos was a free agent with no apostolic status, and his activity in Corinth or any part of Paul's mission-field presented no threat to Paul's authority, but it was different with Peter. Doubt could easily have been cast on Paul's commission by any one who was so minded – he had received it, by his own account, in a vision shared by no one else – whereas Peter's apostolic credentials were unquestionable. If he said something which differed from Paul's teaching, which was more likely to be right? That the Corinthian Christians had a special interest in Peter is indicated by a reference which Paul makes to "the other apostles and the brothers of the Lord and Cephas"[35] – singling the last-named out specifically (1 Corinthians 9: 5). The point of the reference is that those men, un-

33. Chloe (of whom nothing is otherwise known) seems to have been head of the household or owner of the house.

34. He was *en route* for Rome to help with the reconstruction of the church there, after receiving news of Claudius's death on October 13, A.D. 54, according to G. Edmundson, *The Church in Rome in the First Century* (London, 1913), pp. 80, 84. Cf. T. W. Manson, *Studies in the Gospels and Epistles* (Manchester, 1962), pp. 38–40.

35. How any one could infer from this wording that "Cephas" was not reckoned among the "apostles" is difficult to comprehend, but see W. Schmithals, *The Office of Apostle in the Early Church*, E.T. (London, 1971), pp. 80–82.

like Paul, were accompanied by their wives on their missionary journeys, a fact of which, in Peter's case, the Corinthians may have been aware from experience.[36]

If Peter did not visit Corinth in person, then some others may have visited the city and church in his name, and tried to impose his authority to a degree which he himself would not have countenanced. What the Corinthian Christians were pressed to accept on Peter's authority is uncertain, but they may have been urged to observe the food-restrictions in the Jerusalem decree.[37] Paul speaks of himself as laying the foundation of Corinthian Christianity and of others coming along and building further courses on it: "let each man take care how he builds upon it", he adds in a note of warning (1 Corinthians 3: 10). As for apostolic credentials, Corinth is one place where Paul has no need to present his: the existence of the Corinthian church is evidence enough of his commission – "the seal of my apostleship in the Lord", he tells them (1 Corinthians 9: 2).

But there were others in the church of Corinth, Paul's visitors told him, who had loftier ideas than those associated with the names of leading servants of the exalted Christ: they claimed the patronage of Christ himself – not in the sense in which all Christians might do so but in a partisan sense. In Paul's eyes this was the most outrageous manifestation of party spirit: "Is Christ divided?" he asks indignantly (1 Corinthians 1: 13). What can be said of those people whose slogan was "I belong to Christ"?

## 9. "Men of knowledge" at Corinth

The Corinthian church presents us with an example of the subtle changes which the gospel was apt to undergo when it was transplanted to a Gentile environment. Concepts and terms which originally had one meaning tended to take on another meaning from their new surroundings. Paul, for instance, regarded the indwelling Spirit in the followers of Jesus as the firstfruits of the heritage of glory which would be theirs in fulness in the resurrection age. For some of his Corinthian converts, on the other hand, the possession of the Spirit, the heavenly essence, was the all-important matter: the crowning achievement of Jesus was his impartation of the Spirit. His crucifixion was significant not so much for the reason given by Paul as for its being the means by which he outwitted and overcame the "principalities and powers" which were hostile to men and would have prevented them from enjoying the heavenly gift. But now that they had received the heavenly gift, they

36. There is an "undesigned coincidence" here with Mark 1: 30 f., where Peter appears as a married man.

37. Cf. C. K. Barrett, "Thing Sacrificed to Idols", *NTS* 11 (1964–65), pp. 138–153, especially pp. 149 f.

had "arrived"; the coming kingdom of which Paul spoke was already theirs.[38] What could the hope of bodily resurrection add in the way of bliss to those who knew themselves to be here and now "men of the Spirit"?[39] If Paul still retained his traditional Jewish belief in a future resurrection of the body, there was no reason why they should take over this belief from him; they were more thoroughly emancipated. Paul did express a clearer insight, they conceded, when he spoke occasionally of believers having died and risen again with Christ in their baptism: [40] that was all the resurrection they needed. Let others know the exalted Christ as he was proclaimed to them by Paul or Apollos or Peter: they were in direct touch with him by the Spirit and had no need of human intermediaries. We shall not be far wrong if we identify the men who argued thus with the "Christ party" at Corinth.[41]

The same attitude manifests itself in the exaggerated estimate placed by some Corinthian Christians on the more spectacular and ecstatic "spiritual gifts" or *charismata*, especially glossolalia. Paul did not rule out glossolalia as a phenomenon inspired by the Spirit, but he was anxious to convince his Corinthian friends that there were other *charismata* which, while not so impressive as glossolalia, were much more helpful in building up the Christian fellowship. Glossolalia in itself was not peculiar to Christianity: Greece had long experience of the utterances of the Pythian prophetess at Delphi and the enthusiastic invocations of the votaries of Dionysus. Hence Paul insists that it is not the phenomenon of "tongues" or prophesying in itself that gives evidence of the presence and activity of the Holy Spirit, but the actual content of the utterances. Taking what may be intended as two extreme examples, he points out that such an utterance as "Jesus is Lord" is self-evidently prompted by the Holy Spirit, whereas such an utterance as "Jesus is anathema" – perhaps the kind of utterance which he had once tried to force Palestinian believers to take upon their lips [42] – was equally self-evidently prompted by a spirit of a very different order.[43]

38. Cf. 1 Corinthians 4: 8.
39. Cf. 1 Corinthians 15: 12.
40. Cf. Romans 6: 4 f. (where, however, the rising with Christ seems to be future as well as present); Colossians 2: 11–13.
41. Cf. T. W. Manson, *Studies in the Gospels and Epistles*, p. 207. This is a quite different account of the Christ party from that propounded by F. C. Baur in his epoch-making article "Die Christuspartei in der korinthischen Gemeinde", *Tübinger Zeitschrift für Theologie* 5 (1831), Heft 4, pp. 61–206 (reprinted in *Ausgewählte Werke in Einzelausgaben*, ed. K. Scholder, i [Stuttgart, 1963], pp. 1–76). Baur looked on the Christ party (to which he found a further reference in 2 Corinthians 10: 7) as comprising judaistic adherents of Peter who wished to stress their relationship to the Christ who had appointed and commissioned Peter and his colleagues.
42. Acts 26: 11.
43. 1 Corinthians 12: 3. Another, but less probable, explanation is that some

It would be anachronistic to call these "men of the Spirit" Gnostics; that is a term best reserved for adherents of the various schools of Gnosticism which flourished in the second century A.D. Their doctrine, however, might permissibly be described as "incipient Gnosticism". From Paul's Corinthian correspondence one can at least appreciate "into how congenial a soil the seeds of Gnosticism were about to fall".[44] The "men of the Spirit" at Corinth certainly set much store by wisdom (*sophia*) and knowledge (*gnōsis*), reckoning these qualities (as Paul tells them) by current secular standards, whereas (he maintained) in the gospel of Christ crucified God had turned these standards upside down and made them look foolish. The knowledge which they cultivated, if it was not accompanied by Christian love, could not build up the Christian community or strengthen its fellowship. It carried with it a temptation to despise fellow-Christians who were thought to be less enlightened and to treat with impatience their immature scruples in such matters as food and sex. They themselves regarded the body as a temporary provision and held that bodily actions were morally and religiously indifferent.

Paul, the most liberal and emancipated of first-century Christians, could go a long way with these "men of knowledge". He agreed with them that the flesh of animals which had been sacrificed to pagan deities was none the worse for that, and that Christians might say grace over it and eat it with a good conscience; but, unlike them, he was always prepared voluntarily to restrict his liberty in such matters if its exercise might harm the conscience of a less emancipated Christian.

On the other hand, while food was ethically and spiritually a matter of indifference, sexual relations were not: they had profound and lasting effects on the personalities of those involved.[45] The "men of knowledge" had a saying, "Food for the stomach and the stomach for food, but God will destroy both one and the other"[46] — and they were inclined to add as a corollary: "Sex for the body and the body for sex". But the corollary was inadmissible, according to Paul: food and stomach would alike perish, it was true, but sexual relationships affected not the body only but the whole person, and the person would not share the fate of the mortal body. Not long

Gentile Christians were so exclusively devoted to the heavenly Christ whose presence they enjoyed by the Spirit that they anathematized any reference to the earthly Jesus who suffered humiliation and death.

44. R. Law, *The Tests of Life* (Edinburgh, 1909), p. 28.

45. Cf. D. S. Bailey, *The Man-Woman Relation in Christian Thought* (London, 1959), p. 10.

46. 1 Corinthians 6: 13. Possibly RSV is right in placing the closing quotation-mark after "... the stomach for food", in which case "but God will destroy both one and the other" is Paul's comment on their saying.

after he left Corinth he had occasion to send his converts there a letter, now lost (which may be conveniently referred to as "Corinthians A"), urging them not to tolerate fornication and certain other vices within their fellowship,[47] but it is plain that they found it difficult to put his advice into practice, for in one subsequent letter after another he had to repeat it, not simply by way of general exhortation but with reference to specific cases. It was clearly no easy matter even for regenerate Christians to break free from the besetting sin of their city, especially when some "enlightened" members of their community kept assuring them that it was not really a sin at all.

How far some of these "enlightened" people were prepared to go appears from an incident which was reported to Paul by one or more of the visitors from Corinth who called on him at Ephesus, and to which he reacted vigorously. A member of the Corinthian church had begun to cohabit with his father's wife. Whether the father was alive or dead is not made clear, but even in permissive Corinth such a relationship was generally regarded as going too far, and its existence within the membership of the church must inevitably damage the church's reputation. That was bad enough, but even worse was the fact that many members of the church were disposed to be proud of this situation, looking on it as a rather fine assertion of Christian liberty, setting at naught the inhibitions of Jewish law and pagan convention alike. Such conduct, if tolerated within the church, would corrupt the whole fellowship, said Paul, as surely as a little leaven would leaven the whole batch of dough. The offender must be disowned, excluded from the membership of the church, for the church's health and also for his own ultimate salvation.[48]

## 10. "Weaker brethren" at Corinth

It was not only against the perversion of Christian liberty into licence that Paul had to put the Corinthian church on its guard. Some of its members, perhaps by reaction against the pervasive immorality of Corinthian life, or in anticipation of the ascetic Gnosticism of the second century, thought it wise to abstain from marriage and impose a severe regimen on the body. Others had scruples about eating the flesh of animals which had been sacrificed to idols, to a point where they would make careful inquiries about any meat offered to them in case it had been so used and, in case of doubt, would abstain from meat. Such people would be disposed to listen sympathetically to critics of Paul who disapproved of what

47. It is referred to in 1 Corinthians 5: 9–11.
48. 1 Corinthians 5: 1 ff.

they considered to be his regrettable laxity in this and other matters relating to food.

While Paul was foremost in restricting his liberty for the sake of Christian charity, and recommended his example in this regard to his converts, he insisted that such restrictions must be voluntarily self-imposed, and saw in any attempt to impose them from without a threat to the grace of the gospel and the freedom of the Spirit. His policy in this regard comes to expression in the replies which he gave to a number of questions from the church of Corinth sent to him during his Ephesian ministry.

# CHAPTER 24

# Corinthian Correspondence

## 1. The Corinthians' letter to Paul

PAUL DEALT WITH THE NEWS HE RECEIVED FROM CHLOE'S PEOPLE and other visitors in the letter which has come down to us as 1 Corinthians. Since this had been preceded by an earlier letter, no longer extant,[1] which may conventionally be called "Corinthians A", our 1 Corinthians may for certain purposes be referred to as "Corinthians B".

Paul not only sent letters; he received them. None of the letters he received has survived; this is our loss, because if we had access to them they would probably be found to throw some light on passages in his own letters which are obscure to us because of our ignorance of the persons and circumstances mentioned in them.

But we do at least know something about one letter which he received – a letter from his friends and followers at Corinth, brought to him in Ephesus by three members of the Corinthian church (Stephanas, Fortunatus and Achaicus).[2] In this letter they assured him that they observed all the "traditions" which he had delivered to them,[3] and asked a series of questions to which he replied one by one in the second (and major) part of 1 Corinthians (chapters 7–16). Some of the questions were perhaps stimulated by things which Paul had said in "Corinthians A".[4]

(a) *Observing the traditions.* The "traditions" which the Corinthians assured Paul they continued to observe included basic articles of faith and practice, which Paul himself had "received" before he "delivered" them to his converts.[5] (The verbs "receive" and "deliver" in this kind of context are practically technical terms for the passing on of tradition from one individual or generation to the next.) These traditions were summed up as "the tradition of Christ",[6] which comprised (i) a summary of the Christian message, expressed as a confession of faith, with special emphasis

1. Cf. 1 Corinthians 5: 9–11 (see p. 262).
2. 1 Corinthians 7: 1; 16: 17.
3. 1 Corinthians 11: 2.
4. See J. C. Hurd, Jr., *The Origin of 1 Corinthians* (London, 1965).
5. Cf. 1 Corinthians 11: 23; 15: 3.
6. Cf. Colossians 2: 6, 8.

on the death and resurrection of Christ; (ii) various deeds and words of Christ; (iii) ethical and procedural rules for Christians. Much of this, as has been suggested above, was imparted to Paul during his first visit to Jerusalem after his conversion,[7] and he imparted it in turn to his converts.

When the Corinthians told him that they maintained these traditions, he commended them; but added that he was reliably informed that there were some which they had forgotten.[8] The growth of a spirit of division among them was something which he did not commend: this manifested itself not only in the development of rival schools of thought but in social cleavages which took a particularly unpleasant form at the Lord's table, and made a mockery of their claim to have fellowship there with their Lord and with one another. The memorial bread and wine were taken in the course of a fellowship meal to which each member or family made a contribution, but instead of sharing what had been brought, the rich ate their own food and the poorer members made do with the little they could afford, so that, as Paul said, "one is hungry and another is drunk" (1 Corinthians 11: 21). Such selfish conduct was an outrage on the sacred occasion; those who participated in such an unworthy spirit, far from deriving any grace from their participation, were eating and drinking judgment upon themselves.

It is in this context that Paul gives us the earliest account which we have of the institution of the communion meal (1 Corinthians 11: 23–26):

> For I received from the Lord what I also delivered to you, that the Lord Jesus on the night when he was betrayed took bread, and when he had given thanks, he broke it, and said, "This is my body which is for you. Do this in remembrance of me." In the same way also the cup, after supper, saying, "This cup is the new covenant in my blood. Do this, as often as you drink it, in remembrance of me." For as often as you eat this bread and drink the cup, you proclaim the Lord's death until he comes.[9]

The last clause, "until he comes", is in all probability an integral part of what Paul "received". It may hark back to Jesus' saying in the upper room that the next time he ate the passover or drank the fruit of the vine would be in the consummated kingdom of God;[10] but in any case it reflects the eschatological significance of the meal in the early church. It not only commemorated Jesus' passion but anticipated his parousia: indeed, it may have been regarded as a "prophetic action" helping to ensure the fulfilment of the prayer

7. See pp. 84 ff., 100 f.
8. 1 Corinthians 11: 17 ff.
9. See pp. 283 ff.
10. Cf. Luke 22: 16; Mark 14: 25.

*maranā-thā* ("Our Lord, come!") which appears to have had its original setting at the Lord's table.[11]

It is in his reply to the Corinthians' letter, in fact, that Paul quotes most of the sayings of Jesus which are to be found in his writings. In answering their questions about marriage, he adduces Jesus' prohibition of divorce;[12] in defending his own apostolic freedom, he invokes his ruling "that those who proclaim the gospel should get their living by the gospel";[13] in giving advice to a Christian invited to a meal in a non-Christian home he echoes Jesus' injunction to the seventy disciples to eat what is set before them wherever they are offered hospitality.[14]

Another aspect of the tradition which he delivered to the Corinthians was the gospel account of the death, burial and resurrection of Christ, with a summary of the occasions on which he had appeared in resurrection to one and another. Paul had reason to know that this tradition, too, was being taken with insufficient seriousness by those members of the church of Corinth who denied any such thing as a future resurrection.[15] They had no thought of denying the past resurrection of Christ, but Paul reminds them of the tradition to this effect which they had received from him and insists that the past resurrection of Christ and the future resurrection of his people are so completely bound up with each other – Christ's resurrection being the presentation of the first fruits and that of his people the completed harvest – that to give up belief in the latter logically demands giving up belief in the former, with consequent collapse of the Christian faith.[16]

The questions raised in the Corinthians' letter covered a wide range: marriage and related subjects, food sacrificed to idols, spiritual gifts in the church, the relief fund which they had heard he was organizing for their fellow-believers in Jerusalem. These questions or groups of questions are readily identifiable because Paul introduces his answers to them one by one with the phrase "Now concerning".

(*b*) *Questions about marriage.* The sexual laxity which was part of the Corinthian way of life, and from which even the church in Corinth was not immune, made some members of the church feel that sexual relations, even within a marriage already contracted, were best avoided altogether. Those who felt like this may have been confirmed in their sentiment by the consideration that the ap-

11. It has a eucharistic setting in *Didache* 10: 5. See O. Hofius, "Bis dass er kommt", *NTS* 14 (1967–68), pp. 439 ff.
12. 1 Corinthians 7: 10 f. (cf. Mark 10: 5–12); see p. 106.
13. 1 Corinthians 9: 14 (cf. Matthew 10: 9 f./Luke 9: 3 f.); see p. 107.
14. 1 Corinthians 10: 27 (cf. Luke 10: 8); see p. 108.
15. See pp. 306 ff.
16. 1 Corinthians 15: 12–19.

proaching end of the age ruled out the long-term planning which was incumbent on those who undertook the responsibilities of family life. They summed up their view in the statement: "It is well for a man not to touch a woman" [17] – with which some of them at least confidently expected Paul to agree. They knew of his preference for the celibate life, and thought that he would applaud this preference in his converts. The Paul of later tradition does indeed applaud this preference: in the apocryphal *Acts of Paul* he gets into trouble because his female converts, if betrothed, refuse to be married or, if married, discontinue normal relations with their husbands.[18] But the historical Paul takes quite a different line. He surprises his Corinthian correspondents because, after quoting their counsel of perfection as though he approved of it, he immediately adds a "nevertheless" which explodes it. Monogamy, he says, not celibacy, is the norm for Christians,[19] even if there were no higher motive for it than the avoidance of fornication, which was his correspondents' aim. (This is said for the sake of the *ad hominem* argument; it does not mean that Paul could see no higher motive for marriage than the avoidance of fornication.)[20] Unless one had a special vocation – a *charisma*, as he calls it[21] – for celibacy, any attempt to adopt this condition was contrary to nature and would expose them to the very kind of temptation which they abhorred. Paul goes as far as he can with his converts in either the ascetic or the libertarian direction, until he reaches a point where he calls a halt, and profoundly qualifies his foregoing concession.[22]

As for the idea that husband and wife should refrain from sexual union, Paul concedes that they may do so, for a limited period, if both are agreed on it. He will not countenance a unilateral abstention: that would be defrauding the other party of his or her rights. After the agreed period of abstinence they should resume normal relations: to adopt any other course would be to court disaster.

For a Christian husband or wife divorce is excluded by the law of Christ: here Paul has no need to express a judgment of his own, for the Lord's ruling on this matter was explicit. True, Jesus' ruling was given in the context of rabbinical debate and Jewish social

---

17. 1 Corinthians 7: 1b. That this is Paul's quotation of an attitude of the ascetic party in the Corinthian church, not his own dictum, was seen by Origen, *Commentary on 1 Corinthians*, §121 (ed. C. Jenkins, *JTS* 9 [1907–8], pp. 500 ff.).

18. E.g. Thekla, a virgin of Iconium, and Artemilla, wife of the governor of Asia (*New Testament Apocrypha*, E.T., ed. E. Hennecke, W. Schneemelcher, R. McL. Wilson, ii [London, 1965], pp. 355–364, 370–373). See pp. 467 f.

19. See J. M. Ford, "St. Paul the Philogamist", *NTS* 11 (1964–65), pp. 326 ff.

20. J. Klausner does less than justice to Paul on this point; he quite wrongly says that Paul saw marriage as a "necessary evil" (*From Jesus to Paul*, E.T. [London, 1944], pp. 570–572).

21. 1 Corinthians 7: 7.

22. Cf. H. Chadwick, "All Things to all Men", *NTS* 1 (1954–55), pp. 261 ff.

usage, in which the initiation of divorce proceedings was a male prerogative: his ruling against such proceedings was in a part a protection of the underprivileged wife. Paul writes in a Gentile situation, and applies Jesus' ruling to men and women alike: reconciliation, not estrangement, is the course for Christians.

But the Gentile mission might frequently lead to a situation which was not envisaged in Jesus' Palestinian ministry and on which, accordingly, no ruling of his was available. A husband or a wife might be converted to Christianity, while the other party to the marriage remained a pagan. What was to be done about it? If the pagan partner is willing to go on living with the Christian partner, said Paul, good and well. But, it might be asked, would not cohabitation with a pagan pollute the Christian? On the contrary, said Paul; continued cohabitation with a Christian would "sanctify" the pagan, and the children of such a union would share in that "sanctification".[23] Perhaps Paul was guided in this judgment by the principle inherent in an ordinance of the Jewish ceremonial law: "whatever touches the altar shall become holy" (Exodus 29: 37). In rabbinical literature a proselyte after conversion to Judaism is described as being "in holiness".[24] There was also the possibility that the pagan partner might be won for the gospel through the other's witness: such a marriage had missionary potentialities.[25]

On the other hand, the pagan partner might refuse to live with the Christian: what was to be done then? Let it be so, says Paul; do not try to compel non-Christian husbands or wives to stay or return against their will. Better agree to part in that kind of situation than live together in contention. The deserted partner is then no longer bound by the marriage contract.

Although no dominical authority is claimed for this "Pauline privilege", Paul plainly does not consider that it conflicts with Jesus' ruling. He deals with such unprecedented issues as a wise pastor, having regard to the interests of the people concerned and remaining faithful to the spirit and principle of the "law of Christ". Marriage, like the sabbath, was instituted for human beings, and not *vice versa*.

Would it be permissible in that case for the Christian to enter into a new marriage? Probably Paul would give the same answer to that question as he gave to widows and unmarried persons (including those couples who had resolved to live together in virginity):[26] "You will do better if you refrain from marriage, but if

23. 1 Corinthians 7: 14.
24. Mishnah *Yebamôt* 11: 2.
25. Cf. J. Jeremias, "Die missionarische Aufgabe in der Mischehe" in *Neutestamentliche Studien für R. Bultmann*, ed. W. Eltester, *BZNW* 21 (1954), pp. 255 ff.
26. The interpretation of 1 Corinthians 7: 25 ff. ("Now concerning virgins . . .")

you must marry, then marry: it is no sin!" Not only did married people incur secular cares and anxieties from which the unmarried were free: in times of persecution and distress, which Paul saw to be impending, an unmarried man was under less powerful temptation to compromise the faith than a man with family responsibilities, whose wife and children might suffer for his confession as well as himself. Paul is prescribing iron rations for hard times, which presaged the end of the present world-order. Jesus had spoken of a coming crisis when the childless would be counted exceptionally fortunate because of the calamities which it would bring.[27] These were more practical arguments than Paul's remark that ideally much trouble would be avoided if everyone found the celibate life as congenial as he himself did: celibacy, he acknowledged, was for the few who knew themselves called to it.

It is reasonably clear that Paul was a celibate throughout his apostolic career. But what was his actual marital status? He knew of other Christian leaders, from Peter downwards, who were accompanied by their wives on their missionary journeys, and he agreed that they were perfectly entitled to do so, and to have their wives as well as themselves maintained by the churches. Indeed, he claims the same right for himself, if he were minded to avail himself of it, as he is not.[28]

This does not mean that he had a wife, but chose to forgo her company during his apostolic visits to this place and that. We may dismiss such a romantic fantasy as that he married Lydia, the tradeswoman of Philippi, and that she is the "true yoke fellow" whom he asks to help other Philippian women who had co-operated with him in his gospel ministry (Philippians 4: 3).[29] But, granted that he was not married during his apostolic activity, had he ever been married? It may be pointed out that marriage was normal and, indeed, expected in pious Jews when they came of age.[30] True, Jesus had spoken of certain exceptions – those who, as he said, had "made themselves eunuchs for the sake of the kingdom of heaven" (Matthew 19: 12) – among whom he may have included John the Baptist and himself. But Paul was not presumably influenced by considerations of this kind in his pre-Christian days. What then? Was he a widower? Perhaps he was: the question has

is debatable, but the passage is best understood of couples living in a state of permanent but unconsummated betrothal.

27. Luke 23: 29; cf. Mark 13: 17.
28. 1 Corinthians 9: 5 (see pp. 258 f.).
29. Cf. S. Baring-Gould, *A Study of St. Paul* (London, 1897), pp. 213 ff.
30. Judah ben Tema, a rabbi of a later period (second half of the second century A.D.), specified eighteen as the appropriate age for a young man to marry (*Pirqê Abôt* 5: 24).

received a positive answer from Joachim Jeremias, for example.[31] Rather more probable is the view that his wife left him when he became a Christian: that when he "suffered the loss of all things"[32] for the sake of Christ he lost his wife too. This cannot be proved, of course, but if something like this did happen it might explain Paul's specially sympathetic understanding of the domestic situation in which the unconverted partner walks out on the husband or wife who has become a Christian: "in such a case the brother or sister is not bound" (1 Corinthians 7: 15). Paul, for his part, was not "bound" either way: he knew that he could fulfil his commission more wholeheartedly if he remained free from the marriage bond.

(c) *Questions about food.* The issue of food that had been sacrificed to idols could not be considered in isolation in a pagan city like Corinth: it was part of the wider problem of idolatrous associations. The more enlightened members of the church maintained that since "there is no God but one", it followed that "an idol has no real existence" (1 Corinthians 8: 4), and that therefore food was neither better nor worse for coming from an animal which had been sacrificed in a pagan temple. Paul agreed; *nevertheless*, as he pointed out, for many less enlightened Christians an idol had a real existence; it was a demonic power to those who ascribed a measure of reality to it, even if they did not worship it but rather abominated it. In the eyes of such people, the food had been in some sense contaminated by its association with the idol, and if they ate it they might become demon-possessed. Paul shows considerable sympathy with these "weak brethren":[33] he realized, as many of the men of knowledge did not, that to a person who believes in an idol or similar demonic being, it has real substance and power – not independently but none the less effectively.

If an attempt had been made, possibly through the "Peter party" at Corinth, to impose the Jerusalem decree on the church, this would have provided an additional reason for presenting the question to Paul.[34]

Quite apart from the doubtful propriety of subjecting his Gentile churches to the authority of Jerusalem, it was not Paul's way to impose a rule but to help his converts to judge such issues for themselves in the light of basic Christian principles. One of the most important of these principles was to consider the consciences of weaker brethren so as to assist them gently to a better and more

31. J. Jeremias, "War Paulus Witwer?" *ZNW* 25 (1926), pp. 310 ff., with critique by E. Fascher, "Zur Witwerschaft des Paulus und der Auslegung von 1 Cor 7", *ZNW* 28 (1929), pp. 62 ff., and reply by J. Jeremias, "Nochmals: war Paulus Witwer?" *ZNW* 28 (1929), pp. 321 ff.

32. Philippians 3: 8.

33. 1 Corinthians 8: 7, 9–12; 9: 22; Romans 14: 1 ff.

34. See p. 259 with n. 37.

enlightened appreciation of what their faith involved. Otherwise a Christian's freedom was not to be impaired by external restrictions. The Christian was at liberty to buy what he chose for domestic use in the Corinthian meat-market,[35] without scrupulously inquiring whether the meat came from a sacrificed animal or not. Similarly, he was at liberty to accept an invitation to a meal in the home of a pagan acquaintance – again, without making scrupulous inquiries. If, on the other hand, his attention was deliberately drawn to the fact that a particular dish was *hierothyton*,[36] the flesh of a sacrificed animal, as though his response to this information was being treated as a test of his Christian confession, he could properly asked to be excused from eating it.[37]

But some members of the Corinthian church went much farther than buying what might be sacrificed meat at the butcher's or eating it at the table of a pagan neighbour. Such a neighbour might arrange a banquet in a pagan temple: should the Christian accept an invitation to be present?[38] Here it was of little importance that the meat would certainly come from an animal sacrificed to the god worshipped in that temple; it was of great importance that the whole occasion would be under the patronage of the god, and a Christian might well find himself in an atmosphere where some compromise with idolatry was inevitable. Was it conceivable, Paul asks, that the same man should be a partaker of the table of the Lord one evening and of the table of a demon another evening?[39] Nonentities though false gods were, they were demonic powers to their worshippers, and it was hardly possible to take part in a feast in the temple of one of them without being influenced for the worse. Even here Paul does not lay down the law but appeals to his readers' sense of fitness: "I speak as to sensible men; judge for yourselves what I say" (1 Corinthians 10: 15).

In a pagan city it was difficult to avoid all association with

35. The fact that Paul in 1 Corinthians 10: 25 refers to the meat-market as the μάκελλον, a word of Latin origin (*macellum*), suggests that he had the meat-market of Corinth in mind: the *macellum* is mentioned on a fragmentary Latin inscription found near the Lechaeum road, north of the Corinthian agora; see H. J. Cadbury, "The Macellum of Corinth", *JBL* 53 (1934), pp. 134 ff.

36. Paul (and Greek-speaking Jews in general) would call it εἰδωλόθυτον ("sacrificed to an idol"); the more devout term ἱερόθυτον implies that a pagan is speaking (1 Corinthians 10: 28).

37. Paul would limit his liberty voluntarily out of regard for others, but he would not allow others to sit in judgment on his exercise of his liberty or to make their conscience the standard by which his liberty was to be regulated. This is the point of his remark about conscience in 1 Corinthians 10: 29b, 30.

38. The reference to this kind of occasion in 1 Corinthians 8: 10 is illustrated by some papyrus letters from Oxyrhynchus, e.g. "Chaeremon invites you to dine at the table of the lord Sarapis in the Sarapeion [temple of Sarapis] tomorrow, the 15th, at the 9th hour" (Papyrus 110; cf. Papyri 523, 1484, 1755).

39. 1 Corinthians 10: 21.

idolatry, but it was foolish to enter deliberately into such associations when there was no need to do so. Paul reminds them of the disastrous consequences of Israel's association with the Moabites in the apostasy of Baal-peor during the wilderness wanderings, with the implication that now, as then, such idolatry might well involve sexual immorality.[40] "These things", he says, "were written down for our instruction . . .; therefore let any one who thinks that he stands take heed lest he fall" (1 Corinthians 10: 11 f.).

All things might be lawful, as the men of knowledge affirmed, but (Paul added) "not all things are helpful"[41] – least of all attendance at an idolatrous feast in a pagan temple.

(d) *Questions about spiritual gifts.* In the eyes of some Corinthian Christians, the most important manifestations of the indwelling Spirit were spectacular phenomena like speaking with tongues. On this question too Paul's opinion is sought. And once again he starts to answer the question by going as far as he can with the questioners. As for speaking with tongues, he says – yes, I speak with tongues myself, more than any of you, in fact; "*nevertheless*, in church I would rather speak five words with my mind, in order to instruct others, than ten thousand words in a 'tongue'" (1 Corinthians 14: 18 f.).

The physiology of glossolalia was unknown to Paul: it results from the appropriate stimulation of what has been known since 1861 as "Broca's area", the centre for articulate speech in the third frontal convolution of the dominant cerebral hemisphere. What did concern him was its cultivation as a spiritual gift. That it might be a vehicle of the Spirit of Christ he agreed, but this could not be known unless the utterance was interpreted, and the power to interpret glossolalia was itself a spiritual gift. Only when an interpreter was available would glossolalia be helpful to an assembled congregation; otherwise its value was confined to private devotion (as Paul had presumably proved in his personal experience).[42]

Prophecy, on the other hand, was a *charisma* of great value; Paul warmly recommended its cultivation. By prophecy he seems to mean the declaration of the mind of God in the power of the Spirit, in a language understood by speaker and hearers alike – as when a prophetic utterance at Antioch directed that he and Barnabas should be released by the church there for a more extended ministry.[43] A stranger finding his way into a church meeting where

40. Numbers 25: 1–5; Psalm 105: 28b.; cf. G. E. Mendenhall, *The Tenth Generation* (Baltimore, 1973), pp. 105 ff.; A. T. Hanson, *Studies in Paul's Technique and Theology* (London, 1974), pp. 4 ff.
41. 1 Corinthians 10: 23; cf. 6: 12.
42. 1 Corinthians 14: 4a.
43. Acts 13: 2 (see p. 160).

several people were speaking with "tongues" would conclude that they were all mad; but if he found his way there while they were prophesying one by one, he would be convicted in conscience by what he heard and acknowledge that God was present. [44]

Paul uses the analogy of a human body, in which the proper functioning of each part contributes to the health of the whole, to show that in the church, "the body of Christ", a variety of endowments and ministries was necessary for the general well-being. It was foolish, therefore, for too many members of the church to concentrate on the exercise of a few impressive *charismata* when so many more, some of them obscure and unspectacular but none the less valuable, were needed for the common good. This figure of the body was to play an increasingly important part in Paul's thinking about the church and her relation to the risen Lord. [45]

(e) *Questions about the Jerusalem relief fund.* One final question dealt with a practical matter not arising from controversies within the Corinthian church. They had heard that Paul was organizing a relief fund in his Gentile mission-field for the benefit of the Jerusalem church: how did he wish them to set about contributing to it? Let each of you set aside an appropriate sum week by week, said Paul; then, when I come to supervise the collecting of the money, it will be ready and there will be no undignified scramble to raise your contribution. They should appoint their own delegates with written accreditation to take the gift to Jerusalem; he might be going there himself about the same time, in which case they could accompany him. He had given similar instructions to other contributing churches, including the churches of Galatia. [46]

## 2. A painful visit and a stern letter

When Paul sent off this letter – 1 Corinthians or "Corinthians B" – he expected to follow it up with a personal visit. He planned to stay on at Ephesus for a few more weeks at least – until Pentecost (probably A.D. 55). Meanwhile he sent Timothy ahead of him, and asked the Corinthians to make him feel at home among them. [47] After Pentecost he himself would cross the Aegean to Macedonia, [48] visit his churches there, and then make his way south to Corinth, where he hoped to spend the winter. Soon afterwards he modified this plan, and let the Corinthians know that he would visit them twice – once on his way to Macedonia and again on his way back

44. 1 Corinthians 14: 23–25.
45. 1 Corinthians 12: 12–27; see pp. 420 f.
46. 1 Corinthians 16: 1–4; see p. 319.
47. 1 Corinthians 16: 5–11; cf. Acts 19: 22 and perhaps Philippians 2: 19.
48. The situation in Macedonia may have changed with the death of Claudius in A.D. 54; at any rate Paul felt it would now be safe to return there (see p. 236).

from there.[49] After the second of these visits he would set sail in the spring for Palestine, along with delegates of the churches which were contributing to the Jerusalem relief fund.

A number of factors made it impossible for this modified plan to be carried out. One of these was news of further trouble in the church of Corinth, which compelled Paul to pay it an urgent visit. The letter recently received by the church had evidently not been so effective as Paul had hoped in checking those tendencies of which he expressed disapproval, and when Timothy arrived he was quite unable to enforce Paul's directions. It may indeed have been Timothy who brought back the news which made Paul decide that nothing would serve but a direct confrontation with the church. A confrontation it proved to be – a painful experience for Paul and his converts alike. The opposition to Paul came to a head, and one member of the church in particular took the lead in defying his authority. The others took no effective action in Paul's defence, and Paul, deeply humiliated, left Corinth.[50]

But he could not leave the Corinthian situation as it was: he composed a stinging letter to the church – "out of much affliction and anguish of heart and with many tears" (2 Corinthians 2: 3 f.) – and sent it to Corinth by the hand of Titus, a stronger personality, probably, than Timothy. We may call this letter "Corinthians C"; it is doubtful if any part of it survives.[51] When Titus set off with it, Paul immediately began to be sorry that he had sent it. Its severe tone might produce the desired effect, but it might on the other hand exacerbate the situation. In it he assured the Corinthians of his love for them, but demanded that they give evidence of the love which they professed for him by acknowledging his apostolic authority and taking disciplinary measures against the man who had defied it. He assured Titus, as he gave him the letter to take to Corinth, that the Corinthian Christians were sound at heart, and that they would give proof of their true quality by gladly rendering the obedience which the letter demanded. He now had to wait and see if his confident assurance was well founded or not.

### 3. Temporary reconciliation

On his return to the province of Asia he was assailed by severe depression, and also, it appears, by extreme external danger.[52] The

49. 2 Corinthians 1: 15 f.

50. This was the "painful visit" of 2 Corinthians 2: 1.

51. It has been widely held that part at least of this letter survives in 2 Corinthians 10–13 (a view first propounded by A. Hausrath, *Der Vier-Capitel Brief des Paulus an die Corinthier* [Heidelberg, 1870], and popularized by J. H. Kennedy, *The Second and Third Letters of St. Paul to the Corinthians* [London, 1900]), but this is rendered improbable by 12: 18, which seems clearly to refer back to 8: 6, 16–19.

52. 2 Corinthians 1: 8 ff.; see pp. 295 ff., 310.

danger subsided, but the anxiety remained. He went to the district around Troas,[53] in the north-west of the province, hoping to greet Titus there on his return by sea from Corinth. While he waited for Titus, he found many encouraging opportunities for evangelism, but his mind was so unsettled that he could not take proper advantage of them. He waited probably until navigation across the Aegean had ceased for the winter, and since he now knew that Titus would have to take the land-route through Macedonia, he himself set out for Macedonia, still a prey to "fightings without and fears within" (2 Corinthians 7: 5).

But then Titus met him, and brought good news from Corinth.[54] The severe letter had been completely effective: the Corinthian Christians were stung to such a pitch of indignation in their zeal to vindicate themselves in Paul's eyes and assure him of their loyalty that they were now in danger of going to the opposite extreme in making a scapegoat of the man who had been foremost in defying Paul's authority. There were still some complaints that Paul's changes of travel plans were disconcertingly abrupt and unforeseen, but the general mood was one of reconciliation. Titus was delighted with their attitude and shared his delight with Paul. Paul immediately sent a further letter, "Corinthians D" – our 2 Corinthians (or at least 2 Corinthians 1–9) – in which he expressed his response to Titus's news in an outpouring of open-hearted affection. He explains that his one reason for sending Titus instead of coming back himself was his desire not to cause them further pain. He urges them to forgive the offender because his demand for disciplinary action against him was due to no personal resentment but to a resolve to test the church's love and obedience. Now that they had satisfied him on this score, they should extend full friendship and fellowship to the offender; otherwise the dejection which he was suffering as a result of their unconcealed disapproval might be his undoing – and theirs.[55]

The sense of euphoria which Titus's news had engendered in Paul encouraged him to wear his heart on his sleeve and enlarge on the hardships and the splendours of his apostolic service. To be a minister of the new covenant, with its message of liberation and life, was more glorious by far than to be a minister of the old covenant, even were that minister Moses himself, not to speak of some contemporaries of Paul who proclaimed the continuing validity of the law in the gospel age.[56] Paul's feeling of relief and relaxation

53. The phrase in 2 Corinthians 2: 12, εἰς τὴν Τρῳάδα , might refer to the port of Troas (as in Acts 20:6) or to the Troad, the district in which it lay. See p. 217 with n. 21.
54. 2 Corinthians 7: 6 ff.
55. 2 Corinthians 2: 5–11.
56. 2 Corinthians 3: 7 ff.; see p. 200.

encouraged him also to raise afresh the question of the collection for Jerusalem. During the period of strained relations it had not been expedient to mention this. Now, however, he tells the Corinthians how generously the Macedonian churches, despite their deep poverty and recent endurance of persecution, have given to this fund. He mentions, too, that he has been boasting to the Macedonians about the promptness with which the Corinthian church and other Achaian churches have got their contributions ready. He will soon be on his way to Corinth with representatives of the Macedonian churches, carrying those churches' donations; but meanwhile, to make sure that the Corinthian donation will indeed be ready, he is sending Titus back to them with two other friends, highly reputed among the churches for their impartiality and probity, to help them to complete what has been so well begun – the gathering together of the sums of money already set aside for this purpose by individuals or households.[57]

### 4. Challenge to Paul's authority

But this second visit of Titus to Corinth was not so happy as the former one. Some members of the church may have felt that, for all his insistence on the voluntary character of the gift for Jerusalem, Paul was really putting them on the spot, placing them in a situation in which they had no choice but to make a generous contribution if they were not to lose face – and make Paul lose face – before the representatives of other churches.

A new feeling of resentment showed itself among some members of the church, and it was fostered by certain visitors to Corinth who did their best to undermine Paul's prestige in his converts' eyes. Our knowledge of these visitors, and of the atmosphere of the church at the time of their visit, is derived solely from 2 Corinthians 10–13, which may have been sent to Corinth a little later than chapters 1–9, and could be called "Corinthians E".[58] Since Paul had no need to identify those visitors in writing about them to the Corinthians, it is not surprising that conflicting opinions about their character are held today. One view, first put forward by Wilhelm Lütgert in 1908, is that they were Gnostics of ecstatic temperament and libertine ethics.[59] But since they claimed to be

57. 2 Corinthians 8: 1–9: 15.
58. Cf. C. K. Barrett, *The Second Epistle to the Corinthians* (London, 1973), pp. 243 ff.
59. W. Lütgert, *Freiheitspredigt und Schwarmgeister in Korinth: ein Beitrag zur Charakteristik der Christuspartei* (Gütersloh, 1908); cf. W. Schmithals, *Gnosticism in Corinth*, E.T. (Nashville/New York, 1971). See also G. Friedrich, "Die Gegner des Paulus im 2. Korintherbrief", in *Abraham unser Vater: Festschrift für O. Michel*, ed. O. Betz, etc. (Leiden, 1963), pp. 181 ff.; D. Georgi, *Die Gegner des Paulus im 2. Korintherbrief* (Neukirchen, 1964); C. K. Barrett, "Paul's Opponents in II Corinthians",

"Hebrews" and invoked the authority of the "superlative apostles", it is more likely that they came from Judaea. They represented themselves as "men of the Spirit", no doubt, but that does not make them Gnostics: the issue between Paul and them was not *gnōsis*, not spiritual gifts, but Paul's apostolic *exousia*, his authority and liberty.[60]

If, like some earlier visitors to the Corinthian church, they brought credentials signed by the Jerusalem leaders, Paul had the task of exposing the hollowness of their pretensions without overtly questioning the authority or *bona fides* of those who recommended them. He was concerned to avoid the slightest appearance of a breach between his Gentile mission and the Jerusalem church. It was not always easy to avoid the appearance of such a breach, when the authority of Jerusalem was so vigorously asserted in opposition to his own. The interlopers argued that no teaching could be validated unless it was authorized by Jerusalem. If Paul acted in independence of Jerusalem, he lacked the commission of Christ which was primarily vested in Jerusalem and which they accordingly inherited; to cut oneself loose, as Paul did, from the source of spiritual authority was to "walk according to the flesh" (2 Corinthians 10: 2). If the church of Corinth wished to enjoy the blessings of the Spirit, it must acknowledge the authority of Jerusalem.

In Paul's mind, these arguments did not affect his personal status so much as the truth of the gospel and the nature of the church. If his ministry bore the stamp of divine approval, if the Corinthian church was the seal of his apostleship, then the opposition of those intruders was opposition not merely to him but to the Lord who commissioned him, to the Spirit who empowered him, and to the gospel which he proclaimed: theirs was therefore "another Jesus,[61] . . . a different Spirit, . . . a different gospel" (2 Corinthians 11: 4). They might invoke the authority of the "superlative apostles"[62] – it is not certain whether this is their own designation of the Jerusalem leaders or Paul's ironical summing-up of their portrayal of those leaders. (Even if none of the twelve was actually resident in Jerusalem by this time, Jerusalem would still be regarded as their

---

*NTS* 17 (1970–71), pp. 233–254; J. J. Gunther, *St. Paul's Opponents and their Background* (Leiden, 1973).

60. Cf. E. Käsemann, "Die Legitimität des Apostels", *ZNW* 41 (1942), pp. 33–71.

61. According to D. Georgi (*Die Gegner des Paulus*, p. 286), this "other Jesus" was presented as the "man of the Spirit" ( θεῖος ἀνήρ ) *par excellence*; this cannot be disproved, but there is no evidence for it. It is just as possible that they preached a *theologia gloriae* as against Paul's *theologia crucis*. See also D. W. Oostendorp, *Another Jesus* (Kampen, 1967).

62. Greek ὑπέρλιαν ἀπόστολοι (2 Corinthians 11: 5; 12: 11).

home base; and James was permanently there.) But they themselves were apostles of a very different kind. In so far as they were entitled to be so called, they were "apostles" or messengers of the Jerusalem church, whether they carried out their instructions to the letter or (as is possible) exceeded them. But they were usurping the functions of "apostles of Christ" – men who, like Paul, were directly commissioned by the risen Christ to undertake pioneer evangelism and to plant churches, and whose commission was sealed, as Paul's was at Corinth, by the visible fruit of their labours. Far from being messengers of Christ, however, those others were false apostles in disguise, no true servants of Christ but servants of Satan. Instead of pioneering a mission-field of their own (as true apostles of Christ would have done), they preferred to be parasites on "other men's labours" (2 Corinthians 10: 15).

They boasted of their impeccable Israelite pedigree and pointed in support of their claims to "visions and revelations of the Lord" (2 Corinthians 12: 1). Paul makes no attempt to refute these claims, because they are really irrelevant to the issue; but if such credentials impress the Corinthians, he himself can produce more impressive ones.[63] What is more to the point – though he is ashamed to have to say it (for his own converts might have been expected spontaneously to defend him against his detractors) – he has endured far more hardships in the discharge of his ministry than they have done.[64] If they assert their authority among the Corinthian Christians by lording it over them and living at their expense, Paul will exercise his apostolic freedom by tending his converts with paternal care and spending and being spent for them.

These intruders were not judaizers in the narrower sense; they did not try to impose legal observances on Gentile believers. They simply conceived it as their mission to impose the authority of the mother church over the Christian world. It was nothing to them that this contravened the agreement over which the Jerusalem leaders had shaken hands with Paul and Barnabas some years previously; if the "superlative apostles" were so blind to their own best interests, they themselves would secure for them the status which was their due. For a time they clearly made some headway at Corinth. Ten or eleven years later their policy must have collapsed in any case; the dispersal of the Jerusalem church at the time of the Jewish revolt against Rome which broke out in A.D. 66 put an end to such authority as that church had enjoyed throughout the Gentile mission-field. But there never came a time during Paul's life, so far as can be known, when he could feel that the cause of gospel

63. See pp. 134 ff.
64. 2 Corinthians 11: 23 ff.

liberty had finally triumphed at Corinth. "Paul, who learnt at Corinth what it is to be weak in Christ, shows there perhaps more clearly than elsewhere his full stature of Christian intelligence, firmness, and magnanimity." [65]

65. C. K. Barrett, "Christianity at Corinth", *BJRL* 46 (1963–64), p. 297.

# CHAPTER 25

# Baptism and the Lord's Supper in Pauline Thought

B APTISM AND THE LORD'S SUPPER WERE TWO CHRISTIAN institutions which Paul "received" from those who were in Christ before him, and he "delivered" them as a matter of course to the churches of his Gentile mission field.

## 1. Baptism

Since John the Baptist distinguished his own baptism in water – a "baptism of repentance for the remission of sins" (Mark 1: 4) – from the baptism in the Spirit to be administered by the stronger one who was to come after him, it might have been expected that, when the first Christians experienced the outpouring of the Spirit from the day of Pentecost onward, they would discontinue water baptism as having been superseded by something better. In fact they did not: they continued to baptize converts in water "for the remission of sins" (cf. Acts 2: 38), but this baptism was now part of a more comprehensive experience which took character especially from the receiving of the Spirit.[1]

This was the situation which Paul inherited, but his thinking and practice integrated the water and Spirit baptism more closely together. According to the narrative of Acts 19: 1–7, when he met twelve "disciples" at Ephesus who had received John's baptism – for the remission of sins, presumably – but who knew nothing of the Holy Spirit, he concluded that their baptism was defective. He therefore baptized them afresh, "into the name of the Lord Jesus", and laid his hands on them, whereupon they gave audible evidence of having received the Spirit.

That Paul himself at his conversion was baptized and so had his sins washed away is the testimony of Acts 22: 16 (cf. 9: 18). When

---

1. See p. 210. The sequence of the component elements in Christian initiation varies from one occasion to another in Acts. Peter's hearers in Jerusalem on the day of Pentecost repent, are baptized, and receive the Spirit (2: 38, 41); the Samaritans evangelized by Philip believe and are baptized "into the name of the Lord Jesus", but do not receive the Spirit until apostolic hands are laid on them (8: 12, 14–17); Cornelius and his household receive the Spirit while they are still listening to the message and are then baptized (10: 44–48).

in his letters he reminds his Christian readers of the meaning of their baptism he associates his own baptism with theirs: "all of us who were baptized into Christ Jesus were baptized into his death" (Romans 6: 3); "in one Spirit we were all baptized into one body" (1 Corinthians 12: 13).[2] At the same time he gives baptism – theirs and his – a new depth of meaning. Baptism, in Paul's teaching, initiates believers into their state of being "in Christ", so that his historical death and resurrection become part of their spiritual experience; the baptism in the Spirit which the risen Lord then effects incorporates them into one body with him – or, as Paul puts it to the Galatians, "as many of you as were baptized into Christ have put on Christ ... you are all one in Christ Jesus" (Galatians 3: 27 f.). Paul, who had learned so clearly the religious inadequacy of the old circumcision, was not the man to ascribe *ex opere operato* efficacy to another external rite; it was the impartation of the Spirit in response to faith that made the convert a new creation. We must beware of forcing Paul's thought and terminology into the mould of twentieth-century Christian rationalism, but if it be realized that repentance and faith, with baptism in water and reception of the Spirit, followed by first communion, formed one complex experience of Christian initiation, then what is true of the experience as a whole may be predicated of any element in it. We may make logical distinctions between this and that element, but such distinctions need not have been present to the minds of Paul's Corinthian converts who knew that they had been "washed, . . . sanctified, . . . justified in the name of the Lord Jesus Christ and in the Spirit of our God" (1 Corinthians 6: 11). It is unlikely that they dissociated the washing from their baptism in water, but it was the divine action in their lives that gave their baptism effective meaning and caused Paul to use what has been called the language of sacramental realism.[3]

Christians could no more be immunized by baptism (or the eucharistic meal) against divine judgment on their unfaithfulness than the Israelites during the wilderness wanderings were protected by their "baptism" in the cloud and in the sea (or their partaking of bread from heaven and water from the rock) from the consequences of their idolatry and immorality (1 Corinthians 10: 1–11). At the same time, the baptism of Christians constituted the

2. J. D. G. Dunn, however, makes a sharp distinction between Spirit-baptism and water-baptism: in 1 Corinthians 12: 13, he says, "Paul is thinking of baptism in the Spirit; he is not speaking about water at all" (*Baptism in the Holy Spirit* [London, 1970], p. 129). On the relation and distinction between water-baptism and baptism with the Spirit see Karl Barth, *Church Dogmatics* iv, 4, E.T. (Edinburgh, 1969), pp. 32 ff. *et passim*.

3. Cf. D. A. Tappeiner, "Hermeneutics, the Analogy of Faith and New Testament Sacramental Realism", *EQ* 49 (1977), pp. 40–52.

frontier between their old unregenerate existence and their new life
in Christ: it marked their death to the old order and their rising
again to the new order, so that for a baptized Christian to go on in
sin was as preposterous as it would be for an emancipated slave to
remain in bondage to his former owner (Romans 6: 1–4, 15–23) or
for a widow to remain subject to "the law of her husband"
(Romans 7: 1–6). Paul knew himself to have been in bondage to sin
before his conversion in the sense that he was in bondage to the law
which (without his realizing it at the time) led him into sin; the
bondage to sin which many of his Gentile converts had experienced
took a different form. When Paul appeals to the logic of baptism, he
means that the power of the Spirit, which is the source and stay of
the new life, enables the believer to shake off the old bondage,
however its form might have varied from one to another.

Paul gives his readers no ground for supposing that baptism
makes no practical difference or that it is an optional extra in Christian life. He takes it for granted that all believers have been
baptized,[4] just as he takes it for granted that they have all received
the Spirit.[5] When he thanks God that he baptized none but a
handful of his Corinthian converts, saying that Christ did not send
him to baptize but to preach the gospel, he is not belittling the importance of baptism.[6] He indicates rather that by leaving the work
of baptizing to others he avoided giving any one ground to charge
him with setting up a church or party of his own. It was into
Christ's name – that is, as followers of Christ, not of Paul – that his
converts were baptized or, as the Colossian Christians are told, it
was with Christ that they were "buried . . . in baptism, in which
you were also raised with him through faith in the working of God,
who raised him from the dead" (Colossians 2: 12). While Paul does
not say of the baptismal tradition, as he does of the eucharistic
tradition, that he received it "from the Lord",[7] he probably implies
that he did so receive it.

What had happened in the experience of individual believers, incorporated by baptism into the new community, is applied in
Ephesians 5: 25 f. to the community as such when Christ is said to
have given himself up for her, "that he might sanctify her, having
cleansed her by the washing of water with the word"[8] – the

4. On the other hand, D. W. B. Robinson concludes from 1 Corinthians 1:
13–17 "that Paul regarded water-baptism as ultimately an *adiaphoron*, a matter of
indifference. This would be consistent with everything he says about the non-
essential character of ordinances of the flesh" ("Towards a Definition of Baptism", *Reformed Theological Review* 34 [1975], p. 14). Cf. J. D. G. Dunn, *Baptism in
the Holy Spirit*, pp. 117–120.
5. Cf. Romans 8: 9 (see p. 209).
6. Cf. 1 Corinthians 1: 13–17.
7. Cf. 1 Corinthians 11: 23.
8. Similar language is used in Titus 3: 5 f. for "the washing [ λουτρόν , as in

"word" or utterance being either the pronouncing of the holy name over the persons being baptized or (more probably) the response in which they confessed their faith and invoked the name of the Lord.[9]

## 2. The Lord's Supper

Paul's references to the Lord's Supper are fewer than his references to baptism; they are confined to 1 Corinthians. Few as they are, however, they show how this institution, like that of baptism, was integrated in his thinking with the concept of the believing community as the body of Christ.

When he tells the Corinthians that he "received from the Lord" the account of what Jesus did and said "on the night when he was betrayed" (1 Corinthians 11: 23), he does not say when or where he received it. He received it "from the Lord" in the sense that it is in the crucified and exalted Lord that all true Christian tradition has its source, as it is by him that it is perpetually validated.[10] The probability is that he received it at the outset of his Christian career, even before he went up to Jerusalem to make the acquaintance of the leaders of the mother-church – that he learned it, in fact, from the disciples in Damascus, if it was in their fellowship that he first took the memorial bread and wine.

Paul's record of the institution of the Lord's Supper is the earliest one we have: a comparison of it with the others – that in Mark 14: 22–25 (reproduced, with minor changes, in Matthew 26: 26–29)[11] and the shorter and longer forms which are conflated in Luke 22: 17–20[12] – indicates that at an early date variations appeared in the transmission of the dominical words. In the form known to Paul "This is my body" is augmented by "which is for you"; "This is my covenant blood, which is poured out for many" becomes "This cup is the new covenant in my blood", and the bread-word and

---

Ephesians 5: 26] of regeneration and renewal in the Holy Spirit, which God poured out upon us richly through Jesus Christ our Saviour".

9. On Pauline baptism see also O. Cullmann, *Baptism in the New Testament*, E.T. (London, 1950), pp. 23 ff.; G. W. H. Lampe, *The Seal of the Spirit* (London, 1951), pp. 3 ff.; G. R. Beasley-Murray, *Baptism in the New Testament* (London, 1962), pp. 127 ff.; D. E. H. Whiteley, *The Theology of St. Paul* (Oxford, 1964), pp. 166 ff.; R. Schnackenburg, *Baptism in the Thought of St. Paul*, E.T. (Oxford, 1964); G. Wagner, *Pauline Baptism and the Pagan Mysteries*, E.T. (Edinburgh/London, 1967).

10. Cf. O. Cullmann, "*Kyrios* as Designation for the Oral Tradition concerning Jesus", *Scottish Journal of Theology* 3 (1950), pp. 180 ff.; *The Early Church* (London, 1956), pp. 66 ff.

11. In Matthew's version the statement about the cup, "and they all drank of it" (Mark 14: 23) becomes a command on the Lord's lips, "Drink of it, all of you", and to the clause "which is poured out for you" there is added an epexegetic phrase, "for the remission of sins" (Matthew 26: 28).

12. On the textual problem of Luke 22: 17–20 see B. M. Metzger, *A Textual Commentary on the Greek New Testament* (London/New York, 1971), pp. 173–177.

cup-word alike are followed by the injunction "Do this in remembrance of me" (which is appended to the bread-word only in the longer Lukan form).[13] The memorial purpose of the meal is thus made quite explicit, and when Paul adds, "as often as you eat this bread and drink the cup, you proclaim the Lord's death until he comes", he does justice also to the forward-looking perspective which was present in the original setting.[14] But the variations make no material difference to the central intention: of the institution narrative Paul might have said, much as he said of his sharing the basic facts of the gospel with the other apostles, "Whether then it was I or they, this is what we delivered; this is what you received".[15]

Paul's distinctive contribution to eucharistic doctrine lies in his emphasis on the meal as an occasion of communion (*koinōnia*) and in his interpretation of the bread-word, "This is my body", to include Christ's body corporate.

When he warns the Corinthian Christians against participation in idolatrous feasts, he draws an analogy between what happens there and what happens in the eucharist, in order to show the absurdity of thinking they can "drink the cup of the Lord and the cup of demons" (1 Corinthians 10: 21). "The 'cup of blessing' [16] over which we say a blessing, is it not a participation (*koinōnia*) in the blood of Christ? The bread which we break, is it not a participation in the body of Christ? Because there is one bread", he adds, "we who are many are one body, for we all partake of the one bread" (1 Corinthians 10: 16 f.). Communion with Christ, which they enjoyed together at his table, excluded communion with a pagan divinity at *his* table; and such communion with a pagan divinity excluded communion with Christ.

But their membership in the body of Christ could be violated at

---

13. After the cup-word in 1 Corinthians 11: 25 the memorial command takes the form: "Do this, as often as you drink it, in remembrance of me". It is improbable that this meant, "Do this in order that God may remember me by speeding my parousia and consummating his kingdom", as J. Jeremias argued (*The Eucharistic Words of Jesus*, E.T. [Oxford, 1955], pp. 159 ff.); it is even less probable that the memorial command marks a change or reinterpretation of the original intention of the Jerusalem rite, as was held by H. Lietzmann, *Mass and Lord's Supper*, E.T. (Leiden, 1953 ff.), pp. 145 ff., 172 ff., 204 ff.

14. See p. 265.

15. Cf. 1 Corinthians 15: 11.

16. The "cup of blessing" was a common Jewish expression for the cup of wine taken at the end of a meal, perhaps because it was the signal for saying grace after meat. The blessing said over the cup expresses thanks to God (the verb in 1 Corinthians 10: 16 is εὐλογέω , synonymous with εὐχαριστέω used in 11: 24). In Jewish usage it took the form, "Blessed art thou, O Lord our God, King of the universe, who createst the fruit of the vine"; the eucharistic blessing may have been given a more explicitly Christian content, like "We give thee thanks, our Father, for the holy vine of David thy servant, which thou hast made known to us through Jesus thy Servant; thine be the glory for ever" (*Didache* 9: 2).

his own table by an unbrotherly attitude or conduct towards fellow-members of his body. When they broke the bread which was the token of the body of Christ they not only recalled his self-oblation on the cross but proclaimed their joint participation in his corporate body. If, then, they denied in practice the unity which they professed sacramentally in the eucharist, they ate and drank unworthily and so profaned the body and blood of the Lord; if they ate and drank "without discerning the body" they ate and drank judgment upon themselves.[17] To eat and drink "without discerning the body" meant quite simply to take the bread and cup at the same time as they were treating their fellow-Christians uncharitably in thought or behaviour. So realistically does Paul regard such "unworthy" participation that he warns those who are guilty of it that sickness or death may befall them by way of self-incurred judgment.[18] Eucharistic participation in Christ, like baptismal incorporation into Christ, is no solitary matter: both involve sharing the common life in the body of Christ with all other believers, and carry with them serious ethical corollaries which Christians ignore at their peril.[19]

17. 1 Corinthians 11: 27, 29.
18. 1 Corinthians 11: 30.
19. On the Lord's Supper in Paul cf. A. J. B. Higgins, *The Lord's Supper in the Early Church* (London, 1952), pp. 64 ff.; D. E. H. Whiteley, *The Theology of St. Paul*, pp. 178 ff.; C. K. Barrett, *The First Epistle to the Corinthians* (London, 1968), pp. 231–238, 262–277.

# CHAPTER 26

# Ephesus: Open Door and Many Adversaries

## 1. Paul comes to Ephesus

AFTER HIS SHORT VISIT TO PALESTINE AND SYRIA IN THE SPRING
of A.D. 52, Paul made his way back to Ephesus by land.
This time no obstacles or prophetic prohibitions prevented
him from completing his westward journey through Asia Minor.
On the way he is said to have passed through "the Galatic region
and Phrygia", but as nothing is said of his undertaking evangelism
there but only of his "strengthening all the disciples" (Acts 18: 23),
the area indicated is probably much the same as that which he
traversed with Silas and Timothy on the earlier occasion, called
"the Phrygian and Galatic region" in Acts 16: 6. Then he went on
to Ephesus by way of the "upper country" (Acts 19: 1), which may
mean that, instead of taking the main road by the Lycus and
Maeander valleys, he travelled by a more northerly road and approached Ephesus from the north side of Mount Messogis (modern
Aydi Dağlari).[1] (Another suggestion is that the expression simply
refers to the hinterland of Ephesus, as when we say "up
country".)[2]

The province of Asia, as has been mentioned already, was formed from the kingdom of Pergamum when Attalus III died in 133
B.C. and left his territory to the senate and people of Rome. It comprised the regions of Moesia, Lydia, Caria, Lycia and Western
Phrygia. On its coast and off-shore islands there had been Ionian
Greek settlements from time immemorial.[3] In the first half of the
sixth century B.C. the mainland settlements were incorporated by
Croesus into his expanding kingdom of Lydia: when he was
overthrown by Cyrus in 546 B.C. they passed under Persian con-
trol. After an abortive revolt in 498 B.C., they regained their liberty
for some decades following the repulse of Xerxes' invasion of
Greece in 480–479 B.C., but reverted to Persian rule by the King's
Peace of 387 B.C.[4] They were liberated again by Alexander in 334

1. Cf. W. M. Ramsay, *St. Paul the Traveller and the Roman Citizen* (London,
[14] 1920), pp. 265 f.
2. Cf. K. Lake and H. J. Cadbury, *BC* i. 4, pp. 236 f.
3. They appear as "Javan" in the table of nations in Genesis 10: 4.
4. Otherwise called the Peace of Antalcidas (Xenophon, *Hellenica* v. 1. 33).

B.C. and after his death were ruled by one or another of the succession dynasties: the chief cities, however, enjoyed a considerable measure of civic autonomy, and continued to do so under the Romans.

Of these Ionian settlements the most illustrious was Ephesus, at the mouth of the Caÿster (modern Kücük Menderes). There had been a Carian settlement here before the Ionians came, devoted to the cult of the great Anatolian mother-goddess in her local manifestation.[5] The Ionian colonists intermingled with their Carian predecessors, and shared in the worship of the great goddess. Her name Artemis is pre-Greek. She first appears in Greek literature as mistress and protectress of wild life;[6] in Greece proper she was worshipped as the virgin-huntress. The temple of Artemis at Ephesus housed the many-breasted image of the goddess, which was believed to have "fallen from the sky" (Acts 19: 35) and to be therefore of divine workmanship. An earlier temple was burned down in 356 B.C. – on the night, it was said, when Alexander the Great was born – by a young man who explained that he had done this to perpetuate his name in history. It must be confessed that he succeeded in his aim; his name, Herostratus, is known to us solely for this act of arson.[7] A new temple, more magnificent than the one it replaced, was built soon afterwards and ranked as one of the seven wonders of the world. The city prided itself on its designation "Temple Warden (neōkoros) of Artemis";[8] and on the fact that the cult of the great goddess had spread out into the whole Greek world and even beyond its frontiers: the silversmith Demetrius might well speak of her as worshipped by "all Asia and the world" (Acts 19: 27).[9] Magnificent as the temple was – four times as large as the Parthenon in Athens, supported by 127 columns, each of them sixty feet high, and adorned by Praxiteles and other great sculptors of antiquity[10] – it has almost completely disappeared; only its founda-

5. The Carians were one of the non-Greek populations of south-west Asia Minor; the Carians or Carites of 2 Kings 11: 4, 19 (related to the Philistines) were probably so called because they came from there. The mother-goddess was given a variety of names – Ma in Cappadocia, Cybele or the Great Mother in Pessinus (from which her image was taken to Rome in 204 B.C.).

6. Homer (*Iliad* xxi. 470 f.) calls her πότνια θηρῶν, Ἄρτεμις ἀγροτέρη ("mistress of wild beasts, Artemis of the wilds"); Aeschylus (*Agamemnon* 134 ff.) pictures her indignant concern for injured wild things. See W. K. C. Guthrie, *The Greeks and their Gods* (London, 1950), pp. 99 ff.

7. Strabo, *Geography* xiv. 1. 22; Plutarch, *Life of Alexander* 3. 3.

8. Cf. Acts 19: 35. In *CIG* 2972 Ephesus is given this title ( νεωκόρος τῆς Ἀρτέμιδος ).

9. In *RE* ii, cols. 1385 f., mention is made of 33 places where she was worshipped. An inscription of A.D. 161 records her fame "not only in her own home territory . . . but also among both Greeks and barbarians" (*British Museum Inscriptions* iii. 482B).

10. Cf. Pliny, *Nat. Hist.* xxxvi. 95–97, 179.

tions remain, and these were located with difficulty by J. T. Wood in 1869 in a marsh at the foot of the hill of Ayasoluk (now Selçuk).[11]

The chief remains of Hellenistic and Roman Ephesus stand about a mile and a half south and south-west of the temple site. Although the city was a seaport in New Testament times, it now stands seven miles inland because of the silt carried down by the Caÿster. From the top of the theatre one can still discern the outline of the ancient harbour (rather as in aerial photography), now a marshy waste at the end of the Arcadian Way.[12] The theatre, built into the western slope of Mount Pion (Panayirdag) in the city centre, is reckoned to have accommodated over 25,000 people.

Pergamum remained the titular capital of the province, as it had been of the kingdom of the Attalids, but Ephesus was the greatest and most populous city – the greatest trading centre, says Strabo, of all the Asian cities west of the Taurus.[13] Ephesus, Pergamum and the other Greek city-states of the province formed a confederation (the *koinon* of Asia); the representatives of the cities who served on its council were known as the Asiarchs. The Roman administration of the province exercised its authority through regular assizes (*agoraioi*) held in nine or more of the cities and presided over by the proconsul. Liaison was maintained between the municipality and the provincial government by the city secretary (*grammateus*) or chief executive officer.

To this great city, then, Paul came in the late summer of A.D. 52 and stayed there for the best part of three years, directing the evangelization of Ephesus itself and of the province as a whole. Plainly he was assisted in this work by a number of colleagues – like Epaphras, who evangelized the Phrygian cities of the Lycus valley (Colossae, Laodicea and Hierapolis)[14] – and so effectively did they work that, as Luke puts it, "all the residents of Asia heard the word of the Lord, both Jews and Greeks" (Acts 19: 10). Indeed, the Christian history of the area continued unbroken from those years until the Graeco-Turkish exchange of populations in 1923.

## 2. Luke's "pictures" of Paul in Ephesus

Luke does not appear to have been with Paul at any point during his Ephesian ministry, and we have no connected account of these years, for all their importance in the expansion of the Gentile mis-

11. Cf. J. T. Wood, *Discoveries at Ephesus* (London, 1877).
12. The Arcadian Way was named in honour of the Emperor Arcadius (A.D. 395–408), under whom it was repaired.
13. Strabo, *Geography* xii. 8. 15; xiv. 1. 21–25.
14. Cf. Colossians 1: 7; 2: 1; 4: 12 f.; see pp. 407.

Ephesus: The theatre (see p. 293)

Caesarea: The theatre (see p. 354)

sion. Nor have we any correspondence between Paul and his converts at Ephesus which could help us to reconstruct his experiences
with them as the Corinthian letters help us to reconstruct his experiences with the church of Corinth. But the vividness of some of
the Ephesian episodes reported by Luke has suggested to many
readers that he was indebted to eyewitness reports of these.[15]

A New Testament scholar of the present day has compared
Luke's literary style to "a lecture with lantern-slides; the pictures
are shown one after another illustrating the story the lecturer wants
to tell while he makes the transition from one plate to another by
some general remarks".[16] Nowhere in Acts is this analogy more apt
than in the account of Paul's Ephesian ministry (Acts 19: 1–41).

(a) *Disciples at Ephesus.* The first of these "pictures" has as its
subject Paul's encounter, shortly after his arrival in Ephesus, with a
dozen men whom Luke calls "disciples" (Acts 19: 1–7). When he
uses the term "disciples" in this absolute way, Luke normally
means "disciples of Jesus"; that this is what these men were is implied by the question which Paul put to them: "Did you receive the
Holy Spirit when you believed?" He assumed that they were
believers – believers in Jesus, that is to say – but suspected that
there was something deficient in their Christian experience, and
discovered that they knew nothing of the Holy Spirit. Further inquiry showed that the only baptism of which they knew was John's:
in this they resembled Apollos. Perhaps they acquired such
knowledge of the Way as they possessed from some person or persons who, like Apollos, added an acquaintance with the story of
Jesus to an initial reception of John's baptism. It was not necessarily in Ephesus that they had been baptized: John's followers may
conceivably have carried his teaching as far north as Asia Minor,
but these disciples could have come in touch with his teaching and
baptism elsewhere, possibly in Palestine. We are reminded once
more of the scantiness of our knowledge of the dissemination of the
gospel in various forms from its homeland to other regions.

Paul impressed on these disciples the preparatory character of
John's ministry. Their understanding of John's ministry itself was
defective if they did not know of his testimony to the one who was to
come after him and administer baptism with the Holy Spirit.
Apollos had made what could be recognized as a Christian commitment, and Luke's statement that he was "fervent in spirit" (Acts
18: 25) may mean that he was "bubbling over with the Spirit"[17] –

15. E.g. Aristarchus (in whose company Luke appears in Colossians 4: 10, 14;
cf. also Acts 20: 4 f.; 27: 2) could have described the riot in the Ephesian theatre
(cf. Acts 19: 29).

16. W. C. van Unnik, "The 'Book of Acts' the Confirmation of the Gospel",
*Novum Testamentum* 4 (1964), p. 35.

17. The Greek phrase is identical with that used by Paul in Romans 12: 11,

an experience far exceeding anything that these disciples knew. Accordingly Paul had them baptized "into the name of the Lord Jesus" and laid his hands on them, whereupon they received the Spirit and gave audible evidence of their doing so by glossolalia and prophecy. This is the only instance of re-baptism in the New Testament: there is no suggestion that this had been required of Apollos. The apostles themselves and their fellow-disciples, some of whom had received John's baptism, had no need to be baptized afresh because the Spirit came upon them spontaneously at Pentecost, but baptism with the imposition of hands was apparently judged necessary to induce the pentecostal experience in these disciples of Ephesus. Their baptism betokened their full and intelligent commitment to the Christ whose significance was made plain to them by Paul. Paul, it has been validly pointed out, "was one of the greatest assets" for the Jerusalem church,[18] for either by his personal action (as here) or under his influence (as when Priscilla and Aquila instructed Apollos) versions of the gospel which were defective by Jerusalem standards were brought into conformity with the line maintained in common by Paul and the leaders of the mother-church.

(b) *Transference to the lecture-hall of Tyrannus.* Luke's second "picture" is of Paul's expulsion from the synagogue after enjoying its hospitality for three months. The synagogue authorities in Ephesus appear to have accommodated him rather longer than did their colleagues in most other cities visited by Paul. In Ephesus, indeed, the opposition to Paul's "arguing and pleading about the kingdom of God" in the synagogue is not said to have come from the authorities themselves but from some unspecified persons who "were stubborn and disbelieved, speaking evil of the Way before the congregation"[19] (Acts 19: 8 f.). The opposition, at any rate, was sufficiently powerful and vocal to make Paul withdraw from the synagogue. He took his converts and fellow-Christians with him, and they found another meeting-place in the lecture-hall of one Tyrannus. It may be wondered whether it was his parents or his pupils who first called him Tyrannus. His pupils evidently attended his lectures in the cooler hours of the day and then teacher and pupils alike went home towards noon for their siesta; according to the Western text of Acts 19: 9 it was "from the fifth hour to the tenth" – from 11 a.m. to 4 p.m. – that Paul had the use of his hall

where he urges his Christian readers to be "fervent in the Spirit". See J. D. G. Dunn, *Baptism in the Holy Spirit* (London, 1970), p. 88.

18. A. A. T. Ehrhardt, *The Framework of the New Testament Stories* (Manchester, 1964), p. 94.

19. For "before the congregation ( πλήθους )" Codex D, the principal witness to the Western text in Acts, has the fuller reading, "before the multitude ( πλήθους ) of the Gentiles".

and held public debate there. Whatever be the textual basis for the Western reading, the statement is quite probable, although it says much for the staying-power of Paul's hearers as well as of Paul himself if they frequented the lecture-hall daily during the heat of the day for two years. Paul for his part seems to have spent the early morning, and possibly the evening, in manual labour: "these hands", he later reminds the elders of the Ephesian church, "ministered to my necessities, and to those who were with me" (Acts 20: 34).

(c) *Magical arts*. In Shakespeare's *Comedy of Errors*, Antipholus of Syracuse comes to Ephesus and refers to the city's reputation as a centre for the learning and practice of magical arts:

> They say this town is full of cozenage,
> As, nimble jugglers that deceive the eye,
> Dark-working sorcerers that change the mind,
> Soul-killing witches that deform the body,
> Disguised cheaters, prating mountebanks,
> And many such-like liberties of sin.[20]

Its reputation in this respect is indicated by the fact that the phrase "Ephesian writings" (*Ephesia grammata*) [21] was commonly used in antiquity for documents containing spells and formulae like the lengthy magical papyri in the London, Paris and Leiden collections or small amulets (like the mottoes in Christmas crackers) to be rolled up and placed in small cylinders or lockets worn round the neck or elsewhere about the person. [22] One of the latter, in the Princeton University collection of papyri, begins with an odd series of letters arranged in a special pattern:

ZAGOURĒPAGOURĒ

AGOURĒPAGOUR

GOURĒPAGOU

OURĒPAGO

URĒPAG

RĒPA

ĒP

P

20. Act 1, Scene 2, lines 97 ff.

21. Anaxilas, "The Harp-maker", quoted by Athenaeus, *Deipnosophists* xii. 548c; Plutarch, *Table-Talk* vii. 5. 706e; Clement of Alexandria, *Stromateis* v. 242. 45. 2.

22. Cf. K. Preisendanz, *Papyri Graecae Magicae*, i-ii (Leipzig, 1928–31), for a collection of such documents.

– after which comes the petition: "Sovereign and good angels, deliver . . . the son of Sophia from the fever which has him in its grip, this present day, this very hour, now now, quickly quickly." [23] The carefully arranged pattern with which the amulet begins may represent an effort to express the name of some divinity or demon. The great magical papyri are full of such real or imagined names. These documents have come down to us from all over the Near East, but Ephesus was specially renowned for them.

It was not unnatural that in such a setting Paul himself should be regarded as a magician of sorts: kerchiefs and aprons which he wore while engaged in manual labour were taken and applied to various sick and possessed people and proved remarkably beneficial. The virtue, naturally, did not reside in the pieces of cloth or leather but in the faith of those who used them as medicaments. Others looked upon the name of Jesus, so frequently on Paul's lips, as a potent spell, and tried to invoke it as such. The Paris magical papyrus contains such an invocation, "I adjure you by Jesus the god of the Hebrews",[24] and we have evidence of the similar use of other Jewish names, including the divine names Sabaoth, Iao and Iabe.

The last two are attempts at reproducing the ineffable name of the God of Israel. A name of which very few knew the pronunciation, or were permitted to utter it if they did, was by all the standards of magic a name of great power. It was believed that one of the few men to possess the secret was the Jewish high priest, who uttered it when he laid the people's sins on the head of the scapegoat in the court of the Jerusalem temple on the annual day of atonement.[25] It is not surprising then that some strolling Jewish exorcists should give themselves out as members of a high-priestly family. Luke mentions the seven sons of Sceva, billed as a "Jewish high priest", who undertook to exorcize a demon with the words: "I exorcize you by Jesus whom Paul proclaims" (Acts 19: 13 f.). But the demon-possessed man turned on them with such ferocity that they counted themselves fortunate to escape with their lives. In the eyes of the public this served only to emphasize the power of the name of Jesus: it was too dangerous a name to be invoked by any who did not know the right way to use it. In no other city which figures in Luke's narrative could such an incident seem so natural as in Ephesus.

23. Edited by B. M. Metzger in *Papyri in the Princeton University Collections*, ed. A. C. Johnson and S. P. Goodrich, iii (Princeton, 1942) § 159, pp. 78 f.; cf. his popular account, "St. Paul and the Magicians", *Princeton Seminary Bulletin* 38 (1944), pp. 27 ff., where he describes the amulet as "a first-hand specimen of the same sort of magical craft which Paul encountered at Ephesus".

24. Preisendanz, *Papyri Graecae Magicae*, i, P IV (Pap. Bibl. Nat. suppl. gr. 574), lines 3018 f.

25. Mishnah *Yoma* 6: 2.

But the power of the name of Jesus was manifested in the way of which Paul approved when several practitioners of magic were converted to Christianity and renounced their magical arts. They gave practical proof of the change which they had experienced by publicly divulging their secret spells (thus depriving them of their potency) and burning their papyrus scrolls, the value of which was estimated at 50,000 drachmae.

(d) *Demonstration in the theatre.* The most vivid of all the Ephesian episodes reported by Luke describes the riotous assembly in the great theatre of the city. The success of Paul's evangelistic activity meant a diminution in the number of worshippers of the great goddess Artemis, and a consequent diminution in the income of those craftsmen who depended heavily on the Artemis cult for the sale of their wares. Among these craftsmen the silver-smiths held a leading place. The president of the guild of silversmiths at Ephesus, Demetrius by name, called a meeting of his fellow-craftsmen and set before them the seriousness of the situation on the religious and economic planes alike. Demetrius and his colleagues, says Luke, found a ready sale for "silver shrines of Artemis" – miniature sanctuaries representing the goddess (perhaps with her attendant lions) in a niche: her devotees would purchase these and dedicate them in the temple. No silver miniatures of this kind have survived, although silver replicas of her image and terra-cotta models of her temple are known. An inscription of A.D. 104, half a century later than the present incident, tells how a Roman official presented a silver image of Artemis and other statues to be set up in the theatre.[26] The expression used by Luke of Demetrius is similar to the designation *neōpoios*, literally "shrine-maker", which was actually used of a member of the temple vestry (which seems to have comprised twelve men).[27] Demetrius may have been one of the goddess's vestrymen, then, as well as president of the local guild of silversmiths.

Filled with a sense of outrage at the indignity inflicted on the great goddess by these foreign preachers, the silversmiths and their associates raised the cult-cry, "Great is Artemis of the Ephesians!"[28] Their indignation spread to the populace, who rushed to the theatre and demonstrated there. They laid hands on two of Paul's companions, Gaius and Aristarchus, and dragged them to the theatre with them.[29] Paul himself was about to go there

26. The inscription is bilingual (Greek and Latin); see A. Deissmann, *Light from the Ancient East*, E.T. (London, [2] 1927), pp. 112 f.

27. Cf. E. L. Hicks, "Demetrius the Silversmith: An Ephesian Study", *Expositor*, series 4, 1 (1890), pp. 401 ff.

28. The Western text says that they "ran into the square" and raised the cult-cry there.

29. Perhaps Gaius of Derbe and Aristarchus of Thessalonica, if the final letter

too and do what he could to appease the crowd, but some of the Asiarchs of Ephesus who were well-disposed to him warned him to do no such thing.

The Jews of Ephesus felt very uneasy about the turn of events. Although they had no part in Paul's activity, it was well known that they were no believers in Artemis, and a pro-Artemis demonstration might well develop into an anti-Semitic rampage, the more so because Paul himself was so evidently a Jew. A leading member of the Jewish community, Alexander by name, tried to gain the attention of the crowd and dissociate his community from Paul and the other missionaries; but the crowd, recognizing him to be a Jew, howled him down and for two hours kept up the cry, "Great is Artemis of the Ephesians!"

At last the city secretary, thoroughly alarmed, secured something like silence and warned his fellow-Ephesians that the consequences of their riotous assembly might be very serious. The Roman administration of the province would not tolerate such behaviour, and might well deprive them of their civic privileges. The honour and renown of the great goddess were not at stake: the men with whom they were indignant had committed no sacrilege. If they had any charge to being against Paul or the others, let them make use of the law-courts. Matters of concern to the city should be dealt with at a regular meeting of the *ekklēsia* or civic assembly and not at an unruly gathering like this. (That the regular meetings of the assembly were held in the theatre is indicated by the inscription of A.D. 104 mentioned above, for it was during a meeting of the assembly that the silver image of Artemis and the other statues were to be set up there.) [30] The secretary had good reason to be concerned: he was "perhaps the most influential individual in the city",[31] but for that very reason the Romans would hold him specially responsible for the citizens' conduct.

### 3. Dangers at Ephesus

This could have been a dangerous situation for Paul, although the impression given by Luke is that, thanks to the city secretary's forceful interposition, it passed off more quietly than might have been feared. Paul's friends Gaius and Aristarchus appear to have taken little harm apart from a rough handling, unless those are right who see in Paul's description of Aristarchus as his "fellow-prisoner" (Colossians 4: 10) an allusion to a period of imprisonment experienced by Aristarchus (presumably in Paul's company)

---

of Μακεδόνας is due to dittography before the initial letter of συνεκδήμους (Acts 19: 29).

30. See p. 293, n. 26.

31. W. M. Ramsay, *HDB* i. p. 723 (*s.v.* "Ephesus").

about this time – an unnecessary supposition. But if Paul was not seriously endangered on this occasion, there were other occasions during these years which put him in peril of his life. When arguing with the Corinthian intelligentsia about the resurrection hope, for example, he asks: "What do I gain if, humanly speaking, I fought with beasts at Ephesus?" (1 Corinthians 15: 32). The phrase "humanly speaking" is equivalent to "figuratively speaking" and shows that his fighting with beasts is not to be taken literally (although the author of the second-century *Acts of Paul* did take it literally and told an engaging tale of Paul's encounter in the arena with a lion which he had previously befriended – and baptized!).[32] But if the language is metaphorical, for what kind of experience would such a metaphor have been suitable? Then, at a later date, there is the reference in 2 Corinthians 1: 8–10 to a mortal peril which he had recently endured in the province of Asia: death had seemed so imminent and certain that no escape appeared possible, so that when he did nevertheless escape, he greeted his deliverance as a miracle performed by "God who raises the dead". It is possible that this peril was an illness which nearly proved fatal;[33] but it is rather more probable that it was due to human hostility, and that certain circumstances made it advisable not to enter into unnecessary detail about it in writing.

In this connexion political events in the province may have some relevance. The proconsul of Asia at the time when Nero succeeded his stepfather Claudius in the principate (October 13, A.D. 54) was Marcus Junius Silanus, member of a distinguished Roman family allied by marriage to the imperial house. Silanus was the first casualty of the new principate: Nero's mother Agrippina had him poisoned. This was done without Nero's knowledge or approval; but Agrippina bore a grudge against Silanus's family, and seized the earliest opportunity of getting him out of the way. Moreover he was, like Nero himself, a great grandson of Augustus and there was some muttering to the effect that, since Nero was not a direct heir (Claudius's own son Britannicus had a prior claim), the people would be better off with Silanus as emperor.[34]

Agrippina entrusted the work of getting rid of Silanus to two members of the imperial civil service in proconsular Asia – an

32. Cf. *New Testament Apocrypha*, E.T., ed. E. Hennecke, W. Schneemelcher, R. McL. Wilson, ii (London, 1965), pp. 370–373. It is not absolutely true to say, as some have done, that a Roman citizen could not be condemned to the lions: for exceptionally serious offences this sometimes happened, but by being so condemned he lost his citizenship, so that, strictly speaking, a Roman citizen could not be *exposed* to the lions (*Digest* xxviii. 1. 8. 4). See p. 469.

33. So C. H. Dodd, "The Mind of Paul: I" in *New Testament Studies* (Manchester, 1953), p. 68.

34. Tacitus, *Annals* xiii. 1. 1–3; Dio Cassius, *History* lxi. 6. 4 f.

official of equestrian rank named Publius Celer and a freedman named Helius, both of whom became increasingly influential in the following years.[35] When the city secretary of Ephesus told the demonstrators in the theatre that the law-courts were available if they had any specific accusation to bring against Paul or his companions, he added, "and there are proconsuls" (Acts 19: 38). The proconsul of Asia presided at the provincial assizes, but why should the secretary speak of "proconsuls" in the plural? One possibility is that the incident took place in the interval between the murder of Silanus and the arrival of his successor. The secretary would scarcely have referred to Celer and Helius as proconsuls, even if they did discharge some of the proconsul's administrative duties in the interregnum; in the absence of one recognizable proconsul he may have used the generalizing plural: "there are such people as proconsuls" (NEB).

The theory has been propounded that Silanus had befriended Paul, possibly acquitting him when he was prosecuted at the assizes on a charge of temple-robbery, and that this fact worked to Paul's detriment after the fall of Silanus. But why should Paul have been accused of temple-robbery? It has been suggested that his organizing of the Jerusalem relief fund may have been regarded by the leaders of the Jewish communities in Ephesus and other Asian cities as an encroachment on the collection of the annual temple-tax for the maintenance of the temple in Jerusalem.[36] Roman law specifically authorized the collection of this tax and its conveyance to Judaea: indeed, in that very province of Asia, a little over a century before, the Roman governor Lucius Valerius Flaccus allegedly prevented the export of the tax to Judaea and had to stand trial in Rome in 59 B.C. on this and other charges of financial malpractice.[37]

But the temple-tax was collected from Jewish communities; Paul's relief fund was launched for contributions from Gentile churches. Even so, it could have been argued that Paul's Gentile converts were potential proselytes and hence potential contributors to the temple tax, so that, by detaching them from possible adherence to Judaism and encouraging them to contribute to the maintenance of the Jerusalem church, Paul was in effect robbing the Jerusalem temple. If this charge was included in the general ac-

35. Celer was prosecuted for extortion in the province in Asia in A.D. 57 but Nero prevented sentence from being passed on him (Tacitus, *Annals* xiii. 33. 1 f.); Helius was left in charge of Rome and Italy during Nero's tour of Greece (A.D. 66–68) and was later put to death by Galba (Suetonius, *Life of Nero* 23. 1; Dio Cassius, *History* (*Epitome* lxiv. 3. 4).

36. G. S. Duncan, *St. Paul's Ephesian Ministry* (London, 1929), pp. 103–107, 249.

37. Cicero, *Pro Flacco* 66 ff.; cf. Josephus, *Ant.* xvi. 162–165 for Augustus's edict (12 B.C.) authorizing provincial Jews (*inter alia*) to send money to Jerusalem.

cusation of temple violation pressed against Paul on his next visit to Jerusalem,[38] and if it was likely to be raised at Rome when his case was referred to the emperor's jurisdiction, Luke may have had a strong apologetic reason for making no explicit reference to the Jerusalem fund, despite the important part that it played in Paul's strategy.[39] (It has been pointed out that when the city secretary in Ephesus assured the crowd in the theatre that Paul and his friends had committed no sacrilege, the term he used had the literal sense of "temple-robbing";[40] but whatever the precise meaning of the word might be, on his lips it could refer only to the temple and cult of Artemis and so would be irrelevant to the present question.) If a charge of "temple-robbery" was preferred against Paul, it could well have been initiated by Ephesian Jews.

Paul indicates in the course of one of his letters to Corinth that alongside the wide-open opportunities for gospel witness at Ephesus there were "many adversaries" (1 Corinthians 16: 9). There are hints here and there that some of these "adversaries" were persons of influence in the local Jewish community. When, a year or two after his departure from Ephesus, he had an opportunity of talking to the leaders of the Ephesian church during a break in his last voyage from the Aegean to Palestine, he reminded them of the trials which he had had to endure in their city "through the plots of the Jews" (Acts 20: 19). Luke, to whom we are indebted for this information, was probably present at this meeting and heard what was said. It is Luke also who tells us that the hue and cry against Paul during his last visit to Jerusalem, which almost led to his being lynched on the spot, was raised by the "Jews from Asia" who were present for the feast of Pentecost (Acts 21: 27 ff.). And Alexander the coppersmith who, according to 2 Timothy 4: 14, did Paul "great harm", may be identical with that Alexander who tried to dissociate the Jewish community of Ephesus from Paul in the minds of the assembled rioters in the theatre. It is not clear whether the "great harm" was done in Ephesus itself or elsewhere. (Was he, for example, a leader of those Asian Jews who stirred up such trouble for Paul in Jerusalem?)[41]

If – and the *if* must be emphasized – Paul was arraigned on this charge before Junius Silanus and was acquitted, his opponents may have judged that they had a better chance of success when Silanus was removed. If their second attempt procured a conviction, this

38. See p. 356.
39. On the reference to "alms and offerings" in Acts 24: 17 see p. 345, 357.
40. These men, he said, "are neither temple-robbers ( ἱερόσυλοι ) nor blasphemers of our goddess" (Acts 19: 37).
41. The Alexander of 1 Timothy 1: 20 appears to have been a renegade (or at least a libertine) Christian and so presumably to be distinguished from the Alexander of Acts 19: 33.

298 PAUL: APOSTLE OF THE FREE SPIRIT

could have led to "so deadly a peril" as Paul speaks of having undergone in Asia – a peril from which he did not think he could escape with his life. The invocation of his legal rights as a Roman citizen could have sealed his fate more certainly in this situation, if it became known at Rome that he had been protected by Silanus. But all this is a matter of hypothesis.

It was most probably in the period of the Ephesian ministry that Priscilla and Aquila "risked their necks" for Paul's life, as he expresses it in Romans 16: 4. His reference to this incident is (for us, whatever it may have been for the original readers) tantalizing in its brevity and vagueness; but it clearly points to an occasion when Paul himself was in mortal danger, and his two friends hazarded their own lives in an effort to help him. In the same context (Romans 16: 7) he mentions Andronicus and Junias (or Junia if a woman is meant), notable members of the apostolic circle, whom he describes as his "fellow-prisoners". When and where had they shared an imprisonment with Paul, if not at Ephesus? [42]

### 4. Ephesian imprisonment?

This opens the much-canvassed question whether Paul had to endure a term of imprisonment, or even more than one, during his Ephesian ministry. When in 2 Corinthians 11: 23–27, written shortly after the end of his Ephesian ministry, Paul enumerates the hardships and hazards which he has experienced in the course of his apostolic service thus far, he includes among them "many imprisonments". Like much else in this catalogue, the reference to these imprisonments brings home to us the immensity of the gaps in our knowledge of Paul's career. The narrative of Acts mentions only one occasion before this period when Paul was imprisoned: that was when he and Silas were locked up overnight in the town jail at Philippi. We have no direct evidence that he was ever imprisoned at Ephesus, but the possibility cannot be excluded. The tower on a spur of Mount Coressus (Bülbüldağ) called St. Paul's Prison has no acceptable claim to this designation, which nevertheless may reflect some tradition of his imprisonment in Ephesus; but we cannot be sure how old the tradition is. Such a tradition might be reflected also in the note at the end of the Marcionite prologue to the Epistle to the Colossians, stating that it was written by the apostle while in bonds at Ephesus, but this may be little more than a slip: [43] the companion prologue to Philemon gives

42. This imprisonment must have been before A.D. 57; the imprisonment which Aristarchus shared with Paul, according to Colossians 4: 10, may (if "fellow-prisoner" is to be understood literally) have belonged to a later date (see p. 360).

43. A. von Harnack suggested that *ab Epheso* ("from Ephesus") was a corruption of *per Epaphram* ("by Epaphras") (*The Origin of the New Testament*, E.T. [London, 1925], p. 168).

that epistle a Roman provenance, and Philemon and Colossians were certainly sent together from the same place at the same time.

The theory of one or more Ephesian imprisonments has been taken up within the past century by a number of scholars who have postulated such a setting for some of Paul's "captivity epistles": [44] G. S. Duncan, for example, dated Philippians during a short imprisonment preceding Paul's assumed acquittal by Silanus, [45] and P. N. Harrison dated Philemon and Colossians (or at least what he took to be its authentic nucleus) "during a brief period of house arrest by friendly Asiarchs . . . , to keep Paul out of the reach of fanatical Jews, and avert a riot". [46] These datings, especially the latter, are doubtful.

Despite all these uncertainties arising from the scantiness of our information, we can say that the evangelization of proconsular Asia was one of the most fruitful phases of Paul's missionary career and that his experiences during these years – especially, perhaps, the deadly peril towards the end, from which he was so unexpectedly delivered – had a profound effect on Paul's inner life.

44. E.g. by H. Lisco, *Vincula Sanctorum* (Berlin, 1900); A. Deissmann, "Zur ephesinischen Gefangenschaft des Apostels Paulus" in *Anatolian Studies presented to Sir W. M. Ramsay*, ed. W. H. Buckler and W. M. Calder (Manchester, 1923), pp. 121 ff., and *Paul*, E.T. (London, 1926), pp. 16 ff.; W. Michaelis, *Die Gefangenschaft des Paulus in Ephesus* (Gütersloh, 1925), and *Einleitung in das Neue Testament* (Bern, 1946), pp. 205 ff.; G. S. Duncan, *St. Paul's Ephesian Ministry* (London, 1929); M. Dibelius, *Paul*, E.T. (London, 1953), p. 81.

45. G. S. Duncan, *St. Paul's Ephesian Ministry*, pp. 106, 108–111.

46. P. N. Harrison, *Paulines and Pastorals* (London, 1964), p. 75.

# CHAPTER 27

# Paul and the Life to Come

## 1. Background of thought

THE SPIRITUAL CRISIS WHICH PAUL UNDERWENT TOWARDS THE
end of his Ephesian ministry as a result of his almost
miraculous escape from what seemed imminent death has
been described by one of the greatest New Testament students of
the twentieth century "as a sort of second conversion". It is pointed
out in defence of this view that in the letters which can be dated
after this crisis there is "a change of temper": controversies are conducted in a more tolerant spirit, there is a readier acceptance of his
apostolic hardships, a greater appreciation of the values of family
life and "a sustained emphasis on the idea of reconciliation".[1] It is
probably impossible to draw such a sharp line between Paul's attitude to life before this crisis and his attitude after it: if the judgment expressed in an earlier chapter is maintained, that 2
Corinthians 10–13 ("Corinthians E") followed and did not precede
chapters 1–9 ("Corinthians D"), then Paul was capable of quite
sharp and ironical polemic after his "second conversion".

Nevertheless, on a broad view of Paul's spiritual development,
the thesis can, in general, be sustained; and there is one area of his
thinking in which the effect of the crisis can be discerned with
special clarity – his thinking about the life to come.

Paul's detailed views of the life to come before his conversion cannot be established with complete certainty. There was a wide variety of opinions in this field current in the Judaism of his time – much
wider than has been commonly supposed. In Jewish literature of
the period between 200 B.C. and A.D. 100, it has been pointed out:

> statements on an immortality of the soul which excludes the resurrec-
> tion of the body are almost as common as those which explicitly state
> the resurrection of the body, and the same proportions can be asserted
> for statements on the soul's life after death without exclusion of the
> body and texts which state the resurrection without explicit reference to
> the body.[2]

1. C. H. Dodd, "The Mind of Paul: I", *New Testament Studies* (Manchester,
1953), p. 81. See p. 391.
2. H. C. C. Cavallin, *Life after Death: Paul's Argument for the Resurrection of the Dead*

300

It is plain that Paul inherited the belief in a coming resurrection of the body which was widespread among the Pharisees, but it should not be assumed too readily that the Pharisaic doctrine of resurrection at the beginning of the first century A.D. was uniform, or that it can be deduced without more ado from later rabbinical teaching. The belief in resurrection appears to have been one of the principal points of theological difference between the Pharisees and the Sadducees:[3] the narrative of Acts records how Paul, appearing before the Sanhedrin after his arrest in Jerusalem, threw the apple of discord among its members by declaring that as a Pharisee born and bred he stood on trial for "the hope of the resurrection of the dead" (Acts 23: 6). Still more explicitly, he is said to have declared before Felix that he held the hope, shared by his accusers – by his *Pharisaic* accusers, of course – "that there is to be a resurrection of good and wicked alike" (Acts 24: 15). It is curious – though it may be accidental – that in Paul's letters there is no clear reference to the resurrection of the wicked.

The twofold resurrection is commonly believed to be first attested in Daniel 12: 2 – "many of those who sleep in the dust of the earth will wake, some to everlasting life, and some to the reproach of eternal abhorrence". But it is possible to render these words otherwise: "many who sleep in the dust of the earth will wake, and these are (destined) to everlasting life; but those (the others, who do not wake) are (destined) to the reproach of eternal abhorrence"[4] (cf. Proverbs 10: 7, "the memory of the righteous is for a blessing, but the name of the wicked will rot").

Josephus's account of the Pharisees' teaching is based on inside information, but it suffers from his eagerness to assimilate it to the Greek outlook, especially in *Antiquities* xviii. 14: "They believe that souls have power to survive death and that there are rewards and punishments under the earth for those who have led lives of virtue or vice: eternal imprisonment is the lot of evil souls, while the good souls receive an easy passage to a new life." Nothing here would cause much offence to a Platonist. In his earlier work, his *Jewish War*, Josephus had spoken more explicitly of the Pharisees' belief in resurrection: "They hold that every soul is incorruptible, but that

---

in *1 Corinthians 15*, Part 1 (Lund, 1974), p. 200, as quoted by M. J. Harris, "Resurrection and Immortality: Eight Theses", *Themelios*, n.s. 1 (1975–76), p. 52. Cf. G. W. E. Nickelsburg, *Resurrection, Immortality and Eternal Life in Intertestamental Judaism* (Harvard Theological Studies 26, 1972): M. Hengel, *Judaism and Hellenism*, E.T., i (London, 1974), pp. 196–202.

3. Cf. Mark 12: 18 ff.

4. Cf. S. P. Tregelles, *Remarks on the Prophetic Visions of the Book of Daniel* (London, 1852), pp. 165 ff.; B. J. Alfrink, "L'idée de résurrection d'après Dan., XII, 1. 2", in *Studia Biblica et Orientalia*, i = *Analecta Biblica* 10 (Rome, 1959), pp. 221 ff. Even the commoner interpretation implies a resurrection of many, but not of all.

the soul of the good alone passes *into another body*, while the souls of the wicked suffer eternal punishment".[5] Here it appears that the bodily resurrection of the righteous only is contemplated – although an uninitiated Greek or Roman reader might well have taken Josephus's words to imply a belief in metempsychosis. Later in the *Jewish War* the Pharisaic belief finds fresh expression, where Josephus represents himself as trying to dissuade his comrades at Jotapata from committing suicide to avoid falling into the hands of the Romans: "those who depart this life in accordance with the law of nature [which would be violated by suicide] . . . win eternal renown; . . . their souls, remaining spotless and obedient, are allotted the most holy place in heaven whence, in the revolution of the ages, they return to find a new habitation in pure bodies".[6]

The varieties of expectation among religious Jews in the last two centuries B.C. are well illustrated by the intertestamental literature. Ben Sira thinks that posterity's remembrance of a good man's virtues is the most desirable immortality:[7] the author of Wisdom, influenced by Greek thought, thinks in terms of the survival of souls – especially of "the souls of the righteous" which "are in the hand of God", so that no evil can befall them.[8] The martyrs in 2 Maccabees – an epitome of the history of Jason of Cyrene – look forward to their resurrection in the same bodies as those in which they suffer, with their mutilated members restored;[9] in 4 Maccabees – like Wisdom, a product of Alexandrian Jewry – the same martyrs use the language of Stoicism and exemplify the supremacy of Right Reason over physical pain and death.[10]

From the second century B.C., however, the idea of the Garden of Eden (Paradise) as a place of bliss for the righteous and of Gehinnom as a place of fiery punishment for the wicked after death took hold of popular imagination among the Jews – partly, no doubt, under the influence of Iranian belief, in which fire is a means of testing at the last judgment.[11] In Pharisaism the fire of Gehinnom for the ungodly is not always purely penal; according to the school of Shammai those whose merits and demerits were evenly balanced had first to purge their sins in its flame and only so enter into Paradise.[12] This implies the idea of some sort of personal survival between death and resurrection.

In a couple of Jewish apocalypses dating from the end of the first

5. Josephus, *BJ* ii. 163.
6. Josephus, *BJ* iii. 374.
7. Cf. Ecclesiasticus 44: 1 ff.
8. Wisdom 3: 1 ff.
9. 2 Maccabees 7: 11.
10. 4 Maccabees 5: 15 ff.
11. *Yasna* 47: 6; 51: 9.
12. TB *Rosh ha-Shanah* 16b (a *baraitha*, i.e. a saying handed down from the tannaitic period, A.D. 70–200).

century A.D. the souls of the dead, or at least of the righteous dead, are kept in store-chambers or treasuries between death and resurrection.[13]

The Qumran texts speak plainly enough of eternal life for the righteous and annihilation for the wicked, but throw no clear light on the question of resurrection. Those who hold fast to God's house "are destined for eternal life and all the glory of man (? the glory destined for man) is theirs"; [14] the disobedient "have no remnant or survival" [15] but suffer the doom of the antediluvian sinners who "perished and became as though they had never been".[16] The men of Qumran looked forward to the day of requital when God would "render to man his reward".[17] His elect would inherit the lot of the holy ones – indeed, in their community life they anticipated this inheritance, for God had "joined their assembly to the sons of heaven, to be a council of the community, a foundation of the building of holiness, an eternal plantation for all time to come".[18] They are "adorned with God's splendour and will enjoy many delights with everlasting peace and length of days".[19] When the last battle between good and evil is fought, "there shall be eternal deliverance for those belonging to the lot of God and destruction for all the nations of wickedness".[20] But just how the godly pass from mortal life, or from a martyr-death, to their state of endless bliss is not so clear.

If we could be sure that the men of Qumran were Essenes, then we might associate the former's expectation of eternal bliss with Josephus's statement that the latter look for the soul, consisting of the finest ether, to be released from the bonds of the flesh and enjoy an elysian retreat.[21] His description of this retreat is not unlike the oasis in which, according to one of the Qumran hymns, the godly man finds his abode – "beside a fountain of streams in an arid land, . . . beside a watered garden [in a wilderness]".

No [one shall approach] the well-spring of life
   or drink the waters of holiness
      with the everlasting trees
      or bear fruit with [the planting] of heaven

13. Of all the dead, apparently, in 4 Ezra 7: 32, 75–101 and 2 Baruch 21: 23; of the righteous dead in 2 Baruch 30: 2.
14. CD 3, l. 20 ("the glory of man [Heb. '*ādām*]" may refer to Adam's glory in Eden).
15. CD 2, ll. 6 f.
16. CD 2, l. 20.
17. 1 QS 10, l. 18.
18. 1 QS 11, ll. 7–9.
19. 1 QH 13, ll. 17 f.
20. 1 QM 15, ll. 1 f.
21. Josephus, *BJ* ii. 154 ff.

who seeing has not discerned
and considering has not believed
in the fountain of life.[22]

But Josephus's tendency to conform Jewish beliefs and practices to those rendered respectable by Greek philosophy counsels caution once more in taking his information *au pied de la lettre*. Hippolytus, whose account of the Essenes in the ninth book of his *Philosophoumena* largely follows Josephus but seems to be indebted to a further source, says that in addition to the immortality of the soul they believed in the resurrection of the body: the soul, he says, is regarded by the Essenes as imperishable, resting after death in an airy and well-lighted place, until it is rejoined by the resurrected body on the day of judgment.[23] Our ignorance of Hippolytus's additional source prevents us from adequately evaluating his information where it contradicts that of Josephus, but a certain suspension of judgment is plainly the wise course to adopt.

## 2. New perspective

Whatever Paul's earlier position on immortality may have been, it was decisively modified by his conversion to Christianity. This conversion resulted immediately and inevitably from his vision of the risen Lord, who called him to be his apostle. What he had previously refused to admit – that the crucified Jesus had been raised from the dead by the power of God, as the earlier apostles maintained – was now borne in upon him by testimony too compelling to be doubted. Jesus was therefore the Messiah, the Son of God, the highly exalted Lord – but, more especially for our present purpose, with Jesus' rising from the dead the expected resurrection had begun to take place. What had been for Paul previously the resurrection *hope* was now, so far as Jesus was concerned, more than a hope; it was a *fait accompli*. Since God had raised Jesus from the dead, he would assuredly raise all his people in due course – more specifically, at Jesus' parousia, his advent in glory.[24] At least, he would raise those of them who had passed through death before the parousia – whether they belonged to the patriarchs and prophets of the old age or to believers of the new age. But many believers of the new age would not require to be raised from the dead, for they would still be alive at the parousia. Here and now believers of the new age continued to live in mortal bodies, but inwardly they already enjoyed a foretaste of the coming resurrection life – eternal life – because they were united by faith to the risen Christ, incor-

22. 1 QH 8, ll. 4 ff.
23. Hippolytus, *Philosophoumena* (= *Refutation of all Heresies*) ix. 18 ff.
24. Cf. 1 Thessalonians 4: 14; 1 Corinthians 6: 14; 2 Corinthians 4: 14, etc.

porated in him. This incorporation was effected by the Spirit of
Christ whom they had received, and by his power the life of the
risen Christ was already imparted to all his people. In baptism, indeed, they had died with Christ and been buried and raised with
him; at his advent they would share his manifested glory, but by
the indwelling Spirit they were able to anticipate the hope of glory
and live in the good of it.[25] It was no mere intimation of
immortality that they thus received; it was an initial experience of
immortality, though the full experience must await the parousia.
Here and now they knew that "Christ, once raised from the dead,
will never die again: death no longer has dominion over him"
(Romans 6: 9); and what was true of him must be true of his people
who through him possessed as the gift of God the life of the age to
come. "If the Spirit of him who raised Jesus from the dead dwells
within you" – so Paul's argument runs – "then he who raised
Christ Jesus from the dead will give life to your mortal bodies also
through his indwelling Spirit" (Romans 8: 11).

These last quotations from Paul's writings express the full
maturity of his understanding; but, while we can trace a progression in his thought and language on this subject, his central belief
and teaching do not appear to have undergone any essential change
throughout his Christian career.

The main body of Paul's correspondence that has been preserved
to us comes from a period lasting not more than from ten to twelve
years. So short a period may see but little development in some
men's careers when they have reached this stage of life, but Paul's
life during these years was so full of intense activity and, latterly, a
spell of enforced inactivity, coupled with an ever deepening
awareness of what it meant to be Christ's apostle among the Gentiles, that it would be surprising if his experiences had no influence
at all on his outlook on the future.

### 3. The Thessalonians' problem

At the beginning of this period Paul founded the church in
Thessalonica. Circumstances beyond his control, however, forced
him to leave the city before he had given his converts all the
teaching he believed they required. He had at least taught them to
wait expectantly for Jesus' appearance from heaven to deliver them
from the end-time outpouring of wrath on the ungodly;[26] and such
expectant waiting implied their survival to witness this great event.
But in the weeks and months that followed Paul's departure some
of his converts died. The death of believers before the parousia was

25. Cf. Romans 5: 2; 6: 4; Colossians 1: 27; 2: 11 f.; 3: 1–4.
26. Cf. 1 Thessalonians 1: 9 f.; see p. 226.

something that the Thessalonian church had not been prepared for, and a problem was thereby created in their minds on which they sought enlightenment. They seem, in fact, to have put two questions to Paul:

(a) At Christ's parousia, what will be the lot of those believers in him who have died before he comes?

(b) When may the parousia be expected?

In answering the former question Paul assures them that those of their number who have died before the parousia will suffer no disadvantage when it take place; "we who are left alive until the Lord comes shall not forestall those who have fallen asleep". On the contrary, when the Lord descends from heaven with the shout of command, the archangel's voice and the trumpet blast, those who respond to his summons first will be the dead in Christ; when they rise at his call, brought to life with him who died and rose again, "then we who are left alive shall join them, caught up in clouds to meet the Lord in the air" (1 Thessalonians 4: 14–18). This assurance is conveyed to them "by the word of the Lord" – on the authority of an utterance of Jesus himself (whether given before his death or subsequently we need not now inquire). The language and imagery are those associated with Old Testament theophanies of redemption and judgment – we may think of the trumpet blast which calls home the dispersed of Israel in Isaiah 27: 13 and the clouds of heaven on which one like a son of man is brought to the Ancient of Days in Daniel 7: 13 – but what is here communicated in these terms is new and distinctively Christian. Because Jesus died and rose again, those who die believing in him cannot fail to rise with him; and all his people must live forever with him.

As for the latter and more general question, *when* the parousia would take place, Paul does little more than repeat the words of Jesus, that it would come unexpectedly, "like a thief in the night".[27] The call to the people of Christ therefore is to "keep awake and sober" – "for God has not destined us for wrath, but to obtain salvation through our Lord Jesus Christ" (1 Thessalonians 5: 1–9).

## 4. The resurrection of the dead

Paul's best-known contribution to the subject is his reply to those members of the church of Corinth who held, as he put it, that there was "no resurrection of the dead" (1 Corinthians 15: 12). In these people's eyes the doctrine of the reanimation of corpses, as they

27. Cf. Matthew 24: 43; Luke 12: 39; also Revelation 16: 15.

took it to be, was perhaps an uncongenial Jewish superstition which was a handicap to the acceptance of the Christian message by thoughtful Gentiles. It was a pity, they thought, that Paul had not been able to disencumber himself of this as he had of so many other Jewish peculiarities. Happily, they themselves were more completely emancipated.

What these Corinthians positively believed about the life to come is more difficult to determine. They may simply have believed in the inherent immortality of the soul, or in some kind of assumption into glory at death or at the parousia; but there are hints elsewhere in Paul's correspondence with them that they held what has been described as an "over-realized eschatology". Earlier in this letter he tells the Corinthian Christians, ironically, that they have "arrived" ahead of time: "You have come into your fortune already. You have come into your kingdom – and left us out. How I wish you had indeed won your kingdom; then you might share it with us!" (1 Corinthians 4: 8). Presumably they thought that with the gift of the Spirit they had received all that the religious man could desire. One suggestion is that they anticipated the outlook of Prodicus, a second-century Gnostic, whose followers claimed to be "by nature sons of the first God" and therefore "royal sons far above the rest of mankind".[28]

If a gnostic link is sought, a more promising one may be provided by the *Epistle to Rheginus*, a short Valentinian treatise on resurrection, included in the "Jung papyrus" (one of the Nag Hammadi codices) and published for the first time in 1963.[29] According to this document,

> The Saviour swallowed up death. . . . For he laid aside the world that perishes. He changed himself into an incorruptible *aeon* and raised himself up, after he had swallowed up the visible by the invisible, and he gave us the way of our immortality. But at that time, as the apostle said, we suffered with him, and we rose with him, and we went to heaven with him. But if we are made manifest in this world wearing him, we are his beams and we are encompassed by him until our setting, which is our death in this life. We are drawn upward by him like beams by the sun, without being held back by anything. This is the spiritual resurrection which swallows up the "psychic" together with the fleshly.[30]

28. Clement of Alexandra, *Stromateis* iii. 30; cf. R. M. Grant, *A Historical Introduction to the New Testament* (London, 1963), pp. 204 ff.

29. *De Resurrectione (Epistula ad Rheginum)*, ed. M. Malinine, H.-Ch. Puech, G. Quispel, W. Till (Zürich/Stuttgart, 1963).

30. Jung codex, p. 45, ll. 14 ff. The word "psychic" in the last sentence (Jung codex, p. 46, l. 1) is Gk ψυχική , (feminine in agreement with ἀνάστασις , "resurrection"), taken over unchanged into Coptic – the same adjective as Paul uses of the present "natural" body in 1 Corinthians 15: 44, 46.

The first editors of this document interpreted its contents in terms of an over-realized eschatology such as that for which Hymenaeus and Philetus are reprobated in 2 Timothy 2: 17 f.: "they have shot wide of the truth in saying that our resurrection has already taken place, and are upsetting people's faith". (Presumably the new life in Christ into which they had already entered was all they desired.) More recently Dr Malcolm Lee Peel has pointed out that there is an element of not-yet-realized eschatology in the document: bodily death must be undergone even by the elect, and it is followed by resurrection, albeit a spiritual resurrection.[31] But when the transformation which follows death is described as a spiritual resurrection, the word "resurrection" is used in an extended sense, one which it does not bear in the New Testament. If the deniers of the resurrection at Corinth held some form of incipient Gnosticism (a possible, though not a necessary, view), they may have anticipated some such view as that expressed in the *Epistle to Rheginus*, for the "spiritual resurrection" envisaged in the *Epistle* might for Paul hardly have been a resurrection in the true sense of the word. In this "spiritual resurrection" it is the inward and invisible "members" that ascend, clothed in a new and spiritual "flesh", for which the appearance of Moses and Elijah on the mount of transfiguration is cited as a precedent.

For Paul, the past resurrection of Christ involved a coming resurrection for his people, and it would be a bodily resurrection, as his was. True, the immortal resurrection body would be of a different order from the present mortal body; it would be a "spiritual" body whereas the present body was a "natural" body – *sōma psychikon*, a body animated by "soul". This language is bound up with his distinction between life "in Adam", who in Genesis 2: 7 is described as "a living soul", and life "in Christ", who in resurrection has become "a life-giving spirit" (1 Corinthians 15: 45). But in this argument Paul goes beyond the assurance he had given to the Thessalonian Christians a few years earlier. Then, he declared that those who survived to the parousia would enjoy no advantage over the faithful departed; now he affirms, and that on the strength of a special revelation, a "mystery" newly disclosed,[32] that those who survive will then undergo an instantaneous transformation, so that they too will be adapted to the conditions of the resurrection age. We may compare and contrast the expectation found later in the first century in the Apocalypse of Baruch where the bodies of the dead, raised without change of form in order to receive equitable judgment, are thereafter transformed in accor-

31. M. L. Peel, *The Epistle to Rheginos* (London, 1969), pp. 143 ff.; cf. also his paper "Gnostic Eschatology and the New Testament", *Novum Testamentum* 12 (1970), pp. 141 ff.
32. 1 Corinthians 15: 51.

dance with the verdict — those of the justified being clothed in angelic glory, while those of the condemned waste away in torment.[33] According to Paul, the dead — that is to say, the dead in Christ, who alone of the dead come into his purview here — will rise in bodies which are not liable to corruption, while the living will exchange mortality for immortality.[34] To much the same effect he tells his friends at Philippi that from heaven "we await a Saviour, the Lord Jesus Christ, who will change our lowly body and make it like his body of glory" (Philippians 3: 20 f.). Basic to his thinking throughout is the conviction that Christ and his people are so vitally and permanently united that his triumph over death must be shared with them, not only in sacramental anticipation but in bodily resurrection.

## 5. What happens at death?

But in all this nothing has been said about a question which, to our way of thinking, is of the essence of this topic of immortality: what happens at death? Not until 2 Corinthians does Paul approach this question, so far as his extant correspondence is concerned. This may have been due in part to his expectation that he would survive until the parousia. In the nature of the case he could not *know* that he would survive until then, but in his earliest references to the subject he associates himself with those who will survive: "we who are left alive until the Lord comes shall not forestall those who have died" (1 Thessalonians 4: 15) — "those who have died" are mentioned in the third person but the survivors are mentioned in the inclusive first person plural. In 1 Corinthians 6: 14 the first person plural is used of those who will experience resurrection: "God not only raised our Lord from the dead; he will also raise us by his power" — but here no distinction is drawn between those who have died and those who will still be alive, for Paul is emphasizing that the body comes within the scope of God's redemptive purpose and that present bodily actions have therefore a serious relevance for the future state of Christians; by "us" he means "us Christians" in the most general sense. No significant shift of perspective is involved in 1 Corinthians: "we shall not all die, but we shall all be changed", for at the parousia "the dead will

33. 2 Baruch 49: 1 ff.
34. It is doubtful if J. Jeremias's distinction can be maintained throughout, between the perishable or corruptible ( φθαρτόν ) putting on the imperishable or incorruptible ( ἀφθαρσία ) as referring exclusively to the dead, and the mortal ( θνητόν ) putting on immortality (ἀθανασία) as referring exclusively to the living ("Flesh and Blood cannot inherit the Kingdom of God", *NTS* 2 [1955–56], pp. 151 ff.).

rise immortal and we [the living also] shall be changed" (1 Corinthians 15: 51 f.).

It is when we come to 2 Corinthians that we are conscious of a change of perspective on Paul's part. Probably not more than a year separated the writing of the two letters, but the experiences of that year affected Paul profoundly. In addition to the "fightings without and fears within" to which he refers in 2 Corinthians 7: 5, there was one specially serious danger which overtook him in proconsular Asia, one from which he could see no way out but death.[35] Confrontation with death was no new thing for Paul: "I die daily", he could say some months before this trouble befell him (1 Corinthians 15: 31). But on this occasion he felt like a man who had received the death-sentence. On earlier occasions the way of escape had presented itself along with the danger, but no such way could be discerned this time, so that when at last, beyond all expectation, escape did come, Paul welcomed it as little short of resurrection from death.

Paul had frequently experienced the risk of death before, but never before had he faced for a period what he believed to be certain death. Whatever other changes this experience occasioned in his outlook, it modified his perspective on death and resurrection. For one thing, he henceforth treats the prospect of his dying before the parousia as more probable than otherwise. This change would no doubt have come about in any case with the passage of time, but it was precipitated by his affliction in Asia. Be it noted, however, that while it affected his personal perspective, the "deferment of the parousia" caused no such fundamental change in his thought as it is sometimes held to have caused in the thought of the church as a whole.[36] Now it is as a personal confession of faith that he says: "we know that he who raised the Lord Jesus to life will with Jesus raise us too, and bring us to his presence, and you [who are still alive] with us" (2 Corinthians 4: 14).

But, if death before the parousia was now the more probable prospect for Paul, what would be his state of existence (if any) between death and the parousia? As we have seen, this question did not exercise him before (so far as can be judged from his extant writings); now in 2 Corinthians he tackles it. But in tackling this question he could appeal to no "word of the Lord" as he had done when clearing up the Thessalonians' difficulty, nor had he any special revelation to guide him as when he unfolded to the Corinthians the "mystery" that the parousia would witness the transformation of living believers as well as the resurrection of those who had fallen asleep. Nonetheless he speaks with confidence: "we

35. 2 Corinthians 1: 8 f.; see pp. 274, 295 ff.
36. On this subject see S. S. Smalley, "The Delay of the Parousia", *JBL* 83 (1964), pp. 41–64.

know", he says (2 Corinthians 5: 1). But what do "we know"? Not simply that for the believer to depart is to be "with Christ", which is "better by far", as he puts it in Philippians 1: 23, but that, for this to be so, some kind of new embodiment is necessary at death – and his assurance is that such embodiment is available.

Paul evidently could not contemplate immortality apart from resurrection; for him a body of some kind was essential to personality. Our traditional thinking about the "never-dying soul", which owes so much to our Graeco-Roman heritage, makes it difficult for us to appreciate Paul's point of view. (Except when immortality is ascribed to God himself in the New Testament, it is always of the resurrection body that it is predicated, never of the soul.) It is, no doubt, an over-simplification to say that while for the Greeks man was an embodied soul, for the Hebrews he was an animated body; yet there is sufficient substance in the statement for us to say that in this as in other ways Paul was a Hebrew born and bred. For some, including several of his Corinthian converts, disengagement from the shackle of the body was a consummation devoutly to be wished; but if Paul longed to be delivered from the mortality of this present earthly "dwelling", it was with a view to exchanging it for one that was immortal; to be without a body of any kind would be a form of spiritual nakedness or isolation from which his mind shrank. But he sees the resurrection principle to be already at work in the people of Christ by the power of the Spirit who indwells them; in some sense the spiritual body of the coming age is already being formed: while the "outward man" wastes away under the attrition of mortal life and the hardships of apostolic service, the inward man experiences daily renewal,[37] so that physical death will mean no hiatus of disembodiment but the immediate enjoyment of being "at home with the Lord".[38]

It is in 2 Corinthians 5: 1–10 that Paul makes his most personal contribution to the subject of immortality. The number of articles and monographs devoted to the interpretation of this passage is beyond counting, and shows no sign of abating. Without waiting for the parousia, Paul begins by stating his assurance that "if the earthly frame that houses us today should be demolished, we have a building from God, a house not made by human hands, eternal, and in heaven" (2 Corinthians 5: 1). What is in these words called a "building" is afterwards described in terms of a garment: "we

37. 2 Corinthians 4: 16.
38. 2 Corinthians 5: 8. See M. J. Harris, "2 Corinthians 5: 1–10: Watershed in Paul's Eschatology?" *Tyndale Bulletin* 22 (1971), pp. 32–57, and *The Interpretation of 2 Corinthians 5: 1–10 and its Place in Pauline Eschatology* (unpublished Ph.D. thesis, University of Manchester, 1970). For the hope of an earlier (or immediate) resurrection and entrance into glory for martyrs cf. T. E. Pollard, "Martyrdom and Resurrection in the New Testament", *BJRL* 55 (1972–73), pp. 240–251.

yearn to have our heavenly habitation put on over this one" – since, of course, "being thus clothed, we shall not find ourselves naked" (5: 2 f.). But whether building or garment is spoken of, it is a body – the new, immortal body – that is meant: "we do not want to have the old body stripped off. Rather our desire is to have the new body put on over it, so that our mortal part may be absorbed into life immortal. God himself has shaped us for this very end; and as a pledge of it he has given us the Spirit" (5: 4 f.).

It is difficult to distinguish the new body to which Paul here looks forward from the spiritual body to be received when the last trumpet sounds, according to the teaching of 1 Corinthians 15. Attempts have indeed been made to explain the heavenly body as a corporate entity, the body of Christ[39]; but believers have already "put on Christ" (Galatians 3: 27), and the Pauline concept of the body of Christ and believers' membership in it is related to the present mortal existence rather than to the life to come. If, however, the new body referred to here is the spiritual body of 1 Corinthians 15, Paul no longer thinks of waiting until the parousia before he receives it. Nor is it a merely temporary integument that he hopes to receive at death, pending his investiture with the resurrection body at the parousia; it is the *eternal* "housing" which God has prepared for him and his fellow-believers, and of which the present gift of the Spirit is an anticipatory guarantee. So instantaneous is the change-over from the old body to the new which Paul here envisages that there will be no interval of conscious "nakedness" between the one and the other.[40] The change-over takes place, as he says in 1 Corinthians 15: 52, "in a moment, in the twinkling of an eye" – only there the split-second transformation takes place at the parousia, whereas here Paul seems to imply that for those who do not survive until the parousia the new body will be immediately available at death. If he does not say so quite explicitly, this may be because he has received no clear revelation to this effect.

Perhaps Paul's pre-Christian conception of the life to come had little to say about the state of affairs between death and resurrec-

---

39. Cf. J. A. T. Robinson, *The Body* (London, 1952), pp. 76 ff.; R. F. Hettlinger, "2 Corinthians 5. 1–10", *Scottish Journal of Theology* 10 (1957), pp. 174 ff.; E. E. Ellis, *Paul and his Recent Interpreters* (Grand Rapids, 1961), pp. 35 ff.; M. E. Thrall, *Greek Particles in the New Testament* (Leiden, 1962), pp. 82 ff. (revised in her Cambridge Bible Commentary volume, *I and II Corinthians*, 1965, pp. 142 ff., where a distinction is made between the "building from God" in verse 1 and the "heavenly dwelling" of verse 2); A. E. Harvey, *Companion to the New Testament* (Oxford/Cambridge, 1970), p. 583.

40. The tension created by the postulated interval between death and resurrection might be relieved today if it were suggested that in the consciousness of the departed believer there is no interval between dissolution and investiture, however long an interval might be measured by the calendar of earth-bound human history.

tion. The dead were dead, and that was that, but they would be brought back to life by the power of God on the resurrection day.

But, for Paul the Christian, the resurrection of Christ made a vital difference to this pattern. For Christ, having died, had already been brought back to new life by the power of God, and by faith-union with him his people were already enabled to share the power of his resurrection and walk in newness of life. Was it conceivable that those who were united, right now in mortal life, with the risen and ever-living Christ, should have this union interrupted, even temporarily, by bodily death? We have it on Dr Samuel Johnson's authority that a man's expectation of imminent execution "concentrates his mind wonderfully",[41] and it may have been precisely such expectation that concentrated Paul's mind on this question in the months preceding the writing of 2 Corinthians, to the point where he reached the conclusion set forth in this fifth chapter. It was not the nature of the resurrection body that caused him chief concern, although he could not conceive of conscious existence and communication with his environment in a disembodied state. What he craved, and received, was the assurance that absence from this earthly body would mean being "at home" with the Lord, without any waiting interval. The immediate investiture with the new body is valued only as a means of realizing and enjoying a closer nearness and a fuller communion with the Lord than had been possible in mortal life. Therefore, says he, "we never cease to be confident" and meanwhile we "make it our ambition, wherever we are, at home or away, to be acceptable to him" (2 Corinthians 5: 6, 9). Appearance before the tribunal of Christ, to give account of deeds done in mortal body, is still a future certainty; so also is the participation of the people of Christ in their Lord's glory when he is manifested – that "revelation of the sons of God" for which, according to Romans 8: 19, "the created universe waits with eager expectation". The coming consummation is in no way diminished, but those eschatological features which are realized in life on earth at present do not cease to be realized in the interval between death and the final consummation; they continue indeed to be more intensely realized than is possible during life on earth. Paul's last word on the immortality of men and women of faith is the logical outworking of his teaching on their union with the living Christ.

41. "Depend upon it, Sir, when a man knows he is to be hanged in a fortnight, it concentrates his mind wonderfully" (J. Boswell, *Life of Johnson*, ed. G. B. Hill and L. F. Powell, iii [Oxford, 1934], p. 167). And perhaps it was actually from a judge's lips that Paul "received the sentence of death" of which he speaks in 2 Corinthians 1: 9.

# CHAPTER 28

# Farewell to Macedonia and Achaia

## 1. Paul looks west

T OWARDS THE END OF THE EPHESIAN MINISTRY, SAYS LUKE, "PAUL resolved in the Spirit to pass through Macedonia and Achaia and go to Jerusalem, saying, 'After I have been there, I must also see Rome' " (Acts 19: 21). That Paul did make such plans about this time is corroborated in detail by what he himself says in his letters; yet there is a difference in emphasis between Luke and Paul. Luke has Rome in view as the goal of his narrative, and underlines this rôle of Rome by making it Paul's own goal. Paul himself bears witness in his letter to the Roman Christians, written shortly after this time, of his long-cherished and often frustrated desire to visit their city: "I am eager to preach the gospel to you also who are in Rome" (Romans 1: 15). But in this letter Paul makes it plain that he has no intention of making a prolonged stay in Rome. For one thing, to settle in Rome, where there was already a thriving Christian community, would involve him in "building on another man's foundation" [1] – something which formed no part of his policy (we know what his attitude was to those who came into his own mission-field and built on *his* foundation).[2] For another thing, Rome in his mind was a halting place, or at best an advance base, on his way to Spain, where he planned to repeat the programme which he had just completed in the Aegean world (Romans 15: 23 f.):

> But now, since I no longer have any room for work in these regions, and since I have longed for many years to come to you, I hope to see you in passing as I go to Spain, and to be sped on my journey there by you, once I have enjoyed your company for a little.

The statement that he "no longer has any room for work in these regions" throws light on Paul's conception of his task. There was certainly much room for further work in the area already evangelized by Paul, but not (as he conceived it) work of an apostolic nature. The work of an apostle was to preach the gospel where it had not

1. Romans 15: 20.
2. Cf. 1 Corinthians 3: 10 ff.

314

been heard before and plant churches where none had existed before. When those churches had received sufficient teaching to enable them to understand their Christian status and responsibility, the apostle moved on to continue the same kind of work elsewhere. So Paul travelled along the Roman highways, the main lines of communication, preaching the gospel and planting churches in strategic centres. From those centres the saving message would be disseminated; thus Thessalonica served as a base for the further evangelization of Macedonia, Corinth for Achaia and Ephesus for proconsular Asia.[3] Paul's time was limited, and there was much ground to cover, if the prophecy of Jesus was to be fulfilled, that before the final consummation "the gospel must first be preached to all the nations" (Mark 13: 10).[4] If Spain beckoned to him as his next mission-field, that was probably because the other lands bordering on the Mediterranean (including the North African coast west of Cyrenaica) were already being evangelized. Narbonese Gaul (the present-day Provence), part of which had been colonized by Ionian Greeks centuries before and still maintained close links with the Aegean world, came to be regarded as falling within the sphere of the churches of Asia.[5] But Spain, the oldest Roman province in the west [6] and a bastion of Roman civilization in that part of the world, had not yet heard the gospel and so must be evangelized as quickly as possible.

But Spain differed in one material respect from the provinces which Paul had evangelized thus far: they were Greek-speaking, but Spain was Latin-speaking. Paul would not have been entirely unfamiliar with Latin.[7] He knew it to be the language of the Roman army and had heard it spoken in such Roman colonies as Philippi and Corinth,[8] even if his work was carried out chiefly among Greek-speaking residents in those cities. When he claimed

3. Cf. R. Allen, *Missionary Methods: St. Paul's or Ours?* (London, 1927), pp. 18 ff.

4. On the authenticity of this logion see W. G. Kümmel, *Promise and Fulfilment*, E.T. (London, 1957), pp. 84–86; G. R. Beasley-Murray, *A Commentary on Mark Thirteen* (London, 1957), pp. 40–45; for its relevance to Paul's conception of his mission see J. Munck, *Paul and the Salvation of Mankind*, E.T. (London, 1959), pp. 38–40, 48 f.

5. Massilia (Marseilles) was founded by Phocaeans from the Ionian coast of Asia Minor *c.* 600 B.C. The close association of the churches of Lyons and Vienne in the Rhone valley with their Asian mother-churches is seen in the letter which they sent "to the churches of Asia and Phrygia" describing their suffering in A.D. 177 (Eusebius, *Hist. Eccl.* v. 1. 1 ff.) and in the appointment soon afterwards of Irenaeus, an Asian Christian, to be their bishop in succession to the martyred Pothinus.

6. Spain was taken over by Rome and organized as two provinces in 197 B.C.

7. Cf. A. Souter, "Did St. Paul speak Latin?" *Expositor*, series 8, 1 (1911), pp. 337–342.

8. His Corinthian friends Gaius (Titius Justus) and Erastus were probably Latin-speaking.

his citizen rights, he may have done so in the Latin form: *ciuis Romanus sum.*[9] But to visit a country where Latin was the medium of communication, and to preach the gospel acceptably in that language, required special preparation. This may explain Paul's statement in his letter to the Christians of Rome that he had by this time preached the gospel "from Jerusalem and as far round as Illyricum" (Romans 15: 19).[10] The idea of visiting the nearest Latin-speaking territory to his existing mission-field and undertaking evangelism there may have been in his mind when he expressed the hope to his Corinthian friends that, with the increase of their faith, he might have an opportunity to "preach the gospel in the lands beyond you" (2 Corinthians 10: 15 f.). The precise reference of these words may be unclear – they might point to his further plans to visit Rome on the way to Spain – but what he says to the Romans is plainer: by the time he wrote to them from Corinth at the beginning (probably) of A.D. 57 he had carried the gospel as far west as Illyricum.

Illyricum was the Latin name of the province bordering on the Adriatic Sea. The Greek name of the territory was Illyria, but in Greek usage Illyria stretched farther south than Roman Illyricum, including Dyrrhachium, one of the western termini of the Via Egnatia[11] (which lay within the Roman province of Macedonia). The Illyrians originally spoke an Indo-European vernacular, belonging to the same group as the languages of modern Albania. Illyricum came under Roman control in the course of the second century B.C. In 59 B.C. it was allocated to Julius Caesar along with Cisalpine (and later Narbonese) Gaul as part of his proconsular province. Under Augustus its northern frontier was extended to the Danube (*c.* 9 B.C.). In consequence of a rebellion some years later, which was put down by Tiberius, adopted son and heir-designate of Augustus, the northern part, Pannonia, was detached and became a separate province (A.D. 9); the southern part continued to be known as Illyricum but also bore the name Dalmatia (which it receives in 2 Timothy 4: 10). It was an imperial province, governed by a *legatus pro praetore* with legionary troops under his command. In the early years of the principate of Tiberius the legionary troops were employed to good purpose in road-construction which opened up the mountainous interior of Illyricum.

Had Paul used the form Illyria, his language could be adequately

9. Cf. Acts 16: 37; 23: 25.

10. A. S. Geyser, "Un essai d'explication de Rom. XV. 19", *NTS* 6 (1959–60), pp. 156–159, argues that these words are an echo of the general apostolic commission of Acts 1: 8 and do not indicate the specific geographical limits of Paul's missionary activity thus far. That "Illyricum" should be another way of saying "the end of the earth" in this context seems most improbable.

11. Cf. N. G. L. Hammond, "The Western Part of the Via Egnatia", *JRS* 64 (1974), pp. 185–194.

explained as indicating an extension of his Macedonian ministry as far west as Dyrrhachium; it is his use of the Latin form Illyricum that suggests his crossing the frontier into the Roman province of that name, and a reason for his doing so – to familiarize himself with a Latin-speaking environment – lies ready to hand. But apart from his bare mention of Illyricum, nothing is known of his visit there.

## 2. *After Ephesus*

The period following Paul's completion of his Ephesian ministry is summed up by Luke in the briefest possible terms (Acts 20: 1–3a):

> After the uproar [over the alleged threat to the cult of Ephesian Artemis] ceased, Paul sent for the disciples and having exhorted them took leave of them and departed for Macedonia. When he had gone through these parts and had given them much encouragement, he came to Greece. There he spent three months . . .

But the interval between his leaving Ephesus (probably in the summer of A.D. 55) and his spending three months in Greece (that is, in the province of Achaia and more particularly in Corinth) appears to have been considerably longer than could be gathered from Luke's summary; eighteen months, indeed, would not be an excessive estimate. The earlier part of the period forms the setting for some of the correspondence mentioned or preserved in our 2 Corinthians, with its travelling to and fro between Corinth, Macedonia and the province of Asia. Room must then be found for Paul's journey to western Macedonia and Illyricum.

There are, moreover, allusions in the Pastoral Epistles to visits paid to other places in the Greek world which, in the opinion of some students of these documents, can best be fitted into this period. The criticism and exegesis of the Pastoral Epistles are beset by too many problems for certainty to be attainable about these allusions, but some of the visits, it is urged, could be more reasonably accommodated in this phase of Paul's career than relegated to the limbo period following his two years under house-arrest in Rome.[12] For example, the reference in Titus 3: 12 to his plan to winter in Nicopolis (a Roman colony founded by Augustus in Epirus to commemorate his victory at Actium) has been related, very precariously, to his visit to Illyricum, on the ground that, being on the west coast of Greece, Nicopolis would provide convenient winter-quarters on his return from Illyricum.[13]

12. Cf. J. A. T. Robinson, *Redating the New Testament* (London, 1976), pp. 67–84, and *Can we trust the New Testament?* (London, 1977), pp. 65 f.
13. Cf. G. S. Duncan, *St. Paul's Ephesian Ministry* (London, 1929), pp. 217 ff.

Even more precariously, it has been asked if Paul could have spoken of having no more "room for work in these regions" if Crete remained unevangelized – the implication being that his travels during the period before he expressed himself in those terms to the Roman Christians included a visit to Crete in the company of Titus, whom he left behind to continue the missionary work they had started together and to organize church life in the island (Titus 1: 5).[14] But, inadequate though our knowledge of his travels during this period is, it is very difficult to fit a Cretan visit into them.

In so far as we can trace Paul's movements from the close of his Ephesian ministry, they may be tabulated, very tentatively, as follows:[15]

A.D.

| | | |
|---|---|---|
| 55 | Spring | Painful visit to Corinth; Paul sends severe letter ("Corinthians C") by the hand of Titus |
| | Summer | Deadly peril in Asia; Paul leaves Ephesus |
| | Late summer | In Troas |
| | October | Paul leaves Troas for Macedonia, meets Titus, sends letter of reconciliation ("Corinthians D") |
| 55–56 | Winter-spring | In Macedonia; news of interlopers at Corinth; Paul sends letter of rebuke ("Corinthians E") |
| 56 | Summer | In Illyricum |
| | Autumn | In Macedonia (?) |
| 57 | January-March | In Corinth |

14. According to J. M. Gilchrist, "Crete must have been evangelized by now, or Paul writes nonsense in Romans 15: 23" (*The Authorship and Date of the Pastoral Epistles* [unpublished Ph.D. thesis, University of Manchester, 1966], p. 189); he dates the evangelization of Crete and the mission of Titus in this period. J. V. Bartlet saw the mission of Titus as the sequel to Paul's brief contact with Crete during his voyage to Rome in A.D. 59 (Acts 27: 7–13): the Letter to Titus was written "*after* Paul's arrival in Rome, and after he had left Titus behind in Crete, where his ship had tarried for a time at Fair Havens" ("The Historic Setting of the Pastoral Epistles", *Expositor*, series 8, 5 [1913], p. 327).

15. Cf. G. S. Duncan, "Chronological Table to illustrate Paul's Ministry in Asia", *NTS* 5 (1958–59), pp. 43 ff.

*3. The collection for Jerusalem*

One fact emerges clearly from those letters of Paul which can be dated in this period – that he was greatly taken up during these months with the completion of the contributions to the Jerusalem fund made by his churches in Macedonia and Achaia. It would be difficult to exaggerate the importance which Paul attached to this work and to the safe conveyance of the money to Jerusalem in the hands of delegates of the contributing churches.

At an earlier stage in Paul's career he and Barnabas had a meeting with the leaders of the Jerusalem church at which it was agreed that those two men, who had already made a good beginning with the work of Gentile evangelization, should continue to prosecute it, while the Jerusalem leaders would concentrate their missionary activity on Jews. The Jerusalem leaders added a special request that Barnabas and Paul should continue to remember "the poor"[16] – a request which is best understood against the background of the famine relief which the church of Antioch had sent to the Jerusalem believers by the hand of Barnabas and Paul. In reporting this request Paul adds that this was a matter to which he himself paid special attention. It was in his mind throughout his evangelization of the provinces to east and west of the Aegean, and in the closing years of that period he applied himself energetically to the organizing of a relief fund for Jerusalem in the churches of Galatia, Asia, Macedonia and Achaia.

We first learn about this fund from the instructions given to the Corinthian Christians in 1 Corinthians 16: 1–4; they had been told about it and wanted to know more. From what he says to them we learn that he had already given similar instructions to the churches of Galatia – presumably in the late summer of A.D. 52, when he passed through "the Galatic region and Phrygia" on his way from Judaea and Syria to Ephesus (Acts 18: 22 f.). Thanks to Paul's Corinthian correspondence, more details are known about the organizing of the fund in Corinth than in any of the other contributing churches.

If Paul's instructions to his converts in Corinth had been carried out, then each householder among them would have set aside a proportion of his income week by week for some twelve months, so that the church's contribution would have been ready to be taken to Jerusalem in the spring of the following year by the delegates appointed by the church for that purpose. The tension which developed soon afterwards between many of the Corinthian Christians and Paul perhaps occasioned a falling off in their enthusiasm for this good cause. Next time Paul wrote to them about

16. Galatians 2: 10 (see p. 156 f.).

it (in the aftermath of the reconciliation resulting from the severe letter which he sent to them by Titus) he expressed the assumption that they had been setting money aside for the fund systematically ever since they received his instructions, and told them how he had been holding up their promptness as an example to the Macedonian churches. But when one reads between the lines, it is plain that he had private misgivings on this score; hence he sent Titus back to Corinth with two companions [17] to help the church to complete the gathering together of its contributions "so that you may be ready, as I said you would be; lest if some Macedonians come with me and find that you are not ready, I should be humiliated – to say nothing of you – after my confident boasting" (2 Corinthians 9: 3 f.). As we have seen, some of them probably felt that this was a subtle way of putting irresistible pressure on them: he was "crafty", they said, and got the better of them "by guile" (2 Corinthians 12: 16).

At the time when Paul sent Titus and his companions to Corinth to see about this matter, he himself was in Macedonia, helping the churches of that province to complete their share in it. The political situation which made it impossible for Paul to stay in Macedonia five or six years previously had now passed; perhaps the change of emperor in A.D. 54 had something to do with this. [18] Even so, the Macedonian churches had been passing through a period of unspecified trouble as a result of which they were living at bare subsistence level, if that; and Paul felt that he could hardly ask them to contribute to the relief of fellow-Christians who were no worse off than themselves. But they insisted on making a contribution, and Paul was greatly moved by this token of divine grace in their lives (2 Corinthians 8: 2–4):

> for in a severe test of affliction, their abundance of joy and their extreme poverty have overflowed in a wealth of liberality on their part. For they gave according to their means, as I can testify, and beyond their means, of their own free will, begging us earnestly for the favour of taking part in the relief of the saints –

and the secret of their generosity, he adds, was that, having given themselves to the Lord, they took it as a matter of course that their property (such as it was) was equally at his disposal. He pays the Macedonian Christians this tribute in a letter to the Corinthians in order to encourage the latter to give as generously from their com-

---

17. 2 Corinthians 8: 18 f., 22; they are not named, and it is fruitless to speculate on their identity. Since Origen's day at least (cf. Eusebius, *Hist. Eccl.* vi. 25. 6) one of them ("the brother whose praise in the gospel is spread through all the churches") has frequently been identified with Luke, but this is quite doubtful.

18. See p. 236.

parative affluence as the Macedonians gave from their destitution.

Paul makes one further reference to this relief fund in his extant letters, and this reference is particularly informative, because it comes in a letter to a church which was not of Paul's planting and which therefore was not involved in the scheme and indeed had no prior knowledge of it. Writing to the Roman Christians to prepare them for his intended visit to their city on the way to Spain, he tells them that the business of this relief fund must be completed before he can set out on his westward journey (Romans 15: 25–28):

> At present, however, I am going to Jerusalem with aid for the saints. For Macedonia and Achaia have been pleased to make some contribution for the poor among the saints at Jerusalem; they were pleased to do it, and indeed they are in debt to them, for if the Gentiles have come to share in their spiritual blessings, they ought also to be of service to them in material blessings. When therefore I have completed this, and have "sealed" this fruit to them, I shall go on by way of you to Spain.

The members of the Jerusalem church are the "saints" *par excellence*, being at once the faithful remnant of Israel and the nucleus of the people of God in the new age. If Gentile believers can also be called "saints", it is because they have become "fellow citizens with the saints" of Jewish stock and with them "members of the household of God" (Ephesians 2: 19). The solidarity of Jewish and Gentile Christianity, in particular the strengthening of fellowship between the church of Jerusalem and the Gentile mission, was a major concern of Paul's, and his organization of the relief fund was in large measure designed to promote this end. He knew that many members of the Jerusalem church looked with great suspicion on the independent direction taken by his Gentile mission: indeed, his mission-field was repeatedly invaded by men from Judaea who tried in one way or another to undermine his authority and impose the authority of Jerusalem. But in denouncing them Paul was careful not to give the impression that he was criticizing the church of Jerusalem or its leaders. On the other hand, many of his Gentile converts would be impatient of the idea that they were in any way indebted to the church of Jerusalem. Paul was anxious that they should recognize their substantial indebtedness to Jerusalem. He himself had never been a member of the Jerusalem church and denied emphatically that he derived his gospel or his commission from that church, yet in his eyes that church, as the mother-church of the people of God, occupied a unique place in the Christian order. If he himself were cut off from fellowship with the Jerusalem church, his apostolic activity, he felt, would be futile. Such was the part that Jerusalem played in his thinking that, when he indicates to the Roman Christians the limits of his ministry up to the time of writing, he says that he has preached the gospel "from Jerusalem and as far round as Illyricum" (Romans 15: 19). That he should mention Illyricum as the easternmost limit thus far is natural; but why should he name Jerusalem as the place where he began? [19] According to his own account in the letter to the Galatian churches, he began his ministry in Damascus and Arabia. [20] Yet for Paul in measure, as for Luke absolutely, [21] Jerusalem is the starting-place of the gospel; perhaps both of them recognized in this the fulfilment of the oracle preserved in Isaiah 2: 3 and Micah 4: 2:

> out of Zion shall go forth the law,
>     and the word of the LORD from Jerusalem.

Paul certainly had much more regard for Jerusalem than Jerusalem had for Paul.

As for the suspicions entertained in the Jerusalem church about Paul and his Gentile mission, what would be more calculated to allay those suspicions than the manifest evidence of God's blessing on that mission with which Paul planned to confront the Jerusalem believers – not only the monetary gift which would betoken the Gentile churches' practical interest in Jerusalem but living representatives of those churches, deputed to convey their contributions? Writing to his friends in Corinth Paul holds out to them the prospect that their Jerusalem fellow-Christians will be moved to a deep feeling of brotherly affection for them "because of the surpassing grace of God in you" (2 Corinthians 9: 14). That all suspicions would in fact be allayed was not a foregone conclusion – Paul asks the Roman Christians to join him in prayers that his "service for Jerusalem may be acceptable to the saints" (Romans 15: 31) – but if this would not allay them, nothing would.

Perhaps Paul envisaged this appearance of Gentile believers with their gifts in Jerusalem as at least a token fulfilment of those Hebrew prophecies which spoke of the "wealth of the nations" as coming to Jerusalem and of the brethren of its citizens as being brought "from all the nations as an offering to the LORD" on his "holy mountain" (Isaiah 60: 5; 66: 20). [22] But if Paul had those prophecies in mind, perhaps the Jerusalem leaders had them in mind also, and drew different conclusions from them. In the original context, the wealth of the nations is a tribute which the Gentiles bring to Jerusalem in acknowledgment of her supremacy. In Paul's eyes the contributions made by his converts to the Jerusalem relief fund constituted a voluntary gift, an expression of

19. Cf. F. F. Bruce, "Paul and Jerusalem", *Tyndale Bulletin* 19 (1968), pp. 3–25.
20. Galatians 1: 17.
21. Cf. Luke 24: 47, 52 f.; Acts 1: 4, 8, 12; 2: 5, 14, etc.
22. Cf. Isaiah 2: 1 ff.; Zephaniah 3: 9 f.

Christian grace and gratitude, but it is conceivable that the recipients looked on them rather as a tribute due from the Gentile subjects of the Son of David.[23]

There was, moreover, an intensely personal element in Paul's concern for this relief fund. The Gentile delegates were to bring their offerings to Jerusalem, but the Gentile delegates themselves were Paul's own offering, presented not so much to the mother-church as to the Lord who, many years before, had called Paul to be his apostle to the Gentiles. A major phase of Paul's apostleship had now come to an end; before he embarked on a new phase he would render an account of his stewardship thus far. He looked on his stewardship as a "priestly service" and desired that "the offering of the Gentiles", the fruit of that service which he was about to "seal" in Jerusalem, might be "acceptable, sanctified by the Holy Spirit" (Romans 15: 16). There were those who stigmatized his Gentile converts as unclean because they were uncircumcised and therefore excluded from the people of God; Paul knew that their hearts had been purified by faith, that they had been washed, sanctified and justified "in the name of our Lord Jesus Christ and in the Spirit of our God" (1 Corinthians 6: 11). They were thus fitted to be a "pure offering" to that God whose name, through the Gentile mission, had now become "great among the nations", as another Hebrew prophet had put it (Malachi 1: 11).

Paul had no thought of presenting this offering anywhere but in Jerusalem. To Jerusalem, then, he took a representative group of his Gentile converts. It may even have been in his mind to render the account of his apostolic stewardship and re-dedicate himself for the next phase of his ministry in those very temple precincts where, years before, the Lord had appeared to him in a vision and sent him "far away to the Gentiles" (Acts 22: 21).[24] His converts could not accompany him into the temple, but there in spirit he could consummate "the offering of the Gentiles" who had believed through his witness hitherto, and seek grace and strength for the future.

He may indeed have hoped that on a later occasion, when his contemplated evangelization of Spain was completed in its turn, he might visit Jerusalem again with a fresh offering of Gentiles from the western Mediterranean and render a further account, perhaps the final account, of his stewardship. This, as we know, was not to be; but Paul could not know what his impending visit to Jerusalem had in store for him. He did foresee the possibility of trouble; hence he bespoke the prayers of the Christians in Rome that he might "be

---

23. Cf. K. Holl, "Der Kirchenbegriff des Paulus in seinem Verhältnis zu dem der Urgemeinde", *Gesammelte Aufsätze zur Kirchengeschichte* ii (Tübingen, 1928), pp. 44 ff., especially pp. 58 ff.

24. See p. 144.

delivered from the unbelievers in Judaea" (Romans 15: 31). But the present visit to Jerusalem might well witness a partial anticipation of the rôle which Jerusalem was to fill in the end-time. For Jerusalem was not only the place from which the gospel set out; it was also to be the place from which the crowning phase of God's saving plan for the world would be displayed.[25]

Even the "unbelievers in Judaea", from whom Paul half-expected some opposition,[26] might nevertheless be impressed by the visible testimony of so many representative believers from the Gentile lands in their midst.[27] We know that at the very time when Paul was preparing to sail for Judaea with his converts and their gifts, he was pondering the relation, in the divine programme, between his Gentile mission and the ultimate salvation of all Israel: this also is a subject on which he lays bare his thought in his letter to the Romans.[28] This letter was sent from Corinth, where he was the guest of his friend Gaius at the beginning of A.D. 57, shortly before his departure for Judaea. If, in telling the Romans about the collection for Jerusalem, he refers only to the contributing churches in Macedonia and Achaia, that was probably because these two provinces were uppermost in his thought and action at the time. He had colleagues in Asia Minor who could be entrusted with completing the arrangements for gathering the contributions in the churches there.

In the letter to the Romans, however, he sets this matter of the collection for Jerusalem, with the problem of Jerusalem itself, in the context to which, in his judgment, they properly belong – the context of God's saving purpose for mankind.

25. Cf. Romans 11: 26, "The Deliverer will come from Zion" (a conflated quotation of Psalm 14: 7/53: 6 and Isaiah 59: 20); see p. 335.
26. Romans 15: 31.
27. Cf. also K. F. Nickle, *The Collection: A Study in Paul's Strategy* (London, 1966); D. Georgi, *Die Geschichte der Kollekte des Paulus für Jerusalem* (Hamburg, 1965).
28. Romans 9–11, especially 11: 13 ff.

# CHAPTER 29

# The Gospel According to Paul

## 1. Righteousness by faith

WHEN PAUL, HAVING COMPLETED THE AEGEAN PHASE OF HIS ministry, sent a letter to the Christians in Rome to prepare them for his intended visit to the imperial city *en route* for Spain, he judged it appropriate to devote the main body of the letter to a systematic exposition of the gospel as he understood and proclaimed it. Although he had no thought of settling down in Rome and building on a foundation which he himself had not laid, he hoped to have an opportunity to preach the gospel in Rome during his limited stay, so as to "reap some harvest" there as well as elsewhere in the Gentile world. "for", he adds, "I am not ashamed of the gospel" (meaning, I make my boast in the gospel): "it is the power of God for salvation to every one who has faith, to the Jew first and also to the Greek; for in it God's way of righteousness is revealed through faith for faith, as it is written, 'He who through faith is righteous shall live' " (Romans 1: 16 f.).[1]

The words of Habakkuk 2: 4b ("the righteous shall live by his faith") had been quoted earlier by Paul, with this same emphasis, in Galatians 3: 11: "it is evident that no man is justified before God *by the law*; for 'He who *through faith* is righteous shall live'." The words are quoted in Galatians in the course of a running argument, whereas in Romans they introduce Paul's exposition of the gospel and serve as its text. The gospel which, as Paul insists in writing to the Galatians, is the only gospel worthy of the name, is the same gospel as he sets forth in Romans, but its presentation in Romans is more orderly and detailed, for now he does not write under the pressure of such passionate anxiety as he felt for his new-born children in the Galatian churches who were being persuaded to embrace, instead of the gospel which they had first accepted, a different gospel, which was in fact no gospel at all. The relation between the two documents has been summed up in frequently-quoted words by J. B. Lightfoot:

---

1. Cf. C. K. Barrett, "I am Not Ashamed of the Gospel", in *Foi et Salut selon S. Paul = Analecta Biblica* 42 (1970), pp. 19–50. Habakkuk 2: 4b is quoted also (with part of its context) in Hebrews 10: 37 f., where the emphasis is closer to that of the original oracle.

The Epistle to the Galatians stands in relation to the Roman letter, as the rough model to the finished statue; or rather, if I may press the metaphor without misapprehension, it is the first study of a single figure, which is worked into a group in the latter writing. To the Galatians the Apostle flashes out in indignant remonstrance the first eager thoughts kindled by his zeal for the Gospel striking against a stubborn form of Judaism. To the Romans he writes at leisure, under no pressure of circumstances, in the face of no direct antagonism, explaining, completing, extending the teaching of the earlier letter, by giving it a double edge directed against Jew and Gentile alike. The matter, which in the one epistle is personal and fragmentary, elicited by the special needs of an individual church,[2] is in the other generalised and arranged so as to form a comprehensive and systematic treatise.[3]

In Galatians Paul has insisted that men and women are justified in God's sight by faith in Christ, not by keeping the law, and that this justification is bestowed on them by God as a gift of grace, not as a reward of merit. In Romans he sets this teaching in a wider context but gives it the same fundamentally important position as it had in Galatians. The argument that the doctrine of justification by faith is a "subsidiary crater" in the volcano of Pauline theology, that it is a weapon first fashioned and used by him in his polemic against the judaizing invaders of his Galatian mission-field,[4] is put out of court by his more dispassionate emphasis on it in the systematic exposition of the gospel which he now imparts to the Roman Christians.[5] Indeed, as has been said already,[6] the doctrine was implicit in the logic of Paul's conversion, which revealed to him in a flash the inadequacy of the law, to which he had hitherto been devoted, as a basis for acceptance with God. In that same flash he was assured of his acceptance with God on another basis – the basis of God's pardoning grace, blotting out the sin of one who was quite unfit for his service because, as he says, "I persecuted the church of God" (1 Corinthians 15: 9), and calling him into his service. Only so was it possible for him to introduce himself to the Romans as one who had received through Christ "grace and apostleship to bring

2. Rather, by the special needs of a particular group of churches.
3. J. B. Lightfoot, *St. Paul's Epistle to the Galatians* (London, 1865), p. 49. The more leisurely and literary character of Romans appears, for example, in the use it makes of the *diatribe* style, as when an objection is placed in the mouth of an imagined critic and answered with devastating finality.
4. A. Schweitzer, *The Mysticism of Paul the Apostle*, E.T. (London, 1931), pp. 219–226; cf. W. Wrede, *Paul*, E.T. (London, 1907), pp. 122 ff.; W. Heitmüller, *Luthers Stellung in der Religionsgeschichte des Christentums* (Marburg, 1917), pp. 19 f.
5. Cf. E. Käsemann, *Perspectives on Paul*, E.T. (London, 1971), pp. 60 ff.; G. Bornkamm, *Paul*, E.T. (London, 1971), pp. 115 ff.; R. Y. K. Fung, *The Relation between Righteousness and Faith in the Thought of Paul* (unpublished Ph.D. thesis, University of Manchester, 1975).
6. See p. 188.

about the obedience of faith for the sake of his name among all the nations" (Romans 1: 5).

## 2. The universal need

He sets the scene for the exposition of his gospel by emphasizing the universal need for such a message if there is to be any hope for mankind. Mankind is affirmed to be morally bankrupt in God's sight. In this respect Gentiles and Jews, for all the differences between them, stand on one level.

The moral bankruptcy of the Gentiles was not difficult to establish. Among the Jews a literary form had already been standardized, as can be seen in the Alexandrian book of Wisdom and the Letter of Aristeas, underlining the depravity of "that hard pagan world". Paul takes up this form and adapts it to his own purpose, tracing in the pagan predicament the outworking of a process of divine retribution in history. The root of the trouble was idolatry, he says – the worship of created things instead of the Creator.[7] Nor was idolatry an innocent error: the true knowledge of God was accessible to all in his works of creation, so that those who chose not to give him the unique allegiance which was his due had no excuse to plead. From idolatry sprang all the other forms of deviancy, including in particular those sexual perversions which in Jewish eyes were the most offensive feature of pagan misconduct. The principle of retribution[8] is seen in God's giving men up to the natural consequences of their freely chosen course of action, to a point where their conscience has become so insensitive that they not only enjoy such behaviour but actually produce moral arguments in support of it.

This picture is paralleled not only in other Jewish literature but also in contemporary pagan literature. Greek and Roman moralists could condemn current trends as roundly as Paul, but that does not absolve them from their share in the general guilt, as he sees the situation. In condemning others they condemned themselves, for they were guilty of practices and attitudes not so different in principle from those which they deplored in others.[9] And if the moralist

---

7. Cf. Wisdom 14: 12, "the idea of making idols was the beginning of fornication, and the invention of them was the corruption of life".

8. Cf. G. Bornkamm, "The Revelation of God's Wrath", E.T. in *Early Christian Experience* (London, 1969), pp. 47–70.

9. Paul's contemporary Seneca might provide a good example: he wrote so effectively on the good life that a Christian rigorist like Tertullian could describe him as "often one of us" (*De anima*, 20), he exalted the great moral virtues, he exposed hypocrisy, he preached the equality of all men, he acknowledged the pervasive character of sin, he practised and inculcated daily self-examination, he ridiculed vulgar idolatry, he assumed the rôle of an ethical guide – yet he too often

who sat in judgment on the pagan world was a Jew, not a Gentile, he was in no better case. His responsibility was the greater, since he had received the knowledge of God not only in the works of creation and the inner voice of conscience but in the special revelation given in the law of Israel. If he did not keep the law which he had received, he was the more guilty: Gentiles who regulated their lives by the limited sense of right and wrong which they had "by nature" would win greater approval than Jews who, having the much fuller unfolding of God's will in the law, failed nevertheless to live by it.[10] It was a matter of common report that the conduct of some Jews in the Gentile world brought the name of their God into disrepute (we may think of the Roman Jews whose embezzlement of a donation destined by a wealthy proselyte for the Jerusalem temple led to the expulsion of Jews from Rome by the Emperor Tiberius in A.D. 19).[11] For all the religious privileges received in the course of Jewish history – privileges not to be despised by any Jew – Jews were as morally bankrupt in God's sight as Gentiles: "there is no distinction, since all have sinned and fall short of the glory of God" (Romans 3: 22 f.).

### 3. The way of salvation

If there is to be any salvation for either Jews or Gentiles, then, it must be based not on ethical achievement but on the grace of God. What Jews and Gentiles need alike, in fact, is to have their records blotted out by an act of divine amnesty and to have the assurance of acceptance by God for no merit of their own but by his spontaneous mercy. For this need God has made provision in Christ. Thanks to his redemptive work, men may find themselves "in the clear" before God; Christ is set before them in the gospel as the one who by his self-sacrifice and death has made full reparation for their sins. The benefits of the atonement thus procured may be appropriated by faith – and only by faith. Thus God, without abandoning his personal righteousness, accepts all believers in Jesus as righteous in his sight, regardless of whether they are Jews or Gentiles.[12]

The example of Abraham is instructive: it was by faith that even he found acceptance with God. "Abraham believed God", says scripture, "and it was reckoned to him as righteousness" (Genesis 15: 6). Nor is Abraham an isolated instance; David similarly

tolerated in himself vices not so different from those which he condemned in others.
10. Romans 2: 12–16, 26–29.
11. Romans 2: 21–24; cf. Josephus, *Ant.* xviii. 81 ff.
12. Romans 3: 21–30.

proclaims the blessedness of "the man against whom the Lord will not reckon his sin" (Psalm 32: 1 f.).[13] As for Abraham, it is important to observe that his faith was reckoned to him as righteousness long before he was circumcised: this shows that the way of righteousness by faith is in no way dependent on circumcision, but is open to Gentiles as well as Jews. Abraham is thus the spiritual father of all believers, irrespective of their racial origin. And the testimony that his faith was reckoned to him as righteousness means that to all who believe in God, whose saving power has been manifested in the death and resurrection of Christ, their faith will similarly be reckoned as righteousness.[14]

So then, believers in God receive his gift of righteousness, and with it they receive also peace, joy and the hope of glory. Above all, they receive his Spirit to indwell and empower them, and by the Spirit their hearts are flooded with the love of God. With all these blessings, with God himself as their exceeding joy, they can cheerfully endure the afflictions that beset the life of faith. And as for the hope of glory, if God's love, demonstrated in the self-giving death of Christ, has reconciled them to himself, much more will the risen life of Christ, and their participation in his risen life, ensure their salvation at the last judgment.[15]

Once they were involved in the old solidarity of sin and death, when they lived "in Adam" and shared the fruits of his disobedience. Now that old solidarity has been replaced by the new solidarity of righteousness and life, by which men and women of faith are incorporated "in Christ". The old humanity is being dissolved; the new humanity, headed by Christ, the "last Adam", is taking shape, and the obedience of the last Adam will accomplish more in blessing than the disobedience of the first Adam accomplished in disaster.[16] "For certainly", as John Calvin puts it, "Christ is much more powerful to save than Adam was to ruin." [17]

The law of Moses has nothing to do with this change of

13. The coincidence of the verb "reckon" in Genesis 15: 6 and Psalm 32: 2 suggested a joint interpretation of the two texts, in accordance with the rabbinical exegetical principle of *gezerah shawah*, "equal category" (another instance appears in the two texts linked by the common term "cursed", adduced in Galatians 3: 10–14; see pp. 181 f.). On the relation between the two texts quoted in Romans 4: 3–8 see A. T. Hanson, *Studies in Paul's Technique and Theology* (London, 1974), pp. 52 ff.

14. Romans 4: 1–25.

15. Romans 5: 1–11.

16. Cf. K. Barth, *Christ and Adam*, E.T. (Edinburgh, 1956); J. Murray, *The Imputation of Adam's Sin* (Grand Rapids, 1959); R. Bultmann, "Adam and Christ according to Romans 5", in *Current Issues in New Testament Interpretation: Essays in Honor of O. A. Piper*, ed. W. Klassen and G. F. Snyder (New York, 1962), pp. 143–165; C. K. Barrett, *From First Adam to Last* (London, 1962).

17. J. Calvin, *Commentary on the Epistle of Paul the Apostle to the Romans* (Strasbourg, 1540), E.T. (Edinburgh, 1961), pp. 114 f.

relationship; it was introduced in order that man's latent sinfulness might be brought into the open, expressing itself visibly in concrete transgressions of specific commandments. This in fact is what happened; the law brought about an increase of sin, "but where sin increased, grace abounded all the more" (Romans 5: 20).[18]

### 4. Freedom from sin

Let no one argue that therefore sin should go on increasing, even in the believer's life, in order that grace might abound still more. (Paul had probably met people, even among his own converts, who argued like this.) Such an argument betrays a complete failure to grasp the meaning of the gospel and the life of faith. Believers in Christ have entered on a new life: "how can we who died to sin still live in it?" (Romans 6: 2). That is the practical significance of their incorporation with Christ by baptism: death with Christ to the old existence, resurrection with Christ to "newness of life" (Romans 6: 4). Instead of being enslaved to sin, as they formerly were, believers are now emancipated from sin.

If sin be personified as a slave-owner, his slaves are bound to obey his orders while they are alive, but when they have died, these orders have no further relevance for them. Or, to change the figure slightly, when slaves are purchased from their former owner by a new master who sets them free, their former owner has no more authority over them. Sin has no longer any authority over believers; they now belong to God, who has liberated them from their former bondage. Sin was a harsh master who dealt out death as his wages; God, by contrast, bestows on his people the free gift of eternal life in Christ. For one who by faith has been united to Christ to live in sin is a moral contradiction in terms.

### 5. Freedom from law

The law might declare the will of God, but could not impart the power to do it or break the thraldom of sin. It was therefore possible to be under law, recognizing its divine majesty and authority, and under the control of sin at the same time. But the same act of grace that broke the chains of sin simultaneously freed those who were under the constraint of law. A dangerous doctrine, many must have thought; but Paul makes his meaning plain: the grace of God liberates those who are bound by sin, but law can never do so: paradoxically, law may serve to bind the chains of sin more securely on the sinner.[19]

18. See p. 195.
19. See pp. 193 f.

The analogy of the marriage bond is evoked by way of illustration. Referring to contemporary code and practice, whether Roman or Jewish (but more probably Jewish than Roman), Paul points out that a wife is legally bound to her husband until death parts them. In the analogy of the slave-owner and his slave, the slave-owner was sin, the slave, now emancipated, was the believer. In the present analogy, the believer corresponds to the wife, set free through death-with-Christ from the tie which bound her to her former husband, the law. Now that this tie has been broken, the believer is free to enter into union with Christ. While the law stimulated the very sins it forbade, those who are united to Christ produce the fruit of righteousness and life. The analogy has its difficulties,[20] but the situation which it is intended to illustrate belongs to real life; in particular, Paul himself had enjoyed the experience of liberation from the law so as henceforth to "serve not under the old written code but in the new life of the Spirit" (Romans 7: 6).

With awareness of the law comes consciousness of sin. This fact is enshrined in the primaeval story of the fall: the first human pair enjoyed a carefree existence until the commandment came which forbade them to eat the fruit of the tree of knowledge: the commandment was speedily followed by the temptation to break it and so, as Eve said, the tempter "beguiled me, and I ate" (Genesis 3: 13). The same truth was seen by Paul in the history of the race: the giving of the law was designed to show men the path to life, but in the event (because of the weakness of the human nature on which it operated) it increased the sum-total of sin and so led to death. So also, in the experience of the individual under the law (dramatically described by Paul in the first person singular), life was carefree until the law was brought to his attention; then the awareness of such a commandment as "Thou shalt not covet" immediately stimulated all kinds of covetousness. The commandment is good, but sin exploits it to a bad end: as with Eve, so once again, "sin, finding a point of vantage in the commandment, beguiled me and by it brought about my death" (Romans 7: 11).

Man under the law lives in a state of tension. He knows what is right; he approves what is right; but he lacks the power to do what is right. Another power at work within him, the power of indwelling sin, compels him against his will to disobey the divine law. He longs for deliverance from this uncongenial power, but finds none until it comes to him through Christ. Until then, "I of myself serve the law of God with my mind, but with my flesh I serve the law of sin" (Romans 7: 25b).

20. In the "parable" it is the husband who dies, leaving his wife free to marry another man; in the real situation, it is the believer (corresponding to the wife) who dies in relation to the law (corresponding to the husband). See pp. 193 f.

### 6. Freedom from death

But when the deliverance through Christ is experienced, there is no need to continue any more in this condition of penal servitude. For those who are in Christ receive his Spirit, and the Spirit of Christ sets in motion a new power – the principle of life – which frees them from the dictation of indwelling sin. Those whose lives are directed by the Spirit are now able to fulfil the requirements of God as they could never have done under the law. In the very sphere which sin dominated – the sphere of human nature – Christ won the victory over sin and broke its domination, and this victory is made effective in his people's experience by the Spirit. The Spirit imparts a new power, which triumphs over the old sinful propensities; the Spirit maintains the new life-in-Christ in being and action here and now, as on a coming day he will transform the mortality of believers' present bodies into immortality. The Spirit, thus directing their lives, enables believers to live as the freeborn sons of God; it is he who prompts them spontaneously to call God "Father". "When we cry 'Abba! Father!' it is the Spirit himself bearing witness with our spirit that we are children of God" (Romans 8: 15 f.).[21] The day is coming when the children of God, liberated from all that is mortal, will be manifested to the universe in the glory for which they were created; and on that day all creation will be liberated from the frustration under which it groans at present and will share the glorious freedom of the children of God.

For that day all creation longs, as the children of God also do, but amid their present restrictions they have the help and intercession of the Spirit, and the assurance that he co-operates in all things for their good,[22] since their good is God's own purpose for them. God's purpose, which cannot fail, is to invest with final glory all those who from eternity were the objects of his foreknowledge and foreordaining grace and whom, in the fulness of time, he called as his people and blessed with his gift of righteousness.

Paul concludes this phase of his argument with a call to confident trust in God. God is on the side of his people; the once crucified and eternally exalted Christ is their advocate in God's presence, and from his love no power in the universe, here or hereafter, can separate them.[23]

21. On the word "Abba" see pp. 208 f.
22. The NEB rendering of Romans 8: 28 ("and in everything, as we know, he [the Spirit] co-operates for good with those who love God") marks the revival of an ancient and attractive interpretation which has received too little attention; cf. M. Black, "The Interpretation of Romans 8: 28", in *Neotestamentica et Patristica: Eine Freundesgabe O. Cullmann zu seinem 60. Geburtstag überreicht*, ed. W. C. van Unnik = *Novum Testamentum Supplement* 6 (Leiden, 1962), pp. 166 ff.
23. Romans 8: 31–39.

## 7. *Israel and the Gentiles in God's saving purpose*

At the outset of the letter Paul had said that God's way of righteousness on the ground of faith was presented in the gospel "to the Jew first and also to the Greek" (Romans 1: 16). But it was a matter of common knowledge that Jews for the most part had not accepted the gospel, whereas Gentiles had embraced it in large numbers. Some might argue that the Jews' refusal to accept it frustrated the divine purpose. But Paul rejects this conclusion. It has, he points out, been a recurring feature of Israel's history that some members of the nation had responded to the call of God, while others (usually the majority) had been disobedient. The gospel had been plainly set before the Jewish people of Paul's day, as the messages of the prophets had been set before their ancestors, so none could say that they had not heard it. Even so, there remained a chosen remnant of Jewish believers in Christ, and as in earlier days so now it was in the faithful remnant that the hope of the people's future was embodied.

If the order of proclamation was "to the Jew first and also to the Greek", the order of acceptance was "by the Gentile first and (then) also by the Jew". Paul set a high estimate on his ministry as apostle to the Gentiles since through this ministry not only were the Gentiles blessed directly but the Jews would be blessed indirectly. The spectacle of Gentiles in large numbers enjoying the blessings of the gospel would one day stir the Jews to jealousy and move them to claim a share for themselves in those blessings – the blessings which indeed fulfilled the promises made to Abraham and the other patriarchs of Israel. Perhaps the sight of so many Gentile believers coming to Jerusalem with their gifts would precipitate this response at the heart of their corporate life. Their present phase of "hardening" or unresponsiveness to the gospel was partial and temporary – partial, because some Jews (like Paul himself) had already believed, and temporary, because in due course they would all believe. Through the bringing in of the full quota of Gentiles "all Israel will be saved" (Romans 11: 26).[24]

There may be in this discussion (as perhaps in other discussions in this letter) a more direct application to the circumstances of the Roman Christians than appears on the surface. The church of Rome was founded on a Jewish base. Probably up to the time of Claudius's expulsion edict of A.D. 49 all Roman Christians were of Jewish birth. When, after a few years, the edict became a dead letter and Jews made their way back to Rome, the Christian com-

24. An important monograph on Romans 9–11 is J. Munck, *Christ and Israel*, E.T. (Philadelphia, 1967); cf. also H. L. Ellison, *The Mystery of Israel* (Exeter, 1966).

munity in the city was reconstituted, but now it included an increasing proportion of Gentiles as well as Jews; and the Gentile members may have tended to look patronizingly on their Jewish brethren as poor relations, mercifully salvaged from the wreck of Israel. Paul deprecates such an assumption of superiority, and describes the relation of Gentiles and Jews in terms of the analogy of an olive-tree – an analogy which may have been the more telling because one of the Roman synagogues was called the Synagogue of the Olive.[25] The olive tree in this analogy is the true Israel, the people of God; the branches are its individual members. Because of unbelief some of the branches were cut out, and their place was taken by branches from a wild olive or oleaster – Gentile believers – who were grafted on to the stock of Israel to share its vitality and nourishment.[26] But these newly engrafted branches had no cause for pride: by faith they had been grafted in, but by unbelief they would be cut out like many of the original branches. By now the analogy with horticultural practice has been strained to the limit,[27] but the link snaps completely when Paul says that God can graft the original branches which were lopped off back on to their parent tree, to derive life from it anew. Paul seriously expects such a miracle of grace in the spiritual realm, and illustrates it by what would be a miracle in the natural realm. If Gentiles, by the grace of God, have become members of the true Israel, how much more may Jews, by that same grace, be restored to membership in it.

Paul's own sympathies were manifestly engaged in this matter,[28] but he does not present his forecast of Israel's restoration as the product of wishful thinking but as the substance of a "mystery"[29] – an aspect of the divine purpose formerly concealed but now divulged. This "mystery" was in fact implicit in that "revelation of Jesus

25. Romans 11: 17–24. For the suggestion of a link with the Roman Synagogue of the Olive cf. W. L. Knox, *St. Paul and the Church of Jerusalem* (Cambridge, 1925), pp. 254, 258.

26. Israel is described in Jeremiah 11: 16 as having been "a green olive tree, fair with goodly fruit". It is quite conceivable that proselytes to Judaism were compared to branches removed from a fruitless wild olive and grafted on to this good olive tree.

27. Paul concedes that the process he describes is "contrary to nature" (Romans 11: 24). But it appears to have been practised in Roman times, to judge from Paul's contemporary Columella, according to whom, when an olive tree produces badly, a slip of a wild olive is grafted on to it, so as to give new vigour to the olive (*De re rustica*, v. 9. 16).

28. A. von Harnack thought that in arguing for the salvation of "all Israel" (Romans 11: 26), after drawing a careful distinction between the wider, empirical Israel and the faithful remnant which constituted the genuine Israel (Romans 9: 6 f.), Paul had let his heart run away with him: "the Jew in himself was still too strong" (*The Date of the Acts and of the Synoptic Gospels*, E.T. [London, 1911], p. 61).

29. Romans 11: 25.

Christ" on the Damascus road by which Paul received his vocation to preach him to the Gentiles. The fulness of this implication was something which he could not have grasped at the time, but in the course of his apostolic experience it became increasingly plain to him. His own apostolic ministry was the means in the divine purpose for the accomplishment of this "mystery". Isaiah in his day had been cleansed and sent by God to people whose hearts were "hardened" against his message by their very hearing of the message (Isaiah 6: 9 f.); [30] so Paul had been cleansed and sent by God, not directly to the people whose hearts were hardened against the message, but to convey that message and its saving benefits to others so that the people with hardened hearts might begin to covet those benefits for themselves and at last embrace the message with which the benefits were bound up. Thus the history of salvation would be consummated, and Paul had a distinctive part to play as God's chosen instrument in bringing about this consummation. In the light of the initiatory revelation and its progressive unfolding in his ministry he knew himself to be, under God, a figure (as has been said already) of eschatological significance.[31]

Moreover, now that this mystery was revealed, it illuminated certain prophetic sayings which, as now became clear, were to find their fulfilment in this welcome dénouement. Quoting the Septuagint version of Isaiah 59: 20, he says:

The Deliverer will come from Zion,
  he will banish ungodliness from Jacob –

except that, where the Septuagint says "for Zion's sake",[32] Paul says "from Zion", deriving this perhaps from Psalm 14: 7 (= 53: 6), "O that deliverance for Israel would come out of Zion!" Then he adds, echoing Jeremiah's oracle of the new covenant, "and this will be my covenant with them, when I take away their sins" (Romans 11: 26 f.).[33]

Paul, that is to say, associates the consummation of God's plan of blessing for Israel, for which his own ministry was paving the way, with a manifestation "out of Zion" of Israel's divine Redeemer – identical, perhaps, with the parousia itself. If this is so, then the "life from the dead" of which Israel's acceptance is to be the im-

30. Luke represents Paul as quoting the Isaianic passage to the leaders of the Roman Jews (Acts 28: 25–27); cf. its citation and application in the gospel tradition (Mark 4: 12; John 12: 39 f.). See p. 375.
31. Cf. J. Munck, *Paul and the Salvation of Mankind*, E.T. (London, 1959), pp. 40 ff. *et passim*.
32. MT says "he will come *to Zion* as Redeemer".
33. Cf. Isaiah 59: 21 and 27: 9 (LXX) for language to much the same effect.

mediate precursor (Romans 11: 15) could be the resurrection harvest.

What is emphasized above all, however, is God's good will towards all men, Jews and Gentiles alike. If, at an earlier stage of his argument, Paul has concluded that "there is no distinction, since all have sinned" and stand alike in need of God's grace, now he concludes that "there is no distinction between Jew and Greek, . . . for God has consigned all to disobedience, that he may have mercy upon all" (Romans 10: 12; 11: 32).

### 8. The Christian way of life

Paul follows up his exposition of the gospel with practical exhortations. In view of all that God has done for his people in Christ, their lives should be devoted to his service. They are fellow-members of the body of Christ, and should discharge their respective functions for the well-being of the whole. In all their relations with others, let them show the forgiving mercy of Christ. In this last injunction, Paul shows his familiarity with the teaching of Jesus which has been preserved for us in the Sermon on the Mount. Although these words of his antedate the earliest of our Gospels, yet he knew much of their content in an earlier form.

He next calls on his readers to render all due obedience to the civil authorities; in their own sphere they too are servants of God.[34] This injunction may be a generalization of Jesus' ruling, "Render to Caesar the things that are Caesar's" (Mark 12: 17); but whereas Jesus' ruling was given in response to a question designed to face him with a dilemma in the delicate situation of Judaea under Roman control, no such political delicacy was involved in Paul's advice to the Christians of Rome. The very positive assessment of imperial administration which he expressed reflects his own happy experience of this administration in the provinces, as in the judgment of Gallio. Paul was not so unrealistic as to suppose that the established powers would always protect the interests of the gospel: he would have assented as readily as Peter and his companions to the declaration that, when they encroached on the things that are God's, "we must obey God rather than men" (Acts 5: 29). There is no reason to suppose that he had abandoned the outlook of 2

---

34. Romans 13: 1–7. Among many treatments of this passage, mention may be made of O. Cullmann, *The State in the New Testament*, E.T. (London, 1955), pp. 50 ff., 95 ff.; C. D. Morrison, *The Powers That Be* (London, 1960); A. Strobel, "Furcht, wem Furcht gebührt", *ZNW* 55 (1964), pp. 58–62 (where reference is made to a *senatus consultum* of A.D. 53 [cf. Tacitus, *Annals* xii. 60; Suetonius, *Life of Claudius*, 12. 1] granting special fiscal powers to imperial procurators); J. Kallas, "Romans xiii. 1–7: An Interpolation", *NTS* 11 (1964–65), pp. 365–374 (where the authenticity of the paragraph is denied).

Thessalonians 2: 3–12, according to which the established order of government would one day be swamped by the force of lawlessness, demanding divine honours for itself.[35] But while the established order prevailed, discharging its divinely conferred functions, protecting right and restraining wrong, it should receive the prompt obedience of Christians. The payment of taxes, for example, was part of their service to God – part, indeed, of their "spiritual worship" (Romans 12: 1).

The one debt that Christians should owe to others is the debt of love. Again following the precedent of Jesus, Paul sums up all the commandments of the law in the words: "Thou shalt love thy neighbour as thyself" (Leviticus 19: 18).[36] "Love does no wrong to a neighbour; therefore love is the fulfilling of the law" (Romans 13: 10). When law is summed up in these terms, the meaning of "law" has been transformed: it is no longer enforced from without but impelled from within, by the operation of the Spirit of Christ.[37] The law of love is thus the law of Christ.

Paul warns of ominous times impending: it is the more necessary for Christians to keep alert in mind and live as befits their calling, to "put on the Lord Jesus Christ" (Romans 13: 14) – that is, to have those graces reproduced in their lives which were seen in their perfection in his.

Then comes a call for special gentleness and consideration to be shown to fellow-Christians, especially to those who are "weak in faith" and unemancipated in conscience. There are matters such as food-restrictions and the observance of special days on which Christians do not see eye to eye. Those who have no scruples in such matters should not despise those who have; and those who have scruples should not sit in judgment on those who have none. "Let every one be fully convinced in his own mind" (Romans 14: 5).[38] It is to God that each believer must ultimately render his account, and it is to God that he is responsible for his conduct here and now. Christian liberty is a precious thing, not to be limited by any man's dictation, but it should not be asserted at the expense of Christian charity. Christ, his people's supreme exemplar, always considered the interests of others before his own;[39] therefore his people, while subject to none in respect of their liberty, should be subject to all in respect of their charity.[40]

35. See p. 231.
36. Cf. Mark 12: 31; Luke 10: 27; Galatians 5: 14.
37. When Paul says, of love and the rest of the fruit of the Spirit, that "against such there is no law" (Gal. 5: 23b), he may be applying a tag from Aristotle (*Politics* iii. 8. 2, 1284a) to mean that such things are outside the scope of law.
38. Cf. P. S. Minear, *The Obedience of Faith* (London, 1971). He finds the purpose of the letter set out in the injunctions of Romans 14: 1–15: 13; see p. 389.
39. Romans 15: 3.
40. For the allusion to Luther see p. 202 with n. 36.

### 9. Final greetings

Paul then tells the Roman Christians of his impending visit to Jerusalem with his converts and their gifts and of his intention then to set out for Spain and stay a little time with them on the way.[41] He asks them to give a welcome to Phoebe, a minister of the church in the port of Cenchreae, who may have been the bearer of the letter;[42] he sends greetings to a number of friends whom he had come to know in various places and who were now resident in Rome;[43] he sends greetings also from his companions who were with him as the letter was about to be despatched, including Gaius his host and Erastus the city treasurer, and from "all the churches of Christ" (Romans 16: 16). "All the churches of Christ" – that is, the churches of Paul's own mission-field – were represented by their delegates who had come to Corinth to join Paul in sailing to Judaea,[44] where they were to deliver their churches' gifts to their brethren in Jerusalem.[45]

41. See p. 314.
42. See p. 384.
43. On the destination of Romans 16 see pp. 385 ff.
44. Cf. Acts 20: 4 (see p. 339).
45. Two recent and highly distinguished commentaries on Romans are those by C. E. B. Cranfield, *The Epistle to the Romans*, 2 volumes (Edinburgh, 1975-), and E. Käsemann, *An die Römer* (Tübingen, 1973), E.T. in preparation.

# CHAPTER 30

# Last Visit to Jerusalem

## 1. The voyage to Judaea

A MONG THE TRAVELLING COMPANIONS WHO JOINED PAUL IN
Corinth, or its Aegean port of Cenchreae, ready to sail
with him to Judaea, Luke mentions Sopater of Beroea, the
son of Pyrrhus; Aristarchus and Secundus from Thessalonica;
Gaius of Derbe and Timothy (originally from Lystra), and
Tychicus and Trophimus from the province of Asia [1] (the latter of
whom was a Gentile Christian from Ephesus). [2] It would be unwise
to attach sinister importance to the absence of a Corinthian name
from Luke's list. The list may not be exhaustive; it may be confined
to those who had travelled to Corinth from other places to join
Paul. Paul had been spending several weeks with Gaius, his host,
and other Corinthian friends; moreover, he had just told the
Roman Christians how Macedonia and Achaia had resolved to
contribute to the Jerusalem relief fund. [3] Achaia, for Paul, meant
Corinth and the places around it, and there is no breath of a
suggestion in his letter to the Romans that "Achaia" had not
carried out its resolve. We should, indeed, consider the possibility
that (in spite of some grumblings over Paul's "craftiness" [4] in
sending Titus to help with the organizing of their contribution) the
Corinthian church asked Titus to convey their gift to Jerusalem; if
so, the omission of the name of Titus here is of a piece with its omission throughout the whole narrative of Acts. [5]

1. Acts 20: 4.
2. Acts 21: 29.
3. Romans 15: 26.
4. 2 Corinthians 12: 16.
5. One explanation of Luke's silence about one who was such a trusted lieutenant of Paul's is that Titus was Luke's brother; cf. W. M. Ramsay, *St. Paul the
Traveller and the Roman Citizen* (London, 1895), p. 390; *Luke the Physician and Other
Studies* (London, 1908), pp. 17 f.; A. Souter, "A Suggested Relationship between
Titus and Luke", *Expository Times* 18 (1906–7), p. 285, and "The Relationship
between Titus and Luke", *ibid.*, pp. 335 f. But if this relationship is maintained,
then the possibility that Luke is the "brother" of 2 Corinthians 8: 18 f. (see p. 320)
is ruled out: Paul's purpose in sending this "brother" along with Titus was that he
should be an independent guarantor of the probity of the administration of the
relief fund, and this purpose would have been frustrated if critics had been given
an opportunity to draw attention to a blood-relationship between the two. Nothing
could have been better calculated to foster already existing suspicions.

Most of the party set sail from Cenchreae at the appointed time, when the Aegean was open for navigation after the winter. Paul, however, got wind of a plot against his life on board the ship by which he had arranged to sail; accordingly, he changed his plans, went north to Philippi, and found a ship at Neapolis, the port of Philippi, bound for Troas, on which he and Luke embarked "after the days of Unleavened Bread" (Acts 20: 6). In A.D. 57 the festival of Unleavened Bread fell probably during the week April 7–14.[6] Paul hoped to be in Jerusalem for Pentecost, which would begin in the last week of May, but the realization of this hope would depend on the availability of suitable shipping.

They reached Troas in five days; the prevailing winds probably made the voyage longer than that from Troas to Neapolis which they had completed in two days about eight years previously.[7] At Troas they found the rest of their company, who had sailed from Cenchreae, waiting for them; and there they remained for a week. Either the ship from Neapolis was going no farther than Troas, in which case they had to wait for a ship going in the direction they wished to take, or it was to sail farther south and call at various points along the west coast of Asia Minor, but had to stay some days at Troas (as it did also at some later ports of call) unloading its cargo and taking on a fresh one.

We are informed about the stages of this voyage in considerable detail, since the narrator himself was on board and kept a diary which was later embodied in the published edition of Acts.[8]

In Troas there was a small community of Christians, formed perhaps during Paul's distracted and interrupted evangelization of the city and its neighbourhood a year or two before.[9] Paul and his friends enjoyed the company of these Christians while they remained at Troas, especially during the evening before their departure (a Sunday), when they met to break bread and Paul went on talking to them until midnight. Luke remembered the occasion vividly because a young man of the community in Troas, Eutychus by name, was overcome by sleep while Paul was talking and fell down from the third-floor window-ledge where he had been sitting. He was knocked unconscious by the fall and his friends feared that he was dead, but Paul hurried downstairs and embraced him (perhaps applying some form of artificial respiration) and assured the others, to their great relief, that Eutychus was still alive.

Next day the ship set sail, with most of the company aboard

6. W. M. Ramsay therefore concludes that "the company left Philippi on the morning of Friday, April 15" (*St. Paul the Traveller*, p. 289); but this depends on the assumption that a ship was waiting for them the day after the festival ended.
7. Acts 16: 11 f.; see p. 218.
8. See p. 218 with n. 25.
9. 2 Corinthians 2: 12 f.; see p. 275.

(Luke included), but Paul went by land across the peninsula to Assos (Behramkale). Perhaps he wanted to delay his departure from Troas until the last minute to make sure that all was well with Eutychus, and then took a road which he knew from his previous visits to those parts, in the certainty that he would reach Assos in time to board the ship there, since it would have to round Cape Lectum (Bababurun).

At Assos, then (where the harbour, with its ancient breakwater, is still in use), he was taken on board, and the ship continued on its way, putting in at Mytilene (on the east coast of the island of Lesbos), then (after negotiating the channel between Chios and the Anatolian mainland) at Samos, and the following day at Miletus, on the south shore of the Latonian Gulf, at the mouth of the Maeander. (Between Samos and Miletus the Western text inserts a mention of the promontory of Trogyllium.) [10]

At Miletus the ship was due to stay in harbour for a few days, so Paul sent an urgent message to Ephesus, some thirty miles distant, asking the leaders of the church there to come and see him at Miletus. He could not risk going to Ephesus himself, as the ship might have left Miletus before his return. He had deliberately chosen to travel by a ship which made the straight run from Chios to Samos, across the mouth of the Ephesian Gulf, so as to be sure of reaching Jerusalem by Pentecost, if this were possible. At the same time he could not be so near as he was to Ephesus without making some effort to get in touch with his friends there.

Nothing is said of Christians in Miletus, although presumably, like other cities in the province, it had "heard the word of the Lord" in the course of Paul's Ephesian ministry. [11] The existence of a Jewish community in the city is attested by an inscription in the theatre, allocating a section of the seats to Jews and God-fearers. [12]

When the Ephesian leaders arrived Paul greeted them. Luke has preserved a summary of what he said to them – a summary of which Percy Gardner said that among all the Pauline discourses in Acts this "has the best claim of all to be historic". While it is "altogether in the style of the writer of *Acts*", yet, he said, it "offers phenomena which seem to imply that he was guided by memory in the composition". [13] Paul lays a solemn charge on his hearers, who are variously described as elders, shepherds and overseers

10. This Western reading was adopted by the Byzantine text (cf. Acts 20: 15, AV). Trogyllium or Trogyllia is a promontory jutting out from the mainland to the south-east of Samos, forming a strait less than a mile wide.

11. Acts 19: 10.

12. Cf. A. Deissmann, *Light from the Ancient East*, E.T. (London,[2] 1927), pp. 451 f. The God-fearers are here called θεοσεβεῖς.

13. P. Gardner, "The Speeches of St. Paul in Acts", in *Cambridge Biblical Essays*, ed. H. B. Swete (Cambridge, 1909), pp. 401, 403. See also J. Dupont, *Le discours de Milet: le testament de saint Paul* (Paris, 1962).

(bishops),[14] beseeching them to take care of their fellow-Christians and protect them against dangers which threatened them from without and within, following the example which Paul himself had set them during the years that he had spent with them. He himself would never see them again, but God would supply them with all the resources necessary for their pastoral ministry.

This is the only Pauline speech in Acts which is addressed to Christians, so it is not surprising that it presents, to a far greater degree than any of the other Pauline speeches, features of affinity with the letters of Paul. In particular, here only in Acts is explicit mention made of the saving efficacy of the *death* of Christ. "Feed the church of God", says Paul, "which he purchased with the blood of his beloved one"[15] (Acts 20: 28). It is fruitless to argue that this is just a "turn of phrase" introduced by Luke "to give the speech a Pauline stamp";[16] the context in which the words appear confirms the judgment of C. F. D. Moule:

This is Paul, not some other speaker; and he is not evangelizing but recalling an already evangelized community to its deepest insights. In other words, the situation, like the theology, is precisely that of a Pauline epistle, not of preliminary evangelism.[17]

From Miletus the ship continued on its way to the islands of Cos and Rhodes in the Dodecanese, and then put in at Patara, a port on the Lycian coast of south-west Asia Minor.[18] From here it may have been proceeding farther east along the south coast of the peninsula, but it could no longer serve the purpose of Paul and his companions, so they transferred at Patara to another ship bound for Phoenicia. This ship sailed in a south-easterly direction from Patara to Tyre, passing Cyprus on the port side, and laid up in the harbour at Tyre for seven days, while it discharged its cargo. At Tyre, as previously at Troas, the party seized the opportunity of

14. Acts 21: 17, 28; see p. 172.

15. Literally, "his own one": Gk. διὰ τοῦ αἵματος τοῦ ἰδίου, where τοῦ ἰδίου is better construed as possessive genitive by τοῦ αἵματος than as being in attributive concord with it.

16. H. Conzelmann, *The Theology of St. Luke*, E.T. (London, 1960), p. 201.

17. C. F. D. Moule, "The Christology of Acts", in *Studies in Luke-Acts: Essays in honor of P. Schubert*, ed. K. E. Keck and J. L. Martyn (Nashville/New York, 1966), p. 171. Professor Moule makes a sharp distinction between "preliminary" or primary evangelism and the counselling of those already evangelized; cf. his "Jesus in the New Testament Kerygma", in *Verborum Veritas: Festschrift für G. Stählin*, ed. O. Böcher and K. Haacker (Wuppertal, 1970), pp. 15 ff.

18. The Western text of Acts 21: 1 makes the party go on in the same ship from Patara to Myra, and trans-ship there (perhaps under the influence of 27: 5, where Paul changes ship at Myra on his way from Caesarea to Rome).

fellowship with local Christians. The origins of the church of Tyre
are nowhere expressly recorded, but they belong almost certainly to
the evangelization of Phoenicia by dispersed Hellenistic Christians
from Jerusalem after Stephen's death.[19] When the week was up, all
the members of the Tyrian church, with their wives and children,
escorted their temporary visitors to the beach, where they bade
each other farewell with prayer.

Their next port of call was Ptolemais (Akko), where the ship
which they had boarded at Patara may have reached its terminus.
They spent a day with the church there, and then went on to
Caesarea, whether by land or sea is not said explicitly. Probably
they had several days in hand before the onset of Pentecost, so they
were able to relax with their friends at Caesarea, after quite a tiring
voyage, before going up to Jerusalem.

At Caesarea Paul had an opportunity of renewing old acquaintance and introducing his new friends to those whom he had known
in earlier days. The Christian community in Caesarea had grown
since the conversion of Cornelius and his household;[20] it received
an accession of strength when Philip the evangelist (one of the seven
Hellenistic leaders in the Jerusalem church while Stephen was
alive) made his home there and brought up his family of four gifted
daughters, each one a prophet.[21] (Half a century later, after
Philip's migration to Phrygia, some of his daughters lived on into
old age and were highly reputed as informants on persons and
events from the early days of Palestinian Christianity.)[22]

At the end of their stay in Caesarea they were accompanied by
some of their fellow-believers from that city, and also by Mnason, a
Cypriot by origin and a foundation-member of the mother
church,[23] who was to be their host in Jerusalem. It was important
to find a Jerusalem Christian willing to be host to so many Gentile
Christians, but Mnason, a Hellenist, readily undertook this
ministry. Perhaps the Caesarean Christians made themselves
responsible for this arrangement. If Mnason was in a position to accommodate the party during their visit to Jerusalem, the Jerusalem
church was not completely denuded of Hellenists after the dispersion which followed Stephen's death. To Jerusalem, then, they
came, mounted perhaps on mules or donkeys[24] (the distance from
Caesarea is 64 miles or over 100 kilometres).

19. Cf. Acts 11: 19.
20. Cf. Acts 10: 44 ff.
21. Acts 21: 8 f.; cf. 8: 40.
22. Cf. Polycrates of Ephesus and Proclus (c. A.D. 190), as quoted by
Eusebius, *Hist. Eccl.* iii. 31. 2–5.
23. Acts 21: 16; this is probably the sense of his designation ἀρχαῖος μαθητής ,
"a disciple from the beginning( ἀρχή )".
24. Cf. W. M. Ramsay, *St. Paul the Traveller*, p. 302.

## 2. Premonitions of trouble

Before he started the voyage, Paul foresaw that this visit to Jerusalem would be fraught with hazards. The misgivings at which he hinted in his letter to the Romans were confirmed by prophetic utterances in one Christian community after another in the ports at which he and his companions put in during their voyage. "The Holy Spirit testifies in every city", he told his Ephesian friends at Miletus, "that imprisonment and afflictions await me" (Acts 20: 23). Some of the Christians at Tyre urged him "through the Spirit" – that is, under prophetic inspiration – "not to go on to Jerusalem" (Acts 21: 4). And at Caesarea he had a visit from Agabus of Jerusalem, the prophet who, some twelve years earlier, had come to Antioch and foretold the famine that hit Palestine with special severity shortly afterwards. On this occasion Agabus, in the tradition of the great prophets of Israel, accompanied his prediction with a symbolic action (Acts 21: 11):

> he took Paul's girdle and bound his own feet and hands, and said, "Thus says the Holy Spirit, 'So shall the Jews at Jerusalem bind the man who owns this girdle and deliver him into the hands of the Gentiles'."

If his words have been precisely recorded, then they did not tally completely with the event: it was the Gentiles who bound Paul, after snatching him from his Jewish assailants. But their main drift was plain enough: Paul's life would be endangered if he persisted in going on to Jerusalem. His friends therefore begged him to give up any thought of carrying out his plan to visit the city with the delegates of the Gentile churches: they could perfectly well hand over the gifts which they had brought, and their hospitality during their stay in Jerusalem was assured.

Paul, however, was as sure of divine guidance in resolving to go to Jerusalem as his friends and well-wishers were in beseeching him not to go. When they saw that his mind was made up, and that nothing would shift him, they left off trying to dissuade him and said "The Lord's will be done" (Acts 21: 14). In these words there may be an echo of Jesus' submission to the will of God in Gethsemane[25] – a conscious echo, so far as Luke was concerned, for there is a recognizable literary parallel between his account of Jesus' "setting his face to go to Jerusalem"[26] in the first part of his history and Paul's last journey to Jerusalem in the second part. To the repeated passion-predictions in the Gospel correspond the

25. Mark 14: 36/Luke 22: 42.
26. Luke 9: 51.

repeated forecasts of trouble for Paul in Acts, and in both sequences there is the same insistence on the fulfilment of the divine purpose.[27] Thus Luke's emphasis on Paul's "going to Jerusalem under the constraint of the Spirit" (Acts 20: 22) is consistent with Paul's contemplation of his visit to Jerusalem in Romans 15: 15–32 as something which was necessary to seal "the priestly service of the gospel of God" which he had discharged thus far.

### 3. James and the elders

Paul had asked the Roman Christian to join him in praying that the relief fund which he had organized for Jerusalem might be "acceptable to the saints" (Romans 15: 32). This prayer at least appears to have met with an affirmative answer.[28] Writing as one of Paul's companions, Luke says that the brethren in Jerusalem gave them a cordial welcome. The day after their arrival in the city (Acts 21: 18–20):

Paul went in with us to James; and all the elders were present. After greeting them, he related one by one the things that God had done among the Gentiles through his ministry. And when they heard it, they glorified God.

So well they might, for what Paul told them by word of mouth was corroborated by the presence of so many of his Gentile converts, representatives of hundreds if not thousands more; it was corroborated also (although Luke, for reasons best known to himself, passes this over in silence) [29] by the gifts which, presumably on this occasion, they handed over to James and his fellow-elders on behalf of the churches which they represented.

27. Cf. Mark 8: 31; 9: 31; 10: 33 f., with the δεῖ of divine necessity and the repeated emphasis on the Son of Man's being handed over to the Gentiles – a note echoed in the prophecy of Agabus (Acts 21: 11).

28. But see A. J. Mattill, "The Purpose of Acts: Schneckenburger reconsidered", in *Apostolic History and the Gospel*, ed. W. W. Gasque and R. P. Martin (Exeter, 1970), p. 116: "the biggest shock to Luke was the refusal of the Jerusalem church to accept Paul's collection, thereby symbolizing their break with the Pauline mission" (he refers to O. Cullmann, "Dissensions within the Early Church", *Union Seminary Quarterly Review* 22 [1967], pp. 83–92).

29. J. Knox, pointing out that Luke had a good first-hand source for this part of his narrative, concludes (rightly) that his soft-pedalling the nature and purpose of the collection must have been deliberate. He explains this by the consideration that the collection was designed as a peace-offering to the Jerusalem church, whereas Luke's picture of peaceful relations between that church and the Gentile mission ever since the apostolic council of Acts 15 excluded any occasion for such a peace-offering at this later stage, so that in his narrative the offering had to be "separated entirely from its original context" (*Chapters in a Life of Paul* [London, 1954], p. 71). What seems to me a more probable explanation is suggested above on p. 297.

On earlier occasions when the church of Jerusalem figures in any detail in Paul's letters or Luke's narrative, the apostles, or some of them, play a leading part; this time they are conspicuously absent. Probably Peter and his colleagues had left Jerusalem to engage in missionary activity in the lands of the Jewish dispersion, leaving the mother-church to be cared for by James the Just and a college of elders – perhaps the sanhedrin of the true remnant of Israel, as they considered themselves to be. If James occupied the position of *primus inter pares* among them that the high priest occupied in the official Sanhedrin, this might account for the later legend that he wore garments of priestly type and had the right to enter the sanctuary.[30]

While James and his colleagues greeted Paul as a brother and were impressed by the record of his achievement among the Gentiles, they were afraid that his presence in Jerusalem might be the signal for trouble. Apart from the hostility which was inevitably felt towards such a renegade by the Jewish religious establishment, many members of the church, described as "zealots for the law" (Acts 21: 20), disapproved of his missionary policy and of the freedom with which he treated the law and the traditions of Israel. It was bad enough that he should so resolutely refuse to impose the law and the traditions on his Gentile converts, but it was rumoured that he even advised Jewish Christians of the dispersion to cease observing their ancestral customs, including the circumcision of their children. James and the other elders appear not to have believed these rumours and indeed, while it is easy to see what gave rise to them, it is equally easy to see that they were distortions of the truth. Some people cannot readily distinguish between the essential and the non-essential: if they abandon an old order for a new one, they feel it necessary to give up everything associated with the old order – neutral or even helpful features as well as others. But this is to exchange a positive form of legal obligation for a negative form. Thus, at the opposite extreme from those Jewish Christians in Jerusalem who followed the ancient customs as a matter of course there may have been others elsewhere who discontinued them on principle. Paul's policy was different from both. Truly emancipated souls are not in bondage to their emancipation. Paul conformed to the customs or departed from them according to the company, Jewish or Gentile, in which he found himself from time to time, making the interests of the gospel the supreme consideration.[31] In Jewish company he would naturally observe the Jewish food laws, from common courtesy, not to speak of Christian

30. So Hegesippus as quoted by Eusebius (*Hist. Eccl.* ii. 23. 6); cf. A. A. T. Ehrhardt, *The Apostolic Succession* (London, 1953), pp. 63 ff.; F. F. Bruce, *The Spreading Flame* (London, 1958), p. 151 with n. 3.
31. 1 Corinthians 9: 19–23.

charity, nor would he outrage Jewish sentiment by violating the sanctity of holy days, however much for his own part he esteemed all days alike.[32] True, he was dismayed when he heard that his Galatian converts had begun to "observe days, and months, and seasons, and years" (Galatians 4: 10); but they were Gentiles, and had no good reason for adopting the Jewish sacred calendar, least of all for adopting it by way of religious obligation. Once Paul had himself inherited the observance of that calendar by way of religious obligation, but he had learned as a Christian to enjoy complete freedom with regard to its observance or non-observance.

It is certain that in Jerusalem, of all places, he would live as a practising Jew, if only out of consistency with his declared policy, to "give no offence to Jews or to Greeks or to the church of God" and to "try to please all men in everything I do, not seeking my own advantage, but that of the many, that they may be saved" (1 Corinthians 10: 32 f.). There were few "Greeks" in Jerusalem, but both the Jews and the church of God in that city would be scandalized if he failed to observe the "customs".

But if Paul claimed liberty of action for himself in such matters, why would he deny it to other Jewish Christians? Provided they shared his attitude to the traditional practices of Israel as no longer divine requirements but as voluntary actions which might be undertaken or omitted as expediency directed, they might freely go on with them. It was no more necessary for them than for Paul to be in bondage to their emancipation. If they wished, for what seemed to them to be good and proper reasons, to circumcise their children, Paul would remember that he had circumcised Timothy for what seemed to himself to be good and proper reasons.[33] His letters give us no indication of his advice in these respects to Jewish Christians, except that Jewish Christians and Gentile Christians alike should respect each other's scruples – or lack of scruples.

Not that the leaders of the Jerusalem church would have been altogether happy about Paul's libertarian attitude to these questions; they would probably have disapproved of Jewish Christians who voluntarily discontinued the "customs". They felt that they themselves had made all the concession that was called for in the Jerusalem decree which exempted *Gentile* Christians from circumcision, while stipulating a certain minimum of "necessary things" which they should observe.[34] Of this concession they now reminded Paul, as though to reassure him that they had no thought of imposing the "customs" on his Gentile converts.[35] (The possibility should be recognised that they perhaps insufficiently

32. Romans 14: 5 f.
33. Acts 16: 3; see pp. 214 ff.
34. Acts 15: 28.
35. Acts 21: 25.

informed about Paul's increasing reservations about the Jerusalem decree.) [36]

As for the rumours and misrepresentations which were circulating about Paul in Jerusalem, they had a practical proposal to
put to him – one which, they hoped, would effectively squash them.
Four members of the church had undertaken a Nazirite vow, and
the time had now come to discharge it. This involved the cutting or
shaving of their hair, which had been allowed to grow long for the
duration of the vow, and the presentation of an appropriate offering
in the temple.[37] There were some unspecified circumstances which
made it necessary for them to undergo ceremonial purification
before their vow could be discharged; this purification involved the
delay of a week.[38] If Paul would associate himself with these men,
share in their purificatory ceremony and pay the expenses incurred
in the discharge of their vow, this would be a demonstration to all
that he was a practising Jew.

Paul probably did not share the optimistic naïveté of his
Jerusalem brethren, but if the course of action they suggested
would save them from the embarrassment of being associated in the
public eye with such a dubious character as he was reputed to be,
there was no reason why he should not fall in with their plan. There
is no ground for the idea that they pressed it on Paul as a subtle
way of humiliating him.[39] As for the propriety of a Nazirite vow, he
himself had undertaken one at Corinth five years before.[40] To pay
the expenses of others who had undertaken such a vow was regarded as an act of pious charity;[41] certainly neither Paul nor
(probably) the four Nazirites took part in this ceremony as a means
of acquiring merit before God. It was an outward and visible sign of
thanksgiving to God for answered prayer.

## 4. Paul taken into custody

Whatever effect Paul's visit to the temple with the four Nazirites
had on the many "zealots for the law" in the church of Jerusalem, it
brought Paul himself into the very danger against which he had

36. See p. 270.
37. See Numbers 6: 1–21; Mishnah *Nazir* (according to *Nazir* 6: 3 "a Nazirite
vow that is vowed without a fixed duration is binding for thirty days").
38. Numbers 6: 9 f.; Mishnah *Nazir* 6: 6.
39. Or worse; cf. A. J. Mattill (*loc. cit.*, pp. 115 f.): "As Luke watched the riot in
the Temple, the suspicion dawned upon him that Judaizers had drawn Paul into
an ambush by luring him into the Temple."
40. Acts 18: 18 (see p. 255).
41. It was an act of piety on the part of the elder Herod Agrippa to pay the expenses of many Nazirites (Josephus, *Ant.* xix. 294). His daughter Bernice undertook a thirty days' Nazirite vow shortly before the outbreak of war in A.D. 66
(Josephus, *BJ* ii. 310–314).

been forewarned by friends in Tyre, Caesarea and elsewhere.
Pentecost was coming on, and Jews from the dispersion had arrived
in Jerusalem to celebrate the festival. Among them were some Jews
from Ephesus and the neighbourhood, who had come to know Paul
well by sight during his residence in proconsular Asia, and who disapproved of him and all his works. They had seen him in Jerusalem
with an Ephesian whom they recognized – Trophimus, one of his
Gentile converts. Now, at the end of the Nazirites' week of purification, they found Paul in the temple precincts with them –
presumably in the Court of Israel [42] – and raised a hue and cry
against him, charging him with violating the sanctity of the temple
by taking Gentiles within forbidden bounds.

The outer court of the temple, enclosed by Herod the Great, was
called the court of the Gentiles because Gentiles were free to enter
it. This was the area which Jesus had "cleansed" during Holy
Week, in protest against those encroachments upon it which
diminished its use as "a house of prayer for all the nations" (Mark
11: 15–17). But Gentiles were prohibited, on pain of death, from
trespassing beyond the barrier which separated the outer court
from the inner courts, the sacred area proper. Inscriptions in Greek
and Latin were fastened at intervals to this barrier, warning Gentile
visitors against proceeding farther.[43] This was the one type of
offence for which the Romans allowed the Jewish authorities to
retain capital jurisdiction; they authorized the death penalty in this
regard even when the offender was a Roman citizen, so careful were
they to conciliate Jewish religious susceptibilities.[44] Had there been
any foundation for the charge against Paul, his Roman citizenship
would not have saved him from the consequences.

The immediate result of the Asian Jews' outcry was that the surrounding crowd turned on Paul and dragged him out of the court of
Israel down into the outer court, where they continued to beat him
up. The temple police closed the gates leading from the outer court
into the inner courts, so that the sanctity of the sacred area might
not be outraged by the crowd's unseemly violence. In the outer
court Paul could not have survived the violence long, but timely action was taken by the Roman garrison posted in the Antonia fortress, which overlooked the temple precincts from the north-west
and communicated with the outer court by two flights of steps.[45] As

42. Paul, as a Jew, could enter the court of Israel but, as a layman, he could not
penetrate farther. Trophimus, as a Gentile, could go no farther than the court of
the Gentiles.

43. Josephus, *BJ* v. 194; for the text of one of these inscriptions in Greek (found
in 1871 by C. S. Clermont-Ganneau) see *OGIS* 598; for another (discovered over
60 years later) see J. H. Iliffe, "The ΘΑΝΑΤΟΣ Inscription from Herod's
Temple", *QDAP* 6 (1938), pp. 1 ff.

44. Josephus *BJ* vi. 124–126.

45. Josephus *BJ* v. 243 f.

soon as the military tribune in charge of the garrison got wind of the tumult, which was now spreading into the city, he sent a detachment of soldiers down the steps into the midst of the rioters; they dragged Paul away from his assailants and carried him shoulder-high back up the steps, to prevent the assailants from pulling him down. At the top of the steps stood the military tribune, Claudius Lysias by name, who formally arrested Paul and ordered him to be handcuffed to two soldiers and taken into the fortress.

It was impossible to make sense of the crowd's excited accusations, but Paul had plainly done something to infuriate the people. The tribune jumped to the conclusion that he was an Egyptian adventurer who, some three years before, had appeared in Jerusalem claiming to be a prophet, and led a band of followers to the Mount of Olives. There he told them to wait until, at his word of command, the walls of Jerusalem would fall down flat; then they would march in, overthrow the Roman garrison and take possession of the city. The procurator Felix sent a body of troops against them who killed some, took others prisoner, and dispersed the rest. The Egyptian discreetly vanished.[46] The feelings of those whom he had duped would not be friendly towards him; now, thought the tribune, he had reappeared and the people were venting their rage on him.

He was therefore surprised when Paul, before he could be taken into the fortress, addressed him in educated Greek and asked permission to speak to the crowd. Paul assured him that he was no Egyptian, but a Jew from Tarsus, "a citizen of no mean city" (Acts 21: 39). The tribune gave him the permission which he sought, and from his vantage-point at the top of the steps, flanked by the soldiers to whom he was handcuffed, Paul secured the crowd's attentive silence for a time by addressing them in their Aramaic vernacular.

He told them of his own zeal for God and strict devotion to the ancestral law, and explained why he had adopted the course which he now followed. As his speech is summarized by Luke, it emphasizes those aspects in Paul's story which might make a special appeal to such hearers – his upbringing in Jerusalem, his education at the feet of Gamaliel, his fanatical persecution of "the Way", the part played in his conversion and call by Ananias of Damascus, "a devout man according to the law", and the subsequent confirmation of his call in the Jerusalem temple itself, where the risen Lord appeared to him in a vision and sent him "far away to the Gentiles" (Acts 22: 3–21).[47]

At this last word the crowd remembered its grievance and the

46. Josephus, *BJ* ii. 261 ff.; *Ant.* xx. 171 f.
47. See p. 144.
48. Acts 22: 25–28.

hubbub broke out afresh, so that the tribune, despairing of finding
out the cause of the trouble except by examining his prisoner under
torture, had Paul taken into the fortress and gave orders for him to
be scourged. Both Greek and Roman legal systems had the idea
that people were more likely to tell the truth under torture, or the
threat of it, but Greek law generally exempted freemen from such
treatment, and Roman law exempted Roman citizens. Accordingly, as Paul was being tied up for the lash, he asked the centurion in
charge of the operation if it was permissible to scourge a Roman
citizen, especially one against whom no crime had been proved in
open court. The centurion suspended the arrangements for scourging and went to the tribune with the news that the man was a
Roman citizen. The tribune, in some alarm, sent in haste to ask
Paul if this was true. On being assured that it was, the tribune looked at him doubtfully. "I know how much it cost *me* to acquire the
citizenship", he said – perhaps with the implication that Paul, who
must by now have presented a very dishevelled appearance, did not
look as if he had one denarius to rub against another. "Ah", said
Paul; "I was *born* a citizen." The tribune was duly impressed.[48]

A Roman citizen must be treated in accordance with due legal
procedure. Evidently Paul was being charged with an offence
against Jewish law, and the Sanhedrin was the proper body to deal
with such an offence. Paul, therefore was brought before the
Sanhedrin, which was presided over at this time by a high priest of
very doubtful reputation, Ananias the son of Nedebaeus (A.D.
47–58).[49] But until a charge was formally made and it was ascer-
tained whether or not the Sanhedrin had jurisdiction in the case,
the tribune maintained his responsibility for Paul. If witnesses had
come forward to say that they had seen Paul take a Gentile into the
inner courts, then the case would certainly have fallen within the
competence of the Sanhedrin – but throughout the long drawn out
proceedings, from first to last, no such witnesses were forthcoming.
Paul might declare that in Christ the middle wall of partition
between Jew and Gentile had been broken down,[50] but he knew
that the material wall of partition in the temple still stood, and he
would have thrown away his hopes of getting safely out of
Jerusalem and visiting Rome and Spain if he had done such a crazy
thing as the Asian Jews alleged when they raised the hue and cry
against him.[51]

49. Josephus tells how Ananias appropriated the tithes that should have gone to
the rank and file of the priests (*Ant.* xx. 205–207); rabbinical tradition preserved a
popular song lampooning his gluttony (TB *Pesaḥim* 57a). He was murdered by
Zealots in A.D. 66 (*BJ* ii. 441 f.).

50. Ephesians 2: 14 (see p. 434).

51. J. Klausner, extraordinarily, suggests that nevertheless he may have done it
(*From Jesus to Paul*, E.T. [London, 1944], p. 400).

Since no accusers presented themselves before the Sanhedrin at this stage, Paul took the opportunity to say a word himself. He started off inauspiciously, with a rebuke to the high priest for conduct unbefitting the president of the supreme court of Israel, but when he had apologized to the dignitary (if not to the man),[52] he began again and enlisted the good will of the Pharisaic members of the court by declaring that the whole issue on which he stood before them rested on the hope of resurrection. The resurrection of Jesus, authenticated to Paul on the Damascus road when he received the call to his present ministry, was bound up in his mind with the general hope of resurrection which he shared with all the Pharisees. In the absence of a clear charge against Paul on which they could adjudicate, the Sadducees and Pharisees in the Sanhedrin fell to arguing about the resurrection, the Pharisees feeling that a man who was so sound on this fundamental doctrine could not be altogether bad.

## 5. Paul sent to Caesarea

At last the tribune, finding that no progress was being made with his problem of how to deal with this inconvenient Roman citizen, had him taken back to the fortress. Meanwhile Paul's enemies, seeing that there was no legal way of getting him into their hands, plotted to assassinate him next time he was brought before the Sanhedrin. Paul's nephew learned about this plot – this is the only reference we have in any New Testament document to any relative of Paul, and a tantalizingly fleeting one it is [53] – and obtained access to Paul in the fortress and told him what was afoot. Paul arranged for him to tell the tribune what he had discovered. This made the tribune's mind up. He could no longer take personal responsibility for Paul's safety. There were issues here with which he could not cope: if any one was to cope with them, let it be the provincial governor.

Accordingly he sent Paul off by night, under armed guard, to Caesarea, where the governor had his headquarters. When the party reached Antipatris (Rosh ha'Ayin) next morning, the foot-soldiers returned, leaving seventy light-armed cavalry to escort Paul on the remaining 27 miles to Caesarea. With Paul the tribune sent a letter to the governor, explaining the circumstances and representing his own rôle in the best light: he had rescued Paul

52. "I did not know, brethren, that he was the high priest" (Acts 23: 5) might mean, "I did not think that a man who behaved so illegally [as to order him to be struck across the mouth] could possibly be the high priest".

53. The young man's mother, Paul's sister, presumably lived in Jerusalem, which may imply that more members of the family than Paul himself came to Jerusalem from Tarsus in Paul's boyhood (see p. 43).

Rome: Appian Way (see p. 374)

HIC·HABITASSE·PRIVS·SANCTOS·COGNOSCERE·DEBES
NOMINA·QVISQVE·PETRI·PARITER·PAVLIQVE·REQVIRIS
DISCIPVLOS·ORIENS·MISIT·QVOD·SPONTE·FATEMVR
SANGINIS·OB·MERITVM·ⅭRISTVMQE·PER·ASTRA·SECTI
AETHERIOS·PETIERE·SINVS·REGNAQVE·PIORVM
ROMA·SVOS·POTIVS·MERVIT·DEFENDERE·CIVES
HAEC·DAMASVS·VESTRAS·REFERAT·NOA·SIDRA·LAVDS

Rome: Inscriptions from the Church of St. Praxedis and the
Church of St. Sebastian (see p. 452)

from his assailants in the temple, he said, "having learned that he was a Roman citizen" (Acts 23: 27).

The governor read the letter, asked Paul which province he came from, and had him kept in custody in his headquarters at Caesarea – the official praetorium which had been built by Herod as his palace. The governor himself would henceforth take charge of the proceedings.

Paul had good reason to ask for the prayers of the Roman Christians that he might "be delivered from the unbelievers in Judaea" (Romans 15: 31). Delivered he was, but in circumstances which involved the loss of his freedom for the next four years at least, and the postponement of his plan to visit Rome. So ended his last visit to Jerusalem.

# CHAPTER 31

# Caesarea and the Appeal to Caesar

## 1. Paul and Felix

CAESAREA, WHERE PAUL WAS TO SPEND THE NEXT TWO YEARS, was built by Herod the Great between 20 and 9 B.C., on the site formerly called Strato's Tower, in order to serve as the principal Mediterranean port of his kingdom. Because of the lack of natural harbours along the coast south of the Bay of Haifa, he had an elaborate artificial harbour constructed here, enclosed by a semicircular breakwater, together with several other installations (excavated in 1956 and the following years) such as the temple of Augustus (in whose honour the city received its name), a magnificent theatre and a hippodrome.[1] From the outset it was a predominantly Gentile city, and for this reason the Roman governors of Judaea from A.D. 6 onwards found it a more congenial place for their normal residence than Jerusalem. Herod's palace in Caesarea served them as their headquarters (*praetorium*). The name of an earlier governor of Judaea, Pontius Pilate, was found in a Latin inscription in the theatre when it was being excavated in 1961; there Pilate's official title is given as "prefect" (*praefectus*).[2] It has been thought that the title *procurator* came to be used of the governor of Judaea from A.D. 44 onwards (although *procurator* is the title which Tacitus gives to Pilate).[3]

The procurator who took Paul into custody at Caesarea, Marcus Antonius Felix, was not the typical Roman provincial governor. Prefects or procurators of third-grade provinces like Judaea belonged regularly to the equestrian order (whereas proconsuls of senatorial provinces and legates of imperial provinces were drawn from the nobility, the senatorial order). But Felix was a freedman (*libertus*), who had once been a slave in the household of Antonia,

---

1. Josephus, *BJ* i. 408–415; *Ant.* xvi. 136–141. See L. I. Levine, *Caesarea under Roman Rule* (Leiden, 1975), and *Roman Caesarea: An Archaeological-Topographical Study* (Jerusalem, 1975); C. T. Fritsch (ed.), *Studies in the History of Caesarea Maritima*, i (Missoula, Montana, 1975).
2. The inscription was first published by A. Frova, *Istituto Lombardo di Scienze e Lettere: Rendiconti* (Milan, 1961), pp. 419–434; cf. A. Degrassi, *Atti della Accademia Nazionale dei Lincei: Rendiconti* (Rome, 1964), pp. 59–65; it runs: *[Dis Augusti]s Tiberieum [. . . Po]ntius Pilatus [praef]ectus Iuda[ea]e [fecit d]e[dicauit].*
3. Tacitus, *Annals* xv. 44. 4.

daughter of Mark Antony and Octavia, widow of Drusus (Tiberius's brother) and mother of the Emperor Claudius. His brother Pallas, who was likewise one of Antonia's emancipated slaves, rose to a position of high responsibility and opportunity under Claudius, as chief accountant of the public treasury (*praepositus a rationibus*) – chancellor of the exchequer, one might say. It could well have been his influence that helped to procure for Felix the governorship of Judaea,[4] but Felix had considerable native ability, coupled with personal qualities which won for him the entrée into the most exalted families. Each of his three successive wives was of royal birth: one was a granddaughter of Antony and Cleopatra,[5] and his third wife, whom he had married by the time his path crossed Paul's, was Drusilla, the youngest daughter of Herod Agrippa the elder and sister of Agrippa II and Bernice.

From a statement of Tacitus it has been inferred that before being appointed to succeed Ventidius Cumanus as procurator of Judaea in A.D. 52, Felix had occupied an administrative post under Cumanus in Samaria (which was part of the province of Judaea).[6] During this period he seems to have won the confidence of Jonathan the son of Ananus (Annas), an influential ex-high priest, who pressed for Felix's appointment as procurator of Judaea when he was in Rome on a deputation to voice Jewish grievances against Cumanus.[7] It is to Tacitus that Felix owes the unfavourable reputation of having "exercised the power of a king with the mind of a slave";[8] but allowance must be made for the prejudice with which Tacitus would contemplate the exaltation of a man of such humble origins. Felix's entry upon his procuratorship of Judaea coincided with the emergence of a new body of terrorists (*alias* freedom fighters), the *sicarii* or dagger-men, who mingled with crowds at festivals and the like and stabbed Jewish "collaborationists" and others of whom they disapproved. One of their first victims was the ex-high priest Jonathan.[9] The ruthless vigour with which Felix put down these and other liberationist movements raised his credit in Rome, and even when Pallas fell from favour in the imperial household in A.D. 55, shortly after Nero's accession,[10] Felix remained in office in Judaea for four more years.

This, then, was the man to whom Paul was sent by the military

---

4. Suetonius, *Life of Claudius*, 28; Tacitus, *Annals* xii. 53 f.; *History* v. 9.

5. Suetonius, *Life of Claudius*, 28. 1; Tacitus, *History* v. 9.

6. Tacitus, *Annals* xii. 54. 3 ("Judaea was divided: the Samaritans came under Felix and the Galilaeans under Cumanus").

7. Josephus, *BJ* ii. 243–247; *Ant.* xx. 131–137, 162.

8. Tacitus, *History* v. 9.

9. Josephus, *BJ* ii. 254–257; *Ant.* xx. 160–166, 186–188.

10. Tacitus, *Annals* xiii. 14. 1.

tribune in Jerusalem, and who henceforth had the responsibility of investigating the complaints against him.

Proceedings against Paul were now taken up by the Sanhedrin. Five days after Paul's arrival in Caesarea, a deputation from that body came down to state their case before Felix. With them they brought an orator named Tertullus to present it in the conventional terms of forensic rhetoric. Luke quotes the exordium of Tertullus's speech rather fully; it is a fair example of the *captatio beniuolentiae* employed in addressing such an official (Acts 24: 2 ff.):

> Your excellency! It is thanks to you that we enjoy unbroken peace; it is due to your provident care that, in every way and in every place, improvements are made for the good of this nation. We welcome this, sir, most gratefully. And now, not to take up your valuable time, I crave your indulgence for a brief statement of our case.

Then followed the indictment, asserting, as it passed from the more general to the more particular, that Paul was a perfect plague, a fomenter of discord among Jews throughout the Roman Empire, and a ringleader of the sect of the Nazarenes,[11] and that he had attempted to profane the temple. He was caught in the act while committing this last offence, but when the Jewish authorities had arrested him in accordance with their special jurisdiction in such matters, the military tribune had, with unwarranted force, snatched him from their hands.[12]

It is doubtful if the procurator of Judaea had any competence to take up the general complaints, which were probably designed to prejudice his mind against Paul. The particular charge of temple profanation was a grave one, but there was a serious defect in its presentation: no witnesses were produced to substantiate it. Paul was not slow to point this out when Felix invited him to reply to the accusations (Acts 24: 10 ff.):

> Realizing that you have been governing this nation for many years, I make my defence with confidence. As you may ascertain, it is not more than twelve days since I went up to worship at Jerusalem. They did not find me disputing with any one or stirring up a crowd, either in the temple or in the synagogues or anywhere in the city. Neither can they produce evidence for the charges which they now bring against me. This much I admit: according to the Way – the "sect" of which they speak – I worship the God of our fathers. I believe everything laid down in the law

11. They were so called presumably because they were followers of Jesus the Nazarene (Jesus of Nazareth), but the term (Hebrew *noṣrîm*) could have been understood to mean "observant ones".

12. It is only in the Western text of Acts 24: 7 (preserved in TR; cf. AV) that this reference to Lysias is included in Tertullus's speech, but a good case can be made out for its genuineness.

or written in the prophets, sharing the same hope in God as my accusers cherish, that there will be a resurrection of just and unjust alike. So I always train myself to maintain a clear conscience before God and men.

After an absence of several years I came to bring alms and offerings for my nation. They found me in the temple purified, discharging this service, without any crowd or disturbance. But it was some Jews from the province of Asia who stirred up the trouble, and they ought to be here before you to state whatever charge they have to lay against me. In their default, let my accusers themselves say of what offence they found me guilty when I was brought before the Sanhedrin, unless it lay in my open assertion as I stood among them: "the real issue of my trial before you today is the resurrection of the dead".

If Paul drew attention to the absence of the potential witnesses for the prosecution, the procurator decided that another material witness was absent, from whom he might expect a more impartial account than the accusers or the defendant were likely to give. Accordingly, having listened to the Sanhedrin's charge and to Paul's reply, he adjourned proceedings – perhaps with the Latin formula *Amplius*: "When Lysias the tribune comes down", he said, "I will decide your case."

Luke's formulation of Paul's defence contains the only reference to the Jerusalem relief fund in the record of Acts, and includes some other features of interest. Apart from the insistence that no evidence was produced to substantiate the allegation that he had violated the sanctity of the temple, the contents of the speech might well have a greater relevance to Paul's later appearance before the supreme tribunal in Rome than to his present appearance before the procurator of Judaea, and the same thing might indeed be said of the more general terms of Tertullus's indictment. This raises the long-debated question of the relation between Acts and Paul's trial in Rome. If it can no longer be held that Luke actually wrote his record to brief the counsel for the defence, or otherwise to serve as a document in the case,[13] the possibility remains that some material of this kind was used as source-material in the composition of Acts. Charges, expressed or implied, that Paul was a disturber of the peace in the provinces, that he had diverted to a sectarian interest money which ought to have gone to the maintenance of the temple

13. See for various arguments more or less to this effect M. Schneckenburger, *Ueber den Zweck der Apostelgeschichte* (Bern, 1841), with A. J. Mattill, Jr., "The Purpose of Acts: Schneckenburger reconsidered", in *Apostolic History and the Gospel*, ed. W. W. Gasque and R. P. Martin (Exeter, 1970), pp. 108–122; also M. V. Aberle, "Exegetische Studien: 2. Ueber den Zweck der Apostelgeschichte", *Theologische Quartalschrift* 37 (1855), pp. 173 ff.; D. Plooij, "The Work of St. Luke: A Historical Apology for Pauline Preaching before the Roman Court", *Expositor*, series 8, 8 (1914), pp. 511–523; "Again: The Work of St. Luke", *ibid*. 13 (1917), pp. 108–124; J. I. Still, *St. Paul on Trial* (London, 1923); G. S. Duncan, *St. Paul's Ephesian Ministry* (London, 1929), p. 97.

or to the relief of the Judaeans as a whole, and that he was propagating a new cult which (despite Gallio's ruling) had no right to share the protection extended by Roman law to the Jewish religion, would have been relevant indeed in a hearing before the emperor, however little they may have fallen within the jurisdiction of Felix.

We may suppose that Felix did hold a further hearing at which Claudius Lysias was present to give his evidence, although no record of it has been preserved. Even so, nothing that Claudius Lysias could have said would have helped the case against Paul, and if Felix had had regard simply to the legalities of the situation, he might have discharged Paul there and then. But he postponed such action – hoping, says Luke, that Paul (or his associates) might try to persuade him by bribery to do what it was in any case his duty to do. The fact that Paul had so recently come to Jerusalem with "alms and offerings" may have suggested to Felix that Paul had access to sources of supply from which Felix himself might derive some financial profit. Stringent as Roman laws against bribery were,[14] they were not sufficient to make many provincial governors resist the opportunities for quick enrichment which their office presented, and Felix was not the man to let such opportunities pass – modest as they were in comparison with those which his brother Pallas was able to exploit in Rome.[15] His hopes of a bribe from Paul or his friends, however, were not realized, so Paul remained undischarged.

## 2. Paul's associates

Meanwhile, it may be asked, what happened to the Gentile Christians who had accompanied Paul to Jerusalem? Two of them seem to have stayed on in Judaea, Luke and Aristarchus; perhaps they went to Caesarea so as to be near Paul and perform what services they could for him.[16] The others probably made their way home as quickly and unobtrusively as they could: the turn of events which they had witnessed in Jerusalem may well have frustrated the realization of Paul's hopes that his Gentile churches would find that the collection forged a bond of affection between them and

14. As early as 122 B.C., within twelve years from the acquisition of the province of Asia, the *lex Acilia repetundarum* was enacted against extortion and venality on the part of provincial governors, and a standing court (*quaestio*) was instituted to deal with such offences.

15. So wealthy were Pallas and another of Claudius's freedmen, Narcissus (see p. 386), that one day, when Claudius was complaining that there was so little money in the privy purse, he was advised in jest that he should get these two to take him into partnership (Suetonius, *Life of Claudius* 28. 3).

16. They accompanied Paul when he set sail for Rome from Caesarea (Acts 27: 2)

their Judaean brethren. Whether the Judaean brethren in their turn felt more closely drawn to their Gentile fellow-Christians "because of the surpassing grace of God" manifested in their generous gift (2 Corinthians 9: 14) we have no means of knowing.

Neither have we any means of knowing if the Jerusalem church or its leaders exerted themselves at all on Paul's behalf when they saw the predicament into which their well-meant counsel had brought him. Probably they felt relieved when they heard that he had been taken to Caesarea. This last visit of Paul's to Jerusalem had followed the pattern of earlier visits: trouble had broken out once more. It would really be best if Paul never came to Jerusalem again. Now that he was in Caesarea, under Roman guard, he was probably out of immediate danger, but in any case there was little that they could do for him. Moreover, the high priest and Sanhedrin were engaged in prosecuting him, and it would be unwise to do anything which might unnecessarily attract their hostile attention. It is easy to credit the Jerusalem church and its leaders with unworthy motives, but some attempt should be made to appreciate the extremely difficult situation in which they found themselves. If they still took seriously their commission to evangelize their fellow-Jews (and there is no reason to suppose that they had ceased to do so), any public association with Paul would have been a major handicap to its prosecution. It is possible, indeed, that this association was one of the grounds for the illegal execution of James the Just at the instance of the high priest Ananus II during the interregnum in the procuratorship which followed the death of Festus (A.D. 62).[17]

## 3. Two years in Caesarea

As for Paul himself, there are several scholars who hold that it was from Caesarea that some, if not all, of his "captivity epistles" were sent.[18] We have seen that an Ephesian provenance has been postulated for some of them;[19] but whereas an Ephesian

17. Josephus, *Ant.* xx. 200.

18. Cf. E. Lohmeyer, *Die Briefe an die Philipper, an die Kolosser und an Philemon* (Göttingen, [13] 1964), pp. 3 f., 14 f., 41; L. Johnson, "The Pauline Letters from Caesarea", *Expository Times* 68 (1956–57), pp. 24–26; J. J. Gunther, *Paul: Messenger and Exile* (Valley Forge, 1972), pp. 91 ff.; J. A. T. Robinson, *Redating the New Testament* (London, 1976), pp. 57 ff. W. G. Kümmel thinks Caesarea rather more probable than Rome as the setting for the Colossians group, but finds the case more evenly balanced for Philippians (*Introduction to the New Testament*, E.T. [London, 1966], pp. 235, 245); B. Reicke argues more positively for a Caesarean provenance for the Colossians group but against it for Philippians ("Caesarea, Rome and the Captivity Epistles", in *Apostolic History and the Gospel*, ed. W. W. Gasque and R. P. Martin, pp. 277–286).

19. See p. 299.

imprisonment is but an inference (however reasonable) from ambiguous data, there is no doubt that Paul did undergo an imprisonment in Caesarea. In Philippians 1: 13 he says that it has become
known throughout the whole *praetorium* that his imprisonment is for
Christ's sake. He was certainly kept under guard in the *praetorium* at
Caesarea, and this might be the *praetorium* which he mentions in
writing to the Philippians; however, *praetorium* is a word with
several meanings. Apart from its use to designate the praetorian
guard in Rome, it meant the commanding officer's headquarters in
a military camp, or the headquarters of a provincial governor (like
the legate of Syria or the procurator of Judaea) who had troops under his command. It does not seem to have been used of the proconsular headquarters in a province like Asia which had no standing
army.[20]

As for the other group of captivity epistles – Philemon,
Colossians and Ephesians – we have to consider Paul's request to
Philemon to get the guest-room ready for him, since he hopes to be
released and to pay him a visit: [21] is it likely that he thought of
going back to proconsular Asia if he were set free from his
Caesarean imprisonment? It is just conceivable, if he thought of
taking the long land-route to Rome, instead of the more direct
sea-route, but not very probable. Reference has been made above to
the "unnecessary supposition" that it was at Ephesus that
Aristarchus was his fellow-prisoner, as he calls him in Colossians 4:
10.[22] Since he appears to have been with Paul at Caesarea, was it
there that he shared his imprisonment? Possibly; but he went in
due course with Paul to Rome, and could have shared his imprisonment *there*.

All that Luke tells us of Paul's tedious period of custody in
Caesarea is that from time to time Felix called him to his presence
for conversation. For, strange as it appears, Felix, according to
Luke, had "a rather accurate knowledge of the Way" (Acts 24: 22).
Nothing that is otherwise known about Felix prepares the reader
for this statement, but it must be linked with his marriage to the
youngest daughter of the elder Herod Agrippa. Indeed, the
Western text says quite explicitly that it was Felix's wife "who asked to see Paul and hear him speak, so wishing to satisfy her he summoned Paul".

At this time Drusilla was not yet twenty years old. As a small girl
she had been betrothed to the crown prince of Commagene, but the

20. References to a *praetorianus* in three Latin inscriptions found on a road near
Ephesus (*CIL* iii. 6085, 7135, 7136) do not imply the presence of a *praetorium* at
Ephesus: this *praetorianus* was an ex-member of the praetorian guard who was now
discharging police duties as a *stationarius* on that road.

21. Philemon 22.

22. See pp. 294 f., 298

marriage did not take place because he refused to embrace Judaism. Then her brother, the younger Agrippa, gave her in marriage to Azizus, king of Emesa (Homs) in Syria, who was prepared to make the necessary sacrifice. But when she was still only sixteen, Felix – with the help, says Josephus, of a Cypriot magician named Atomos – persuaded her to leave her husband and become his third wife. (There was no question of *his* becoming a Jew in order to marry her.) [23] She bore Felix one son, Agrippa by name, who met his death in the eruption of Vesuvius in A.D. 79. [24]

Thus summoned to take part in religious discussion with this extraordinary couple, Paul not only expounded the Christian faith and its relation to Judaism but also emphasized the ethical implications of his message – righteousness, self-control and future judgment. When Felix felt that the conversation was taking too personal a turn for his comfort, he dismissed Paul for the time being, but recalled him repeatedly – perhaps as a change from the boredom of official life. Caesarea, we may suppose, did not provide much in the way of diversion, but the acrimonious communal strife between its Jewish and Gentile residents gave him increasing trouble, and led at last to his recall.

Although Caesarea had the constitution of a Gentile city, its Jewish residents believed that they were entitled to *isopoliteia* – equal civic rights with their Gentile neighbours – because the city's royal founder was a Jew. The dispute about these rights led to rioting between the two communities, and when Felix's troops intervened to put down the rioting, they did so in a way which, the Jews believed, favoured the Gentile cause against theirs. This exacerbated the strife, and Felix sent the leaders of the two communities to Rome to make their representations before the emperor. The upshot was that the Jews' claim to *isopoliteia* was disallowed[25] – a grievance which became one of the factors leading to the Jewish revolt against Rome in A.D. 66 – but at the beginning of the investigation Felix was summoned to Rome and relieved of his procuratorship. He suffered nothing worse than this because of the continuing influence of his brother Pallas who, although he had been dismissed from the civil service four years previously, retained

23. Josephus, *Ant.* xix. 354 f.; xx. 139–143. Felix, playing on his own name, is said to have promised her every "felicity" if she married him; one can but hope that he kept his promise.

24. Josephus, *Ant.* xx. 143 f.

25. This is rather more probable than Josephus's statement (*Ant.* xx. 183 f.) that Nero annulled the *isopoliteia* which the Caesarean Jews already possessed. Cf. E. Schürer, *The History of the Jewish People in the Age of Jesus Christ*, new E.T., i (Edinburgh, 1973), pp. 465 ff.; M. Stern, "The Province of Judaea", in *The Jewish People in the First Century*, i. ed. S. Safrai and M. Stern (Assen, 1974), pp. 367 f.

considerable personal power because of his great wealth and his contacts with the people who mattered.[26]

Felix had earned the disapproval of the Jews in his province for a variety of reasons and, most recently, for what was interpreted as his anti-Jewish action in Caesarea. There was not much he could do to redress the balance, but at least he need not annoy the Sanhedrin gratuitously by releasing Paul. "If you release this man, you are not Caesar's friend" was an argument which had been used effectively with one of his predecessors,[27] so Felix, "desiring to do the Jews a favour, left Paul in prison" (Acts 24: 27).

### 4. A new procurator

Felix was succeeded as procurator by Porcius Festus,[28] who inherited the responsibility of coming to a decision about Paul. He was probably quite inexperienced in Jewish affairs and, unlike Felix, he had no Jewish wife through whom he could acquire "a rather accurate knowledge of the Way". The new governor's inexperience could easily be exploited to Paul's disadvantage, especially if he endeavoured at the outset of his period of office to establish good relations with the high priest and Sanhedrin. This was precisely what Festus did. A few days after his arrival in Judaea he went up to Jerusalem to make their acquaintance, and after the appropriate exchange of civilities they raised the question of Paul (no doubt among other matters which Felix had left in an unsatisfactory state). Festus agreed to re-open the case, so a deputation from the Sanhedrin came down to Caesarea to restate their charges against Paul. As before Felix, so now before Festus, Paul returned a direct negative to each of their charges. His situation was precarious. If the governor found that a *prima facie* case had been made out against him on the ground of sacrilege, he might have been handed over forthwith to the Sanhedrin's jurisdiction. The governor's *imperium* was such that he was not necessarily bound by his predecessor's finding, even if that finding had been placed on record. But Paul's accusers probably overplayed their hand by charging him further (as they had done before Felix) with offences

26. When Pallas was dismissed from office he had sufficient influence to stipulate that neither his past conduct nor his personal accounts should be open to inspection (Tacitus, *Annals* xiii. 14. 2). The fact that Drusilla was sister to the younger Agrippa, who was *persona grata* at the imperial court, may also have been helpful to Felix.

27. The chief priests' warning to Pilate at the trial of Jesus (John 19: 12).

28. Festus's accession to the procuratorship may have been the occasion for the striking in A.D. 59 of a new provincial coinage – the last before A.D. 66 (see F. W. Madden, *History of Jewish Coinage* [London, 1864], p. 153; A. Reifenberg, *Ancient Jewish Coins* [Jerusalem, ² 1947], p. 27). The date of Felix's dismissal and Festus's arrival is discussed in E. Schürer, *HJP* i (1973), p. 465, n. 42.

against the imperial peace; this was something which belonged to Roman jurisdiction and not to theirs.

However, in his desire to ingratiate himself with the Jewish leaders, Festus proposed to transfer the inquiry to Jerusalem, where the alleged sacrilege had been committed; he himself would continue to keep it under his own control. He no doubt regarded this as a reasonable proposal, but Paul did not think it reasonable at all. If Festus began by making one concession to the Sanhedrin, he might well go on to make more, and each concession would expose Paul to further peril. Festus might even treat the Sanhedrin as his *consilium*, his *ad hoc* advisory body, as his *imperium* entitled him to do.[29] There was one course open to Paul as a Roman citizen to avoid this particular peril, even if it was a course which might be attended by perils of its own. It was not, he assured Festus, that he wished to circumvent the law of Rome or escape the due reward of anything he had done. If he were in fact guilty cf a capital crime, as his accusers maintained, he was prepared to suffer the supreme penalty; but if there was no substance in their charges, he must not be placed in their power. Let Roman justice decide. As Festus was Caesar's representative, the tribunal before which Paul stood was Caesar's, but since Paul had not sufficient confidence in the provincial tribunal, he appealed to the supreme tribunal: "I appeal to Caesar", he declared (Acts 25: 11).

## 5. Appeal to Caesar

The citizen's right of appeal (*prouocatio*) to the emperor appears to have developed from the earlier right of appeal in republican times to the sovereign Roman people. According to Dio Cassius,[30] Octavian in 30 B.C. was granted the right to judge on appeal (*ekklēton dikazein*, in which A. H. M. Jones recognized the Greek equivalent of *ex prouocatione cognoscere*).[31] It was in this period, too, that the *lex Iulia de ui publica* (mentioned above) was enacted.[32] This law forbade any magistrate vested with *imperium* or *potestas* to kill, scourge, chain or torture a Roman citizen, or even to sentence him *aduersus prouocationem* ("in the face of an appeal") or prevent him from going to Rome to lodge his appeal there within a fixed time.[33] Professor Jones concluded that, from the date of this enactment, a

29. Cf. A. N. Sherwin-White, *Roman Society and Roman Law in the New Testament* (Oxford, 1963), p. 67.

30. *History* li. 19. Seven years later he received in addition life-long *tribunicia potestas*, which authorized him on *appellatio* to veto the action of any other magistrate in Rome itself and within a mile of its walls; but this is irrelevant to the present issue.

31. *Studies in Roman Government and Law* (Oxford, 1960), p. 96.

32. See p. 38.

33. *Digest* xlviii. 6, 7; Paulus, *Sententiae* v. 26. 1.

Roman citizen anywhere in the empire was protected against summary magisterial punishment (*coercitio*), although the provincial magistrate might deal with cases which involved a plain breach of established statute law (which Paul's case manifestly did not).[34] By the beginning of the second century A.D. it evidently became the regular practice for Roman citizens in the provinces, charged with offences *extra ordinem* (not covered by the standard code of procedure), to be sent to Rome almost automatically, without going through the formality of appealing to Caesar.[35] But there seems to have been a gradual erosion of the citizen's privileges with the steady increase in the number of citizens throughout the empire as the second century advanced[36] – a tendency which reached its climax in A.D. 212 with the extension of the franchise to all freeborn provincials under Caracalla. In this as in other respects, when we think historically and not theologically, the picture given in Acts is true to the dramatic date of the book; the case of Paul's appeal fits in with what we know of conditions in the late fifties of the first Christian century, and Luke's account of it is worthy to be treated as a substantial contribution to the available evidence.

It was with some relief that Festus heard Paul's appeal to Caesar: he himself would now be quit of the responsibility of adjudicating in a case where he knew himself to be out of his depth. One responsibility remained, however: he had to send to Rome along with the accused man an explanatory statement (*litterae dimissoriae*) outlining the nature of the case and its history up to date. In drafting this statement he was glad to have the timely aid of one who was reputed to be an expert in Jewish religious affairs.

Not long after Paul's appeal, the younger Agrippa and his sister Bernice came to Caesarea to pay their respects to the new procurator. After the death of his father, Herod Agrippa I, in A.D. 44 the younger Agrippa, then seventeen years old, was judged by Claudius and his advisers too immature to be appointed king of the Jews in his place, but he was given a less unmanageable district farther north to rule with the title of king, and at the present time his kingdom comprised the former tetrarchies of Philip and Lysanias, east and north of the Lake of Galilee, together with the

34. *Studies in Roman Government and Law*, p. 59.

35. The best-known instance is Pliny the Younger's reference, in his letter to Trajan about Christians in his province of Bithynia (*c.* A.D. 112), to some whom, because they were Roman citizens, he marked down to have their case referred to the capital (*Epistles* x. 96. 4).

36. In A.D. 177 the Roman citizens among the Christians rounded up in the Rhone valley were not sent to Rome for trial: they were kept in prison until a ruling was obtained from Marcus Aurelius, and even after he had ruled that they should be beheaded (instead of being put to death by torture, like the others), one of them, Attalus, was exposed to the wild beasts at the mob's insistence (Eusebius, *Hist. Eccl.* v. 1. 44, 50). See p. 295, n. 32.

cities of Tiberias and Tarichaeae west of the Lake, and Julias in Peraea, with their surrounding villages. His capital was Caesarea Philippi (now Banyas), which he renamed Neronias as a compliment to the Emperor Nero. In addition to his royal dignity, he enjoyed from A.D. 48 to 66 the privilege of appointing (and deposing) the high priests of Israel.[37]

After the normal exchange of courtesies, Festus acquainted Agrippa with his problem. The charges against Paul, he said, seemed to revolve around "one Jesus, who was dead, but whom Paul asserted to be alive" (Acts 25: 19). Agrippa's interest was immediately aroused and he expressed a desire to meet Paul. Festus was only too glad to arrange an interview, and next day Paul was brought before Festus, Agrippa, Bernice and other notabilities.

The speech which Paul made, according to Luke, in response to Agrippa's invitation to him to state his case, is as carefully adapted to this setting as his speech to the turbulent crowd in the temple court is to that setting. Luke, indeed, takes this speech as the opportunity to present Paul's *apologia pro vita sua*. He is no doubt true to life when he portrays Paul as unable to maintain complete objectivity in his statement. As Paul warms to his theme that the gospel to which he is dedicated consists of "nothing but what the prophets and Moses said would come to pass" (Acts 26: 22), he invites Agrippa to endorse the logic of his argument; Agrippa laughs off the invitation with the remark that Paul will not get him to play the part of a Christian as easily as that. But Agrippa agreed with Festus that Paul could not reasonably be convicted on any of the serious charges brought against him. Indeed, said the king, Paul might have been discharged on the spot had he not appealed to Caesar, but for Festus to prejudge the issue now by releasing him would have been impolitic, if not *ultra vires*. But Agrippa presumably gave Festus the help he required in drafting the *litterae dimissoriae*.

Paul did not appeal to Caesar while Felix was in office, presumably because Felix had virtually decided on his innocence and was simply postponing his formal acquittal and release. One day, Felix's procrastination would come to an end and Paul would be discharged and be able to carry out his long-cherished plan of travelling to Rome and the west. So Paul might have hoped. But with the recall of Felix and his supersession by Festus a new and dangerous situation was developing for Paul; hence his momentous decision.

From what we know of Paul, we may be sure that the uppermost consideration in his appeal to Caesar was not his own safety, but

37. Josephus, *BJ* ii. 220, 223, 247, 252; *Ant*. xv. 407; xviii. 132, 194, 354; xix. 360, 362; xx. 9–12, 104, 138, 159; *Life* 38.

the interests of the gospel. Seven or eight years previously he had experienced the benevolent neutrality of Roman law in the decision of Gallio, proconsul of Achaia, that there was nothing illegal in his preaching.[38] He might reasonably expect a similarly favourable verdict from the supreme court in Rome. Not only so: even a man of smaller intelligence than Paul must have realized that the consideration which moved Gallio would not be valid much longer. Gallio had ruled in effect that what Paul preached was a variety of Judaism, and therefore not forbidden by Roman law. But, thanks in large measure to Paul's own activity, it would soon be impossible to regard Christianity as a variety of Judaism, since it was now manifestly more Gentile than Jewish. A favourable hearing from the emperor in Rome might win recognition for Christianity, if not as the true fulfilment of Israel's ancestral religion (which Paul believed it to be), at least as a permitted association (*collegium licitum*) in its own right.[39] Besides, if Caesar in person heard Paul's defence, what might the outcome not be? [40] The younger Agrippa had politely declined to admit the logic of Paul's argument, but Gentiles had regularly shown themselves more amenable to the gospel than Jews, and a Roman emperor might be more easily won than a Jewish client-king. It would be precarious to set limits to Paul's high hopes, however impracticable they may appear to us in retrospect.

But would Caesar hear the case in person? This would not follow from the fact that it was to Caesar that Paul appealed. According to Tacitus, Nero announced at the beginning of his principate that he would not judge cases *in propria persona*, as his predecessor Claudius had done; and indeed, during his first eight years he generally delegated them to others.[41] A. N. Sherwin-White is thus right in saying: "If Paul came to trial some time after the period of two years mentioned in Acts 28: 30, it is probable that his case was heard by someone other than the Princeps." [42] This "someone other" might be the *praefectus praetorio*, "representing the Emperor

---

38. Acts 18: 12 ff.; see pp. 253 ff.

39. Or rather, as a series of local *collegia licita*. The frequently used phrase *religio licita* does not appear to have been a technical term of Roman law; it was used by Tertullian (*Apology* 21. 1) to describe the status of Judaism in the Roman Empire. On *collegia licita* as the approved term (*Digest* xlvii. 42) see E. Schürer *HJP* II. ii, p. 260; S. Safrai and M. Stern (ed.), *The Jewish People in the First Century*, i, p. 460. On attempts by later apologists to win such recognition for Christianity see S. L. Guterman, *Religious Toleration and Persecution in Ancient Rome* (London, 1951), p. 12.

40. Does this consideration lie behind the request for prayer that Paul may be enabled "boldly to proclaim the mystery of the gospel" (Ephesians 6: 19 f.)?

41. Tacitus, *Annals* xiii. 4. 2. It was evidently a new departure for Nero when in A.D. 62 he personally judged the case of Fabricius Veiento (Tacitus, *Annals* xiv. 50. 2).

42. *Roman Society and Roman Law in the New Testament*, p. 112.

in his capacity as the fountain of justice, together with the assessors and high officers of the court".[43] But this is a matter on which we have no information.

---

43. W. M. Ramsay, *St. Paul the Traveller and the Roman Citizen* (London,[14] 1920), p. 357. On the death of Afranius Burrus in A.D. 62, he was succeeded by Ofonius Tigellinus and Faenius Rufus as joint-prefects for the next three years, Tigellinus being the more powerful of the two. If Paul did indeed have his appeal heard by one of the prefects of the praetorian guard, it would make a substantial difference whether it was the relatively honest Burrus or the despicable Tigellinus.

# CHAPTER 32

# "And So We Came to Rome"

## 1. Embarkation for Italy

SINCE PAUL WAS A PRISONER, HE HAD TO BE SENT TO ROME UNDER guard. When a suitable opportunity came along, he was put in charge (together with some other prisoners) of "a centurion of the Augustan Cohort,[1] named Julius" (Acts 27: 1). The centurion had a number of soldiers under his command to assist him in the discharge of his duties.

Theodor Mommsen, followed by W. M. Ramsay, inferred from these words that Julius was a member of the corps of *frumentarii* – a corps of centurions who served as liaison officers between Rome and the armies in the imperial provinces, and who might well undertake as an additional duty the escorting of prisoners from the provinces to Rome.[2] There is, however, no evidence that the *frumentarii* acted as liaison officers or imperial police before the principate of Hadrian (A.D. 117–138);[3] their original duty, as their name implies, was the organization of the transport of grain (*frumentum*) to Rome.

The transport of grain from Egypt, the chief granary of Rome, was of the highest importance: the shipping fleet devoted to it was organized for the service of the Roman state "as early as the Ptolemaic period."[4] It was indeed in a vessel belonging to this service that the greatest part of Paul's voyage to Rome was completed. The ship in which Paul and the others embarked at Caesarea was bound in the opposite direction to that by which he and his companions had come to Palestine two years before; it was making in the first instance for the south-west coast of Asia Minor, but had to sail east and north of Cyprus, under the lee of the island, the prevailing wind being west or north-west. The ship put in at

---

1. "Augustan" (*Augusta*) was "a title of honour very frequently bestowed upon auxiliary troops" (*HJP*, new E.T., i [Edinburgh, 1973], p. 364 f.).
2. T. Mommsen, *Gesammelte Schriften*, vi = *Historische Schriften*, iii (Berlin, 1910), pp. 546 ff.; W. M. Ramsay, *St. Paul the Traveller and the Roman Citizen* (London, ¹⁴1920), pp. 315, 348.
3. Cf. A. N. Sherwin-White, *Roman Society and Roman Law in the New Testament* (Oxford, 1963), p. 109.
4. M. Rostovtzeff, *The Social and Economic History of the Roman Empire* (Oxford, 1926), p. 595.

Myra, a port some miles east of Patara; it was then to sail north along the west coast of Asia Minor until it reached Adramyttium, on the mainland opposite Lesbos, which was its home port. At Myra, however, the centurion transferred his charges to a vessel of the Alexandrian grain-fleet, bound for Italy, with a considerable number of passengers on board.[5] With a steady wind from the west, the best route from Alexandria to Italy was by Myra, which was in fact one of the chief ports serving the grain-fleet. The sequel shows that the centurion exercised considerable authority on board this vessel; he may well have been a *frumentarius* in the earlier sense of the term.

The description of the voyage to Italy is a masterpiece of vivid narrative. Martin Dibelius, drawing special attention to the literary and stylistic features of the narrative, pointed to the defects in "the older school of criticism, which thinks only of the event and not of the account".[6] Equally defective would be an approach which thought only of the account and not of the event. True, the classical student will readily discern in this narrative a well-established literary form which can be traced back to Homer's *Odyssey*, and the Old Testament student will trace some affinities with Jonah's Mediterranean voyage.[7] But attention must also be paid to the detailed contents of the narrative, which has been described (and justly so) as "one of the most instructive documents for the knowledge of ancient seamanship".[8]

Paul was accompanied on the voyage by his friends Luke and Aristarchus. Luke's personal participation has given us an account of the voyage in the first person plural. Perhaps he signed on as ship's doctor. Aristarchus may have been entered on the passenger

5. Two hundred and seventy-six (passengers and crew together), according to the majority reading of Acts 27: 37; "about seventy-six", according to Codex B and the Sahidic version. The larger number is the more probable on textual grounds; Josephus set sail for Rome in A.D. 63 in a ship which had 600 on board (*Life*, 13 ff.).

6. M. Dibelius, *Studies in the Acts of the Apostles*, E.T. (London, 1956), p. 107. For a critique of a much more radical assessment of the voyage-narrative than Dibelius's see R. P. C. Hanson, "The Journey of Paul and the Journey of Nikias: An Experiment in Comparative Historiography", *Studia Evangelica* iv = *Texte und Untersuchungen* 102 (Berlin, 1968), pp. 315–318.

7. There is a notable Homeric echo in the language about running the vessel aground in Acts 27: 41, including the use of the classical but obsolete word ναῦς. The jettisoning of the cargo, etc., in Acts 27: 18 f. is described in language reflecting the LXX version of Jonah 1: 5. The narrative contains several other literary reminiscences.

8. H. J. Holtzmann, *Handcommentar zum Neuen Testament* (Freiburg-im-Breisgau, 1889), p. 421; see also A. Breusing, *Die Nautik der Alten* (Bremen, 1886). Another informative document from antiquity is Lucian's dialogue *The Ship*, which describes a voyage made by a vessel of the Alexandrian grain-fleet which set out for Italy but was forced by stormy weather to put in at Sidon and then at Piraeus.

list as Paul's servant, or he may even have shared his status as a prisoner under guard: we do not know.

Paul's genius for friendship manifested itself at an early stage in the voyage. He so won the confidence of the centurion that by the time the ship on which they had embarked at Caesarea put in at Sidon he was allowed to go ashore on parole and visit his friends. Not only is Luke's account of the voyage instructive in the matter of ancient seamanship; it is valuable also for its depicting of Paul's personality in those trying circumstances which are apt to bring out a man's real quality.

## 2. Storm at sea

From Myra the going was slow and difficult, because of the strong north-west wind that was blowing. The ship did not put into port at Cnidus (on the Carian promontory of Triopium), which they reached several days after setting out from Myra, but ran for the eastern extremity of Crete (Cape Salmone) and sailed under the lee of that island (along its south coast). The first convenient shelter after rounding Cape Salmone was Fair Havens (*Kaloi Limenes*), where they put in and waited for the wind to change. Two leagues farther west lies Cape Matala, beyond which the south coast of Crete trends suddenly to the north and would provide no more protection against a north-west wind.[9]

While they waited, they held a ship's council, in which Paul – perhaps because he was an experienced traveller – was invited to participate. The safe season for Mediterranean navigation was now at an end: Luke mentions that "the fast" – that is, the Jewish day of atonement – "had already gone by" (Acts 27: 9). In A.D. 59 the Day of Atonement fell on October 5, and the dangerous season for sailing had set in three weeks before.[10] It was plain therefore that they could not complete the voyage to Italy before winter; the question was therefore debated where they should stay until winter was past. Paul strongly urged them to stay where they were in Fair Havens; there was a neighbouring town, Lasea,[11] where accommodation might be available for the ship's company. He foresaw danger and disaster if they sailed farther.

The pilot and shipowner, however, thought that they should

9. Cf. J. Smith, *The Voyage and Shipwreck of St. Paul* (London, [4] 1880), pp. 75 f. This work remains of unsurpassed value for its stage-by-stage annotation of the narrative of the voyage.

10. Cf. Vegetius, *De re militari*, iv. 39 (the dangerous season for navigation lasted from September 14 to November 11; after that, all navigation on the open sea ceased for the winter).

11. Variously spelt; cf. the forms Lasos and Alos in Pliny, *Nat. Hist.* iv. 12. It has been identified with a ruined site to the east of Fair Havens; cf. T. A. B. Spratt, *Travels and Researches in Crete*, ii (London, 1865), pp. 7 f.

make for the more commodious and better protected harbour of Phoenix (modern Phineka),[12] some 36 miles (60 kilometres) west of Cape Matala. The centurion took their advice, and his vote seems to have been the decisive one. Soon after this decision was taken, the wind changed, and it appeared as if they might gain the winter quarters they had in mind. But they had scarcely rounded Cape Matala when the wind changed again: a typhonic north-easter, known to sailors as Euraquilo, rushed down upon them from Mount Ida and drove them out to sea.[13] They soon ran under the lee of the small island of Cauda (Gavdos), some 23 miles to the south-west, and made speedy and timely use of the brief spell of shelter thus afforded – hauling the dinghy on board (it was normally towed astern), undergirding the ship and letting down the drift-anchor.[14] There was great danger that, if Euraquilo continued blowing with gale force, it would drive them into the Greater Syrtis, the quicksands west of Cyrene. But with the drift-anchor dragging astern and the storm-sail set on the foremast, it was possible for the ship to be laid-to on the starboard tack (with her right side to the wind) and drift slowly, at a rate of about one and a half knots, in a general direction of eight degrees north of west. All the movable baggage and spare gear were thrown overboard, followed after a day or two by the mainyard. At a later stage the wheat cargo itself had to be jettisoned.

The storm raged for many days on end, blotting out the sky, so that they had neither sun by day nor stars by night to guide them. It was thus impossible to fix an accurate course, or even to reckon the passage of time with any precision. The ship was no doubt leaking badly, and they "could not tell which way to make for the nearest land, in order to run their ship ashore, the only resource for a sinking ship; but unless they did make the land, they must founder at sea."[15] Hunger and thirst were fast reducing their stamina; they had but little appetite in this desperate plight, quite apart from the difficulty of preparing food and the possibility that what food they had was spoiled or lost. Sooner rather than later, it seemed, the ship was bound to go down with all on board.

There is no implication in Luke's narrative that Paul did not share the general pessimism of the rest on board who abandoned all

12. This identification, formerly much disputed, may now be taken as established; cf. R. M. Ogilvie, "Phoenix", *JTS*, n.s. 9 (1958), pp. 308 ff.

13. Cf. C. J. Hemer, "Euraquilo and Melita", *JTS*, n. s. 26 (1975), pp. 100 ff. The word is a hybrid, from Greek εὖρος , "east wind" (or south of east), and Latin *aquilo*, "north wind"; the wind is familiar today as the *gregale*.

14. Cf. E. Haenchen, *The Acts of the Apostles*, E.T. (Oxford, 1971), pp. 703 f., following J. Renié, "Summisso vase (Acts 27, 17)", *Recherches de Science Religieuse* 35 (1948), pp. 272 ff.

15. J. Smith, *Voyage*, p. 117.

hope of survival. He had faced death before and was inwardly prepared for it: his ambition, as he put it on another occasion, was "that with full courage now as always Christ will be honoured in my body, whether by life or by death" (Philippians 1: 20). This was more important even than bearing witness in Rome, which indeed he had been divinely assured early in his Jerusalem imprisonment he would yet do. It was he who had uttered the warning at Fair Havens that the result of proceeding with the voyage would be "much loss, not only of the cargo and the ship, but also of our lives" (Acts 27: 10). That was the voice of practical common sense, not of special revelation. But after ten or twelve days of drifting he experienced a night-vision in which it was revealed to him not only that he himself would survive to bear his witness before Caesar but that for his sake the lives of all his shipmates would be spared. (It is doubtful if Luke intended a contrast with Jonah, whose presence on board endangered the lives of all *his* shipmates.)

The fresh confidence with which he himself was thus inspired he endeavoured to impart to the others. This ship would be lost, he told them, but they themselves would be saved, "though we have to be cast ashore on some island"[16] (Acts 27: 26). Sure enough, during the fourteenth night after they left Fair Havens the sound of breakers off a rocky coast gave warning of approaching land, and successive soundings confirmed this. The sailors therefore dropped four anchors from the stern to serve as a brake until daylight showed them where they were. In the morning they slipped anchor and ran the ship into a creek with a sandy beach. What they could not know was that in the creek the ship "would strike a bottom of mud graduating into tenacious clay, into which the fore part would fix itself and be held fast, whilst the stern was exposed to the force of the waves".[17] After the strains and stresses to which the hull had been exposed it could not survive this fresh battering for long, and soon began to break up. The centurion issued a *sauve qui peut* order, and all reached land in safety.

### 3. Winter in Malta

Only when they landed did they find out where they were – on Malta. The name of the island was originally given by Phoenician sailors, in whose language *meliṭa* meant "refuge", and as that word occurs in Hebrew with the same meaning, Paul at any rate would recognize how apt the name was.[18]

As Luke has given a vivid portrayal of Paul's helpfulness on board the storm-tossed ship – keeping his head when all about him

16. Which island is not said, but if they had no hope of a landfall on Sicily, Malta was the next best hope (though Paul would not have known this).

17. J. Smith, *Voyage*, p. 144.

were losing theirs, sharing with his shipmates his divinely-imparted assurance that no life would be lost, urging them to eat something in view of the exertions which they would have to make in getting ashore from the wreck — so after the landing he pictures him as a practical man, co-operating with others in necessary work. The hospitable islanders light a fire to enable the ship's company to warm and dry themselves; Paul knows (unlike many theologians) that a fire will not continue to burn unless it is fed with fuel, and he joins in gathering sticks to keep it going. When one of the "sticks" turns out to be a snake, torpid through cold, which turns and fastens on his wrist when the heat thaws it,[19] the Maltese conclude that he has committed some crime against heaven, and that Nemesis, having failed to drown him, has caught up with him by means of the snake.[20] When Paul shakes off the snake and has plainly taken no harm, they change their minds and conclude that he is a god in disguise.

Paul was neither a god nor a superman, but his presence was a blessing to many of the islanders during the winter. He was still a prisoner, of course, but there was little danger that he or the other prisoners would escape from Malta before the next navigation season set in. He cured the father of Publius, the "first man" of Malta,[21] who was suffering from fever and dysentery, and many other Maltese who had ailments of various kinds came to him and Luke for treatment, so that, by the time they were ready to sail to Italy, they were loaded with gifts from their grateful patients.[22]

18. The identity of the Melita of Acts 28: 1 with Malta has been challenged most recently by A. Acworth, "Where was St. Paul shipwrecked? A Re-examination of the Evidence", *JTS*, n. s. 24 (1973), pp. 190 ff. He identifies it with Mljet, off the Yugoslav coast near Dubrovnik, taking "the sea of Adria" (Acts 27: 27) to be the Adriatic Sea. There is ample evidence that the central Mediterranean was then known as the sea of Adria (Hadria): Strabo, for example, says that "the Ionian Sea is part of what is now called the Sea of Hadria" (*Geography* ii. 5. 20) and Josephus's ship, bound for Rome in A.D. 63, foundered in the midst of the sea of Adria and he was picked up by a ship of Cyrene bound for Italy (*Life*, 15). C. J. Hemer has given Acworth's argument what appears to be a conclusive answer in his article "Euraquilo and Melita", *JTS*, n. s. 26 (1975), pp. 100 ff.

19. There are no venomous snakes in Malta today. Luke calls the snake a viper ( ἔχιδνα ); whether there were vipers there in the first century cannot be determined. W. M. Ramsay suggested that the snake was the non-poisonous *Coronella austriaca*, which resembles a viper (*Luke the Physician and Other Studies* [London, 1908], pp. 63 ff.).

20. The *Palatine Anthology* (vii. 290) contains an epitaph on a man who, having escaped a storm at sea, was overtaken by Nemesis in exactly this way on the coast of Libya.

21. The title "first man of the Maltese" is inscriptionally attested both in Greek (*CIG* 5754; cf. Addenda, p. 1251) and in Latin (*CIL* x. 7495).

22. A. von Harnack pointed out that "the whole story of the abode of the narrator in Malta is displayed in a medical light" (*Luke the Physician*, E.T. [London, 1907], p. 179).

### 4. Rome at last!

The voyage to Italy was completed at the beginning of spring in another ship of the Alexandrian state service, which had wintered in Malta. It put in at Syracuse and Rhegium and then set its passengers ashore at Puteoli (modern Pozzuoli), in the Bay of Naples. There was a Christian group there, with whom Paul was allowed to stay for seven days – presumably because Julius had business which detained him in the area for that length of time. Puteoli was the chief port of arrival in Italy of merchant shipping from the eastern Mediterranean. If Julius was a *frumentarius* in the original sense, he could well have had to deal with the landing and storage of the ship's cargo. (In addition to the Christian group in Puteoli, there had been a Jewish community there for the best part of a century.) [23]

The remainder of the journey to Rome was completed by road; from Capua northward they travelled along the Via Appia. But news of Paul's arrival in Italy had reached Rome already – no doubt the Christians in Puteoli had sent the message – and he and his friends were still thirty or forty miles distant from the capital [24] when they were met by Roman Christians who had walked out to greet them and escort them for the remainder of their journey. Their presence and welcome brought great encouragement to Paul. "And so", says Luke, "we came to Rome" (Acts 28: 15).

In Rome, according to the Western text of Acts 28: 16, the prisoners (including Paul) were handed over to an official called the *stratopedarchos*, the "camp-commandant". One witness to the Old Latin version of Acts [25] (which is based on the Western text) translates this title by *princeps peregrinorum*. The existence of an official so designated is attested by an African inscription of Trajan's time; [26] he was evidently commandant of the *castra peregrinorum* on the Caelian hill [27] – the headquarters of legionary officers on furlough in Rome (and also, from the second century, of *frumentarii* in their later rôle as liaison officers). But the rendering *princeps peregrinorum* may be no more than an intelligent guess; the *stratopedarchos* could have been the commandant of some other camp – the *castra praetoria*, for example, the headquarters of the praetorian

23. Cf. Josephus *BJ* ii. 104; *Ant.* xvii. 328.

24. At Appii Forum, about 43 miles (72 km) south of Rome on the Via Appia, and at Tres Tabernae, another halting stage ten miles farther north along the road. Cicero (*Ad Atticum* ii. 10) mentions them both together.

25. The thirteenth-century Codex *gigas*.

26. *Comptes-rendus de l'Académie des Inscriptions et Belles-Lettres* (Paris, 1923), p. 197, quoted by T. R. S. Broughton in *The Beginnings of Christianity*, ed. F. J. F. Jackson and K. Lake, i. 5 (London, 1933), p. 444, n. 3.

27. Mommsen and Ramsay thought the reference in Acts 28: 16 was to this official (see p. 368, n. 2).

guard near the Viminal Gate, at the north-east corner of the city. The praetorian camp-commandant (*princeps castrorum*) would have been a much less exalted person than the prefect of the praetorian guard (*praefectus praetorio*), who was a very powerful officer of state.[28] In any case, the longer Western reading of Acts 28: 16, which mentions the *stratopedarchos*, cannot certainly be accepted as part of the original text, but all forms of the text agree that Paul "was permitted to stay by himself with the soldier who guarded him". According to the last sentence in Luke's record, he stayed thus for two full years "at his own expense" or "in his own hired dwelling" (the Greek phrase may be translated either way). That is to say, he remained under house-arrest, guarded by a soldier, instead of being detained in the praetorian headquarters or any other "camp".[29] He was thus able to receive visitors from near and far and discharge his apostolic ministry, even in this restricted situation, without let or hindrance.

Among the visitors whom he received at an early stage of his detention Luke mentions a deputation of leading Roman Jews. Their debate with Paul forms the final word-picture of Luke's narrative, plainly with programmatic intent. They manifested prudent reserve in disclaiming any previous knowledge of Paul: they had received no communication from Judaea to his discredit, they assured him. They manifested the same prudent reserve in disclaiming any first-hand acquaintance with Christianity: "we desire to hear from you what your views are", they said; "for with regard to this sect we know that everywhere it is spoken against" (Acts 28: 22). The debate completes the pattern of Jewish refusal of the gospel coupled with Gentile acceptance of it, which has recurred earlier in Acts. Paul speaks the definitive last word, after quoting the text from Isaiah 6: 10 about dull minds, deaf ears and closed eyes (a widespread early Christian *testimonium* of Jewish unbelief):[30] "Take knowledge, then, that this salvation of God has been sent to the Gentiles; *they* will listen to it" (Acts 28: 28).

## 5. *Unanswered questions*

Luke's perspective on Paul's apostleship and Gentile mission is

28. Sejanus had occupied the post for the greater part of the principate of Tiberius; it was under him that the nine praetorian cohorts were concentrated in Rome (Tacitus, *Annals* iv. 2). There were usually two collegiate prefects, but Sejanus and (under Nero) Burrus held the office alone. In Pliny, *Epistles* x 57, Trajan directs Pliny (when legate of Bithynia) to send a prisoner in chains to the prefects of the praetorian guard.

29. The Western text of Acts 28: 16 adds expressly that Paul was allowed to live "outside the camp" (but there may be a theological nuance here, derived from the LXX of Exodus 33: 7 or Leviticus 16: 27; cf. Hebrews 13: 11).

30. Cf. Mark 4: 11 f.; John 12: 40. See p. 335.

different from Paul's own. But the depth of our ignorance about the sequel to Paul's arrival in Rome when Luke takes his leave of us is ample testimony to the value of his record for the period that it covers. What, for example, were Paul's relations with the Christians of Rome during his two years' house-arrest? Since they began so happily on the Appian Way, how did they continue? And what happened at the end of this period?

Some assure us quite confidently that it ended with Paul's trial, conviction and execution; others, that it ended with his release – either through acquittal after trial, or because the case went against his accusers by default.

That Paul was executed at the end of the two years was contended over sixty years ago by J. Vernon Bartlet.[31] He argued that the prosecutors gave notice within the statutory time-limit (which he supposed, in the light of later usage, was eighteen months) of their intention to proceed with the case; that they arrived in Rome early in A.D. 62 and successfully prosecuted Paul; that he was condemned to death as a disturber of the peace of the provinces; that the earliest readers of Acts would know from Nero's record, without having to be told explicitly, what the outcome of the prosecution would be (the more so in view of the Jewish sympathies of Poppaea Sabina, whose influence over Nero was then approaching its peak); and that in fact there are ominous overtones in Agrippa's remark to Festus: "He might have been released if he had not appealed to Caesar" (Acts 26: 32).

If Paul was executed in A.D. 62, then his martyrdom was not, as is commonly supposed, an incident in the imperial attack on the Christians of Rome which followed the great fire of the year 64. This, of course, is no argument against dating his execution in 62, if the evidence points in that direction. But if Paul's two years' detention was followed immediately by his conviction and execution, Luke's failure to mention it is very strange.

Alternatively we have the view variously propounded by W. M. Ramsay, Kirsopp Lake, and H. J. Cadbury, that the case never came to trial because the prosecutors failed to appear within the statutory period.[32] This suggestion has some antecedent plausibility. If the Sanhedrin had failed to persuade Felix and

31. J. V. Bartlet, "Two New Testament Problems: 1. St. Paul's Fate at Rome", *Expositor*, series 8, 5 (1913), pp. 464 ff.

32. Cf. W. M. Ramsay, "The Imprisonment and Supposed Trial of St. Paul in Rome", *Expositor*, series 8, 5 (1913), pp. 264 ff., reprinted in *The Teaching of Paul in Terms of the Present Day* (London, 1913), pp. 346 ff. (the article to which Bartlet's article mentioned in the immediately preceding footnote was a reply); K. Lake, "What was the End of St. Paul's Trial?" *Interpreter* 5 (1908–9), pp. 147 ff.; H. J. Cadbury, "Roman Law and the Trial of Paul", *Beginnings of Christianity* i. 5, pp. 297 ff., especially pp. 326 ff.

Festus of the soundness of their case against Paul, in spite of all the local pressure that could be brought to bear on the procurator of Judaea, they would be even less likely to succeed in Rome. Roman law was apt to be severe on frivolous prosecutors. On the other hand, no prosecution would be so frivolous as one in which the prosecutors failed to appear; and Roman law insisted that they must appear.

The statutory period of eighteen months, which was assumed by Bartlet on his side (provisionally) and by Ramsay and Cadbury on theirs, turns out on examination to be based on the wrong dating of a papyrus which records an imperial edict fixing a time-limit of eighteen months for ciminal cases submitted to the emperor from the provinces, whether by way of appeal or by reference as to a court of first instance. This document was first published towards the end of last century; Ramsay's attention was drawn to it by J. S. Reid. But, as Mommsen recognized, the edict belongs to the third century,[33] and the "appeal" which it has in view is the later procedure of *appellatio* against a sentence already passed, not the first-century procedure of *prouocatio*, which prevented the court of first instance from trying the case at all.[34] In fact, there does not appear to be first-century evidence for any procedure permitting a case to lapse automatically by default. What evidence there is suggests that everything was done to compel the appearance of prosecutors and defendants and to prevent the abandonment of charges. A prosecutor who did not appear in court within a reasonable time would probably be penalized, but that would not imply the automatic discharge of the defendant.

The prolongation of Paul's stay in Rome over two full years could have been due to congestion of court business as much as anything else; and if indeed he was discharged without his coming to trial, this (as A. N. Sherwin-White points out) would probably have been the result of an act of *imperium* on Caesar's part. "Perhaps Paul benefited from the clemency of Nero, and secured a merely casual release. But there is no necessity to construe Acts to mean that he was released at all."[35] From the account of Paul's

33. T. Mommsen, *Römisches Strafrecht* (Leipzig, 1899), pp. 469, n. 1, 472, n. 5, 473, n. 1. The document (*BGU* ii. 628 recto) is reproduced by Cadbury, *Beginnings of Christianity* i, 5. pp. 333 f., and by H. Conzelmann, *Die Apostelgeschichte* (Tübingen, 1963), pp. 157 f. Bartlet recognized its third-century date; he refers to "eighteen months, which to judge from the third century usage was the limit for capital charges sent on appeal from the provinces" (*Expositor*, series 8, 5, pp. 466 f.).
34. The distinction is made plain by A. H. M. Jones, *Studies in Roman Government and Law* (Oxford, 1960), p. 57.
35. A. N. Sherwin-White, *Roman Society and Roman Law in the New Testament*, p. 109.

night vision at sea, in which he was assured that he would stand
before Caesar,[36] Luke probably intends his readers to infer that
Paul's appeal did at length come up for hearing, whatever the outcome was.

Since the evidence of Acts fails us here, we must look elsewhere in
our quest for further data relating to Paul's Roman captivity and its
aftermath.

36. Acts 27: 23 f.

# CHAPTER 33

# Paul and Roman Christianity

## 1. Jews and Christians in Rome

"THE ROMANS HAD EMBRACED THE FAITH OF CHRIST, ALBEIT according to the Jewish rite, although they saw no sign of mighty works nor any of the apostles." [1] So wrote the anonymous fourth-century Latin commentator on Paul, whom by tradition and for convenience we call Ambrosiaster, in the preface to his exposition of the Epistle to the Romans. By his time [2] the Romans as a whole had "embraced the faith of Christ", but when the faith of Christ was first embraced in Rome those who professed it formed a tiny minority of the city's population. Even so, the preface as a whole suggests that Ambrosiaster had access to a reliable tradition about the origin of Roman Christianity and more particularly about the Jewish milieu in which it arose. The tradition of the Roman church claims the apostles Peter and Paul as joint-founders,[3] but the scanty evidence that we have confirms Ambrosiaster's testimony that Christianity came to Rome before any apostle was seen in the city.

The beginnings of the Jewish community in Rome should probably be dated not long after the establishment of diplomatic relations between Rome and the Hasmonaean regime in Judaea about the middle of the second century B.C.[4] Its numbers were greatly augmented after the incorporation of Judaea in the Roman Empire in 63 B.C. and Pompey's triumph two years later. When Cicero, in 59 B.C., was defending Lucius Valerius Flaccus in Rome against the charge of having hindered the conveyance of the temple-tax to Jerusalem during his proconsulship of Asia, he lowered his voice dramatically at one point so as not to be overheard by the Jews outside the court-room, "for you know", he explained confidentially to the jury, "how numerous they are and

---

1. Edited by H. J. Vogels in *CSEL* lxxxi. 1 (Vienna, 1966), p. 6.
2. He wrote during the Roman episcopate of Damasus (A.D. 366–384); cf. A. Souter, *The Earliest Latin Commentaries on the Epistles of St. Paul* (Oxford, 1927), pp. 42 f.
3. Cf. Irenaeus, *Against Heresies* iii. 3. 1; Gaius of Rome as quoted by Eusebius, *Hist. Eccl.* ii. 25. 7; Dionysius of Corinth as quoted by Eusebius, *Hist. Eccl.* ii. 25. 8.
4. Cf. 1 Maccabees 8: 17 ff.; 12: 1 ff.; 14: 16 ff., 40.

how clannish, and how they can make their influence felt".[5] This
was rhetorical exaggeration, but it exaggerated a situation with
which his hearers were acquainted. By the beginning of the Christian era, it is estimated, the Jews of Rome numbered between
40,000 and 60,000.[6]

Our knowledge of the Jews of Rome is derived not only from contemporary literary sources but also from the study of six Jewish
catacombs, three of which – one on the Via Portuensis (the
Monteverde catacomb), one on the Via Appia, and one on the Via
Nomentana – have supplied specially valuable information.[7] No
Jewish synagogue from the imperial period has yet been excavated
in Rome, but the names of eleven are known from inscriptions.[8]
Apart from the synagogue of the Olive Tree, which has already
been mentioned,[9] some took their names from the districts where
they were situated (like the synagogues of the Campenses and
Suburrenses),[10] from the places from which their members
originally came (like that of the Tripolitani),[11] or from patrons (like
those of the Augustenses and Agrippenses).[12] The synagogue of the
Hebrews, in Rome as in Corinth,[13] may have been so called
because the services were conducted in Hebrew.

A public scandal within the Jewish community in A.D. 19
brought about its expulsion from Rome by decree of the Emperor
Tiberius.[14] Four Jews persuaded a wealthy Roman proselyte,
Fulvia by name, to make a munificent gift to the Jerusalem temple
but they misappropriated it. This was the kind of scandal that Paul
had in mind when he said that the name of the God of Israel was
blasphemed among the pagans because of his worshippers'
behaviour.[15] But in a few years the Jews of Rome were as numerous
as ever.

    5. Cicero, *Pro Flacco* 66. See p. 296.
    6. Cf. H. J. Leon, *The Jews of Ancient Rome* (Philadelphia, 1960), pp. 135 f. (see
p. 30 above).
    7. Cf. H. J. Leon, *The Jews of Ancient Rome*, pp. 46 ff.
    8. Cf. H. J. Leon, *The Jews of Ancient Rome*, pp. 135 ff. A fourth-century syn-
agogue was excavated at Ostia in 1963; it had been erected on the site of a late
first-century synagogue. Cf. M. F. Squarciapino, "The Synagogue at Ostia",
*Archaeology* 16 (1963), pp. 194 ff.
    9. See p. 334.
    10. From the Campus Martius (on the left bank of the Tiber) and the Suburra
(a heavily populated district between the Quirinal and Viminal hills).
    11. Either from Tripolis in North Africa or from Tripolis in Phoenicia.
    12. The synagogue of the Augustenses was presumably named in honour of the
emperor; that of the Agrippenses either after his minister and son-in-law M. Vip-
sanius Agrippa (63–12 B.C.) or after the elder Herod Agrippa (10 B.C.–A.D. 44).
    13. See p. 250.
    14. Cf. Josephus, *Ant.* xviii. 81–84; cf. Tacitus, *Annals* ii. 85. 5; Suetonius, *Life of
Tiberius* 36. Four thousand Jews were sent to Sardinia to take part in the military
suppression of brigandage in that island. See p. 328.
    15. Romans 2: 24.

Claudius, at the beginning of his principate, found the imperial peace troubled by disturbances in Jewish communities here and there throughout the empire – pre-eminently in Egypt but also, it appears, in Rome. He tried to deal with the troubles in Rome by placing restrictions on Jewish communal activities [16] but eight years later [17] took the drastic step of expelling the Jews from Rome – an expulsion which had repercussions, as we have seen, on Paul's missionary activity at the time in Macedonia and Achaia, especially in his forming a lifelong friendship with two of the refugees, Priscilla and Aquila. [18]

According to Suetonius, writing seventy years after the event, the reason for this expulsion was the persistent rioting in which the Roman Jews were involved "at the instigation of Chrestus" (*impulsore Chresto*). [19]

This is usually (and probably rightly) interpreted as the earliest indication we have of the arrival of Christianity in Rome. It is not a certain interpretation: Chrestus was a common enough slave-name. But if the reference were to an otherwise unknown Chrestus, Suetonius would probably have said *impulsore Chresto quodam* ("at the instigation of one Chrestus"). The form of words he uses points to a well-known bearer of the name, and the common confusion between *Christus* and *Chrestus* (which by this time were homophones in Greek) makes it easy to suppose that Christ is meant. We cannot readily think that "Christ" is here used in the sense of "Messiah", as though the reference were to some kind of messianic dispute in the Jewish community, with no necessary involvement of Jesus of Nazareth: *Christus* (or *Chrestus*) was not current in Latin paganism in that sense. This in itself would rule out Robert Eisler's fantasy that Simon Magus is meant, [20] quite apart from the absence of evidence that Simon made messianic claims. It is most likely that Suetonius had in mind the well-known *Christus* (or *Chrestus*) – well-known, that is, as the founder of the *Christiani* (or *Chrestiani*). [21] True, the natural implication of his words is that this man was actually in Rome during the principate of Claudius, stirring up dis-

---

16. Dio Cassius, *History* lx. 6: "he forbade them to meet together in accordance with their ancestral way of life".

17. The date indicated by Orosius (*History* vii. 6. 15 f.), A.D. 49, is probably accurate enough, although Orosius confuses the issue by referring to a non-existent account of Josephus.

18. See pp. 235, 250.

19. Suetonius, *Life of Claudius* 25. 4.

20. Cf. R. Eisler, *Iesous basileus ou basileusas*, ii (Heidelberg, 1930), p. 706; *The Messiah Jesus and John the Baptist* (London, 1931), p. 581.

21. He mentions them in his *Life of Nero* (16. 2) as men addicted to "a novel and mischievous superstition", on whom exemplary punishment was inflicted. See p. 442.

orders within the Jewish community.[22] Perhaps Suetonius understood his source in this sense; he did not take as much trouble to verify his chronology as did his contemporary Tacitus, who knew that Christ was executed in the principate of Tiberius.[23] The disorders may have arisen in the Jewish community because of the recent arrival in its midst of disciples of Jesus.

One thing seems clear from other evidence – that Roman Christianity was originally Jewish, and Jewish of a nonconformist stamp. As late as the first quarter of the third century, Christian practice in Rome, to judge by the manual of church order (the so-called *Apostolic Tradition*) associated with the name of Hippolytus, was characterized by features derived from Jewish nonconformity;[24] hence Ambrosiaster's qualification of primitive Roman Christianity as being "according to the Jewish rite".

Who first brought Christianity to Rome is unknown. It has sometimes been thought that there is a special significance in Luke's including among those who listened to Peter's preaching in Jerusalem on the first Christian Pentecost "visitors from Rome, both Jews and proselytes" (Acts 2: 10); but nothing is said in that context which would help us to decide whether any of those believed his message or, if so, whether any of them took it back to Rome. In the normal course of travel, however, the gospel was bound to be carried to Rome sooner rather than later, and in the first instance by Jewish believers.

Another thing that seems clear is this: Priscilla and Aquila, who had left Italy because of Claudius's edict of expulsion shortly before they met Paul in Corinth,[25] appear to have been Christians already. Paul nowhere calls them his children in the Lord or implies in any way that they were converts of his.

It may be that the reminder to the recipients of the Epistle to the Hebrews of the "former days" when they were exposed to affliction and public abuse and "joyfully accepted" the plundering of their property (Hebrews 10: 32–34) is an allusion to events in Rome in A.D. 49.[26] But the Roman destination of this "epistle" is itself speculative (however reasonable)[27] and should not be treated as

22. Cf. R. Graves and J. Podro, *Jesus in Rome* (London, 1957), pp. 38 ff.
23. Tacitus, *Annals* xv. 44. 4.
24. See especially Hippolytus, *Apostolic Tradition* 20: 5, where the purificatory bath prescribed on Maundy Thursday for candidates for baptism on Easter Day presents affinities with nonconformist Judaism of the Essene variety; cf. R. J. Zwi Werblowsky, "On the Baptismal Rite according to St. Hippolytus", *Studia Patristica* iv = *Texte und Untersuchungen* 54 (1957), pp. 93 ff.; M. Black, *The Scrolls and Christian Origins* (London, 1961), pp. 91 ff.
25. Acts 18: 2; see pp. 250 f.
26. See F. F. Bruce, *The Epistle to the Hebrews* (Grand Rapids, 1964), pp. 267 ff.
27. Cf. A. von Harnack, "Probabilia über die Adresse und den Verfasser des Hebräerbriefs", *ZNW* 1 (1900), pp. 16 ff.

though it provided evidence on which to base further speculations.

If there were Gentile Christians in Rome before A.D. 49, they would not be affected by the emperor's edict, but we have no indication that there were any. Eight years later, however, the situation was quite different.

## 2. Gentile Christians in Rome

Too much weight should not be laid in this connexion on the interesting case of Pomponia Graecina, the wife of Aulus Plautius, conqueror of Britain. Tacitus reports that in A.D. 57 this lady was charged with "foreign superstition" and was brought, in accordance with Roman tradition, before a family court, over which her husband presided. She was acquitted of the charge.[28] Nothing in this report suggests that the "foreign superstition" was Christianity. One commentator on Tacitus remarks, with reference to the statement that she wore mourning for forty years, that "the retirement and sobriety of a Christian might well appear a kind of 'perpetual mourning' to the dissolute society of the Neronian period".[29] But Tacitus says quite explicitly that this mourning was due to the murder, fourteen years previously, of her kinswoman Livia Julia, at the instigation of the Empress Messalina.[30] If she wore mourning for forty years in all, she lived on into the principate of Domitian (A.D. 81–96).

A stronger reason for associating Pomponia with Christianity than Tacitus's report about the "foreign superstition" is the evidence that, by the end of the second century, some members of her family (the *gens Pomponia*) were Christians. The Cemetery of Callistus by the Appian Way, one of the oldest Christian catacombs in Rome, contains inscriptions of this period commemorating members of that family, one of whom bore the name Pomponius Graecinus.[31] But even from this we cannot infer with any assurance that Pomponia Graecina was a Christian four or five generations earlier.

For this same year (A.D. 57) we have, however, much more positive evidence for the state of Christianity in Rome, in Paul's letter to the Roman Christians. Paul makes it plain that Gentile as well as Jewish believers are included in "all God's beloved ones in Rome, saints by calling", to whom his letter is addressed (Romans 1: 7). Whether by this time they outnumbered their Jewish

28. Tacitus, *Annals* xiii. 32. 3–5.

29. H. Pitman (ed.), *Cornelii Taciti Annalium Libri XIII-XVI* (Oxford, 1904), Notes, pp. 29 f.

30. Cf. Dio Cassius, *History* lx. 18. 4.

31. Cf. H. Leclercq, "Aristocratiques (Classes)", in *DACL* i. 2 (Paris, 1907), columns 2847 f.

brethren in the city is uncertain, but Paul finds it necessary to warn them not to give themselves airs as though it were due to some superior merit of theirs that they were enrolled among the people of God when so many natural descendants of Abraham had declined to be so enrolled.[32]

### 3. The organization of Roman Christianity

Why does Paul address his letter "to all God's beloved ones in Rome, saints by calling" and not "to the church of God which is in Rome" (following the precedent, say, of his Corinthian letters)? We cannot infer forthwith that there was no church in Rome organized on a city-wide basis. The letter to the Philippians is addressed not to the church at Philippi but "to all the saints in Christ Jesus who are at Philippi, with the bishops and deacons" (Philippians 1: 1), but that does not preclude us from speaking of the church in Philippi. Indeed, the addition of the "bishops and deacons" implies a well-administered church, and when Paul, thanking the Philippian Christians for a gift, recalls a time when, as he says, "no church entered into partnership with me in giving and receiving except you only" (Philippians 4: 15), he makes it explicitly clear that he regarded them as a church. "The saints and faithful brethren in Christ at Colossae" to whom another Pauline letter is sent (Colossians 1: 2) are not expressly called a church,[33] but they were evidently as much one as the sister "church of the Laodiceans" (Colossians 4: 16), the more so as the Christian community at Colossae, like those in the other cities of the Lycus valley, appears to have been planted by one man, Paul's colleague Epaphras (Colossians 1: 7; 4: 12 f.).[34]

If it is doubtful whether there was one centrally administered church in Rome, this is not simply because the Christians there are not called a church, but rather because of the probabilities of the situation together with the evidence of Paul's letter. On the one hand, he expected that his letter would reach all the Roman Christians,[35] but it is unlikely that he thought of a single occasion when they would all hear it read together. Perhaps Phoebe carried it from one house-church to another.[36]

The Christians in Rome appear at this time to have met as

32. Romans 11: 12 ff. (see p. 334).
33. The Christian community in Colossae included smaller groups ("churches") meeting in the houses of Nympha (Col. 4: 15) and Philemon (Philemon 2).
34. See p. 408.
35. Cf. "all" in Romans 1:7.
36. Cf. P. S. Minear, *The Obedience of Faith* (London, 1971), p. 23.

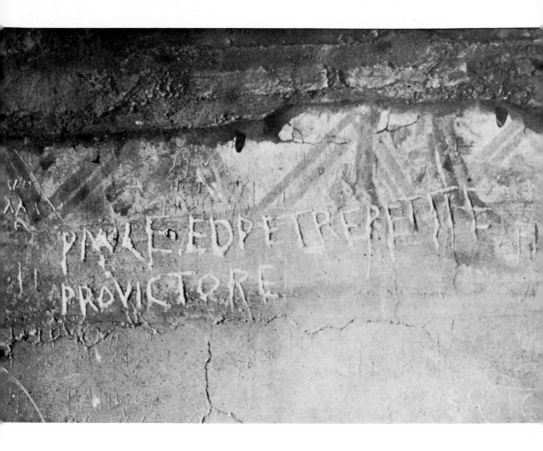

Rome: Catacombs of St. Sebastian: graffiti invoking Peter and Paul (see p. 452)

Rome: St. Paul-Without-the-Walls: façade and porch, showing
statue of Paul (see p. 451)

groups in house-churches or other local meeting-places. Some of the Jewish Christians may still have counted themselves as adherents of one or another of the Jewish synagogues. The time was fast approaching when they would no longer be able to maintain a foot in either camp, so to speak, but some were not disposed to sever their connexion with the synagogue until they were compelled to do so. This was perhaps the situation of the group addressed in the Epistle to the Hebrews. They had come to faith in Christ several years before the time at which this document was written (*c.* A.D. 63)[37] and had endured considerable persecution in consequence. But they were not willing to burn their boats and identify themselves irrevocably with Christ and his people, whom the synagogue as an institution had by now repudiated, to exchange the security of a *collegium licitum* for the uncertainty involved in a fellowship which enjoyed no such protection. Hence the urgency of the unknown writer's call to them: "let us go forth to him outside the camp, bearing the stigma that attaches to his name" (Hebrews 13: 13).

## 4. Evidence of the greetings in Romans 16

The Roman destination of the Epistle to the Hebrews cannot, however, be taken for granted. This must be said also of the destination of the last chapter of the Epistle to the Romans, in which Paul sends greetings by name to twenty-six individuals and five households or house-churches, in view of the weighty arguments which have moved many exegetes to ascribe an Ephesian destination to it.[38] But two general points may be made.

First, Paul was not in the habit of sending personal greetings to members of a church with which he was well acquainted. The only other letter in which he sends personal greetings is that to the Colossians. He had not himself visited the church of Colossae, but he had met elsewhere one or two people who were now resident in Colossae (Nympha and Archippus, for example)[39] and he sends greetings to them by name, knowing that others in the church would not wonder why they were not mentioned (which might very

37. If it was addressed to a Jewish Christian group in Rome, then Hebrews 12: 4 ("... you have not yet resisted to the point of shedding your blood") seems to preclude a date after the Neronian persecution of A.D. 64/65.
38. Cf. T. W. Manson, *Studies in the Gospels and Epistles* (Manchester, 1962), pp. 234 ff.; he names D. Schulz in *Theologische Studien und Kritiken* 2 (1829), pp. 609 ff., as the first to suggest an Ephesian destination for Romans 16. For the Roman destination cf. C. H. Dodd, *The Epistle to the Romans* (London, 1932), pp. xvii ff., 236 ff.; H. W. Schmidt, *Der Brief des Paulus an die Römer* (Berlin, 1963), pp. 250 ff.; W. G. Kümmel, *Introduction to the New Testament*, E.T. (London, 1966), pp. 224 ff.
39. Colossians 4: 15, 17 (with the latter verse cf. Philemon 2).

well happen if he sent personal greetings to some members of the church in Corinth or Ephesus and not to others). So, in view of the ease of travel throughout the Roman world of Paul's day and the fact that all roads led to Rome, it was but natural that many people whom Paul had met in other places should now be resident in Rome (including Epaenetus, his first convert in the province of Asia)[40] and that he should send his personal greetings to them and to others of whom he had heard, without risk of causing offence to those whom he had never met and who were unknown to him even by name.

Second, a number of the names of people to whom these greetings are sent are better attested at Rome than at Ephesus. This is largely due to the much larger number of inscriptions available from Rome than from Ephesus; in any case it is, for the most part, the names and not the individuals that are well attested at Rome. (Such a name as Urbanus, occurring in Rom. 16: 9, immediately bespeaks an association with the *urbs*.)

To come to particulars, greetings are sent, among others, to "those in the Lord who belong to the household of Narcissus" (Romans 16: 11). This Narcissus has been commonly identified with Tiberius Claudius Narcissus, a wealthy freedman of the Emperor Tiberius, who exercised great influence under Claudius but was executed at the instance of Agrippina soon after Nero's accession in A.D. 54.[41] His goods being confiscated, his slaves and retainers would pass into the imperial household, being distinguished from other groups in that household by the additional designation *Narcissiani*. Paul's greetings may have been intended for Christians among those *Narcissiani*. We have no idea, of course, how he would know, or know of, members of the *Narcissiani*. But if the tentative identification is right, these were certainly "saints in Caesar's household" and may have been among those so described whose greetings are sent by Paul to the church of Philippi (Philippians 4: 22).

Another group of "saints in Caesar's household" has been tentatively identified in "those who belong to the household of Aristobulus", to whom Paul sends greetings in Romans 16: 10. Aristobulus was a name particularly common in the Herod family. One Herodian of that name, a younger brother of the elder Agrippa (and called after their ill-fated father), lived in Rome as a private citizen and, like his brother, enjoyed the friendship of Claudius.[42] If

40. Romans 16: 5.
41. Tacitus, *Annals* xiii. 1. 4; Dio Cassius, *History* lx. 34; cf. Juvenal, *Satire* 14. 329. This identification was made (*inter alios*) by J. Calvin (*Commentary on the Epistle of Paul the Apostle to the Romans* [Strasbourg, 1540], E.T. [Edinburgh, 1961], p. 323). See p. 358, n. 15. For *Narcissiani* cf. *CIL* iii. 3973, vi. 15640.
42. Cf. Josephus *BJ* i. 552; ii. 221; *Ant.* xviii. 133, 135, etc.

he bequeathed his property to the emperor, then his slaves too would pass into the imperial household and be distinguished as *Aristobuliani*. But we do not know that he bequeathed his property to the emperor, although such an action would be not at all unprecedented. It could then be more than a mere coincidence that the next person to whom Paul sends greetings bears the name of Herodion. Paul calls Herodion his "kinsman", meaning probably a fellow-Christian of Jewish birth. [43]

Two other Christian groups are identified by the mention of several of their members by name. They are (first) "Asyncritus, Phlegon, Hermes, Patrobas, Hermas and the brethren who are with them" (verse 14) and (next) "Philologus, Julia, Nereus and his sister, and Olympas, and all the saints who are with them" (verse 15). In the former group the name Patrobas will remind the reader of Tacitus's *Histories* that Nero had an influential and unpopular freedman called Patrobius, [44] of which Patrobas is an abbreviated form: the Christian Patrobas was conceivably a dependent of Nero's Patrobius. [45] The name Hermas (an abbreviation of Hermagoras, Hermodorus, Hermogenes or the like) was common enough: a generation or two later it was borne by another Roman Christian, the author of the very popular *Shepherd*. [46] Roman ecclesiastical tradition, as far back as the fourth century, gives the name Nereus to a Christian of the last decade of the first century who, with his companion Achilleus, was associated with Flavia Domitilla, niece of the Emperor Domitian, after whom the Cemetery of Domitilla on the Via Ardeatina is named. [47] (This cemetery incidentally, contains burying-places of Christian members of the *gens Aurelia* bearing the cognomen Ampliatus, a name appearing in Romans 16: 8.) [48] In the latter group Philologus and Julia may have been husband and wife or (like another pair mentioned in the same list) brother and sister. Julia's name suggests some association with the imperial household. It is

43. Gk. συγγενής . Others whom Paul so designates in this chapter are Andronicus and Junia(s) (verse 7) and Lucius, Jason and Sosipater (verse 21).

44. Tacitus, *Histories* i. 49; ii. 95; he was executed under Galba, according to Dio Cassius, *History (Epitome)* lxiv. 3. 4.

45. J. B. Lightfoot, *St. Paul's Epistle to the Philippians* (London, 1868), p. 177.

46. An allegorical work, composed about the beginning of the second century, which had the same sort of vogue in the church of the generations following as John Bunyan's *Pilgrim's Progress* once had in the English-speaking world.

47. The tomb of the martyrs Nereus and Achilleus was marked by an epitaph set up by Pope Damasus. The *Acts of Nereus and Achilleus* should be dated in the fifth century; cf. H. Leclercq, "Nérée et Achillée", *DACL* xii. 1 (Paris, 1935), columns 1111 ff. For Flavia Domitilla see Dio Cassius, *History (Epitome)*, lxvii. 14; for her cemetery see H. Leclercq, "Domitille (Cimetière de)", *DACL* iv. 2 (Paris, 1921), columns 1404 ff.

48. Cf. H. Leclercq, "Ampliatus (Cubiculum d')", *DACL* i. 2 (Paris, 1907), columns 1712 ff.

remarkable, indeed, how many names occurring in Romans 16: 5–15 are found on inscriptions as names of members of the imperial household, though community of name is no evidence for identity of person.

Then we note at the head of the greetings a reference to Priscilla (or Prisca, as Paul regularly calls her) and Aquila, together with "the church in their house" (verses 3–5a). Since they left Italy when Claudius expelled all Jews from Rome, there is nothing surprising in their return to the capital when the expulsion edict had lapsed. True, when last they were mentioned by Paul (1 Corinthians 16: 19) they were still in Ephesus, to which they had gone with him from Corinth; but Paul's departure from Ephesus may have been their cue to go back to Rome. Their return, indeed, could have been connected with Paul's own plan to visit Rome as soon as possible,[49] and in any case it is to be expected that they would keep in touch with Paul by letter or otherwise. As they accommodated a Christian congregation in their house in Ephesus, so they did also in Rome. As for Epaenetus, Paul's first Asian convert, to whom he sends greetings immediately after greeting Priscilla and Aquila (verse 5b), he may well have attached himself to those two and accompanied them on their return to Rome.

The inclusion among those greeted by name of Andronicus and Junias (or possibly the feminine Junia) raises interesting questions – not only because Paul claims them as kinsfolk and fellow-prisoners but even more so because he says that they are "of note among the apostles" and "were in Christ before me" (verse 7). They must have been very early Christians if they were Christians before Paul, and if their being "of note among the apostles" implies not merely that they were well known to the apostles but that they were in some sense apostles themselves, what does this mean? Perhaps they were among the five hundred and more to whom on one occasion the risen Christ appeared; J. B. Lightfoot hinted (he was too cautious to do more) that they could have been among the visitors from Rome who heard Peter preach in Jerusalem on the day of Pentecost.[50]

As for "Rufus, eminent in the Lord" (verse 13), mention has already been made of the possible implication of his coincidence in name with one of the sons of Simon of Cyrene.[51] If these greetings were sent to Rome by Paul, and the Gospel of Mark was written a few years later for the Christians in Rome, the possibility that one and the same Rufus is meant in both documents becomes almost a probability.

The impression given by these greetings is of a decentralized

49. Cf. O. Michel, *Der Brief an die Römer* (Göttingen,[13] 1966), p. 341.
50. J. B. Lightfoot, *St. Paul's Epistle to the Philippians*, p. 17. See p. 382.
51. See p. 148.

Christian community in Rome – indeed, the word "community" may be more a spiritual interpretation than a practical fact. The various groups may have differed one from another in outlook, not to speak of differences in outlook within any one group. The Pauline understanding of the gospel was probably fostered especially in the house-church which enjoyed the hospitality of Priscilla and Aquila. One scholar has identified elsewhere in the letter to the Romans evidence of five different outlooks among the potential readers, with special reference to being strong or weak in faith and adopting various attitudes towards debatable aspects of Christian conduct such as observance of certain days or avoidance of certain foods, and various attitudes, also, towards fellow-Christians taking a different line in these matters.[52] This correlation cannot be established in any thorough-going way. Paul was certainly aware of differences in attitude and practice which might set up tensions if brotherly consideration were not exercised; this is why he urges all the groups so earnestly to give one another the same welcome as they had all received from Christ, "for the glory of God" (Romans 15: 7). Thus a sense of spiritual unity would be fostered.

But if Paul found the Roman Christians decentralized in organization, he did little to centralize them in this way; indeed, had he wished to do any such thing, his opportunities were limited. And half a century after his coming to Rome the evidence of Ignatius and Hermas is that the Roman church was still less centralized than many other churches were by that time: it was not yet organized under the administrative authority of a single bishop.[53]

## 5. Evidence of the letter to the Philippians

Our uncertainty regarding the Roman destination of some New Testament documents is matched by our uncertainty regarding the Roman provenance of others. Paul's "prison epistles" have traditionally been dated during his Roman captivity but we have seen that, for some of them at least, an Ephesian or Caesarean provenance has been defended.

If the "saints in Caesar's household" whose greetings are sent to

52. P. S. Minear, *The Obedience of Faith*, pp. 8 ff.
53. The evidence of Ignatius is especially conclusive. He is obsessed with the importance of the bishop's office, and insists on it in six out of his seven letters, so that his silence about it in his letter to the Romans calls for explanation. The most probable explanation is that when he wrote (c. A.D. 110) the Roman church was still without a monarchical bishop. There is no tone of episcopal authority in the letter of Clement of Rome to the Corinthians (c. A.D. 96); Hermas, not long afterwards, speaks of no rule in the Roman church but that of the "elders who preside over the church" (*Shepherd*, Vision 2. 4. 3; 3. 9. 7).

the Philippian church were Roman Christians, as seems most probable, then it is in Rome also that we may most naturally seek the *praetorium* throughout which, according to Philippians 1: 13, it was generally known that Paul's imprisonment was for Christ's sake. (It has been argued by some students that the Epistle to the Philippians as we have it comprises more than one letter sent by Paul to his friends in Philippi,[54] and this possibility should be kept in mind, even if it does run counter to "bibliographical probability".)[55] Of all the possible meanings of *praetorium*, the most appropriate in this context is "praetorian guard". The praetorian guard was the emperor's personal bodyguard, and since Paul by his appeal had placed himself at the emperor's disposal it was natural that the soldiers who had charge of him in his lodgings, relieving one another in succession, should be drawn from the praetorian guard. Few of those soldiers had ever come across a man like Paul before, and each of them would quickly learn what had brought him to Rome.

Not only the praetorian guard, but "all the rest", says Paul, had come to know the reason for his imprisonment – "all the rest" meaning, probably, all those who were in any way concerned with arrangements to be made for the eventual hearing of his case.

Moreover, the fact that Paul, despite the conditions of his house-arrest, was able to preach the gospel freely to all who came to see him encouraged many other Christians in Rome to bear witness more boldly than they had done before, so that Paul's coming to Rome had in every way worked for the advance of the gospel in the city. Not that this advance was consistently promoted in a spirit of co-operation with Paul; the differences in outlook among the various groups of Christians in Rome meant that some groups were less sympathetic to Paul than others: some, in fact, were downright antipathetic. So much may be gathered from Paul's own words that, while some preached Christ in a spirit of good will, counting themselves as his friends and partners, others did so in a spirit of envy and rivalry, with no worthier motive than to rub salt into his wounds, to add to the sense of frustration which he might well feel in his restricted situation. But Paul reacts in a spirit of contented relaxation: what mattered was that Christ was being proclaimed, whether from worthy or unworthy motives – "and in that," he says, "I rejoice" (Philippians 1: 15–18).

54. Polycarp in his *Letter to the Philippians* (3: 2) reminds them how Paul "in his absence wrote letters to you". For the composite view see E. J. Goodspeed, *Introduction to the New Testament* (Chicago, 1937), pp. 90–96; F. W. Beare, *A Commentary on the Epistle to the Philippians* (London, 1959), pp. 2–5, 100–102, 150. W. G. Kümmel, on the other hand, finds "no sufficient reason to doubt the original unity of the transmitted Philippians" (*Introduction to the New Testament*, E.T., p. 237).

55. For the expression see F. G. Kenyon, *The Bible and Modern Scholarship* (London, 1948), pp. 37 etc.

This is a far cry from the anathema which he invoked on those trouble-makers who, several years earlier, had invaded his Galatian mission-field and taught "a different gospel" to his converts there. True, his ill-wishers in Rome were not intruding into a sphere which was not their own, and it is not suggested that there was anything defective or subversive in the content of their preaching; even so, Paul has recognizably mellowed and manifests more of the "meekness and gentleness of Christ" than he was able to do when he invoked those qualities in his remonstrance with disaffected members of the Corinthian church.[56] Perhaps his two years of imprisonment at Caesarea, followed by his present house-arrest in Rome, had taught him new lessons in patience.

For there was no way of knowing how long he would remain under house-arrest, or when he would be summoned to appear before Caesar. He more than half expected that when he did appear, the outcome would be favourable: many friends, in Rome and Philippi and elsewhere, were praying for this, and he was convinced that for the welfare of his converts and the furtherance of the gospel his acquittal and release would be desirable.[57] If he had his own preference alone to consult, he was not so sure: it would be "far better" for him to set out on his last journey and be at home "with Christ" (Philippians 1: 23). It was difficult for him to choose between the two; happily, the choice was not his, and his prayer was that, one way or the other, Christ would be glorified.[58]

## 6. *Evidence of the letter to the Colossians*

At this stage the relevance of the letter to the Colossians to Paul's stay in Rome must be viewed as quite uncertain. But if this letter was indeed sent from Rome it is necessary to take account of the implication of the final greetings in which Paul names Aristarchus, Mark ("the cousin of Barnabas") and Jesus surnamed Justus as the only men of Jewish birth who are with him at the time as "fellow-workers for the kingdom of God" – men, he adds, who "have been a comfort to me" (Colossians 4: 10 f.). He has other companions who are of Gentile origin,[59] but no other "men of the circumcision" apart from Timothy, whose name is coupled with his own in the initial salutation of the letter.[60] This language may point, as J. B. Lightfoot thought, to the "antagonism of the converts from the Circumcision in the metropolis"[61] and could be related to

56. 2 Corinthians 10: 1.
57. Philippians 1: 19.
58. Philippians 1: 20.
59. Colossians 4: 12–14.
60. Technically (but only technically), Timothy could be included among the "men of the circumcision" since Paul had circumcised him (Acts 16: 3); see p. 214.

Paul's mention, in writing to the Philippians, of those who "proclaim Christ out of partisanship" (Philippians 1: 17).

Of the three Jewish Christians whom Paul names, Jesus surnamed Justus is mentioned nowhere else. Aristarchus, who is here described as "my fellow-prisoner", had come with Paul to Rome, and may at this time have been sharing his house-arrest.[62] The reference to Mark is of special interest, as his path and Paul's had not crossed, so far as the records inform us, since the day that Barnabas took Mark and set sail with him from Syrian Antioch to Cyprus after Paul's refusal to have him a second time as a missionary adjutant.[63] Second-century tradition links Mark with Rome, more particularly in association with Peter. [64]

One way of reconstructing the situation which brought Mark to Rome is to suppose that, shortly after the return of Jews to the city about the year 54, Peter, accompanied by Mark, paid his first visit to Rome to help the Christian members of the Jewish community to re-establish their identity and witness.[65] By the time of Paul's writing to the Roman Christians at the beginning of A.D. 57 Peter, and probably Mark, had left the city; but Mark came back from time to time to maintain contacts with Jewish believers in Rome, and was paying one of these visits at the time when Paul wrote to the Colossians. While Paul had looked on Mark with a critical eye at one time, it is good to observe that now he includes him among the men who had proved a "comfort" to him.[66] Mark no doubt had matured first under the wise and sympathetic guidance of Barnabas and then as aide-de-camp to Peter; and, as we have noted already, Paul for his part had mellowed.

But the question of a Roman provenance for the letter to the Colossians requires an examination of the companion letter to Philemon.

61. J. B. Lightfoot, *St. Paul's Epistles to the Colossians and to Philemon* (London, 1875), p. 236; cf. his *St. Paul's Epistle to the Philippians*, pp. 16 ff.

62. See p. 360.

63. See p. 212.

64. According to Papias (c. A.D. 130), as quoted by Eusebius (*Hist. Eccl.* iii. 39. 15), "Mark became Peter's interpreter and wrote accurately all that he remembered of the words or deeds of the Lord – not, however, in order". Towards the end of the second century the anti-Marcionite prologue to Mark's Gospel says that "after Paul's departure he committed this Gospel to writing in the parts of Italy". About the same time Clement of Alexandria (as quoted by Eusebius, *Hist. Eccl.* ii. 25) and Irenaeus (*Against Heresies* iii. 1. 2) write to similar effect.

65. Cf. T. W. Manson, *Studies in the Gospels and Epistles* (Manchester, 1962), pp. 38 ff.; see p. 258 above with n. 34.

66. Colossians 4: 11.

# CHAPTER 34

# The Letter to Philemon

P AUL'S LETTER TO PHILEMON IS SHORT ENOUGH TO BE REPRODUCED
in full, in a fairly free translation.

Paul, prisoner of Christ Jesus, and Timothy our brother, to Philemon,
our dear friend and fellow-worker, with our sister Apphia and our fellow-
soldier Archippus, and the church that meets in your house: grace and
peace be yours from God our Father and our Lord Jesus Christ.

I always thank God, my dear friend, when I remember you in my
prayers, for I hear good news of the love and loyalty which you show to
our Lord Jesus and all his holy people. So I pray that your Christian
liberality, springing as it does from your faith, may lead you effectively
into the experience and appreciation of every blessing which we have as
fellow-members of Christ. Your love has brought me great joy and comfort, my dear brother; you have refreshed the hearts of God's people.

That is why I am making this request of you; I am making it for love's
sake, although I could quite well exercise my authority in Christ's name
and *command* you to do the proper thing. Yes, I could command you as
Paul, ambassador[1] of Christ Jesus; but I don't do that: I prefer to ask you
a favour as Paul, *prisoner* of Christ Jesus.

The request I am making is for my son. My son? Yes, my son; I have
acquired one here, prisoner though I am. His name is Onesimus –
profitable by name and profitable by nature. I know that in former days
you found him quite profitable, but now, I assure you, he has learned to
be true to his name – profitable to you, and profitable to me.

Well, I am sending him back to you, though it is like tearing out my
very heart to do so. My own inclination is to keep him here with me, and
then he could go on serving me while I am a prisoner for the gospel's sake
– serving me as your representative. But I do not want to do anything
without your consent; I do not want the good turn you are doing me
through his service to be done by you willy-nilly, but on your free initiative.

For aught I know, this was why you and he were separated for a short
time, so that you might have him to yourself for ever, no longer as a slave,
but something much better than a slave – a dear brother, very dear
indeed to me, and surely dearer still to you, since he is now yours not only
as a member of your household but as a fellow-believer in the Lord. You
look on me as your partner, don't you? Well, Onesimus is my represen-

---

1. Taking πρεσβύτης ("old man") in the sense of πρεσβευτής "ambassador").

tative; give him the welcome you would give me. Has he done you any wrong? Does he owe you something? Never mind; put that down on my account. Here is my I.O.U., written with my own hand. "I will make it good. *Signed*: Paul."

(I scarcely need to remind you, of course, of the debt that *you owe me*; it is to me that you owe your very life!)

Yes, my dear brother, let me have this *profit* from you as a fellow-Christian. Refresh my heart in the name of Christ, to whom we both belong.

I write like this because I have every confidence in your obedience; I know you will do more than I say. And, by the way, please get the guest-room ready for me; I hope I shall soon be restored to you, thanks to your prayers.

Epaphras, my fellow-prisoner for the sake of Christ Jesus, sends you his greetings; so do my fellow-workers Mark, Aristarchus, Demas and Luke.

May the grace of our Lord Jesus Christ be with your spirit, all of you.

It is admittedly question-begging to discuss the letter to Philemon in the context of Paul's Roman imprisonment. Two questions, in fact, are begged: Was this letter written by Paul, and was it written in Rome?

## 2. Authorship

Was it written by Paul? Most critics have been content to leave the Pauline authorship intact. The letter is too short for the most efficient computer to yield a significant analysis of its style and vocabulary.[2] If its authenticity is questioned, it is questioned mainly on account of the close association between this letter and Colossians, which some find it difficult to accept as Pauline. For Colossians and Philemon were plainly written at the same time and place, sent to the same place, carried by the same messengers. Practically the same companions of Paul send their greetings in both; of the six who do so in Colossians, five do so in Philemon. Apart from these, Archippus is mentioned in both; and in both Onesimus arrives at the same time as the letters.

Ernest Renan was so convinced of the genuineness of Philemon that for its sake he was willing to admit the genuineness of Colossians. "The Epistle to the Colossians", he wrote, "though full of eccentricities, does not embrace any of those impossibilities which are to be found in the Epistles to Titus and to Timothy. It furnishes even many of those details which reject the hypothesis [of its pseudonymity] as false. Assuredly of this number is its connec-

2. Cf. A. Q. Morton, *The Times*, April 24, 1963 ("there seems no reason to exclude it from the works of Paul").

tion with the note to Philemon. If the epistle is apocryphal, the note is apocryphal also; yet few of the pages have so pronounced a tone of sincerity; Paul alone, as it appears to us, could write that little masterpiece."[3]

But Renan was a romantic, and would have been reluctant as such to abandon the authenticity of Philemon; a real biblical critic must be made of sterner stuff. And such was Ferdinand Christian Baur, in whose eyes only the letters to the Galatians, Corinthians and Romans were authentically Pauline.

"What", asks Baur, "has criticism to do with this short, attractive, graceful and friendly letter, inspired as it is by the noblest Christian feeling, and which has never yet been touched by the breath of suspicion?"[4] Yet, he goes on, apostolic authorship cannot be taken for granted even here; and since the other "captivity epistles" to which Philemon is so clearly related are not Pauline, it follows that this epistle is not Pauline; it is, in fact (says Baur), a Christian romance in embryo, comparable in this respect to the *Clementine Homilies*. The *Clementine Homilies* show how "Christianity is the permanent reconciliation of those of who were formerly separated by one cause or another, but who by a special arrangement of affairs brought about by Divine Providence for that very purpose, are again brought together; through their conversion to Christianity they know each other again, the one sees in the other his own flesh and blood."[5] So the Epistle to Philemon suggests that perhaps Onesimus and his master were separated for a short time in order that the latter might thenceforth have Onesimus to himself for ever, no longer as a slave, but as a dear brother.

W. C. van Manen, who rejected the authenticity of all thirteen Pauline epistles (including even the four "capital letters" which Baur admitted), added to Baur's arguments against the genuineness of Philemon some considerations of his own. For one thing, the ambiguity of the direction speaks against Pauline authorship, since the epistle is addressed by Paul and Timothy to three individuals and a household church, while the bulk of it is a personal letter from Paul to Philemon. "This double form . . . is not a style that is natural to any one who is writing freely and untrammelled, whether to one person or to many ."[6] More probably the unknown author has modelled his composition on the letter of the younger Pliny to his friend Sabinianus, interceding on behalf of a freedman of the latter who has offended his patron and has sought

3. E. Renan, *Saint Paul*, E.T. (London, 1889), p. x.
4. F. C. Baur, *Paul*, E.T., ii (London, 1875), p. 80.
5. Baur, *Paul*, E.T., ii, p. 83.
6. W. C. van Manen, article "Philemon, Epistle to", *Encyclopaedia Biblica*, iii (London, 1902), column 3695.

Pliny's good offices to bring about a reconciliation.[7] The author of Philemon makes the freedman into a slave, and rewrites the letter so as to portray the ideal "relations which, in his judgment, that is according to the view of Pauline Christians, ought to subsist between Christian slaves and their masters, especially when the slaves have in some respect misconducted themselves, as for example by secretly quitting their master's service".[8]

Such a combination of hypercriticism and naïveté is easily recognized for what it is. There is no need to propound such far-fetched explanations of a document which, in the judgement of most critics as of most general readers, bears a much more probable explanation on its face – namely, that is is a genuine letter of Paul, concerning a slave called Onesimus, who somehow needs the apostle's help in restoring good personal relations between him and his master, and that Paul quite naturally takes the opportunity at the beginning and end of the letter to send greetings to other members of the household. Because of what they regard as the transparent genuineness of this epistle, several scholars who are unable to accept the whole of Colossians as Pauline feel constrained nevertheless to salvage some of it for the apostle – enough, at least, to keep Philemon company.[9]

### 3. Place of writing

But even if it was written by Paul, was it sent from Rome? Here, debate has fastened on two points: (a) the length of the journey that Onesimus must have made from his master's home to the place where Paul was in custody, and (b) Paul's request for the preparation of the guest-room in view of his expectation of an early release and a visit to the Lycus valley. Do these two points suggest that Paul was fairly near the Lycus valley at the time (say in Ephesus, about 100 miles away) or much farther distant (say in Rome, more than 1,000 miles away)?

The case has been debated one way and the other, by none more ably than by Principal G. S. Duncan and Professor C. H. Dodd. Principal Duncan's argument for Ephesus, because it was so much nearer to Colossae than Rome was, was answered by Professor Dodd, who thinks the remoter city the more probable. Principal Duncan replied to Professor Dodd, but the question remains unresolved.

7. Pliny, *Epistle* ix. 21. For translations see J. B. Lightfoot, *St. Paul's Epistle to the Colossians and to Philemon* (London, 1879), pp. 318 f.; J. Knox, *Philemon among the Letters of Paul* (London, [2]1960), pp. 16 f.; E. M. Blaiklock, *From Prison in Rome* (London, 1964), pp. 71 f.
8. *Encyclopaedia Biblica*, column 3696.
9. Cf. P. N. Harrison, "Onesimus and Philemon", *Anglican Theological Review* 32 (1950), pp. 268 ff. See pp. 409 f.

With regard to Onesimus's choice of a place of refuge, "only in the most desperate circumstances", says Principal Duncan, "such as the letter gives us no reason to assume, would a fugitive from justice have undertaken over unknown and dangerous roads a journey of a thousand miles by land, together with two sea voyages extending over some five days, especially when comparatively near at hand there was a city with which he was no doubt already familiar, and which was of sufficient size to afford him all the security that he was likely to require." [10]

With regard to the visit proposed by Paul in verse 22, Principal Duncan goes on to say:

> How natural such a visit would be at a time when his activities, temporarily interrupted by imprisonment, were directed towards the evangelisation of Asia: not far from him as he lay at Ephesus were those churches in the Lycus valley which in some indirect way no doubt owed their origin to his missionary-work in the province, but which he had never so far visited, and in at least one of which, Colossae, the conditions gave him grave cause for anxiety. On the other hand, how unlikely was he to contemplate such a visit, let alone give thought to the provision of a lodging there, when he lay a prisoner at Rome . . . From Rome he meant, not to turn back to the Lycus valley, but to advance into Spain. [11]

To the argument that Onesimus was more likely to have fled to neighbouring Ephesus than to distant Rome, Professor Dodd says:

> This seems plausible. But a moment's reflection may convince us that we are here talking of things about which we know nothing. We cannot know either what was in Onesimus's mind or what his opportunities for travel may have been. If we are to *surmise*, then it is as likely that the fugitive slave, his pockets lined at his master's expense, made for Rome *because* it was distant, as that he went to Ephesus because it was near. But this meeting of the runaway slave with the imprisoned apostle is in any case an enigma. Did he mean to go to Paul? Or was he taken to him? Or was it the long arm of coincidence that brought about such an improbable meeting? No secure argument can be based upon an incident which we cannot in any case explain. [12]

To the argument that Paul's request for a lodging at Colossae comes more naturally if he was at Ephesus at the time than if he was at Rome, he says:

---

10. G. S. Duncan, *St. Paul's Ephesian Ministry* (London, 1929), pp. 72 f.; cf. P. N. Harrison, "Onesimus and Philemon", p. 271.

11. *St. Paul's Ephesian Ministry*, pp. 74 f.; cf. P. N. Harrison, "Onesimus and Philemon", p. 281.

12. C. H. Dodd, "The Mind of Paul", in *New Testament Studies* (Manchester, 1953), p. 95.

This is a real point in favour of the Ephesian hypothesis. At the same time we do not know that Paul would have held to his intention in the greatly changed circumstances. Like all practical men, he was open to change his mind, as in fact we know both from Acts and from the Epistles he not infrequently did. On the Roman hypothesis, the emergence of the Colossian heresy may well have led Paul to plan a visit to Asia before setting out on further travels, whether or not the plan was ever fulfilled.[13]

These arguments of Professor Dodd, first publicly voiced in a lecture delivered in the John Rylands Library, Manchester, were taken up by Principal Duncan soon after they appeared in print in the Library's *Bulletin* (1934). On the first score Principal Duncan added little to what he had said before (apart from a footnote reference to J. Pongrácz's suggestion that the temple of Artemis would have afforded a place of refuge for Onesimus at Ephesus); on the second score he conceded that Paul might have changed his plans during his Roman imprisonment and decided to visit Colossae. "But long before he could have arrived at that remote and unimportant town in the Lycus valley, must we not allow for the eager news preceding him of his release, his journeyings eastwards, his subsequent arrival at Ephesus or some such centre in Asia? That one so situated should bespeak quarters at Colossae suggests the air-mindedness of the twentieth century rather than the rigorous conditions, which Paul himself knew so well (2 Corinthians 11: 25 ff.), of travel in the first."[14]

On this last point it may be said that long before the air-minded twentieth century most readers of the epistle, including some who experienced travel conditions not noticeably less rigorous than those which Paul had to endure in the first century, took it for granted that Paul did from Rome bespeak quarters at Colossae. More important: it was not only the Colossian heresy that caused Paul concern. The developing situation in the province of Asia, as Paul learned of it from Epaphras and other visitors, may well have seemed to him to call urgently for his presence there as soon as he regained his freedom (if indeed he did regain it). In other parts of the province than the Lycus valley Paul's opponents were exploiting his enforced absence to his detriment and (as he saw it) to the detriment of his converts and the cause of the gospel. Even if things had not yet come to the pass described in 2 Timothy 1: 15, where "all who are in Asia" are said to have turned away from him, the beginnings of this trend could certainly be traced during Paul's custody in Rome, if not earlier.

One slight pointer to Rome as the place of origin might be the in-

13. *Ibid.*
14. G. S. Duncan, "The Epistles of the Imprisonment in Recent Discussion", *Expository Times* 46 (1934–35), p. 296.

clusion of Luke and Mark among Paul's companions at the time of writing. Luke was with Paul at Rome; we have no evidence that he was with him at Ephesus. Mark is traditionally associated with Rome, not with Ephesus.[15] But this pointer, if such it be, is far from conclusive.

Defenders of the view that the letter and its companion letters were composed during Paul's imprisonment at Caesarea could point out that Luke was very probably with Paul at that time; but (in spite of Lohmeyer's arguments)[16] Caesarea hardly comes into the picture. One could understand Onesimus making his way to Ephesus because it was near, or working his passage to Rome because it was distant; but why should he go to Caesarea?

The place from which the Epistle to Philemon was written cannot, in fact, be determined from a study of this letter alone. It must be determined, if at all, by taking into account the evidence of the letters with which this one is most closely associated – in the first instance, the letter to the Colossians. When we look at Philemon by itself, the arguments for Ephesus are weighty. But when we take Philemon and Colossians together, these arguments are outweighed by the arguments for Rome as the place from which Colossians was written. This question calls for separate treatment.

## 4. The case of Onesimus

The picture sometimes given of Paul's meeting Onesimus as a fellow-prisoner is rather misleading. Principal Duncan is quite right in emphasizing "how very radically Paul's condition of imprisonment in Rome must have changed for the worse if, following on two years spent in his own hired house (Acts 30), he was reduced to sharing the same prison-cell as a fugitive slave."[17] But there is no need to conjure up any such picture in our minds. The situation is more intelligible if we think of Paul as still living under house-arrest in his lodgings – albeit hand-cuffed to his military guard, and therefore technically a prisoner (verses 1, 9) or "in chains" (verses 10, 13) – when Onesimus came to him.

In this case we might consider a suggestion made many years ago by Professor E. R. Goodenough.[18] He pointed out that Athenian law permitted a slave in danger of his life to seek sanctuary at an altar, and that that altar might be the hearth of a private family.

---

15. A visit by Mark to the province of Asia is implied in Colossians 4: 10, but after the despatch of the letter to the Colossians.

16. E. Lohmeyer, *Der Kolosser– und der Philemonbrief* (Göttingen, [11] 1957).

17. *St. Paul's Ephesian Ministry*, p. 73.

18. E. R. Goodenough, "Paul and Onesimus", *Harvard Theological Review* 22 (1929), pp. 181 ff.

The head of the family was then obliged to give the slave protection while he tried to persuade him to return to his master; he would no doubt use his good offices to try to mollify the master's wrath. If the slave refused to return, the householder's duty was to put the slave up for auction and hand over the price received for him to his former master. This provision survived in Egypt under the Ptolemies, and well into Roman imperial times, since it influenced Ulpian's legislation early in the third century A.D. Philo, who knew the Egyptian practice, modified the Deuteronomic law of the fugitive slave [19] to conform with it.[20]

Goodenough explained the case of Onesimus in terms of this provision, but found it necessary then to suppose that Paul was free at the time, and that the reference to his being "in bonds" might be figurative.[21] But if the apostle was under house-arrest in his own lodgings, might not the place where he lived count as a "hearth" or "altar" within the meaning of the law – always supposing that Onesimus did avail himself of this legal provision?

There is no way of deciding how in fact Onesimus made his way to Paul. Perhaps Epaphras of Colossae, the evangelist of the Lycus valley (Colossians 1: 7), who was on a visit to Paul at the time (Colossians 4: 12) and who is indeed described as Paul's "fellow-prisoner" in Philemon 23, brought him to Paul because he knew that Paul would help him in his predicament. We cannot be sure. We may be quite wrong in supposing that Onesimus was a runaway slave in the usual sense of the word. It could, I suppose, be argued that his master sent him to Paul to fulfil some commission, and that Onesimus overstayed his leave – *amore Pauli*, perhaps (why not?) – and had to have a note of excuse from Paul begging pardon for his unduly long absence. Our ignorance of the details being what it is, the possibilities which might be canvassed are numerous.

The letter throws little light on Paul's attitude to the institution of slavery. We get more formal teaching on this subject in the "household tables" of Colossians and Ephesians, and in remarks in

19. The Deuteronomic law runs as follows: "You shall not give up to his master a slave who has escaped from his master to you; he shall dwell with you, in your midst, in the place which he shall choose within one of your towns, where it pleases him best; you shall not oppress him" (Deuteronomy 23: 15 f.). This is unparalleled in the legislation of the ancient Near East, where severe sanctions (even the death penalty, as in Law 16 of Hammurabi's code) were imposed on anyone harbouring a runaway slave. The Israelites had good reason to know that God cared for runaway slaves. To Paul this enactment carried divine authority; even so, he would not invoke it without Philemon's consent, preferring Philemon to act like a Christian of his own free will.

20. Philo, *On the Virtues*, 124; see F. H. Colson's notes in the Loeb edition of Philo, viii (London/Cambridge, Mass., 1939), pp. 238 f., 447 f.

21. He also cast doubt (p. 182, n. 7) on the identity of Philemon's Onesimus with the Onesimus of Colossians 4: 9.

other letters.[22] What this letter does is to bring us into an atmosphere in which the institution could only wilt and die. When Onesimus is sent to his master "no longer as a slave, but as a dear brother", formal emancipation would be but a matter of expediency, the technical confirmation of the new relationship that had already come into being. If the letter were a document on slavery, one could illustrate it copiously by accounts of the conditions of slavery under the Roman Empire, including an advertisement of 156 B.C. quoted by Professor Moule in his commentary on Colossians and Philemon, in which information is requested about a runaway slave and a description is given not only of the slave himself but of the goods which he had on him when last seen.[23]

## 5. Three questions

If the letter is not primarily a sociological document, what is it? We may gain a clearer idea of its nature and purpose if we ask three specific questions:

(a) *What is Paul asking for?*
(b) *Did he get it?*
(c) *Why was the letter preserved?*

Although formally these are three questions, materially they are parts of one comprehensive question, covering the character of the document and its place in the New Testament. It will help us, moreover, to find an answer to this comprehensive question and the more specific questions which make it up if we look at one of the most important and fascinating books ever written on this epistle – a book which deals not only with these major questions but also with a number of subsidiary ones.

In 1935 Professor John Knox, formerly of the University of Chicago and later of Union Theological Seminary, New York, published a little book entitled *Philemon among the Letters of Paul*. The edition was a small one, and the book did not receive the attention which it deserved. In 1959 it appeared in a new and slightly enlarged edition. Meanwhile Professor Knox's views on Philemon had received wider currency in his introduction and commentary on the epistle in *The Interpreter's Bible*.[24]

22. Colossians 3: 22–4: 1; Ephesians 6: 5–9; 1 Corinthians 7: 21–23; 1 Timothy 6: 1 f. (cf. 1 Peter 2: 18–21).
23. C. F. D. Moule, *The Epistles of Paul the Apostle to the Colossians and to Philemon* (Cambridge, 1957), pp. 34 ff.; cf. E. J. Goodspeed and E. C. Colwell, *Greek Papyrus Reader* (Chicago, 1935), no. 59.
24. *The Interpreter's Bible* xi (New York, 1955), pp. 555 ff.

The milieu in which Professor Knox's work took shape was the Chicago New Testament school led by the late Edgar J. Goodspeed. Goodspeed himself pioneered the view that the *corpus Paulinum* of ten epistles (that is, lacking the three Pastorals) was edited and published at Ephesus about the end of the first century A.D., and that the document which we call the Epistle to the Ephesians was composed by the editor to serve as an introduction to the *corpus*.[25] Other members of the Chicago school undertook supporting studies with a bearing on the central thesis, and Professor Knox's book belongs to this category.

He accepts the general Goodspeed position and asks the pertinent question: Why was Philemon included among the letters of Paul? His answer, briefly, is that Philemon mattered supremely to a man who played a prominent part in the publication of the *corpus Paulinum*. Who was that man? It was Onesimus.

The argument runs thus. When Ignatius, bishop of Syrian Antioch, was on his way to Rome to be thrown to the wild beasts, about A.D. 110 or shortly after, the name of the bishop of Ephesus was Onesimus.[26] "What of that?" it might be asked. Onesimus was a common enough name – especially a common enough slave-name. "Profitable" or "Useful" was a name bestowed on many slaves in accordance with a well-known principle of nomenclature, not because a slave was actually profitable or useful, but in the fond hope that the attachment of this name of good omen to him would make him so. Why, then, should one connect the Onesimus who was bishop of Ephesus about A.D. 110 with the Onesimus who figures in the letter to Philemon between fifty and sixty years earlier?

Because, says Professor Knox, Ignatius in his letter to the church of Ephesus shows himself familiar with the Epistle to Philemon; it is one of the rare places in patristic literature where the language of our epistle is clearly echoed. Not only so, but the part of Ignatius's letter to Ephesus where the language of Philemon is echoed is the part in which Bishop Onesimus is mentioned – the first six chapters. In these six chapters the bishop is mentioned fourteen times;[27] in the remaining fifteen chapters he is not mentioned at all, apart from one general reference: "obey the bishop and the presbytery with an undisturbed mind." [28]

This consideration is impressive, if not conclusive. But there is

25. E. J. Goodspeed, "The Place of Ephesians in the First Pauline Collection", *Anglican Theological Review* 12 (1929–30), pp. 189 ff.; *Introduction to the New Testament* (Chicago, 1937), pp. 210 ff., 222 ff.; *The Meaning of Ephesians* (Chicago, 1933); *The Key to Ephesians* (Chicago, 1956). See pp. 425 ff.

26. Ignatius, *To the Ephesians* 1: 3.

27. Including three times by name (1: 3; 2: 1; 6: 2).

28. Ignatius, *To the Ephesians* 20: 2.

one point which I find particularly impressive. In verse 20 of our epistle Paul, playing on the meaning of Onesimus's name, says, "Yes, my dear brother, let me have this *profit* from you (*onaimēn sou*) as a fellow-Christian". And Ignatius seems to echo this expression with the intention of making the same play on words when he says to the Christians of Ephesus, "May I always have *profit* from you (*onaimēn hymōn*), if I am worthy".[29]

This indeed does not demand the identification of the two Onesimi; it could simply be that the name of the contemporary bishop of Ephesus reminded Ignatius of the Onesimus of Philemon; as the earlier Onesimus, formerly unprofitable, was henceforth going to be as profitable as his name promised, so the second Onesimus was eminently worthy of his "well-loved name".[30] But the identification is not impossible; it is (I should say) not improbable. Whether the Epistle to Philemon was written about A.D. 61, or some six years earlier (as those think who date it in the course of Paul's Ephesian ministry), a lad in his later teens or early twenties when Paul wrote it would be in his seventies by the time of Ignatius's martyrdom — not an incredible age for a bishop in those days.

Professor Knox is not so convincing, when he makes Paul say, "The request I am making is for my son,[31] whom I have begotten here in prison as Onesimus" — as though Onesimus were the new "Christian" name given him by his father in the faith.[32] This idea is too far-fetched; not only, as has been said, was Onesimus a common slave-name, but Paul would not designate the young man by a name which his master would not recognize.

Apart from this, what has the possible identification of Paul's Onesimus with the bishop of Ephesus whom Ignatius knew to do with the preservation of the Epistle to Philemon among the letters of Paul? This, says Professor Knox: if (as the Goodspeed school believes) Ephesus was the place where the *corpus Paulinum* was edited about the end of the first century, then the Onesimus of

29. *To the Ephesians* 2: 2 (Ignatius's ὀναίμην ὑμῶν [plural] catches up Paul's ὀναίμην σου [singular]).

30. Knox argues (*Philemon among the Letters of Paul*, pp. 89 ff.) that Ignatius's reference to the Ephesian church's "well-loved name" (1: 1) is an allusion to the name of its bishop, in whom the church was embodied: "I received in the name of God your whole community in Onesimus" (1: 3).

31. "I appeal to you for my child" (*Philemon among the Letters of Paul*, p. 14). "Is Paul appealing *on behalf of* Onesimus? Or is he simply asking *for* Onesimus? . . . Paul, with all possible delicacy, is asserting a claim upon Onesimus" (pp. 19 f.), i.e. he is asking that Onesimus be given (back) to him.

32. *Philemon among the Letters of Paul*, p. 21; he alludes (p. 90) to Ignatius's mention of "thy [singular] well-loved name, which you [plural] have acquired by your righteous nature, according to faith and love in Christ Jesus" (*To the Ephesians* 1: 1).

Ignatius's letter was probably already bishop of Ephesus and in a position of responsibility in relation to the editing of the *corpus*. Why should he not have been the editor himself? In that case we need look no farther for the reason for the careful preservation of the epistle to Philemon. But if Onesimus was editor of the *corpus Paulinum*, then (according to the Goodspeed school) he would have been the author of the Epistle to the Ephesians. If that were so, Paul certainly did a wonderful piece of work the day he won Onesimus for Christ!

Professor Knox raises another interesting question. To whom is the Epistle to Philemon addressed? To Philemon, of course, is the natural answer. Yes, but not so fast. It is addressed not to Philemon alone; it is addressed to "our dear fellow-worker Philemon, our sister Apphia and our comrade Archippus, and the church in your house" – "your" in the singular. This is a place where it is useful to follow the Authorized and Revised Versions and retain the distinction between the singular and plural pronouns of the second person: "the church in thy house". In whose house? The house of the person who is addressed in the second person singular from verse 4 to verse 24 of the epistle – Onesimus's owner. And who was he? Philemon, again, is the natural answer – the person first mentioned among the addressees in verse 1 (just as the real author of the epistle is the person first mentioned among the senders in verse 1).

But Professor Knox does not think so. Onesimus's owner, according to him, was not Philemon but Archippus, the third addressee.[33] Why should Philemon have been Onesimus's owner any more than Archippus? Confirmation that Archippus was Onesimus's owner is sought in the cryptic reference to Archippus in Colossians 4: 17, where Paul bids the Colossian church tell Archippus to see to it that he fulfils the ministry he has received "in the Lord". What Paul is doing there is enlisting the support of the Colossian church in persuading Onesimus's master to do what Paul wants him to do.

Who then was Philemon? He was overseer of the churches of the Lycus valley, who lived at Laodicea. Paul arranged that the epistle should be delivered to Philemon first because he could use his influence with Archippus; this was the "epistle from Laodicea" which Paul asked the church of Colossae to procure and read (Colossians 4: 16).[34]

What can be said of this reconstruction? It is quite probable that the cryptic reference to Archippus's ministry had something to do

33. *Philemon among the Letters of Paul*, pp. 49 ff.
34. Goodspeed held this view of the letter from Laodicea, but he made Archippus and Onesimus, as well as Philemon, live at Laodicea (*Introduction to the New Testament*, pp. 109 ff.).

with the "letter from Laodicea", since it comes immediately after the injunction to procure and read that letter. But one thing is certain: after the extraordinary delicacy with which Paul makes his plea for Onesimus in the letter to Philemon, it would be an incredibly flat-footed action to put pressure on Onesimus's owner by name in another letter which was to be read aloud at a church meeting where the owner would presumably be present.[35] The reference to Onesimus in Colossians 4: 9, on the other hand, is unobtrusive: "Along with Tychicus I am sending Onesimus, my trusty and well-loved brother, who is one of yourselves." No one could take exception to that, although doubtless it would add just a little more weight to Paul's plea in the letter to Philemon. But there was no need to put on the spot a man to whom Paul was writing separately and saying, "I know you will do more than I say"; any attempt to put him on the spot before the church of Colossae would go far to neutralize the effect of Paul's diplomacy in the letter to Philemon.

And it would if anything be still more disastrous for Paul to direct that the letter to Philemon should be read aloud to the assembled church at Colossae. True, in the letter to Philemon Paul sends greetings to "the church that meets in your house" as well as to Philemon, Apphia and Archippus – but that does not mean that the private contents of verses 4–22 were to be divulged even to the household church with which these three were associated, let alone the city church of Colossae.

What Archippus's ministry was, which had to be publicly enjoined on him in Colossians 4: 17, must be a matter of speculation; but there is no good reason to suppose that it is relevant to our understanding of the letter to Philemon. Nor was Archippus Onesimus's owner. It is unlikely that this idea would have occurred to any one but for a desire to link the burden of the letter to Philemon with the ministry laid on Archippus in Colossians 4: 17. The first person addressed in the letter to Philemon would naturally be the head of the house;[36] Apphia and Archippus would naturally be members of his family – his wife and his son perhaps. It was, then, in Philemon's house that the household church of verse 1 met, and when Paul goes on to say, "I am making this re-

35. According to Goodspeed, he would not be present: "If he were in Colossae, why should the Colossians have to 'tell' him? He would be present at the meeting of the church and would hear the message without being told" (*Introduction to the New Testament*, p. 112).

36. "It is evident that Philemon's house is meant" (E. J. Goodspeed, *Introduction to the New Testament*, p. 111). C. F. D. Moule rightly regards the fact that Philemon's name comes first, together with the phrase κατ' οἶκόν σου ("at thy house") as "fatal to the theory that Archippus is primarily the one addressed" (*Colossians and Philemon*, pp. 16 f.).

406

quest of you" (verse 9), it is to Philemon that the request is addressed. It is Philemon who is Onesimus's master; the traditional title of the epistle is no misnomer.

### 6. Three answers

We return to our three specific questions.

(a) *What is Paul asking for?* He is asking Philemon of Colossae, one of his own converts,[37] not only to pardon his slave Onesimus and give him a Christian welcome, but to send him back so that he can go on helping Paul as he had already begun to do. Paul would have liked to keep Onesimus with him, but would not do so without Philemon's express and willing consent – not only because it would have been illegal to do so, but also, and especially, because it would have involved a breach of Christian fellowship between himself and Philemon.

(b) *Did he get it?* Yes; otherwise the letter never would have survived. That it survived at all is a matter calling for comment, but if Philemon had hardened his heart and refused to pardon and welcome Onesimus he would certainly have suppressed the letter.

(c) *Why was the letter preserved?* Not only because it accomplished its purpose so far as Philemon was concerned, but also because Onesimus treasured it as his charter of liberty. And there is much to be said for the view that Onesimus did not remain a private Christian, but became in due course one of the most important figures in the life of the province of Asia – bishop of Ephesus, no less. It was in his lifetime that the corpus of Pauline letters was first collected and published, and wherever and by whomsoever this work was carried out, Onesimus (if he was bishop of Ephesus) could scarcely fail to get to know about it, and he would make sure that *his* Pauline letter found a place in the collection.

37. If Philemon of Colossae was Paul's convert, how is it that Paul apparently knew the Colossian church only by hearsay (Colossians 1: 4 ff.; 2: 1)? It has been suggested to me by Professor E. W. Goodrick of Multnomah School of the Bible, Portland, Oregon, that the "upper country" through which Paul passed on his way to Ephesus (Acts 19: 1; see p. 286 above) included the Lycus valley. If so, he might have met Philemon on his journey and won him for Christ, although the actual evangelization of Colossae and neighbouring cities was carried out, a little later, by Paul's colleague Epaphras. Alternatively, he might have met Philemon elsewhere, e.g. in Ephesus: we do not know.

# CHAPTER 35

# Principalities and Powers

## 1. The gospel in the Lycus valley

COLOSSAE, PHILEMON'S HOME CITY, WAS SITUATED IN PHRYGIA, on the south bank of the river Lycus (modern Çürüksuçay), a tributary of the Maeander (modern Menderes). It lay on the main road from Ephesus to the Euphrates, and accordingly finds mention in the itineraries of the armies of Xerxes and Cyrus the Younger, which marched along this road. Herodotus, in the fifth century B.C., speaks of it as "a great city of Phrygia" [1]; Xenophon, at the beginning of the following century, describes it as "a populous city, wealthy and large" [2]. But later in the pre-Christian era it diminished in importance with the growth of neighbouring Laodicea and Hierapolis, and at the beginning of the Christian era Strabo calls it a small town [3]. The site is now deserted, but the town of Honaz (formerly a Byzantine fortress and seat of an archbishopric) lies three miles to the south-east. In New Testament times its population comprised indigenous Phrygians and Greek settlers, together with a number of Jewish colonists who settled in Phrygia from the time of Antiochus III (early second century B.C.) onwards.

The western region of Phrygia in which Colossae and the other cities of the Lycus valley lay formed part of the kingdom of Pergamum, which was bequeathed to the Roman senate and people in 133 B.C. by Attalus III, the last ruler of that kingdom, and reconstituted by them as the province of Asia.

Christianity was introduced to the Lycus valley during the years of Paul's Ephesian ministry (c. A.D. 52–55). So vigorously was evangelization prosecuted during those years that, according to Luke, not only the people of Ephesus but "all the residents of Asia heard the word of the Lord, both Jews and Greeks" (Acts 19: 10). While this work was directed by Paul, he was assisted by a number of colleagues, and through their activity churches were planted in some areas of the province which Paul was unable to visit personal-

---

1. Herodotus, *History* vii. 30.
2. Xenophon, *Anabasis* i. 2. 6.
3. Strabo, *Geography* xii. 8. 13 (πόλισμα ).

ly. Among these were the churches of Colossae, Laodicea and Hierapolis, which appear to have been planted by Paul's colleague Epaphras; this may be inferred from Paul's references to him in Col. 1: 7 f.; 4: 12 f.

Within five years from Paul's departure from Ephesus, he found himself under house-arrest in Rome. Here, for a period of two years, he was able to receive visitors in his lodgings without difficulty.[4] One of these visitors was Epaphras, the evangelist of the Lycus valley. He brought Paul news of the progress of the churches in that region. Much of his news was encouraging, but there was one disquieting feature: at Colossae in particular there was a strong tendency among the Christians to embrace a form of teaching which (although they themselves had no suspicion of this) threatened to subvert the gospel of grace which they had recently believed and to replace their Christian liberty with spiritual bondage. To safeguard them against this threat Paul sent them the Epistle to the Colossians.

## 2. Authorship and date

The statements in the foregoing paragraph are based on several assumptions – two in particular: (a) that the letter to the Colossians has Paul for its author; (b) that it was written during his imprisonment in Rome.

(a) Authorship. On the point of authorship, Paul and Timothy are named together in the opening salutation as senders of the letter. It has been shown that most of the epistles in which Timothy's name is conjoined in this way with Paul's present some common literary features which mark them off from other letters in the corpus Paulinum; a natural explanation of this would be that in these letters Timothy served the apostle as his amanuensis.[5]

But it has been urged against the Pauline authorship of this epistle that such a gnostic heresy as it presupposes could not have emerged before the second century A.D. There would be substance in this argument if the "Colossian heresy" exhibited the traits of fully developed Valentinianism or one of the other gnostic systems described by Irenaeus and Hippolytus or reflected in the Nag Hammadi papyri. But, as compared with such second-century systems, the "Colossian heresy" must be recognized as an incipient form of gnosticism. Evidence has indeed been forthcoming in increasing

4. It was about this time (A.D. 60) that the Lycus valley suffered an earthquake which devastated Laodicea (Tacitus, Annals xiv. 27. 1); we are not told how it affected Colossae.

5. Cf. W. C. Wake, "The Authenticity of the Pauline Epistles: A Contribution from Statistical Analysis", Hibbert Journal 47 (1948–49), pp. 50 ff., especially p. 54. See also pp. 16, 443 f.

measure of the currency of incipient forms of gnosticism in the first century, especially in areas where Judaism found itself involved in dominant trends of Hellenistic and Oriental thought.

Some other arguments that have been brought against the Pauline authorship of Colossians boil down to the feeling that the author of Galatians, Corinthians and Romans could not have adapted himself as the writer of Colossians does to the situation with which this epistle deals. But this is seriously to underrate Paul's intelligence and versatility. The man whose settled policy it was to be "all things to all men" for the gospel's sake (1 Corinthians 9: 22 f.) was perfectly capable of confronting what he regarded as the false *gnōsis* and worldly *askēsis* taught at Colossae with the true *gnōsis* and spiritual *askēsis* of Christ. For all his opposition to the "Colossian heresy", he readily takes up its characteristic terminology with a view to showing that the truth which it attempts to convey and only succeeds in distorting is perfectly embodied in Christ, the manifested "mystery of God" (Colossians 2: 2).

It was pointed out some years ago by Dr. Henry Chadwick [6] that Paul in this epistle is doing two things at once: he is acting as the apologist for Christianity to the intellectual world of paganism at the same time as he is defending gospel truth within the church. His employment for apologetic purposes of the technical terms of the "Colossian heresy" in what has been called a "disinfected" sense[7] goes some way to account for the differences in vocabulary which have been discerned between this epistle and Ephesians on the one hand and the Galatian, Corinthian and Roman epistles on the other.

Some scholars – notably H. J. Holtzmann,[8] Charles Masson[9] and (most recently) P. N. Harrison[10] – recognizing indubitably Pauline elements in Colossians, have tried to explain the presence of elements felt to be un-Pauline by supposing that Paul wrote a shorter Epistle to the Colossians. This shorter epistle, the hypothesis proceeds, was drawn upon by the Paulinist who wrote Ephesians; and the same Paulinist subsequently inserted substantial interpolations into the genuine Colossians in his own "inimitable style",[11] thus producing our present enlarged Colossians. Holtzmann attempted in this way to account for the curious phenomenon that, in passages common to Colossians and

6. H. Chadwick, "All Things to All Men", *NTS* 1 (1954–55), pp. 261 ff., especially pp. 270 ff.

7. H. Chadwick, "All Things to All Men", pp. 272 f.

8. H. J. Holtzmann, *Kritik der Epheser- und Kolosserbriefe* (Leipzig, 1872).

9. C. Masson, *L'Epître de Saint Paul aux Colossiens* (Neuchatel/Paris, 1950), pp. 83 ff.

10. P. N. Harrison, *Paulines and Pastorals* (London, 1964), pp. 65 ff.

11. *Paulines and Pastorals*, p. 75. According to Harrison, the original letter consisted of Colossians 1: 1–6a, 6c–9a; 1: 26–2: 2a; 2: 5, 6; 3: 2–13; 3: 17–4: 18.

Ephesians, sometimes the one epistle and sometimes the other seems to be earlier. But A. S. Peake's criticism of Holtzmann's argument – "the complexity of the hypothesis tells fatally against it"[12] – is equally valid against its more recent formulations.

P. N. Harrison incorporates with his formulation of this hypothesis the view which he takes over from E. J. Goodspeed that Ephesians was written by Onesimus; Onesimus, he concludes, was also the interpolator of Colossians.[13] Two of the most substantial interpolations which Harrison discerns are the passages in Colossians 1: 9b–25 and 2: 8–23, largely because of the high proportion of *hapax legomena* which they contain. But the argument from *hapax legomena* is precarious when applied to these two passages, since in the former liberal use is made of liturgical formulae, while the latter is above all others the passage in which the vocabulary of the "Colossian heresy" seems to be taken over and used in a "disinfected" sense.

In a more recent study Bishop Eduard Lohse agrees that the thought of Colossians exhibits Pauline features, but finds differences between its theology and that of the major Pauline letters which rule out Paul as its direct, or even indirect author. These differences pervade the non-polemical as well as the polemical parts of the letter; they affect Christology, ecclesiology, eschatology and baptismal doctrine, and are ascribed to the emergence of a "Pauline school tradition" which was based probably in Ephesus. Colossians, however, belongs to a relatively early phase of this tradition: its conception of the church, for example, is earlier than that of Ephesians, and its understanding of the ministry more primitive than that of the Pastoral Epistles. One might say, indeed, that on Bishop Lohse's own showing, Colossians is here in line "with the major Pauline epistles, which occasionally also mention teachers, prophets, and ministers of the word along with the apostle, but as the same time describe teaching as the entire community's duty which every Christian, by virtue of the charisma bestowed on him, may and should fulfill".[14] This last statement goes beyond the evidence of the major epistles, where "he who teaches" exercises one of the "gifts that differ according to the grace given to us" (Romans 12: 6 f.). The question "Are all teachers?" (1 Corinthians 12: 29) expects the answer "No". Yet the primitiveness of the understanding of the ministry in Colossians

---

12. A. S. Peake, *Critical Introduction to the New Testament* (London, 1909), p. 52.
13. *Paulines and Pastorals*, pp. 70, 77.
14. E. Lohse, *A Commentary on the Epistles to the Colossians and to Philemon*, E.T. (Philadelphia, 1971), pp. 177–183 *et passim*. The exhortation to the Colossian Christians to "teach and admonish one another" (Colossians 3: 16) should not be pressed to imply that there was no specialized teaching gift in that church.

may well serve as a positive argument for a date within the apostle's lifetime.

(b) *Date.* As for the question whether Paul's imprisonment at the time of writing Colossians (Colossians 4: 3, 18) was his Roman imprisonment or an earlier one, reference has been made elsewhere to two criteria which, in default of more explicit evidence, may help to determine the relative dating of the Pauline epistles.[15] These criteria have to do with the development of Paul's thought in certain fields. Here it is all too easy to argue in circles, determining the development of his thought from the order of his epistles, and then determining the order of his epistles from the development of his thought. But if we can establish some definite progression of thought on the basis of those epistles which can be dated on independent evidence, we may be able sometimes to suggest where, along the line of progression thus established, the other epistles should most probably be placed. Even so, we must beware of imagining that we can assume anything in the nature of linear progression when we are dealing with a mind like Paul's.

The two criteria mentioned are Paul's progression of thought in relation to (i) the eschatological hope and (ii) and the church as the body of Christ.

The former of these criteria does not take us very far with Colossians. In this epistle there is none of the apocalyptic picture-language which we find in the Thessalonian epistles [16] and in some degree in 1 Corinthians 15: 51 ff., but the certainty of the parousia as the hope of the people of Christ is as clear as ever: "When Christ who is our life appears, then you also will appear with him in glory" (Colossians 3: 4). This is very much in line with Romans 8: 18–25, where the revealing of the sons of God in glory is the consummation for which the universe waits with longing expectancy; and the portrayal of Christ in Colossians 1: 20 as the one through whom God plans to reconcile the universe to himself is in line both with that passage in Romans and with Philippians 2: 10 f., where the divine purpose is said to be that every knee should bow in Jesus' name and every tongue confess that he is Lord.

Much more decisive for the dating of Colossians is the other criterion – Paul's conception of the Church as the body of Christ. A comparison of the setting forth of this conception in Colossians with its setting forth in 1 Corinthians and Romans suggests that Colossians marks a more advanced stage in Paul's thinking on the subject than do 1 Corinthians and Romans. More will be said about this later in this chapter; suffice it to note here that, whereas

15. F. F. Bruce, "The Epistles of Paul", in *Peake's Commentary on the Bible*, ed. M. Black and H. H. Rowley (London, [2] 1962), pp. 928 ff.

16. E.g. 1 Thessalonians 4: 16 f.; 2 Thessalonians 1: 7; 2: 3–12; see pp. 231, 306.

in 1 Corinthians and Romans the common life of Christians is compared to the interdependence of the various members of a body, the head (or a particular part of the head) being one member among others,[17] in Colossians (and Ephesians) Christ is viewed as the head of the body. This more advanced stage in Paul's thinking may reflect his reaction to the Colossian heresy; at any rate, it is difficult to date it during his Ephesian ministry, about the same time as 1 Corinthians and earlier than Romans. It follows that an Ephesian imprisonment is out of the question as the setting of Colossians; and if an Ephesian imprisonment is out, we have to think of either Caesarea or Rome. As between these two alternative, Rome is the more probable on all counts.[18]

This argument would, of course, be rebutted if the theory of two stages in the composition of Colossians were accepted; P. N. Harrison, for example, assigns all the occurrences of "head" and "body" in the epistle to the interpolator, and is thus able to date the genuine nucleus in Paul's Ephesian ministry, "during a brief period of house arrest by friendly Asiarchs (Acts 19: 31), to keep Paul out of the reach of fanatical Jews, and avert a riot".[19] But the bibliographical improbability of this theory is such that it could be favourably considered only if powerful evidence were forthcoming in its support – and for such evidence we seek in vain.[20]

## 3. The "Colossian heresy"

We have no formal exposition of what is commonly called the "Colossian heresy"; its character must be inferred from the counter-arguments presented in our epistle.

But, it may be asked, do these counter-arguments point to the existence of a "Colossian heresy"? Paul puts the Romans and the Philippians on their guard against certain false teachings and malpractices (Romans 16: 17–20; Philippians 3: 2, 18 f.) without necessarily implying that such things had actually invaded the churches of Rome and Philippi; might he not be doing the same thing in Colossians? "Were there", in short (as Professor Morna Hooker has asked), "false teachers in Colossae?" She suggests, not that Paul is forewarning the Colossian Christians against false teachers who might infiltrate their ranks, but that he is arming them against the pressures of contemporary society with its prevalent superstitions, just as "a Christian pastor in twentieth

17. Cf. 1 Corinthians 12: 16–21.
18. If Ephesus is excluded as the place of origin for Colossians, it is by the same token excluded for Philemon (see p. 399).
19. *Paulines and Pastorals*, p. 75 (see p. 299).
20. It is not easy to see why the allegedly genuine nucleus of Colossians should have been written at all.

century Britain might well feel it necessary to remind those in his care that Christ was greater than any astrological forces".[21]

The answer to Professor Hooker's question must in large measure be a subjective one: as I read the letter, the impression made on me makes me answer, "Yes; there were false teachers in Colossae."[22]

Basically, their teaching seems to have been Jewish. This appears from the part played in it by legal ordinances, circumcision, food regulations, the sabbath, new moon and other prescriptions of the Jewish calendar. But it was not the more straightforward Judaism against which the churches of Galatia had to be put on their guard. That Judaism was probably introduced into the Galatian churches by emissaries from Judaea; the Colossian heresy was more probably a Phrygian development in which a local variety of Judaism had been fused with a philosphy of non-Jewish origin – an early and simple form of gnosticism.

The synagogues of Phrygia appear to have been peculiarly exposed to the influence of Hellenistic speculation and consequent tendencies to religious syncretism.[23] When the gospel was introduced to the region, a Jewish-Hellenistic syncretism would find little difficulty in expanding and modifying itself sufficiently to fit the general framework of the Christian story, and the result would be something not unlike the Colossian heresy as we can reconstruct it from Paul's reply to it.

In this heresy a special place was apparently given to angels, as agents both in creation and in the giving of the law.

As for the angelic agency in creation, one form of this belief appears in Philo.[24] Another form seems to be attested by Justin Martyr, who refers to certain Jewish teachers who held that the words "let us make man" (Genesis 1: 26) and "as one of us" (Genesis 3: 22) imply "that God spoke to angels, or that the human frame was the workmanship of angels" – whereas Justin held that the plural pronoun "us" denoted the Father and the Son.[25] We

21. M. D. Hooker, "Were there False Teachers in Colossae?" in *Christ and Spirit in the New Testament: Studies in Honour of C. F. D. Moule*, ed. B. Lindars and S. S. Smalley (Cambridge, 1973), pp. 315–331.

22. For an inquiry into their teaching see G. Bornkamm, "Die Häresie des Kolosserbriefes", in *Das Ende des Gesetzes: Paulusstudien = Gesammelte Aufsätze* i (Munich, 1952), pp. 139–156, E.T., "The Heresy at Colossae", in *Conflict at Colossae*, ed. F. O. Francis and W. A. Meeks (Missoula, 1975), pp. 125–140.

23. The statement sometimes quoted in this connexion from TB *Shabbath* 147b, to the effect that the wines and baths of *Prugita* had separated the ten tribes from their fellow-Israelites, is of doubtful relevance: *Prugita* may be Phrygia, but it may not.

24. Cf. H. Chadwick, "St. Paul and Philo of Alexandria", *BJRL* 48 (1965–66), pp. 286–307, especially p. 303.

25. Justin, *Dialogue with Trypho* 62.

may compare the statement in the *Treatise on the Three Natures*, discovered among the Nag Hammadi texts: "Some [Jewish sects] say that God is the creator of that which exists; others say that he created through his angels."[26]

The angelic agency in the giving of the law is mentioned by Paul in his letter to the Galatians and by two other New Testament writers; it is attested in contemporary Jewish literature, as well as earlier in the Book of Jubilees and later in rabbinical commentaries.[27] In the Colossian heresy the keeping of the law was regarded as a tribute of obedience due to those angels, and the breaking of the law incurred their displeasure and brought the law-breaker into debt and bondage to them. Hence they must be placated not only by the legal observances of traditional Judaism but in addition by a rigorous asceticism.

The angels through whom the law was given are described as "elemental beings" (*stoicheia*), a term already used in the same sense in Galatians 4: 3, 9. But they are not only elemental beings but dominant ones as well – principalities and powers, lords of the planetary spheres, sharers in the divine plenitude (*plērōma*) and intermediaries between heaven and earth. Since they controlled the lines of communication between God and man, all revelation from God to man and all worship from man to God could reach its goal only by their mediation and with their permission. Christ himself, it was evidently held, had to submit to their authority on his way from heaven to earth, if not indeed also on his way back from earth to heaven.

All this was presented as a form of advanced teaching for a spiritual élite. The Christians of Colossae were urged to go in for this progressive wisdom and knowledge (*gnōsis*), to explore the deeper mysteries by a series of successive initiations until they attained perfection (*teleiōsis*). Christian baptism was but a preliminary initiation; those who wished to proceed farther along the path of truth must put off all material elements by pursuing an ascetic regimen until at last they became citizens of the spiritual world, the realm of light.

Bishop Lightfoot, in his commentary on Colossians and Philemon (1875), traced this species of Judaizing *gnōsis* back to the Essenes,[28] to whom he devoted three dissertations at the end of the

26. See G. Quispel's account in *The Jung Codex*, ed. F. L. Cross (London, 1955), p. 62; he suggested that the treatise was by Heracleon. Cf. also *Genesis Rabba* 8: 8 on Genesis 1: 26: "When Moses came to the words, 'Let us [plural] make man', he said, 'Lord of the world! What an opportunity is thus given to the heretics to open their mouths!' He answered, 'Write! He who wishes to go astray may go astray'."

27. Cf. Galatians 3: 19; Acts 7: 53; Hebrews 2: 2; see p. 192 with n. 9.

28. J. B. Lightfoot, *Saint Paul's Epistles to the Colossians and to Philemon* (London, 1875), pp. 73 ff.

commentary,[29] thus reverting to a subject which he had already broached ten years earlier in his dissertation on "St. Paul and the Three" in his commentary on Galatians.[30]

Quite apart from the relevance of his dissertations on the Essenes to the theme of Colossians, Lightfoot shows his characteristic sobriety and accuracy of scholarship in his description of the Essenes and their doctrines – as may be seen on the one hand by the contrast between his account and that of C. D. Ginsburg's essay on *The Essenes, their History and Doctrines*, published in 1864,[31] and now on the other hand in the light of the vastly increased knowledge of the Essenes or a related group available to us from the Qumran texts. In the light of these texts, too, Lightfoot's further thesis of a strong Essene element in Ebionitism is reinforced.[32]

In relating the Colossian heresy to the Essenes Lightfoot argues (a) that Essene Judaism was "gnostic", characterized by the intellectual exclusiveness and speculative tenets of gnosticism; (b) that this type of Jewish thought and practice had established itself in that area of Asia Minor in the apostolic age; (c) that the Colossian heresy was a brand of gnostic Judaism, because (i) it was clearly Jewish in its basis and (ii) it was marked by several distinctive features of gnosticism: an intellectual élite (which insisted on wisdom, knowledge, etc.), cosmogonic speculation (with emphasis on angelic mediation, the *plērōma*, etc.), asceticism and calendrical regulations.[33]

More recently many of these features reappear in a catalogue of specific points of contact between the Qumran texts and the Colossian heresy.[34] Professor W. D. Davies, for example, enumerates among these points of contact features of phraseology,[35] calendrical niceties, sabbath regulations, food distinctions, asceticism, and emphasis on wisdom and knowledge,[36] involving a special

29. "The Name Essene" (pp. 349 ff.); "Origin and Affinities of the Essenes" (pp. 355 ff.); "Essenism and Christianity" (pp. 397 ff.).

30. J. B. Lightfoot, *Saint Paul's Epistle to the Galatians* (London, 1865), pp. 292 ff.

31. Reprinted with another of his treatises in C. D. Ginsburg, *The Essenes: Their History and Doctrine/The Kabbalah: Its Doctrines, Development and Literature* (London, 1955).

32. Cf. O. Cullmann, "Die neuentdeckten Qumran-Texte und das Judenchristentum der Pseudoclementinen" in *Neutestamentliche Studien für R. Bultmann*, ed. W. Eltester = *BZNW* 21 (Berlin, 1954), pp. 35 ff., and "The Significance of the Qumran Texts for Research into the Beginnings of Christianity", in *The Scrolls and the New Testament*, ed. K. Stendahl (London, 1958), pp. 18 ff.; H. J. Schoeps, *Urgemeinde, Judenchristentum, Gnosis* (Tübingen, 1956), pp. 69 ff.

33. *Saint Paul's Epistles to the Colossians and to Philemon*, pp. 73 ff.

34. Cf. W. D. Davies, "Paul and the Dead Sea Scrolls: Flesh and Spirit", in *The Scrolls and the New Testament*, ed. K. Stendahl, pp. 157 ff., especially pp. 166 ff.

35. E.g. "his body of flesh", attested in Colossians 1: 22 (τῷ σώματι τῆς σαρκὸς αὐτοῦ, cf. Colossians 2: 11) and in 1 Qp Hab 9, 1. 2 (big'wiyyat b'sārô).

36. With Colossians 2: 18, "taking his stand on visions" (ἃ ἑώρακεν ἐμβατεύων)

understanding of the world, of angelology, of the "spirit of truth" and the "spirit of error", and so forth.

Even so, we cannot without more ado identify the Colossian heresy as a variety of Essenism or of the Qumran doctrine. For one thing, we miss in the letter to the Colossians any reference to an insistence on ceremonial washings, which appear to have played an important part among the Essenes in general and at Qumran in particular. When baptism is mentioned in Colossians, it is mentioned not as the true counterpart to heretical ablutions but in connection with the "circumcision made without hands" (Colossians 2: 11 f.) – perhaps by way of showing that the literal rite of circumcision has been superseded by the work of Christ. Instead, therefore, of talking of specifically Essene influence in the Colossian heresy, it might be better to use the wider term recently popularized by Principal Matthew Black and talk of the influence of "nonconformist Judaism" or "Jewish nonconformity".[37]

Behind Colossians, and some other areas of New Testament literature, several scholars have discerned a gnostic myth of Iranian origin which they believe to have been current in the Near East around the time when Christianity first appeared.[38] The reflection of this myth in a New Testament document is usually sufficient to stamp it as post-apostolic – sufficient especially, if the document in question belongs to the *corpus Paulinum*, to stamp it as non-Pauline

---

Professor Davies compares the description in 1 QM 10, ll. 10 ff., of

> "the people of the saints of the covenant
>     instructed in the laws and learned in wisdom,
> who have heard the voice of Majesty
>     and have seen the angels of holiness,
> whose ears have been unstopped,
>     and who have heard profound things".

The meaning of the Greek phrase was considerably illuminated in 1913 by the publication of a group of inscriptions from Claros, on the Ionian coast of Asia Minor, where the verb ἐμβατεύειν denotes a sequel to initiation, meaning something like "to tread the sacred area", "to have access to the inmost shrine". Cf. W. M. Ramsay, *The Teaching of Paul in Terms of the Present Day* (London, 1913), pp. 286 ff.; A. D. Nock, *Essays on Religion and the Ancient World*, i (Oxford, 1972), p. 342; M. Smith, *The Secret Gospel* (London, 1974), pp. 98 f., where the phrase is translated "[beings] he saw [when] going in [to the heavens]", in a context which makes one wonder if the "Colossian heresy" may not have had something to do with an inchoate phase of *merkābāh* mysticism (see p. 135, n. 2).

37. M. Black, *The Scrolls and Christian Origins* (London, 1961), p. 166.

38. See in particular R. Reitzenstein, *Das iranische Erlösungsmysterium* (Bonn, 1921); for the application to the New Testament, especially to Colossians and Ephesians, cf. H. Schlier, *Christus und die Kirche im Epheserbrief* (Tübingen, 1930); E. Käsemann, *Leib und Leib Christi* (Tübingen, 1933); R. Bultmann, *Theology of the New Testament*, E.T., i (London, 1952), pp. 164 ff., ii (London, 1955), pp. 133 ff., 149 ff.

or at least deutero-Pauline. One distinctive feature of this myth is the association or identification of Primal Man with the Redeemer-Revealer who comes from the realm of light to liberate exiles from that realm who have been imprisoned in material bodies in the lower world of darkness, by imparting to them the knowledge of the truth. Much of the material on the basis of which this myth has been reconstructed – especially Mandaean and Manichaean literature – is later than the apostolic age, and is at least as likely to have been influenced by the New Testament as to have exercised an influence upon it. It is possible to defend the thesis that Primal Man and the Redeemer-Revealer are nowhere brought together in gnosticism except under the influence of the gospel, and one might even hazard the guess that one of the earliest attempts to re-state the gospel in terms of such a gnostic myth can be detected in the Colossian heresy.

## 4. The cosmic Christ

The whole elaborate structure of the Colossian heresy is condemned by Paul as so much specious make-believe. Far from representing a more advanced grade of religious truth than that proclaimed in the apostolic preaching, it was at every point inconsistent with that preaching. A system in which the planetary powers played so prominent a part must needs enthrone fate in place of God. If we may judge by the analogy of parallel systems, Christ was probably held to have relinquished successive portions of his authority to the planetary powers as he passed through their spheres on his way to earth, and if (as the Colossian heresy seems to have taught) it was these powers that made him suffer on the cross, that would be regarded as conclusive proof of their superiority to him.

Paul's reply to this "human tradition" (Colossians 2: 8) is to set over against it the tradition of Christ – not merely the tradition which stems from the teaching of Christ but the tradition which finds its embodiment in him.[39] Christ, he says, is the image of God, the one who incorporates the plenitude of the divine essence, so that the elemental spirits have no share in it at all. And those who are members of Christ realize their plenitude in him; they need not seek, for they cannot find, perfection anywhere else. It is in Christ that the totality of wisdom and knowledge is concentrated and made available to his people – not to an élite only, but to all. And he is the sole mediator between God and mankind.

39. Cf. O. Cullmann, "The Tradition", in *The Early Church* (London, 1956), pp. 55 ff.

Far from the angels playing a part in creation, Christ is the one through whom all things were created, including the principalities and powers which figured so prominently in the Colossian heresy. Why should people who were united by faith with the creator of these powers think it necessary to pay them tribute? Again, far from these powers demonstrating their superiority to Christ, his death and resurrection reveal him as their conqueror. When on the cross they flung themselves upon him with hostile intent, he not only repelled their attack but turned the cross into the triumphal chariot before which he drove them as his vanquished foes.[40] Why then should those who through faith-union with him shared his death and resurrection go on serving those elemental spirits which Christ had conquered? The Colossian heresy, with all its tabus, was no syllabus of advanced wisdom; it bore all the marks of immaturity. Why should those who had come of age in Christ go back to the apron-strings of infancy? Why should those whom Christ had set free submit to this yoke of bondage?

In his reply to the Colossian heresy, Paul develops the doctrine of the cosmic Christ more fully than in his other epistles. Adumbrations of it certainly appear in some of his other epistles. To Paul there was "one Lord, Jesus Christ, through whom are all things and through whom we exist" (1 Corinthians 8: 6); this Christ was "the power of God and the wisdom of God" (1 Corinthians 1: 24), and God through the Spirit had revealed to his people that hidden wisdom, decreed before the ages for their glory, through ignorance of which the cosmic powers[41] had crucified the Lord of glory and thus accomplished their own overthrow (1 Corinthians 2: 6–10). And the liberation from such hostile forces procured by Christ in his death was not to be restricted to his people alone, but would in due course reach out to the whole cosmos (Romans 8: 19–22). But what is suggested in passing in 1 Corinthians and Romans is expounded more fully and systematically in Colossians. (This, it may be added, is a further indication that Colossians is later than these two epistles.)

The language in which Paul portrays Christ as the one in whom and for whom the universe was created, and in whom all things hold together, is generally recognized nowadays to be based on an early Christian hymn or confession in which Christ is celebrated as the Divine Wisdom.[42]

---

40. Colossians 2: 15.

41. The "archons of this age" in 1 Corinthians 2: 8 are probably identical with the "*kosmokratores* of this darkness" in Ephesians 6: 12. For Paul's understanding of them see pp. 422 f.

42. On the structure of these verses see E. Lohmeyer, *Die Briefe an die Philipper, an die Kolosser und an Philemon* (Göttingen, [8] 1930), p. 41; E. Käsemann, "A

A Wisdom Christology can be traced in various strands of first-century Christianity, the most notable evidence of it in the New Testament being Colossians 1: 15–17, John 1: 1–3 and Hebrews 1: 1–3, three mutually independent passages. The root of this Christology, on which Paul and the Fourth Evangelist and the writer to the Hebrews alike drew, must be primitive indeed; and in view of the presence of what form critics call "wisdom sayings" among the *verba Christi* in the Synoptic Gospels, it is not too hazardous to suggest that Christ's occasional speaking in the rôle of Divine Wisdom is a major root of the Wisdom Christology of the Apostolic Age.

One Old Testament passage in particular has influenced those New Testament contexts in which Christ, as the Wisdom of God, is said to have created all things, and that is Proverbs 8: 22 ff., where Wisdom personified speaks in the first person as the beginning of God's way, his darling first-born child and his assessor when he created the world. The wording of this passage underlies the description of Christ in Colossians 1: 15 as "the first-born of all creation" and in Colossians 1: 18 as "the beginning" (*archē*). Later rabbinical exegesis adduced the word "beginning" in Proverbs 8: 22 – "the beginning (Heb. *rē'šît*) of his way" – to explain the "beginning" (Heb. *rē'šît*) of Genesis 1: 1; that is to say, the "beginning" in which God created heaven and earth was Wisdom (identified with the Torah). This analogy explains the curious use of the preposition *en* in Colossians 1: 16a ("in him were all things created") where we might have expected the *dia* ("through") of agency; the "in" is the "in" of Genesis 1: 1: if "in the beginning God created heaven and earth", Christ, as the Wisdom of God, is the beginning "in" whom all things were created.[43]

But the hymn of Colossians 1: 15–20 celebrates Christ not only

Primitive Christian Baptismal Liturgy", in *Essays on New Testament Themes*, E.T. (London, 1964), pp. 149 ff.; R. P. Martin, *Colossians: The Church's Lord and the Christian's Liberty* (Exeter, 1972), and *Colossians and Philemon* (London, 1974), pp. 55 ff. Professor Martin accepts that verses 15–20 "form a compact, self-contained hymn written in praise of the cosmic Christ, the Lord of creation and redemption" (*Colossians: The Church's Lord and the Christian's Liberty*, p. 39). M. D. Hooker is not convinced that there was a previously existent "hymn", but suggests that the passage "may . . . have been developed and formulated . . . in order to demonstrate that both creation and redemption are completed in Christ because he has replaced the Jewish Law" ("Were there False Teachers in Colossae?", pp. 316 f., 329). J. M. Robinson has proposed that Colossians 2: 9–15 should be regarded as "clearly a baptismal homily on the anti-gnostic kerygmatic hymn in Col. 1: 15–20" ("From Paulinism to Early Catholicism", *Interpretation* 10 [1956], p. 349). The present state of the question is reviewed in detail and judiciously assessed by P. Benoit, "L'hymne christologique de Col 1, 15–20", in *Christianity, Judaism and Other Greco-Roman Cults: Studies for Morton Smith at Sixty*, ed. J. Neusner, i (Leiden, 1975), pp. 226–263.

43. Cf. C. F. Burney, "Christ as the ΑΡΧΗ of Creation", *JTS* 27 (1925–26),

as head of the old creation but as head of the new creation; this is the subject of the second strophe, beginning in verse 18. In the new creation, too, Christ is the "beginning", not this time as the "first-born of all creation" but as "first-born from the dead" – i.e. by resurrection.[44] If in relation to the old creation he is "head" of every principality and power (Colossians 2: 10) in the sense of being their author and ruler, in relation to the new creation he is "head" of his body the church, not simply in the sense of ruler or origin but in the sense that he is so vitally united with his people that the life which they now live is derived from the life which he lives as first-born from the dead. The cosmos is not called his body, and to envisage an earlier form of the hymn in which the cosmos, and not the church, was so called is an unwarranted exercise of the imagination.[45]

Whatever form the hymn originally had, the description of Christ as "the head of the body, the church" (Colossians 1: 18) is most probably Pauline. All our evidence points to Paul as the originator of this way of expressing the church's vital unity with the church's Lord, "the head, from whom the whole body, nourished and knit together through the joints and ligaments, grows with a growth that is from God" (Colossians 2: 19). This, as we have seen, marks an advance on the use of this terminology in 1 Corinthians and Romans, where the church is "the body of Christ" (1 Corinthians 12: 27) or "one body in Christ" (Romans 12: 5), but Christ is not spoken of as the church's head.

A great variety of theories have been advanced regarding the source of the conception of the church as the body of Christ. Jewish,[46] Gnostic[47] and Stoic[48] antecedents have been suggested. But most probably we have to do with a survival of the Hebrew concept of corporate personality.[49] Christ and his people are so

---

pp. 160–177. Paul's exegesis of Proverbs 8: 22 in this sense antedates by nearly 200 years its earliest rabbinical exponent, the third-century Hoshaiah (*Genesis Rabba* 1: 1 on Genesis 1: 1). For the Greek background of ἀρχή see A. A. T. Ehrhardt, *The Beginning* (Manchester, 1968).

44. Cf. Revelation 1: 5.

45. In Colossians 1: 18 and 2: 10 there is probably the same kind of oscillation between the literal sense of "head" and its secondary sense of "origin" as appears in 1 Corinthians 11: 3 ff. Mention may also be made here of W. L. Knox's improbable argument that, under the influence of Hellenism, Paul moved from apocalyptic to cosmogony, from Christ as Omega to Christ as Alpha (*St. Paul and the Church of the Gentiles* [Cambridge, 1938], pp. 90 ff.).

46. Cf. W. D. Davies, *Paul and Rabbinic Judaism* (London, 1948), pp. 53 ff.

47. Cf. H. Schlier, *Christus und die Kirche im Epheserbrief* (Tübingen, 1930), pp. 37 ff.; E. Käsemann, *Leib und Leib Christi* (Tübingen, 1933). (Both these scholars have modified their views since these monographs were published.)

48. Cf. W. L. Knox, *St. Paul and the Church of the Gentiles*, pp. 160 ff.

49. Cf. A. Schweitzer, *The Mysticism of Paul the Apostle*, E.T. (London, 1931), pp. 115 ff.; E. Best, *One Body in Christ* (London, 1955), pp. 93 ff., 203 ff.

conjoined that on occasion Christ and his people together can be called "Christ".[50] This is not the only phase of Paul's thought where oscillation between individual and corporate personality can be traced; but this phase was probably impressed indelibly on his mind when on the Damascus road he heard the challenge of the voice from heaven: "Saul, Saul, why do you persecute me?" (Acts 9: 4). Not that Paul immediately interpreted these words in terms of head and body, as Augustine later did; [51] but the truth which they expressed is the truth which Paul expressed in Colossians (and Ephesians) when he speaks of the church as the body of Christ, drawing life and all other resources from him who is her head.

The advance from the language of simile in 1 Corinthians and Romans to the real interpersonal involvement expressed in the language of Colossians and Ephesians may have been stimulated by Paul's consideration of the issues involved in the Colossian heresy. Far from being subject to the principalities and powers, he argued, Christ was their author and ruler by the twofold claim of creation and conquest. But as he was head of the old creation, so by his resurrection from the dead he was head of the new creation too; and as Paul had already repeatedly spoken of the church as the body of Christ, Christ's headship over the church could readily be conceived as an organic relationship, in which Christ exercised the control over his people that the head of a body exercises over its various parts. In this way not only is the living fellowship between the members of the church brought out (as in the earlier epistles referred tò) but so is the dependence of all the members on Christ for life and power, and his supremacy is vindicated against a system of thought which threatened to cast him down from his excellency. In consequence "body" is used in Colossians and Ephesians in correlation with "head" rather than (as in the earlier epistles) with "spirit"; but this is no valid argument against identity of authorship.

## 5. The defeat of demonic powers

"Christ crucified, . . . the power of God and the wisdom of God" (1 Corinthians 1: 23 f.), the message preached to the Corinthians, is the message which Paul proclaims as the answer to the Colossian heresy. How foolish it was to pay tribute to the angelic powers through which the law was given, as though they controlled the way from God to man and back from man to God! That way was now controlled by Christ, who had subjugated these powers and

---

50. Cf. 1 Corinthians 12: 12 ("as the body is one and has many members, and all the members of the body, being many, are one body, so also is Christ").
51. "Membris adhuc in terra positis caput in caelo clamabat" (*Sermons* 279. 1).

reduced them to the status of "weak and beggarly elemental spirits" (Galatians 4: 9).

The lords of the planetary spheres may play but little part in the world-outlook of man today – although the number of readers of the popular press who accept the invitation to "plan with the planets" suggests that they perhaps play a larger part than we think. Yet man today is unprecedentedly aware of powerful and malignant forces in the universe which he does not hesitate to call "demonic". He feels that they are operating against his welfare but that he is quite unable to master them, whether by individual strength or by united action. They may be Frankenstein monsters of his own creation; they may be subliminal horrors over which he has no conscious control. He knows himself to be involved in situations from which his moral sense recoils – but what can he do about them? If he and his fellows are puppets in the hand of a blind and unfriendly fate, what difference does it make whether they resist and be crushed immediately, or acquiesce and be crushed a little later? [52]

To this mood of frustration and despair Paul's answer would be his answer to the Colossian heresy. To be united to Christ, he would say, is to be liberated from the thraldom of demonic forces, to enjoy perfect freedom instead of being the playthings of fate.

Indeed, archaic as some of Paul's terminology is, his essential message is easily translated into the language of today. Whatever others might think, in his mind the principalities and powers were no longer the archons who governed the planetary spheres; he has "demythologized" them to stand for all the forces in the universe opposed to Christ and his people. Rudolf Bultmann has pointed out that "in our day and generation, although we no longer think mythologically, we often speak of demonic powers which rule history, corrupting political and social life. Such language", he continues, "is metaphorical, a figure of speech, but in it is expressed the knowledge, the insight, that the evil for which every man is responsible individually has nevertheless become a power which mysteriously enslaves every member of the human race." [53] It may be suggested that this knowledge, this insight, was present to Paul's

52. Cf. A. D. Galloway, *The Cosmic Christ* (London, 1951), p. 28; J. S. Stewart, "On a Neglected Emphasis in New Testament Theology", *Scottish Journal of Theology* 4 (1951), pp. 292 ff.; G. H. C. Macgregor, "Principalities and Powers", *NTS* 1 (1954–55), pp. 17 ff.

53. R. Bultmann, *Jesus Christ and Mythology*, E.T. (London, 1960), p. 21. Cf. the treatment of "Beliar" in H. H. Rowley, *The Relevance of Apocalyptic* (London, [3] 1963), pp. 177 f. On the subject in general see also G. B. Caird, *Principalities and Powers* (Oxford, 1956); H. Schlier, *Principalities and Powers in the New Testament*, E.T. (Freiburg/London, 1961); E. G. Rupp, *Principalities and Powers* (London, 1964).

mind and expressed by him in terms of the principalities and powers which, he affirmed, were unable to separate believers "from the love of God in Christ Jesus our Lord" (Romans 8: 39).

# CHAPTER 36

# The Quintessence of Paulinism

"THE QUINTESSENCE OF PAULINISM" WAS CHOSEN BY A. S. PEAKE as the title of a lecture which he delivered in the John Rylands Library, Manchester, on October 11, 1916 – a penetrating exposition of the thought and teaching of Paul.[1] The same title is chosen for this chapter because it is a fitting description of the first-century document which has been preserved for us in the New Testament canon as the Epistle to the Ephesians. This document in large measure sums up the leading themes of the Pauline letters, and sets forth the cosmic implications of Paul's ministry as apostle to the Gentiles.

## 1. Introductory questions

No fresh contribution is offered here to the problem of the authorship of Ephesians. Suffice it to say, with G. B. Caird, that the epistle, "if not by Paul, is a masterly summary of Paul's theology by a disciple who was capable of thinking Paul's thoughts after him"[2] – to which one may add a note of surprise that such a disciple has left no other trace, with the observation that Paul's Roman imprisonment provides the most plausible *dramatic* life-setting for the letter.

1. Published in *BJRL* 4 (1917–18), pp. 285 ff., and subsequently in J. T. Wilkinson (ed.), *Arthur Samuel Peake* (London, 1958), pp. 116 ff.
2. G. B. Caird, *The Apostolic Age* (London, 1955), p. 133; cf. his New Clarendon Bible commentary, *Paul's Letters from Prison* (Oxford, 1976), pp. 9 ff. According to S. H. Hooke, Ephesians, "if not by Paul, certainly belongs to the Pauline exposition of the glory" (*Alpha and Omega* [Welwyn, 1961], p. 256). P. N. Harrison adds that the author of Ephesians "knew how to put into words, and so make explicit, thoughts which are implicit in Paul's other letters, but nowhere else so explicit as here" (*Paulines and Pastorals* [London, 1964], p. 35). The case against Pauline authorship is presented most substantially by C. L. Mitton, *The Epistle to the Ephesians* (Oxford, 1951); cf. his more popular commentary, *Ephesians* (London, 1976). Pauline authorship is defended by E. Percy, *Die Probleme der Kolosser- und Epheserbriefe* (Lund, 1946), and A. van Roon, *The Authenticity of Ephesians* (Leiden, 1974). See further the two opening papers, "The Case for the Pauline Authorship" by J. N. Sanders (pp. 9 ff.) and "The Case against the Pauline Authorship" by D. E. Nineham (pp. 21 ff.) in F. L. Cross (ed.), *Studies in Ephesians* (London, 1956); also H. J. Cadbury, "The Dilemma of Ephesians", *NTS* 5 (1958–59), pp. 91 ff.; R. P. Martin, "An Epistle in Search of a Life-Setting", *Expository Times* 79 (1967–68), pp. 297 ff.

Ephesians is not an easy document for New Testament students to come to terms with. Markus Barth calls it "a stranger at the door"[3] of the Pauline corpus. E. J. Goodspeed speaks of it as "the Waterloo of commentators"[4] – an ambiguous expression. More promisingly, he describes the epistle as "a great rhapsody of the Christian salvation".[5] It reads, he says, "like a commentary on the Pauline letters"[6] – which is true, but a trifle odd in a work which, a few lines previously, has referred to it as "a mosaic of Pauline materials".[7] A mosaic made up of fragments of a man's writings is not best calculated to provide a commentary on them.

In a book published in 1966 mention is made of an unnamed writer who, "anxious to preserve Ephesians for Paul", says that "Ephesians may look like a compilation of Pauline phrases, but if looked at as a whole it has a unity". "So", say the authors of the book, "has a pile of stones, no matter what kind or by whom brought together – if looked at as a unity."[8] The analogy is inexact: the structural unity of Ephesians is not like that of a pile of stones but much more like that of its own "building fitly framed together" (2: 21). Such a careful literary structure, indeed, is no proof of Pauline authorship; one could well imagine its being used as an argument *against* Pauline authorship. But an elaborately constructed work like this, with its own inner unity, a work which Samuel Taylor Coleridge could characterize as "the divinest composition of man",[9] cannot properly be compared to a cairn, or even to a mosaic painstakingly pieced together with fragments from other Pauline epistles.

## 2. Relation to other Pauline letters

"In form", says Goodspeed, "it is an encyclical."[10] This is a

3. M. Barth, *The Broken Wall* (London, 1960), p. 9; see also his massive commentary in the Anchor Bible: *Ephesians*, 2 volumes (Garden City, N.Y., 1974).

4. E. J. Goodspeed, *The Meaning of Ephesians* (Chicago, 1933), p. 15.

5. *The Meaning of Ephesians*, p. 3.

6. *The Meaning of Ephesians*, p. 9.

7. *The Meaning of Ephesians*, p. 8.

8. A. Q. Morton and J. McLeman, *Paul: The Man and the Myth* (London, 1966), pp. 27 f.

9. S. T. Coleridge, *Table Talk*, May 25, 1830; see H. N. Coleridge (ed.), *Specimens of the Table Talk of the late Samuel Taylor Coleridge* (London, 1835), p. 88. "The Epistle to the Ephesians", Coleridge said on this occasion, "is evidently a catholic epistle, addressed to the whole of what might be called St. Paul's diocese. . . . It embraces every doctrine of Christianity; – first, those doctrines peculiar to Christianity, and then those precepts common to it with natural religion."

10. *The Meaning of Ephesians*, p. 3. Goodspeed's own view, in which he was followed by the "Chicago school" and P. N. Harrison, was that Ephesians was composed by the first editor of the Pauline corpus to serve as an introduction to it. See p. 402.

widely held view, and some support is given to it by the textual
phenomena of the salutation with which it commences, which
throw doubt on the originality of the words "at Ephesus".[11]
Perhaps we may call it a general letter to Gentile Christians, more
particularly in the province of Asia – Gentile Christians who (like
the readers of 1 Peter) needed to be shown what was involved in
their recent commitment to the way of Christ. The personal notes
at the end of Ephesians link it with Colossians,[12] and provide
formal justification for considering the two epistles in the same
historical context.

Even apart from these personal references, Ephesians has other
close links with Colossians, material as well as verbal. If in
Colossians the cosmic rôle of Christ has been unfolded, Ephesians
considers the implications of this for the church as the body of
Christ – what is the church's relation to Christ's cosmic rôle, to the
principalities and powers, to God's eternal purpose? This change of
perspective from Christ to the church goes far to explain the
different nuances with which such keywords as "fulness" (plērōma)
and "mystery" (mystērion) are used in Ephesians as compared with
Colossians.

Ephesians has manifest affinities also with 1 Corinthians; in particular, it universalizes the teaching about the church which in the
earlier epistle is applied to the life of one local congregation.

Nor should its relation to certain parts of Romans be overlooked.
If Paul in Romans emphasizes that "there is no difference"
between Jew and Gentile (Romans 3: 22; 10: 12), either "in
Adam" or "in Christ", Ephesians emphasizes that all the spiritual
blessings which are available to men "in the heavenly realm in
Christ Jesus" are accessible on an equal footing to Jews and Gentiles alike (Ephesians 1: 3, etc.). If Paul in Romans magnifies his
office as apostle to the Gentiles (Romans 11: 13) [13] and tells how he
has discharged this ministry, winning obedience from the Gentiles
"from Jerusalem and as far round as Illyricum" (Romans 15:
15–21), Ephesians presents him as "a prisoner for Christ Jesus on

11. The reference to Ephesus is omitted by $P^{46}$ (the oldest extant Pauline
manuscript) and by the principal witnesses to the Alexandrian text-type. See B.
M. Metzger, A Textual Commentary on the Greek New Testament (London/New York,
1971), p. 601.

12. The reference to Tychicus in Ephesians 6: 21 f. is practically a verbatim
reproduction of Colossians 4: 7 f.

13. He magnifies his office because it will be the indirect means of the conversion of his fellow-countrymen; apostle to the Gentiles though he is, he has closely
at heart the spiritual welfare of his Jewish kith and kin (see p. 334). On the relation
between Ephesians and Romans 9–11 see H. Chadwick, "Die Absicht des
Epheserbriefes", ZNW 51 (1960), pp. 145 ff., especially p. 148. He suggests that
Ephesians was designed to bring the whole Gentile mission, in all its streams (cf.
p. 18), under the aegis of Paul's unique apostleship.

behalf of you Gentiles" (Ephesians 3: 1) and sees an astounding token of divine grace in the fact that Paul, of all people, has been chosen "to preach to the Gentiles the unsearchable riches of Christ" (Ephesians 3: 8).[14]

In the light of such affinities between Ephesians and other outstanding letters in the Pauline corpus, it is not so easy to accept the view, expounded principally by Heinrich Schlier, that Ephesians is indebted for its dominant themes to gnostic sources and only in two or three instances to the common stock of primitive Christianity.[15] This thesis calls for serious study and evaluation, but I find it much less cogent than the interpretation of Ephesians as an exposition of dominant themes of Paul's ministry.

## 3. Salvation by grace through faith

Among dominant Pauline themes justification by faith is the one that comes most readily to many minds. Luther's discovery of justification by faith in the writings of Paul, and his use of it as a touchstone to determine, if not the genuineness, at least the value of everything handed down as sacred scripture, has, I think, made it difficult for many of his followers to see much else in Paul, and has inclined them to dismiss as non-Pauline, or at best as deutero-Pauline, any document in the Pauline corpus in which justification by faith does not play the central part that it does in Galatians and Romans. How does Ephesians fare in this regard? Certainly justification by faith is not a central theme in Ephesians, but it underlies the argument of the epistle, so much so that it is assumed rather than expressed, apart from Ephesians 2: 8 f.: "by grace you have been saved through faith; and this is not your own doing, it is the gift of God – not because of works, lest any one should boast."

This salvation by grace through faith implies the justification of the ungodly, the more so as the readers who had experienced it, whether Gentiles or Jews by birth, were formerly "dead in their trespasses and sins" and "by nature children of wrath" (as truly as

14. Cf. the similar sentiment in 1 Corinthians 15: 9 f.

15. H. Schlier, *Christus und die Kirche im Epheserbrief* (Tübingen, 1930). From the common stock of Christian language about Christ's saving work, he points out, come statements about Christ's giving himself up for his people (Ephesians 5: 2, 25) and about God's raising him from the dead and putting all things beneath his feet (Ephesians 1: 20, 22). For the rest, Schlier derives from the world of gnostic thought the concepts of the redeemer's ascent to heaven, the heavenly wall, the heavenly man, the church as the body of Christ, the body of Christ as a heavenly building, and the heavenly bridal union. See the summary of his thesis by K. L. Schmidt in *TDNT* iii, *s.v.* ἐκκλησία , pp. 509 ff., abridged in *The Church* (Bible Key Words, London, 1950), pp. 15 ff.

those whose moral bankruptcy is exposed in Romans 1: 18–3: 20). While Paul usually speaks of salvation in terms of its fulfilment at the parousia, he presents it as a past event in Romans 8: 24. The emphasis in Ephesians 2: 8 f. is precisely the point that Paul has made in Romans 3: 27 ("Then what becomes of our boasting? It is excluded. On what principle? On the principle of works? No, but on the principle of faith") and in 1 Corinthians 1: 30 f. (God "is the source of your life in Christ Jesus, whom God made our wisdom, our righteousness and sanctification and redemption; therefore, as it is written, 'Let him who boasts, boast in the Lord' ").

### 4. The parousia

Less prominence is given to the parousia, the manifestation of Christ in glory. This theme is plain enough in Colossians (cf. Colossians 3: 4, "When Christ who is our life appears, then you also will appear with him in glory"), but in Ephesians it is present only by implication. When, for example, the purpose of the church's hallowing and cleansing is said to be its presentation to Christ "in glory, without spot or wrinkle" (Ephesians 5: 26 f.), this presentation is most naturally contemplated as coinciding with the parousia, as it certainly does elsewhere in the Pauline corpus. The parousia is also "the day of redemption" against which, according to Ephesians 4: 30, the people of Christ are sealed with the Holy Spirit.[16]

### 5. The Holy Spirit

This brings us to a major Pauline doctrine which is undoubtedly dominant in Ephesians – the doctrine of the Holy Spirit. Central as it is to Paul's teaching, this doctrine is practically absent from Colossians,[17] and in view of the affinity between Colossians and Ephesians it is all the more striking to note its dominance in Ephesians.

In the New Testament in general the presence of the Holy Spirit is a sign that the last days have come, in accordance with the words of Joel 2: 28 quoted by Peter in Jerusalem on the first Christian Pentecost: "And in the last days it shall be, God declares, that I will pour out my Spirit upon all flesh . . ." (Acts 2: 16 ff.). The presence of the Spirit, moreover, is the witness that Jesus was indeed the Messiah, the one who (in John the Baptist's words) would

16. Cf. Ephesians 1: 14 (see p. 209 above).
17. The Spirit is mentioned incidentally in Colossians 1: 8 ("your love in the Spirit"), and his inspiration is implied in the reference to "spiritual songs" in Colossians 3: 16.

baptize with the Holy Spirit; in other words, the new era which Jesus' passion and triumph inaugurated is the age of the Spirit to which the prophets pointed forward. This emphasis on the Spirit's vindicating witness to Jesus as Messiah and Lord pervades the New Testament; it is found in Acts,[18] in the Johannine Gospel [19] and Epistles,[20] and in 1 Peter.[21] It is found also in Paul, in whose eyes the age of the Spirit has superseded the age of the Torah.[22]

But in addition to the general early Christian teaching on the Spirit, which Paul had received, he makes at least two distinctive contributions: (a) the Holy Spirit is the present earnest of coming resurrection and glory [23] and (b) it is in the Holy Spirit that the people of Christ have been baptized into one corporate entity.[24] Both of these contributions, expounded in Paul's "capital" epistles (those to the Romans, Corinthians and Galatians), are emphasized in Ephesians.

(a) *The earnest of the Spirit.* The Holy Spirit is called in Ephesians "the Holy Spirit of promise" (Eph. 1. 13). This does not mean, as the RSV and NEB render it, that he is "the promised Holy Spirit" (true though that is, as witness Acts 1: 4 f.; 2: 33); the context rather indicates that to those whom he indwells the Holy Spirit is himself the promise of resurrection life and all the heritage of glory associated with it. The *locus classicus* for this view of the Spirit is Romans 8: 9 ff. There "the Spirit of him who raised Jesus from the dead" will "quicken" the mortal bodies of those who believe in Jesus. He is "the Spirit of adoption" in the sense that he enables believers to realize their privileges and responsibilities as sons of God against the day when they will be publicly revealed as such. This "revelation of the sons of God" (for which, as Paul says, all creation eagerly waits in order to share "the liberty of the glory of the children of God") is called our "adoption as sons, the redemption of our bodies". And of this consummation believers here and now possess the "first fruits" in the form of the Spirit. To the same effect Paul in 2 Corinthians 5: 5, where he speaks of believers' coming investiture with their "heavenly dwelling", says: "He who has prepared us for this very thing is God, who has given us the Spirit as a guarantee (*arrhabōn*)."

This insistence that the Spirit is for believers their "first fruits" or "guarantee" appears in Ephesians 1: 13, where they are reminded

18. Acts 2: 33; 5: 32.
19. John 15: 26; 16: 8–10, 14 f.
20. 1 John 5: 7 f.
21. 1 Peter 1: 12.
22. Romans 7: 6; 8: 2, 4; 2 Corinthians 3: 3 ff.; Galatians 3: 2 ff.; see p. 200 above.
23. Romans 8: 10 ff., especially verse 23; 2 Corinthians 1: 22; 5: 5.
24. 1 Corinthians 12: 13 (see p. 210).

– Gentiles as well as Jews – that on believing in Christ they were "sealed" with the Holy Spirit of promise, who is "the guarantee (*arrhabōn*) of our inheritance, pending God's redemption of his own possession". (This collocation of "seal" and "guarantee" in reference to the Spirit has already occurred in 2 Corinthians 1: 22: "God has sealed us and set the guarantee of the Spirit in our hearts.")[25] Again, in Ephesians 4: 30 the warning is given: "do not grieve the Holy Spirit of God, in whom you were sealed for the day of redemption" – here, as in Ephesians 1: 14, the "redemption" is identical with "the redemption of our bodies" mentioned in Romans 8: 23.

When this sealing is regarded as taking place has been debated with some animation, but most probably it coincides with the occasion indicated in 1 Corinthians 12: 13: "in one Spirit we were all baptized into one body – Jews or Greeks, slaves or free – and all were watered with one Spirit".

(*b*) *The unity of the Spirit.* This quotation of 1 Corinthians 12: 13 brings us to Paul's other distinctive contribution to the doctrine of the Spirit, for it is summed up there. This baptism in the Spirit – Christ himself being the baptizer, in fulfilment of John the Baptist's prophecy[26] – is not simply an individual experience; it is the divine act by which believers in Christ are incorporated into his body. Elsewhere Paul speaks of being "baptized into Christ" (Galatians 3: 27; Romans 6: 3) or "putting on Christ" (Galatians 3: 27; Romans 13: 14) with the plain implication that incorporation into Christ is involved, but it is in 1 Corinthians 12: 13, quoted at the end of the foregoing paragraph, that the Spirit's part in this experience finds expression. And the i's of 1 Corinthians 12: 13 are dotted and its t's crossed in Ephesians 4: 3, where the readers are enjoined to be sure to "keep the unity of the Spirit in the bond of peace". This "unity of the Spirit" is the unity of the body of Christ into which the people of Christ are brought by his Spirit for, in the words which immediately follow, "there is one body and one Spirit" (Ephesians 4: 4). [27]

In Ephesians 2: 19 ff. the church is portrayed rather as a building than as a body (although, just as architectural language is used of the body in Ephesians 4: 12–16, so biological language is

25. See p. 209, n. 25; cf. for a full treatment of the subject G. W. H. Lampe, *The Seal of the Spirit* (London, 1951).

26. Mark 1: 8; John 1: 33; Acts 1: 5; 11: 16 and (by implication) 19: 1–6.

27. The "unity ( ἑνότης ) of the Spirit" which the readers are charged to keep is not, of course, the fact that there is one Spirit (which cannot be affected by anything they do or fail to do); it is a consequence of that fact. Ephesians 4: 4–6 to some extent echoes 1 Corinthians 12: 4–6; both passages include the coordinated "Spirit . . . Lord . . . God". The repeated "one" in Ephesians 4: 4–6 anticipates the later eastern creeds; cf. R. R. Williams, "Logic *versus* Experience in the Order of Credal Formulae", *NTS* 1 (1954–55), pp. 42 ff.

used of the building in Ephesians 2: 21); but here too it is "in the Spirit" that the building takes shape, as the individual components are bonded together by Christ the "corner-stone". Here too it is in that same "one Spirit" that Jewish and Gentile believers together have common access to the Father (cf. Romans 5: 2), or (by a change of figure) constitute a holy dwelling-place or temple for God (an idea anticipated in 1 Corinthians 3: 16 f.).

## 6. *The new man*

These concepts of the body of Christ and the temple of God are interwoven with the concept of the "new man". In a mingling of the architectural and biological figures, we read in Ephesians 4: 13 ff. of the full-grown man (*anēr teleios*), "the measure of the stature of the fullness of Christ", which is the climax of the church's development as the body of Christ is built up, growing up to match him who is its head. Christ as the second man, the last Adam, the head and embodiment of the new creation, meets us in Romans 5: 12–19 and 1 Corinthians 15: 20–28, 42–50. When believers' putting on Christ is mentioned in Romans 13: 14 and Galatians 3: 27, this (as we have seen) is not so much a question of personal *imitatio Christi* as of incorporation into Christ. So, when Colossians and Ephesians speak of putting on the new man, "who is being renewed in knowledge after the image of his creator" (Colossians 3: 10), "created after the likeness of God in true righteousness and holiness" (Ephesians 4: 24),[28] the new man is Christ himself – not Christ in isolation from his people, but Christ *in* his people, the same Christ as Paul has in mind when he tells his Galatian converts that he endures birth-pangs over them "until Christ be formed" in them (Galatians 4: 19).

When we bear these earlier Pauline references in mind, there is no need to look to extraneous sources for the concept of the "new" of "perfect" man. Neither need we be surprised that the church in Ephesians is the church universal rather than the local congregation.

28. Cf. the "new man" of Ephesians 2: 15, who comprises former Jew and former Gentile in one. There, as in Ephesians 4: 24, the "new man" is the καινὸς ἄνθρωπος , whereas in Colossians 3: 10 he is the νέος ἄνθρωπος . But no difference in meaning can be pressed here between καινός and νέος , for in Ephesians 4: 23 putting on the καινὸς ἄνθρωπος is equivalent to ἀνανεοῦσθαι ("being renewed") in the spirit of their mind, while in Colossians 3: 10 the verb ἀνακαινόω is used for the renewal of the νέος ἄνθρωπος With the new man we must compare the "inner man" ( ἔσω ἄνθρωπος ) of Romans 7: 22 and 2 Corinthians 4: 16, who appears also in Ephesians 3: 16. It is in the παλαιὸς ἄνθρωπος of Romans 6: 6 and the ἔσω ἄνθρωπος of Romans 7: 22 that we find the source of the "new man" concept, not in the gnostic "redeemer" myth (cf. J. Horst in *TDNT* iv. p. 565, n. 79, *s.v.* μέλος ).

Ephesians, as has been said above, universalizes the church doctrine of 1 Corinthians, but the universal principle which finds clear expression in Ephesians is already latent in 1 Corinthians, which is addressed not only to "the church of God that is in Corinth" but also to "all those who in every place call on the name of our Lord Jesus Christ" (1 Corinthians 1: 1). The oneness of the church is bound up with the fact that there is one Spirit, one Lord and one God; it follows that there is one people of Christ, indwelt by the one Spirit, confessing the one Lord and through him worshipping the one God, and comprising indifferently those who were formerly separated as Jews on the one hand and Gentiles on the other.

There are plainly to be recognized in the New Testament elements of what our German colleagues call *Frühkatholizismus* – incipient catholicism. Chief among these elements is the conception of the church throughout the world as a unity, which characterizes Ephesians. But it has been too generally accepted as axiomatic that incipient catholicism has no place in authentic Paulinism, so that any document in which it appears, even if it bears Paul's name, cannot be a genuine epistle of Paul.[29]

Like so many other theological axioms, this one calls for scrutiny, and under scrutiny it loses something of its plausibility. We might *a priori* have expected Paul to think of Christians throughout his mission field as forming a unity. "Israel after the flesh" did not exist only in local synagogues; it was an ecumenical reality. The synagogue in any place was the local manifestation of the whole "congregation of Israel". The same situation governed the new Israel.

What we should have expected *a priori* is confirmed by the evidence in the "capital" epistles that Paul had a deep concern for Christian unity – not only the unity of his own Gentile mission but

---

29. Thus E. Käsemann says that "in the New Testament it is Ephesians that most clearly marks the transition from the Pauline tradition to the perspectives of the early Catholic era"; he compares the epistle in this respect with Acts ("Ephesians and Acts", in *Studies in Luke-Acts: Essays in Honor of Paul Schubert*, ed. L. E. Keck and J. L. Martyn [Nashville, 1966], pp. 288 ff.). On this point H. Küng takes issue with Käsemann and others in *The Structures of the Church*, E.T. (London, 1965), pp. 135 ff., especially 142 ff., charging them with establishing a New Testament canon within the received canon by relegating to an inferior status anything that savours of "early Catholic decadence". S. C. Neill points out that in German Protestant theology the term *Frühkatholizismus* is used "always as a term of reproach" (*The Interpretation of the New Testament* [London, 1964], p. 160). It is noteworthy that when the former Lutheran scholar H. Schlier, author of *Christus und die Kirche im Epheserbrief*, became convinced that incipient catholicism and other features commonly labelled "accretions" were part and parcel of apostolic Christianity, he not only joined the Roman Catholic Church but found it possible to regard Ephesians as an authentic epistle of Paul; cf. his commentary, *Der Brief an die Epheser* (Düsseldorf,[5] 1965), pp. 22 ff.

the unity which embraced his Gentile mission on the one hand with the Jerusalem church and the Jewish mission on the other.[30]

Moreover, all Christians, according to Paul, were baptized "into Christ", not merely into a local fellowship. All who were baptized into Christ (and had thus "put on" Christ) inevitably formed part of one spiritual entity. In baptism they had been united with Christ in his death, to rise with him in the likeness of his resurrection and so "walk in newness of life" (Romans 6: 3–5). They had, in other words, become members of the body of Christ, baptized into it "in one Spirit". The Christians in Corinth are reminded that they are Christ's body, and individually members thereof (1 Corinthians 12: 27); similarly those in Rome are told that "we" (that is, not the Roman Christians alone but the Roman Christians in fellowship with Paul and others), "though many, are one body in Christ, and individually members one of another" (Romans 12: 5).[31] To Paul's way of thinking Christ could no more be divided between the several congregations than he could be divided between the factions within the congregation at Corinth. The explicit appearance of the church universal in Colossians and more particularly in Ephesians is a corollary of Paul's understanding of the phrase "in Christ" and all that goes with it.

Language such as Paul uses to the Corinthian and Roman Christians about membership in the body of Christ could not be locally restricted, even if the occasions that called forth the "capital" epistles directed its application to the requirements of local fellowship. All believers – in Corinth and Rome, in Jerusalem and Ephesus, and everywhere else – had together died with Christ and been raised with him; as participators in his risen life they could not but constitute one Christian fellowship.

## 7. From darkness to light

This experience of passing in Christ from death to life may also be expressed in terms of passing from darkness to light, and it is so expressed in Ephesians 5: 7–14. "Once you were darkness, but now you are light in the Lord", the readers are told, in language which has affinities elsewhere in the Pauline corpus,[32] as also in the Johannine writings [33] and in the Qumran literature. The point is driven home by the quotation of the tristich:

30. An evident token of this is his collection for the Jerusalem "saints" (see pp. 321 ff).
31. Cf. the similar use of μέλη ("members") in Ephesians 4: 16, 25; 5: 30.
32. Cf. 1 Thessalonians 5: 6; Colossians 1: 12.
33. Cf. John 3: 19 ff.; 12: 35 ff.; 1 John 1: 7; 2: 8 ff.

Awake, O thou that sleepest,
And from the dead arouse thee,
And Christ shall dawn upon thee.

Although this is introduced by the phrase "Therefore it (he) says", as though it were holy writ, it is no precise Old Testament quotation, and has often been regarded as part of an early Christian baptismal hymn. The rhythm, it has been said, is similar to that of initiation formulae used in various mystery cults,[34] but the content is entirely Christian.[35] In the context of Ephesians 5: 14, where the light reveals all things as they truly are, these words constitute a call to the sinner to abandon his old course and embrace a new way of life; they express the experience which, according to Paul, is sacramentally realized in baptism: "we were buried with him through baptism into death, in order that, as Christ was raised from the dead through the Father's glory, so we too should walk in newness of life" (Romans 6: 4).

### 8. The broken wall

Emphasizing the equal incorporation within the Christian community of Jews and Gentiles – two groups which had previously been estranged from each other – Ephesians says that Christ "has made both one and has broken down the middle wall of partition" – the breaking down of this wall being otherwise described as his removal of the hostility between the two groups, his annulling of "the law consisting of commandments, ordinances and all" (Ephesians 2: 14 f.). [36]

It is a commonplace with British commentators on Ephesians to suppose that this "middle wall of partition" may have been suggested by the barrier which separated the inner courts of the Jerusalem temple from the court of the Gentiles, a barrier which Gentiles were forbidden to penetrate on pain of death.[37] German commentators, on the other hand, are more inclined to think of the

34. Cf. the metre (not the substance) of the Attis initiation formula quoted by Firmicus Maternus, *De errore profanarum religionum* 18: 1:

ἐκ τυμπάνου βέβρωκα,

ἐκ κυμβάλου πέπωκα,

γέγονα μύστης ᾿Αττεως

("I have eaten from the drum, I have drunk from the cymbal, I have become an initiate of Attis"). A similar Eleusinian formula is quoted by Clement of Alexandria, *Exhortation to the Greeks* 2. 14.

35. On this see K. G. Kuhn, "The Epistle to the Ephesians in the Light of the Qumran Texts", E.T. in *Paul and Qumran*, ed. J. Murphy-O'Connor (London, 1968), pp. 115 ff.

36. With this annulment of the law cf. the statement in Romans 10: 4 that "Christ is the end of the law" (see pp. 190 ff.).

37. E.g. J. A. Robinson, *St. Paul's Epistle to the Ephesians* (London, 1904), pp. 59 f. (On the barrier see Josephus, *BJ* v. 194.)

barrier which, in some gnostic texts, separates the world beneath from the upper world of light.[38]

Without examining the question whether this concept in its gnostic form was current as early as the first century A.D.,[39] we may ask which of the two barriers provides the more apt analogy to the thought of Ephesians 2: 14. The barrier in the temple was a vertical one; the "iron curtain" of the gnostic texts was horizontal. The division in view in Ephesians 2: 14 is not a division between the upper and lower world; it is a division between two groups of people resident in this world, and is therefore more aptly represented by a vertical barrier than by a horizontal one – the more so as the two groups which were kept apart by this "middle wall of partition" are exactly the same two groups as were kept apart by the barrier in the Jerusalem temple.

It may indeed be asked, as it is by Martin Dibelius,[40] if the readers of Ephesians 2: 14 would have understood such an allusion. Perhaps not; but would they have understood a gnostic allusion any better? There is in any case no emphasis on a material barrier. But whatever the readers may or may not have understood, the writer may well have had at the back of his mind that temple barrier which played an important part in the chain of events through which Paul became (to quote Ephesians 3: 1) "the prisoner of Christ Jesus in behalf of you Gentiles". For, according to Acts 21: 27 ff., Paul's arrest came about because he was charged with aiding and abetting illegal entry by a Gentile through the temple barrier. The charge could not be sustained when it came to court, as no witnesses were forthcoming, but Paul was not released; he remained in custody, first in Caesarea and then in Rome. That literal "middle wall of partition", the outward and visible sign of the ancient cleavage between Jew and Gentile, could have come very readily to mind in this situation.

This is further suggested by the emphasis laid a few lines later on the common access to the Father which Jewish and Gentile believers in Christ now enjoy "in one Spirit".[41] The barrier which formerly kept Gentiles at a distance from the God of Israel has been abrogated, and even Jewish believers have now more unimpeded

38. E.g. H. Schlier, *Der Brief an die Epheser*, pp. 126 ff., following his treatment of "die himmlische Mauer" in *Christus und die Kirche im Epheserbrief*, pp. 18 ff.

39. This question is especially provoked when attempts are made to reconstruct the concept of the heavenly wall (or other gnostic concepts) on the basis of Mandaean texts which are several centuries later than the New Testament age.

40. M. Dibelius, *An die Kolosser, An die Epheser, An Philemon* (Tübingen, 1953), p. 69; cf. H. Schlier, *Christus und die Kirche im Epheserbrief*, p. 18. E. J. Goodspeed sees the temple barrier here, but considers that its figurative use in this context was suggested by its actual destruction in A.D. 70 (*The Meaning of Ephesians*, p. 37).

41. Ephesians 2: 18, 21.

access to God in this "holy sanctuary" of living men and woman than was available to them in the earthly temple where, in accordance with their status, they had to maintain a respectful distance. For the barrier which excluded Gentiles from the inner courts was not the only barrier there. There was a further succession of barriers in the inner precincts, barring various groups of Israelites from nearer access. Beyond the court of the women Jewish women might not proceed; beyond the court of Israel Jewish laymen might not proceed. Into the court of the priests and the outer compartment of the holy house itself priests and Levites might enter in the performance of their prescribed duties, but the heavy veil which curtained off the inner compartment barred all access to the throne-room of God's invisible presence except to the high priest when he entered it annually on the Day of Atonement with sacrificial blood. His direct access then was an occasion for soul-affliction; in the spiritual sanctuary of Ephesians 2: 21 the direct access to God which all believers enjoy is an occasion for gladness and praise. This direct access is a major theme of the Epistle to the Ephesians and the Epistle to the Hebrews alike; but whereas the barrier which Hebrews uses as an illustration is the veil which hung before the holy of holies, that which is more probably envisaged in Ephesians is the one which forced Gentiles to keep their distance.

## 9. The heavenly ascent

Something more in the nature of the horizontal barrier may, however, be discerned in another passage in Ephesians. In Ephesians 4: 8–10 there is a remarkable commentary in what we have now learned to call *pesher* style on the words of Psalm 68: 18. "When he ascended on high", the quotation runs (turning the second person of the original into the third), "he led captivity captive and gave gifts to men."

The context of Psalm 68 seems to portray a triumphal procession ascending the sacred hill of Zion: the conquering hero is followed by a train of captives and his route is lined by his exultant fellow--citizens. The temple singers acclaim him as victor, and tell how he has "received gifts among men" – a reference, probably, to the tribute paid him by the vanquished. Or the leader of the triumphal procession may be no human conqueror but Yahweh himself, his invisible presence betokened by the ark of the covenant, safe home from leading Israel into battle and now being carried up to its shrine at the head of the procession. In this case the tribute of subject nations is paid direct to the God of Israel.

Whichever of these interpretations of the Psalm be preferred, it is not in terms of its historical setting that verse 18 is expounded in

Ephesians 4: 8–10. Even if the historical setting had been taken into account, an acclamation of the God of Israel or of his anointed king would have been equally appropriate for the present application of the words to the one who was "born of the seed of David according to the flesh but appointed Son of God in power, according to the Spirit of holiness, by the resurrection from the dead" (Romans 1: 3 f.). What is most striking is that, instead of the Massoretic and Septuagint reading, "*received* gifts among men", a reading is here chosen which agrees with the Aramaic Targum and the Syriac version: "*gave* gifts to men". In the Targum this is interpreted of Moses ascending Mount Sinai to receive the tables of the law and deliver them as God's gift to men. But in Ephesians it is interpreted of Christ's ascent on high and his bestowal thence upon his church of the ministers or ministries necessary for its growth to maturity.

It is in the exposition of Psalm 68: 18 that a horizontal barrier is possibly implied. This is the barrier between "the lower parts of the earth" and the upper world, "far above all the heavens", which Christ broke when he ascended. But if it is implied, no particular stress is laid on it. On the verb "ascended" in the Psalm the comment is made:

> What does this mean if not that he first of all *descended* into the lower parts of the earth? He who *descended* is the same who *ascended* far above all the heavens, in order to fill the universe.

In this exposition the crucial question is whether by "the lower parts of the earth" the earth itself is indicated (as being "lower" in relation to the world above), or the underworld (as being "lower" in relation to the earth). It is not possible to reach complete certainty. Comparison with Romans 10: 6 f., where (in a *pesher* exegesis of Deuteronomy 30: 12–14) ascending into heaven is contrasted with descending into the abyss, suggests the latter interpretation; comparison with John 3: 13 (and the Gospel of John has special affinities with the Epistle to the Ephesians) suggests the former, for in John 3: 13 the Son of Man's ascent into heaven is paralleled by his coming down from heaven (that is, to earth). Traditionally the passage has been interpreted of the *descensus ad inferos* and the harrowing of hell, and the "leading captivity captive" has been understood in this sense; but in Ephesians the "leading captivity captive" appears simply in the quotation from the psalm, playing no part in the following exegesis. If there is any implied significance in the quotation of the words, they might refer to the despoiling of principalities and powers described in Colossians 2: 15. But this was effected on the cross, not in Hades. On the whole, "the earth" in the phrase "the lower parts of the earth" is best construed as genitive of definition – that is, earth itself is the "lower" realm into which Christ is here said to have descended. But the point of the reference to his successive descent and ascent, which is not affected by our resolution one way or another of this *crux interpretum*, is that by this twofold movement Christ fills the universe, upper and lower realms alike, with his presence.[42]

## 10. The divine mystery

One of the most interesting points of affinity between Ephesians and the Qumran texts lies in the idea of the "mysteries" of God. These "mysteries" are not *arcana*; they have been revealed, but even when they are revealed they remain mysteries until they are interpreted in terms of their fulfilment. The pattern of *rāz* ("mystery") and *pesher* ("interpretation") in the Aramaic sections of Daniel, where the former requires the latter to complete and explain it, reappears in the Qumran texts (pre-eminently in commentaries) and in the New Testament.[43] Paul, for example, speaks of himself and his fellow-apostles as "stewards of the mysteries of God" (1 Corinthians 4: 1) – servants of God called to proclaim that what had been "promised beforehand through his prophets in the holy scriptures" (Romans 1: 2) was now accomplished, and was made plain by the fact of that accomplishment, being embodied in Christ and the gospel.

But Paul speaks not only of the mysteries in the plural, but also (comprehensively) of "the mystery" in the singular, for all the revelation of God has been consummated in Christ. So in Colossians 2: 2 f. he speaks of his desire that his readers and the other churches in the Lycus valley may attain "the knowledge of God's mystery – that is, of Christ himself – in whom all the treasures of wisdom and knowledge are hidden" (but no longer hidden from those who have attained this knowledge). This mystery is unfolded in the gospel; so the doxology at the end of Romans mentions "my gospel and the proclamation concerning Jesus Christ, according to the revelation of the mystery which was shrouded in silence in eternal ages but has now been made manifest, and through prophetic writings, according to the commandment of the eternal God, made known to all the nations for the obedience of faith" (Romans 16: 25 f.).

As one called to make known among the Gentiles "the unsearchable riches of Christ" (Ephesians 3: 8) Paul might well ap-

---

42. How evenly balanced is the evidence for either view may be illustrated by a series of entries in *TDNT*. In Vol. i, pp. 522 f., *s.v.* ἀναβαίνω , J. Schneider argued for the "lower realm" being earth itself; in Vol. iv, pp. 597 f., *s.v.* μέρος he acknowledges a change of mind, having been persuaded thereto by F. Büchsel's entry on κατώτερος in Vol. iii, pp. 640 f.

43. Cf. F. F. Bruce, *Biblical Exegesis in the Qumran Texts* (London, 1960), pp. 7 ff.

preciate the honour of being entrusted with the stewardship of such a "mystery", nor is it surprising that at times he concentrates on some aspect of the gospel specially related to his own ministry and speaks of it as a mystery. In Colossians 1: 26 f., for example, he calls the subject-matter of his ministry "the mystery which has been kept hidden from ages and generations but has now been made manifest to the people of God, to whom God has been well pleased to make known what is the glorious wealth of this mystery among the Gentiles, which is Christ in you [even in you Gentiles], the hope of glory". That Gentiles would come to worship the God of Israel was a theme of Old Testament expectation; in Romans 15: 9–12 Paul reproduces a catena of passages from the Law, the Prophets and the Psalms to this effect. But that Gentiles should have the Messiah of Israel, now the exalted Lord, dwelling in their hearts by faith as the living hope of coming glory – this was something completely uncontemplated before: it was bound up with Paul's own Gentile apostolate and was the subject of a new revelation. Similarly in Ephesians 3: 9 the substance of this mystery now for the first time divulged is said to be "that the Gentiles should be joint heirs, fellow-members of the one body, sharers of the promise conveyed in Christ Jesus through the gospel". Not the Gentiles without the Jews, or even in preference to the Jews, but the Gentiles on the same basis as the Jews – Gentiles and Jews alike being reconciled to God "in one body through the cross" (Ephesians 2: 16). [44]

Moreover, the full unveiling of the mystery of God, in the Qumran texts and in the New Testament, illuminates his ultimate purpose. In Ephesians 3: 9–11 the unfolding of the mystery hidden in God from ages past brings to light the purpose for which he has created the church, his "fellowship of reconciliation" – it is that through the church his many-coloured wisdom might be made known to all created beings, to "principalities and powers in the heavenly realm . . . according to the eternal purpose which he conceived in Christ Jesus our Lord". And this eternal purpose, thus subserved by the church and due to be realized in the "fulness of the times", is concisely stated in Ephesians 1: 9 f.: it is to bring all things together under the headship of Christ.

In 1 Corinthians 2: 6 ff. Paul tells the Corinthian Christians that, for all their self-styled wisdom, he has to feed them with milk and not with solid food, because they are not yet spiritually mature. This immaturity was due not to deficiency in *gnōsis* (of which they

44. Goodspeed (*The Meaning of Ephesians*, p. 12) suggests strangely that when Ephesians was written the Jewish-Gentile question was no longer actual, but that "under this old form the writer puts forth his appeal for unity among the Greek churches in the face of the rising sects". This is reading into the text what is not there in preference to reading out of it what is there.

had plenty of a kind), but to deficiency in *agapē*. "Nevertheless", he goes on, "to those who are mature we do impart wisdom . . . God's wisdom in a mystery, the hidden wisdom ordained before the world for our glory . . . as it is written:

What eye never saw, what ear never heard,
What never entered the heart of man,
What God prepared for those who love him –

these are the things which God has revealed to us by the Spirit."[45]

If we ask where in the Pauline corpus this divine "wisdom in a mystery" is imparted, we should direct our attention to the letter to the Ephesians.[46]

---

45. This quotation in 1 Corinthians 2: 9 is introduced by "as it is written" as though it were scripture. It bears some resemblance to Isaiah 64: 4, on which indeed it may ultimately be based, but that is not its immediate source. Origen in his *Commentary on Matthew* 27:9 (cf. Jerome on Isaiah 64: 4 and Ambrosiaster on 1 Corinthians 2: 9) says the words appear in the *Secrets* (or *Apocalypse*) of *Elijah*, but they do not occur in the fragment of that (probably post-Pauline) work which has survived. They are frequently quoted in the early centuries A.D., especially by gnostic writers, because they lent themselves readily to a gnostic interpretation (of which the wording of 1 John 1: 1 might be a deliberate rebuttal). In some late second-century documents they are ascribed to Jesus (cf. *Acts of Peter* 39; *Gospel of Thomas* 17). See also E. von Nordheim, "Das Zitat des Paulus in 1 Kor 2, 9 und seine Beziehung zum koptischen Testament Jakobs", *ZNW* 65 (1974), pp. 112–120 (this Coptic work is a christianized version of a Jewish testament, from which, it is suggested, Paul may have quoted), with reply by H. F. D. Sparks, "1 Kor 2, 9 a quotation from the Coptic Testament of Jacob?" *ZNW* 67 (1976), pp. 269–276.

46. Cf. H. Schlier, *Der Brief an die Epheser*, pp. 21 f.

# CHAPTER 37

# The Last Days of Paul: History and Tradition

## 1. Persecution under Nero

OUR QUEST FOR FURTHER DATA BEARING ON PAUL'S ROMAN captivity and its aftermath has not been particularly fruitful. If the "captivity epistles" at which we have looked were indeed sent from Rome, they suggest that Paul was about to have an opportunity of declaring "the mystery of Christ", for the sake of which he was in custody, and was anxious that his friends should pray for him, that he might "declare it boldly" (Colossians 4: 3 f.; Ephesians 6: 19 f.). He hoped also, through their prayers, to be released and to pay a further visit to the provinces of Asia and Macedonia.

It is probable that Paul's appeal did come up for hearing at the end of his two years in Rome. But we have no direct information about the outcome.

That Paul's life was brought to an end in Rome by the executioner's sword may be confidently accepted, but tradition associates his execution with the persecution of Christians in Rome which followed the great fire of A.D. 64 – at least two years after the latest probable date for the hearing of his case.

During the night of July 18/19 in A.D. 64, a fire broke out at the north-east end of the Circus Maximus. The colonnade of shops which stood round the outer face of the Circus was full of inflammable wares; the conflagration secured a hold there and, fanned by the wind, raged for five days until, of the city's fourteen divisions, three were completely destroyed and seven severely damaged.[1]

Although Nero, who was at Antium (Anzio) when the fire broke out, hurried back to Rome and instituted energetic relief measures, rumour alleged that he had set the city on fire in order to "re-mould it nearer to the heart's desire". Tired at last of being the target for the finger of popular suspicion, he looked around for scapegoats. Tacitus, who is our most reliable authority for these events, continues the story thus:

1. Cf. Tacitus, *Annals* xv. 38 ff.

441

Therefore, to scotch the rumour, Nero substituted as culprits, and punished with the utmost refinements of cruelty, a class of men, loathed for their vices, whom the crowd styled Christians. Christus, from whom they got their name, had been executed by sentence of the procurator Pontius Pilate when Tiberius was emperor; and the pernicious superstition was checked for a short time, only to break out afresh, not only in Judaea, the home of the plague, but in Rome itself, where all the horrible and shameful things in the world collect and find a home.

First of all, those who confessed were arrested; then, on their information, a huge multitude was convicted, not so much on the ground of incendiarism as for hatred of the human race. Their execution was made a matter of sport: some were sewn up in the skins of wild beasts and savaged to death by dogs; others were fastened to crosses as living torches, to serve as lights when daylight failed. Nero made his gardens available for the show and held games in the Circus, mingling with the crowd or standing in his chariot in charioteer's uniform. Hence, although the victims were criminals deserving the severest punishment, pity began to be felt for them because it seemed that they were being sacrificed to gratify one man's lust for cruelty rather than for the public weal.[2]

The same occasion is probably referred to briefly by Suetonius in his *Life of Nero*, when he says:

Punishment was inflicted on the Christians, a class of men addicted to a novel and mischievous superstition.[3]

Some interesting questions are raised by Tacitus's account, which may point to tensions within the believing community. We cannot be sure whether those who first "confessed" pleaded guilty to the charge of arson or to the charge of being Christians, nor can we be sure what kind of information they provided which led to the arrest of the "huge multitude". Christians were generally disliked for what their neighbours regarded as anti-social attitudes, and some of the simpler souls among them may well have thought – and said – that the fire raging through the city was the beginning of the conflagration which was to consume the current world-order and usher in the reign of the saints. The ferocity and malignity of Nero's attack caught the Christians of Rome unawares, but "the patience and faith of the saints"[4] enabled them to stand firm and survive the attack.

## 2. *Evidence from the Pastoral Epistles?*

If a firm and acceptable date and life-setting for the Pastoral

2. Tacitus, *Annals* xv. 44. 3–8.
3. Suetonius, *Life of Nero* 16. 2.
4. Revelation 13: 10.

Epistles could be established, their evidence might prove to be relevant. Even when their Pauline authorship is admitted *simpliciter*, there is not complete unanimity on their location in Paul's career. J. Vernon Bartlet's argument for placing all three in the period before Paul's appeal came up for hearing appears never to have convinced any one but himself.[5] As for placing them in the period following Paul's postulated release at the end of his two years in Rome, it is no argument against this to describe it as "a flight into *terra incognita*";[6] Paul's fortunes at the end of those two years constitute a *terra incognita*, whatever form they took; and we have to make the best of this frustrating fact.

If the Pastoral Epistles are not Paul's composition as they stand, but represent *disiecta membra* of Paul's correspondence and instruction, collected by one or more of his friends and disciples, and given a continuous form by the provision of editorial transitions, then it is not necessary to date all the authentically Pauline material in them at the same time (and the same is true of P. N. Harrison's "fragment" hypothesis).[7] Some of the passages might then belong to earlier phases of Paul's career, others to the last phase, like the passage beginning "I am now ready to be poured out as a libation; the time of my release is at hand" (2 Timothy 4: 6) and probably the reference to Onesiphorus (2 Timothy 1: 16–18).

C. F. D. Moule published a "reappraisal" of the problem of these epistles in 1965. Recognizing on the one hand the difficulties in the way of accepting the Pastoral Epistles as completely Pauline in the customary sense, and on the other hand the improbabilities inherent in the "fragment" hypothesis, he suggested that for those letters Paul employed as his amanuensis a man whom he could trust with much greater discretion than could be allowed to any ordinary amanuensis – namely, Luke. The non-Pauline elements in them would then reflect Luke's thought rather than Paul's. Greatest freedom was given to Luke for 1 Timothy, which (on Professor Moule's hypothesis) was written shortly before Paul's release from his Roman imprisonment, when Paul wanted to send a message to Timothy in a hurry while he himself was particularly busy with preparations for leaving Rome and perhaps with completing judicial formalities just preceding his release. Certainly the Pastoral Epistles have more in common with Acts in matters of

5. J. V. Bartlet, "The Historic Setting of the Pastoral Epistles", *Expositor*, series 8, 5 (1913), pp. 28 ff., 161 ff., 256 ff., 325 ff. especially pp. 326–339. J. A. T. Robinson dates them even earlier (see p. 317, n. 12; p. 446, n. 15).

6. Cf. M. Dibelius and H. Conzelmann, *The Pastoral Epistles*, E.T. (Philadelphia, 1976), pp. 3, 15 f., 126 f., 152 ff. The first known writer so to date them was evidently Eusebius (*Hist. Eccl.* ii. 22. 2–8).

7. P. N. Harrison, *The Problem of the Pastoral Epistles* (Oxford, 1921), pp. 93 ff., 115 ff.; cf. his *Paulines and Pastorals* (London, 1964), pp. 106 ff.

style and church polity than have Paul's earlier letters. In view of the homogeneity of the Pastoral Epistles in style and vocabulary, the reference in 2 Timothy 4: 11 to Luke as the only member of Paul's inner circle present with him at the time of writing may lend some support to Professor Moule's reappraisal.[8]

This reappraisal assumes that Paul was released at the end of his two years in Rome and returned for some time to the Eastern Mediterranean, revisiting his friends in the provinces of Macedonia and Asia and conducting a missionary campaign in Crete, where Titus was left behind to consolidate the converts.

Similar conclusions are defended by J. N. D. Kelly in his *Commentary on the Pastoral Epistles* (1963). He argues that, since Paul's death cannot be dated before the Neronian persecution of A.D. 64/65 and the following years, and since it is difficult to see how his house arrest could have lasted until then, it is most reasonable to infer that he was released after the expiry of the two years, and after a further spell of missionary activity was arrested again and imprisoned in Rome for the second and last time. This is certainly a plausible – perhaps the most plausible – reconstruction of the course of events, although some would not share Dr. Kelly's confidence that Paul's "martyrdom cannot in any case be placed earlier than A.D. 64".[9]

### 3. Release and second imprisonment?

It is clear that no dogmatic statements are justified when the sequel to Paul's first imprisonment is under discussion. Tradition affirms rather confidently that he was released, but Eusebius, who first records this tradition explicitly, introduces it with the expression "report has it".[10] It should be recognized, moreover, that release on the one hand and execution on the other do not exhaust the possibilities. A third possibility is that his *libera custodia* may have given place to a much stricter confinement, such as P. N. Harrison thinks he was enduring at the time when Onesiphorus took so much trouble to track him down.[11] A fourth possibility is that he may have been exiled. Clement of Rome, writing some thirty years after Paul's death, includes exile among his sufferings.[12] This suggests that there was an early tradition of exile – unless Clement, with rhetorical exaggeration, is talking loosely of Paul's en-

8. C. F. D. Moule, "The Problem of the Pastoral Epistles: A Reappraisal", *BJRL* 47 (1964–65), pp. 430 ff.; cf. A. Strobel, "Schreiben des Lukas? Zum sprachlichen Problem der Pastoralbriefe", *NTS* 15 (1968–69), pp. 191 ff.
9. J. N. D. Kelly, *A Commentary on the Pastoral Epistles* (London, 1963), p. 9.
10. Eusebius, *Hist. Eccl.* ii. 22. 2 ( λόγος ἔχει).
11. P. N. Harrison, *Problem*, pp. 127 ff.; cf. J. N. D. Kelly, *Commentary*, p. 170.
12. 1 Clement 5: 6.

forced departure from one city after another in the course of his apostolic ministry. If exile in the proper sense is meant, when was he supposed to have been exiled, and what was supposed to be the place of his exile? It would be odd if it was Spain – if Paul, having achieved his ambition of visiting Rome by the unforeseen means of being sent there under armed guard to have his appeal heard in Caesar's court, later achieved his ambition of preaching in Spain by the unforeseen means of exile.[13]

If he was released or exiled, he was arrested and imprisoned a second time in Rome, and this time the conditions of his imprisonment were much more stringent than before. Such a stringent imprisonment probably forms the setting for the one mention of Rome in the Pastoral Epistles. Referring to a wholesale defection from loyalty to him in proconsular Asia, Paul goes on (2 Timothy 1: 16–18):

> May the Lord grant mercy to the household of Onesiphorus, for he often refreshed me; he was not ashamed of my chains, but when he arrived in Rome he searched for me eagerly and found me – may the Lord grant him to find mercy from the Lord on that Day – and you well know all the service he rendered at Ephesus.

Onesiphorus appears to have been an Ephesian Christian who had proved very helpful during Paul's ministry in his home city, and who at a later date had occasion to visit Rome and sought Paul out in circumstances where to do so involved not only trouble and possible loss of face, but no doubt danger too. It is usually inferred from the language of this passage that Paul was no longer enjoying the *libera custodia* of Acts 28: 16 ff. but undergoing more severe restraint. It was not so easy now to discover Paul's whereabouts in Rome: P. N. Harrison, describing Onesiphorus's resolute quest for his old friend, draws a moving and vivid picture of "one purposeful face in a drifting crowd".[14] The circumstantiality and incidental nature of this personal reference bespeak a genuine Pauline reminiscence.

On the hypothesis of Paul's release and second Roman imprisonment, his case came up again for hearing – he was prosecuted (with due regard to his Roman citizenship) on the charge, it may be, of

13. Cf. J. J. Gunther, *Paul: Messenger and Exile* (Valley Forge, 1972), pp. 144 ff., for the view that this is precisely what happened (see also L. P. Pherigo, "Paul's Life after the Close of Acts", *JBL* 70 [1951], p. 278). Apollonius of Tyana is said to have been exiled to Spain (Philostratus, *Life of Apollonius* iv. 47).

14. P. N. Harrison, *Problem*, p. 127. To delete "in Rome" as a gloss, because its retention stands in the way of a hypothesis one wishes to maintain (cf. G. S. Duncan, *St. Paul's Ephesian Ministry* [London, 1929], pp. 188 f., 193 f.) is an impermissible procedure; the phrase constitutes a solid piece of evidence.

being a leader of the Christians and also of being a persistent disturber of the peace of the provinces. This may be the setting of another passage in the Pastoral Epistles (2 Timothy 4: 16 f.):

> At my first defence no one took my part; all deserted me. May it not be charged against them! But the Lord stood by me and gave me strength to proclaim the word fully, that all the Gentiles might hear it. So I was rescued from the lion's mouth.

Dr. Kelly understands his "first defence" as the *prima actio* or preliminary investigation. This had gone more favourably for Paul than he might have dared to hope: he was not discharged but remanded in custody for a further investigation, the verdict being *Amplius*.[15] Not only so, but the hearing gave Paul a welcome opportunity of proclaiming the gospel at the heart of the imperial system, to the cosmopolitan audience present in court.[16]

Why no one stood by him is not said: if the general persecution of Christians in Rome had broken out, this would provide cause enough. If Onesiphorus receives special commendation for his courage in visiting Paul in prison, to stand by Paul in court at that time would have called for exceptional courage.

For the time being, then, Paul was saved from Nero's malice: "rescued from the lion's mouth", as he puts it.[17] But only for the time being: the *secunda actio* was held in due course, and this time the verdict was "guilty", and the sentence, death by the sword. Paul's last words have been preserved in 2 Timothy 4: 6–8:

> I am now ready to be poured out as a libation; the time of my release is at hand. I have fought the good fight, I have finished the race, I have kept the faith. Henceforth there is laid up for me the crown of righteousness, which the Lord, the righteous judge, will award to me on that Day, and not only to me but also to all who have loved his appearing.[18]

### 4. Clement of Rome

We turn now to early evidence outside the New Testament.

The earliest is that provided by Clement of Rome, and it does not add much to our sum of positive knowledge. The letter which, as foreign secretary of the Roman church, he wrote about A.D. 96 in the name of that church to the church of Corinth, begins by war-

15. Cf. J. N. D. Kelly, *Commentary*, p. 218. J. A. T. Robinson thinks that *Felix's* pronouncement of *Amplius* (see p. 357) is referred to (*Redating the New Testament* [London 1976], p. 74; cf. *Can we trust the New Testament?* [London, 1977], pp. 65 f.).
16. See pp. 366 f.
17. 2 Timothy 4: 17.
18. Cf. J. N. D. Kelly, *Commentary*, pp. 207–210, 218.

THE LAST DAYS OF PAUL: HISTORY AND TRADITION

ning the latter church of the terrible effects of jealousy and envy. Seven examples are given from the Old Testament; then Clement continues:

> But, to leave the examples of former days, let us come to those who were athletes in the days nearest to our own. Through jealousy and envy the greatest and most righteous pillars of the church were persecuted, and maintained their athletic contest unto death. Let us set before our eyes the good apostles. Peter, on account of unrighteous jealousy, underwent not one or two but many toils and, having thus borne witness, he made his way to his allotted place of glory. Paul, on account of jealousy and strife, showed the way to the prize of endurance; seven times he wore fetters, he was exiled, he was stoned, he was a herald both in the east and in the west, he gained the noble renown of his faith, he taught righteousness throughout the whole world and, having reached the limit of the west, he bore testimony before the rulers, and so departed from the world and was taken up into the holy place – the greatest example of endurance. [19]

In a rhetorical essay of this kind we do not expect the precision which is properly looked for in a work whose primary purpose is the supplying of historical information. Clement is not imparting to the Corinthians facts which they did not know, but drawing morals from facts which, in general outline at least, were common knowledge to him and them. Indeed, even to us he does not say anything concrete about Paul's later life to supplement the narrative of Acts from the point where it breaks off. That Paul bore his testimony before the rulers could have been an inference from the record of Acts, as well as being a reminiscence of the risen Lord's prophecy about Paul to Ananias of Damascus: "he is a chosen instrument of mine to carry my name before the Gentiles and kings and the sons of Israel" (Acts 9: 15).[20] But what was "the limit (Gk. *terma*) of the west" that Paul reached? From the standpoint of one who, like Clement, lived and wrote in Rome, would it not indicate some place west of Rome, presumably Spain? Perhaps it would, but even so we cannot be sure that Clement knew for a fact that Paul did go to Spain; if he meant Spain, he might simply have been making an inference from Paul's statement of his plans in Romans 15: 24, 28.

On the other hand, we must give serious attention to the argument for translating the phrase not by "the limit of the west" but by "the goal in the west" – Paul's western goal. Amid so many other athletic terms, *terma* might well be intended in the sense of

---

19. 1 Clement 5: 1–7.
20. There might also be an echo here of the dominical warning in Mark 13: 9 (Matthew 10: 18).

"goal". But even if we take Clement to mean Paul's western goal, the phrase is not unambiguous. For Luke, Paul's western goal was Rome, but for Paul himself it was not Rome but Spain. P. N. Harrison, who argues persuasively for the meaning "goal", goes on to say: "the goal of this race was certainly not Spain, but Rome, from whatever point in the world-stadium one happened to be regarding it." [21] That, however, is going too far, when we consider that in Paul's own programme Rome was but a temporary station on his way farther west, or at best an advance base for the evangelization of Spain. Yet it is readily conceivable that, to a Christian of a later generation, in the light of Paul's martyrdom at Rome, Rome would naturally suggest itself as the "goal" of his race; and it might easily be inferred from Clement's language that Paul's western "limit" or "goal" was the place where he "bore testimony before the rulers, and so departed from this world".

As for the *time* of Paul's martyrdom, Clement may be thought to say something with a bearing on this when he goes on:

> To these men of holy life was gathered together a great multitude of the elect, who through their endurance amid many indignities and tortures because of jealousy presented to us a noble example. . . .[22]

That this is a reference to the persecution of Christians in Rome under Nero is hardly to be doubted: with Clement's "great multitude" may be compared Tacitus's almost identical wording.[23] If we took Clement's language *au pied de la lettre* it would imply that Peter and Paul had suffered martyrdom before the persecution which followed the great fire and, so far as Paul is concerned, that he was executed on conviction some time after the end of his two years' house arrest in Rome. But, although Moffatt and others were inclined to deduce this from Clement's language,[24] to insist on it demands from him an exactitude in the use of terms which he probably did not intend. Moreover, "these men of holy life" should not be restricted to Peter and Paul, mentioned in the immediately preceding sentences; they include the Old Testament heroes of endurance who are listed before Clement turns to "the good apostles". The most that can safely be said is that Clement bears witness to Paul's death at Rome under Nero.[25]

21. P. N. Harrison, *Problem*, p. 107. J. N. D. Kelly, on the other hand, says that Clement's phrase "in a Roman writer could only mean Spain" (*Commentary*, p. 10).

22. 1 Clement 6: 1.

23. Where Clement says πολὺ πλῆθος, Tacitus has *multitudo ingens*.

24. Cf. J. Moffatt, *Introduction to the Literature of the New Testament* (Edinburgh, ³1918), pp. 313, 416 f.

25. Eusebius (*Hist. Eccl.* iii. 1. 3) indicates that Origen bore similar witness in the third volume of his commentary on Genesis.

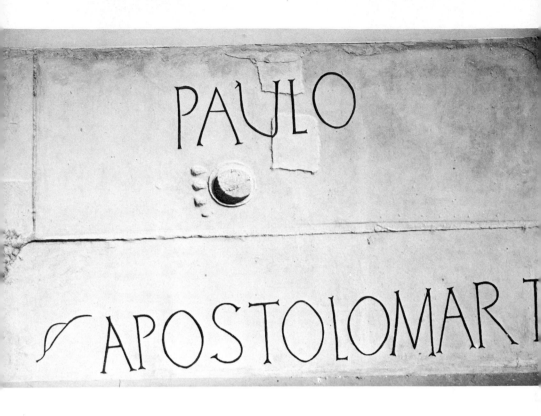

Rome: St. Paul-Without-the-Walls: inscription above Paul's
tomb (see p. 451)

Rome: Tre Fontane: Church of St. Paul, exterior (see p. 450)

## 5. The Muratorian canon

The Muratorian fragment is a Latin list of New Testament books drawn up in Rome towards the end of the second century, a corrupt seventh- or eighth-century manuscript of which was discovered and published by Cardinal L. A. Muratori in 1740. After its account of the Gospels, the list has this to say about Acts:

> Then the "Acts of all the Apostles" were written in one book. Luke tells the "most excellent Theophilus" that the various incidents took place in his presence, and indeed he makes this quite clear by omitting the passion of Peter, as well as Paul's journey when he set out from Rome for Spain.

The author takes Paul's Spanish journey for granted. There is no indication that he had any independent evidence of this; in itself, the mention of this journey could be nothing more than an inference from Romans 15: 24, 28. But since it is mentioned along with "the passion of Peter", another source is indicated – the apocryphal *Acts of Peter*.[26]

This gnostic work was probably composed about A.D. 180, shortly before the Muratorian list was drawn up. It is extant only in fragments in various languages. The best known fragment is the Vercelli manuscript (in Latin), which begins by describing Paul's departure from Italy by sea for Spain, and goes on to recount Peter's controversy in Rome with Simon Magus, ending with a description of Peter's crucifixion.[27] It looks as if the Muratorian compiler is trying (ineptly) to explain why the contents of the *Acts of Peter* do not appear in the canonical Acts. If we are right in identifying the *Acts of Peter* as the source of his reference to Paul's departure for Spain, it is not an authority which inspires great confidence, although it may reflect Roman tradition in the latter half of the second century.[28]

As for the fourth-century authors who report Paul's release from his first Roman imprisonment – Eusebius, Jerome,[29] etc. – they

---

26. For the dependence of the Muratorian statement on this document cf. T. Zahn, *Introduction to the New Testament*, E.T. ii (Edinburgh, 1909), pp. 62 f., 73 ff. See further A. A. T. Ehrhardt, *The Framework of the New Testament Stories* (Manchester, 1964), pp. 18, 35.

27. Cf. *New Testament Apocrypha*, E.T., ed. E. Hennecke, W. Schneemelcher, R. McL. Wilson, ii (London, 1965), pp. 279 ff.

28. Cf. J. B. Lightfoot, *Biblical Essays* (London, 1893), pp. 423 ff.; G. Edmundson, *The Church in Rome in the First Century* (London, 1913), pp. 160 f.; M. Dibelius and W. G. Kümmel, *Paul*, E.T. (London, 1953), p. 152, for more positive assessments.

29. See p. 444; Jerome, *De uiris illustribus* 5.

were merely repeating inferences of their predecessors, and doing so with proper caution: Eusebius, as we have seen, says that "rumour has it" that he resumed his ministry of preaching after his first appearing before Caesar. Our literary sources, therefore, leave us with a verdict of "not proven" in this regard.

### 6. The Ostian Way

The hypothesis which is provisionally entertained here is that Paul was released after his appeal was heard by the supreme court, and subsequently arrested a second time, imprisoned, put on trial, sentenced to death and beheaded. On this hypothesis, his execution was most probably an incident in Nero's persecution of the Roman Christians, and to be dated in or shortly after the year 65.

One way or the other, it is scarcely to be doubted that Rome was the place where he was executed. As regards the more precise location of his death or burial, our earliest witness is the Roman presbyter Gaius, at the end of the second century. In the course of a controversial correspondence with the Phrygian Montanist Proclus, Gaius says that, if Proclus can invoke in support of his views the names of distinguished early Christians (Philip and his daughters, and others) whose tombs can still be pointed out in the province of Asia, *he* can improve on that, for (says he) "I can point out the trophies of the apostles: for if you will go to the Vatican hill or to the Ostian Way, you will find the trophies of those who founded this church".[30] By "the apostles" Gaius meant Peter and Paul, claimed by the Roman church as its joint founders. By "trophies"[31] he means monuments (*memoriae*) marking the traditional sites either of the martyrdom or of the burial of the two apostles – probably the latter, since he is countering Proclus's claim to show the *tombs* of early Christians in *his* homeland. In any case, that Peter and Paul were actually buried at the places mentioned became a matter of general belief, on the strength of which the Constantinian basilica of St. Paul Outside the Walls was built on the Ostian Way and that of St. Peter on the Vatican hill.

Paul was beheaded, tradition asserts, at Aquae Salviae (now Tre Fontane) near the third milestone on the Ostian Way.[32] By Gaius's

30. As quoted by Eusebius, *Hist. Eccl.* ii. 25. 7; cf. iii. 31. 4.

31. Greek τροπαῖα, monuments set up by the victorious army on a battle-field to mark their triumph.

32. Cf. (Greek) *Acts of Peter and Paul*, 80 (*Acta Apostolorum Apocrypha*, ed. R. A. Lipsius, i [Leipzig, 1891], p. 214). A memorial chapel was built on the spot in the fifth century; above it stands the present-day church of St. Paul at Tre Fontane. According to these *Acts*, Paul was executed beneath a stone pine ( στρόβιλος ); in 1875 Trappists, excavating behind the chapel, found a number of fossilized pine-cones with a mass of Neronian coins (R. Lanciani, *Pagan and Christian Rome* [London, 1895], pp. 156 f.).

time a monument had been erected on the reputed site of his tomb, about a mile nearer the city (as one was erected on the Vatican hill, probably in the time of Marcus Aurelius, *c.* A.D. 160, to commemorate Peter).[33] On the same site Constantine built a small basilica in Paul's honour (*c.* A.D. 324); this was replaced at the end of the fourth century by a larger one, which survived substantially until it was destroyed by fire during the night of July 15/16, 1823. The present basilica was reconsecrated by Pope Pius IX on December 10, 1854.[34] Some details of the substructure were preserved in sketches made by the architect of the new building, Virgilio Vespignani, when a new *confessio* was constructed in front of the altar, instead of behind it (where the *confessio* in the old basilica had been).[35]

The floor of the *confessio* underneath the high altar is formed by two slabs, discovered in 1835 during the excavations preceding the erection of the present basilica – one bearing the inscription PAVLO and the other completing it with a second line of letters, APOSTOLO MART ("To Paul, apostle and martyr"). The lettering belongs to the fourth century, and has been assigned by some epigraphists to a Constantinian date. There are several indications that the two slabs are no longer in their original position: it has been suggested that at one time they stood upright, alongside each other, so as to present one line of writing, or even at right angles, forming two of the four sides of the apostle's *memoria*.[36]

It is a point in favour of the authenticity of the site that Paul's *memoria*, like Peter's, was located in a pagan necropolis, not the environment which later piety would have chosen.

## 7. The Appian Way

Mention should be made of what was for a time a rival tradition – not for the site of Paul's martyrdom but for that of his burial. In the *Calendar of Philocalus* (A.D. 354) and thence in the earlier part of the *Liber Pontificalis* (*c.* A.D. 530) Peter and Paul are associated with the site later occupied by the basilica of St. Sebastian on the Appian Way.[37] In the *Depositio Martyrum* included in the former

---

33. Cf. H. Lietzmann, *Petrus und Paulus in Rom* (Berlin, [2] 1927); J. M. C. Toynbee and J. B. Ward-Perkins, *The Shrine of St. Peter and the Vatican Excavations* (London, 1956).

34. Cf. E. Kirschbaum, *The Tombs of St. Peter and St. Paul*, E.T. (London, 1959), pp. 165 ff.

35. E. Kirschbaum, *op. cit.*, pp. 168 ff. The *confessio* is the chamber around the tomb together with the shaft connecting it with the altar.

36. E. Kirschbaum, *op. cit.*, pp. 179 ff. MART is an abbreviation of the dative MARTYRI.

37. A magisterial examination of this rival tradition is provided by H. Chadwick, "St. Peter and St. Paul in Rome: The Problem of the Memoria Apostolorum ad Catacumbas", *JTS*, n. s. 8 (1957), pp. 30 ff.

document, an entry under June 29 (III Kal. Iul.) mentions that the
remains of Peter were deposited *in Catacumbas* in the consulship of
Tuscus and Bassus (A.D. 258), a date probably denoting the establishment of an apostolic *memoria* and cult on this spot. (This
general area was then known as *Ad Catacumbas*, "By the Hollows".
Since the underground galleries there were the only early Christian
cemeteries known in the Middle Ages, the term "catacombs" was
extended from these cemeteries to denote others which were discovered from the sixteenth century onwards.) Paul is mentioned
along with Peter in this entry for June 29, but in association with
the Ostian Way, not with the *Catacumbae*. The text of the entry,
however, is probably corrupt and originally mentioned three cultic
sites – Peter's on the Vatican hill, Paul's on the Ostian Way, and
Peter and Paul's together at the *Catacumbae*.[38] Certainly the belief
that Paul's remains as well as Peter's were deposited at the *Catacum-*
*bae* is attested by a large number of *graffiti* on the site, of the later
third and early fourth centuries, invoking the names of Peter and
Paul and mentioning *refrigeria* (cultic meals) held there in their
honour. The hymn *Apostolorum Passio*, dating from the mid-fourth
century and traditionally ascribed to Ambrose of Milan, describes
how on June 29 the martyrdom of Peter and Paul was commemorated at three sites – the Vatican hill, the Ostian Way and the
Appian Way.[39] This attempt to meet the competing claims of rival
sites was judged unsatisfactory: when Pope Damasus (A.D.
366–383), in the course of restoring the Christian cemeteries of
Rome, turned his attention to the Memoria Apostolorum ad
Catacumbas, he indicated what was henceforth to be the official
line in a metrical inscription set up in the Basilica Apostolorum
which was built over the *memoria*:˙

> Here you must know that the saints formerly dwelt, whosoever you
> are who ask for the names of Peter and Paul. These disciples were sent

38. The text as it has been transmitted runs:

> III KAL. IVL.   Petri in Catacumbas
>                 et Pauli Ostense Tusco et Basso consulibus

On the basis of the *Martyrologium Hieronymianum* this can be restored somewhat as
follows:

> III KAL. IVL.   Petri in Vaticano
>                 Pauli uero in uia Ostensi
>                 utrumque in Catacumbas Tusco et Basso consulibus.

Cf. L. Duchesne (ed.), *Liber Pontificalis* i (Paris, 1886), p. cv.
39. Tantae per urbis ambitum
    Stipata tendunt agmina;
    Trinis celebratur uiis
    Festum sacrorum martyrum.

from the east, as we readily admit, but because of the merit of their blood they followed Christ through the stars and reached the ethereal bosom and the realms of the holy ones; and Rome has acquired the prior right to claim them as *her* citizens. Let Damasus thus record your praises, ye new constellations.[40]

The latter part of this inscription affirms that the two apostles' martyrdom in Rome gives the church of that city a superior right to speak with apostolic authority, even though they belonged originally to the east. But the opening couplet means: "their bodies once lay here, but are here no longer." These words, with their implication of a transference of the two bodies from the Appian Way to the Vatican hill and the Ostian Way respectively, represent an attempt to harmonize the conflicting traditions and divert the attention of pious pilgrims to the Constantinian basilicas. Some students of later days, beginning apparently with John Pearson, seventeenth-century bishop of Chester,[41] envisaged a temporary translation of the apostles' bodies from the original sites to the Appian Way because of the circumstances of the persecution under Valerian (A.D. 258), when Christians were forbidden to hold their ordinary public meetings and access to their cemeteries was prevented. But this harmonistic reconstruction of two separate traditions, the one enjoying official approval and the other popular favour, has no independent evidence in its support.

In the mid-third century the Roman Christians who wished to honour the apostles at the site of their tombs may not have had easy access to the Vatican hill or to the Pauline *memoria* on the Ostian Way, whereas there were fewer hindrances to their doing so *ad Catacumbas*. But why choose that particular spot? We do not know: there may already have been a popular tradition of the apostles' burial there; it may have been revealed to someone in a vision that this was where their bodies lay. Whatever the origin of the tradition was, it strongly influenced popular devotion for early a century. But it was bound to weaken after the erection of the Constantinian basilicas in honour of Peter and Paul. The cult of the apostles on the Appian Way was increasingly displaced by that of St. Sebas-

40. Hic habitasse prius sanctos cognoscere debes,
    Nomina quisque Petri pariter Paulique requiris.
    Discipulos Oriens misit, quod sponte fatemur;
    Sanguinis ob meritum, Christumque per astra secuti
    Aetherios petiere sinus regnaque piorum:
    Roma suos potius meruit defendere ciues.
    Haec Damasus uestras referat noua sidera laudes.
41. J. Pearson, *Annales Cyprianici*, p. 62, *ad annum* 258, printed in *Sancti Caecilii Cypriani Opera*, ed. John Fell (Oxford, 1682), according to H. Chadwick, *JTS*, n. s. 8 (1957), p. 41, n. 2.

tian, who is said to have been buried in their vicinity late in the third century; and Damasus eased the situation by explaining that while the bodies of Peter and Paul had indeed once lain by the Appian Way, they now lay on the sites covered by their respective basilicas.

### 8. Paul in Roman memory

These, however, are relatively unimportant matters compared with the real memorials to Paul in Rome – those which he might have been gratified, though surprised, to foresee. The church and city of Rome have not forgotten their association, brief and limited as it was, with the apostle to the Gentiles. Although Paul himself makes it plain that Roman Christianity flourished years before he first visited the city, the Roman church has claimed him as one of its two apostolic founders. Clement of Rome, as we have seen, appeals to the example of Peter and Paul.[42] Ignatius of Antioch, writing to the Christians at Rome a decade or two later, will not lay commands on them, as Peter and Paul did; they were apostles, he is "a convicted criminal" – although they were no more than that in Roman law.[43] Dionysius of Corinth (c. A.D. 170), writing to Pope Soter, sees a special bond between the churches of Corinth and Rome in that each was founded by Peter and Paul and profited by the teaching of both apostles.[44] (While Paul would have deprecated nomination as one of the founders of the Roman church, he must have turned in his grave at the suggestion that Peter was joint-founder with him of the Corinthian church!) Gaius of Rome points to the "trophies" of Peter and Paul as the most illustrious material monuments of Roman Christianity. Irenaeus of Lyons, about the same time, reviewing the churches which were founded by apostles, gives pride of place to that "very great, very ancient and universally known church founded and organized at Rome by the two most glorious apostles Peter and Paul",[45] and adds that they committed the episcopate in that church to Linus.[46] This is in keeping with early tradition which names Peter and Paul as founders not only of the church of Rome but also of the Roman succession of bishops. Irenaeus's informant may have been Hegesippus,[47] although Irenaeus himself was in sufficiently close touch with the Roman

42. See p. 447.
43. Ignatius, *Letter to the Romans* 4: 3.
44. As quoted by Eusebius, *Hist. Eccl.* ii. 25. 8.
45. Irenaeus, *Against Heresies* iii. 3. 1.
46. *Ibid.*, iii. 3. 2.
47. According to Eusebius (*Hist. Eccl.* iv. 22. 1–3), Hegesippus (a mid-second-century Palestinian Christian) drew up an early succession-list of Roman bishops. For Irenaeus's dependence on Hegesippus see J. B. Lightfoot, *The Apostolic Fathers* i. 1: *S. Clement of Rome* (London, 1890), pp. 202 f., 327 ff.

church to know directly what its local tradition was. Down to the middle of the third century the two apostles are regularly conjoined as joint founders of the Roman church; even Eusebius, in the fourth century, can on occasion name them in a Roman context in the order Paul-Peter [48] (although in his Chronicle he mentions Peter only: "After Peter Linus was the first to occupy the Roman see").[49] Later still in that century Damasus, as we have seen, lays claim on behalf of the Roman church to their joint prestige.

But, as C. H. Turner put it, "in transcribing a catalogue it was easier to use one name than two, and as soon as the habit grew up of including the name of the Apostle-founder as the first of the list rather than as a title at the head of it, . . . the use of a single name was dictated by the principle that there could only be one bishop at a time." [50] The naming of Peter alone is first attested in Hippolytus, who calls Pope Victor (c. A.D. 190) "thirteenth from Peter"[51] – although this leaves Peter outside the numbered episcopal list. The first to attach dogmatic significance to the name of Peter alone at the head of the Roman list is Cyprian, bishop of Carthage (died A.D. 258).[52] So Paul's contribution to early Roman Christianity was in practice increasingly overlooked. To be sure, Paul with the sword of the Spirit stands in the forecourt of St. Peter's, alongside Peter with the keys of the Kingdom, just as Peter faces Paul in front of St. Paul's Outside the Walls – more congenial associates in death, perhaps, than they were in life. But there may be a symbolical fitness, it has sometimes been said, in the location of St. Paul's basilica *outside* the walls. Paul might have understood and approved; he was well accustomed to being odd man out. It would be pleasant to think that such a minister of reconciliation as Paul was there in spirit in March, 1966, when his namesake Paul VI and Michael Ramsey chose his basilica for the signing of their Common Declaration, asking their respective communions to engage in "a serious dialogue based upon the Holy Gospels and ancient common traditions".[53]

48. Eusebius, *Hist. Eccl.* iii. 2. 1; 21. 1.
49. Eusebius, *Chronicon*, Year of Abraham 2084 = Nero 14 (i.e. A.D. 67).
50. C. H. Turner, *Catholic and Apostolic* (London, 1931), p. 225; see also his essay "Apostolic Succession" in *Essays on the Early History of the Church and the Ministry*, ed. H. B. Swete (London, 1921), pp. 93–214, especially pp. 141 f.
51. As quoted anonymously by Eusebius, *Hist. Eccl.* v. 28. 3. That the quotation is from Hippolytus was maintained by J. B. Lightfoot, *The Apostolic Fathers* i. 2 (London, 1890), p. 379, and A. von Harnack, *Chronologie der altchristlichen Literatur*, ii (Leipzig, 1897), pp. 224 f.
52. Cyprian, *De unitate ecclesiae* 4; *Epistles* 43. 5; 70. 3; 73. 7, etc.
53. Cf. A. M. Ramsey, *Canterbury Pilgrim* (London, 1974), p. 10. Paul might have raised his eyebrows at the use of the plural "Gospels", but he would have approved of "ancient common traditions" if they were such as he delivered to his converts at Thessalonica and Corinth (2 Thessalonians 2: 15; 1 Corinthians 11: 2).

# CHAPTER 38

# Concluding Reflections

## 1. Paul's personality

WHAT KIND OF MAN WAS PAUL?
So far as external features are concerned, we gather only that, in the estimation of candid friends, he was impressive neither in appearance nor in speech.[1] We have already discussed the humiliating disability which may have had an adverse effect on one or both of these.[2] More important, however, are his qualities of mind and spirit.

By his own account, he grew up a zealot for the ancestral traditions of his people;[3] and when those traditions were displaced in his life by another cause, he was no less zealous in the promotion of this new cause. The zeal which he had shown as a persecutor of the church he continued to show as a builder of what he had once tried to destroy, as a bondslave of the Lord whom he had formerly repudiated. For the sake of this Lord everything that he had once valued was discounted as so much refuse;[4] the one-time rigorist made himself the most versatile and adaptable of men in order to bring others to acknowledge the same Lord as he did; everything was subordinated to the propagation of the good news of his grace and to this cause all his talents and energies were dedicated.

Something of Paul's native impetuousness is apparent in his epistolary style. His letters were regularly dictated to an assistant. At times the torrent of his thought rushes forward so swiftly that it outstrips the flow of his words, and his words have to leap over a gap now and then so as to catch up on his thought. How the scribe managed to keep up with his words we can only surmise. Time and again Paul starts a sentence that never reaches a grammatical end, for before he is well launched on it a new thought strikes him and he turns aside to deal with that. When he comes back on to the main track, the original start of the sentence has been forgotten. All this means that Paul is not the smoothest of authors, or the easiest

1. Cf. 2 Corinthians 10: 10.
2. See pp. 135 f.
3. Galatians 1: 13 f.
4. Philippians 3: 8.

to follow, but it does give us an unmistakable impression of the man himself. He has something worth saying, and in saying it he communicates something of himself; there is nothing artificial or merely conventional about the way he says it. And what he has to say is so important – for readers of the twentieth century as much as for those of the first – that the effort to understand him is abundantly rewarding.

Dr. Samuel Johnson described one of his acquaintances as an "unclubbable" man.[5] That is the last adjective that anyone who knew Paul would use of him. He was eminently "clubbable", sociable, gregarious. He delighted in the company of his fellows, both men and women. The most incredible feature in the Paul of popular mythology is his alleged misogyny. He treated women as persons: we recall his commendation of Phoebe, the deacon of the church in Cenchreae, who had shown herself a helper to him as to many others,[6] or his appreciation of Euodia and Syntyche of Philippi who worked side by side with him in the gospel.[7] The mainstream churches of Christendom, as they inch along towards a worthier recognition of the ministry of women, have some way to go yet before they come abreast of Paul.[8]

The range of his friendship and the warmth of his affection are qualities which no attentive reader of his letters can miss. There are scores of people mentioned in the New Testament who are known to us, by name at least, simply because they were friends of Paul. And in his friends he was able to call forth a devotion which knew no limits. Priscilla and Aquila risked their lives for him in a dangerous situation.[9] Epaphroditus of Philippi overtaxed his strength and suffered an almost fatal illness in his anxiety to be of service to the imprisoned apostle.[10] Timothy readily surrendered whatever personal ambitions he might have cherished in order to play the part of a son to Paul and help him in his missionary activity, showing a selfless concern for others that matched the apostle's own eagerness to spend and be spent for them.[11]

As a pious Jew, Paul would have thought of his death as the final offering he could make to God, an offering which would expiate his sins and crown his piety. As a Christian, he continued to look upon his death as an offering to God, but preferred now that it should be

5. Mme D'Arbley (Fanny Burney), *Diary*, i (London, 1842), p. 66: he called Sir John Hawkins "a most unclubbable man".

6. Romans 16: 1 f.

7. Philippians 4: 2 f.

8. Even if he asks them to keep their heads veiled when praying or prophesying, the veil is the sign of their authority to play a responsible part in church life.

9. Romans 16: 3 f.

10. Philippians 2: 25–30.

11. Philippians 2: 19–22.

credited to his converts' account rather than to his own. For example, if some contribution was necessary to complete the faith of the Philippian Christians, a libation to be poured out upon their sacrifice, so to speak, then let the outpouring of Paul's life be that libation. Charles Wesley in later days could voice the aspiration:

> Ready for all thy perfect will,
>   My acts of faith and love repeat,
> Till death thy endless mercies seal,
>   And make the sacrifice complete.

Paul was aware of the same aspiration, but with one modification: let *his* death make *their* sacrifice complete.[12]

Nothing can surpass the spontaneous expression of the tenderness which he feels for his Galatian friends when they are being led astray from freedom back to spiritual bondage: "my little children, for whom I suffer birth-pangs all over again until Christ be formed in you!" (Galatians 4: 9). It is his affection and concern for them that explains the indignation with which he explodes against those who are misleading them, placing a yoke of slavery on their necks – the same order of indignation as earlier found expression in Jesus' stern words about any one who upset "one of these little ones": "Better for him that a millstone were hung round his neck and he were cast into the sea" (Luke 17: 2). "Who is weak, and I am not weak?" asks Paul. "Who is tripped up, and I am not indignant?" (2 Corinthians 11: 29).

Paul wants to see his converts bound together in heart by the same strong affection as he feels for them. The faith which saves, he tells the Galatians, is the "faith that works through love" (Galatians 5: 6). Through this same love they are called to "serve one another" and so "fulfil the law of Christ" (Galatians 5: 13; 6: 2). Paul has no place for the solitary life as an ideal; for all his apostolic energy he would have scouted the suggestion that "he travels the fastest who travels alone".[13] He emphasizes the fellowship, the togetherness, of Christians in worship and action; they are members one of another, and all together members of Christ.

12. Philippians 2: 17. We may compare his readiness to be himself "accursed and cut off from Christ" if only thus the salvation of his Jewish kinsmen could be achieved (Romans 9: 3).

13. It was not for this reason that he found the celibate life congenial (see p. 269); he does not imply that Peter and others found the company of their wives on their missionary journeys an encumbrance (1 Corinthians 9: 5). The implications of Paul's fondness for compounds with the prefix συν- (e.g. "fellow-worker", "fellow-soldier", etc.) have been studied by several writers; cf. T. R. Glover, *Paul of Tarsus* (London, 1925), pp. 178 ff., 212.

His converts were his pride and joy. When he writes to them he is like a father addressing his children. He commends everything that is praiseworthy in them, where others might have found little enough to commend. He scolds them for their shortcomings, and warns them that if they do not mend their ways he will take a big stick with him next time he comes.[14] But he encourages them for all he is worth, and makes no secret of his consuming desire that they should grow up to be hundred-per-cent Christians, worthy of the honourable name they bear.

If he exercises a father's privilege in this way, he boasts about them to others. When he is organizing the Jerusalem relief fund, he tells the Corinthians about the Macedonians' generosity and boasts to the Macedonians about the Corinthians' promptness.[15] Above all, he hopes that when he gives a final account of his apostolic stewardship to the Lord who commissioned him, he will need do no more than point to his converts and have the quality of his service judged by their faith and life.[16]

Reference to the Jerusalem relief fund brings to mind his extraordinary sense of delicacy where money is concerned. He organized the fund, but insisted that the contributions should be handled and delivered to their destination by individuals appointed by the donors. As for himself, honesty must not only be practised but must be seen to be practised; he knew how convenient a handle involvement in financial affairs provides for suspicion-mongers. It was partly for a similar reason that he refused to accept money from the Corinthian Christians, but partly because of his inbred independence: he much preferred to maintain himself. To express thanks for a gift, even from his dear friends at Philippi, was evidently something which he could not do without a certain embarrassment.[17] It is plain, too, that by maintaining himself and not becoming chargeable to others he wished to set an example to other Christians who, from a conviction that the day of the Lord was just round the corner or for some other reason, thought it was pointless to go on working to earn their daily bread.[18]

Paul strikes us as a man possessed of uncommon strength of will, not easily to be turned aside from the path which he believed it to be his duty to follow. Since the risen Lord had called him to be his apostle to the Gentiles, he had no option but to obey him. He obeyed him right gladly, with utter heart-devotion: the love of Christ constrained him. But even if he had felt otherwise about it,

14. 1 Corinthians 4: 21.
15. 2 Corinthians 8: 1–5; 9: 1–4.
16. 1 Thessalonians 2: 19 f.; Philippians 2: 14–16.
17. Philippians 4: 10–20.
18. 2 Thessalonians 3: 6–13.

he had no option in the matter. He had been conscripted into this service. Never, to be sure, was there a more willing conscript, but he knew himself to be under authority. In other respects he might be allowed freedom of choice: not in this.[19]

When he argues that it is preposterous for people who have been delivered from the bondage of sin to place themselves under it again, it may be thought that he credited his converts with his own strength of will and made insufficient allowance for the pull of old habits, old associations, old environments. The bondage from which he knew himself to have been delivered was the bondage of law, and he had no desire to resume that bondage; but he had not been exposed to the Corinthian way of life and was perplexed when some of his converts found so much difficulty in shaking it off.

Yet he set no limits to the transforming power of the risen Christ, implanted in believers' hearts by the Holy Spirit, and he saw sufficient evidence of that power in action in their lives to know that he was not recommending a hopelessly unpractical ideal. And if we suppose that he was too inclined to measure his converts by the strong-willed character of a man for whom to see that a course was right was to pursue it, let us recall his own testimony that he practised unremitting self-discipline lest, after preaching to others, he might be disqualified himself. For him the Christian life was a strenuous business: he liked to picture it in athletic terms, as a battle to be fought, a race to be run.[20] Instant attainment was out of the question: not before the end of his mortal career would he have reached the goal towards which he pressed, to receive "the prize of God's upward call in Christ Jesus" (Philippians 3: 14). It was a naturally proud man who schooled himself to boast about his humiliations in place of his achievements.

His great concern for his converts was that they should have reproduced in their own lives the character of Christ – the fruit of the Spirit (as he called it) which included such qualities as love, patience, gentleness, meekness and self-control.[21] This concern underlay much of his self-discipline. What was the use of recommending them to cultivate such qualities if they were not at the same time visible in his own life? The lack of these would certainly disqualify him from exhorting others to develop them. Some of them at least – patience and gentleness, for example – did not come to him naturally. Meekness was a distinctive feature in the character of Jesus, but its reproduction in Paul required the taming of his impetuousness by the power of the Spirit and his regular self-discipline. So resolutely, however, did he submit to this taming

19. 1 Corinthians 9: 15–18.
20. 1 Corinthians 9: 24–27.
21. Galatians 5: 22 f.

process that he could not only with a good conscience try to inculcate these Christian graces in others, but could even encourage them to take his own practice as their example.

As an apple-tree does not produce apples by Act of Parliament, but because it is its nature so to do, so the character of Christ cannot be produced in his people by rules and regulations; it must be the fruit of his Spirit within them. Especially in the earlier days of his ministry, Paul appears to have been bewildered by the spectacle of Christians who, instead of rejoicing in the liberty of the Spirit, preferred to be directed by a code of rules. With his own exhilarating experience of spiritual freedom, he could not be content to see his converts going along happily as those for whom "rules are more comfortable to live with than principles".[22] He longed to see them entering more fully into the liberty with which Christ had set them free instead of living like those Pharisees whom the Talmud assigns to the "tell-me-my-duty-and-I-will-do-it" category.[23]

But Paul's personal strength of will was not accompanied, as it is in so many, by impatience with lesser mortals. While he himself had a robust and emancipated conscience, he had warm sympathy with those whose conscience was immature and unenlightened, and he would go to almost any length of self-denial in consideration for his weaker brethren. He deplored the inability or unwillingness of other strong-minded Christians to show them such consideration, and it was pre-eminently in this regard that he pressed his own example on them, urging them to imitate him as he for his part imitated Christ.[24]

His strength of will was matched by unusual physical toughness; in both respects, indeed, he might be compared to Socrates. Here the evidence of Acts corroborates that of his own writings. Luke describes how he was stoned at Lystra, dragged out of the city and left for dead by the roadside, "but as the disciples surrounded him he got up and went into the city, and set out next day with Barnabas for Derbe" (Acts 14: 20). This experience forms one item in the list of hardships which he enumerates in 2 Corinthians 11: 23–27. He is abashed at being put in a position where, in self-defence, he has to present such a catalogue, but the matter-of-fact recital of imprisonments, floggings, shipwrecks, narrow escapes from death and the like that he has been through in the course of his apostolic work tells its own tale of the resilience and staying power of the man who has endured it all. The scars which

22. J. R. W. Stott, *Obeying Christ in a Changing World, 1: The Lord Christ* (London, 1977), p. 24.
23. TJ *B<sup>e</sup>rakôt* 9: 7.
24. 1 Corinthians 10: 32–11: 1. Cf. W. P. DeBoer, *The Imitation of Paul* (Kampen, 1962).

those experiences left he wears with pride: they were the indelible *stigmata* which proclaimed him to be the bondslave of the Lord in whose service he had received them.[25]

Paul would not have interpreted his sustaining of trouble and danger in terms of toughness; in his eyes all this was part of the life of faith, not to be endured as something one would rather be spared but to be embraced with joy as a sure token of acceptance by God and as a strengthening of Christian hope. This attitude belonged to the reversal of all conventional values implicit in the cross of Christ. Paul welcomed such hardships the more gladly as a sharing in the sufferings of Christ and as a means of absorbing in his own person afflictions which would otherwise fall to the lot of his fellow-Christians. As the hardships wore down the outer man, they were at the same time used by God for the renewal of the inner man and the augmenting of his heritage of glory.

Paul was a child of his time, born in the first century A.D. and not earlier or later, born in the Roman Empire and not beyond its frontiers, born a Jew and not a Gentile. He was influenced by his heritage, his environment and his upbringing. Some men and women remain so completely children of their time that practically everything about them can be explained in terms of their cultural conditioning. Not so Paul. Perhaps this is what John Donne had in mind when he said that "Paul was borne a man, an Apostle, not carved out, as the rest, in time; but a fusile Apostle, an Apostle powred out, and cast in a Mold".[26] He belongs to that select company who leave their mark on their time, who mould their contemporaries and exert an influence which stretches far into the future.

Although he was rabbinically trained, his reappraisal of the whole spirit and content of his earlier training was so radical that many Jewish scholars have had difficulty in recognizing him as the product of a rabbinical education. They have found it easier to appreciate the Prophet of Nazareth (who, indeed, was not rabbinically trained) than the apostle to the Gentiles. Paul presents an enigma with which they cannot readily come to terms.[27]

When it dawned on the young Pharisee that God in the fulness of time had sent his Son, that the crucified Jesus was exalted as Lord over all, that as such he had inaugurated a new era which superseded the reign of law, it not only brought about a complete reorientation in his own thought and life, but through him reoriented the

25. Galatians 6: 17.
26. *LXXX Sermons* (London, 1640), no. 46, p. 460.
27. More appreciative Jewish assessments have come from C. G. Montefiore, *Judaism and St. Paul* (London, 1914); H. J. Schoeps, *Paul*, E.T. (London, 1961); S. Sandmel, *The Genius of Paul* (New York, 1970). Cf. also the interesting psycho-analytic study by R. L. Rubinstein, *My Brother Paul* (New York, 1972).

thought and life of a considerable body of mankind. While others in his day took part in the Gentile mission, his contribution was unique and most far-reaching. Paul, more (it appears) than any of the original disciples of Jesus, appreciated the universal implications of his Master's person and work and gave them practical effect. Four themes emphasized in his teaching call for summary mention because they still need to be emphasized.

(a) True religion is not a matter of rules and regulations. God does not deal with people like an accountant, but accepts them freely when they respond to his love, and implants the Spirit of Christ in their hearts so that they may show to others the love they have received from him.

(b) In Christ men and women have come of age, as the new humanity brought into being through his death and resurrection-life. God does not keep his children in leading-strings but calls them to live as his responsible adult sons and daughters.

(c) People matter more than things, more than principles, more than causes. The highest of principles and the best of causes exist for the sake of people; to sacrifice people to them is a perversion of the true order.

(d) Unfair discrimination on the grounds of race, religion, class or sex is an offence against God and humanity alike.

If these lessons are important, it is well to give grateful credit to one man who taught them.

## 2. Paul in the early church

Paul's withdrawal from public activity during the four years following his arrest by Roman auxiliaries in Jerusalem gave his opponents throughout his Gentile mission-field an opportunity which they were not slow to exploit. The evidence of Colossians, if it is to be dated in the context of his Roman imprisonment, speaks for itself; and the Philippian Christians are put on their guard alike against Judaizers (the "mutilation" party) and gnosticizing libertines (Philippians 3: 2, 18 f.). The words of 2 Timothy 1: 15, "You are well aware that all who are in Asia turned away from me", probably relate to the climax of this anti-Pauline trend. What the direction of the "turning away" was we are not told: Phygelus and Hermogenes are singled out for special mention, presumably as leaders of the movement, but no details of their teaching are given. Elsewhere in the same letter another couple, Hymenaeus and Philetus, are accused of deviating from the truth by maintaining an over-realized eschatology – saying, as some of the Corinthians had said before them, that the resurrection had already taken place (2 Timothy 2: 17 f.).[28] It is not even certain that Hymenaeus and Philetus belonged to the province of Asia; the probability that they did so is high, however, if (as seems likely) Hymenaeus is identical with the bearer of that name who, according to 1 Timothy 1: 19 f., had with a certain Alexander "made shipwreck of the faith" and undergone disciplinary action at Paul's hands (by remote control, presumably), "so as to learn not to blaspheme".[29]

A stabilizing influence was apparently introduced into the churches of Asia in the later sixties with the emigration to that province of some forward-looking and liberal-minded Christian leaders from Judaea, including "John, the disciple of the Lord" (as he is called) and Philip of Caesarea with his prophesying daughters. They enjoyed considerable prestige among the Asian Christians, not only while they lived but for some generations after.[30] The presence of such men and women, closely associated as they were with Christian beginnings in Palestine, helped to discourage tendencies to Jewish legalism or libertine gnosticism.

But the one event that more than anything else brought about the collapse of the judaizing mission in Paul's mission-field was the Jewish revolt against Rome in A.D. 66, which led not only to the destruction of the temple and city of Jerusalem four years later but also to the dispersal of the church of Jerusalem. The church of Jerusalem endeavoured to maintain its identity in exile for many generations, but no longer could it issue decrees to be accepted by Gentile Christendom; indeed, contact between it and the Gentile churches was reduced to a minimum. Its ancient prestige was later inherited to some extent by the new church of Jerusalem, the completely Gentile community which established itself in Hadrian's new foundation of Aelia Capitolina, erected on the site of the holy city in A.D. 135 and the following years.

Where the traditions of the original church of Jerusalem were cherished, Paul remained a dubious character, if he was not indeed regarded as the enemy who sowed the tares of antinomianism among the wheat of the new law promulgated by Jesus, the prophet like Moses.[31] But such a picture of Paul was eccentric and uninfluential. Throughout his Gentile mission-field, and beyond it,

---

28. Cf. W. L. Lane, "1 Tim. iv. 1–3: An Early Instance of Over-realized Eschatology", *NTS* 11 (1964–65), pp. 164–167; see also p. 307 above.

29. Cf. the disciplinary action enjoined in 1 Corinthians 5: 4 f.

30. Eusebius quotes to this effect the Phrygian Montanist Proclus (*Hist. Eccl.* iii. 31. 4) and Polycrates, bishop of Ephesus (*Hist. Eccl.* iii. 31. 3; v. 24. 2); cf. Irenaeus, *Against Heresies* iii. 1. 1. All three of these writers belong to the end of the second century.

31. Cf. Matthew 13: 25. He is so portrayed in the Clementine literature, a corpus of third-century writings purporting to come from the apostolic age (see p. 395), in which James the Just and Peter are the fountain-heads of authority in the church; cf. H. J. Schoeps, *Theologie und Geschichte des Judenchristentums* (Tübingen, 1949), pp. 120, 127.

Rome: Tre Fontane: Church of St. Paul, interior (see p. 450)

Page of $P^{46}$ (see p. 466), showing Galatians 6:10–18 and Philippians 1:1. $P^{46}$ is the oldest known manuscript of Paul's letters (c. A.D. 200); it is one of the Chester Beatty biblical papyri in the Chester Beatty Library, Dublin his prestige rose higher than it had often done in his lifetime: churches which owed their first beginnings to his evangelistic energy were proud to acknowledge him as their apostolic founder.

His letters, whether as entire documents or in fragments, were carefully collected. He himself had given a first impetus to this trend in his life-time by encouraging the exchange of letters addressed by him to neighbouring churches and probably by occasionally sending copies of a letter addressed to one community to be read elsewhere. When Clement of Rome wrote in the name of the Roman church to the church of Corinth about A.D. 96, he plainly had access to a copy of the letter which we know as 1 Corinthians, for he quotes it freely, reminding the Corinthian Christians that they should have paid more attention to what their apostolic founder had said to them forty years before.

It may well be that a powerful impetus was given to the collecting of Paul's letters and their publication as a literary corpus by the wider circulation of the second volume of Luke's history – the Acts of the Apostles. If there was any tendency to forget Paul in the regions which he had evangelized, this fascinating record would certainly rekindle interest in him both in those regions and elsewhere.[32]

However that may be, early in the second century an unknown benefactor of all succeeding ages copied at least ten Pauline letters into a codex from which copies were made for use in many parts of the Christian world.[33] From that time forth Paul's letters circulated as a collection and not singly. The second-century writers, whether "orthodox" or "heterodox", who refer to the Pauline letters, knew them in the form of a corpus.

Among the "heterodox" writers the most notable was Marcion, who about A.D. 144 promulgated a canon of Christian scripture, comprising his edition of the Gospel of Luke and ten Pauline epistles (the Pastorals being omitted). Paul, in Marcion's eyes, was the only faithful apostle of Jesus Christ; the original apostles all adulterated his pure gospel with judaizing doctrines. But even the authentic Pauline letters required to be purified of what, according to Marcion, were non-Pauline accretions, such as those passages which assumed the continuing validity of the Old Testament writings. It has been said that Marcion was "the only man of his

32. Cf. E. J. Goodspeed, *Introduction to the New Testament* (Chicago, 1937), pp. 210 ff.

33. Cf. G. Zuntz, *The Text of the Epistles* (London, 1954), pp. 14 ff., 276 ff.; he thinks of Alexandria as the place where this work was done, in view of its apparent "dependence upon the scholarly Alexandrian methods of editorship" (p. 278). An Ephesian setting for the compilation of the corpus was envisaged by E. J. Goodspeed (*Introduction to the New Testament*, pp. 217 ff.); cf. C. L. Mitton, *The Formation of the Pauline Corpus of Letters* (London, 1955), pp. 44 ff. See also p. 402 above.

age who understood Paul, and even in his understanding of him he misunderstood him".[34] Although his peculiar teachings were repudiated by the church, his edition of the Pauline corpus influenced the subsequent transmission of their text in several ways.[35]

Our oldest known surviving copy of the Pauline letters is a papyrus codex in the Chester Beatty collection in Dublin ($P^{46}$ in the recognized list of Greek New Testament manuscripts). It belongs to the end of the second century and contains the shorter Pauline corpus of ten letters (excluding the Pastorals) together with the Epistle to the Hebrews. In Egypt, from which the Chester Beatty biblical papyri came, Hebrews was regarded as a Pauline letter as early as A.D. 180 [36] (the Roman church, to one group in which Hebrews was probably sent in the first instance, knew better).

Throughout catholic Christendom, then, by the last quarter of the second century, Paul's memory was venerated and his writings were canonized.[37] But this did not mean that his teaching was understood. The tendency to subject Christian life to regulations was too powerful, and when, as happened from time to time, someone appeared who really grasped Paul's intention, the effect was liable to be revolutionary. Many of the fathers would not have thought it possible that Paul really meant what he said about Christians being no longer under law but under grace.[38] Naturally, too, when the historical context of his more polemical passages had been forgotten it was difficult to follow his strategy as he waged war on two fronts simultaneously, going as far as he could, first with this line of thought among his converts and then with that, until he

34. Cf. A. von Harnack, *Marcion: Das Evangelium vom fremden Gott* (Leipzig, 1921), pp. 230 ff.; 2nd edition = *Texte und Untersuchungen* 45 (1924), pp. 199 ff.; this (with its supplement *Neue Studien zu Marcion* = *Texte und Untersuchungen* 44, Part 4 [1923]) remains the most important work on Marcion. See also R. S. Wilson, *Marcion: A Study of a Second-Century Heretic* (London, 1933); J. Knox, *Marcion and the New Testament* (Chicago, 1942); E. C. Blackman, *Marcion and his Influence* (London, 1948). See p. 19.

35. In some quarters Marcion's devotion to Paul raised questions about Paul in orthodox minds: Tertullian, for example, calls him "Marcion's apostle" or "the apostle of the heretics" (*Against Marcion* iii. 5. 4; v. 14. 9) – not indeed disparagingly, but in *ad hominem* argument; he speaks of him also as "my apostle" (v. 1. 8), but not in Marcion's exclusive sense. See also C. K. Barrett, "Pauline Controversies in the Post-Pauline Period", *NTS* 20 (1973–74), pp. 229–245.

36. Cf. Clement of Alexandria, as quoted by Eusebius, *Hist. Eccl.* vi. 14. 2 f. See also C. P. Anderson, "The Epistle to the Hebrews and the Pauline Letter Collection", *Harvard Theological Review* 59 (1966), pp. 429–438.

37. In their response to Marcion the catholic churchmen named thirteen Pauline letters, not ten only, and writings of other apostolic men in addition to Paul; a fourfold Gospel and not one single record; with the Acts of the Apostles as the link joining the Gospel and the Epistles. See F. F. Bruce, *The Spreading Flame* (London, 1958), pp. 228 ff.

38. See T. F. Torrance, *The Doctrine of Grace in the Apostolic Fathers* (Edinburgh/London, 1948).

reached. the point where the interposition of a "But . . ." substantially modified what had appeared to be a wholesale concession. One ironical result of this failure to place Paul's arguments in their contemporary setting was that the apostle who had been criticized by moralists in his lifetime as an antinomian was highly esteemed by their spiritual successors as an ascetic.[39]

### 3. Paul in fiction and legend

Early in the second half of the second century A.D. a presbyter in the province of Asia gathered together legends and traditions about Paul from the whole area of the apostle's activity from Damascus to Rome, drew on his own imagination to provide them with the necessary continuity, and issued the work as the *Acts of Paul*. His purpose was to honour the apostle's memory, but his colleagues and superiors disapproved of what he had done – finding fault either with the general idea of such a work of fiction, or with some of its contents which encouraged beliefs or practices which they found unacceptable – and deposed him from his office. He affirmed that he had compiled the work *amore Pauli*, "for love of Paul", but the worthiness of the motive could not compensate, to their way of thinking, for the objectionable nature of the product.

Our information about the author's unfrocking comes from Tertullian of Carthage who, writing later in the same century, warns those who allow a teaching ministry for women in the church that they should not invoke the authority of this work, since it was condemned by competent authority.[40] The particular section of the work referred to is the episode of Paul and Thekla. Thekla was a legendary convert of the apostle's who, at his instance, broke off her engagement and for a time shared his apostolic ministry, experiencing a miraculous deliverance from martyrdom. The Paul of this episode acts inconsistently with the Paul of the Pastoral Epistles: whereas the Pastoral Epistles "permit no woman to teach" and condemn those "who forbid marriage" (1 Timothy 2: 12; 4: 3), Paul in these *Acts* discourages Thekla from matrimony but encourages her to cultivate her gift as a teacher. It may have been in the inculcation of celibacy and general asceticism that the Asian church leaders recognized heretical tendencies in the *Acts of Paul*, for such tendencies were manifesting themselves just then in the new Montanist movement.[41]

It is in this section of the *Acts of Paul* that we came upon a pen-portrait of the apostle which has sometimes been thought, because

39. See M. F. Wiles, *The Divine Apostle* (Cambridge, 1967), pp. 94 ff. *et passim*.
40. Tertullian, *De baptismo* 17.
41. Cf. A. von Harnack, *The Origin of the New Testament*, E.T. (London, 1925), pp. 35 ff., for the influence of Montanism on the canonizing process.

of its vigorous and unconventional character, to reflect a persistent local recollection. Paul is on his way to Iconium with two companions –

> And a man named Onesiphorus, who had heard that Paul had come to Iconium, went out with his children Simmias and Zeno and his wife Lectra to meet Paul, that he might receive him to his house. Titus had told him what Paul looked like; thus far Onesiphorus had not seen him in the flesh, but only in the spirit. He went along the royal road that leads to Lystra,[42] and stood there waiting for him, and looked at those who came, comparing them with Titus's description. And he saw Paul coming, a man small of stature, with a bald head and crooked legs, in a good state of body, with eyebrows meeting and nose somewhat hooked, full of friendliness; for now he appeared like a man, and now he had the face of an angel.[43]

Despite the impression of realism which this pen-portrait makes, it has been suggested that it belongs to a literary tradition – the tradition of which Alcibiades's description of Socrates is an early expression. Alcibiades's description is to a large extent quite unflattering – Socrates is portrayed as a Silenus or a satyr in outward appearance – but his conversation is inexpressibly captivating: within the unprepossessing exterior there was a treasure "so divine and golden, so wholly beautiful and wonderful, that I simply had to do as Socrates bade me".[44] Robert Eisler argued that the description of Paul belonged to the same *genre* as the imaginative description of Jesus in the so-called *Letter of Lentulus*.[45] But these parallels are not so close as to carry conviction, and the possibility remains – it can be no more than that – that Sir William Ramsay was not mistaken in saying that "this plain and unflattering account of the Apostle's personal appearance seems to embody a very early tradition".[46]

While Tertullian disapproved of the *Acts of Paul*, his contemporary Hippolytus of Rome seems to have accepted the work – not indeed as holy writ (it was never intended to receive such recognition) but as a genuine record of events. Hippolytus was the greatest scholar of his day in western Christendom but his scholarship did not prevent him from taking, apparently, as factual truth what we

---

42. The royal road "is obviously the Roman road built by Augustus from [Pisidian] Antioch to Lystra" (W. M. Ramsay, *The Church in the Roman Empire before A.D. 170* [London,[5] 1897], p. 32).

43. *New Testament Apocrypha*, E.T., ed. E. Hennecke, W. Schneemelcher, R. McL. Wilson, ii (London, 1965), pp. 353 f. The reference to "the face of an angel" is reminiscent of Stephen in Acts 6: 13.

44. Plato, *Symposium* 215 A–222 B.

45. R. Eisler, *The Messiah Jesus and John the Baptist* (London, 1931), pp. 393 ff.

46. W. M. Ramsay, *The Church in the Roman Empire*, p. 32.

should regard as one of the most patently legendary incidents in the book – the story of Paul's confrontation in the arena with a lion which he had befriended and baptized.[47]

The legend of Androcles and the lion is well enough known to-day, thanks mainly to Bernard Shaw, but in the mid-second century something very like it was told of Paul himself. This probably arose from a literalistic interpretation of Paul's reference to his having "fought with beasts at Ephesus" (1 Corinthians 15: 32) or of his later claim to have been "rescued from the lion's mouth" (2 Timothy 4: 17). The story was recorded quite circumstantially in the *Acts of Paul* and Hippolytus, treating it quite seriously, adduces it in his *Commentary on Daniel* as a parallel to the story of Daniel in the lions' den: "If we believe that, when Paul was condemned to the circus, the lion which was set upon him lay down at his feet and licked him, why should we not also believe what happened in the case of Daniel?"[48] – a precarious apologetic indeed!

In Rome, too, legend embellished the story of Paul. It was told, for example, how he was taken to Naples to see the tomb of the poet Virgil, who died in 19 B.C., and wept over him: "What a convert I would have made of you", said he, "had I found you still alive, greatest of poets!"[49] The record of his martyrdom in particular was adorned with miraculous accessories. As he was led to the place of execution, says one apocryphal work, he saw a woman named Perpetua, blind in one eye, who burst into tears as he pass-ed. He asked her to lend him her kerchief. The soldiers who were conducting him laughed at her, but she adjured them by the emperor's well-being to tie it round Paul's eyes and return it to her after his death. When they did so, she put it on again, all bloodstained as it now was, and immediately the sight of her blind eye was restored.[50]

Reliefs in the church of St. Paul at Tre Fontane commemorate the legend that the apostle's head bounced on the ground three times when it was severed, and at each place there welled forth one of the three springs from which the place is named.

## 4. Paul's perennial influence

Such legends represent an unsophisticated attempt to emphasize

47. *New Testament Apocrypha*, E.T., ii, pp. 369–373; see p. 295 above.
48. Hippolytus, *Commentary on Daniel*, iii. 29.
49.      Ad Maronis mausoleum
         Ductus, fudit super eum
            Piae rorem lacrimae:
         "Quem te", inquit, "reddidissem,
         Si te vivum invenissem,
            Poetarum maxime!"
50. Cf. (Greek) *Acts of Peter and Paul*, 80. (See p. 450, n. 32.)

the greatness of Paul. But his true greatness is attested by the abiding power of his liberating message. Time and again, when the gospel has been in danger of being fettered and disabled in the bonds of legalism or outworn tradition, it has been the words of Paul that have broken the bonds and set the gospel free to exert its emancipating power once more in the life of mankind.

(a) *Augustine*. In the summer of A.D. 386 the thirty-two year old Augustine sat weeping in the garden of his friend Alypius at Milan. He had been for two years Professor of Rhetoric in that city, and had every reason to be satisfied with his professional career thus far, yet he was conscious of a deep inner dissatisfaction. He was almost persuaded to begin a new life, but lacked the resolution to break with the old. As he sat, he heard a child singing in a neighbouring house, *Tolle, lege! Tolle, lege!* ("Take up and read! Take up and read!"). Taking up the scroll which lay at his friend's side – a copy of Paul's letters, as it happened – he let his eye fall on what we know as the closing words of Romans 13: "not in revelling and drunkenness, not in debauchery and licentiousness, not in quarrelling and jealousy; but put on the Lord Jesus Christ, and make no provision for the flesh, to gratify its desires." "No further would I read," he says, "nor had I any need; instantly, at the end of this sentence, a clear light flooded my heart and all the darkness of doubt vanished away." [51]

The colossal influence which Augustine, "the greatest Christian since New Testament times" [52] (as one patristic scholar has called him), has exercised on the thought of succeeding ages can be traced directly to the light which flooded into his mind as he read the words of Paul.

(b) *Luther and the Reformation*. In 1513 Martin Luther, Augustinian monk and Professor of Sacred Theology in the University of Wittenberg in Saxony, endeavoured to prepare a course of lectures on the Psalms while his mind was preoccupied with the agonizing endeavour to "find a gracious God". He was struck by the prayer of Psalm 31: 1, "in thy righteousness deliver me". But how could God's *righteousness* deliver him? The righteousness of God was surely calculated rather to condemn the sinner than to save him. As he thought about the meaning of the words, his attention was more and more directed to Paul's statement in Romans 1: 17 that in the gospel "the righteousness of God is revealed through faith for faith; as it is written, 'He who through faith is righteous shall live'" (Habakkuk 2: 4). The result of his study is best told in his own words:

---

51. Augustine, *Confessions* viii. 29.
52. A. Souter, *The Earliest Latin Commentaries on the Epistles of St Paul* (Oxford, 1927), p. 139.

I had greatly longed to understand Paul's epistle to the Romans, and nothing stood in the way but that one expression, "the righteousness of God", because I took it to mean that righteousness whereby God is righteous and acts righteously in punishing the unrighteous. . . . Night and day I pondered until . . . I grasped the truth that the righteousness of God is that righteousness whereby, through grace and sheer mercy, he justifies us by faith. Thereupon I felt myself to be reborn and to have gone through open doors into paradise. The whole of Scripture took on a new meaning, and whereas before "the righteousness of God" had filled me with hate, now it became to me inexpressibly sweet in greater love. This passage of Paul became to me a gateway into heaven.[53]

The consequences of Luther's grasp of the liberating gospel according to Paul are writ large in history.

It may well be that, since Augustine and Luther both found Paul to speak so helpfully to their own respective spiritual conditions, there has been an unwarranted tendency to ascribe to Paul the same kind of inward conflict before his conversion that they experienced before theirs.[54] But what should be emphasized is that Paul's gospel of salvation by divine grace has a living relevance not only to people who, like him, supposed they had attained a satisfactory standard of righteousness by law-keeping but also to those who, in one way or another, have known themselves to fall far short of such a standard and have suffered agonies of conscience as a result. The gospel according to Paul is not a message for one kind of temperament or one type of experience only. The Wesley brothers had a very different background and experience from Augustine and Luther, but it was Paul who spoke to their condition too.

(c) *The Wesleys and the Evangelical Revival.* In John Wesley's wellknown account of the event which is usually called his conversion, but which he himself later described (in Pauline language) as the occasion when he exchanged "the faith of a *servant*" for "the faith of a *son*",[55] he tells how, in the evening of Wednesday, May 24, 1738, he "went very unwillingly to a society in Aldersgate Street [London], where one was reading Luther's preface to the Epistle to the Romans. About a quarter before nine", he goes on, "while he was describing the change which God works in the heart through faith in Christ, I felt my heart strangely warmed. I felt I did trust in Christ, Christ alone for salvation: And an assurance was given me,

53. *Gesamtausgaben seiner lateinischer Schriften* (Wittenberg, 1545); cf. *Luthers Werke* (Weimar edition, 54 [1928], p. 186). See E. G. Rupp, *The Righteousness of God* (London, 1947), pp. 129 ff.; J. Atkinson, *The Great Light* (Exeter, 1968), pp. 19 f.

54. Cf. K. Stendahl, "The Apostle Paul and the Introspective Conscience of the West", *Harvard Theological Review* 56 (1963), pp. 199–215. See p. 196 above.

55. J. Wesley, *Journal*, i (London, 1872), pp. 76 f., footnotes. The language is Pauline; cf. Galatians 4: 3–7.

that he had taken away *my* sins, even *mine*, and saved *me* from the law of sin and death."[56]

If there is one event more than another that marked the birth of the evangelical revival of the eighteenth century, it was that. "The inextinguishable blaze which burned so brightly throughout the remainder of the century and beyond was nourished in the warmed heart of this one man at Aldersgate Street."[57] But similar awakenings were being experienced by others around the same time, and it is remarkable in how many of them Paul had a determinant part to play. A week before John's awakening, his brother Charles came for the first time upon Luther's commentary on Galatians, and "found him nobly full of faith". Later in the same day, he records, "I spent some hours this evening in private with Martin Luther, who was greatly blessed to me, especially his conclusion of the second chapter. I laboured, waited, and prayed to feel 'who loved *me* and gave himself for *me*'."[58] Four days later, his prayer was answered.

But another phase of Pauline thought made a powerful contribution to the evangelical revival – the phase expounded in the early 1670s by Henry Scougal in *The Life of God in the Soul of Man*.[59] This treatise was well known to the Wesleys: their mother recommended it to them as "an excellent good book' and "as an acquaintance of mine many years ago". John Wesley had a copy with him in Savannah, Georgia, and Charles in his Oxford days gave a copy to his fellow-student George Whitefield. It was the reading of this book that brought about Whitefield's conversion in 1733: it showed him, in his own words, "that they who know anything of religion know it is a vital union with the Son of God – Christ formed in the heart. O what a ray of divine life", he adds, "did then break in upon my soul!"[60] In thus describing what happened to him, he echoes Scougal's own language: "true religion is a union of the soul with

56. J. Wesley, *Journal*, i, p. 103.

57. A. S. Wood, *The Inextinguishable Blaze* (London, 1959), p. 113.

58. C. Wesley, *Journal*, i (London, 1849), p. 90. In his quotation from Galatians 2: 20 he lays (following Luther) the same emphasis on the personal pronoun *me* as his brother does in his reference to Romans 8: 2.

59. Henry Scougal (1650–78) was elected Professor of Divinity in King's College, Aberdeen, in 1673 and died of consumption five years later. He wrote *The Life of God in the Soul of Man* probably during the year 1672–73, when he was parish minister of Auchterless in Aberdeenshire. It was published anonymously in 1677; a number of further impressions and editions appeared within the following century. The edition used here is that issued by the Inter-Varsity Press (London, 1961), with a foreword by D. J. Innes.

60. Sermon preached in 1769 (quoted by D. J. Innes in his foreword to the 1961 reissue of Scougal, p. 12); cf. G. Whitefield, *Journals*, i (Banner of Truth edition, London, 1960), pp. 46 f. Whitefield was nineteen years old when he underwent this experience.

God, a real participation of the divine nature, the very image of God drawn upon the soul, or, in the apostle's phrase, it is 'Christ formed within us'." [61] The "apostle's phrase" comes from that letter to the Galatians which so emphasizes justification by faith, apart from legal works: Paul tells his Galatian friends how he endures birth-pangs on their behalf "until Christ be formed in you" (Galatians 4: 19). It was perhaps the combination of these two aspects of Paulinism – the initial pardoning grace of God and the progressive inward work of the Spirit – that gave the evangelical revival its deep and lasting effect: concentration on the one without the other leads to a lop-sided form of religion.

(d) *Barth and the Theology of Crisis.* To come to more recent times, one of the most epoch-making theological publications of the twentieth century was Karl Barth's exposition of the Epistle to the Romans, first issued in August 1918 when he was pastor of Safenwil in Canton Aargau, Switzerland. "The reader", he said in his preface, "will detect for himself that it has been written with a joyful sense of discovery. The mighty voice of Paul was new to me: and if to me, no doubt to many others also. And yet, now that my work is finished, I perceive that much remains which I have not yet heard . . .". [62] But what he had heard he wrote down, and others heard it too. He compared himself to a man who, clutching in the dark at a rope for guidance, finds that he has pulled on a bell-rope, making a sound fit to wake the dead. [63] The Catholic theologian Karl Adam said that the first edition of Barth's *Römerbrief* fell "like a bombshell on the theologians' playground". [64] The repercussions of that explosion are with us still, nearly sixty years later.

(e) *Paul and democratic liberty.* It can be argued that, in those parts of the world where the democratic process has been specially indebted to the Reformation and the evangelical revival, Paul has exercised an indirect influence because of his direct influence on those movements. This was the judgment of Sir Thomas Taylor, a distinguished Scottish lawyer and churchman, who was a careful student both of Pauline theology and of the democratic process.

Justification by Faith means that salvation depends not on sacraments, not on what is done or not done by any priest or presbyter, but on the simple response of the believing heart to the Word of God in Jesus Christ. Observe what this really means; it is not just a theological figment. At one stroke it cuts at the root of the whole vast system of sacerdotalism, with its associated doctrine of works – penance, pil-

61. *The Life of God in the Soul of Man* (1961 reissue), p. 16.
62. K. Barth, *The Epistle to the Romans*, E.T. (Oxford, 1933), p. 2.
63. K. Barth, *Die Lehre vom Worte Gottes* (Munich, 1927), preface.
64. K. Adam, in *Das Hochland*, June 1926, as quoted by J. McConnachie, "The Teaching of Karl Barth", *Hibbert Journal* 25 (1926–27), pp. 385 f.

grimage, fasting, purgatory, and all the rest. The Church is no longer a
hierarchy of clergy performing indispensable rites for its members; no
longer a caste of priests endued with mysterious, not to say magical
powers at the word of a bishop; but the priesthood of all believing
men, and a ministry authorised by the call of the Holy Spirit, by due
examination of life and doctrine, and by the consent of the people concerned. Here you have the beginning of Scottish democracy, here and
nowhere else. Accept this doctrine of Justification by Faith and the
layman, the common man, John the Commonweal, at one stride comes
into the centre.[65]

Sir Thomas referred particularly to "Scottish democracy" because
he was addressing the General Assembly of the Church of Scotland
convened to commemorate the quatercentenary of the Scottish
Reformation; but his wise words have a wider reference. Paul looked forward to the day when the racial, religious, sexual and social
prejudices or discrimination to which on principle he denied any
place in the Christian fellowship would be banished from the whole
new creation. And he placed a higher valuation on human personality than social or political democracy could ever do when he
insisted that the weaker members of the community should receive
special consideration because each of them, however insignificant
in other respects, was "the brother (or sister) for whom Christ
died" (1 Corinthians 8: 11). Campaigner for spiritual liberty that
he was, he gave one thing precedence even over liberty, and that
one thing was love. But spiritual liberty is not really diminished by
love; both together are imparted by the Spirit, and to serve in love is
perfect freedom. In this, as in so many other respects, Paul has
remained unsurpassed in his insight into the mind of Christ.

65. T. M. Taylor, *The Heritage of the Reformation* (Edinburgh, 1960), pp. 6 f. John
the Commonweal ("Iohne the Common-weill") is a character in Sir David Lind-
say's *Satyre of the Thrie Estaitis* (1552).

# Chronological Table

| | Christian history | Roman history |
|---|---|---|
| | | 14–37 Tiberius emperor |
| c. 28–30 | Public ministry of Jesus | |
| c. 33 | Conversion of Paul | |
| c. 35 | Paul's first post-conversion Jerusalem visit | |
| 35–46 | Paul in Cilicia and Syria | |
| | | 37–41 Gaius emperor |
| | | 41–54 Claudius emperor |
| 46 | Paul's second Jerusalem visit | |
| 47–48 | Paul and Barnabas in Cyprus and Galatia | |
| ? 48 | *Letter to the Galatians* | |
| 49 | Council of Jerusalem | 49 Jews expelled from Rome |
| 49–50 | Paul and Silas travel from Syrian Antioch through Asia Minor to Macedonia and Achaia | |
| 50 | *Letters to the Thessalonians* | |
| 50–52 | Paul in Corinth | 51–52 Gallio pro-consul of Achaia |
| Summer 52 | Paul's third Jerusalem visit | |
| | | 52–59 Felix procur-ator of Judaea |
| 52–55 | Paul in Ephesus | 54–68 Nero emperor |
| 55–56 | *Letters to the Corinthians* | |
| 55–57 | Paul in Macedonia, Illyricum and Achaia | |
| early 57 | *Letter to the Romans* | |
| May 57 | Paul's fourth (and last) Jeru-salem visit | |
| 57–59 | Paul's imprisonment in Caesarea | 59 Festus suc-ceeds Felix as procurator of Judaea |
| September 59 | Paul's voyage to Rome begins | |
| February 60 | Paul's arrival in Rome | |
| 60–62 | Paul under house-arrest in Rome | |
| ? 60–62 | *Captivity Letters* | 62 Death of Fes-tus; Albinus procurator of Judaea |
| | | July 64 Fire of Rome |
| ? 65 | Paul visits Spain | |
| ? | *Pastoral Letters* | |
| ? 65 | Death of Paul | |

# Select Bibliography

This is a select and partial bibliography. Some of the most important literature on Paul is to be found in commentaries on his epistles or exegetical monographs. Other important studies of his life and thought appear in works on early Christian history and theology or on contemporary Graeco-Roman civilization, not to mention contributions to periodicals and *Festschriften*. References to such important studies have been given here and there in footnotes throughout this volume.

Alexander, A. B. D., *The Ethics of St. Paul* (Glasgow, 1910)

Allen, R., *Missionary Methods: St. Paul's or Ours?* (London, 1927)

Bacon, B. W., *The Story of St. Paul* (London, 1905)

Bacon, B. W., *Jesus and Paul* (London, 1921)

Bandstra, A. J., *The Law and the Elements of the World: An Exegetical Study in Aspects of Paul's Teaching* (Kampen, 1964)

Barclay, W., *The Mind of St. Paul* (London, 1958)

Barrett, C. K., *From First Adam to Last: A Study in Pauline Theology* (London, 1962)

Baur, F. C., *Paul: His Life and Works*, E.T., 2 volumes (London, 1875)

Beare, F. W., *St. Paul and his Letters* (London, 1962)

Betz, H.-D., *Der Apostel Paulus und die sokratische Tradition* (Tübingen, 1972)

Bornkamm, G., *Paul*, E.T. (London, 1971)

Buck, C. H., and Greer, T., *St. Paul: A Study of the Development of his Thought* (New York, 1969)

Bultmann, R., "Paul" (1930), "Romans 7 and the Anthropology of Paul" (1932), and "Jesus and Paul" (1936), E.T. in *Existence and Faith* (London, 1964), pp. 130–172, 173–185 and 217–239

Bultmann, R., "The Theology of Paul" in *Theology of the New Testament*, E.T., i (London, 1952), pp. 185–352

Cerfaux, L., *Christ in the Theology of St. Paul*, E.T. (Edinburgh/London/New York, 1959)

Cerfaux, L., *The Church in the Theology of St. Paul*, E.T. (Edinburgh/London/New York, 1959)

Davies, W. D., *Paul and Rabbinic Judaism* (London, 1948)

Deissmann, A., *Paul: A Study in Social and Religious History*, E.T. (London, 1926)
Dibelius, M., and Kümmel, W. G., *Paul*, E.T. (London, 1953)
Dodd, C. H., *The Meaning of Paul for Today* (London, 1920)
Dodd, C. H., "The Mind of Paul" in *New Testament Studies* (Manchester, 1953), pp. 67–128
Drane, J. W., *Paul: Libertine or Legalist?* (London, 1975)
Duncan, G. S., *St. Paul's Ephesian Ministry* (London, 1929)
Dungan, D. L., *The Sayings of Jesus in the Churches of Paul* (Oxford, 1971)
Ellis, E. E., *Paul's Use of the Old Testament* (Edinburgh, 1957)
Ellis, E. E., *Paul and his Recent Interpreters* (Grand Rapids, 1961)
Ellis, E. E., and Grässer, E. (ed.), *Jesus und Paulus: Festschrift für W. G. Kümmel* (Göttingen, 1975)
Enslin, M. S., *The Ethics of Paul* (Nashville/New York, [2]1962)
Enslin, M. S., *Reapproaching Paul* (Philadelphia, 1972)
Foakes-Jackson, F. J., *The Life of Saint Paul* (London, 1927)
Fraser, J. W., *Jesus and Paul* (Appleford, 1974)
Fridrichsen, A., *The Apostle and his Message* (Uppsala, 1947)
Furnish, V. P., *Theology and Ethics in Paul* (Nashville, 1968)
Glover, T. R., *Paul of Tarsus* (London, 1925)
Grant, M., *Saint Paul* (London, 1976)
Gunther, J. J., *Paul: Messenger and Exile* (Valley Forge, 1972)
Gunther, J. J., *St. Paul's Opponents and their Background* (Leiden, 1973)
Hanson, A. T., *Studies in Paul's Technique and Theology* (London, 1974)
Haughton, R., *The Liberated Heart* (London, 1975)
Hugedé, N., *Saint Paul et la Culture Grecque* (Geneva, 1966)
Hunter, A. M. *Paul and his Predecessors* (London, [2]1961)
Hunter, A. M., *Interpreting Paul's Gospel* (London, 1954)
Jüngel, E., *Paulus und Jesus* (Tübingen, 1962)
Käsemann, E., *Perspectives on Paul*, E.T. (London, 1971)
Kennedy, H. A. A., *St. Paul's Conception of the Last Things* (London, 1904)
Kennedy, H. A. A., *St Paul and the Mystery Religions* (London, 1913)
Klausner, J., *From Jesus to Paul*, E.T. (London, 1944)
Knox, J., *Chapters in a Life of Paul* (London, 1954)
Knox, W. L., *St. Paul and the Church of Jerusalem* (Cambridge, 1925)
Knox, W. L., *St. Paul and the Church of the Gentiles* (Cambridge, 1939)
Kuss, O., *Paulus: Die Rolle des Apostels in der theologischen Entwicklung der Urkirche* (Regensburg, 1971)
Lake, K., *The Earlier Epistles of St. Paul* (London, 1911)
Lake, K., *Paul: His Heritage and Legacy* (London, 1934)
Longenecker, R. N., *Paul, Apostle of Liberty* (New York, 1964)

Longenecker, R. N., *The Ministry and Message of Paul* (Grand Rapids, 1971)

Machen, J. G., *The Origin of Paul's Religion* (New York, 1921)

Manson, T. W. (ed.), *On Paul and John* (London, 1963)

Meeks, W. A. (ed.), *The Writings of St. Paul* (New York, 1972)

Michel, O., *Paulus und seine Bibel* (Gütersloh, 1929)

Mitton, C. L., *The Formation of the Pauline Corpus of Letters* (London, 1955)

Montefiore, C. G., *Judaism and St. Paul* (London, 1914)

Munck, J., *Paul and the Salvation of Mankind*, E.T. (London, 1959)

Murphy-O'Connor, J. (ed.), *Paul and Qumran* (London, 1968)

Nock, A. D., *St. Paul* (London, 1938)

Ogg, G., *The Chronology of the Life of Paul* (London, 1968)

Paley, W., *Horae Paulinae* (London, 1790)

Pohlenz, M., *Paulus und die Stoa* (Darmstadt, 1964)

Prat, F., *The Theology of St. Paul*, E.T. (London, 1957)

Ramsay, W. M., *St. Paul the Traveller and the Roman Citizen* (London, [14]1920)

Ramsay, W. M., *Pauline and Other Studies in Early Christian History* (London, 1906)

Ramsay, W. M., *The Cities of St. Paul: Their Influence on his Life and Thought* (London, 1907)

Ramsay, W. M., *The Teaching of Paul in Terms of the Present Day* (London, 1913)

Ridderbos, H., *Paul: An Outline of his Theology*, E.T. (Grand Rapids, 1975)

Rigaux, B., *Letters of St. Paul*, E.T. (Chicago, 1968)

Sanders, E. P., *Paul and Palestinian Judaism* (London, 1977)

Sandmel, S., *The Genius of Paul: A Study in History* (New York, 1970)

Schmithals, W., *Paul and James*, E.T. (London, 1965)

Schnackenburg, R., *Baptism in the Thought of St. Paul*, E.T. (Oxford, 1964)

Schoeps, H. J., *Paul: The Theology of the Apostle in the Light of Jewish Religious History*, E.T. (London, 1961)

Schrenk, G., *Studien zu Paulus* (Zürich, 1954)

Schütz, J. H., *Paul and the Anatomy of Apostolic Authority* (Cambridge, 1974)

Schweitzer, A., *Paul and his Interpreters*, E.T. (London, 1912)

Schweitzer, A., *The Mysticism of Paul the Apostle*, E.T. (London, 1931)

Scott, C. A. A., *Christianity according to St. Paul* (Cambridge, 1927)

Scott, C. A. A., *Footnotes to St. Paul* (Cambridge, 1935)

Scott, C. A. A., *St. Paul: The Man and the Teacher* (Cambridge, 1936)

Scroggs, R., *The Last Adam: A Study in Pauline Anthropology* (Oxford, 1966)

Scroggs, R., *Paul for a New Day* (Philadelphia, 1976)

Sevenster, J. N., and van Unnik, W. C. (ed.), *Studia Paulina in honorem J. de Zwaan* (Haarlem, 1953)

Souter, A., *The Earliest Latin Commentaries on the Epistles of St. Paul* (Oxford, 1927)

Stacey, W. D., *The Pauline View of Man* (London, 1956)

Stendahl, K., *Paul Among Jews and Gentiles* (Philadelphia, 1976)

Stewart, J. S., *A Man in Christ: The Vital Elements of St. Paul's Religion* (London, 1935)

Thackeray, H. St. J., *The Relation of St. Paul to Contemporary Jewish Thought* (London, 1900)

van Unnik, W. C., *Tarsus or Jerusalem: The City of Paul's Youth*, E.T. (London, 1962)

Vos, G., *The Pauline Eschatology* (Grand Rapids, ²1952)

Wagner, G., *Pauline Baptism and the Pagan Mysteries*, E.T. (Edinburgh/London, 1967)

Weinel, H., *St. Paul: The Man and his Work*, E.T. (London, 1906)

Weiss, J., *Paul and Jesus*, E.T. (London/New York, 1909)

Whiteley, D. E. H., *The Theology of St. Paul* (Oxford, 1964)

Wikenhauser, A., *Pauline Mysticism: Christ in the Mystical Teaching of St. Paul*, E.T. (Freiburg/Edinburgh/London, 1960)

Wiles, M. F., *The Divine Apostle: The Interpretation of St. Paul's Epistles in the Early Church* (Cambridge, 1967)

Wilson, T., *St. Paul and Paganism* (Edinburgh, 1927)

Wrede, W., *Paul*, E.T. (London, 1907)

Ziesler, J. A., *The Meaning of Righteousness in Paul* (Cambridge, 1972)

# Index